The Dragon Variation

The Dragon Variation

Sharon Lee & Steve Miller

THE DRAGON VARIATION

Local Custom copyright © 2000 by Sharon Lee & Steve Miller, *Scout's
Progress* copyright © 2000 by Sharon Lee & Steve Miller, *Conflict of Honors*
copyright © 1988 by Steve Miller & Sharon Lee

Liaden Universe® is a registered trademark

A Baen Book

Baen Publishing Enterprises
P.O. Box 1403
Riverdale, NY 10471
www.baen.com

ISBN: 978-1-4391-3369-9

Cover art by Alan Pollack

First Baen printing, June 2010

Distributed by Simon & Schuster
1230 Avenue of the Americas
New York, NY 10020

Library of Congress Cataloging-in-Publication Data

Lee, Sharon, 1952-
  The dragon variation / by Sharon Lee & Steve Miller.
    p. cm.
  ISBN 978-1-4391-3369-9 (trade pbk.)
  1. Science fiction, American. I. Miller, Steve, 1950 July 31- II. Lee, Sharon,
1952- Local custom. III. Lee, Sharon, 1952- Scout's progress. IV. Lee,
Sharon, 1952- Conflict of honors. V. Title.
  PS3562.E3629D73 2010
  813'.54--dc22

                                    2010011766

Printed in the United States of America

10 9 8 7 6 5 4 3 2

CONTENTS

HERE, THERE BE DRAGONS . . .

Not, granted, the sort of Dragons you're probably thinking of—scaled treasure-hoarders of legend, or leather-winged devourers of Thread.

Not exactly, anyway.

Our Dragons are human. Oh, they fly—they're pilots, mostly— and they hoard treasure in the form of spaceships. They're charismatic and dangerous; good friends and bad, bad enemies.

The Dragons we're talking about are the members of Clan Korval, and "here" is the planet Liad.

Why Dragons? you ask.

Good question.

In Liaden culture, each clan has a sigil—a hallmark, if you will—which is part and parcel of the clan's identity. Each delm— head of clan—wears a ring bearing the Clan's mark, and is formally addressed by the clan's name. Korval's clan mark is an image of a dragon, wings half-furled, hovering protectively over a well-leafed tree. To Liadens, applying liberal social wit, members of Clan Korval become Dragons; its delm, Korval Him-or-Herself.

Liad . . .

Liaden society, you understand, is very formal, and is generally codified in a multi-volume work known as the *Liaden Code of Proper Conduct*. Being Dragons, Korval has . . . limited use for such stringent social confines. They are not dishonorable, generally, nor are their manners anything but nice.

But they do tend to consider the Code more on the order of guidelines, rather than law.

So, Dragons.

This omnibus is titled *The Dragon Variation*. A "variation" in chess is a new angle built on an established and well-studied line of attack. Variations are often the purview of a Romantic—the sort of chess player who sacrifices order for elegance; and plays from their heart. Such a line of play is not for the timid, since it depends upon flying in the face of custom—and on risking one's heart.

We need to stop here and explain ourselves a little.

One of the great joys that the Liaden Universe® holds for us, its authors, is its very *size*. Make no doubt about it, the universe is **big**.

How big, you might ask.

Big enough for love, to paraphrase Mr. Heinlein. Big enough for war, and for reconciliation. Big enough for multiple entrances and storylines that range from thrillers, to battle tales, to quiet love stories. Big enough for all of that—and big enough for fun.

We've mentioned *fun* before, in the prologue to another book. We're mentioning it again, now, because, to us, fun is serious.

When we were just getting started in the collaboration biz, we made a promise to each other. We promised that we would keep on writing as long as it was fun. That was in 1984, so you can see that we're easily amused. We also believe that readers have more fun with stories that are written by authors who are enjoying themselves. And, yes, we do think you're are smart enough to tell. And big-hearted enough to care.

Regarding world-building choices, we agreed straight off that— while the Liaden Universe® would be exciting and strange, with wars to fight, aliens to decipher, and wrongs to right— people would fall in love. That doesn't sound like so much of an artistic decision nowadays, but back in the early-to-mid 80s, it was something of a radical notion in science fiction.

Mind you, the idea of mixing romance into a genre plot wasn't original with us. Dorothy Sayers used romance to excellent effect in the exemplary Peter Wimsey mysteries, to which Sharon introduced Steve. Steve returned the favor by introducing Sharon to Georgette

Heyer. Romance, after all, is part of being human—of being *people*.

And so it is with the Liaden Universe®; because the other thing we agreed on is that stories are about people.

That said, the three novels in this omnibus are, yes, romances. *Local Custom* and *Scout's Progress* are essentially Regency Romances set on an alien world— Space Regencies, if you will, and our bow to Georgette Heyer, acknowledging all that she taught us, as writers and as readers.

Conflict of Honors is our tribute to Peter Wimsey, who did what duty demanded, and was never afraid to cry.

The Dragon Variation also lays the groundwork of Liaden culture and the larger trading universe of which it is a part. Taken together, these three novels are an on-ramp to the Liaden Universe®, taking you in slowly, before . . . just before . . . the trouble begins.

Over the next several months, Baen will be releasing three more Liaden Universe® reprint omnibi: *The Agent Gambit* (including *Agent of Change* and *Carpe Diem*); *Korval's Game* (including *Plan B* and *I Dare*) and *The Crystal Variation* (including *Crystal Soldier*, *Crystal Dragon*, and *Balance of Trade*). The novels run the gamut from Space Regencies to Space Opera. All are character-driven; all were fun to write and, we hope, fun to read.

In addition to the reprints, Baen has-or-will-be publishing three more Liaden Universe® novels: *Fledgling*, and *Saltation*, the story of Theo Waitley; and *Mouse and Dragon*, the sequel to *Scout's Progress*, which appears in this omnibus.

If this is your first encounter with a Liaden Universe® book— welcome. If you're an old friend, stopping by for a revisit—we're very glad to see you.

Thank you.

Sharon Lee and Steve Miller
Waterville, Maine
November 2009

LOCAL CUSTOM

CHAPTER ONE

Each person shall provide his clan of origin with a child of his blood, who will be raised by the clan and belong to the clan, despite whatever may later occur to place the parent beyond the clan's authority. And this shall be Law for every person of every clan.

**—From the Charter of the Council of Clans
Made in the Sixth Year After Planetfall,
City of Solcintra, Liad**

"NO?" HIS MOTHER ECHOED, light blue eyes opening wide.

Er Thom yos'Galan bowed hastily: Subordinate Person to Head of Line, seeking to recoup his error.

"Mother," he began, with all propriety, "I ask grace . . ."

She cut him off with a wave of her hand. "Let us return to 'no.' It has the charm of brevity."

Er Thom took a careful breath, keeping his face smooth, his breath even, his demeanor attentive. Everything that was proper in a son who had always been dutiful.

After a moment, his mother sighed, walked carefully past him and sat wearily in her special chair. She frowned up at him, eyes intent.

"Is it your desire, my son, to deny the clan your genes?"

"No," said Er Thom again, and bit his lip.

"Good. Good." Petrella, Thodelm yos'Galan, drummed her fingers lightly against the chair's wooden arm, and continued to gaze at him with that look of puzzled intensity.

"Yet," she said, "you have consistently refused every possible contract-alliance the head of your line has brought to your attention for the past three years. Permit me to wonder why."

Er Thom bowed slightly, granting permission to wonder, belatedly recognizing it as a response less conciliatory than it might be, given the gravity of circumstances. He glanced at his mother from beneath his lashes as he straightened, wondering if he would now receive tuition on manners.

But Petrella was entirely concentrated upon this other thing and allowed the small irony to pass uncriticized.

"You are," she said, "captain of your own vessel, master trader, pilot—a well-established *melant'i*. You are of good lineage, your manner is for the greater part, pleasing, you have reached your majority and capably taken up the governing of the various businesses which passed to you upon your thirty-fifth name day. It is time and past time for you to provide the clan with your child."

"Yes," murmured Er Thom, because there was nothing else to say. She told him no more than the Law: Every person must provide the clan with a child to become his heir and to eventually take his place within the clan.

His mother sighed again, concern in her eyes. "It is not so great a thing, my child," she offered with unlooked-for gentleness. "We have all done so."

When he remained speechless, she leaned forward, hand extended. "My son, I do not wish to burden you. Necessity exists, but necessity need not be oppressive. Is there one your heart has placed above others? Only tell me her name and her clan, negotiations will be initiated . . ." Slowly she sank back into the chair, hand falling to her knee. "Er Thom?"

"Mother," he murmured miserably, eyes swimming as he bowed. "I ask grace . . ."

✿ ✿ ✿

GRACE, AFTER ALL, had not been forthcoming. He had scarcely expected it, with him tongue-tangled and kittenish as a halfling. His mother had no time to waste upon baseless sentiment, not with her illness so hard upon her. She had granted grace to one child already—and those genes lost to Clan Korval forever by reason of her leniency.

So there was to be no grace given Petrella's second child and the hope of Line yos'Galan. Er Thom wondered at himself, that he had dared even ask it.

Wondering still, he turned down the short hallway that led to his rooms and lay his hand against the lockplate. Late afternoon sun bathed the room beyond in thick yellow light, washing over the clutter of invoices and lading slips on his work table, the islands of computer screen, comm board and keypad. The message waiting light was a steady blue glow over the screen.

Er Thom sighed. That would be the file on his wife-to-be, transferred to him from his mother's station. Duty dictated that he open it at once and familiarize himself with the contents, that he might give formal acquiescence to his thodelm at Prime Meal this evening.

He went quietly across the hand-loomed imported rug, thoughts carefully on the minutiae he would need to attend to, so he might stay on Liad for the duration of his marriage, as custom, if not Law, demanded. Another master trader would have to be found for *Dutiful Passage,* though Kayzin Ne'Zame, his first mate, would do very well as captain. The upcoming trip would require re-routing and certain of their regular customers notified personally . . . He pushed the window wide, letting the mild afternoon breeze into the room.

Behind him, papers rustled like a startled rookery. Er Thom leaned out the window, hands gripping the sill, eyes slightly narrowed as he looked across the valley at the towering Tree.

Jelaza Kazone was the name of the Tree—Jela's Fulfillment— and it marked the site of Korval's clanhouse, where Er Thom had spent his childhood, constant companion and willing shadow of his cousin and foster-brother, Daav yos'Phelium.

Er Thom's eyes teared and the Tree broke into an hundred glittering shards of brown and green against a sky gone milky bright. The desire to speak to Daav, to bury his face in his brother's shoulder and cry out against the unfairness of the Law was nearly overmastering.

Compelling as it was, the desire was hardly fitting of one who kept adult *melant'i*. Er Thom tightened his grip on the sill, feeling the metal track score his palms, and closed his eyes. He would *not* go to Daav with this, he told himself sternly. After all, the younger man was facing much the same necessity as Er Thom—and Daav lacked even a parent's guidance, his own mother having died untimely some five Standard Years before.

Eventually the compulsion passed, leaving him dry-mouthed and with sternness at least awakened, if not full sense of duty.

Grimly, he pushed away from the window, marched across the room and touched the message-waiting stud.

The screen flickered and the lady's likeness appeared, his mother being no fool, to waste time fielding dry fact when fair face might easily carry the day.

And she was, Er Thom thought with detached coolness, very fair. Syntebra el'Kemin, Clan Nexon, was blessed with classic beauty: Slim brows arched over wide opal-blue eyes fringed with lashes long enough to sweep the luscious curve of her cheekbones. Her skin was smooth and flawlessly golden; her nose petite; her mouth red as clemetia buds. She looked at him coyly from the screen, dark hair pulled back and up, seductively displaying tiny, perfect ears.

Er Thom swallowed against a sudden cold surge of sickness and glanced away, toward the window and the Tree, towering into twilight.

"It is—not possible," he whispered and ground his teeth, forcing his eyes back.

Beautiful, serene and utterly Liaden—even as he was utterly Liaden—Syntebra el'Kemin beckoned from the depths of the screen.

That the rest of her person would be as guilesome as her face, he knew. *Knew.* He should in all honor seek out his mother and kneel at her feet in gratitude. Nothing in the Law said that the lady must be comely. Indeed, Korval's own law required merely that a contract-spouse be a pilot, and of vigorous Line—all else as the wind might bring it.

Lower lip caught tight between his teeth, Er Thom stared into the lovely face of his proposed wife, trying to imagine the weight of her hair in his hands, the taste of her small, rosy-gold breasts.

"No!"

The chair clattered back and he was moving, pilot-fast, through the adjoining kitchenette to his bedroom. Fingers shaking, he snatched open his jewel-box, spilling rubies, pearls and other dress-gems carelessly aside. His heart clenched for the instant he thought it gone—and then he found it, stuffed into a far corner, half-hidden by a platinum cloak pin.

A scrap of red silk no longer than his hand, that was all. That, and a length of tarnished, gold-colored ribbon, elaborately knotted into a fraying flower, through which the red silk had been lovingly threaded.

"It is not possible," he whispered again, and lay his cheek against the tarnished flower, blinking back tears that might stain the silk. He swallowed.

"I will not wed."

Fine words, the part of him that was master trader and a'th-odelm and heir to the delm jeered. *And what of duty to the Clan, not to mention the Law and, easing of one's mother's pain?*

If there is one your heart has set above all others . . . his mother pleaded from memory and Er Thom's fingers clenched convulsively on the scrap of silk. She would never—he dared not—It was against everything: Code, custom, clan—duty.

He took a deep breath, trying to calm his racing thoughts. The clan required this thing of him, the clan's dutiful child, in balance for all the clan had thus far given him. It was just. The other—was some strange undutiful madness that should after so many years have passed off. That it remained in this unexpectedly virulent form told a tale of Er Thom yos'Galan's sad lack of discipline. He would put the madness aside once and forever, now. He would burn the silk and the tawdry ribbon, then he would read the file on Syntebra el'Kemin, bathe and dress himself for Prime Meal. He would tell his parent—

Tears overflowed and he bowed his head, fingers tenderly bracketing the red and gold token.

Tell his parent what? That for three years, steadfast in his refusal of all prospective spouses he had likewise taken no lover nor even shared a night of bed-pleasure? That new faces and old alike failed to stir him? That his body seemed to exist at some distance from where he himself lived and went about the work that the clan required of him? That food tasted of cobwebs and wine of vinegar and duty alone forced him to eat sufficient to fuel his cold, distant body?

Tell his mother that, Er Thom thought wretchedly, and she would have him to the Healers, quick as a blink.

And the Healers would make him forget all that stood in the way of duty.

He considered forgetfulness—such a little bit of time, really, to be erased from memory, and so very—long—ago.

The thought sickened him, nearly as much as the face of the woman his mother proposed to make his wife.

He blinked his eyes and straightened, slipping the rag of silk and the frazzled ribbon into his sleeve-pocket. Carefully, he put his jewelry back into the box and lowered the heavy carved lid.

In the office, he saved Syntebra el'Kemin's data to his pending file, and left a message for his mother, expressing regret that he would not be with her for Prime.

Then he quit the room, shrugging into the worn leather jacket that proclaimed him a pilot.

The papers on his worktable rustled irritably in the breeze from the open window and across the valley the first stars of evening glittered just above the Tree.

CHAPTER TWO

∞∞∞∞∞∞∞∞∞∞∞∞∞∞∞∞∞∞∞∞∞∞∞∞∞∞∞∞∞∞∞∞∞∞∞

The giving of nubiath'a, *the parting-gift, by either partner signals the end of an affair of pleasure. The person of impeccable* melant'i *will offer and accept* nubiath'a *with gentleness and grace, thereafter referring to the affair by neither word nor deed.*

—Excerpted from the *Liaden Code of Proper Conduct*

"**I SURMISE THAT** the lady is a two-headed ogre—and ill-tempered, besides?" Daav yos'Phelium splashed *misravot* into a crystal cup and handed it aside.

"Another face entirely," Er Thom murmured, accepting the cup and swirling the contents in counterfeit calm, while his pulses pounded, frenzied. "The lady is—very—beautiful."

"Hah." Daav poured himself a cup of the pale blue wine and assayed a sip, black eyes quizzing Er Thom over the crystal rim.

"Your mother, my aunt, exerts herself on your behalf. When shall I have the felicity of wishing you happy?"

"I have not—that is—" Er Thom stammered to a halt and raised his cup to taste the wine.

In general, he was not as fond of *misravot* as was his brother, finding the burnt cinnamon taste of the wine cloyed rather than refreshed. But this evening he had a second sip, dawdling over it, while his mind skipped in uncharacteristic confusion from this thought to that.

He sighed when at last he lowered the cup, and raised his head to meet his brother's clever eyes.

"Daav?"

"Yes, *denubia*. How may I serve you?"

Er Thom touched his tongue to his lips, tasting cinnamon. "I— am in need. Of a ship."

One dark eyebrow arched. "Is it ill-natured to recall," Daav wondered, "that you are captain of a rather—substantial—ship?"

"A quicker ship—smaller," Er Thom said swiftly, suddenly unable to control his agitation. He spun away and paced toward the game table, where he stood looking down at the counterchance board, dice and counters all laid to hand. Had things been otherwise, he and Daav might even now be sitting over the board, sharpening their wits and their daring, one against the other.

"There is a matter," he said, feeling his brother's eyes burning into his back. He turned, his face open and plain for this, the dearest of his kin, to read. He cleared his throat. "A matter I must resolve. Before I wed."

"I see," Daav said dryly, brows drawn. "A matter which requires your presence urgently off-world, eh? Do I learn from this that you will finally assay that which has darkened your heart these past several *relumma*?"

Er Thom froze, staring speechless at his brother, though he should, he told himself, barely wonder. Daav was delm, charged with the welfare of all within Clan Korval. Before duty had called him home, he had also been a Scout, with sensibilities fine-tuned by rigorous training. How could he not have noticed his brother's distress? It spoke volumes of his *melant'i* that he had not taxed Er Thom with the matter before now.

"Have you spoken to your thodelm of this?" Daav asked quietly.

Er Thom gave a flick of his fingers, signaling negative. "I— would prefer—not to have the Healers."

"And so you come on the eve of being affianced to demand the

Delm's Own Ship, that you may go off-planet and reach resolution."
He grinned, for such would appeal to his sense of mischief, where it
only chilled Er Thom with horror, that necessity required him to fly
in the face of propriety.

"You will swear," Daav said, in a surprising shift from the Low
Tongue in which they most commonly conversed to the High
Tongue, in the mode of Delm to Clanmember.

Er Thom bowed low: Willing Obedience to the Delm. "Korval."

"You will swear that, should you fail of resolution by the end of
this *relumma*, you shall return to Liad and place yourself in the care
of the Healers."

The current *relumma* was nearly half-done. Still, Er Thom
assured himself around a surge of coldness, the thing ought take no
longer. He bowed once more, acquiescence to the Delm's Word.

"Korval, I do swear."

"So." Daav reached into the pocket of his house-robe and
brought out a silver key-ring clasped with an enameled dragon.
"Quick passage, *denubia*. May the luck guide you to your heart's
desire."

Er Thom took the ring, fingers closing tightly around it as his
eyes filled with tears. He bowed gratitude and affection.

"My thanks—" he began, but Daav waved a casual hand, back in
the Low Tongue.

"Yes, yes—I know. Consider that you have said everything
proper. Go carefully, eh? Send word. And for the gods' love leave me
something to tell your mother."

"GOOD-NIGHT, SHANNIE." Anne Davis bent and kissed her
son's warm cheek. "Sleep tight."

He smiled sleepily, light blue eyes nearly closed. "'night, Ma,"
he muttered, nestling into the pillow. His breathing evened out
almost at once and Anne experienced the vivid inner conviction that
her child was truly asleep.

Still, she hung over the truckle-bed, watching him. She extended
a hand to brush the silky white hair back from his forehead, used
one careful finger to trace the winging eyebrows—his father's look

there, she thought tenderly, though the rest of Shan's look seemed taken undiluted from herself, poor laddie. But there, she had never hankered after a pretty child. Only after her own.

She smiled softly and breathed a whisper-kiss against his hair, unnecessarily fussed over the quilt and finally left the tiny bedroom, pulling the door partly shut behind her.

In the great room, she settled at her desk, long, clever fingers dancing over the computer keyboard, calling up the student work queue. She stifled a sigh: Thirty final papers to be graded. An exam to be written and also graded. And then a whole semester of freedom.

More or less.

Shaking her head, she called up the first paper and took the light-pen firmly in hand.

She waded through eight with the utter concentration that so amused her friends and enraged her colleagues, coming back to reality only because a cramped muscle in her shoulder finally shouted protest loudly enough to penetrate the work-blur.

"Umm. Break-time, Annie Davis," she told herself, pulling her six-foot frame into a high, luxurious stretch. Middling-tall for a Terran, still her outstretched fingers brushed the room's ceiling. *Bureaucratic penny-pinchers,* she thought, as she always did. *How much would it have cost to raise the ceiling two inches?*

It was a puzzle without an answer and having asked it, she forgot it and padded into the kitchen for a glass of juice.

Shan was still asleep, she knew. She sipped her juice and leaned a hip against the counter top, closing her eyes to let her mind roam.

She had met him on Proziski, where she had been studying base-level language shift on a departmental grant. Port Master Brellick Gare himself, a friend of Richard's, had invited her to the gala open house, sugaring the bait with the intelligence that there would be "real, live Liadens" at the party.

Brellick knew her passion for Liaden lit—Liadens themselves were fabulously rare at the levels in which Terran professors commonly moved. Anne had taken the bait—and met her Liaden.

She had seen him first from across the room—a solemn, slender young man made fragile by Brellick Gare's bulk. The introduction had been typically Gare.

"Anne, this is Er Thom yos'Galan. Er Thom, be nice to Anne, okay? She's not used to parties." Brellick grinned into her frown. "I'd show you around myself, girl-o, but I'm host. You stick close to this one, though, he's got more manners than a load of orangutans." And with that he lumbered off, leaving Anne to glare daggers into his back before glancing in acute embarrassment toward her unfortunate partner.

Violet eyes awash with amusement looked up into hers from beneath winging golden brows. "What do you suppose," he asked in accented Terran, "an orangutan is?"

"Knowing Brellick, it's something horrible," Anne returned with feeling. "I apologize for my friend, Mr. yos'Galan. There's not the slightest need for you to—*babysit* me."

"At least allow me to find you a glass of wine," he said in his soft, sweet voice, slipping a slim golden hand under her elbow and effortlessly steering her into the depths of the crowd. "Your name is Anne? But there must be something more than that, eh? Anne what?"

So she had told him her surname, and her profession and what she hoped to discover on Proziski. She also let him find her not one but several glasses of wine, and go in with her to dinner and, later, out onto the dance floor. And by the time the party began to thin it had seemed not at all unnatural for Er Thom yos'Galan to see her home.

He accepted her invitation to come inside for a cup of coffee and an hour later gently accepted an invitation to spend the night in her bed.

She bent to kiss him then, and found him unexpectedly awkward. So she kissed him again, patiently, then teasingly, until he lost his awkwardness all at once and answered her with a passion that left them both shivering and breathless.

They hadn't gotten to the bed, not the first time. The rickety couch had been sturdy enough to bear them and Er Thom surprised again—an experienced and considerate lover, with hands, gods, with hands that knew every touch her body yearned for, and gave it, unstinting.

Time and again, he came back to her lips, as if to hone his skill. When at last she wrapped her legs around him and pulled him into her, he bent again and put his mouth over hers, using his tongue to echo each thrust until her climax triggered his and their lips were torn apart, freeing cries of wonder.

"Oh, dear." Anne set the juice glass aside, moving sharply away from the counter and wrapping her arms around herself in a tight hug. "Oh, dear."

He was gone, of course. She had known he would go when the trade mission had completed its task, even as she would go when her study time had elapsed.

But it had been glorious while it had lasted—a grand and golden three-month adventure in a life dedicated to a calm round of teaching and study and research.

Shan was the living reminder of that grand adventure—of her own will and desire. She had never told Er Thom her intention to bear his child, though it seemed she told him everything else about herself. Shan was hers.

She sighed and turned, half-blind, to put the glass properly in the rack to be washed. Then she went into the great room and shut the computer down, shaking her head over the double work to be done tomorrow.

Crossing the room, she made certain the door was locked. Then she turned off the light and slipped into the bedroom, to spend the rest of the night staring at the invisible ceiling, listening to her son breathe.

ER THOM had not come to Prime.

Oh, he had sent word, as a dutiful child should, and begged her pardon most charmingly. But that he should absent himself from Prime Meal on the day when he was to have agreed at last to wed could not fail to infuriate.

And Petrella was furious.

Furious, she had consigned the meal composed of her son's

favorite dishes to the various devils of fifteen assorted hells, and supped on a spicy bowl of *gelth*, thin toast and strong red wine, after which she had stumped off to her office on the arm of Mr. pak'Ora, the butler, and composed a sizzling letter to her heir.

She was in the process of refining this document when the comm-line buzzed.

"Well?" she snapped, belatedly slapping the toggle that engaged the view-screen.

"Well, indeed." Her nephew, Daav yos'Phelium, inclined his head gravely. "How kind of you to ask. I hope I find you the same, Aunt Petrella?"

She glared at him. "I suppose you've finally stirred yourself to call and allow me to know your *cha'leket* my son has dined with you and that you are now both well into your cups and about to initiate a third round of counterchance?"

Daav lifted an eyebrow. "How delightful that would be! Alas, that I disturb your peace for an entirely different matter."

"So." She eyed him consideringly. "And what might that matter be?"

Daav shook his dark hair out of his eyes, the barbaric silver twist swinging in his right ear.

"I call to allow you to know that my *cha'leket* your son has gone off-world in the quest of resolving urgent business."

"Urgent business!" She nearly spat the words. "There is a contract-marriage dancing on the knife's edge and he goes off-planet?" She caught a hard breath against the starting of pain in her chest and finished somewhat more calmly. "I suppose you know nothing about the alliance about to be transacted with Clan Nexon?"

"On the contrary," Daav said gently, "I am entirely aware of the circumstance. Perhaps I have failed of making myself plain: The delm has allowed Er Thom yos'Galan the remainder of the *relumma* to resolve a matter he presents as urgent."

"What is urgent," Petrella told him, "is that he wed and provide the clan with his heir. This is a matter of Line, my Delm, and well you know it!"

"Well I know it," he agreed blandly. "Well I also know that any clan wishing to ally itself with Korval may easily accommodate half-a-*relumma*'s delay. However, I suggest you begin inquiry among our cousins and affiliates, in order to identify others who may be available to wed the lady and cement the alliance with Clan Nexon."

"For that matter," Petrella said spitefully, "it happens that the delm is yet without issue."

Daav inclined his head. "I shall be honored to review the lady's file. But ask among the cousins, do." He smiled, sudden and charming. "Come, Aunt Petrella, every trader knows the value of a secondary plan!"

"And why should I have a secondary when the prime plan is all-important? You are meddling in matters of Line, my Delm, as I have already stated. Chapter six, paragraph twenty-seven of the Code clearly outlines—"

Daav held up a hand. "If you wish to quote chapter and page to me, Aunt, recall that I have the longest memory in the clan."

She grinned. "Could that be a threat, nephew?"

"Now, Aunt Petrella, would I threaten you?"

"Yes," she said with a certain grim relish, "you would."

"Hah." His eyes gleamed with appreciation, then he inclined his head. "In that wise, aunt, and all else being in balance—ask among the cousins—feel free to contact Mr. dea'Gauss, should the enterprise put you out of pocket. In the meanwhile, the delm is confident of the return of Er Thom yos'Galan by *relumma*'s end. As you should be."

Petrella said nothing, though she wisely refrained from snorting.

Daav smiled. "Good-night, Aunt Petrella. Rest well."

"Good-night, child," she returned and cut the connection.

CHAPTER THREE

"Of course you are my friend—my most dear, my beloved . . ." Shan el'Thrasin leaned close and cupped her face in his two hands, as if they were kin, or lifemates.

"I will love you always," he whispered, and saw the fear fade from her beautiful eyes. Achingly tender, he bent and kissed her.

"I will never forget . . ." she sighed, nestling her face into his shoulder.

"Nor will I," he promised, holding her close as he slipped the knife clear. No whisper of blade against sheath must warn her, he told himself sternly. No quiver of his own pain must reach her; she was his love, though she had killed his partner. He would rather die than cause her an instant's distress.

The knife was very sharp. She stirred a little as it slid between her ribs, and sighed, very softly, when it found her heart.

—From "The Trickster Across the Galaxy: A Retrospect"

"JERZY, YOU'RE A DOLL," Anne said gratefully.

Her friend grinned from the depths of the comm-screen and shook his head. "Wrongo. *He's* the doll. I love this kid. Name the price; I gotta have him."

Anne laughed. "Not for sale. But I'll let you watch him tonight. Purely as a favor to you, understand." She sobered. "How about letting me do a favor in return? We're getting a little top-heavy, here."

"What're you, Liaden? Take some advice and skip that meeting. Go home, eat something sexy, glass of wine, play yourself a lullaby and go to sleep. Tomorrow's your study day, right? Jerzy will deliver kid latish in the a.m. If I don't decide to steal him, instead."

"Jerzy—"

"Enough, already! Seeya tomorrow." The screen went blank.

Anne sighed, closed the line at her end and sat looking at the screen long after the glow had faded into dead gray.

There had to be a better way, she thought, not for the first time. Certainly, there were worse ways than the path she was pursuing— the Central University creche leapt forcibly to mind, with its sign-in sheets and its sign-out sheets and its tidy rows of tidy cribs and its tidy, meek babies all dressed in tidy, identical rompers. Horrible, antiseptic, unloving place—just like the other one had been.

She was doing all right, she assured herself, given the help of friends like Jerzy. But she hated to impose on her friends, good-natured as they were. Even more she hated the hours she was of necessity away from her son, so many hours a day, so many days a week. She was growing to resent her work, the demands of departmental meetings, class preparations. Her research was beginning to slack off—fatal in the publish-or-perish university system. Her allotted study days more and more often became "Shan days" while she tried to cram the work that needed to be done into late nights and early mornings, using her home terminal to the maximum, piling up user fees she could have easily avoided by using her assigned terminal at the Research Center.

Abruptly, she stood and began to gather her things together. Her own mother had been a pilot, gone six months of every local year, leaving her son and daughter in the care of various relatives and, one year, at the New Dublin Home for Children.

Anne shuddered, scattering a careful stack of data cards. That had been the worst year. She and Richard had been sequestered in separate dorms, allowed one comm call between them every ten days. They had found ways to sneak away after lights-out, to hold hands and talk family talk. But sneaking away was against the rules, punishable, when they were inevitably caught, by hard labor, by imposed silence, by ostracism. The year had seemed forever, with their mother's ship long overdue, and Anne certain it was lost . . .

She looked down at her clenched fists, puzzled. It had all been so long ago. Her mother had died three years ago, peacefully in her bed. Richard was a pilot in his own right, and his last letter had been full of someone named Rosie, whose parents he was soon to meet. And Anne was a professor of comparative linguistics, with several scholarly publications to her name, teaching a Liaden Lit seminar that was filled to capacity every session.

Anne shook her head and wearily bent to pick up the scattered cards. Jerzy was right; she was tired. She needed a good meal, a full night's sleep. She'd been pushing things a little too hard lately. She needed to remember to relax, that was all. Then, everything would be fine.

WEARILY, Er Thom climbed the curving marble staircase that led to the Administrative Center for University's Northern Campus. It was slightly warmer in the building than it had been outside, but still cool to one used to Liad's planetary springtime. He left his leather pilot's jacket sealed as he approached the round marble counter displaying the Terran graphic for "Information."

A Terran woman of indeterminate years came to the counter as he approached. She had a plenitude of dark hair, worn carelessly loose, as if fresh-tousled from bed, and her shirt was cut low across an ample bosom. She leaned her elbows on the pinkish marble and grinned at him.

"Hi, there. What can I do for you?" she asked, casually, and with emphasis on "you".

He bowed as between equals—a flattery—and offered a slight smile of his own.

"I am looking for a friend," he said, taking extreme care with the mode-less and rough Terran words. "Her name is Anne Davis. Her field is comparative linguistics. I regret that I do not know the name of the department in which she serves."

"Well, you're on the right campus, anyhow," the woman said cheerfully. "You got her ident number, retinal pattern, anything like that?"

"I regret," Er Thom repeated.

She shook her head so the tousled dark curls danced. "I'll see if it flies, friend, but it's not much to go on with the size of the faculty we've got . . ." She moved away, muttering things much like her counterparts in the East and West offices had muttered. A few meters down-counter she stopped and began to ply the keypad set there, frowning at the screen suspended level with her eyes. "Let's see . . . Davis, Davis, Anne . . ." She turned her head, calling out to him over her shoulder. "Is that 'Anne' with an 'e' or not?"

He stared at her, unable to force his weary mind to analyze and make sense of the question. "I—beg your pardon."

"Your friend," the clerk said, patiently. "Does she spell her name with an 'e' or without an 'e'?"

An "e" was the fifth letter of the Terran alphabet. Surely, he thought, half-panicked, surely he had at some time seen Anne's written name? He closed his eyes, saw the old-fashioned ink pen held firmly in long, graceful fingers, sweeping a signature onto the mauve pages of an ambassadorial guest book.

"A—" he spelled out of memory for the clerk's benefit. "n, n, e. D, a, v, i, s."

"Hokay." She turned back to her board as Er Thom opened his eyes, feeling oddly shaken.

The clerk muttered to herself—he paid her no mind. Terran naming systems, he thought distractedly, Terran alphabet, and, gods help him, a Terran woman, bold and brilliant—*alien*. But a woman still, with Terran blood in her and genes so far outside the Book of Clans that—

"Okay!"

Er Thom shook himself out of his reverie as the clerk's cry of jubilation penetrated, and stepped forward.

"Yes?"

She looked up at him, lashes fluttering, and he saw that she was not so young as he had thought. Cosmetics had been used to simulate the dewy blush of first youth across her cheek and her eyes were artfully painted, with silver sequins sprinkled across her lashes. Er Thom schooled his face to calm politeness. Local custom, he reminded himself sternly. As a trader he dealt with local custom in many guises on many worlds. So on this world faces were painted. Merely custom, and nothing to distress one.

"Don't know if this is your friend or not," the woman was saying, "but she's the only Davis in Comparative Ling. Wait a sec, here's the card." She frowned at it before handing it over. "Lives in Quad S-two-seven-squared. You know where that is?"

"No," he said, clutching the card tightly.

The woman stood, leaning over the counter to point. Her breasts flattened against the marble, and swelled toward the margin of the low-cut blouse. Er Thom turned to look along the line of her finger.

"Go back out the way you came," she told him, "turn right, walk about four hundred yards. You'll see a sign for the surrey. Go down the stairs and hit the summonplate. When the surrey comes, you sit down and code in *this* right here, see?" She ran her finger under a string of letters and numbers on the card he held.

"Yes, I see."

"Okay. Then you lean back and enjoy the ride. The surrey stops, you get out and go upstairs. You'll be in a big open space—Quad S. Best thing to do then is either ask one of the residents to help you find the address or go to the Quad infobooth, punch up your friend's code—that's right under the name, there—and tell her to come get you. Clear?"

"Thank you," said Er Thom, bowing thanks and remembering to give a smile. Terrans set great store by smiles, where a Liaden person would merely have kept his face neutral and allowed the bow to convey all that was necessary.

"That's Okay," said the woman, flashing her silvered lashes. "If your friend's not home, or if it turns out it's *not* your friend, come on back and I'll see if I can help you some more."

There was an unmistakable note of invitation there. Hastily, Er Thom reviewed his actions, trying to determine if he had inadvertently signaled a wish for her intimate companionship. As far as he could determine, he had indicated no such thing, unless the smile was to blame. Bland-faced, he bowed once more: gratitude for service well-given, nothing else.

"Thank you," he said, keeping his voice carefully neutral. He turned on his heel and walked away.

Behind him, the Information clerk watched him wistfully, twining her fingers in her hair.

THE SURREY RIDE was longer than he had expected from the clerk's explanation. Er Thom sat rigid in the slippery plastic chair, clutching the thin plastic card and occasionally looking down at it.

"Anne Davis," the Terran letters read. "ID: 7596277483ZQ." He committed the ID to memory, then the Quad code, department number and assignment berth. It did not take long; he had a good head for cargo stats, manifest numbers and piloting equations. After checking himself three times, he put the card in his belt-pocket with infinite care and tried to relax in the too-large, Terran-sized seat, hands tightly folded on his knee.

It had been a weary long trip from Liad to University—three Jumps, which he had taken, recklessly, one after the other, pushing the reactions and the stamina of a master pilot to their limits. And at the end of that reckless journey, this endless day of searching, campus to campus, through a bureaucracy that spanned an entire planet—

To this place. Very soon now he would see Anne—speak to her. He would—for the last time in his life—break with the Code and put his *melant'i* at peril.

He would speak to one to whom he had given *nubiath'a*. The heart recoiled, no matter that necessity existed. Necessity *did* exist— his own, and shame to him, that he use his necessity to disturb the peace of one who was not of his clan.

A tone sounded in the little cab, and a yellow light flashed on the board. "Approaching Quad S. Prepare to disembark," a man's pleasant voice instructed him.

Er Thom slid forward on the seat as the surrey slowed. He was on his feet the instant the door slid open and had run halfway up the automated stairs by the time it closed behind him.

The local sun was setting, bathing the tall buildings that enclosed the quad in pale orange light. Er Thom stopped and looked about him, spinning slowly on one heel, suddenly and acutely aware of his empty hands. It was improper of him to go giftless to an evening call; he had not thought.

There must be shops, he thought. *Mustn't there?*

A group of four tall persons was crossing the Quad a few yards to his right. He stretched his legs to catch them, fishing in his belt for the plastic card.

His dilemma produced a slight altercation among three of his potential aides. It seemed that there were several ways to arrive at the dwelling indicated; the question addressed was which of several was the "best" way. Er Thom stood to one side, having rescued his card from one gesticulating well-wisher, and tried to cultivate patience. He heard a low laugh and turned to look at the fourth member of the party, a shortish Terran male—though still a head taller than Er Thom—with merry dark eyes and a disreputable round face.

"Listen to that bunch and you'll get lost for sure," he said, dismissing his companions with a flutter of his fingers. "I live a couple halls down from your friend's place. I don't guarantee it's the *best* way, but if you follow me, I can get you there."

"Thank you," said Er Thom, with relief. "And—I regret the inconvenience—if there would be a shop selling wine?"

"Oh, sure," said his guide, turning left. "There's the Block Deli, right where we get the lift. Step this way, and keep an eye out for falling philosophers."

CHAPTER FOUR

Relations between Liad and Terra have never been cordial, though there have been periods of lesser and greater strain. Liad prefers to thrash Terra roundly in the field of galactic trade—a terrain it shaped—while Terra gives birth to this and that Terran-supremacist faction, whose mischief seems always to stop just short of actual warfare.

**—From "The Struggle for Fair Trade,"
doctoral dissertation of Indrew Jorman,
published by Archive Press, University**

THE SURREY'S *ding* woke her; she got a grip on her briefcase and went up the autostairs in a fog.

On the Quad, the sharp night breeze roused her and she stopped to stretch cramped leg and back muscles, staring up into a sky thick with stars. It was a very different night sky than Proziski's, with its gaggle of moons. She and Er Thom had counted those moons one night, lying naked next to each other on the roof of the unfinished Mercantile Building, the end of a bolt of trade-silk serving as coverlet and mattress. She liked to think Shan had come from that night.

She shook her head at the laden sky and took one last deep breath before turning toward the block that held her apartment.

She walked past the darkened deli and rode the lift to the seventh floor, trying to remember if she had eaten the last roll that morning for breakfast. She recalled a cup of coffee, gulped between feeding Shan and getting him ready for his trip to Jerzy's place. She remembered having to go back for her notes for the afternoon's lecture.

She didn't remember eating breakfast at all, and she had been too busy with a promising research line to break off for lunch . . .

Anne sighed. *You need a keeper,* she told herself severely. The lift door cycled and she stepped out into the hallway.

A slim figure turned from before her door and began to walk toward her, keeping scrupulously to the center of the hall, where the lights were brightest. Anne hesitated, cataloging bright hair, slender stature, leather jacket—

"Er Thom." She barely heard her own whisper, hardly knew that she had increased her stride, until she was almost running toward him.

He met her halfway, extending a slim golden hand on which his amethyst master trader's ring blazed. She caught his fingers in hers and stood looking down at him, wide mouth curved in a smile no dimmer than the one he had treasured, all this time.

"Er Thom," she said in her rich, lilting voice. "I'm so very happy to see you, my friend."

Happy. What a small word, to describe the dazzling, dizzying joy that threatened to engulf him. He hung onto her hand, though it would have been more proper to bow. "I am—happy—to see you, also," he managed, smiling up into her eyes. "They keep you working late . . ."

She laughed. "A departmental meeting—it dragged on and on! I can't imagine what they found to talk about." She sobered. "Have you been waiting long?"

"Not very long." Hours. He had despaired a dozen times; walked away and returned two dozen . . . three . . . He showed her the bag he held. "Are you hungry? I have food, wine."

"My thoughtful friend. *Starved.* Come in." She tugged on his hand, turning him back toward the anonymous door that marked her dwelling place. "How long are you stopping, Er Thom?"

He hesitated and she looked at him closely.

"More than just today? Don't tell me that stupid meeting has kept me away for half your visit!"

"No." He smiled up at her. "I do not know how long I am staying, you see. It depends upon—circumstances."

"Oh," she said wisely, "*circumstances.*" She let go his hand and lay her palm against the door's lockplate. With a grand, meaningless flourish, she bowed him across the threshold.

Just within and to one side, he stopped to watch her cross the room, past the shrouded half-chora to the wall-desk, where she lay her briefcase down with a sigh. It struck him that she moved less gracefully than he recalled, and nearly gasped at the sharpness of his concern.

"Anne?" He was at her elbow in a flicker, searching her face. "Are you well?"

She smiled. "Just tired, my dear—that absurd meeting." She reached out, touching his cheek lightly with the tips of her fingers. "Er Thom, it's so good to see you."

He allowed the caress. Kin and lifemates alone touched thus: face-to-face, hand-to-face. He had never told her so; he did not tell her now. He turned his face into her palm and felt the icy misery in his chest begin to thaw.

"It is good to see you, also," he murmured, hearing the pounding of his heart, wanting—wanting . . . He shifted slightly away and held up the bag. "You are tired. I will pour you wine—is that proper?— and you will sit and rest. All right? Then I will bring you some of this to eat." He pointed to a dark alcove to the right. "That is the kitchen?"

She laughed, shaking her head. "That's the kitchen. But, my friend, it can't be proper to put a guest to work."

"It is no trouble," he told her earnestly. "Please, I wish to."

"All right," she said, astonished and bewildered at the way her eyes filled with tears. "Thank you. You're very kind."

"Rest," he murmured and disappeared into the kitchen corner. The light came on, adding to the dim illumination of the living area. Anne sighed. There were signs of neglect everywhere: dust, scattered books and papers, discarded pens. Under the easy chair a fugitive rubber block crouched, defiant.

She turned her back on it deliberately, pulled off her jacket and curled into a corner of the couch, long legs under her, head resting on the back cushions. She heard small sounds from the kitchen as Er Thom opened and closed cabinets. The air filtering unit thrummed into sluggish life . . .

"Anne?"

She gasped, head jerking up. Er Thom bit his lip, violet eyes flashing down to the glass he held and back to her face.

"I am inconvenient," he said solemnly, inclining his head. "Perhaps I may come again to see you. When you are less tired. Tell me."

"No." Her changeable face registered guilt, even panic. "Er Thom, I'm sorry to be a bad host. I'd like you to stay. Please. You're not *inconvenient*—never that, my dear. And if you leave now and your circumstances mesh, then you might not be able to come again. You could be gone again tomorrow."

He set the glass aside, caught the hand she half-extended and allowed himself to be drawn down to sit beside her.

"Anne . . ." Fascinated, he watched his fingers rise to her cheek, stroke lightly and ever-so-slowly down the square jaw line to the firm chin.

"All will be well," he said, soothing her with his voice as if she were a child instead of a woman grown. "I will be here tomorrow, Anne. Certainly tomorrow. And you—my friend, you are exhausted. It would be wrong—improper—to insist you entertain me in such a case. I will go and come back again. Tomorrow, if you like. Only tell me."

Her eyes closed and she bent her head, half-hiding her face from him. He held onto her hand and she did not withdraw it, though her free hand stole upward, fingers wrapping around the pendant at the base of her throat.

Er Thom's eyes widened. She wore the parting-gift, even now; touched it as if it were capable of giving comfort. And he, he here by her, *touching* her, speaking on terms that would lead any to assume them lovers, if not bound more closely still.

The magnitude of his error staggered; the cause that had brought him here suddenly showing the face of self-deception. He should never have given Anne *nubiath'a*.

He should never have sought her out again . . .

"Er Thom?" She was looking at him, dark brown eyes large in a face he thought paler than it might be.

"Yes, my friend?" he murmured and smiled for her. Whatever errors were found in this time and place were solely his own, he told himself sternly. Anne, at least, had behaved with utmost propriety.

"I—I know that I'm not very entertaining right now," she said with a tentativeness wholly unAnne-like, "but—unless you have somewhere else you need—would rather be—I'd *like* you to stay."

"There is no other place I wish to be," he said—and that was truth, gods pity him, though he could think of a dozen places he might otherwise be needed, not forgetting his mother's drawing room and the bridge of the trade ship orbiting Liad.

He picked up the wineglass and placed it in her hand as he rose. "Drink your wine, my friend. I will be back in a moment with food."

IT WAS SOME TIME LATER, after the odd sweet-spicy food was eaten and the wine, but for the little remaining in their glasses, was drunk, before she thought to ask him.

"But, Er Thom, what are you doing on University? Another trade mission? There isn't anything to trade for here, is there?"

"To trade for? No . . ." He took a sip of the sticky yellow wine, then, with sudden decision, finished the glass.

"I am not here to trade," he told her, watching as if from a distance as his traitor body slid closer to her on the sofa and his hand lifted to fondle her hair. "What I am doing is seeing you."

She laughed softly as she set aside her glass. "Of course you are," she murmured, gently mocking.

She did not believe him! Panic galvanized him. She *must* believe, or all he had meant to accomplish by this mad breaking with custom was gone for naught. The Healers would take him, and reft him of distress, and it would be forgot, unknown, lost in a swirl of blurry dreaming . . .

His fingers tightened in her hair, pulling her down as he tipped his face up to hers, hungrily, despairingly.

She came willingly, as she ever had, her mouth firm and sweet on his, calling forth the desire, the need, that had been touched by no other, before or since. The need that burned away names, clans and duty, leaving only she . . . and he.

LATER YET, and she asleep. Er Thom shifted onto an elbow, letting the light from the living area fall past his shoulder and onto her.

A Liaden would not count her beautiful. He believed that even among Terrans she was considered but moderately attractive. Certainly her face was too full for Liaden taste, her nose too long, her mouth too wide, her skin merely brown, not golden. And while chestnut was a very pretty color for hair, Anne wore hers with an eye to ease of care.

The rest of her was as strange to the standard of beauty he acknowledged: Her breasts, brown as her face and rosy brown at the very tips, were round and high, larger than his hand could encompass. She was saved from being top-heavy by the width of her hips, flaring unexpectedly from a narrow waist, and she moved with a pilot's smooth grace. Her hands were long-fingered and strong— musician's hands—and her voice was quite lovely.

He thought of the face of the latest proposed to him: Properly Liaden, well-mannered and golden. A person who understood duty, who would do as she was bid by her delm. And who would very properly rebuke Er Thom yos'Galan, should he but reach out a finger to trace the line of her cheek, or lay his lips against hers.

But I do not want her! he thought, plaintive, childish, undutiful— strange. As strange as lying here in this present, in a too-large bed, his arms about a woman not of his kind, who expected him to sleep next to her the night full through; to be there when she awoke . . .

Carefully, he slid down until his eyes were on a level with her closed eyes. For a long while, he stared into her unbeautiful, alien face, watching—guarding—her sleep. Finally, he moved his head to kiss her just-parted lips and said at last the thing he had come to tell her, the thing which must not be forgotten.

"I love you, Anne Davis."

His voice was soft and not quite steady, and he stumbled over the Terran words, but it hardly mattered. She was asleep and did not hear him.

CHAPTER FIVE

Melant'i—A Liaden word denoting the status of a person within a given situation. For instance, one person may fulfill several roles: Parent, spouse, child, mechanic, thodelm. The shifting winds of circumstance, or 'necessity,' dictate from which role the person will act this time. They will certainly always act honorably, as defined within a voluminous and painfully detailed code of behavior, referred to simply as 'The Code.'

To a Liaden, melant'i is more precious than rubies, a cumulative, ever-changing indicator of his place in the universal pecking order. A person of high honor, for instance, is referred to as "a person of melant'i," whereas a scoundrel—or a Terran—may be dismissed with "he has no melant'i."

Melant'i may be the single philosophical concept from which all troubles, large and small, between Liad and Terra spring.

—From *A Terran's Guide to Liad*

LATE IN THE MORNING, loved and showered and feeling positively decadent, Anne stood in front of the tiny built-in vanity. A few brush-strokes put her shower-dampened hair into order, and she smiled into her own eyes as her reflected fingers found and picked up her pendant.

"Anne?"

She turned, transferring her smile to him. An elfin prince, so Brellick had described him, enticing Anne to meet a real, live Liaden. And elfin he was: Slim and tawny and quick; hair glittering gold, purple eyes huge in a beardless pointed face; voice soft and seductively accented.

The eyes right now were very serious, moving from her hand to her face.

"Anne?" he said again.

"Yes, my dear. What can I do for you?"

"Please," he said slowly, gliding closer to her. "Do not wear that."

"Don't wear—" She blinked at him, looked down at the fine golden chain and pendant seed-pearls, artfully blended with gold-and-enamel leaves to look like a cluster of fantasy grapes.

This is a misunderstanding, she told herself carefully; *a problem with the words chosen.* Er Thom's command of Terran tended to be literal and uneasy of idiom—much like her careful, scholar's Liaden. It made for some interesting conversational tangles, now and then. But they had always been able to untangle themselves, eventually. She looked back into his eyes.

"You gave this to me," she said, holding it out so he might see it better. "Don't you remember, Er Thom? You gave it to me the day *Dutiful Passage*—"

"I remember," he said sharply, cutting her off without a glance at the pearls. He lay a hand lightly on her wrist.

"Anne? Please. It was—it was given to say good-bye. I would rather—may I?—give you another gift."

She laughed a little and lay her hand briefly over his.

"But you won't be here long, will you? And when you leave again, you'll have to give me another gift, for another good-bye . . ." She laughed more fully. "My dear, I'll look like a jewelry store."

The serious look in his eyes seemed to intensify and he swayed closer, so his hip grazed her thigh.

"No," he began, a little breathlessly. "I—there is a thing you must hear, Anne, and never forget—"

The doorbell chimed. Anne glanced up, mouth curving in a curious smile, and raised her fingers to touch his cheek.

"That's Jerzy," she said, laying the pendant back in its carved ivory box. She moved past him toward the living room. "Er Thom, there's someone I want you to meet."

He stood still for a moment, running through a pilot's calming exercise. Then, he went after her.

The man who was coming in from the hallway was not large as Terrans go; he was, in fact, a bit under standard height for that race, and a bit under standard weight, too. He had rough black hair chopped off at the point of his jaw and a pale face made memorable by the thick line of a single brow above a pair of iron-gray eyes. He was carrying a cloth sack over one shoulder and a child on the opposite hip. Both he and the child were wearing jackets; the child also wore a cap.

"Jerzy delivers kid latish in the a.m., as promised. Notice the nobility of spirit which would not allow me to steal him, though I was tempted, ma'am. Sore tempted."

"You're a saint, Jerzy," Anne said gravely, though Er Thom heard the ripple of laughter through her words.

"I'm a lunatic," the young man corrected, bending to set the child on his sturdy legs. He knelt and pulled off the cap, revealing a head of silky, frost-colored hair, and unsealed the little jacket, much hampered by small, busy hands.

"Knock it off, Scooter. This is hard enough without you helping," he muttered and the child gave a peal of laughter.

"Help Scooter!" he cried.

Jerzy snorted. "Regular comedian. Okay, let's get the arms out . . ."

"I can do that, you know," Anne said mildly, but Jerzy had finished his task and stood up, sliding the bag off his shoulder and stuffing the small garments inside.

"And have you think I don't know how to take care of him? I want him back, you know. Say, next week, same time?"

"Jerzy—"

But whatever Anne had meant to say to her friend was interrupted by a shriek of child-laughter as young Scooter flung himself hurly-burly down-room, hands flapping at the level of his ears. Er Thom saw the inexpert feet snag on the carpet and swooped forward, catching the little body as it lost control and swinging him up to straddle a hip.

The child laughed again and grabbed a handful of Er Thom's hair.

"Good catch!" Jerzy cried, clapping his palms together with enthusiasm. "You see this man move?" he asked of no one in particular and then snapped his fingers, coming forward. "You're a pilot, right?"

"Yes," Er Thom admitted, gently working the captured lock of hair loose of the child's fingers.

The young man stopped, head tipped to one side. Then he stuck out one of his big hands in the way that Terrans did when they wanted to initiate the behavior known as "shaking hands." Inwardly, Er Thom sighed. Local custom.

He was saved from this particular bout with custom by the perpetrator himself, who lowered his hand, looking self-conscious. "Never mind. Won't do to drop Scooter, will it? I'm Jerzy Entaglia. Theater Arts. Chairman of Theater Arts, which gives you an idea of the shape the department's in."

An introduction. Very good. Er Thom inclined his head, taking care that the child on his hip did not capture another handful of hair. "Er Thom yos'Galan Clan Korval."

Jerzy Entaglia froze, an arrested expression on his forgettable face. "yos'Galan?" he said, voice edging upward in an exaggerated question-mark.

Er Thom lifted his eyebrows. "Indeed."

"Well," said Jerzy, backing up so rapidly Er Thom thought *he* might take a tumble. "That's great! The two of you probably have a lot to talk about—get to know each other, that kind of stuff. Anne—seeya later. Gotta run. 'Bye, Scooter—Mr. yos'Galan—" He was gone, letting himself out the door a moment before Anne's hand fell on his shoulder.

"Bye, bye, bye!" the child sang, beating his heels against Er Thom's flank. He wriggled, imperatively. "Shan go."

"Very well." He bent and placed the child gently on his feet, offering an arm for support.

The boy looked up to smile, showing slanting frosty eyebrows to match the white hair, and eyes of so light a blue they seemed silver, huge in the small brown face. "Shank you," he said with a certain dignity and turned to go about his business.

He was restrained by a motherly hand, which caught him by a shoulder and brought him back to face Er Thom.

"This is someone very important," she said, but it was not clear if she was talking to the boy or to himself. She looked up, her eyes bright, face lit with such a depth of pride that he felt his own heart lift with it.

"Er Thom," she said, voice thrilling with joy, "this is Shan yos'Galan."

"yos'Galan?" He stared at her; looked down at the child, who gazed back at him out of alert silver eyes.

"yos'Galan?" he repeated, unable to believe that she would—without contract, without the Delm's Word, without—He took a breath, ran the pilot's calming sequence; looked back at Anne, the joy in her face beginning to show an edge of unease.

"This is—our—child?" he asked, trying to keep his voice steady, his face politely distant. Perhaps he had misunderstood. Local custom, after all—and who would so blatantly disregard proper behavior, *melant'i, honor* . . .

Relief showed in her eyes, and she nearly smiled. "Yes. Our child. Do you remember the night—that horrible formal dance and it was so hot, and the air conditioning was broken? Remember, we snuck out and went to the roof—"

The roof of the yet-unfinished Mercantile Building. He had landed the light-flyer there, spread the silk for them to sit on as they drank pilfered wine and snacked on delicacies filched from a hors d'ouevre tray . . .

"Fourteen moons," he whispered, remembering, then the outrage struck, for there was no misunderstanding here at all, and no local custom to excuse. "You named this child *yos'Galan*?" he demanded, and meant for her to hear his anger.

She dropped back half-a-step, eyes going wide, and her hands caught the boy's shoulders and pulled him close against her. She took a deep breath and let it sigh out.

"Of course I named him yos'Galan," she said, very quietly. "It is the custom, on my homeworld, to give a child his father's surname. I meant no—insult—to you, Er Thom. If I have insulted you, only tell me how, and I will mend it."

"It is improper to have named this child yos'Galan. How could you have thought it was anything else? There was no contract—"

Anne bowed her head, raised a hand to smooth the boy's bright hair. "I see." She looked up. "It's an easy matter to change a name. There's no reason why he shouldn't be Shan Davis. I'll make the application to—"

"No!" His vehemence surprised them both, and this time it was Er Thom who went back a step. "Anne—" He cut himself off, took a moment to concentrate, then tried again, schooling his voice to calmness. "Why did you not—you sent no word? You thought I had no reason to know that there was born a yos'Galan?"

She moved her hands; he was uncertain of the meaning, the purpose, of the gesture. The child stayed pressed against her legs, quiet as stone.

"I wanted a child," she said, slowly. "I had decided to have a child—entirely my own choice, made before I met you. And then, I did meet you, who became my friend and who I—" Again, that shapeless gesture. "I thought, 'why shouldn't I have the child of my friend, instead of the child of someone I don't know, who only happened to donate his seed to the clinic'?" She moved her head in a sharp shake.

"Er Thom, you were leaving! We had been so happy and—is it wrong, that I wanted something to remind me of joy and the friend who had shared it? I never thought I'd see you again—the universe is wide, my brother says. So many things can happen . . . It was only for my joy, my—comfort. Should I have pin-beamed a message to Liad? How many yos'Galans are there? I didn't think—I didn't think you'd *care*, Er Thom—or only enough to be happy you'd given me so—so fine a gift . . ." She bent her head, but not before he'd seen the tears spill over and shine down her cheeks.

Pity filled him, and remorse. He reached out. "Anne . . ."

She shook her head, refusing to look at him, and Shan gave a sudden gasp, which quickly became a wail as he turned to bury his face against her legs. She bent and picked him up, making soothing sounds and stroking his hair.

Er Thom came another step forward, close enough to touch her wet cheek, to lay his hand on the child's thin shoulder.

"Peace, my son," he murmured in Liaden while his mind was busy, trying to adjust to these new facts, to a trade that became entirely altered. He thought of the proposed contract-marriage that must somehow be put off until he had done duty by this child—*his* child—a half-bred child, gods—whatever would he say to his mother?

"No!" Anne jerked back, holding the sobbing child tightly against her. Her face was ashen, her eyes shadowed with some dire terror.

"Anne?"

"Er Thom, he is *my* son! He is a Terran citizen, registered on University. *My* son, of whom your clan was never told—for whom your clan doesn't care!"

Harsh words, almost enough to strike him to anger again. But there, Terrans knew nothing of clans.

"The clan knows," he said softly, telling her only the truth, "because I know; cares because I care. We are all children of the clan; ears, eyes and heart of the clan."

The fear in her eyes grew, he saw her arms tighten about Shan, who put out renewed cries.

Whirling, Anne carried him into the bedroom.

SHE STAYED IN THE BEDROOM a long time, soothing Shan and convincing him to lie down in his little pull-out bed. She sat by him until he fell asleep, the tears dried to sticky tracks on his cheeks.

When she knew he was sleeping deeply, she rose and pulled the tangled blankets straight on her own bed. She strained her ears for a sound—any sound—from the next room. The apartment was filled with silence.

Go away! she thought fiercely and almost at once: *Don't go!* She shook her head. He would go, of course; it was the nature of things.

They would resolve this misunderstanding; she would change her son's surname and he would be easy again. They would be friends. But sooner or later Er Thom would go, back to his round of worlds and trade-routes. She would take up again the rhythm of her hectic life . . .

There was no sound from the living room. Had he gone already? If he was still here, why hadn't he come to find her?

She glanced at the pull-out, stepped over to make sure the bed-bars were secure, then she took a deep breath and went into the living room.

He was sitting on the edge of the sofa, hands folded on his lap, bright head bent. At her approach he stood and came forward, eyes on her face.

"Anne? I ask pardon. It was not my intent to—to cause you pain. My temper is—not good. And it was a shock, I did not see . . . Of course you would not know that there are not so many yos'Galans; that a message sent to me by name, to Liad or to *Dutiful Passage,* would reach me. I am at fault. It had not occurred to me to leave you my beamcode . . ." *And who leaves such*, he asked himself, *for one who has taken* nubiath'a?

She tried a small smile; it felt odd on her face. "Maybe this time you can leave me the code, then. I'll contact you, if something—important—happens. All right?"

"No." He took her lifeless fingers in his, tried to massage warmth into them. "Anne, it cannot continue so—"

She snatched her hand away. "Because he's named yos'Galan? I'll change that—I've said I would! You have no right—Er Thom—" She raised her hand to her throat, fingers seeking the comfort that no longer hung there; she felt tears rising.

"Er Thom, don't you have somewhere else you need to be? You came here for a purpose, didn't you? Business?" Her voice was sharp and he nearly flinched. Instead, he reached up and took her face between his hands.

"I came to see you," he said, speaking very slowly, as clearly and as plainly as he knew how, so there could be no possible misunderstanding. "I came with no other purpose than to speak with you." Tears spilled over, soaking his fingertips, startling them both.

"Anne? Anne, no, only listen—"

She pulled away, dashing at her eyes.

"Er Thom, please go away."

He froze, staring at her. Would she send him away with all that lay, unresolved, between them? It was her right, certainly. He was none of her kin, to demand she open her door to him. But the child was named yos'Galan.

Anne wiped at her face, shook her head, mouth wobbling.

"Please, Er Thom. You're—my dear, we're still friends. But I don't think I *can* listen now. I'm—I need to be by myself for a little while . . ."

Reprieve. He licked his lips.

"I may come again? When?"

The tears wouldn't stop. They seemed to come from a hole in her chest that went on and on, forever. "When? I don't—this evening. After dinner." *What was she saying?* "Er Thom . . ."

"Yes." He moved, spinning away from her, plucking his jacket from the back of the easy chair and letting himself out the door.

For perhaps an entire minute, Anne stared at the place where he had been. Then the full force of her grief caught her and she bent double, sobbing.

CHAPTER SIX

◊◊◊◊◊◊◊◊◊◊◊◊◊◊◊◊◊◊◊◊◊◊◊◊◊◊◊◊◊◊◊◊◊◊◊◊◊◊

Any slight—no matter how small—requires balancing, lest the value of one's melant'i *be lessened*

Balance is an important, and intricate, part of Liaden culture, with the severity of rebuttal figured individually by each debt-partner, in accordance with his or her own melant'i. *For instance, one Liaden might balance an insult by demanding you surrender your dessert to him at a society dinner, whereas another individual might calculate balance of that same insult to require a death.*

Balance-death is, admittedly, rare. But it is best always to speak softly, bow low and never give a Liaden cause to think he has been slighted.

—From *A Terran's Guide to Liad*

IT WAS A CRISP, bright day of the kind that doubtless delighted the resident population. Er Thom shivered violently as he hit Quad S and belatedly dragged on his jacket, sealing the front and jerking the collar up.

Jamming his hands into the fur-lined pockets, he strode off, heedless both of his direction and the stares of those he passed, and only paused in his headlong flight when he found water barring his path.

He stopped and blinked over the glittering expanse before him, trying to steady his disordered thoughts.

The child's name was yos'Galan.

He shivered again, though he had walked far enough and hard enough for the exercise to warm him.

His *melant'i* was imperiled—though that hardly concerned him, so much had he already worked toward its ruination—and the *melant'i* of Clan Korval, as well. A yos'Galan born and the clan unaware? Korval was High House and known to be eccentric—society wags spoke of 'the Dragon's directive' and 'Korval madness'—but even so strong and varied a *melant'i* could scarcely hope to come away from such a debacle untainted.

Er Thom closed his eyes against the lake's liquid luster. Why? Why had she done this thing? What had he done that demanded such an answer from her? So stringent a Balancing argued an insult of such magnitude he *must* have been aware of his transgression—and he recalled nothing.

Abruptly he laughed. Whatever the cause, only see the beauty of the Balance! A yos'Galan, born and raised as Terran, growing to adulthood, building what *melant'i* he might, clan and line alike all in ignorance . . . If Er Thom yos'Galan had been a stronger man, one who knew enough of duty to embrace forgetfulness without once more seeking out the cause of his heart-illness . . . It was, in truth, an artwork of Balance.

But what coin of his had purchased it? If Anne had felt herself slighted, if he had belittled her or failed someway of giving her full honor—

"Hold." He opened his eyes, staring sightlessly across the lake.

"Anne is *Terran*," he told himself, as revelation began to dawn.

There were some who argued that Terrans possessed neither *melant'i* nor honor. It was a view largely popular with those who had never been beyond Liad or Liad's Outworlds. Traders and Scouts tended to espouse a less popular philosophy, based on actual observation.

He himself had traded with persons unLiaden. As with Liadens, there were those who were honorable and those who were, regrettably, otherwise. Local custom often dictated a system strange to Liaden thought, though, once grasped, it was seen to be honor, and consistent with what one knew to be right conduct.

Daav went further, arguing that *melant'i* existed independent of a person's consciousness, and might be deduced from careful observation. It was then the burden of a person of conscious *melant'i* to give all proper respect to the unawakened consciousness and guard its sleeping potential.

Er Thom had thought his brother's view extreme. Until he had met Anne Davis.

He knew Anne to be a person of honor. He had observed her *melant'i* first-hand and at length and he would place it, in its very different strengths, equal to his own. She was not one to start a debt-war from spite, nor to take extreme Balance as bolster for an unsteady sense of self.

Is it possible, he asked himself, slowly, *that Anne named the boy so to honor me?*

The lake dazzled his eyes as the paving stones seemed to move under his feet. He grappled with the notion, trying to accommodate the alien shape, and he grit his teeth against a desire to cry out that *no one* might reasonably think such a thing.

Facts: Anne was an honorable person. There had been nothing requiring Balance between them. The child's name was yos'Galan. Therefore, Anne had meant honor—or at the least no harm—to him by her actions.

He drew a deep breath of chill air, almost giddy with relief, that there was no balancing here that he must answer; that he need not bring harm to her whom he wished only to cherish and protect.

There remained only to decide what must properly be done about the child.

IT WAS MID AFTERNOON. Shan had eaten a hearty dinner, resisted any suggestion of sleep and fell easy prey to *Mix-n-Match*.

Anne shook her head. She'd had to upgrade the set three times already; Shan learned the simple patterns effortlessly, it seemed. He needed a tutor—more time than she could give him, to help him learn at his own rate, to be sure that he received balanced instruction, that he didn't grow bored . . .

"A tutor," she jeered to herself, not for the first time. "Sure, Annie Davis, an' where will ye be getting the means for that madness?"

It was a measure of her uneasiness that she sought comfort in the dialect of her childhood. She shook her head again and went over to the desk, resolutely switching on the terminal. "Get some work done," she told herself firmly.

But her mind would not stay on her work and after half-an-hour's fruitless searching through tangential lines, she canceled the rest of her time and went over to the omnichora.

She pulled the dust cover off and folded it carefully onto the easy chair, sat on the bench, flipped stops, set timings, tone, balance, and began, very softly, to play.

Er Thom was not coming back. Intellectually, she knew that this was so: The abruptness of his departure this morning told its own tale. It was no use trying to decide if this were a good thing or a bad one. She had been trying to resolve that precise point all morning and had failed utterly.

Her hands skittered on the keys, sowing discord. Irritably, Anne raised her hand and re-adjusted the timing, but she did not take up her playing. Instead, she sat and stared down at the worn plastic keys, fighting the terror that threatened to overwhelm her.

It cannot continue so, he insisted in memory and Anne bit her lip in the present. Er Thom was an honorable man. He had his *melant'i*—his status—to consider. Anne had, all unwitting, threatened that *melant'i*—and Er Thom did not think a mere change of Shan's surname would retire the threat.

Liaden literature was her passion. She had read the stories of Shan el'Thrasin compulsively, addictively, searching back along esoteric research lines for the oldest versions, sending for recordings of the famous Liaden *prena'ma*—the tellers of tales. She knew what happened to those foolish enough to threaten a Liaden's *melant'i*.

They were plunged into honor-feud, to their impoverishment, often enough. Sometimes, to their death.

It didn't matter that she loved Er Thom yos'Galan, or what his feelings might otherwise be for her. She had put his status at risk. The threat she posed must be nullified, her audacity answered, and his *melant'i* absolutely reestablished, no matter what hurt he must give her in the process.

He might even be sorry to hurt her, and grieve truly for her misfortune, as Shan el'Thrasin had grieved truly for his beloved Lyada ro'Menlin, who had killed his partner. She had paid fully and Shan had extracted the price, as honor demanded, and then mourned her the rest of his life . . .

She gasped and came off the bench in a rush to go across the room and sweep her son up in a hug.

"Ma no!" yelled that young gentleman, twisting in her embrace.

"Ma, yes!" she insisted and kissed him and rumbled his hair and cuddled him close, feeling his warmth and hearing the beat of his heart. "Ma loves you," she said, fiercely, for all that she whispered. Shan grabbed her hair.

"Ma?"

"Yes," she said and walked with him to the kitchen, back through the living room to the bedroom. "We'll go—someplace. To Richard." She stopped in the middle of the living room and took a deep breath, feeling beautifully, miraculously reprieved. She kissed Shan again and bent down to let him go.

"We'll go to Richard—home to New Dublin. We'll leave tonight . . ." Tonight? What about her classes, her contract? It would be academic suicide—and Er Thom would find her at her brother's house on New Dublin, she thought dejectedly. He would have to find her. Honor required it. Her shoulders sank and she felt the tears rise again.

"Oh, gods . . ."

The door chime sounded.

She spun, some primal instinct urging her to snatch up her son and run.

Shan was sitting on the floor amidst his rubber blocks, patiently trying to balance a rectangle atop a cube. And there was no place, really, to run.

The chime sounded again.

Slowly, she walked across the room and opened the door.

He bowed in spite of the parcels he held, and smiled when he looked up at her.

"Good evening," he said softly, as if this morning had never happened and he had never looked at her with fury in his eyes. "It is after dinner?"

Speechless, she looked down at him, torn between shutting the door in his face and hugging him as fiercely as she had hugged Shan.

"Anne?"

She started, and managed a wooden smile. "It's after Shan's dinner, anyway," she said, stepping back to let him in. "But he's being stubborn about going to bed."

Er Thom glanced over to the boy, absorbed in his blocks. "I see." He looked up at her. "I have brought a gift for our son. May I give it?"

She looked at him doubtfully. Surely he wouldn't harm a child. No matter what he might feel he owed her, surely his own son was safe? She swallowed. "All right . . ."

"Thank you." He offered the smaller of the two parcels. "I have also brought wine." He paused, violet eyes speculative. "Will you drink with me, Anne?"

She caught her breath against sudden, painful relief. It was going to be all right, she thought, dizzily. To drink with someone was a sign of goodwill. It would be dishonorable to ask a feud-partner to drink with one. And Er Thom was an honorable man.

The smile she gave him this time was real. "Of course I'll drink with you, Er Thom." She took the package. "I'll pour tonight. And provide dinner. Are you hungry?"

He smiled. "I will eat if you will eat."

"A bargain." Her laughed sounded giddy in her own ears, but Er Thom did not seem to notice. He was walking toward Shan.

The boy had succeeded in building a bridge of a rectangle across two cubes. Gracefully, Er Thom went to one knee, facing the child across the bridge, and laying down the large parcel.

"Good evening, Shan-son," he said in soft Liaden. Anne swallowed around the lump of dread in her throat, clutched the wine bottle and said nothing.

"Jiblish," Shan said, glancing up from his task with a smile. "Hi!"

"I've brought you a gift," Er Thom pursued, still in Liaden. "I hope that it will please you."

To Shan's intense interest, he removed the wrapping from the package and held out a stuffed animal. It was a friendly sort of animal, Anne thought, with large round ears and rounder blue eyes and a good-natured smile on its pointy face. Shan gave it thoughtful consideration, uttered a crow of laughter and fell upon its neck.

Er Thom echoed the laugh softly and reached out to touch the small brown face. Shan pulled his new friend closer and caught the man's finger in his free hand, crowing again.

Anne quietly turned and went into the kitchen for glasses and for food.

SHE BUSIED HERSELF in the kitchen rather longer than was necessary; cutting the cheese to nibble-size, and the fruit, too. She stood for a ridiculous amount of time, trying to decide which crackers to offer.

Throughout it all relief warred with lingering fear. It went against everything she knew to distrust Er Thom. He was her friend, the father of her son. This morning had been a regrettable misunderstanding—a conflict of custom—and she ought to thank all possible gods, that Er Thom had been able to forgive her assault on his *melant'i*. She would need to be very careful not to threaten him again. Even fondness for a lover could not be expected to stay a Liaden's hand twice . . .

When she finally returned to the living room, it was strangely quiet. Er Thom smiled up at her from his seat against the sofa. Shan was spread out across his lap, head on Er Thom's shoulder, one small hand gripping the stuffed animal's round ear. He was fast asleep.

"Oh, no!" Anne laughed, nearly upsetting the wine glasses on the tray. "My poor friend . . ." She sat the tray down and knelt on the floor next to them, holding out her arms. "I'll put him to bed."

The stuffed animal proved a stumbling block. Even in sleep her son's grip was trojan, but Er Thom patiently coaxed the sleeping fingers open, and offered the liberated toy to Anne. She took it and led the way as Er Thom carried Shan into the bedroom and lay him gently on the pull-out bed.

He waited quietly while she settled both friends comfortably and allowed her to proceed him back into the living room, pulling the door half-closed behind him.

CHAPTER SEVEN

The delm shall be face and voice of the clan, guarding the interests of the clan and treating with other delms in matters of wider interest. The delm is held to be responsible for the actions of all members of his clan and likewise holds ultimate authority over these members. The delm shall administer according to the internal laws of his clan, saving only that those laws do not circumvent the Laws agreed upon by all delms and set forth in this document.

—From the Charter of the Council of Clans

"GO TO LIAD?" Anne set her glass carefully aside. "I have no reason to go to Liad, Er Thom."

"Ah." He inclined his head, keeping his manner in all ways gentle. It had been ill-done to show her his anger; he had not missed the wariness in her face when he had asked entrance this evening. Nor did the continued tension in her shoulders and the unaccustomed care with which she addressed him escape notice. He met her eyes, as one did with a valued friend, and brushed the back of her hand with light fingertips.

"Our child must be Seen by the delm."

She took a slow, deep breath. "I believe," she said with that care which was so different from her usual way with him, "that the matter need not concern your delm. I said this morning that I will change Shan's surname to Davis, and I meant it. I have an early day tomorrow. I'll go to Central Admin and file the request through Terran Census. Three days, at the most, and—"

"No." He caught her hand in both of his, keeping his voice soft with an effort. "Anne, is Shan not the—the child of our bodies?"

She blinked, slipping her hand free. "Of course he is. I told you."

Irritation there, and rightly so. Who was Er Thom yos'Galan to question the word of an equal adult? He bowed his head.

"Forgive me, friend. Most certainly you did tell me. It is thus that the delm's concern is engaged. You have said that the child of our pleasure is yos'Galan. It is the delm's honor to keep the tale of yos'Galans and ensure that the clan—" here he stumbled, sorting among a myriad of words of Terran possibility, all the wrong size or shape to describe the clan's obligations in this matter.

"I've said," Anne stepped into the space his hesitation had created, "that his name will be changed to Davis. In three days, Er Thom, there will be no new yos'Galans for your delm to count."

"You have said he is yos'Galan. Will you unsay it and forswear yourself?" It was not his place to rebuke her, nor any of his concern, should she choose to tarnish her *melant'i*. But his heart ached, for he had taught her to fear him, and now fear forced her to dishonor. "Anne?"

She sighed. "Er Thom, he's the same child, whether his name is Davis or yos'Galan!"

"Yes!" Joy flooded him, so that he caught her hands, laughing with sheer relief, for she did not after all turn her face from honor. "Precisely so! And thus the delm must certainly See him—soon, as you will understand. I shall pilot—you need not be concerned—and the ship is entirely able. To Liad is—"

"Hold it." Her face held an odd mix of emotion—a frown twisted curiously about a smile—and she shook her head, a pet gesture that did not always signal negative, but sometimes also wonder, or impatience, or sadness. She took one of her hands from his and raised it to his face, running her knuckles whisper-soft down his right cheek. Once more, wonderingly, it seemed to him, she shook her head.

"It's really important for your delm to see Shan now?"

Important? It was vital. To be outside the clan was to be outside of life.

"Yes," he told her.

"All right. Then let your delm come here."

"Hah." She was within her right to ask it, though there were few so secure in their *melant'i* as to bid Korval come to them. Er Thom inclined his head.

"It is, you see, that—until his own children are of an age—I am the delm's designated heir. Wisdom dictates that we both not be off-planet at the same time. Your grace would be the clan's delight, could you instead go to Korval."

"You're the delm's heir?" Anne was frowning slightly. "I didn't know that."

There was no reason for her to know; such information was not commonly shared with pleasure-loves. Yet Anne knew much else about him, he realized suddenly. It was possible that only Daav knew more.

"Forgive me. I am a'thodelm—heir to my mother, who is thodelm of yos'Galan. And I am nadelm—named to take the place of the delm, should—necessity—dictate." He paused, biting his lip, and then made her a gift: "The delm is Daav yos'Phelium, who is also my *cha'leket*—you would say, my foster-brother."

"And master trader, and master pilot," Anne murmured, naming the two facets of his *melant'i* she had cause to know well. "That's quite a hat-rack."

His brows twitched together. "Your pardon?"

"I'm sorry," she said, laughing lightly. "An old Terran joke had to do with the number of duties a single person was assigned to perform. Each of the duties was referred to as a 'hat,' and the traditional question was: 'What hat are you wearing today?'"

He stared at her. A joke? But—

"That is *melant'i*," he said, around a sense of wondering bafflement.

"More or less," Anne agreed with a shrug. "It's pretty old—a scholar's joke, you know." She changed the subject abruptly. "If your delm needs to see Shannie *now*, the solution is for you to go home so he can come to University. I certainly can't leave *now*—exam week is just beginning—and I don't have any other reason to go to Liad, Er Thom. Though I'm certain," she added, with a return of that unnatural caution, "that I would *want* to accommodate your delm."

"Of course you would." True enough. Who sane deliberately thwarted Korval? Er Thom reached for his wine, eyes sweeping down the column of her throat, to where her breasts pushed tight against the fabric of her shirt.

"When," he asked softly, dragging his eyes away with an effort and trying to ignore his hammering pulse. "When might you be able to leave University, were you interested in a visit to—to Liad?"

Anne shook her head, sharply, he thought, and seemed to shift her eyes from his face all a-sudden. "I—three weeks. About that, with getting in final grades, and—" She took a hard breath. "Er Thom."

"Yes." He slid nearer to her on the sofa, setting his leg against hers, and raised a hand to stroke one delightful breast through her shirt—deliberately teasing—and felt the quiver of her desire.

Lightly, he smoothed his fingertips across her nipple, feeling it harden as his own passion mounted, hard and demanding. He shifted closer, urgent fingers at the fastening of her shirt.

"Shan—" she began.

"Is asleep," he whispered, and brought his gaze up to her face. "Isn't he?"

Her eyes seem to lose focus—an instant only and he half-swooning with a desire that seemed only to build, and build, until he must—"Anne?"

"Asleep." She was back with him fully, fingers busy with his own clothing. "Er Thom, I need you. Quickly."

"Quickly," he agreed, and the passion built to a wave, hesitated in a pain that became ecstasy as it crashed, engulfing them entirely.

✿ ✿ ✿

"THE RIGHT HONORABLE Lady Kareen yos'Phelium," Mr. pel'Kana announced with unnerving formality, and bowed low.

The lady's brother bit back a curse, spun his chair to face the door and swept his hand across the computer keypad, banishing the files he had been reviewing. The last move was sheer instinct: Kareen never hesitated to busy herself about any bit of business within the clan, a right she claimed as Eldest of Line. That Daav did not agree with this assessment of her *melant'i* barely slowed her and had never, so far as he knew, stopped her.

"Young brother." Kareen paused on the threshold long enough to incline her head—Elder to Younger—and allowed Mr. pel'Kana to seat her.

Inwardly, Daav sighed. True enough, Kareen could give him ten years, but it wearied one that she must always be playing that point. A variation, he thought, would add piquancy to a game of spite and dislike that had become all too predictable. Alas, that Kareen was not imaginative. He moved his hand, catching the servant's attention.

"Wine for Lady Kareen," he murmured.

This done, Mr. pel'Kana quit the room, with, Daav thought, marked relief. The Council of Clans rated Kareen expert in the field of proper action and called upon her often to unravel this or that sticky point of Code. It was to be regretted that she demanded expert's understanding of all she met.

Expert's understanding required that he rise and make his bow, honoring the eldest of Line yos'Phelium, and bidding her graceful welcome.

Daav thrust his legs out before him and crossed them at the ankle. Lacing his fingers over his belt buckle, he grinned at her in counterfeit good-humor.

"Good-day, Kareen. Whatever can you want from me now?"

She allowed the merest twitch of a brow to convey her displeasure at being addressed in the Low Tongue, and lifted her glass, pointedly tasting the wine.

Setting the glass aside, she met his eyes.

"I have lately been," she murmured, still in the mode of Elder

Sibling to Younger, "at the house of Luken bel'Tarda, in the cause of visiting my heir."

Kareen's heir was six-year-old Pat Rin, recently fostered into the house of bel'Tarda by the delm's command. An imperfect solution, as the delm had admitted to his *cha'leket*, and one that had enraged Kareen unseemly.

Daav inclined his head. "And how do you find our cousin Luken?"

"Shatterbrained to a fault," his sister replied with regrettable accuracy. "As I had said to you on another occasion, sirrah, Luken bel'Tarda is hardly fit guardian for one of the Line Direct. However," she said, interrupting herself, "that is a different bolt of cloth." She fixed him with a stern eye.

"Cousin bel'Tarda informs me that yos'Galan searches for one of the Clan to enter into contract-alliance with Clan Nexon, in the person of its daughter Syntebra el'Kemin."

"yos'Galan has the delm's leave for this search," Daav said lazily, moving his hand in a gesture of disinterest. Kareen's mouth tightened.

"Then perhaps the delm is also aware that Thodelm yos'Galan had intended Syntebra el'Kemin as contract-wife for the a'thodelm." It cut very near disrespect, phrased as it yet was in Elder-to-Younger. But Kareen was expert in mode, as well, and kept her tongue nimbly in place.

"The delm is aware of the thodelm's intentions in that regard, yes." He lifted an eyebrow. "Is there some point to this, Kareen?"

"A small one," she said, "but sharp enough to prick interest." She leaned forward slightly in her chair. "The a'thodelm is gone off-planet, not to return before the end of the *relumma*, fleeing, one must conclude, the proposed alliance. Think of the insult to Nexon, that one intended for the contract-room at Trealla Fantrol should be shunted off to make do with—forgive me!—the like of Luken bel'Tarda."

"Luken is an amiable fellow," Daav said calmly. "Though I give you score—thought is not his best endeavor. As for the insult to Nexon—the contract has not yet been written, much less signed. If the lady hoped for an a'thodelm and nets instead a country cousin, still her clan gains ties with Korval, to her honor. I note that she is young, and while Nexon is all very well, it is hardly High House."

"Which matters to Korval not at all," Kareen said, with a touch of acid. "I recall that your own father was—solidly—Low House."

"But a pilot to marvel at," Daav returned, very gently. "So our mother praised him."

Kareen, who was no pilot at all, took a deep breath, visibly seeking calm.

"This does not address," she said after a moment, "how best to deal with the scandal."

Daav straightened slowly in his chair. He met his sister's eyes sternly.

"There will be no scandal," he said, and the mode was Ranking-Person-to-Lesser. "Understand me, Kareen."

"I do not—"

"If I hear one whisper," Daav interrupted, eyes boring into hers, "one syllable, of scandal regarding this, I shall know who to speak with. Do I make myself plain?"

It was to her credit that she did not lower her eyes, though the pulse-beat in her throat was rather rapid. "You make yourself plain," she said after a moment.

"Good," he said with exquisite gentleness. "Is there something else to which you desire to direct your delm's attention?"

She touched her tongue to her lips. "Thank you, I—believe there is not."

"Then I bid you good-day," he said, and inclined his head.

There was a fraction of hesitation before she rose and bowed an entirely unexceptional farewell.

"Good-day."

Mr. pel'Kana met her at the edge of the hallway and guided her away.

Daav waited until he no longer heard her footsteps, then he got up and went across the room to the wine rack. Kareen's glass, full, except for the single sip she had taken, he left on the elbow table by her chair. Mr. pel'Kana would come back presently and take it away.

He poured himself a glass of *misravot* and had a sip, walking to the window and looking out into the center garden. Flowers and shrubs rioted against the backdrop of *Jelaza Kazone*'s massive trunk, threaded with thin stone walkways. Daav closed his eyes against the familiar, beloved scene.

Alone of all the orders he had from his mother, who had been delm before him, the mandate to preserve Kareen's life stood, senseless. It was doubtless some failing of his own vision, that he could not see what use she was to the delm she continually worked to thwart. The best that could be said of her was that she was an assiduous guard of the clan's *melant'i*, but such vigilance paled beside a long history of despite. Daav sighed.

Perhaps, as he grew older and more accustomed to his duties, he would acquire the vaunted Delm's Vision and see what it was his mother had found worth preserving in Kareen.

In the meanwhile, her latest bit of spite was put to rest, at least. Now if only Er Thom would finish with his mysterious errand, return home and mold himself to duty!

Not such an arduous duty, Daav thought, who had lately reviewed Syntebra el'Kemin's file. True, the lady was very young, and her second class pilot's license nothing out-of-the-way. But she would by all accounts make an agreeable enough contract-wife, and like to quickly produce an infant pilot.

Once the new yos'Galan was born, and accepted, and named, then Syntebra el'Kemin was free to return to her clan, richer by the mating-fee and bonus, with her *melant'i* enhanced by having married one of Korval.

Er Thom would likewise be free, to seek out *Dutiful Passage* and pick up his rounds as Korval's master trader.

And Daav would have a new niece or nephew to wonder over and nurture and guide—and a contract-wife to find for himself.

CHAPTER EIGHT

Love is best given to kin and joy taken in duty well done.

—*Vilander's Proverbs*, **Seventh Edition**

THE SOUND OF WATER, splashing and running, brought him from dream to drowse, where he recalled that he lay on Anne's spring-shot sofa, covered over with the blanket from her own bed.

She had left him sometime in the early morning, amid a comedy of untangling limbs and wayward clothing, murmuring that the child had stirred. The blanket she had brought a moment later, and spread carefully on the sofa before bending and kissing him, too quickly, too lightly, on the lips.

"Thank you," she whispered and flitted away.

And for what did she thank him? Er Thom wondered, as the drowse began to thin. For breaking her peace and teaching her fear? Or for being so lost to decency that he twice allowed passion to over-rule right conduct and made fierce, almost savage, love to a woman who was neither pleasure-love, wife, nor lifemate?

He twisted in his uncomfortable nest and inhaled sharply, smelled Anne's scent mingled with the blanket's scratchy, synthetic odor, and felt a surge of longing.

It was to have been so simple. He had only planned to find her, to tell her of his love—that had seemed important. Vital. That done, knowing his truth held by one who treasured it, he thought he might have faced the Healers with calm. And he would have come away from them a fit husband for Nexon's daughter, no impossible might-have-beens shadowing his heart.

Instead, he found a child who must someway be brought to the clan, a woman who seemed etched into his bones, so deep was his desire for her—and no easy solutions at all.

"Hi!" Warm, milk-sweet breath washed his face.

Er Thom opened his eyes, finding them on a level with a serious silver pair, thickly fringed with black lashes.

"*Tra'sia volecta*," he replied, in Low Liaden, as one did with children.

The winging white brows pulled together in a frown.

"Hi!" Shan repeated, at slightly louder volume.

Er Thom smiled. "Good morning," he said in Terran. "Did you sleep well?"

The child—*his* child—gave it consideration, head tipped to one side.

"Okay," he conceded at last, and sighed. "Hungry."

"Ah." The water continued to flow, noisily, nearby: Anne was doubtless in the shower. Er Thom wriggled free of the clinging blanket and stood. "Then I shall find you something to eat," he said and held out a hand.

His son took it without hesitation and the two of them went together into the tiny kitchen.

HE FOUND INSTANT SOY-OATS and made porridge, sprinkling it with raisins from a jar on the cluttered counter. The cold-box yielded milk and juice: Er Thom poured both and stood sipping the juice while he watched his son assay breakfast.

Shan was an accomplished trencherman, wielding his spoon with precision. There were a few, of course unavoidable, spills and splashes, and Er Thom stepped forward at one juncture to help the young gentleman roll up the sleeves of his pajamas, but for the most part breakfast was neatly under way by the time Anne strode into the kitchen.

"Oh, no!" She paused on the edge of the tiny space, laughter filling her face so that it was all he could do not to rush over and kiss her.

"Hi, Ma," her son said, insouciant, barely glancing up from his meal.

Anne grinned. "Hi, Shannie." She looked at Er Thom and shook her head, grin fading into something softer.

"My poor friend. We impose on you shamefully."

He cleared his throat, glancing away on the excuse of finishing his juice.

"Not at all," he murmured, putting the glass into the washer. "The child was hungry—and I was able to solve the matter for him." He met her eyes suddenly. "What should a father do?"

Her gaze slid away. "Yes, well. What a mother should do is grab a quick cup of coffee and then get this young con artist ready to go see his friend Marilla."

"Rilly!" Shan crowed, losing a spoonful of cereal to the table top. "Oops."

"Oops is right," Anne told him, pulling a paper napkin from the wall dispenser and mopping up the mess. "Finish up, Okay? And try to get most of it in your mouth."

"Clumsy Scooter," the child commented matter-of-factly.

"Single-minded Scooter," Anne returned, maneuvering her large self through the small space with deft grace. "Leave eating and talking at the same time to the experts—like Jerzy."

Shan laughed and adjusted his grip on the spoon. "Yes, Ma."

Anne shook her head and pulled her mug out of the wall unit. The acrid smell of chicory-laden synthetic coffee substitute— 'coffeetoot,' according to most Terrans—was nearly overpowering. Er Thom stifled a sigh. Anne loved real coffee. He could easily have brought her a tin—or a case of tins—had he any notion she was reduced to drinking synthetic.

"Done," Shan announced, laying his spoon down with a clatter.

"How about the rest of your milk?" His mother asked, sipping gingerly at her mug.

"There is no need," Er Thom said, quietly, "for you to—cheat yourself of a meal. I can easily tend our child today."

She looked down at him, brown eyes sharp, face tense with reawakened caution. Er Thom kept his own face turned up to hers and fought down the desire to stroke her cheek and smooth the tension away.

"That's very kind of you, Er Thom," she said carefully, "but Rilly—Marilla—is expecting Shan today."

"Then I will take him to her," he replied, all gentleness and reason, "and you may eat before you go to teach your class."

"Er Thom—" She stopped, and, heart-struck, he read dread in her eyes.

"Anne." He did touch her—he *must*—a laying of his hand on her wrist, only that—and nearly gasped at the electrical jolt of desire. "Am I a thief, to steal our son away from you? I am able to care for him today, if you wish it, or to take him to your friend. In either case, we will both be here when you come home." He looked up into her face, saw trust warring with fear.

"Trust me," he whispered, feeling tears prick the back of his eyes. "Anne?"

She drew a deep, shaking breath and sighed it out sharply, laying her hand briefly on his shoulder.

"All right," she said, and gave him a wobbling smile. "Thank you, Er Thom."

"There is no thanks due," he told her, and shifted away to allow her access to the meager cupboards and crowded counter. "Eat your breakfast and I will wash our son's face."

"NOT COMING TODAY?" Marilla looked grave. "He isn't sick, is he, sweetie? Pel said there's a *horrific* flu-thing going through the creche—half the kids down with it and a third of the staff." She sighed, theatrically. "Pel's working a double-shift. Naturally."

"Naturally." Anne grinned, Pel was always finding an excuse to work double-shifts. Marilla theorized—hopefully—a late-shift love-interest. Anne privately thought that Marilla's fits of drama probably grated on her quieter, less demonstrative daughter.

"Shan's in the pink of health," Anne said. "His father's visiting and the two of them are spending some time together."

There, she thought, *it sounds perfectly reasonable.*

Marilla fairly gawked. "His *father,*" she repeated, voice swooping toward the heights. "Shan's father is *visiting* you?"

Anne frowned slightly. "Is that against the law?"

"Don't be silly, darling. It's only that—of course he's fabulously wealthy."

As a matter of fact, Er Thom never seemed at a loss for cash, and his clothes were clearly handmade—tailored to fit his slim frame to perfection. But the jacket he wore most often was well-used, even battered, the leather like silk to the touch.

"Why should he be?" she asked, hearing the sharpness in her voice. "Fabulously wealthy?"

Marilla eyed her and gave an elaborate shrug. "Well, you know—everyone *assumes* Liadens must be rich. All those cantra. And the trade routes. And the clans, too, of course. Terribly old money—lots of investments. Not," she finished, glancing off screen, "that it's any of *my* business."

That much was true, Anne thought tartly, and was immediately sorry. *It's only Marilla,* she told herself, *doing her yenta routine.*

"Rilly, I've got to go. Class."

"All right, sweetheart. Call and let me know your plans." The screen went dark.

My plans? Anne thought, gathering together the pieces of Comp Ling One's final. *What plans?*

DURING HER FREE PERIOD, she banged back into her office for an hour's respite, juggling a handful of mail, the remains of Liaden Lit's exam and a disposable plastic mug full of vending-machine soup.

Dumping the class work into the "Out" basket near the door, she sat down at her desk, pried the top off the plastic mug and began to go through her mail.

Notice of departmental meeting—*another* one? she thought, sighing. Registrar's announcement of deadline for grades. Research Center shutdown for first week of semester break. Request for syllabi for next semester. A card from the makers of *Mix-n-Match*, offering to upgrade Shan's model to something called an *Edu-Board*. A—

Her fingers tingled at the touch—a gritty beige envelope, with "Communications Center" stamped across it in red block letters that dwarfed her name, printed neatly in one corner.

A beam-letter. She smiled and snatched it up, eagerly breaking the seal. A beam-letter meant either a note from her brother Richard or a letter from Learned Doctor Jin Del yo'Kera, of the University of Liad, Solcintra.

The letter slid out of the envelope—one thin, crackling sheet. From Richard then, she decided, unfolding the page. Doctor yo'Kera's letters were long—page upon page of scholarly exploration, answers to questions Anne had posed, questions re-asked, re-examined, paths of thought illuminated . . .

It took her a moment to understand that the letter was not from Richard, after all.

It took rather longer to assimilate the message that was put down, line after line, in precise, orderly Terran, by—by Linguistic Specialist Drusil tel'Bana, who signed herself "colleague."

Scholar tel'Bana begged grace from Professor Davis for the intrusion into her affairs and the ill news which necessity demanded accompany this unseemly breaking of her peace.

Learned Doctor yo'Kera, Scholar tel'Bana's own mentor and friend, was dead, the notes for his latest work in disarray. Scholar tel'Bana understood that work to be based largely, if not entirely, on Professor Davis' elegant line of research, augmented by certain correspondence.

"It is for this reason, knowing the wealth of your thought, the depth of your scholarship, that I beg you most earnestly to come to Liad and aid me in reconstructing these notes. The work was to have been Jin Del's life-piece, so he had told me, and he likened your own work to an unflickering flame, lighting him a path without shadows."

Then the signature , and the date, painstakingly rendered in the common calendar: Day 23, Standard year 1360.

Anne sat back, the words misting out of sense.

Doctor yo'Kera, dead? It seemed impossible that the death of someone she had never physically met, who had existed only as machine-transcribed words on grainy yellow paper should leave her with this feeling of staggering loss.

In the hallway, a bell jangled, signaling class-change in ten minutes. She had an exam to give.

Awkwardly, she folded Drusil tel'Bana's letter and put in her pocket. She gathered up Comp Ling Two's exam booklets, automatically consulting the checklist. Right.

The five-minute bell sounded and she left the office, taking care to lock the door behind her, leaving the vending-machine soup to congeal in its flimsy plastic mug.

CHAPTER NINE

The delm of any given clan, when acting for the Clan, is commonly referred to by the clan's name: "Guayar has commanded thus and so . . ."

To make matters even more confusing, it is assumed all persons of melant'i *will have a firm grounding in Liaden heraldry, thus opening up vast possibilities for double-entendre and other pleasantries. "A hutch of bunnies," will indicate, en masse, the members of Clan Ixin, whose clan-sign is a stylized rabbit against a rising moon. Korval, whose distinctive Tree-and-Dragon is perhaps the most well-known clan-sign among non-Liadens, is given the dubious distinction of dragonhood and a murmured, "The Dragon has lifted a wing," should be taken as a word to the wise.*

—From *A Terran's Guide to Liad*

SHAN ACCEPTED THE SURREY RIDE with the cheerful matter-of-factness that seemed his chiefest characteristic. He settled into the oversized seat next to Er Thom, pulled off his cap and announced, "Jerzy Quad C. C. Three. Seven. Five. Two. A. Four. Nine. C."

Fingers over the simple code-board, Er Thom flung a startled glance at the child, who continued, "Rilly Quad T. T. One. Eight. Seven. Eight. P. Three. Six. T."

"And home?" Er Thom murmured.

"Home Quad S," Shan said without hesitation. "S. Two. Four. Five. Seven. Z. One. Eight. S."

Correct to a digit. Er Thom inclined his head gravely. "Very good. But today we are going elsewhere. A moment, please." He tapped the appropriate code into the board and leaned back, pulling the single shock-strap across his lap and Shan's together and locking it into place.

The child snuggled against his side with a soft sigh and put a small brown hand on Er Thom's knee.

"Who?" he asked and Er Thom stiffened momentarily, wondering how best—

The child stirred under his arm, twisting about to look into his face with stern silver eyes. "Who are you?" he demanded. "Name."

Er Thom let out the breath he had been holding. "*Mirada*," he said, the Low Liaden word for "father." "My name is Er Thom yos'Galan, Clan Korval."

The white brows pulled together. "*Mirada*?" he said, hesitantly.

"*Mirada*," Er Thom replied firmly, settling his arm closer around the small body and leaning back into the awkward seat.

The boy curled once more against his side. "Where we go?"

Er Thom closed his eyes, feeling his son's warm body burning into his side, thinking of Anne, and of love, and the demands of *melant'i*.

"To the spaceport."

DRAGON'S WAY admitted them, hatch lifting silently. Beyond, the lights came up, the life-systems cycled to full, and the piloting board initiated primary self-check.

Shan hesitated on the edge of the piloting chamber, small hand tensing in Er Thom's larger one.

"*Mirada*?"

"Yes, my child?"

"Go home."

"Presently," Er Thom replied, taking half a step into the room.

"Go home *now*," the boy insisted, voice keying toward panic.

"Shan." Er Thom spun and went to his knees, one hand cupping a thin brown cheek. "Listen to me, *denubia*. We shall go home very soon, I promise. But you must first help me to do a thing, all right?"

"Do?" Doubtful silver eyes met his for an unnervingly long moment.

"All right," Shan said at last, adding, "sparkles."

He lifted a hand to touch Er Thom's cheek. "Soft." He grinned. "Jerzy prickles."

Er Thom bit his lip. Jerzy Entaglia would be bearded, Terran male that he was. But why should Er Thom yos'Galan's son be familiar with the feel of an outsider's face?

He sighed, and forced himself to think beyond the initial outrage. Jerzy Entaglia stood in some way the child's foster-father. The success of his efforts in that role was before Er Thom now: Alert, intelligent, good-natured and bold-hearted. What should Er Thom yos'Galan accord Jerzy Entaglia, save all honor, and thanks for a gift precious beyond price?

"Come," he said to his son, very gently. He rose and took the small hand again in his, leading the boy into the ship. This time, there was no resistance.

SHAN SAT ON A STOOL by the autodoc, watching curiously as Er Thom rolled up his sleeve and sprayed antiseptic on his hand and arm.

"Cold!"

"Only for a moment," Er Thom murmured, tapping the command sequence into the autodoc's panel. He looked down at his son and slipped a hand under the chin to tip the small face up. "This may hurt you, a little. Can you be very brave?"

Shan gave it consideration. "I'll try."

"Good." Er Thom went down on one knee by the stool and put his arm around Shan's waist. The other hand he used to guide the child's fingers into the 'doc's sampling unit. "Your hand in here— yes. Hold still now, *denubia* . . ."

He leaned his cheek against the soft hair, raising his free hand to toy with a delicate earlobe, eyes on the readout. When the needle hit the red line, he used his nails, quickly, deftly, to pinch Shan's ear, eliciting a surprised yelp.

"*Mirada!*"

The unit chimed completion of the routine; the readout estimated three minutes for analysis and match. Er Thom came up off the floor in a surge, sweeping Shan from the stool and whirling him around.

"Well done, bold-heart!" he cried in exuberant Low Liaden and heard his son squeal with laughter. He set him down on his feet and offered a hand, remembering to speak Terran. "Shall I show you a thing?"

"Yes!" his son said happily and took the offered hand for the short walk back to the piloting chamber.

BRONZE WINGS SPREAD WIDE, the mighty dragon hovered protectively above the Tree, head up and alert, emerald-bright eyes seeming to look directly into one's soul. Shan took a sharp breath and hung slightly back.

"It is Korval's shield," Er Thom murmured, though of course the child was too young to understand all that meant. He ran his palm down the image. "A picture, you see?"

The boy stepped forward and Er Thom lifted him, bringing him close enough to run his own hand down the smooth enameled surface. He touched the dragon's nose.

"Name?"

"Ah." Er Thom smiled and cuddled the small body closer. "Megelaar."

"Meg'lar," Shan mispronounced and touched the Tree. "Pretty."

"*Jelaza Kazone*," his father told him softly. "You may touch it in truth—soon. And when you are older, you may climb in it, as your uncle and I did, when we were boys."

Shan yawned and Er Thom felt a stab of remorse. A long and busy morning for a child, in truth!

"Would you like a nap?" he murmured, already starting down the hall toward the sleeping quarters.

"Umm," he son replied, body relaxing even as he was carried along.

He was more asleep than awake by the time Er Thom laid him down in the bed meant for the delm's use and covered him with a quilt smelling of sweetspice and mint.

"'Night, *Mirada*," he muttered, hand fisting in the rich fabric.

"Sleep well, my child," Er Thom returned softly, and bent to kiss the stark brown cheek.

On consideration, and recalling his own boyhood, he opened the intercom and locked the door behind him before going back to the autodoc.

"yos'Galan, indeed," he murmured a few moments later, carrying the 'doc's gene-map with him into the piloting chamber.

He sat in the pilot's chair, eyes tracing the intricate pattern revealed in the printout. yos'Galan, indeed. He glanced at the board, fingered the gene-map and looked, with distaste, down at his shirt. He was not accustomed to sleeping in his clothing, and then rousting about, rumpled and unshowered, for half-a-day afterwards.

The board beckoned. Duty was clear. Er Thom sighed sharply and lay the gene-map atop the prime piloting board.

He wanted a shower, clean clothes. What better time than now, with the child, for the moment, asleep?

A shower and clean clothes, he thought, removing his jacket and laying it across the chair's back. Duty could wait half-an-hour.

"ER THOM? . . . Shannie!"

Anne let her briefcase fall as she darted forward, flashing through the tiny apartment: Empty bedroom, dark bathroom, silent kitchen.

"Gone."

Pain hit in a hammer blow, driving the breath out of her in a keen that might have been his name.

Er Thom! Er Thom, you promised . . .

But what were promises, she thought dizzily, where there was *melant'i* to keep? Anne swallowed air, shook her head sharply.

Shan was well, of that she was absolutely certain. Er Thom would not harm a child. She *knew* it.

But he would take his child to Liad. *Must* take his child to Liad. He had asked her to go with him on that urgent mission—and she—she had thought there was an option of saying no.

"Annie Davis, it's a rare, foolish gel ye are," she muttered, and was suddenly moving.

Three of her long strides took her across the common room. She smacked the door open and burst into the hallway at a dead run, heading for the Quad, the surrey station.

And the spaceport.

SHE SHOULD NEVER HAVE TRUSTED HIM, Anne thought fiercely. She should have never let him back into her life. She should have never let him back into her bed. Gods, it had all been an act, put on to lull her fears, so that she would leave Shan with him—she saw it now. And she—she so starved for love, so besotted with a beautiful face and caressing ways, incapable of thinking that Er Thom would do her harm, willing herself to believe he would—or could—stop being Liaden . . .

She flashed down the stairs and out into the Quad, running as if her life depended upon it and, gods, what if he had already gone? Taken her son and lifted, gone into hyperspace, Jumping for Liad—how would she ever find him again? What Liaden would take the part of a Terran barbarian against one who was master trader, a'thodelm, and heir to his delm?

There are not so—very many—yos'Galans, Er Thom murmured in memory, and Anne gasped, speeding toward the blue light that marked the surrey station.

She was halfway across the Quad when they emerged, the boy straddling the man's shoulders. The man was walking unhurried and smooth, as if the combined weight of the child and the duffel bag he also carried was just slightly less than nothing.

"*I'lanta!*" the child cried, and the man swung right.

"*Dri'at!*" the boy called out then and the man obediently went to the left.

Anne slammed to a halt, fist pressed tight against her mouth, watching them cross toward her.

Shan was exuberant, hanging onto the collar of Er Thom's battered leather jacket, Er Thom's hands braceleting his ankles.

"*I'lanta!*" Shan called again, heels beating an abbreviated tattoo against the man's chest.

But Er Thom had seen her. He increased his pace, marching in a straight line, ignoring it entirely when Shan grabbed a handful of bright golden hair and commanded, "*I'lanta, Mirada!*"

"Anne?" The violet eyes were worried. He reached up and swung the child down, retaining a firm hold on a small hand. His other hand lifted and stopped a bare inch from her face, while she stood there like a stump and stared at the two of them, afraid to move. Afraid to breathe . . .

"You're weeping," Er Thom murmured, hand hesitating, dropping, disappearing into a jacket pocket. "My friend, what is wrong?"

She drew a shaky breath, her first in some time, or so it felt, and found the courage to move her hand from before her mouth.

"I came home," she said, hearing how her voice wobbled, "and you were gone."

"Ah." Distress showed, clearly, for a heartbeat. Then Er Thom was bowing, graceful and low. "I am distraught to have caused you pain," he murmured, in Terran, though the inflection was all High Liaden. "Forgive me, that my thoughtlessness has brought you tears."

He straightened and moved Shan forward, relinquishing his hand. "Go to your mother, *denubia*."

"Ma?" The light blue eyes were worried; she felt his uncertainty as if it were her own.

Anne sank to her knees and pulled him close in a savage hug, her cheek against his.

"Hi, Shannie," she managed, though her voice still quavered. "You have a nice day?"

"Nice," he agreed, arms tight around her neck. "Saw Meg'lar. Saw—*spaceport*." He wriggled, proud of himself. "Saw ship and store and—and—"

He wriggled again, imperatively. Anne loosened her grip, found herself looking up into Er Thom's face.

Very solemn, that face, and the violet eyes shadowed so that she longed to reach out and touch him, to beg his pardon for having doubted—

Enough of that, Annie Davis, she told herself sternly. *You touch the man and lose your sense—only see how it happened yestereve.*

"It was necessary that I have clothes," Er Thom said gently, fingers brushing the bag at his hip. "Also, I have arranged that food be delivered to your dwelling—" His hand came up, fingers soothing the air between them. "It was seen that food was in shortage. I mean no offense, Anne."

"No, of course not," she whispered, and cleared her throat. She took Shan's hand and rose, looking down into her friend's beautiful, troubled face. "Er Thom—"

His fingers flickered again—indicating more information forthcoming.

"It is also necessary that I engage a—a *room*. This has not yet been done. If you desire to keep our son by you, I will complete this task." He hesitated, slanting a glance at her face from beneath thick golden lashes.

"I ask—may I visit you this evening? After supper?" He inclined his head. "It will be entirely as you wish, Anne, and nothing else. My word upon it."

"A room?" she repeated, looking at him in astonishment. She took a breath. "Er Thom, how long are you staying here?"

He glanced aside, then back to her face.

"Three weeks, you had said, until you might come to Liad."

"I said no such thing!" she protested, and felt Shan's hand tense in hers. She took another breath, deep and calming. "Er Thom, I am not going—" Then she remembered the letter in her sleeve and the unknown scholar's plea.

"Anne?"

She bit her lip. "I—perhaps—I will—need to go to Liad," she said, suddenly aware that it was cool on the Quad and that she had dashed out without snatching up a jacket. "A friend of mine—a colleague—has died, very suddenly, and I am asked to—" She shook her head sharply. "I haven't decided. The news just came this morning."

"Ah." He inclined his head and murmured the formal phrase of sorrow for a death outside one's own clan: "*Al'bresh venat'i.*"

"Thank you," Anne said and hesitated. "You can stay with us, you know," she heard herself say. "I know that the couch isn't what you're used to . . ." She let the words die out, even as Er Thom's fingers flickered negative.

"I do not think that—would be wise," he said softly, though the glance he spared her was anything but soft. "May I visit you, Anne? This evening?"

"All right," she said, around a surprising tightening of her heart. "For a little while. I have—examinations to grade."

"Thank you." He bowed to her, touched his fingertips to Shan's cheek.

"This evening," he murmured and turned, boot heels clicking on the Quad-stones as he walked back toward the surrey station.

"'Bye, *Mirada*!" Shan called, waving energetically.

Er Thom glanced back over his shoulder and raised a hand, briefly.

"C'mon, Shannie," Anne murmured, looking at her son so she wouldn't have to watch her lover out of sight, as she had done once before. "Let's go home."

CHAPTER TEN

⊗⊘

The most dangerous phrase in High Liaden is coab minshak'a: "Necessity exists."

—From *A Terran's Guide to Liad*

. . . GUIDE THE DELM'S attention to the appended gene-profile for Shan yos'Galan, who has twenty-eight Standard Months.

"The mother of this child is Anne Davis, native of New Dublin, professor of comparative linguistics, Northern Campus, University Central, Terran Sector Paladin.

One regrets that a profile for Professor Davis is not at this time available. Although professional necessities have denied her the opportunity to pursue her own license, she is descended of a line of pilots. Her elder brother, Richard, holds first-class-pending-master; her mother, Elizabeth Murphy, had held first-class, light transport to trade class AAA. The records of these pilots is likewise appended, for the delm's information.

It is one's intention to bring the child with his mother before the delm's eyes on the second day of the next relumma, the earliest moment Professor Davis may be released from the necessities of her work. One implores the delm to See the child welcomed among Korval, to the present joy and future profit of the clan.

One also begs the delm's goodwill for Professor Davis. She is a person of melant'i *who is owed Balance of Korval through the error of the clan's son Er Thom.*

In respect to the delm,

Er Thom yos'Galan."

"Twenty-eight Standard Months?" Daav stared at the screen, torn between disbelief and a woeful desire to laugh. "I should allow that a matter to resolve, indeed!"

On the desk beside the pin-beam unit, Relchin lifted his head and stared daggers of outraged comfort, which tipped the scale firmly to laughter. Daav chucked the big cat under the chin and hit the advance key, calling up the appended gene-map.

"Well, and the child's out of yos'Galan," he admitted to Relchin a moment or two later. "But what's it to do with me if a Terran lady sees a way to combine profit with pleasure? Especially where there's young Syntebra so eager to wed an a'thodelm and do the thing by contract and Code, with no untoward scandals." He skritched the cat absently behind the ears.

"Er Thom wants to buy the Terran lady off, that seems the gist of the thing, don't you think? And he wants the boy for the clan, though as Aunt Petrella and my sister will no doubt both inform us, Shan is *not* a yos'Galan name." He frowned at the gene-map once more.

"Child might well be the devil of a pilot. Er Thom's very good, you know, Relchin. One needs make a push to stay abreast of him— though it won't do to let him know that, of course. The clan is always eager to welcome pilots . . . The matter comes down to the lady's price, as I see it—and the lady's price must be high, indeed, else why did he simply not pay it out of his private account?"

The cat vouchsafed no answer and after a moment Daav called up the records of the lady's brother and mother.

"Adequate, certainly, but the lady herself is no pilot. Who can say but she's no more than a bumble-fingered pretty-face and the child takes all from her? Only see how it is with Kareen, eh, Relchin? Though it must be recalled that yos'Galan, at least, has always bred true."

He was quiet for a time then, absently stroking the cat and staring not at the screen but at a point just above it.

"No, it won't do," he announced at last, snapping out of the chair and striding to the bar. He poured himself some misravot and wandered out into the middle of the room, holding the glass and glaring down at the rug.

"Has Er Thom run mad?" he inquired, perhaps of the cat, which was busily washing its back. "Implore the delm to See a child unacknowledged by yos'Galan? Put the clan into uproar, set thodelm against delm, open vistas untold to Kareen's despite and all for the sake of an untried child and some person named *Anne*—"

He stopped, dropping into a stillness so absolute the cat paused in its ablutions to stare at him out of wide yellow eyes.

"Anne Davis." He sipped wine, pensively, head cocked to a side. "Anne Davis, now." He sighed lightly. "It really is too bad, the things Scout candidates are required to read. But is it the identical Anne Davis, I wonder? And *was* it Anne Davis at all? Certainly it was linguistics—and rather startling in its way. My pitiful memory . . ."

Talking thus to himself, he went back to the desk, set aside the wine and opened a search program. In response to the command query he typed in a rapid half-dozen keywords, struck "go" and leaned back in his chair.

"Now—" he began, looking significantly at the cat.

He got no further. The first chime signaling a match had barely ceased when the second, third, fourth, fifth sounded. There was a pause of less than a heartbeat before the sixth and final match was announced and by that time Daav was blinking in bemusement at the screen-full of information his first keyword had produced.

"Ah yes," he murmured, touching the 'continue' key. "Exactly so."

Anne Davis' list of publications ran two full screens, including the compilation and cross-check of major Terran dialects Daav had half-recalled. He noted the work had been upgraded twice since; the version he had read had been her doctoral paper.

He also noted that the focus of her study had undergone a fascinating shift of direction, the seeds of which were certainly to be found in that earliest work. Yet the intellectual courage required to begin the painstaking sifting and matching of Liaden

and base-Terran, not to forget the language of the enemy—
Yxtrang—seeking commonality . . .

"A concept worthy of a Scout," Daav murmured, ordering the
entire bibliography for his private library with a flash of quick
golden fingers across the board. "Bold heart, Scholar. May the luck
show you fair face."

The biography, accessed next, jibed very well with Er Thom's
letter. Heidelberg Fellow Anne Davis, author of many scholarly
papers (list appended) in the field of comparative linguistics, was
indeed a native of New Dublin in the Terran Sector of Faerie. She
possessed one sibling, Richard Davis, pilot; and was descended of
Elizabeth Murphy, pilot, deceased, and Ian Davis, engineer, also
deceased.

She was listed as the parent of one child, Shan yos'Galan, born
Standard Year 1357.

"And a matter of very public record," Daav commented wryly.
"One begins to comprehend Er Thom's feelings in the matter."

Eyes still on the bio, he reached out and spun the pin-beam
screen around.

"A person of *melant'i*, forsooth," he murmured, frowning at the
letter. "Is it possible he begs a *solving* for the lady? True enough, she
will have no delm to solve for her, and if the child is to come to
Korval . . ." He rescued his wine glass and leaned back in the chair,
staring at the cloud-painted ceiling and sipping.

On the desk, the cat stirred, stretched and walked over the small
gap to the man's lap, leisurely making itself comfortable.

"It may be alliance she wants," Daav murmured, toying with
the cat's ear. "No bad thing, there, Relchin—and Professor Davis in
pursuit of a notion likely to have found approval with Grandmother
Cantra. There's University of Liad, after all, just over the valley
wall—and all the lovely native speakers . . ."

The cat purred and moved its head so the man's fingers were
tickling its chin.

"Simple for you to say so," Daav complained. "*You're* not asked
to solve for one outside the clan! Nor is the coming of this child to
Korval at all regular. What *can* Er Thom have been about?"

But the big cat only purred harder and kneaded Daav's thigh with well-clawed front feet.

"Stop that, brute, or I'll need a medic." Daav sighed. "Perhaps I should travel to University, see the lady and—no." He finished his wine and reached out a long arm to set the glass aside.

"Best to read the letter precisely as written, Relchin, eh? In which manner we must graciously respond to our erring a'thodelm and solicit details upon the nature of Korval's debt to Professor Davis."

So saying, and to the cat's disapproval, he spun the chair around to the pin-beam unit and began to compose his reply.

SHAN MADE A HEARTY dinner and went to bed without demur, a circumstance so unusual that Anne felt his forehead for signs of fever.

There was none, of course, which she had known in that secret pocket of her heart where she also knew if he slept or waked, was calm or distressed. The child was tired, that was all.

"*Mirada* wore you out, laddie, didn't he just?"

"*Mirada*?" Shan's lashes flickered and the slanting brows pulled together. "*Mirada*?

"Later, Shannie," Anne soothed, brushing the white hair back from the broad, brown forehead. "Go to sleep now."

But she had no need to coax; her inner sense told her sleep had already laid its spell.

Out in the great room a few minutes later, she shook her head at the parcels that had been delivered from the local grocer. Gods only knew where the man thought she was going to put all the various goodies he'd ordered, which included two tins of fabulously expensive, real-bean coffee.

"Well, and perhaps some of it will be for himself," she murmured, turning her back on the pile and resolutely picking up the first examination booklet.

She was very nearly half-way through the lot when the doorbell sounded, startling her into a curse.

"Ah, there, Annie Davis," she chided herself as she crossed the room, "always losing yourself inside the work . . ."

"Good evening." Er Thom bowed low as she opened the door—the Bow of Honored Esteem, she thought, frowning slightly. Most usually, he greeted her with the Bow Between Equals. She wondered, uneasily, what the deviation meant.

"Good evening," she returned, with as much calm as she could muster. She stepped aside, motioning him in with a wave of her hand. "Come in, please."

He did, offering the wine he carried with another slight bow. "A gift for the House."

Anne took the bottle, uneasiness growing toward alarm. Er Thom usually brought wine on his visits—a Liaden custom, she understood, which demonstrated the goodwill of the visitor. But he had never before been so formal—so *alien*—in his manner to her.

Clutching the symbol of his goodwill, Anne attempted her own bow—Gratitude Toward the Guest. "Thank you. Will you take a glass with me?"

"It would be welcome," he returned, nothing but stiff formality, with all of her friend and her lover hid down in the depths of his eyes. He moved a graceful hand, showing her the cluttered worktable and piles of exam booklets. "I would not, however, wish to interrupt your work."

"Oh." She stared at the desk, then at the clock on the shelf above it. "My work will take me another few hours," she said, hesitantly. "A break now, for a few moments, to drink wine with—with my friend . . ." She let it drift off, biting her lip in an agony of uncertainty.

"Ah." Something moved across his face—a flicker, nothing more. But she knew that he was in some way relieved. Almost, she thought he smiled, though in truth he did nothing more than incline his head.

"I suggest a compromise," he said softly. "You to your worktable and I to stow the groceries. The wine may wait until—friends—are able."

"Stow the groceries?" She blinked at him and then at the pile of boxes. "All that stuff won't fit in my kitchen, Er Thom. I'd hoped some was for you."

Surprisingly, he laughed—sweet, rare sound that it was—and she found herself smiling in response.

"A cargo-balancing exercise, no more." He reached out and slipped the bottle from her grasp. "I shall contrive. In the meanwhile, you to your examinations, eh?"

"I to my examinations," she agreed, still smiling like a fool, absurdly, astonishingly relieved. "Thank you, Er Thom."

"It is nothing," he murmured, moving off toward the pile.

He paused briefly to take off his jacket and drape it over the back of the easy chair before continuing on to the kitchen.

Ridiculously light of heart, Anne went back to her desk and opened the next blue book.

TRUE TO HIS WORD, Er Thom found room for every blessed thing in the boxes, then neatly folded the boxes and slid them into the thin space between the coldbox and the washer.

He used the few extra minutes Anne needed to finish grading her last paper to rustle up some of the freshly-foraged foodstuffs and carry the snack, with wine and glasses, into the great room.

"That looks wonderful!" Anne said, eyeing the tray of cheese and vegetables and sauce with real appreciation. She smiled at Er Thom and stretched high on her toes to work out the kinks, fingers brushing the ceiling, as always.

"Blasted low bridge," she muttered, as she always did. "How much could it cost to add an extra two inches of height?"

"Quite a bit, I should think," Er Thom replied seriously. "Two inches on such a scale of building very soon becomes miles." He moved his shoulders, studiously watching the wine he was pouring into the glasses, rather than the delightful spectacle of her stretching tall and taut above him. "And *cantra*."

Anne grinned. "I expect you're right, at that. But it's a nuisance to always be bumping my fingers on the ceiling tiles."

She sank down into a corner of the sofa and took the glass he offered her. "Thank you, my dear, for all your labors on my behalf."

For a moment he froze, panicked that she might somehow know of the plea he had made on her behalf to Daav—Then he shook himself, for of course she only meant the task this evening, which was in truth nothing to one accustomed to balancing the holding pods of a starship.

"You are welcome," he said, since she seemed to wish hear him say it, and was rewarded by her smile.

Carefully, he sat on the opposite end of the sofa, striving to ignore the way his blood heated with her nearness, the shameful desires that clamored for ascendancy over honor and *melant'i* . . . He sipped wine, set the glass gently aside and steeled himself to look up into her face.

"I regret," he said, clearing his throat because his voice had gone unexpectedly hoarse. "I regret very much to have caused you pain, Anne. It was not understood that you would arrive home at an early hour. I erred and I wish you will forgive me."

She blinked. So *that* was the reason for his earlier stiffness. Almost, she reached out to touch his cheek. It was only the memory of the searing, unreasoning passion that the least touch of him awoke that kept her hand resting lightly on her knee.

"I forgive you freely," she said instead, smiling at him warmly. "It was—foolish of me to have panicked that way. You had given me your word and I should have—" Dangerous ground here: Fatal to say that she had *doubted* his word. "—I should have remembered that."

"Ah." He gave her a slight smile in return. "You are kind."

He hesitated then, putting off the moment when he must, in honor, ask what *melant'i* trembled to conceive. And it was not, he admitted to himself, wryly, as he would admit it to Daav, honor's argument that most compelled him. Rather, it was happy circumstance that honor in this instance bent neatly 'round his heart's desire.

He sipped his wine and had a nibble of cheese, all but trembling with desiring her. Sternly, he pushed the passion aside. He had sworn that it would be precisely as Anne wished it, with none of Er Thom yos'Galan's unruly passions to disarm her. There were proposals to be considered here; trade to be engaged upon. He took a deep breath.

"Anne?"

"Yes, love?" The intensity of her gaze betrayed a passion as unruly as his own and almost in that instant of meeting her eyes he was lost again.

Gritting his teeth, he shifted his gaze and swallowed against the flood tide of desire.

"I have a—proposal," he managed, hearing his voice shiver with breathlessness. "If you will hear me."

"All right," she said. Her voice seemed odd, as well, though when he turned to look at her, she had her face averted, watching the wine glass she had set upon the table. "What proposal, Er Thom?"

"I propose—" Gods, his thodelm would berate him and his delm also—perhaps. She was outside the Book of Clans—Terran, Terran, Terran to the core of her. She was bread to nourish him, water to slake him—desire to torment him until he could do nothing else but have her, though it flew in the face of clan and Code and—yes—of kin.

"I propose," he repeated, forcing himself to meet her eyes with a calmness he did not feel, "that we two be wed."

CHAPTER ELEVEN

If fate decrees you'll be lost at sea, you'll live through many a train wreck.

—Terran Proverb

"**WED?**" Astonishment overrode exultation—barely. With the force of both emotions rocking her, she heard her own voice, stammering: "But—I'm not Liaden."

Er Thom smiled slightly, slender shoulders moving in a fluid not-shrug. "And neither am I Terran," he said, with a certain dryness. He half-extended a hand to her, thought better of it and reached instead for his wine glass.

"It would be proper," he murmured, with exquisite care, for who was he to instruct an equal adult in proper conduct? "Proper—and well-intended—for you and I to be bound by contract—wed—at the time our son is Seen by Korval."

Exultation died with an abruptness that was agony. No lover-like words from Er Thom, Anne thought with uncharacteristic bitterness—when had she had even an endearment from him? This was expedience, nothing more. Unthinkable that a man of Er Thom yos'Galan's *melant'i* came home to show his delm a doxy and a bastard when he might, with only a little expense, show instead a wife and legitimate heir. Anne blinked through a sudden glaze of tears and willed herself to believe that the pounding of her heart was caused by anger, not anguish.

"No, thank you," she said shortly, proud that her voice was sharp and even. She turned her head, refusing to look at him, and reached for her glass.

"Hah." His hand—slim golden fingers, one crowned by the carved amethyst ring of a master trader—his hand lay lightly on her wrist, restraining her, waking fire in her belly.

"I have given offense," he murmured, taking his hand away. "My intention was—far otherwise, Anne. Please. What must I do to bring us back into Balance?"

"I'm not offended," she lied, and managed to meet his eyes squarely. "I just don't want to marry you."

Winged golden brows lifted, eloquent of disbelief. "Forgive me," he said gently. "One recalls the joy shared just recently—as well as that which we knew—before . . ."

"Did I say I didn't want to go to bed with you?" Anne snapped, all out of patience with him—and with herself. "Far too much of that, my lad! But lust is less of a reason for marrying than, than because it's—*proper*—and I'm damned if I'll marry for either!" She took a hard breath, barely able to see his face through the dazzle of tears—*angry* tears.

"It's your own notion to be taking Shannie to show your delm, not mine. For all of me he can stay uncounted 'til the end of his days! He's a Terran citizen, which is good enough for quite a number of folk, who manage to have good, long, productive lives and—"

"Anne." He was very close, one knee on the sofa cushion while his hands caught her shoulders, kneading the tight muscles. "*Anne.*"

She gasped, half-choked and lifted a hand to wipe at her eyes. Unaccustomed, she looked up into Er Thom's face, heart melting at the distress in his eyes even as passion flared and took fire at his nearness.

Achingly slow, he lifted a hand, ran light, trembling fingers down her damp cheek, over her lips, purple eyes wide and mesmerizing.

"I love you," he whispered, "Anne Davis."

"No." It was a battle to close her eyes, to deny her body the solace of him. Every thread of her ached to believe that whispered avowal, saving only one small bit of sanity that clamored it was nothing but expediency, still.

"No," she said again, eyes shuttered against him, trembling with need. "Er Thom, stop this. Please."

Instead, she felt warm breath stir the hairs at her temple an instant before his lips pressed there.

"I love you," he said again, wonderful, seductive voice shaking with passion. He stroked her hair back with tender fingers, kissed the edge of her ear. "Anne . . ."

"Er Thom." Her own voice was anything but steady. "Er Thom, you gave me your word . . ."

She could have sworn she felt the jolt go through him, the icy jag of sanity that broke the flaming fascination of desire for the instant he required to jerk back and away, coming to his feet in a blur of motion—and going entirely still, hands firmly behind his back.

"Oh, gods."

Anne shuddered, finding his abrupt absence less easement than added torment. *What* is *this?* she asked herself, for the dozenth time since yesterday. She had felt a rapport with Er Thom yos'Galan almost from the first. But this—*compulsion*—reminded her of the ancient stories of the Sidhe, the Faerie Lords of old Terra, and the enchantments they wove to ensnare mere mortals . . .

Except one sight of Er Thom's sweat-damp face and anguished eyes proved beyond human doubt that if this was enchantment, then he was netted as tightly as she.

She let out the breath she hadn't known she was holding and straightened against the cushions. "Er Thom . . ."

He bowed, effectively cutting her off. "Anne, only think," he said quickly, his accent more pronounced than she had ever heard it. "You say you will be traveling to Liad, that there is duty owed one who has died. What better than to travel with one who is your friend, to guest in the house of your son's kin for as long as you like? Everything shall be as you wish—" He bit his lip and glanced sharply away, then back.

"If you do not wish us to wed, why then, there is nothing more to be said. I—certainly I cannot know your necessities. However, you must know that *my* necessities require our son to show his face to the delm no later than the second day of the next *relumma*—three Standard weeks, as you had said." He moved his hands, showing her palms, fingers spread wide, concealing nothing.

"I tell you all," he said, the pace of his words slowing somewhat. "Anne. I do not wish to wound you, or to frighten you, or to steal our son away from you. But he *must* be brought to the delm. He is yos'Galan! Provision must be made—and yourself! Will you stand alone and without allies, having borne a child to Korval?"

Anne stared, breathless with hearing him out. "Is that—dangerous?" she asked.

"Dangerous?" Er Thom repeated, blankly. He moved a hand, a gesture of tossing aside. "Ah, bah! It is games of *melant'i*. Nothing to alarm one who is prudent." He tipped his head, bit his lip as if unsure how to continue.

"It is prudent to gather allies," he said at last and Anne heard the exquisite care he took now, lest he offend her. "Korval is not negligible, you understand. And the child is yos'Galan. None can deny basis for alliance. The marriage I—wished for—would have brought you immediately into a case of—of—*intended alliance*. You would have been seen to be under the Dragon's wing *now,* rather than waiting upon the trip to Liad and the drawing up of—other—contracts." He took a deep breath, and met her eyes, his own wide and guileless.

"It distresses me to see you in peril," he said, very softly, "when I have the means and the—desire—to give you protection."

"I—see," she managed, around the hammering of her heart. She shook her head in a futile effort to clear it and made a grab for common sense. This was University Central, after all: haven of scholars and students and other servants of odd knowledge and arcane thought.

"No one's likely to come after my head here," she told him, meaning it for comfort and an ease to the distress he showed her plainly, and added a phrase with a flavor of High Liaden: "Thank you for your care, Er Thom."

He hesitated, then bowed acceptance of her decision, or so she thought.

"In three Standard weeks," he said, straightening, "I shall pilot our son and yourself to Solcintra. We shall all three go to the delm and Shan shall be Seen. After, I shall take you to Trealla Fantrol—the house of yos'Galan—where you may guest until your duty to your friend has been completed."

It made sense, even if it was phrased rather autocratically. It solved her transportation and living problems. It solved Er Thom's pressing need to have the newly-discovered yos'Galan added to clan Korval's internal census.

It did *not* solve her disinclination for having the order of her life disrupted for as long as two months while she tried to sort out a colleague's private working notes.

And it certainly did not solve the fact that she would be staying those two months on Liad—in *Solcintra,* called "The City of Jewels" for the standard of wealth enjoyed by its citizens. At—Trealla Fantrol—she might well be Er Thom yos'Galan's honored guest and recipient of every grace the House could provide. But in Solcintra she would be a lone Terran in the company of Liadens, with their fierce competitiveness and Liad-centric ways—

. . . in a society where the phrase, "Rag-mannered as a Terran," enjoyed current—and frequent—usage.

"I had thought perhaps of—not—going to Liad," Anne began, slowly. "It might be just as useful for me to copy my old letters to Jin Del—Scholar yo'Kera—and send them to his colleague. That way she—"

The doorbell chimed—and again, insistent.

"At this hour?" Anne was already moving, unaware that Er Thom had moved with her until he caught her hand, pulling her a step back from the widening door.

"Er Thom—"

"Anne!" Jerzy all but fell into her arms. "You're here! You're *safe*! Gods, gods—the whole damn pantheon! Down at the Quad S Tavern when the news came over—terrified you'd stayed late to grade exams—too stupid to find a call box—" He sagged against her shoulder and let a theatrical sigh shudder through him before he lifted his head to grin at Er Thom.

"Evening, Mr. yos'Galan."

Er Thom inclined his head. "Good evening, Jerzy Entaglia," he said gravely. "Is there a reason why Anne should—not—be safe?"

Jerzy blinked, straightening away from Anne's support and glancing from her to Er Thom. "You didn't hear?" he asked, eyes going back to Anne. "The bulletin, right in the middle of the—" He stared around the room, spied the dark screen. "Guess not. Well, all that exercise for nothing."

"Heard *what*?" Anne demanded. "Jerzy, it's past midnight! If this is one of your—"

"My jokes? No joke." He grabbed her hand, ugly face entirely serious. "Comp Ling's gone. The whole back corner of the Language Block blew sky-high, two hours ago."

PETRELLA YOS'GALAN eyed the child of her deceased twin with a noticeable lack of warmth.

"Felicitations, is it?" she said ill-temperedly. "And to what event does my delm desire me to attach felicity? The continued absence of my heir, perhaps? Or the visit from Delm Nexon this morning, inquiring of that same heir's health? Or shall I find joy in the empty nursery and the absence of a child to continue the Line?"

Daav had a sip of red wine. "Well, certainly you may rejoice in any such that may move you," he said agreeably. "I had only meant to bring tidings of my *cha'leket*'s return on the second day of the next *relumma*."

"Three days later than the delm's deadline," she said with asperity. "As I am certain the delm recalls, having so—long—a memory."

He grinned. "Well-thrown, Aunt Petrella! But as it happens, your heir begged the delm's grace and received the extension, as insisting on the previous timeframe would have considerably inconvenienced the guest."

"Ah, the felicity not only of the return of one's son, but also the inestimable joy of a guest!" Petrella flung her hand high in mock jubilation. "How fortunate for the House, indeed. Is one to know more of the guest, I wonder? For the universe, you understand, is a-bursting with potential guests."

"Why, so it is!" Daav said, much struck by this viewpoint. "I had not considered it thus, but I believe you are correct, ma'am! How piquant, to be sure: An entire universe, panting to guest with Korval!"

"Yes, very good," she returned. "Play the fool, do, and amuse yourself at an old woman's expense. I note that details regarding the guest have not come forth."

He moved his shoulders. "The guest is a scholar of some repute."

"More delight," his aunt said acidly. "A scholar, to our honor! As if there were any more rag-mannered, saving only a—"

"A Terran scholar," Daav interrupted gently. He assayed another sip of the excellent red. "You may wish to remodel the Ambassadorial Suite."

Petrella was staring. "A Terran scholar?"

"Indeed, yes," her nephew said, and amplified: "A scholar who also happens—a mere accident of birth, I assure you!—to be Terran."

Petrella had closed her eyes and allowed herself to slump back into her chair. Daav watched her closely, seeking a sign by which he might know if this sudden sagging were an artifact of her illness or a ploy to divert him.

Petrella opened her eyes. "Er Thom is bringing a Terran scholar to guest in this house," she said, absolutely toneless.

"Correct," replied Er Thom's foster-brother and, when she still glared at him: "He being so scholarly himself, you see."

She snorted. "A master trader may not be an idiot, I allow. However, I confess that this scholarly aspect of my son's nature has heretofore escaped my notice." She waved a hand, and Daav saw sincere weariness in the gesture. "But there—a *cha'leket* will know what none other may guess."

"Exactly so," Daav murmured and finished his wine. Setting the glass aside, he rose and made his bow—affection and honored esteem. "If there is any way in which I may be of service, Aunt, do call. And if you would prefer not to meddle with the Ambassadorial Suite, the scholar may just as easily stay at Jelaza—"

"yos'Galan's guest," the old lady interrupted austerely, "stays in yos'Galan's house."

"Certainly," her nephew said and crossed over to bend and kiss her ravaged cheek and lay a light hand on the sparse, scorched hair. "Don't tire yourself. I am entirely able to assist you."

She smiled her slight, mocking smile and reached up to touch his cheek. "You're a good boy," she said softly, then waved an irritable hand. "Go away. I've work to do."

"Yes, aunt," he said gently and crossed the room with his silent, quick steps, melting down the hallway as if he had no more substance than a shadow.

Petrella sighed and slumped deep in her chair, concentrating on the breath that rasped, painful and hot, through her ruined lungs.

After a time, when she was certain she would not shame herself, she rang the bell for the butler.

CHAPTER TWELVE

The thing to recall about Dragons is that it takes a special person to deal with them at all. If you lie to them they will steal from you. If you attack them without cause they will dismember you. If you run from them they will laugh at you.

It is thus best to deal calmly, openly and fairly with Dragons: Give them all they buy and no more or less, and they will do the same by you. Stand at their back and they will stand at yours. Always remember that a Dragon is first a Dragon and only then a friend, a partner, a lover.

Never assume that you have discovered a Dragon's weak point until it is dead and forgotten, for joy is fleeting and a Dragon's revenge is forever.

—From *The Liaden Book of Dragons*

ER THOM let himself into his stuffy rented quarters, took off his jacket and flung it over the arm of the doubtful sofa. Spacer that he was, he barely noticed the lack of windows, though the rattle of the ventilator grated on senses tuned to catch the barest whisper of life system malfunction.

Surefooted in the dimness, he went across the common room to the pantry and poured a glass of wine from one of the bottles appropriated from *Dragon's Way.*

Honest red wine and none of Daav's precious misravot! he thought, smiling softly. Leaning against the too-high counter, he closed his eyes and sipped.

He had almost lost her.

The thought horrified—and horrified again, for it transpired that on days when Marilla watched Shan, she most usually brought him to Anne's office in the evening, as Rilly went to teach a night class. Dependent upon the child's mood, Anne did sometimes stay late, grading papers, meeting with students, doing "housecleaning." If Er Thom had not had the tending of his son this day . . .

"An accident," Jerzy Entaglia had said, sitting on Anne's sofa and drinking a cup of real coffee. "Just one of those stupid damn things. That's what Admin's saying, anyway." He sighed, looking abruptly exhausted.

"'Course they haven't sorted the rubble yet, or counted the bodies—or even called up the folks who have back-wing offices, just to make sure they're all tucked up, safe and warm." He shook his head. "Likely they'll find huge chunks of a fusion bomb in the wreckage, when they get around to cleaning it up."

"Is there—forgive me," Er Thom had murmured at that point, though it was hardly his place to do so. "Has there been thought of— of a balancing . . . ?"

Jerzy blinked at him.

"An honor-feud, he means," Anne told her friend and shook her head. "It's not too likely, Er Thom. The whole wing went, remember? Not just one person's office. And anyway, how could there be a feud against a language department? We're just a bunch of fuzzy humanities-types. If it were a hard-science department, where they might possibly have gotten onto something someone didn't want them to have—but Languages? You might as well blow up Theater Arts!"

"A notion over-full with glamour," Jerzy announced, with the air of one quoting a passage of Code.

Anne laughed.

"Yah, well, I'm outta here," Jerzy said, levering himself up. "'Night, Anne—Mr. yos'Galan. Lucky thing you were here to take Scooter today." He stuck his big hand out.

Er Thom rose and offered his own, patiently enduring the stranger's touch and the up-and-down motion. Then he rescued his hand and bowed honor for his son's foster-father. "Keep you well, Jerzy Entaglia."

"Thanks," the other man had said. "Same to you."

He'd left then, and Er Thom soon after, to come back to these ragged apartments that were still slightly more spacious than Anne's normal living quarters. He pictured her in Trealla Fantrol, where the guesting suites boasted wide windows and fragrant plants and well-made, graceful furniture.

He pictured her walking the lawns with him, visiting the maze, and Jelaza Kazone—thought of showing her the Tree . . .

She had said she did not wish to wed.

Er Thom opened his eyes, frowning at the clock hung lopsided on the wall opposite.

She had said she did not wish to marry him, but that was not true. She burned for him as he for her and dreaded the day when they would part. He knew it. In his bones he knew it, irrevocably, absolutely, beyond doubt or even question of *how* he knew it.

So, Anne had lied. He was a master trader, after all. He knew prevarication in all its postures, tones and faces. Never before had he had a lie from Anne.

Why now? he wondered, and then recalled that he had taught her to fear him. Very likely the lie was credited to his account—and accurate balance it was.

Still, if she wished to wed and denied him out of fear, the matter might yet be managed. All his skill was in showing folk who had never seen an item why they must yearn to possess it. How much easier a trade, when the one he traded with already desired that which he had to offer—

"Wait."

He came sharply away from the counter and paced into the common room, reaching up to slap at the ill-placed light-switch.

He had offered contract-marriage, he thought agitatedly. It was everything that he *could* offer—though it was extremely irregular and would doubtless require him to fall on his face before his thodelm and cry mercy. Yet, contract-marriage to Anne—especially with the child already fact!—lay within the realm of what was very possible.

Only—contract-marriages very soon expired and the spouses separated—and Anne dreading their eventual separation as much as he.

"How," Er Thom asked the empty room, "if she wishes a life-mating?"

That became a matter for the delm. Giddy as the prospect of spending all his days with Anne Davis might render Er Thom yos'Galan, yet the delm was the keeper of the clan's genes, guardian of the lines' purity, arbiter of alliances. Korval was not as populous as once it had been and the delm might very well have use for Er Thom's genes elsewhere. A lifemating would put him beyond the possibility of future contract-marriages, which left the burden of such alliances to Kareen, which was laughable—and to Daav.

Korval might very well—and with all good cause—deny its son Er Thom the solace of a lifemating.

Or he might be allowed the lifemating—later. After he had done his full duty for the clan—however many years it might take.

"And I hardly able to keep myself from her for one night!" He finished his wine, ruefully. Still, it was out of his hands and firmly in the keeping of the delm, who would decide for the good of the clan and could do nothing at all until Er Thom laid the entire matter before him.

Thinking thus, though in no way comforted, and, indeed, with an unaccustomed dismay for the ways and necessities of the clan, he went back to the pantry for another glass of wine, which he carried with him to the wall desk.

"I shall put the thing before Daav," he said to himself. "He may best advise me of the clan's requirements, and what the delm might decide." And Daav at least, Scout as he had been, would not turn his face in horror from one who professed abiding love for a Terran . . .

Seated on the too-wide chair, booted feet just short of the floor, Er Thom opened the remote unit he had brought with him from the ship and touched the 'on' key.

The message-waiting light blinked in the top right corner, blue and insistent.

So, then. Besides his message to the delm he had also sent word to his first mate, though not—guilt twisted in his stomach—to his mother. *Ever more unruly,* he thought. *Brother, only see what becomes of the one of us who had always been dutiful.*

He touched the access key and a heartbeat later was staring at a brief note from his delm, requesting details of Korval's debt to Respected Scholar Anne Davis and the error which led to this balancing.

"Hah." Er Thom cleared the screen and had a sip of wine, wondering how best to comply with his delm's request. As he put the glass aside, he saw the message light still blinking and touched the access key once more.

Darling, what mad coil have you tangled yourself in? Almost, he could hear Daav's voice through the words on the screen—and smiled. Worse, how am I to do a brother's duty and aid you in ruining yourself unless I Know All? Worse still, I have informed your mother my aunt of your return date and the concomitant arrival of a guest, from which interview I barely escaped with my life. Please believe me willing to die for you, but may I at least know for what cause?

I look forward to making the acquaintance of my new nephew, and of his mother, a lady I have long admired from afar. In preparation for her visit I have ordered and am now reading her entire bibliography, so you see I don't mean to shame you. In the case that you had been unaware of the scope of the lady's work, I most highly commend Who's Who in Terran Scholars *to you.*

In the meanwhile, brother, do not hesitate to call upon me for whatever service I might render. Keep safe. Smooth journey. And may the luck ride your shoulder until we meet again.

All my love,
Daav."

"I love you, too, *denubia*," Er Thom murmured, then grinned. *Who's Who in Terran Scholars*, was it? As it happened, he was aware of the nature of Anne's work, though it would do no harm to read her published papers. His knowledge came from listening to her speak of her theories, her observations, more—he freely admitted!—because the sound of her voice soothed him in some profound, indescribable way than because her theories compelled him.

Still, it was the joke between his cha'leket and himself—that it was Daav who was bookish. What, after all, was a Scout, save a scholar placed in peril? Meantime, Master Trader yos'Galan, with his penchant for statistics and passion for new markets, could most often be found reading a manifest.

Smile fading, Er Thom leaned back, wondering anew how best to put a situation that grew daily more tangled into lines of orderly words, for either delm or *cha'leket*.

He required a plan of action, he thought, sipping his wine thoughtfully. Best perhaps to first soothe Anne's wariness of him, and bring her gently to see that she must of course travel to Liad. Duty to her dead friend was clear, as he was certain she knew. It was fear speaking, when she talked of staying on University and not venturing forth to Liad. And certainly, anyone must be distressed at first encountering Solcintra society, though a guest of Korval would naturally be given all honor due the House. Society was prudent, if not particularly intelligent.

So, then. Anne gentled into making the trip. Shan Seen by the delm and then, gods willing, by Thodelm yos'Galan. He expected his mother would need some gentling herself, but, presented with one already Seen by Korval, she could hardly be churlish enough to refuse to take the child to yos'Galan, mixed blood or pure.

As yos'Galan's guest, Anne could become accustomed to Liad—*and Liad to Anne*, he thought wryly—and fulfill her duty. In the meanwhile, Er Thom would take thought as to how best to present his desires to the delm—and would speak to his *cha'leket* of the matter, face-to-face, over a glass or two, with the warmth of brotherhood between them.

It would do, he decided. It was not precipitate, and it held some promise for success—if he was very careful and played each counter with all the craft and skill in him. He recalled that Daav was a counterchance player to behold, and smiled.

Well, and now that he thought of it, there was a service his brother could perform for him. Er Thom pulled the remote onto his lap. He would write a quick note and then to bed, for he was to rise early and go to mind Shan while Anne went to Central Administration and found what now was required of her, with her place of work destroyed.

CHAPTER THIRTEEN

∽∽∽∽∽∽∽∽∽∽∽∽∽∽∽∽∽∽∽∽∽∽∽∽∽∽∽

There are several million Traders in the galaxy, but only 300 Master Traders registered with the Trade Commission on VanDyk. Until recently, all 300 were Liaden. This has been changing slowly, as Terrans become more successful in the trade arena and able to afford the costly and extensive certification tests.

Terran or Liaden, a Master Trader's work is exacting, requiring intimate knowledge of the regulations of a thousand ports of call, as well as a sure instinct for what will gain a profit at each. Master Traders often chart their ship's course as the trade develops, some running as long as five years between visits to the home port.

Less exalted Traders most usually ply an established route, which has most likely been researched and planned by a Master Trader.

The very best Master Traders are described as cool-headed, analytical, persuasive generalists who are filled with the passion to deal.

—From *A Young Person's Book of Trade*

ER THOM FROWNED at the remote's cramped screen and wondered just how much—and who—Jyl ven'Apon had paid for the privilege of being known as a Master of Trade.

"Lithium, by all gods," he muttered, reaching for the mug of tea set to hand. "An enterprise as substantial as moonbeams, and she begs my hundred cantra buy-in cool as if she has a right! What can she be about? And to claim she enjoys yo'Laney's support—and Ivrex!" He paused, sipping the horrible Terran tea and considering that so-blithe claim of support.

Neither yo'Laney nor Ivrex was master-class, but two solid, substantial traders from solid, substantial clans. By all rights, they should have smelled the overripeness of the scheme even as Er Thom had.

Was ven'Apon's claim of support false, upon which face she was even more foolish than he had suspected? Or was her claim *true*, and she out to lighten as many pouches as possible before she was called to face the Guild Masters and her license—

"*Mirada!*" The demand was punctuated by a bump on his elbow that barely missed sending the mug's contents into orbit.

Carefully, he put the tea aside and turned his chair so he faced his petitioner.

"Shan-son," he said in grave Low Liaden. "How may I serve you?"

The boy looked at him doubtfully, gripping the red plastic keyboard-and-screen unit with both hands.

Er Thom smiled and reached out to stroke the snow-white hair. *Such an odd color,* he thought. *Doubtless it will darken, when he is older . . .*

"My son," he murmured in his careful Terran, "what may I do for you?"

The small face relaxed into a smile and Shan swung the toy onto Er Thom's knees.

"All done," he said with the air of one making himself perfectly clear.

"Ah." Er Thom glanced down at the thing. Dirty white plastic letters spelled out *Mix-n-Match,* against the bright red case. The screen was narrow, and the keys overlarge—to accommodate those too young to possesses fine manipulative skills, Er Thom thought. He touched a key at random.

"This module has been satisfactorily completed," a woman's

bright voice told him. "Please insert upgrade module number *five* to continue progression."

"All done," Shan amplified, leaning cozily against Er Thom's thigh and pointing at the blank screen. "Need new, *Mirada*."

"A moment, if you please," Er Thom replied, putting his left arm around the child's body in a loose hug and adjusting the tiny screen for less glare. "I would like to look at the old . . ."

In very short order he had located and accessed the toy's resident manual, from which he learned that *Mix-n-Match* aimed to teach pattern recognition, eye-hand coordination, improve memory and lay the foundation for understanding of cause and effect. Module four, which Shan had just completed, was rated for the use of children having from 36 to 40 months. Er Thom frowned.

A bit more searching uncovered the module's database, which revealed the fascinating information that Shan's scores were in the ninety-eighth achievement percentile of all those who had completed the module.

"Well done," Er Thom said, touching the power-off and putting the simple computer onto Anne's desk. He bent and gave Shan a hug, rubbing his cheek against the soft, odd-colored hair. "*Ge'shada*, Shan-son. You have done very well, indeed."

Shan wriggled in his embrace. "Gee-shad-a," he announced and laughed.

Er Thom echoed the sound, softly, and let the child go. "Where are the new modules, then, my bright one?"

He had forgotten himself—the question was asked in Low Liaden. But Shan barely hesitated an instant before catching Er Thom's hand and pulling on it.

"Come on, *Mirada*. Needs new."

"So I am told." He stood and allowed himself to be tugged across the room to where Anne's ancient and battered half-chora slept, plastic-shrouded, atop a table made of real wood.

"Here," Shan announced, dropping Er Thom's hand to bend down and paw fruitlessly at the table's single drawer. He sighed gustily and straightened, looking up at Er Thom out of guileless silver eyes. "Stuck."

"I see." He bent and pulled.

The drawer *was* a little sticky, but not to signify. Once opened, however, it proved to be—empty.

"All gone," Shan discovered, peering into the depths. He shook his head. "Oh, well."

Oh, well, indeed, Er Thom thought. *And the child already outpacing the modules . . .*

"Shall I show you how my computer works?" he asked, holding down a hand. Shan took it with his usual lack of hesitation and they went back to Anne's desk.

Er Thom sat in the big chair and lifted the child onto his lap. He filed Jyl ven'Apon's audacious letter away for the moment and pulled the remote closer, adjusting the screen height.

Bintell Products was the manufacturer of *Mix-n-Match,* according to the resident manual.

"It happens," Er Thom murmured to his son, fingers moving over the keys, "that Korval trades with subsidiaries of Bintell Products. We should be able to locate an entire set of modules with very little trouble."

It took a few minutes, with Shan sitting rapt astride his knees, eyes never moving from the screen and the data flickering across it.

"There." He froze the screen, highlighted his choices and called for fuller information.

"I think perhaps we will have this *Edu-Board* for you," he murmured, absently and in Low Liaden. "You find *Mix-n-Match* far too simple, eh? *Edu-Board* has complexity—self-programming, individually-structured learning—yes. I think you will like this extremely, *denubia.*" He issued the order—to be delivered, alas, to Trealla Fantrol, as a special shipment to University would not arrive until several weeks after Shan was on Liad.

"So then." He shut down the goods list and called up his work screen. On his lap, Shan gave a sigh of utter satisfaction.

"Fast," he commented, hand moving toward the remote's keyboard.

Er Thom caught the small, questing fingers in his and squeezed them lightly. "This is mine," he said in firm Terran. "You may watch me do my work, if you like, or you may do something else."

"Watch," his son decided without hesitation, and snuggled his back into Er Thom's chest. "Say—*tell*—me your—work—*Mirada*."

"Ah." He touched keys, accessing the information for *Mandrake,* one of Korval's lesser trade ships. "We must consider how best to utilize Dil Ton sig'Erlan upon this route. He is young, you see, though not entirely untried. Indeed, he may have the ability to achieve master-rank. It is the duty of one already master to give him opportunity to expand himself and hone his talent—but not too quickly. We do not wish to ruin him with too much failure—or with too much success . . ."

He leaned back and Shan did also, so that his head was under Er Thom's chin. The man smiled and lay his arms about the child and closed his eyes, considering Dil Ton sig'Erlan.

There was not much scope for creativity on the Lytaxin run. It was a minor route at best, encompassing a total of seven Outworlds, existing by reason of Korval's ancient ties with Erob, Lytaxin's ascendant clan. Still, there ought to be some way to test sig'Erlan's mettle, to place him out of context and force him into unexpected—

"Hah!" Er Thom opened his eyes, having bethought himself of a certain very odd something that had reposed, undisturbed, these several years in a corner of Korval's third Solcintra warehouse. "I believe that will do nicely, yes." He leaned forward and added the item to *Mandrake's* manifest.

"What you do?" Shan demanded, grabbing at the man's sleeve.

"I have given young sig'Erlan a gift," Er Thom replied, touching the "send" key. "May he reap joy of it."

He smiled and stretched, eye snagging on the time-bar in the upper corner of the remote's screen.

"Are you hungry?" he asked Shan, and received an enthusiastic affirmative.

"Very well." He lifted the child to the floor and stood, offering a hand. "Let us then eat lunch."

THE SKY WAS OF A BLUE just tinged with green and the air was laden with flower-scents.

Daav yos'Phelium sent the sleek groundcar through the various twists and turns of Trealla Fantrol's drive with expert negligence. As he pulled into the carport, he saw Er Thom's mother sitting on the East Patio, taking the sun, a bound book unopened on her lap. He sighed, pushing aside the old sorrow as he walked across the grass toward her.

"Good morning, Aunt Petrella!"

She looked up, making no move to rise from her chair. A bad day, then.

"Good enough, I suppose, for those who have nothing better to do than fidget about in fancy cars."

He grinned. "Ah, but I have much more to do than fidget about! You behold me, in fact, atremble with busy-ness. I have this day received a pin-beam from my brother Er Thom, bidding me purchase in his name a concert-quality omnichora and have it delivered to this house immediately. In my brother's name I have done this thing. It should arrive this afternoon."

She glared at him. "An omnichora?"

"An omnichora," he agreed, with appropriate gravity.

"Er Thom does not play the omnichora," that gentleman's mother announced darkly.

"Ah. Then perhaps it is for the guest," Daav speculated, eyes wide with wholly counterfeit innocence. "It is our duty, you know, Aunt, to arrange all for the comfort and well-being of the guest."

"A lesson in Code, I apprehend," Petrella said scathingly. "Uncounted thanks to the instructor."

Bland-faced, Daav bowed, graciously acknowledging the offered thanks. Petrella sniffed.

"Awake upon all suits, are you? One supposes you know the name of the respected scholar who is to be our guest, but wonders when you will judge it proper to share that information."

"From you, Aunt Petrella, I have no secrets," her nephew told her audaciously. "The scholar's name is Anne Davis."

"Anne Davis," she repeated, mouth tightening. "And Anne Davis is—naturally!—a scholar of the omnichora. Met perhaps at some delightful musical soiree engineered by those who must delight in—"

"I believe," Daav interrupted gently, "that Anne Davis is a scholar of comparative linguistics, attached to the Languages Department based upon University. If you wish, I will forward copies of her publications to your screen—" he bowed, "in order that you may enjoy informed conversation with the guest."

"Yet another lesson in manners! I am quite overcome. In the meanwhile, what has a concert-quality omnichora to do with a scholar of language?"

"Perhaps," Daav offered, ever more gently, "it is an avocation."

Petrella hesitated, considering him out of narrowed eyes. Daav was notoriously—even foolishly—sweet-tempered. Yet that tone of caressing gentleness was clear warning to those who knew him well: Daav hovered on the edge of displeasure, in which state even his *cha'leket* was hard-put to deal with him sanely.

Accordingly, Petrella relented somewhat in her attack and inclined her head. "Perhaps it is, as you say, an avocation. Doubtless we shall learn more when the scholar is with us." She glanced up, moving both hands in the formal gesture of asking. "One cannot help but wonder why the scholar comes to us at all."

There was a small pause.

"My *cha'leket* allows me to know that Scholar Davis had been a friend of Scholar yo'Kera of Solcintra University. Scholar yo'Kera has recently died and duty of friendship calls Scholar Davis to Solcintra."

"I see." An entirely reasonable explanation, saving only that the mystery of Er Thom's acquaintanceship with Scholar Davis remained—deliberately, as Petrella strongly suspected—unresolved.

Still, another measuring glance at her nephew's face argued the best course was to leave the matter until she might have the entire tale, start to finish, from the lips of her heir.

Embracing thus the more prudent course, Petrella inclined her head. "My thanks. Is there anything else one should know beforehand of the guest, so all may be arranged for her comfort and well-being?"

Amusement gleamed in the depths of Daav's dark eyes. He bowed slightly.

"I believe not. Now, if you will excuse me, aunt, I must away. Duty calls."

"Certainly. Give you good day."

"Give you good day, Aunt Petrella." He was gone, noiseless across the blue-green grass.

An omnichora, she thought, watching Daav's car down the drive. *To be delivered this afternoon, by all the gods. And if the guest is an expert in her avocation . . .*

Grumbling to herself, she rang for Mr. pak'Ora.

"An omnichora will be arriving this afternoon. See it situated."

"Situated, Thodelm?"

She drew herself up in the chair, ignoring the pain the effort cost her. "Yes, *situated.* The Bronze Room is said to have good acoustics—put it there. We'll have a music room."

The butler bowed. "Very good, Thodelm," he said, careful of her mood, and left her.

Alone, she fingered her book, but did not open it. Eventually she nodded off in the warm sun and slept so soundly she did not hear either the arrival of the omnichora or of the technician hastily summoned to tend to the Bronze Room's acoustics.

CHAPTER FOURTEEN

The Guild Halls of so-called "Healers"—interactive empaths—can be found in every Liaden city.

Healers are charged with tending ills such as depression, addiction and other psychological difficulties and they are undoubtedly skilled therapists, with a high rate of success to their credit.

Healers are credited with the ability to wipe a memory from all layers of a client's consciousness. They are said to be able to directly— utilizing psychic ability—influence another's behavior; however, this activity is specifically banned by Guild regulations.

—From "The Case Against Telepathy"

THE MUSIC BUILT of its own will, weaving a tapestried wall of sound that shielded her from her weary thoughts.

Er Thom was giving Shan a bath, a project that had been under way when she arrived home, and also appeared to include laundering Er Thom's shirt. After a brief glance into the tiny bathroom and hurriedly exchanged hellos with father and son, Anne had retreated to the great room and, as she so often did in times of stress, to the omnichora.

The music changed direction and her fingers obediently

followed, her mind beyond thought and into some entirely other place, where sound and texture and instinct were all.

Eyes closed, she *became* the music and stayed thus for time unmeasured, until her attention was pricked by a subtle inner-heard unsound: Her son was with her.

Reluctantly, she became apart from the music, lifted her fingers from the keyboard and opened her eyes.

Shan stood beside her in his pajamas, silver eyes wide in his thin brown face. "*Beautiful* sparkles," he breathed.

Anne smiled and reached down to lift him onto her lap. "Sparkles again, is it, my lad? Well, it's a pretty line of chat. All clean, I see. Did your da live, too?"

"Does he see them often?" That was Er Thom, solemn and soft-voiced as ever, though his dark blue shirt was soaked as thoroughly as his hair. He moved his hand in a measured gesture as she glanced over to him. "The—sparkles."

"Who can tell if he sees them now?" Anne replied, ruffling Shan's damp hair. "Ask him where the sparkles *are* and all you'll get is a stare and a point into blank air." She bent suddenly, enclosing the child in a hug. "Ma loves you, Shannie. Sparkles and all."

"Love you, Ma." This was followed by an enthusiastic kiss on her cheek and an imperative wriggle. "Shan go."

"Shan go to bed," his mother informed him, adjusting her grip expertly and standing with him cradled in her arms.

"*Mirada!*"

But if he was hoping for sympathy from that quarter, he got none.

"To bed, as your mother wishes," Er Thom said firmly. "We shall bid you good-night and you shall go to sleep."

Anne grinned at him. "A plan. Even a *good* plan. Let's see how it holds up to practical usage."

"By all means." He bowed, slightly and with amusement, before preceding her across the room and opening the door to the bedroom.

"Not *sleepy!*" Shan announced loudly and tried one more abortive twist for freedom.

"Shannie!" Anne stopped and frowned down into his face. "It's bedtime. Be a good boy."

For a moment, she thought he would insist: He stared mulishly into her face for two long heartbeats, then sighed and leaned his head against her shoulder.

"Bedtime," he allowed. "Good boy."

"Good boy," Anne repeated. She carried him into the bedroom and laid him down next to Mouse.

"Good-night, Shannie. Sleep tight." She kissed his cheek and fussed at the blanket before standing aside to let Er Thom by.

"Good-night, my son," he murmured in Terran, bending to kiss Shan gently on the lips. He straightened and added a phrase in Liaden: "*Chiat'a bei kruzon*"—dream sweetly.

"'Night, Ma. 'Night, *Mirada*."

"Sleep," Er Thom said, gesturing Anne to proceed him.

She did and he followed, closing the door half-way.

In the common room he smiled and bowed. "A plan proved by field conditions. Shall you have wine?"

"Wine would be wonderful," she said, abruptly aware of all her weariness again. She shook her head. "But I'll pour, Er Thom. You're soaked—"

"Not now," he interrupted softly, testing his sleeve between finger and thumb. "This fabric dries very quickly." He ran a quick hand through bright golden locks and made a wry face. "Hair, however—"

Anne laughed. "Adventures in bathing! You didn't need to take that on, my friend. I know Shan's a handful—"

"No more than Daav and I were at his age," Er Thom murmured, leading the way into the kitchenette. "Based on tales which have been told. Though the process by which one may get soup into one's ears seems to have escaped me over time—"

"It's a gift," Anne told him seriously, leaning a hip against the counter.

"As well it might be," he returned, back to her as he ferreted out glasses, corkscrew, and wine bottle.

Anne put her arms behind her, palms flat on the counter, watching his smooth, efficient movements. Her mind drifted somewhat, considering the slim golden body hidden now beneath the dark blue shirt and gray trousers. It was a delightful body: unexpectedly strong, enchantingly supple, entirely, warmly, deliciously male—Anne caught her breath against a throttling surge of desire.

Across the tiny kitchen, Er Thom dropped a glass.

It chimed on the edge of the counter, wine freed in a glistening ruby arc, and surrendered to gravity, heading toward the floor.

In that instant he was moving, hand sweeping down and under, snatching the glass from shattering destruction and bringing it smoothly to rest, upright on the wine-splashed counter.

"Forgive me," he said breathlessly, violet eyes wide and dazzled. "I am not ordinarily so clumsy."

"It could have—happened to anyone," Anne managed, breathless in her own right. "And you made a wonderful recover—I don't think the glass broke. Here—"

Glad of a reason to turn away from those brilliant, piercing eyes, she pulled paper towels out of the wall dispenser and went to the counter to mop up, avoiding his gaze.

"Just a bit of clean up and we're good as new. Though it is a shame about the wine."

"There is more wine," Er Thom replied, voice too near for her peace of mind. She straightened, found herself caught between counter and table and looked helplessly down into his face.

He raised his hands, showing her empty palms. "Anne—"

"Er Thom." She swallowed, mind stumbling. The man could *not* have heard her lustful thinking, she assured herself and in the next heartbeat heard her voice stammering:

"Er Thom, do *you* see sparkles?"

"Ah." He lowered his hands, slowly, keeping them in full view until they hung, open and unthreatening, at his sides. "I am no Healer," he said seriously. "However, you should know—Korval has given many Healers—and—and dramliz as well."

The *dramliz*, for lack of a saner way to bend the language, were wizards, infinitely more powerful than Healers. *Dramliz* talents embraced interactive empathy and took off from there: teleportation, translocation, telekinesis, pyrokinesis, telelocution—every item on the list of magical abilities attributed to any shaman, witch or wizard worth their salt during any epoch in history.

If you believed in such things.

And Shan, Anne thought, somewhat wildly, *sees sparkles.*

"I—see." She took a breath and managed a wobbling smile. "I suppose I should have inquired further into the—suitability of your genes."

It was a poor joke, and a dangerous one, but Er Thom's eyes gleamed with genuine amusement.

"So you should have. But done is done and no profit in weeping over spoiled wine." He stepped back, bowing gently. "Why not go into the other room and—be at ease? I will bring the wine in a moment."

"All right." She slipped past, assiduously avoiding even brushing his sleeve, and fled into the common room.

"OH, IT'S JUST A MESS," she was saying some minutes later in answer to his query. "Admin's being as bitchy as possible. You'd think—oh, never mind." She sighed.

"The best news is that everyone seems to be accounted for—but the cost in terms of people's work! Professor Dilling just stood in a corner during the whole meeting and shook, poor thing. I went over to see if there was something I could do, but he just kept saying, 'Thirty years of research, gone. Gone.'" She sighed again, moving her big hands in a gesture eloquent of frustration, and sagged back into the corner of the sofa.

"But surely," Er Thom murmured, from his own corner, "the computer files—"

"Paper," Anne corrected him, wearily. "Old Terran musical notation—some original sheet music. I'd helped him sort things a couple of times. His office was a rat's nest. Papers, old instruments— wood, metal—all blown to bits. Little, *tiny* bits, as Jerzy would have it." She reached for her wine.

"And your own work?" Er Thom wondered softly.

Anne laughed, though not with her usual ration of humor. "Oh, I'm one of the lucky ones. I lost the latest draft of a monograph I'd been working on—but I've got the draft before that saved down in the belly of Central Comp—some student work, files, study plans— that's the worst of it. The important stuff—the recordings, notes, my letters—is in the storage room I share with Jerzy—all the way over in Theater Arts. I doubt if it even got shook up."

"You are fortunate."

This time her laugh held true amusement. "Paranoid, more likely. I didn't care to have my work sitting about where just anyone could pick it up and read it. As a rule, when I'm working on something, I keep the notes with me—in my briefcase—and I have a locked, triple-coded account in Central Comp." She smiled, wryly. "Welcome to the world of cutthroat academics. Publish or perish, gentlefolk, please state your preference."

"'Who masters counterchance masters the world'" Er Thom quoted in Liaden. He tipped his head. "Central Administration— there are new duties required of you, in the face of this emergency?"

"Not a bit of it!" Anne assured him. "All that is required of us is that we continue precisely as we would have done, had the Languages Department not been—*redecorated*—in this rather extreme fashion. Exams are to be given *on schedule*—Central Admin has located and assigned—alternative—classroom space! Grades are to be filed *on time*—no excuses." She threw her hands up in a gesture of disgust.

"Some of these people lost *everything*! The exams they've already given are buried under a couple of tons of rubble, alongside of the exams still to be given! It was just sheer, dumb luck that I brought my lot home with me last night, or else I'd be trying to issue final grades on the basis of guess-and-golly!"

"Hah." Er Thom sipped his wine. "The explosion—do they know the cause?"

"An accident," Anne said, rubbing her neck wearily. "Which means they don't know. Not," she added, "that they'd tell a bunch of mere professors if they *did* know."

She sipped her wine, eyes closed. Er Thom sat quietly, watching her shuttered face, noting the lines of weariness, hating the demands of necessity.

Tomorrow will be soon enough to speak of the journey to Liad, he told himself. *She is exhausted—wrought.*

He took a sip of wine, wondering if he might properly offer to fetch her a Healer. It struck him as outrageous, that those to whom she owed service had not provided this benefit. To barely miss being blown up with the building where one's work was housed—Healers should have been present at the meeting at Central Administration today, available to any who had need. Had one of his crew been subjected to such stress—

"This is wonderful wine," Anne murmured, opening her eyes. "You never bought this at the Block Deli!"

He smiled. "Alas. It is from the private store of *Valcon Melad'a*—the ship of my brother, which he—lent—to me for this journey."

"Is he going to be a little annoyed with you for drinking up all his good red wine?" she wondered, eyes curiously alert, though the question was nearly idle.

"Daav does not care overmuch for the red," Er Thom told her, with a smile for his absent kin. He moved his shoulders. "We are brothers, after all. How shall it be except that I own nothing that is not his, nor he something that is not also mine?"

"I—see." Anne blinked and had another appreciative sip of wine. "Is he much older than you are?"

"Eh? Ah, no, he is the younger—" He moved his hand, fingers flicking in dismissal. "A matter of a few *relumma*—nothing to signify. You will see, when you have come to be our guest."

It was little enough, and truly he meant to say no more than that, but Anne's mouth tightened and she straightened against the flat cushions.

"I have decided," she said, not quite looking at his face, "that I won't be going to Liad. And neither will Shan."

Without doubt, here was the opening of the trade, which must be answered, at once and fully.

"Ah." Er Thom sipped, delicately, tasting not so much the wine as sorrow, that she forced this now, with her less than able and he with necessity to his arm—and a Master of Trade, besides.

"It is, of course, your decision to make," he murmured, giving her full view of his face, "for yourself. For Shan, it is a different matter, as we have discussed. The delm must Know him. Necessity exists."

It was gentler answer than he would have given any other—by many degrees—and still it seemed to him that her face paled.

"Will you steal my son from me, Er Thom?" Nearly harsh, her voice, and her eyes glittered with the beginnings of anger.

"I am not a thief," he replied evenly. "The child's name is yos'Galan. You, yourself, named him. If there is question of—belonging—the law is clear." He tasted wine, deliberately drawing out the time until he looked back to her.

Her face had indeed paled, eyes bright with tears, mouth grooved in a line of pain so profound that he broke with the trade and leaned forward against all sense, to take her hand in his.

"Anne, there is nothing here for the Council of Clans—there is nothing between we two that must make one of us thief! Shan is our child. What better than we who are both his parents take him before the delm, as is proper and right? And as for declining the journey entire—what of your friend, who has died and left you duty? Surely you cannot ignore that necessity, aside from this other—" He was raving, he thought, hearing himself. What possible right had he to speak to her so? To demand that she embrace duty and turn her face to honor? What—

She snatched her hand away from him, curling it protectively against her breast.

"Er Thom," she said, and her voice shook, though her eyes were steady on his, "I am not Liaden."

"I know," he told her, his own voice barely more than a whisper. "Anne. I know."

For a long moment they sat thus, her eyes pinned to his, neither able to move.

"You're in trouble," she said slowly, and there was absolute conviction in her voice. "Er Thom, why did you come here?"

"To see you—once more," he said, with the utter truthfulness one owes none save kin—or a lifemate. "To say—I love you."

"Only that?"

"Yes."

"You've done those things," Anne said, and the tears were wet on her face, though she never moved her eyes from his. "You can go home now. Forget—"

"The child," he interrupted, hand rising in a sign of negation. "I cannot. Necessity exists." He flung out both hands, imploring, the trade in shambles around him. "Anne, I *am* Liaden."

"Yes," she said softly, putting her hands into his. "I know."

She closed her eyes, long fingers cool against his palms, and he watched her face and wished, urgently, for Daav to be here just now, to show them the safe path out of this desperate muddle that only became more confused with each attempt at repair . . .

"All right." Anne opened her eyes. He felt her withdraw her hands from his with an absurd sense of loss.

"All right," she said again, and inclined her head.

"At the end of the semester, Shan and I will come with you to Liad," she said, intonation formal—a recitation of the conditions of agreement. "Shan will be seen by your delm and we will be the guests of Clan Korval while I help Professor yo'Kera's colleague sort out his notes. When that—duty—is done, my son and I will come home. Agreed?"

He retained enough wit to know he could agree to no such thing. Who was he, to guess what the delm might require? And there was yet that other matter between he and Anne, which the delm must adjudicate . . .

She was watching him closely, eyes sharp, though showing weariness around the corners.

"I hear you," he murmured, matching her tone of formality. He bowed as fully as possible, seated as he was, and looked back up into her face. "Thank you, Anne."

She smiled, dimly, with her face still strained, and reached out toward him. Just shy of his cheek, her fingers hesitated—dropped.

"You're welcome," she said softly, and sighed, all her exhaustion and strain plain for him to see.

"I shall leave you now," he said gently, though he wanted nothing more than to take her in his arms and soothe her, to sit the night through, if need be, and watch that her sleep went undisturbed.

Fighting improper desires, he rose and made his bow.

"Sleep well," he said. "I shall come tomorrow, as I did today, and care for our child while you are away."

"All right." Anne made no move to rise, as if she did not trust herself to do so without stumble. She gave him the gift of another tired smile. "Thank you, Er Thom. *Chiat'a bei kruzon.*"

He bowed, profoundly warmed. "*Chiat'a bei kruzon, denubia,*" he replied and was so lost to propriety that the endearment passed his lips without awaking the least quiver of shame.

CHAPTER FIFTEEN

The Universe adorns
a flawless jewel.
Solcintra.

—**From Collected Poems**
Elabet pel'Ongin, Clan Diot

RELUCTANTLY, Daav lifted his cheek from the comfort of her breast.

"Olwen?"

"Mmm?" she murmured sleepily, raising a hand to push his head down. "Stop *fidgeting*."

"Yes, but I have to leave," he explained, shamelessly nuzzling into her softness.

"You have to leave *now*?" Olwen released him and actually opened her eyes.

"I have uses for you yet, my buck," she told him severely. "I was only just considering which to subject you to next."

He grinned. "You tempt me, never doubt it. But duty is a sterner mistress."

"A hint in my ear, forsooth! Next time you'll not find me so gentle."

"And I with a dozen new bruises to explain," Daav said mournfully. "Ah, well. Those who would seize joy must expect a tumble or two."

"Hah!" Her laugh was appreciative. Rising onto a elbow, she reached out to stroke the hair back from his face, laughter fading as she studied him.

"Old friend." She sighed, touched the silver twist hanging in his ear. "I recall how you earned that," she murmured, "our first time as team-mates. I wish—"

"I know," he said quickly, catching her hand and bringing it to his lips. He kissed her fingertips lightly. "I would still be a Scout, Olwen, if the universe were ordered to my liking. Necessity exists."

"Necessity," she repeated and grimaced—an entirely Scout-like reaction. "Does it occur to you that necessity has killed more Liadens than ever the Yxtrang have?"

"No, are you certain?" He gave her over-wide eyes and a face bright with innocence, winning another laugh.

"I shall formulate a data box and attempt to corroborate my statement, Captain." The laughter faded yet again, and she ran light fingers down his cheek. "Take good care, Daav. Until again."

"Until again, Olwen," he returned gently and slid out of her bed and left her, silently damning necessity.

TWO HOURS until the end of Jump, according to the trip scanner set in the wall.

And after that, Anne thought, *maybe three hours through heavy traffic to setdown in the port.*

Solcintra Port.

"Annie Davis," she told herself, ducking her head to pass through the low doorway connecting the 'fresher unit to the sleeping compartment, "this has not been one of your better ideas."

She did *not* want to go to Solcintra. Yet careful scrutiny of the events leading to her approaching that very place in this lavish, uncannily efficient space-yacht failed to show her how she might have arranged things otherwise.

The conviction that Er Thom was in some sort of trouble

persisted. Pressed, he had admitted to "difficulties" at home—and then hastened to assure her that they were neither "of her making nor solving."

As if, Anne thought grumpily as she pulled on her shirt, *that had any bearing on the matter.*

In the next instant, she allowed that it had every bearing. She simply could not allow him to face his "difficulties" alone.

She paused in the act of sealing her shirt to look into her own eyes, reflected in the low-set mirror.

He came to find me.

That in itself was extraordinary, for surely a man of Er Thom yos'Galan's position might easily call upon powers far beyond those mustered by an untenured professor of linguistics, had he need of aid.

And yet he had come to find *her*—a Terran. Come, so he had it—and would not be pushed from that bald statement—for the sole purpose of saying that he loved her.

The sort of thing, Anne thought, threading her belt around her waist and doing up the buckle, *a man comes to say when he's looked eye to eye at his death.*

She sighed and sat on the edge of the too-short bed to pull on her boots, then stayed there, elbows on knees, staring down at the sumptuous carpet.

"Now, Annie Davis," she murmured, hearing Grandfather Murphy's voice echoing in memory's ear. "Tell the truth, and shame the devil."

And the truth was, she wryly admitted to herself, that she was head over ears in love with the man.

"And will not marry him for propriety's sake, willful, wicked gel that ye are!" the gaffer thundered from life-years and light-years away.

Anne grinned and in the back of her mind, the gaffer laughed. "Well, and who can blame ye? The man might stir himself to a bit of lovemaking, after all."

Though lovemaking was not precisely the problem—or not in the ordinary sense, Anne thought, shaking her head. It was as if the years of separation had multiplied their desire for each other until a touch, a shared glance, a *word* held the potential for conflagration.

The sheer power of the passion—the bone-deep, burning *need* for him was—frightening.

"So why not marry the man?" she asked herself. "You've agreed to everything else he's wanted. Take a bit for yourself and never mind he only asked because it was *proper.*"

Except that he had offered contract-marriage, an arrangement very like a standard Terran cohabitation agreement, with each party going its separate way at the conclusion of the time-limit.

And the thought of letting him go again made her blood cold and her mouth dry and her stomach cramp in agony.

Just how she was going to manage herself upon quitting Liad at the end of semester break had not yet become clear.

I'll think of something, she assured herself, standing and heading for the door to the companionway. *Everything will be all right.*

SHE PAUSED BRIEFLY in the alcove to pay respect to Clan Korval's shield with its lifelike Tree-and-Dragon and to consider yet again the bold, almost arrogant, inscription: *Flaran Cha'menthi.* I Dare.

Not a very conciliatory motto, Anne thought and grinned. The history of Cantra yos'Phelium and her young co-pilot, Tor An yos'Galan, who had used an experimental space drive to bring the people who were now Liadens away from their besieged planet to a fair new world was the stuff of many stories and plays. Pilot yos'Phelium was characterized as a crusty sort who brooked no questioning of her authority. *I Dare* was probably an entirely accurate summation of her philosophy.

Still grinning, she bowed respect to the device and its motto, then reached out to stroke the dragon's muzzle and look into its bright green eyes.

"Keep good watch," she told it, surprised at how earnest her voice sounded. She stroked the dragon once more, fingers lingering on the cool enamel surface, then continued on in search of Er Thom.

✿ ✿ ✿

THEY ENTERED the piloting chamber from opposite doors and Anne noted once more how well-suited he was to this ship. Each doorway that insisted she bend her head for entry framed Er Thom's slender figure like a benediction. The small chairs with their short backs that forced her to bundle her long legs into a ludicrous, adolescent tangle beneath the seat welcomed and enclosed Er Thom as if they had been made for him.

Which, Anne thought wryly, *they very possibly had.*

He bowed now, graceful and smooth, smiling as he straightened.

"Anne. Did you sleep well?"

"Very well," she said, returning his smile and feeling her doubts about the wisdom of this journey begin to slip away. "I missed you."

"Ah." He came closer, fingers stroking her arm, feather-light and enticing, beautiful face tipped up to hers. "The pilot must be vigilant."

"Of course," she murmured, half-tranced by his eyes. She took one careful step back and turned her head toward the board. "About ninety minutes to the end of Jump."

"And another two hours to Solcintra Port," he agreed. "We shall be at Jelaza Kazone by late afternoon." He tipped his head. "Are you troubled, Anne?"

"Nervous," she said and gave him a quick smile. "I don't know much about your *cha'leket* the delm except that he used to be a Scout and that the two of you were raised together. And your mother—"

Here she faltered. The little she had gleaned of Er Thom's mother seemed to indicate the old lady was a high stickler, with, perhaps, a gift for sarcasm. She strongly suspected that Thodelm yos'Galan was not going to find Terran Scholar Anne Davis, the rather irregular mother of her grandson, much to her liking.

"My mother." Er Thom slipped his hand gently under her elbow, as he had done on the occasion of their first meeting, so long ago, and guided her across the pilot's room and into the alcove that served as a kind of snack bar.

"My mother," he repeated, after he ordered them both a cup of tea from the menuboard and they were sitting across from each other at the pull-down table. "You must understand, she is—ill."

"Ill?" Anne blinked at him, teacup halfway to her lips. "Er Thom, if your mother isn't well, it would be—discourteous—of me to insist—"

"You are my guest," he interrupted her softly. "All is as it should be, and no discourtesy attached to you at all, who merely accepted invitation freely offered." He paused to sip tea.

"Several years ago," he said slowly, "a—tragedy—befell the clan. When all was accounted, we had lost the delm—Daav's mother, twin of my mother—and a'thodelm of yos'Galan, my elder brother, Sae Zar."

Anne lowered her cup, eyes wide on his face, but he was staring at some point just beyond his own cup, which was cradled in the net of his fingers.

"Such a blow to the Line Direct could not easily be withstood. Of course, Daav was called home immediately to take up the Ring— and there was myself to—absorb—a'thodelm's duty—but we were neither of us yet full adult and looked to the remaining elder of the Clan to guide us." He sighed.

"Which she was not at first able to do, so desperate was her illness. We feared—for *relumma*—that she would follow sister and son and leave us—a halfling delm, as Daav would have it, and an unschooled thodelm—alone to guide Korval."

"But she didn't die," Anne breathed, unable to take her eyes from his averted face.

"Indeed," he murmured, "she gained strength. To a point. A very specific point, alas, and that more by will than any skill the medics brought. Damage from the radiation had gone too far, taken too much. She is not well. In fact, she is dying. And all the medics and the autodocs can do is somewhat ease the pain of her determination to live." He lifted his cup and drank, eyes still cast aside.

"I'm so terribly sorry," Anne managed and his eyes flashed to hers, brilliantly violet.

"It is not of your blame," he said, softly.

"No," she agreed, "but I still grieve for your grief. Was it—was it an honor-feud?"

"There was nothing honorable in it!" he said sharply, then moved a hand, fingers tracing a formal sign in the air between them.

"Forgive me. It was lies and treachery and outworld conniving and the stupidity of it is the trap was not even set for us! She who told the first tale, the one who set the bait—she had only been awaiting a master trader. One would have done as well as any other. Only ill luck that it was Sae Zar yos'Galan who walked into the place where she waited and lay down his coin for a drink."

"I'm sorry," Anne said again, damning the inadequacy of the phrase. "Were you and your brother very—close?"

"Close?" He tipped his head, frowning. "Ah, I see. Not so—close. Sae Zar was eleven—twelve—Standard years my elder. He brought presents to Daav and me, and took us with him to Port a time or two . . . He was kind, but old, you know, and we but children." He paused.

"There was—vast difference in our estates, you must understand," he said and the impression she had was that he was choosing his words with the utmost care. "It became—necessary—for the delm to provide the clan with another child. The elder child of yos'Phelium had then ten Standard years and it was the delm's wisdom that the new child should have another of—near age—with whom to grow and learn. Thus she commanded her sister my mother to also wed, and then took the child of that union in fostering."

"Which is how you and Daav came to be *cha'lekets*," Anne murmured, shaking her head over this *commanding to wed*. "Er Thom—"

A tone sounded in the piloting chamber—one clear, bright note.

Er Thom stood. "Forgive me. We are about to re-enter normal space, and I must be at the board." He hesitated, flashing her a look from beneath golden lashes. "Would you care to sit with me there?"

A signal honor, Anne knew, to be asked by a master pilot to accompany him at the board. And honor beyond counting, that one who was not even a pilot should be offered that place.

Heart full, she inclined her head.

"I would be honored, Er Thom. Thank you."

"The honor is my own," he returned, which she knew was rote, and thereby sheer nonsense. He bowed and left the alcove then, Anne hard on his heels.

TRAFFIC WAS NOT SO HEAVY as she had imagined—or Delm Korval's pleasure-yacht commanded a clear approach whenever it appeared.

Which, she allowed, upon consideration, might not be so fanciful a notion, after all.

She leaned forward in the acceleration chair that was built all wrong for her size, and watched his face as he worked the board, listening to his matter-of-fact exchange of information with Solcintra Tower. There was nothing hurried in the rapid dance of his fingers over the various keys, toggles and switches—no hurry and no hesitation. Only pure efficiency enveloped by a nearly transcendent concentration.

"You love this," she breathed, barely knowing that she spoke aloud. "Really love this."

Purple eyes flashed to her face. "This—yes. Every liftoff is a privilege. Every homecoming is—a joy."

She was about to answer—and then started, abruptly alert on an utterly different level.

"Shan's awake," she said, rising and moving away. "I'll go and make him presentable."

But Er Thom was fully back in the pilot's beautiful, unfathomable dance and gave no sign that he heard her.

CHAPTER SIXTEEN

Each one of a Line shall heed the voice of the thodelm, head of that Line, and give honor to the thodelm's word. Likewise, the thodelm shall heed the voice of the delm, head of the clan entire, and to the delm's word bow low.

Proper behavior is that thodelm decides for Line and delm decides for clan, cherishing between them the melant'i of all.

—Excerpted from the Liaden Code of Proper Conduct

ER THOM led the way down, Anne coming after, holding Shan's hand. At the edge of the ramp, they were met by a woman in mechanic's coveralls, the Tree-and-Dragon emblem stitched on her sleeve.

"Sir," she murmured, bowing low.

Er Thom barely inclined his head. "There is luggage in the smaller hold to be sent on immediately to Trealla Fantrol," he said in the mode, so Anne thought, of Employer to Employee. "The ship shall at once be inspected and made ready according to its standard bill of orders."

The mechanic bowed, indicating understanding of her orders. "Sir," she said again and stepped aside.

Without further ado, Er Thom moved on, Anne a step still behind him, slowed by the shortness of her son's stride, and her own desire to crane around like a tourist and stare at everything.

"Hi!" Shan announced as they passed the mechanic, which earned him a flash of startled gray eyes and a bow nearly as low as the one given his father.

"Young sir," the woman said swiftly. Her eyes lifted and barely touched Anne's face before she bowed yet again.

"Lady."

Anne blinked, cudgeling her brain for the proper response. Clearly, her *melant'i* in no way approached Er Thom's, whose clan employed the woman. Nor did she have any notion of the relative status of learned scholars to starship mechanics, though she was inclined to think that, on the basis of practical abilities, the mechanic stood several orders above a mere professor of linguistics.

She was saved the necessity of making any decision at all by the arrival of the rest of the woman's crew, to whom she turned with rapid-fire orders. Reprieved, Anne walked over to Er Thom, Shan in tow.

"I need a scorecard," she muttered in Terran, and saw the gleam of a smile in his eyes.

"A guest of the House outranks a hireling of the House," he said softly. "She expected no response. Indeed, it was forward of her to offer greeting, except she was forced to it by this young rogue." He reached down to ruffle Shan's hair.

Anne sighed. "Shannie," she said, without much hope, "don't talk to strangers." She met Er Thom's eyes, adding wryly: "Not that he's ever met a stranger."

He frowned briefly, brows pulling slightly together, then his face cleared. "'Happy the one who finds kin in every port.'"

"Close enough," she allowed. "Except if the other person counts differently there's Hobbs to pay."

"Who is Hobbs?" Er Thom wondered and Anne laughed, shaking her head.

"I'm sorry," she managed after a moment. "Hobbs isn't—anybody—really. A figure of speech, like his brother Hobson, who's generally seen offering a choice." She paused, suddenly taken. "Actually, you may know Mr. Hobson. His choice goes like this: Take my terms or take nothing."

"Hah!" The smile this time was nearer a grin. "We have met." He slid his hand under her elbow, guiding her away from the cold-pad and toward a low building some distance away painted with the Tree-and-Dragon.

"A car awaits us," he said, "and then we may to Daav. In any case, we should clear the field."

As was only prudent, Anne thought. The field was a-buzz with activity. Jitney traffic was heavy, racing between cold-pads and the distant bulk of the main garage. Added to the speedy jitneys were fuel trucks, repair rigs, forklifts and ground-tugs, some with ships in tow.

The Tree-and-Dragon sigil was displayed on every piece of equipment, on every jitney and on several of the ships they passed.

"All this belongs to—to your clan?" Anne asked around a mounting sense of dismay.

He glanced up at her. "This is Korval's primary yard in Solcintra," he murmured. "We maintain three others here, and in Chonselta, two."

It may have been the staggering information that Clan Korval owned no fewer than *six* spaceship maintenance and repair yards that caused the lapse in her usual vigilance. Or it may have been the realization that *rich*, the descriptor she had vaguely attached to Er Thom's financial status, so far understated the matter as to be actually misleading.

Six repair yards, she thought dazedly, allowing herself to be guided through the hurrying traffic. These were not the holdings of a mid-level mercantile clan with a couple near-mythological heroes and a tradeship or two to its credit. This was stupefyingly wealthy, not merely Old House, but High—

"Er Thom," she began, meaning to demand an exact accounting of Clan Korval's melant'i here and now, before she or her son set foot beyond the repair yard's gate. "Er Thom, just precisely where—"

"Sparkles!" Shan shouted, snatching his hand free.

She spun at once, grabbing for him, but he was gone, running as fast as his short legs could carry him, counter-cutting traffic, ignoring the lumbering repair rig entirely.

"Shannie!" She was moving—was caught, snatched aside with sudden, brusque strength—and a slim figure in a leather jacket was past her, running so quickly he seemed to skim the ground.

In the path of the rig, Shan stooped, fingers scrabbling at the blast-sealed tarmac. At the machine's crown, Anne saw the driver frantically slapping at his control board, saw the rig slow—not enough, not nearly enough—

Her terror made the rescue more dramatic than reality, or so Er Thom assured her afterward.

Truth or overheated imagination, she saw the enormous treads bearing the metal mountain inexorably toward her son, tiny and oblivious to his danger.

And she saw Er Thom, swift and unhesitating, flash between Shan and the mountain, catch the boy in his arms and roll away in a shoulder-bruising somersault.

The machine obscured her sight of them for a heart-searing minute, cleared her line of sight and ground, at last, to a halt.

Er Thom was standing, Shan held tightly in his arms, a new white scar showing on the shoulder of his battered brown jacket.

"Is he—?" The driver was shaking, braced against the side of his machine. He lifted eyes half-wild with horror in a face the color of yellow mud. "The child, Lady! By the gods, where is the child?"

"Here." Er Thom walked forward, Shan unnaturally still in his arms, silver eyes stretched wide.

"Compose yourself," Er Thom told the driver, coolly. "No hurt has been taken."

The man closed his eyes and leaned weakly back into the side of the machine. Anne saw his throat work, swallowing anguish.

"Thank gods," he rasped, and abruptly stiffened. Standing away from his support, he made a deep bow that was somewhat marred by his continued trembling.

"Your lordship."

"Yes," Er Thom said, in Employer to Employee, which did not,

Anne thought, finally getting her legs to move, lend itself to warmth. "You are Dus Tin sig'Eva, are you not?"

"Yes, sir," the man said, standing stiffly upright.

Anne made it to Er Thom's side and held out her arms. Shan smiled at her, somewhat unsteadily.

"Hi, Ma," he whispered. Er Thom never turned his head.

"You will call for assistance," he was telling Dus Tin sig'Eva, still in the cool tones of Employer to Employee. "When assistance arrives, you will accept the role of passenger back to your station, where you will report this incident to your supervisor. If you feel need of a Healer, that service will be provided you. In any case, you will be given the rest of this shift and all of your next shift off, with pay. It may be advisable for you to retrain on this piece of equipment."

The man bowed. "Your Lordship," he said, with, Anne thought, staggered relief. Straightening, he turned and swarmed up the ladder into the driver's compartment, to radio for assistance.

At last, Er Thom turned his head.

"And now you, my swift one—" he began in Low Liaden.

Shan shifted sharply in his arms. "Sparkles, *Mirada*!"

Er Thom looked grim. "Sparkles, is it?" he said in ominous Terran.

He swung the child to his feet, keeping a firm grip on one small hand. Anne grabbed the other and held tight. "Show me these sparkles."

Obediently, Shan marched forward, mother and father in tow. Just two steps from the rear of the repair rig, he stopped and bent his head to point with his nose, since neither parent would relinquish a hand.

"There!"

Embedded in the tarmac was a faceted blue gem, sparkling in the brilliant Liaden sunlight.

"Hah. And are these your usual sparkles or something a bit different, I wonder?"

Shan blinked, expression doleful. "Sparkles," he repeated, and tried to yank his hand away from Er Thom. "Shan *go*," he demanded, stamping a foot.

"Shannie!" Anne said warningly, but Er Thom let the small hand free.

"Sparkles!" Shan cried, pointing down at the glittering gem. "More sparkles!" His finger stabbed at a point just over Er Thom's bright head. "Ma sparkles! Jerzy sparkles! Rilly! Everywhere sparkles, but not to touch! This sparkle to touch! Touch this, touch more?"

"Ah." Er Thom went to one knee on the tarmac and looked very earnestly into Shan's face. "Here," he said softly, and to Anne's amazement, pulled off his master trader's ring, the amethyst blazing gloriously purple. "Touch this sparkle, *denubia*."

Shan's fist closed greedily around the big gem. Enthralled, Anne knelt on his other side, letting his hand free, but keeping a firm grip on his shoulder.

"Can you now touch these other sparkles?" Er Thom asked.

There was a long, charged moment as Shan scanned the blank air above Er Thom's head, and extended a cautious, hungry hand.

"Nothing," he said, body losing all its unnatural tenseness at once. His eyes filled with tears, but he only shook his head. "Can't touch *Mirada*."

"Perhaps when you are older," Er Thom said gently, slipping the ring back onto his finger. "In the meanwhile, you see that there are—different sorts—of sparkles, eh? Those you can touch and those you can only see. Can you remember that?"

"Yes," Shan told him, utterly certain.

"Good. Then you must also remember never to run away from your mother again. It was ill-done and caused her pain. This is not how we use our kin, who deserve all of our love and all of our kindness. I am not pleased."

Shan swallowed hard, eyes filling again. "I'm sorry, *Mirada*."

"As is proper, for the fault is yours," Er Thom told him. "But you owe your mother some ease, do you not?"

Woefully, he turned to Anne. "I'm sorry, Ma."

"I'm sorry, too, Shannie," she said. "It was bad to run away like that, wasn't it?"

He nodded, then the tears escaped in a rush and he flung

himself into her arms, burying his face against her neck. "I'm sorry, *sorry!*" he hiccuped, sobbing with such extravagance that Er Thom began to look alarmed.

Anne smiled at him and held up a finger.

"All right," she said, gently rubbing Shan's back, working loose the tight muscles. "I guess that's sorry enough. But you need to do something else for me."

"What?" Shan asked, raising his sodden face.

"Promise you won't run away again."

"I promise," he said and then sighed, tears gone as suddenly as they had appeared. "I won't run away."

"Good," Anne said and set him back so she could stand, remembering to keep a tight grip on his hand. She glanced over at Er Thom, who had also risen.

"Why does he cry like that?" he asked, trouble still showing in his eyes.

Anne grinned. "You can write a note and thank Jerzy. Shan had gotten cranky one day and started to whimper over something and Jerzy told him that if he wanted to be really convincing, he had to *project*—and proceeded to demonstrate. By the time I came in, the two of them were sitting on the floor in the middle of Jerzy's apartment, holding each other and sobbing their hearts out." She shook her head, suddenly serious.

"Are you Okay?" she asked, extending a tentative hand and touching his shoulder. "That was quite a tumble."

"I am fine," he assured her solemnly.

"Your jacket's gotten scarred," she said, fingering the leather briefly before prudence took her hand away.

He glanced negligently at the scrape, shoulders moving. "If that is the worst of the matter then we may make our bow to the luck." He reached down and took Shan's hand.

"In the meanwhile, our car awaits," he said, and led them around the stalled repair rig and away.

CHAPTER SEVENTEEN

The number of High Houses is precisely fifty. And then there is Korval.

—From the Annual Census of Clans

THE LANDCAR was low and sleek and surprisingly roomy. Anne leaned back in a passenger's seat adjusted to accommodate her height, Shan dozing on her lap, and watched Solcintra Port flash by.

She gave an inward sigh of regret for the quickness of the tour as Er Thom guided the car through Port Gate One and into the city proper.

He glanced over at her, violet eyes serious. "Forgive me my necessity," he murmured, "and allow me to show you the Port another day—soon."

She blinked, then inclined her head. "Thank you, Er Thom. I'd like that."

"I, also," he answered and fell silent once more, driving the car with the same effortless efficiency he had demonstrated at the yacht's control board.

Anne settled against the back of her seat and watched him, content to let Solcintra City slip by with only a few cursory glances. Another day, and she would see it all, immerse herself—safely anchored by Er Thom's *melant'i* and knowledge—in all the wonder the City of Jewels could muster.

The car slid effortlessly around a flowered corner, under an ancient archway of shaped stone, negotiated a sweeping curve in a smooth uptake of speed and they were suddenly out of the city and moving through a landscape of plush lawns and wide gardens.

"Soon now," Er Thom said so softly she might have thought he was speaking to himself, except the words were in Terran.

The car accelerated once more, lawns and gardens flickering by—and changing. The houses became larger, set further back from the road, some hidden entirely, marked only by gates and driveways.

Er Thom sent the car right at an abrupt branching of ways. They climbed a sudden hill and a valley stretched before them. At the near end, Anne saw a cluster of trees, glimpsed roof top and chimneys through the leaves.

On the far side of the valley were more trees and, soaring high into the green-tinged, cloudless sky, a—Tree.

"What on—?" She sat forward in the seat, earning a sleepy grumble from Shan. "It *can't* be a tree!"

"And yet it is a tree," Er Thom said, as the car descended the hill to the valley floor. "*Jelaza Kazone*, Korval's Tree, which is at the house of my brother, also called Jelaza Kazone."

Jelaza Kazone, the professorial corner of her mind supplied helpfully, meant "Jela's Peace" or "Jela's Fulfillment." She stared at the impossible tallness of it, and licked lips suddenly gone dry.

"Who is Jela?" she murmured, barely knowing that she asked the question aloud, so absorbed she was by the Tree itself.

"Cantra yos'Phelium's partner, all honor to him, who died before the Exodus."

Anne managed to move her eyes from the Tree—from *Jelaza Kazone*—to Er Thom's profile. "But—'Jela's Fulfillment'? And he never made it to Liad?"

"Ah. But it had been Jela's Tree, you know, and he had made her swear to keep it safe."

"Oh." She eased back slowly, and several minutes passed in

silence, until she said: "So the delm is the dragon who guards the Tree—the *actual* Tree. Your shield isn't an—allegory?"

"Ale—?" He frowned, puzzlement plain. "Your pardon. It—the delm's instruction, when we were children, was that each of us holds the burden of Cantra's promise, and—should there be but one of Korval alive, the life of that one was only to keep the Tree."

Anne sighed, slowly, and shook her head. "It's *the* Tree—Jela's original?"

"Yes," Er Thom murmured, slowing the car as they approached a cluster of low bushes.

"That makes it, what? Nine hundred years old?"

"Somewhat—older, perhaps," he said, flicking a glance at her as he turned into one of those long, mysterious driveways. "We arrive."

Jelaza Kazone, the house, was two stories high, overhung with a sloping roof. A porch girded the second story; chairs and loungers could be seen here and there.

It was, Anne thought in relief, a cozy sort of house, with nothing of the mansion about it, never mind that it was big enough to hold seventy apartments the size of her own on University. Perhaps the benign presence of *Jelaza Kazone*, the Tree, helped make it feel so comfortable.

For the Tree, pinnacle now lost to her sight, grew out of the center of the house.

Questioned, Er Thom told her that the house had been built piece-by-piece as the clan grew, until it now surrounded the Tree on all sides.

"My rooms are—*were*—on the second story, facing the inner court, where the Tree is." The car glided to a soundless stop and Er Thom made several quick adjustments, before turning in his seat to look at her.

"The delm will—very soon—See our child and the clan will rejoice," he said earnestly, taking her hand in his and looking up into her eyes. "Anne. If there is—a thing in your heart—you—are welcomed—to lay it before Korval for—for solving." The pressure of his fingers on hers was hard, nearly painful, and she had the impression he was striving to impart information of paramount importance.

"It is known—forgive me!—that you have none to speak on your behalf. We would not—wish to be—backward—in service to—to the guest." He drew a deep breath and released her hands, looking doubtfully into her eyes.

"I mean no insult, Anne."

"No, of course not," she said gently, while her mind raced. Traditionally, delms solved—spoke for—those of their own clan. For Delm Korval to be willing to speak for someone outside his clan—and a Terran besides!—was something rather extraordinary. Anne inclined her head deeply.

"I am—disarmed—by Korval's graciousness," she said carefully. "You do me great honor. I will not hesitate to bring any worthy matter to the delm's attention."

Er Thom's face relaxed into a smile.

"That is good, then," he said, and glanced down at Shan. "Now, we must wake this sleepy one and take him within."

MASTER DAAV, the stately individual who answered the door-summons informed Er Thom with precision, was in the Inner Court. If the lord and lady and young sir would follow, please?

They did, down a well-lit, wood-paneled hallway, footsteps muffled on bright, thick carpet, past closed doors with ancient china knobs set in the centers. Even Shan seemed awed, and kept close to Anne's side, his fingers clutching at hers.

Rounding a corner, they went down a slightly narrower hall that ended in a glass door. Their guide opened the door with a flourish and bowed them into the Inner Court.

Anne went three steps into the garden and stopped, blinking at the profusion of flowers and shrubs, the riot of bird song and the flutter of jewel-colored insects.

Er Thom continued across the silky grass, glancing this way and that among the unruly flowers.

"Well met, brother!" a cheery voice called from no particular direction.

Er Thom stopped, head tipped to one side. "Daav?"

"Who else? Had you a good trip?"

"Smooth and easy." Er Thom approached the monumental Tree, and lay his palm flat against the silvery trunk as he peered upward into the branches. "It is difficult to converse when I cannot see you."

"Easily solved. Climb yourself up."

"Might you not climb yourself down?" Er Thom inquired. "There are others present and matters that require your attention."

"Ah. You see how it is, brother: My manners have atrophied utterly in your absence."

"*Will* you climb down?" Er Thom demanded, a curious mix of laughter and frustration in his voice. Anne drifted closer, Shan silent and alert at her side.

"I will, indeed," said the Tree cheerfully. "Have a care, *denubia*, and stand away. It would not do for me to fall on you."

There was remarkably little movement among the silent broad leaves. When the lithe dark man dropped from the branches, it was as if he were part of a conjuror's trick: *Now you see him . . .*

"So then." He grinned at Er Thom and opened his arms, heedless of the twig caught in his hair and the smear of green across one wide, white sleeve.

Without hesitation, Er Thom went forward and the two embraced, cheek to cheek.

"Welcome home, darling," the dark-haired man said, his words in Low Liaden carrying clearly to Anne. "You were missed."

The embrace ended and Er Thom stepped back, though his *cha'leket* kept a light hand on his shoulder, thumb rubbing the new scar on the leather jacket.

"Perilous journey, Pilot?"

"A tumble at the Port," Er Thom returned calmly. "Nothing to signify."

"Hah. But there are others present and matters that require my attention—or so recent rumor sings me! Lead on, brother; I am entirely at your disposal."

"Then you must come this way and make your bow to the

guest," Er Thom told him, leading him the way across the grass to Anne.

He extended a hand on which the master trader's ring blazed and laid it lightly on her sleeve. "Anne," he murmured, switching to his accented, careful Terran, "here is my brother, Daav yos'Phelium, Delm Korval."

She smiled at the dark-haired man and bowed acknowledgement of the introduction. "I am happy to meet you, Daav yos'Phelium."

"Korval," Er Thom continued. "This is Anne Davis, Professor of Linguistics."

From beneath a pair of well-marked brows, bright dark eyes met hers, disconcertingly direct before he made his own bow.

"Professor Davis, I am delighted to meet you at last." His Terran bore a lighter accent than Er Thom's; his voice was deeper, almost grainy. He was a fraction taller, wiry rather than slim, with a face more foxy than elfin. A curiously twisted silver loop swung from his right earlobe and his dark brown hair fell, unrelieved by a single curl, an inch below his shoulders.

"And this . . ." Er Thom bent, touching Shan on the cheek with light fingertips. "Korval, I Show you Shan yos'Galan."

"So." Daav yos'Phelium moved, dropping lightly to his knees before the wide-eyed child. He held out a hand on which a wide band glittered, lush with enamel-work. "Good-day to you, Shan yos'Galan."

Shan tipped his head, considering the man before him for a long moment.

"Hi," he said at last, his usual greeting, and brought his free hand up to meet the one the man still patiently offered.

Wiry golden fingers closed around the small hand and Daav smiled. "Did you have a good trip, nephew?"

"Okay," Shan told him, moving forward a half-step, his eyes on his uncle's face. Reluctantly, Anne relinquished her hold on his hand and he took another small step, so he was standing with his toes nearly touching the man's knees.

"Do you see sparkles?" he asked, abruptly.

"Alas," Daav answered, "I do not. Do *you* see sparkles?"

"Yes, but not the kind to touch. *Mirada* on hand has sparkles to touch." He bit his lip, looking earnestly into the man's face.

"You *happen* sparkles," he said plaintively. "Can't *see* sparkles?"

The well-marked brows pulled together. "Happen sparkles?" he murmured.

"He means 'make,'" Anne explained. "You *make* sparkles."

"Ah, do I? I had no notion. Have you brought me a nascent wizard, *denubia*?" This last was apparently to Er Thom.

"Perhaps," that gentleman replied. "Perhaps a Healer. Or perhaps only one who has the gift of knowing when another is happy."

"Not too bad a gift, eh?" He smiled at Shan and then sent his brilliant black gaze to Anne's face.

"If Korval Sees this child, he is of the clan," he said, voice and eyes intently serious. "You understand this?"

Anne nodded. "Er Thom explained that it was—vital—for the delm to—count—a new yos'Galan."

"So? And did Er Thom also explain that what Korval acquires Korval does not relinquish? You have seen our shield."

"The dragon over the tree—yes." She hesitated, looked from his intent face to Er Thom's, equally intent. "Shan yos'Galan is my son," she said to him, voice excruciatingly even. "Whether he is—of—Clan Korval or not."

"Yes," Er Thom said, meeting her gaze straightly, hand half-lifting toward her. "How could it be otherwise?"

"Scholar." Daav yos'Phelium's voice brought her eyes back to his face, which was no less serious than it had been. "Scholar, if you are at all unsure—stand away. There is no dishonor in taking time to be certain."

She stared down at him where he knelt in the grass, holding her son by the hand. Leaf-stained as he was, with his fox-face and bold eyes, lean and tough as a dock-worker—He was beyond her experience: Half-wild and unknown; utterly, bewilderingly different than Er Thom, who was her friend and who—she *knew*—wished her well—and wished to do well for their son.

"It's what we came to do," she said slowly, voice cracking slightly.

She shook her head, as much from a need to break that compelling black gaze as from a desire to deny—anything.

"Shan was to be shown to Delm Korval and then Er Thom could be easy again, and the clan not be—embarrassed—by there being a—rogue yos'Galan loose in the galaxy—one the delm hadn't counted. It was—my error," she explained, looking back to his face. "I—custom on my homeworld is to name the child with the father's surname in—respect. In—*acknowledgement*. I hadn't understood that there would be—complications for Er Thom when I followed my—my world's custom. Having made the error, it is—fitting—that I do what I can to put the error into—context—and repair any harm I may have done."

"Hah." For two long heartbeats, the bold eyes held hers, then he inclined his head.

"So it is done." He extended the hand that bore the broad enameled band and cupped Shan's cheek.

"Korval Sees Shan yos'Galan, child of Er Thom yos'Galan and Anne Davis," he announced. The High Liaden words rang like so many bells across the garden, startling the birds into silence. He bent forward and kissed Shan on the lips before taking his hand away.

"Welcome, Shan yos'Galan. The clan rejoices."

And that, Anne thought, around a sudden and astonishing surge of joy, *is that. I hope Er Thom thinks it was worth all that worry.*

Shan laughed and reached forward on tiptoe to pluck the leaf from his uncle's hair and hold it up for inspection.

"Flower."

"Leaf, I believe," Daav corrected gently. "Quite a nice one." He rose in a single fluid motion, one hand still holding the child and the other sweeping up in a extravagantly wide gesture.

"Thus, matters requiring my attention! Let us go within and have wine—and luncheon, too! For I do not scruple to tell you, brother, that you behold a man who is famished."

"No new sight," Er Thom replied calmly, stepping across to offer an arm to Anne and smiling up into her eyes. "Will you take wine and food before we go on to Trealla Fantrol, friend?"

The sense of joy was dizzying, exhilarating beyond reason, so that it was all she could do not to bend and kiss him, with full measure passion, on the lips. Only the understanding that it would not do—not here—kept her emotion in check.

So instead of kissing him, she smiled at him and slid her arm through his.

"Wine and food sounds delightful," she said warmly and allowed him to lead her into the house.

CHAPTER EIGHTEEN

In an ally, considerations of house, clan, planet, race are insignificant beside two prime questions, which are:
1. Can he shoot?
2. Will he aim at your enemy?

—Excerpted from Cantra yos'Phelium's Log Book

A LIGHT NUNCHEON had been called for, to be brought to the Small Parlor, to which they had repaired. Wine had been poured for each adult—Shan was given a small crystal cup half-filled with citrus punch—and tasted with all due ceremony.

Very shortly after, Er Thom excused himself to place a call to his parent, and left the room. Daav and Shan went to the window, where the man was apparently pointing out sections of shrubbery most likely to yield rabbits, if a boy were patient, and had sharp eyes.

Momentarily left to herself, Anne walked slowly around the room, sipping the slightly tart white wine and trying to absorb everything at once.

The rug—the rug was surely Kharsian wool, hand woven by a single family across several generations. She had seen a hologram of such a priceless treasure once and recognized the signature maroon and cobalt blue among the lesser colors, all skillfully blended to create a riotous garden of flowers, each bloom unique as a snowflake.

At one side of the room, the rug broke and flowed around a hearth of dark gray stone laid with white logs. The mantle that framed the fireplace was of a glossy reddish wood she could not identify, carved with a central medallion slightly larger than her fist. The design tantalized a moment before she named it—a Compass Rose, pure in the smooth red wood.

Turning from the fireplace, she nearly fell over the table and two comfortable-looking chairs. On top of the table was a board, margins painted with fanciful designs. The center of the board was marked into blue and brown squares, bounded by larger borders, like countries. There were twelve countries in all, Anne counted, each containing twelve small squares.

On the table outside the board were four twelve-sided ebony dice. Two shallow wooden bowls likewise sat to hand, each filled with oval pebbles. The pebbles in the right bowl were red; those in the left, yellow.

"Do you play, Professor Davis?" Daav yos'Phelium inquired suddenly from her side.

She glanced up with only a slight start and shook her head. "It's a counterchance board, isn't it?"

"Indeed it is. You must ask my brother to teach you—he's a fiend for the game, you know. And very good, besides." He flashed a smile up into her face, humor crinkling the corners of his eyes. "Although of course it wouldn't do for him to hear I've said so."

Anne laughed. "No, I can see that would be a—bad move."

"Precisely," he agreed, raising his glass. "I've left young Shan scouting for rabbits," he continued after a moment, gesturing toward the window and the child kneeling motionless before it, nose pressed to the glass.

"That should keep him busy until lunch," she said, grinning. "There's a shortage of rabbits on University."

"Ah. Well, there are more than enough here for him to enjoy, never fear it." He tipped his head slightly, black eyes quizzical.

Anne lifted her glass—and brought it down as a low move to the right caught her attention.

"What a beautiful cat!" she breathed.

Daav yos'Phelium turned his head. "Lady Dignity, how kind of you to join us! Come in, do, and give grace to the guest."

The cat paused in her progress across the carpet, considering him out of round blue eyes. After a moment, she sat down, brought up a paw and began to wash her face.

"Wanton," the man said calmly and Anne laughed.

"Lady Dignity?" she asked. "Is she very shy?"

"Merely shatterbrained, I fear, and a great deal set up in her own esteem. She does well in her role, however, so I don't like to complain."

"Her role?" She glanced expressively around her. "Tell me you have mice!"

He laughed—full and rich, a world apart from Er Thom's soft, infrequent laughter. "No, how could I? But she's useful, nonetheless."

Anne looked to where the cat had settled, chicken-fashion, onto the carpet, front paws tucked under creamy chest, blue eyes half-closed within the mask of darker fur.

"She frightens off unwanted guests," she suggested and Daav opened his black eyes wide.

"Isn't that why I keep a butler? No, I will tell you—" He sipped wine, glanced over at the cat, then back to Anne.

"My sister is very proper," he began earnestly, "and I am a great trial to her. She says I have no dignity and I fear she may be correct. Still, scolding will not create what the gods have not provided and I confess I grew tired of being reminded of my deficiency."

He used his chin to point at the drowsing cat. "So I have employed this lady, here, to act in my behalf. Now, whenever my sister demands to know where my dignity is, I can produce her upon the instant."

Anne stared at him, a smile growing slowly, curving her big mouth and lighting her eyes. The smile turned to a chuckle and she shook her head at him in mock severity.

"Your poor sister! I don't expect she was amused."

Daav sighed dolefully, eyes glinting. "Alas, the gods were behindhand in Kareen's sense of fun."

"Daav!" This from Shan, vigilant at the window. "Look, Daav! Cat!"

"Good gods, in *my* garden?" He was gone, moving across the carpet with a quick, silent stride to lean over the boy's shoulder.

Anne drifted over just in time to see an enormous orange-and-white cat slink into the bushes at the base of a small tree.

"Relchin," Daav said. "Doubtless gone birding." He glanced up at Anne. "He never catches any, you know, but the chase does amuse him."

"Exercise," she agreed, seriously.

"Indeed," he murmured and seemed about to say something else, when there was a step at the door.

"Ah, there you are, brother! We were only just wondering when you might return and free us all to dine!" He slid past Anne and crossed the room, blocking her view of Er Thom's face. "How do you find your mother my aunt?"

"A trifle—distressed—today." Er Thom's voice was soft and smooth as always, yet Anne felt apprehension shiver through her as she reached down to take Shan's hand.

"Er Thom, if your mother is not—able—to take on the burden of a guest—" she began, and that quickly he was before her, looking seriously up into her eyes.

"No such thing," he told her, softly, though she was cold with sudden dread. "She sends apology to the guest, that she will be unable to greet you instantly upon your arrival. She looks forward to the pleasure of your company at Prime Meal this evening."

She stared down into his eyes, feeling—*knowing*—that there was something wrong—badly wrong. Er Thom was lying to her. The thought—the surety—shocked her into still wordlessness.

"Anne?" He extended a hand and she caught it tightly, as if it were a thrown rope and she floundering far out of her depth.

"What's wrong?" she demanded, voice raspy and dry. "Er Thom—"

His fingers were firm, giving back pressure for pressure; his eyes never wavered from hers.

"My mother is—inconvenienced," he said patiently. "She is not able to meet you at once, but shall surely do so at Prime." His grip increased, painfully, but she made no move to withdraw her fingers. "You are welcome in my House, Anne. Please."

She held his eyes, his hand, for another heartbeat, trying desperately to plumb the wrongness, identify the ill. At last, defeated, she bowed her head and slid her fingers free.

"All right," she said softly, and raised her head in time to see Daav yos'Phelium's bold black eyes move slowly from her face to Er Thom's.

NUNCHEON PASSED IN A FLURRY of small-talk, of which Er Thom's brother apparently possessed an unending supply. It seemed absurd, Anne thought as she nibbled cheese, that she should have found him strange and formidable scarcely an hour ago. Now, he was merely an amusing young man with a flair for the dramatic and a penchant for telling the most ridiculous stories with an entirely straight face.

He's a bit like Jerzy, really, she thought around a stab of homesickness.

Er Thom's contributions to the conversation were slight: Set-ups for his *cha'leket*'s absurd stories and tolerant corroborations of unlikely events. Mostly, he busied himself with feeding Shan bits of cheese and slices of fruit from the plate he had filled for himself.

Anne, watching surreptitiously, thought Shan accounted for nearly all of the plate's contents, and that Er Thom perhaps had a taste of cheese with his wine. *Worried,* she thought, and wondered how ill his mother was.

When at last nuncheon was over, Daav walked them down the long hall to the door and gave Er Thom another hug.

"Don't keep yourself far," he said and Er Thom smiled—wanly, Anne thought, and caught his brother's arm.

"Come to Prime, do."

Daav's eyes opened wide. "What, tonight?"

"Why not?"

"An excellent question. I shall come in all my finery. In the meanwhile, commend me to your mother."

Er Thom's smile this time was a little less tense. Daav bent to hug Shan and kiss his cheek.

"Nephew. Come and visit me often, eh? I think we shall deal famously."

Shan returned the embrace and the kiss with exuberance, then stood back to wave.

"'Bye, Daav."

The man bowed lightly—as between kin, Anne read. "Until soon, young Shan."

"Professor Davis." The bow he accorded her was of respect. "We shall speak again, I hope. I have read your work, you know, and would welcome a chance to discuss your ideas more fully, if you will grant it."

"That would be pleasant," she told him, returning his bow with one of Respect-to-a-Delm-Not-One's-Own. "I look forward to it."

"Good." His eyes were intent on hers and she felt again that he was utterly beyond her, more alien than she could fathom.

"In the meanwhile," he said, all gentle courtesy, "if there is any matter in which I may serve you, please know that I am entirely at your disposal."

"Thank you," she said, matching his inflection as precisely as possible. "You are gracious and—kind—to a stranger."

For one moment more, the black eyes seared into hers, then he was bowing them gracefully out the door.

"Until Prime," he called, lifting a hand as Er Thom started the landcar. "Keep well, all."

CHAPTER NINETEEN

The best advice for any Terran with a yen to visit the beautiful planet of Liad is: Stay home.

—**From *A Terran's Guide to Liad***

"THE NAME OF THE VALLEY," Er Thom said, deliberately—Anne thought—to cut off any additional questions she might ask, "is *Valcon Berant'a*. Korval's Valley, they say in Solcintra. It was ceded by the passengers to Cantra yos'Phelium and Tor An yos'Galan, for the piloting fee. Jelaza Kazone was built first, of course, after the Tree was planted. Trealla Fantrol—the house of yos'Galan—that came later. It was built as a—sentinel post, you would say—to guard the inroad, to act as first deterrent—and to give warning to the delm."

Anne looked out the window at the lush landscape, turning this burst of information over in her mind. *Valcon Berant'a*? The Liaden name Er Thom had given did *not* mean "Korval's Valley." It meant, she decided after a moment of concentrated thought, 'Dragon's Price,' or perhaps 'Dragon Hoard.'

"A sentinel post," she asked as Er Thom slowed and made the turn into another drive. "Were there wars?"

"Ah, well, in the old times, you know, there were—disharmonies.

Things did not always run smoothly and the Council of Clans did not always agree. Daav says civilized behavior is never to be depended upon." He laughed his soft laugh, so different from his *cha'leket's*. "Do not fear that I ask you to guest in a fortress, friend. Trealla Fantrol has—amenities. Very soon, now . . ."

It was, in fact, a matter of three more minutes and two more twists in the tree-lined drive. The car passed under an arch rich with yellow flowers and entered a sweeping curve.

Er Thom pulled up to the bottom of the stairway and turned the car off. Anne sat and tried not to stare, Shan completely still on her lap.

Trealla Fantrol was a mansion, with a marble stairway and towering granite facade. Windows glittered like diamonds among the gray stone and lawns like plush green velvet sloped away on both sides.

"This is the outpost?" she demanded in a voice that cracked. After the warm hominess of Daav's house . . .

"All of us would live at Jelaza Kazone," Er Thom said quietly, "if we could." He lay a light hand on her arm and immediately took it away.

"Come, allow me to show you and our son to your rooms. I will leave you for a time, so that you might refresh yourselves and rest. One has been engaged to care for our son—Mrs. Intassi, who had been our nurse when we were young. She will arrive before Prime. I shall instruct Mr. pak'Ora to conduct her to you immediately . . ."

Chattering, Anne thought, in no little wonder, as Er Thom came around to her side of car and lifted Shan to his feet. *Er Thom is actually chattering*.

Chattering, he brought them up the marble stairway, through the front door and across the echoing lobby, up the Grand Staircase—each riser hand-carved with a scene from the Great Migration—down an interminable hallway to her room.

"The house has your palmprint on file," he told her as the door slid open. "If you do not find all precisely as you would wish it, only tell me and the deficiency will be corrected." He looked up at her, chatter suddenly broken as his eyes took fire. He glanced away.

"I am sorry to leave you so abruptly, Anne. I—necessity. Later, if you like it, I shall show you the house—and the grounds." He lay a hand on her arm and this time did not remove it so quickly. "My private code is in your computer. If there is—any way—in which I may serve you, do not hesitate . . ."

"All right," she said soothingly and against all sense extended a hand to stroke his cheek, meaning only to ease his nervousness.

As soon as she touched him, she knew it was a mistake; she barely needed to hear the sharp intake of his breath, or see the blaze of his eyes, which echoed the re-awakened blaze of her desire.

Ensorcelled yet again, she looked helplessly into his eyes, her hand trembling against his cheek, unwilling—unable—to move.

It was Er Thom who moved.

A single step, backward, his eyes hot on hers. Her hand fell, lifeless, to her side and he bowed: Esteem and respect.

"I shall return," he said, very softly indeed. "Please. Be at ease in our House."

He turned on his heel and was gone, the door closing behind him with the barest whisper of sound.

HE CAME AS ORDERED to her private parlor, dressed in plain shirt and trousers, with the dust of the Port still on his boots, and made his bow, dutiful and low.

"Mother."

"My son."

Petrella surveyed him from her chair, meaning to make him writhe while she leisurely surveyed the wind-rumpled golden hair, the delicate wing of brow over eyes more purple than blue, the pleasing symmetry of face, and the firm, give-me-no-nonsense mouth. Er Thom, the son who was not her son. Chi's work, this one, returned at last to the mother who bore him on his twelfth name day, when he boarded *Dutiful Passage* as cabin boy.

He had Chi's look, Petrella allowed, which meant her own, since she and her twin had been as like as two seeds in a pod. She knew him to be mannerly and biddable, dutiful to a fault—far different than his volatile *cha'leket*, who looked more changeling than Korval.

"Are that woman and her child in this house?" she demanded abruptly, letting him hear the rasp of her displeasure.

He swayed a bow, discomfited not one whit. "The House is honored by the guesting of Professor Anne Davis," he said in his soft way, "mother of Shan yos'Galan, Seen by Korval."

"Oh, is it?" Petrella straightened to her full height in the chair, preparing to attack.

"Shan yos'Galan," Er Thom continued smoothly, "is the son of Er Thom yos'Galan, and grandson of Petrella yos'Galan." He lifted his head, purple eyes bland. "It would be—gracious—of the thodelm to complete what the delm has begun."

"You *dare*," she breathed, anger filling her with vivid energy. "Is your thodelm a counterchance token, Er Thom yos'Galan, to dance when you choose the tune? Your *cha'leket* the delm has Seen your bastard, has he? You provide an accomplished fact, and I—too weak to protest dishonor—make my bow meekly and am ruled by the whim of an upstarting boy. Think again—*Master Trader*. That child is none of mine."

The firm mouth had tightened somewhat, she noted with satisfaction; the bow he gave her was grave.

"Mrs. Intassi," he murmured, as if all she had said were mere pleasantry, "has been engaged to care for my son. She arrives this afternoon to take charge of the nursery."

For a heartbeat she could only gape at him, then she drew a careful breath, fingers tightening ominously on the arm rests.

"I see. And if your thodelm requires you to engage a house in town in which these delightful arrangements may continue as planned?"

Once again, courteous and grave, he bowed. "Then of course I will remove myself immediately."

And the so-proper contract marriage with Syntebra el'Kemin, Petrella understood from that, would never be consummated. She glared at him, considering her next move.

"Enlighten me," she ordered after a moment. "Precisely where did you meet this—person—who has the honor of being yos'Galan's guest?"

The winged brows twitched—smoothed.

"Professor Davis and I became acquainted on Proziski, at the time when *Dutiful Passage* had been transport for the Liaden contingent of the Federated Trade Mission. Professor Davis had been engaged in field research under a grant from University Central, where she teaches." He paused.

"We met at the port master's rout," he finished gently, "and contracted an alliance of pleasure."

"With so many Liadens by your side, you take a *Terran* as pleasure-love?" She stared at him in disbelief.

The purple eyes sparked—and were shielded immediately by the sweep of long golden lashes. Er Thom said nothing.

"Speak, sirrah! I will know how a son of this House came to so far forget himself as to—"

"It was myself I considered!" he interrupted sharply, and there was no shielding the anger in his eyes now. "She cared nothing for bedding an a'thodelm, or for the daring of coming so near to Korval! She barely cared of *this*—" He flung out his hand, the master trader's ring flashing violet lightnings, "save it said I was competent, and she a lady who admires competence."

"Indeed! You fascinate me. And what did she care for, pray, if not for any of what you are?"

He drew a hard breath, his mouth a tight, straight line. "She cared for who I was," he said quietly, passion seeming spent as quickly as it had been struck. He moved a hand, softening the statement.

"It may have been at first, that I was Liaden, and exotic, and of a form that pleased her. What reasons do *Liaden* lovers need? For me, it was that she gave friendship with no eye to profit, and opened her door and her heart as if I were no less than kin."

"And got your child, to her honor!" Petrella commented caustically. "A strange accident, for one who admires competence."

Er Thom inclined his head. "So I also thought, at first," he said surprisingly. "Anne—Professor Davis—is not, as we have discussed, Liaden. In spite of this, she is a person of honor and meticulous *melant'i*. That her necessity required her to bear my child without proper negotiation is—regrettable. Having bowed to necessity, however, she strove to place honor properly, after the custom of her homeworld, and thus the child is yos'Galan. To the increase and joy of the clan."

Petrella glared. "I *will not be played*, sirrah! Strive to bear it in mind."

"As you say." He bowed obedience and went into stillness, hands loose at his sides, face bland and attentive.

Almost, Petrella laughed, for that was a trick from Chi's bag, designed to unnerve an opponent and force a response—and very often a blunder. She let the silence stretch, teasing his patience. When she spoke at last, her voice was almost mild.

"So, Shan yos'Galan has been Seen by the delm. Tell me, do, what the delm has Seen."

"A child of a little less than three Standard Years," Er Thom said gently, "with pale hair and silver blue eyes, bold and alert. He successfully completes puzzles and match-problems designed to challenge children half again his age. He sees *sparkles*, as he calls them, from which he may interpret another's emotional state."

Petrella stared. "A *Terran*?" she demanded.

Er Thom was seen to sigh. "A *yos'Galan*," he said patiently, "which has given dozens to the Healers and the *dramliz* over the years since the Exodus. Why stare that another child of the Line shows these abilities?"

Petrella closed her eyes. A Terran—blast it all! At best, a half-blood yos'Galan. And already he showed sign of Healer talent? Rare to show so early, certainly. And coupled with the promise of pilot skills—Easy to see the attraction of this irregular child for Delm Korval. Very nearly understandable, that he would risk Thodelm yos'Galan's anger to gain such promise for the clan.

"Professor Davis," Er Thom murmured, "is a scholar of much acclaim in her field. You may wish to read of her work—"

Petrella opened her eyes.

"I have no interest in scholars," she said flatly. "Especially Terran scholars."

There was a moment of electric stillness before Er Thom bowed.

"In that wise," he said softly, "I shall after all engage a house in town. I will not have her shown any dishonor."

"You will not *what*?" Petrella demanded, disbelief in her voice.

"I spoke plainly," Er Thom replied, giving her all his eyes.

She met them, and saw determination—and thus the lines were drawn: Honor to the Terran scholar, or abandon all hope of a more legitimate heir to yos'Galan.

"It's my belief you've run mad," Petrella announced, trading him stare for stare.

He bowed, accepting her judgment with graceful irony.

"So." She moved her shoulders, feeling the edge of exhaustion.

"Very well," she told him crisply. "The Terran scholar is yos'Galan's guest. For a twelve-day. If her business on Liad holds her beyond that, she may guest elsewhere. In the meanwhile, all honor to her."

For a moment, she thought he would not be satisfied with the compromise. Then he bowed acceptance.

"It is heard."

"Good," Petrella snapped. "Let it also be remembered. Go now and leave me in peace. I shall see you and the guest of the House at Prime."

"Yes, Mother," he said, and added, "Daav will be with us, as well."

"Of course he will," she said tiredly. "Go away."

He did, though without alacrity. After all, Petrella thought, he was far too accomplished a player to give her the advantage of seeing him either relieved or dismayed by the outcome of their interview.

Petrella closed her eyes and allowed herself to go limp in the chair, concentrating on her breathing. Her mind wandered a bit, as it tended to do nowadays, rather than face the dreariness of continued pain, and she found herself remembering a long-ago interview with her twin.

"Daav is a forest creature, all eyes and teeth," Chi had murmured, sipping her wine. "He knows the forms, the protocols—but will he bide with them? There's the question." She smiled. "Ah, well. The Scouts will tame him, never fear it. As for your own . . ."

Petrella sipped her wine, waiting with accustomed ease while her twin tidied knowledge into words.

"Your own is—a marvel, considering his place in the Line Direct, son of the Delm's Own Twin—" They shared a glance of amusement for that, before Chi moved her hand and went on.

"He's a sweet-natured child, your Er Thom: mannerly, dutiful and calm. He knows the forms and applies them correctly, with neither rebellion nor irony. From time to time I see him hint Daav—the wonder is my wild thing takes such hinting with grace! But you mustn't fear he is dull—both of them are sharp enough to cut! It is only this attitude of dutiful sweetness that disturbs me, sister—so unlike Korval's more usual attributes . . ."

Petrella remembered that she had laughed, waving away her twin's misgivings.

"What cause to repine, that at last Korval has—through whatever accident!—got itself a biddable child?"

"Biddable—" Chi sipped wine, eyes gazing miles, perhaps worlds, away. She focussed abruptly and gave her wide, ironic smile. "I suspect he may surprise us one day, sister. And I know enough of history to worry how he might go about it. Though I allow when it comes it will doubtless be amusing."

Petrella had laughed again, and refilled her twin's cup with wine, and the talk had moved to other matters.

And now, Petrella thought, eyes opening onto the pain-racked present, *Er Thom has at last surprised.*

She wondered if Chi would have been amused, after all.

CHAPTER TWENTY

If honor be your clothing, the suit will last a lifetime.

—William Arnot

IT WAS QUITE the nicest dress she had ever owned.

Indeed, Anne thought, as she opened the closet, it was the only *formal dress* she possessed, and, hopefully, formal enough for a Liaden dinner party comprised not only of the delm and the delm's heir, but of her lover's thodelm, grandmother of her son.

Until Er Thom yos'Galan, Anne would have laughed at the notion of owning a piece of clothing as extravagant as the luscious green confection she had purchased on Proziski. But—*An ambassadorial affair, with dancing,* Er Thom had said in his soft, sweet way. Would it amuse her to accompany him?

It would have amused her to accompany him to Hell, she recalled ruefully as she took the dress down. She had accepted his invitation with more joy than sense—then spent an entire day—and far too much of her meager personal funds—in pursuit of the green gown.

The delicious fabric swirled round her shoulders, fell and settled, water-smooth, against her skin as she slipped on the matching slippers and turned to face the mirror.

"Oh—my."

The gown still had magic to work, she thought, staring dazedly at the vision in the mirror. The regal lady caught there stared haughtily back, brown skin rich against the pure greenness, chestnut hair glowing, eyes all velvet seduction.

From slim waist to full bosom, the gown was laced with golden chains so delicate they might have been worked at a elf-lord's forge. She had a matching length, provided by the dressmaker, to wear around her throat.

On the occasion of the ambassadorial affair, she had also worn a gold ribbon, threaded through painstakingly-arranged hair. The ribbon was long-lost—and the hair soon woefully disarranged. For the dance had proved insipid and they had left early, smuggling out a napkin filled with delicacies pilfered from an hors d'oeuvre tray and a split of wine offered by a sympathetic waiter.

Dazzling in his own finery, Er Thom had driven them to the Mercantile Building, and pulled the sample bolt from the flitter's boot.

"You mustn't spoil your dress," he had murmured, shaking a prince's ransom worth of lace back from his beautiful hands and spreading the scarlet silk like a blanket . . .

Anne shook herself. "That will do," she informed her reflection sternly, and deliberately turned away.

The vanity had been arranged by the same invisible hands that had unpacked her clothing and carefully put it away.

To the right were her comb, brush and mirror, the black oak veneer battered, the silver-wrapped handles tarnished. To the left sat the chipped lacquer chest that contained her few pieces of jewelry.

Careful of stressed plastic hinges, she lifted the lid and propped it open. Along the back of the box, glowing like a candle in the shiny dark interior, was the carved ivory box that held the necklace Er Thom had given her—"to say good-bye." For a moment, she was tempted to wear that piece tonight, for it was inarguably the most beautiful of her paltry jewels.

He asked you not to wear it, she reminded herself as her fingers touched the exquisitely-carved ivory. With a sigh, she shook her head and fastened the dressmaker's golden chain around her throat instead.

She hung a simple pair of gold hoops in her ears and used plain gold combs to hold her hair back from her face.

The entire effect was a little more austere than she had hoped for, despite the green gown's magic.

Well, she thought wistfully, *and maybe* Er Thom's ma *will pity you, Annie-gel, since it's plain you've no sort of* melant'i *to boast on.*

Or, Er Thom's mother might just as easily take the plainness of her guest's adornment as a personal affront. Anne swallowed against a sudden uprising of butterflies inside her stomach.

"Maybe I'll have a cup of soup and some toast in my room," she said aloud, and with no conviction at all, for that *would* be an insult, and Er Thom's mother well within her rights to avenge it.

Just when she was beginning to think that would be no bad thing, the entrance-chime sounded.

Green dress swirling around her, she left the bedroom, went through the spacious kitchenette and luxurious common room. She paused a moment before laying her hand against the admittance plate, composing her face and trying to calm her racing heartbeat. It would never do for Mr. pak'Ora, come to do butler's duty and guide the guest to the dining room, to see her panting with fright.

Hoping that her face betrayed only serene expectation, she opened the door.

Er Thom bowed, low and eloquent, looked up and smiled into her eyes. "Good evening."

"Good evening," she managed, though her tongue suddenly seemed cleft to the roof of her mouth. She stepped back, motioning him inside with a sweep of her ringless hand. "Please come in."

"Thank you," he said gravely, as if the door weren't coded to his palm as well as hers. He stepped within and the portal in question slid shut behind him.

Er Thom wore the form-fitting dark trousers deemed appropriate formal wear for Liaden males. She knew from experience that the fabric was wonderfully soft to the touch. His wide-sleeved white shirt was silk, or something more precious; the lace frothing at his throat contained by an emerald stickpin. Emeralds glittered in his ears and on his slender hands, half-hidden by more lace.

"Anne?" His gaze warmed her face. "Is there something wrong?"

She shook herself, aware that she had been staring.

"I was just thinking how beautiful you are," she said and felt her face heat, for the man was here to take her to meet his *mother*—

Er Thom laughed his soft laugh and bowed, slightly and with humor.

"And I," he murmured, "was trying most earnestly *not* to think the same of you."

Dear gods, a compliment. She very nearly blinked; rescued the moment with a bow of her own, accepting his admiration.

His eyes gleamed, but he turned a little aside, gesturing around the room.

"Everything is as you wish it? Is there anything else the House may provide for you?"

"Everything is perfectly delightful," she told him soberly. "I'll miss all this elegance, after we go back home." She *did* blink then, seeing him among the wide, comfortable chairs and high-set desk.

"Do you guest Terrans often?"

"Eh?" Winged brows drew together in puzzlement. "I believe you are the first."

"Oh." She bit her lip, then plunged ahead, waving her hand at the room.

"It's just that everything's—*convenient*—for someone who is— of Terran height. I assumed—"

"Ah." Enlightenment dawned in a smile. "My mother has redecorated," he murmured, running his eyes in rapid inventory around the parlor. He looked back to Anne, feeling his blood heat with desire for her even as he forced himself to make civil reply.

"She would have wished to have everything as it should be for the guest," he explained. "Why should you not be comfortable in our house?"

She looked at him doubtfully, then took a breath, the golden laces stretching tight across her delightful bosom.

"Your mother redecorated—*rebuilt*—this whole apartment just so I'd be comfortable for few weeks?"

"Of course," he said reasonably. "Why not?" He moved a hand, drawing her attention away from the subject.

"Mrs. Intassi came to speak with you?" he asked, though he had just come from an interview with that lady. "You have seen the nursery and find it acceptable?"

Anne laughed, head tipped gracefully back. "Your notions of—*acceptable*—" she said, and he heard her unease through the laughter even as she shook her head and made her face more serious.

"The nursery looks lovely. Mrs. Intassi seems—very competent." She hesitated. "It's going to be a little strange—for Shannie and for me, too—to have him sleeping so far away . . ."

"Not so far away," he said softly. "You may visit him whenever you like. The door has your code." Almost, he reached to take her hand; gamesmanship strangled the impulse before it went beyond a finger-twitch.

"Shan is your son," he said, repeating his comfort of the afternoon, and saw the tiny lines of tension around her eyes ease.

Smiling then, he bowed and offered his arm.

"May I escort you to the First Parlor, friend? My mother is eager to make your acquaintance." He slanted a mischievous look into her face, feeling irrationally gay. "Never fear," he told her lightly, "there will be wine close to hand."

She laughed at that and took his arm, resting her hand lightly over his, intertwining their fingers in the way he had taught her.

Just at the door, she checked and looked down into his eyes, her own shaded with trouble, so that he felt his gaiety fade.

"Don't let me make a mistake," she said, fingers tightening around his.

Astonishment held him for half a heartbeat, to be replaced by flaring joy. For here at last was the sign of her intention he had hoped for since she had turned her face from contract-marriage.

Don't let me make a mistake. She placed her *melant'i* in his hands for safekeeping, as if they were kin. Or lifemates.

"Er Thom?" Her eyes were still troubled, doubt beginning to show.

As if she could think that what she asked was any else than his own ardent wish—He stopped himself, recalling that she was Terran and unsure of custom.

Gently, and with extreme caution, he lifted his hand, barely brushing her lips with his fingertips.

"No," he said, solemn despite the burgeoning joy, "I will not let you make a mistake, Anne." A laugh burst free despite his best efforts.

"But if we are late for the Gathering Hour with my mother," he predicted, "nothing may succor either of us!"

HER SON and the guest were late—oh, a few minutes, merely, Petrella allowed, as she settled more comfortably into her chair—but late, nonetheless.

Almost, she had time in their tardiness to imagine herself the victor. To suppose that seeing his Terran tart *here*, in his very home-place, surrounded by all that was elegant, proper and *Liaden* had awakened Er Thom's swooning senses to sanity.

Almost, she began to weigh the wisdom of accepting this child—this *Shan*—to yos'Galan. Not, most naturally, as Er Thom's heir—young Syntebra would doubtless serve them well enough *there*. But it could not be denied that the clan could ill afford to turn away one who was potentially pilot and Healer merely because taint-ed blood ran his veins.

Her hand moved, almost touching the button that would fetch Mr. pak'Ora—and paused.

There were voices in the hall.

Er Thom's murmur came first to her ears. She missed the words, but the cadence was of neither High Liaden nor Low.

The voice that answered him was all too clear; carrying without being shrill, with the hint of such control found in the speech of those trained as *prena'ma*.

"I've sent a message to Drusil tel'Bana," the carrying voice announced in perfectly intelligible Terran, "telling her I'm on-planet and hoping for an early meeting. I'll have to go to her, of course, which means renting a car, if you would give me the name of a—"

"The House," Er Thom's words were now clear, as well, "will provide you a car, friend. And a driver, should you wish."

Oh, and will it? Petrella thought, stiffening against the cushions—but that was only ill-temper, for surely Er Thom owned vehicles enough in his own right that the Terran scholar need never walk.

Honor to the guest, she reminded herself, composing her face into that look of courteous blandness with which one dealt with those not of one's clan.

Asked, she could not have precisely said what portrait imagination had painted of Anne Davis beforehand. Sufficient to its accuracy to say that the woman who crossed the threshold on Er Thom's arm surprised. Entirely.

To be sure, she was a giantess, looming above her tall and shapely escort, but she did not move ill. Indeed, there was that in her stride which seemed peculiarly pilot-like, and her shoulders sat level and easy, as with any person of pride.

Though she was large in all things, Petrella acknowledged her not out of proportion with her height, and of her form there was a pleasing—yet not overcommanding—symmetry.

Her gown suited her figure, and was not—to an old trader's eye—overexpensive. Her plain necklet and earrings, the lack of ostentation in the matter of rings—all this proclaimed her a person who knew her own worth and was neither ashamed of her station nor eager to show herself as more than she was.

The face, to which Petrella now raised her eyes, was large-featured: The nose was too prominent for beauty, the mouth too full, the eyes set a fraction too close, the willful jaw square, the forehead high and smooth. Not a beautiful face, but, rather, an *interesting* face—intelligent and humorous, enlivened by a pair of speaking brown eyes, with a sweetness about the mouth that did much toward balancing the stubborn jaw.

Had Anne Davis been Liaden, Petrella might at this juncture very well admitted to some small portion of interest in her.

But Anne Davis was unremittingly Terran; Er Thom, by guiding her here, was seen to be still in the throes of his madness; and their child, by all that meant winning, must remain a half-bred bastard, unacknowledged by yos'Galan.

With a determination that was surprisingly difficult to rally, Petrella turned a stone-like face toward her son.

"Good evening," she said, chilly and in all of the High Tongue, barely inclining her head.

"Good evening, Mother," he returned gently, bowing respect. He brought the Terran woman forward as if she were some out-world regina and bowed once more.

"I bring you Anne Davis, Professor of Linguistics, mother of my child, guest of the House." He put the woman's hand lingeringly aside, and turned to make his bow to her.

"Anne, here is Petrella, Thodelm yos'Galan, whose child I have the honor to be."

Pretty words, Petrella thought grumpily, *from one who has not also the honor of being obedient.* It surprised her that he gave the introductions in High Liaden, for surely a Terran, no matter how scholarly—

The woman before her bowed with an ease astonishing in one so large, in the mode of Adult to Person of Rank, a choice that charmed by its very lack of innuendo.

"Petrella yos'Galan," she said in her clear, storyteller's voice, "I am glad to meet you. Allow me to thank you at once for the generosity which has admitted me as a guest in your house."

Petrella very nearly blinked. That this graceful acknowledgement was made in High Liaden must amaze, though the delivery was necessarily marred by a rather heavy accent. Still, it was understood that not everyone spoke with the accent of Solcintra, and balancing this was the fact that the sentences had been spoken in proper cadence and with a thoughtfulness indicating the speaker understood her own words, rather than merely repeating what had been learned by rote.

It was necessary to answer grace with grace—her own *melant'i* demanded it, even had there not been this other matter between herself and her son. Petrella inclined her head with full ceremony.

"Anne Davis, I am glad to meet you, as well. Forgive me that I do not rise to greet you more properly."

"Please do not concern yourself," the guest replied. "Indeed, it is your kindness in having myself and my son here when you are so ill that has particularly touched my heart. I wish that we will not be a burden to you."

Petrella was still trying to gauge whether this astonishing speech carried any deliberate offense—given leave to be ill, forsooth!—when Mr. pak'Ora entered to announce the arrival of the delm.

CHAPTER TWENTY-ONE

Liaden clans are primarily social organizations, amended by centuries of ever more exacting usage. Some Terran investigators compare them without amendment to military organizations, perhaps not realizing that the line of command is to some extent fluid, with variation due to considerations of melant'i. *Though the delm is "supreme commander" and the thodelm his "second," an adroit junior with an agenda may at times be as much of an impediment to those commanders as any external enemy.*

—From *The Lectures of a Visiting Professor, Vol. 2*
Wilhemenia Neville-Smythe, Unity House, Terra

"DAAV YOS'PHELIUM, Delm Korval," Mr. pak'Ora informed the room, and stepped aside so the gentleman might pass.

Unhurried and silent, he came across the rug, dressed in much the same way as Er Thom, his dark hair tied neatly at the nape with a length of silver ribbon. Deep and respectful, he made his bow before Petrella yos'Galan's chair.

"Aunt Petrella. Good evening to you."

"Good evening to you, Nephew," the old lady replied, with an inclination of her head, her tone nearly cordial. She lifted a thin, shaking hand, directing the man's attention aside. "I believe you have had the honor of making your bow to yos'Galan's guest."

He made another, nonetheless. "Professor Davis. How good it is to see you again!"

The words were High Liaden, the mode as between equal adults, which was about as friendly as the High Tongue got, Anne thought, returning his greeting with pleasure.

"You are kind," she said, meaning it. "I am glad to see you again, also, sir."

She thought she saw a smile glimmer at the back of his eyes, but before she could be certain, Petrella commanded his attention once more.

"I will also make you known to Er Thom, a'thodelm of yos'Galan, master trader and heir to the delm. I am persuaded you can never have seen his like before."

Her nephew considered her out of bright black eyes, head tipped a little to one side.

"You wrong me, Aunt Petrella," he said after a moment, and with utmost gentleness. "Though it is entirely true that I have never seen his like *anywhere else*." He turned his head, smiling at Er Thom with throat-tightening affection.

"Hello, darling."

Er Thom's smile was no less warm. "Daav. It's good of you to come."

"Yes, let us by all means extol my virtues," his *cha'leket* said with a grin. "Certainly the party has a moment or two at leisure!"

Anne laughed and Daav turned to her, one hand flung out, face comically earnest.

"What! You doubt me virtuous to even that extent?"

"On the contrary," she assured him, with matching earnestness. "I think it very good of you to round out the dinner party—especially when you clean up to such good advantage!"

In her chair, the old lady stiffened. Anne caught the movement from the corner of an eye and half-turned in that direction, worry overcoming fun, and found Daav someway before her.

"Well, you know," he said, still in that tone of bogus gravity, "my aunt has been saying the same of me any time these ten years—have you not, Aunt Petrella?"

"Indeed," the old lady agreed, with, Anne thought, a touch of acid, though her parched face remained as bland as formerly. "It only remains to discover how to influence you to behave in concert with your finery." She shifted abruptly, signaling Er Thom with a wavering fingertip.

"Doubtless, the guest would welcome a glass of wine. Daav, I want you, if you please."

"Certainly," he murmured as Er Thom and the guest walked downroom toward the wine table, "it must always please me to obey you, Aunt Petrella. In the face of such pleasure it does seem churlish to observe that I would welcome a glass of wine, as well."

She merely stared at him, face composed, until she judged the others sufficiently well-embarked on their own conversation to care little of what was being said behind them.

"So," she said at last, meeting his eyes fully. "It comes to my attention that the delm now decides for yos'Galan."

Daav lifted an eyebrow. "I am desolate to be the first before you with the news—the delm decides for Korval."

"And you see nothing that might offend, that the delm should decide—for Korval!—before ever the Line has made decision. I see."

Petrella drew a hard breath, eyes wandering, then stopping where Er Thom stood with his—with yos'Galan's guest—sipping wine and gazing up into her face with such a look of admiration as must give pause—if not actual pain. She brought her attention forcibly back to Daav.

"It is understood," she said, though without any effort to soften her tone, "that the clan must not at this point in its history turn away any who are—never care how irregularly!—of the Line. That the one now offered is likely pilot and perhaps Healer must make him doubly advantageous to the clan. That he is the child of beloved kin must make him more than acceptable to yourself. All this is crystalline." She paused, considering his face, which was merely attentive, black eyes shadowed by long dark lashes.

"However," Petrella continued after a moment, "yos'Galan at present is engaged in a disciplinary matter of no small moment. Respect for authority must be taught in such a way as to leave an indelible impression upon the a'thodelm. It is no less than my duty to the delm, who must at all times be certain his directives *will be* obeyed. I do not know how it is come about that the a'thodelm has become so careless of obedience, but as head of his Line, the fault is mine to correct."

Daav bowed, slightly and gravely. "And young Shan?"

She sighed, fingers tightening on the arms of her chair.

"You will say I am cruel, to use a child as the whip which will humble his parent. But I very much fear, my Delm, that you have Seen a child for Korval who has no other home than—Korval."

"Hah. And this is your last word upon the matter?"

She moved her shoulders, fretfully. "If he learns his lesson well," she said, meaning Er Thom, "perhaps the child may be admitted— eventually. Certainly, the thodelm will do as he pleases, when I am dead. In the meanwhile, however, I will trouble the delm to arrange a fostering for this—Shan. yos'Galan will not have him here."

"Removal of the child at this time will likely distress the guest," Daav commented. "Unless that is also your intention?"

"The guest remains for a twelve-day," Petrella answered calmly. "It is understood that a proper fostering may take even as long as that to arrange. Scholar Davis need experience no grief from an untimely parting."

"You are kind," he observed, in such a tone of bitterness that she raised her eyes in surprise to his face.

His countenance was hidden from her, however, by reason of his bow, which was low and full of respect as always.

"By your leave, Aunt Petrella, I am now in desperate need of wine."

"Go, then," she snapped, pleased to have an excuse to be annoyed with him. "And send my son to me, do."

"TURNABOUT, DARLING!" Daav cried as he approached the couple *tête-à-tête* at the wine table. "You to your mother and I at long last to drink and fashion pretty compliments for the delectation of the guest!"

Er Thom turned, showing a tolerably composed face in which the violet eyes were heated far beyond the prettiest compliment. Anne Davis, her own eyes bright, ventured another of her delightful laughs.

"We've already dealt with the dress and the hair and the hands," she told him gaily. "You shall have to be inventive, sir!"

He smiled at her in appreciation. "But you see, I may admire your abilities in the High Tongue, which are as new to me as our acquaintance, and if Er Thom has not already been delighted with your manner before my aunt, I can only call him a dullard."

"I have never found Anne's manner other than a delight," Er Thom said calmly, while his eyes betrayed him and his brother wondered more and more.

"Best answer the summons quickly, you know," Daav said when a moment had passed and Er Thom made no move to go to his parent. "Try to comport yourself well. Scream, should the pain go beyond you, and I swear to mount a rescue."

Er Thom laughed his soft laugh and bowed gently to his companion. "My mother desires my presence, friend. Allow Daav to bear you company, do. I engage for him that he will not be entirely shatterbrained."

"Bold promises!" Daav countered and Anne laughed. Er Thom smiled faintly and went at last to wait upon his mother.

"Wine is what I believe I shall have," Daav announced, moving toward the table. "May I refresh your glass?"

"Thank you." She came alongside him and held out a goblet half-full of his aunt's best canary.

He shook the lace back from his hand, refilled her glass and took a new one for himself, into which he poured *misravot*. He had just replaced the decanter when the woman beside him spoke, in a very quiet tone.

"Delm Korval?"

He spun, startled by such an address *here*, when more proper solving would call for privacy and time and—

Her face showed confusion at his alacrity; indeed, she dropped back a step, fine eyes going wide as her free hand lifted in a gesture meant, perhaps, to ward him.

"Hah." Understanding came, as it often did to him, on a level more intuitive than thoughtful: She meant courtesy, that was all, and called him by the only title she knew for him. He inclined his head, face relaxing into a smile.

"Please," he said, going into Terran for the proper feel of friendly informality. "Let me be Daav, if you will. Delm Korval is for— formalities." He allowed his smile to widen, showing candor. "Truth told, Delm Korval is a tiresome fellow, always about some bit of business or another. I would be just as glad to be shut of him for an evening."

She smiled, distress evaporating. "Daav, then," she allowed, following him into Terran with just a shade of relief in her voice. "And I will be Anne, and not stodgy Professor Davis."

"Agreed," he said, bowing gallantly. "Though I must hold that I have not yet found Professor Davis stodgy. Indeed, a number of her theories are exciting in the extreme."

She tipped her head. "You're a linguist?"

"Ah, no, merely a captain specialist of the Scouts—retired, alas." He sipped his wine and did not yield to the strong temptation to look aside and see how Er Thom got on.

"My area of speciality was cultural genetics," he told Anne Davis, "but Scouts are all of us generalists, you know—and linguists on the most primitive level. We are taught to learn quickly and to the broad rule of a thumb—" She laughed, softly. "And, truly, there are several languages which I speak well enough to make myself plain to a native of the tongue, yet still could not make available to yourself." He sighed. "My skill as a lexicographer falls short, I fear."

"As does mine," she said. "I've been working forever on a translation guide between High Liaden and Standard Terran." She shook her head, though not, Daav thought, in order to deny anything, unless it was a point made in her own mind. "I'm beginning to think I'm barking up the wrong tree."

Daav took note of the idiom for future exploration. "Perhaps your time on Liad will enlighten you," he suggested.

"Maybe," she allowed, though without observable conviction. "It's just *frustrating*. With the back-language so—" She started, flashing him a conscious look.

"You don't want to hear me rant for hours about my work," she said, smiling and taking a nervous sip of wine. "Professors can bore the ears off of the most sympathetic listener—as my brother often tells me! It would be much safer, if we were to talk about you."

But he was saved from that bit of fancy dancing by the advent of Mr. pak'Ora, come to say that Prime Meal awaited them in the dining room.

CHAPTER TWENTY-TWO

Wicked men obey from fear; good men, from love.

—Aristotle

PRIME WENT OFF without too much event, though Daav fancied he saw Er Thom once or twice hint Anne to the proper eating utensil. Still, there was no harm done, and the attention no more than a dutiful host might without offense offer to a guest of different manner.

Anne had apparently settled upon the more-or-less neutral mode of Adult-to-Adult for her conversation, a point of Code which Petrella was at first inclined to dispute. However, as neither of the remaining party found it beyond them to answer as they were addressed, Adult-to-Adult became the mode of the evening.

There were to have been cards afterwards, but as the guest had never used a Liaden deck, the play was a trifle ragged, and Petrella soon excused herself, pleading, so Daav thought, a not-entirely fictitious exhaustion.

As if this were her cue, Anne also announced an intention of retiring, turning aside Er Thom's offered escort by saying she wished to stop in the nursery for a few moments. Both ladies then quit the drawing room in the wake of Mr. pak'Ora.

And so the brothers were abruptly alone, trading bemused glances across the card table.

"Well," commented Daav, "and to think we shall live to tell the tale!"

Er Thom laughed. "Now I suppose you will make your excuses, as well."

"Nonsense, what would you do with yourself all the long evening if I were to be so craven?"

"There are several hundred invoices awaiting my attention," Er Thom replied with abrupt seriousness, "and a dozen memoranda from my first mate. The evening looks fair to overfull, never fear it."

"Hah. And I wishing to share a glass and a bit of chat . . ."

Er Thom smiled his slow, sweet smile. "As to that—a glass of wine and some talk would be very welcome, brother. The invoices quite terrify me."

"A confession, in fact! Very well—you see to the door, I shall see to the wine. I suppose you're drinking red?"

"Of your goodness." Er Thom was already across the room, pulling the door closed with a soft thud.

"None of my goodness at all, I assure you! The wine is from yos'Galan's cellars." He brought the two glasses back to the table and settled on the arm of a chair, watching as Er Thom gathered in the cards they had spread out for Anne's instruction.

Delm, Nadelm, Thodelm, A'thodelm, Master Trader, Ship, then the twelve common cards, until the three suits—red, blue and black—were all joined again. Absently, Er Thom tamped the deck and shuffled, fingers expert and quick among the gilded rectangles.

Daav sipped *misravot*. "Your mother my aunt appeared some-what—fractious—this evening," he murmured, eyes on the lightning dance of the deck. "How did you find her earlier?"

The shuffle did not waver. "Less inclined to be courteous even than this evening," Er Thom said composedly. "She refused to acknowledge the child, which was not entirely unexpected, though—regrettable. I feel certain that, after she has had opportunity to meet Shan, she will—"

"Thodelm yos'Galan," Daav interrupted neutrally, "has requested that the delm arrange fostering for Shan yos'Galan, child of Korval alone."

The shuffle ended in a snap of golden fingers, imprisoning the deck entire. Daav looked up into his brother's face.

"He will come to me, of course," he said, and with utmost gentleness, for there was that in Er Thom's eyes which boded not much to the good.

"I am—grateful," Er Thom said, drawing a deep breath and putting the cards by. "I point out, however, that such an arrangement will most naturally—distress—Professor Davis."

"Yes, so I mentioned as well." Daav tipped his head slightly, eyes on his brother's set countenance. "Thodelm yos'Galan informs me that the guest remains for only a twelve-day."

"Thodelm yos'Galan is—alas—in error. There are—matters yet to be resolved—but I feel confident that Anne—Professor Davis— will be making a much longer stay."

"Oh, do you?" Daav blinked. "How much longer a stay, I wonder? And what is it to do with Anne—forgive me if I speak too plainly!— should Korval make what arrangements are deemed most suitable for one of its own?"

Er Thom glanced down, found his glass and picked it up. "It is not necessary," he told the sparkling red depths, "that my—our— child be—deprived—of association with his mother. They have been in the habit of spending many hours a day in each other's company. Even so small a separation as Shan's removal to the nursery has caused Anne—anxiety, though certainly he is old enough—" He seemed to catch himself, to shake himself, and brought his gaze up to meet Daav's fascinated eyes.

"My thodelm had suggested I might take a house in Solcintra," he said, with a calm that deceived his cha'leket not at all. "I believe that this course is, at present, wisest. Anne will be more at ease in— a smaller establishment—and may be free to pursue her business at the university. Mrs. Intassi shall continue to care for Shan—"

"And yourself?" Daav murmured.

"I? I should naturally live with my son and—and his mother.

Anne is not—she is not up to line, you know, and depends upon me to advise her."

"Yes, certainly. What of young Syntebra? Shall she be added to your household?"

For a heartbeat Er Thom simply stared at him, eyes blank. Then recollection glimmered.

"Ah. Nexon's daughter." He glanced aside, perhaps to sip his wine. "That would be—entirely ineligible."

"So it would," Daav agreed. "Nearly as ineligible as setting up household with a lady with whom you share no legitimate relationship, save that she has borne you a child outside of contract!"

Er Thom gave him a solemn look. "You had never used to care for scandal."

"And if it were myself," Daav cried, mastering a unique urge to throttle his *cha'leket*, "I should not care now! But this is yourself, darling, on whom I have always depended to lend me credence among the High Houses and untangle me from all my ghastly scrapes! How shall we go on, if both are beyond the Code?"

Er Thom seemed to go suddenly limp; he sagged down onto the arm of the chair, eyes wide and very serious.

"I asked Anne," he said slowly, "to become my contract-wife."

"Did you?" Daav blinked, remembered to breathe. "And she said?"

"She refused me."

And all praise, Daav thought gratefully, *to the Terran scholar!*

"Surely then there is nothing more to be said. If she will not have you, she will not. To talk of sharing houses only ignores the lady's word and belittles her *melant'i*. Certainly, you owe her better—"

"It is my earnest belief," Er Thom interrupted gently, "that she wishes a lifemating. As do I."

It was Daav's turn to stare, and he did, full measure. When he at last spoke again, his voice was absolutely neutral, a mere recitation of the information he had just received.

"You wish a lifemating with Anne Davis."

Er Thom inclined his head. "With all my heart."

"Why?"

The violet eyes were steady as ever, holding his own.

"I love her."

"Hah." Well, and that was not impossible, Daav considered, though Er Thom's passions had not in the past run so very warm. He recalled his brother's eyes, hot on the scholar's face; the care he took to shield her from error during the meal and then after, going so far as to lay out the entire deck and painstakingly delineate each card. Love, perhaps, of a kind. And yet . . .

"It had been three Standard Years since you had seen her," he said evenly. "In all that time—"

"In all that time," Er Thom murmured, "I saw no face that compelled me, felt no desire stir me. In all that time, I was a dead man, lost to joy. Then I saw her again and it was as if—as if it were merely the evening after our last, and I expected, welcomed. Wished-for. Desired."

Oh, gods. It was all he could do to remain perched on his chair-arm, glass held loose while he met his brother's eyes. Within, jealousy had woke, snarling, for Er Thom was *his*, Er Thom's love *his* perquisite, not to be shared with any—

He drew a deep, careful breath, enforcing calm on his emotions. Er Thom was his brother, the being he loved best in all the worlds, his perfect opposite, his balancing point. To wound his brother was to wound himself, and what joy gained, should both be mortally struck?

"This is," he said, and heard how his voice grated. He cleared his throat. "This is the matter you would have brought before the delm?"

Er Thom inclined his head. "It is." His eyes showed some wariness as he looked up.

"I would have—spoken—some time—with my brother before arousing the delm."

"As who would not!" Daav extended a hand across the table, Korval's Ring flaring in the room's light, and felt an absurd sense of relief as Er Thom caught his fingers in a firm, warm grip.

"The delm does not yet take notice," he said earnestly, damning his *melant'i* and the defect of genes that made Kareen unable to take up the Ring. But Kareen would never have Seen young Shan at all and would likely have sent the Terran scholar briskly about her business, richer by neither cantra nor solving, while Er Thom became the victim of whatever punishment spite was capable of framing. He sighed sharply, fingers tight around his brother's hand.

"You must tell me," he said. "Brother—this bringing home of your child—and most especially his mother!—how does this make you ready to contract-wed in accordance with your thodelm's command?"

Er Thom's mouth tightened, though he did not relinquish Daav's hand. "You will think I am mad," he murmured, violet eyes showing a sparkle of tears.

"Darling, we are all of us mad," Daav returned, with no attempt, this once, to make light of the truth. "Ask anyone—they will say the same."

A small smile was seen—no more, really, than a softening of the corners of Er Thom's mouth, a glimmer that dried the sparkling tears.

"Yes," he said softly; "but, you see, I am not entirely in the way of seeming so to myself." He squeezed Daav's hand; relinquished it.

"When I left you, these few weeks ago, it was to accomplish one plan, which I felt *must* be accomplished, after which I—hoped—to be able to show the Healers a calm face and come away from them obedient."

Daav shifted on his chair-arm. "The Healers—that was not necessity, except as you had not accomplished your plan."

"Yes." Er Thom sighed. "And yet necessity did exist. It had been three years, as I said, since I had looked upon a face that pleased me. Three years of—mourning—for she to whom I had given *nubiath'a*. What right had I to bring such business to the contract-room? Nexon's daughter is young, this her first marriage. In all honor, her husband must be attentive, capable of—kindness. I had ought to have had the Healers time a-gone, myself, except I *would not* forget . . ." He drew a hard breath and took up his glass, though he did not drink.

"I went to Anne," he said softly, "to say only that I loved her. It was knowledge I knew she would treasure. Knowledge that I could not allow to be lost entirely to the Healers' arts. It was to have been—a small thing, simply done."

"And the child?" Daav murmured.

Er Thom lifted a hand to rake fingers through his bright hair, a habit denoting extreme distraction of thought, very little seen since he had put boyhood behind him.

"There was no child," he said, and his voice was distracted, as well. "There was no child nor mention of a child, three years ago."

"Hah." Daav glanced down, caught sight of the deck and took it up, then sat holding it in his hand, staring hard at nothing.

"You hunger yet for this lady?" he asked and heard Er Thom laugh, short and sharp.

"Hunger for her? I starve without her! I astonish myself with desire! There is no sound, save her voice; no sensation, save her touch."

Daav raised his head, staring in awe at his brother's face. After a moment, he touched his tongue to his lips.

"Yet she refuses a contract-marriage," he persisted, pitching his voice deliberately in the tone of calm reason. "Perhaps the—depth of your passion—may be—no dishonor to her!—inadequately returned."

"It is returned," Er Thom told him, with the absolute conviction of obsession, "in every particular."

Daav bit his lip. "Very well," he allowed, still calm and reasonable. "And yet unalloyed passion is not the foundation upon which we are taught to build a lifemating. You speak in such terms as make me believe you have indeed erred, by giving *nubiath'a* too soon, before your passions were slaked. In such case, a wiser solving is to go with the lady to the ocean house, indulge yourselves to the full extent of joy, to return home, when you have had your fill—"

"Fill!" Er Thom came to his feet in a flickering surge; instinct brought Daav up, as well, and he met his brother's eyes with something akin to dread.

Er Thom leaned forward, hands flat on the card-table, eyes vividly violet.

"There is no fill," he said, absolutely, utterly flat.

Scouts are taught many tricks in order to ensure the best chance of survival among potentially hostile peoples. Daav employed one such trick now, deliberately relaxing the muscles of his body, letting his mouth soften into a slight smile, his fingers curl half-open. After a moment or two, he had the satisfaction of seeing Er Thom relax, as well, shoulders loosening and eyes cooling even as he sighed and straightened, looking somewhat sheepish.

"Forgive me, denubia," he said softly. "I had never meant to contend against you."

"Certainly not," Daav said gently. "Though I will say it seems a sticky enough coil you plan to lay before the delm." He tipped his head. "Perhaps it would be—illuminating—were I to speak with Anne apart—" He raised a deliberately languid hand, stilling the other's start of protest. "Only to hear what she herself considers of the matter." He tipped his head, offering a smile.

"I shall have to hear it, soon or late, you know."

The smile was answered, faintly. "So you shall."

"Indeed—and tomorrow soon enough, for it is come time—alas!—to make my excuses and leave you to that dreadful pile of invoices." He tipped his head.

"In the meanwhile, promise you will engage no houses in the city—for at least tomorrow, eh?"

"Promised." Er Thom inclined his head and then came around the table to offer his arm.

Arm in arm, they went down the various hallways and across the moon-bathed East Patio. At the car, Er Thom embraced him, and Daav cursed his treacherous muscles, which stiffened, only slightly.

It was enough. Er Thom drew back, staring into his moonlit face.

"You are angry with me." He made some effort to keep his voice neutral, but Daav heard the pain beneath and flung himself into the embrace.

"Denubia, forgive me! My wretched moods. I am not angry—only tired, and such a muddle as you bring the delm must make my head spin!"

"Hah." Er Thom's arms tightened and when Daav asked for his kiss a moment later, he bestowed it with the alacrity of relief.

SHE HAD WANDERED through the beautiful, strange, suite for a time, but her pacing failed to tire her. Finally, she plucked a bound book at random from a shelf and, robe swirling around her, settled into a corner of the wheat-colored sofa, resolving to read until sleep overtook her.

An hour later she was still there, sleepless as ever, pursuing the Liaden words from page to page, resolutely not thinking of how lonely she was, or of how much she missed him, or of—

The door-chime sounded, once.

She was up in a flurry of blue skirts, across the room and hand on the admittance plate before she thought to tighten the sash at her waist—which was not really necessary, after all. The one who stood there had seen all she had to show, many times.

Er Thom bowed and straightened, looking up at her from eyes of molten violet.

"I had come," he said softly, "to make my good-night."

Throat tight, she reached out and took his hand, drawing him inside. The door closed, silent, behind him.

CHAPTER TWENTY-THREE

The guest is sacrosanct. The welfare and comfort of the guest will be first among the priorities of the House, for so long as the guest shall bide.

—Excerpted from the *Liaden Code of Proper Conduct*

DAAV YOS'PHELIUM, fourth of his Line to bear the name; master pilot; Scout captain, retired; expert of cultural genetics; Delm Korval, lay beneath the Hebert 81 DuoCycle, one shoulder braced against the cool stone floor as he worked to loosen a particularly troublesome gasket-seal. Oil dripped from the gasket and he was careful to keep his face stain-free, though neither the thick old shirt he wore nor the scarred leather leggings were so fortunate.

For a time he had worked with only the flutter of bird song from outside the garage for company, and the now-and-again rustle that was rabbits foraging through the dew-sheathed grass. Now, however, he became aware of something different—a deliberate, plodsome rhythm that vibrated through his braced shoulder and into his head.

Attention on the gasket, he wondered briefly if there was an elephant loose on the lawns. He was mildly disappointed, but not really surprised, when a few minutes later the plodding became the harsh click of boot heels striking stone flooring and a sound was vented in the sudden silence that his Scout sensibilities cataloged as a human sigh.

"What," demanded the voice of his sister, speaking in the mode of Elder-Sibling-to-Child, "are you doing under there?"

The gasket-seal at last heeded his promptings and fell free, releasing a minor downpour of oil. He flinched back from the splatter that liberally redecorated his shirt-front and peered around the Hebert's front wheel.

Creamy leather boots met his gaze, striped here and there with light blue grass-stains. The stiff silk trousers that belled over them, falling precisely to the instep, were of an identical cream color. Daav turned his attention back to the gasket.

"Good morning, Kareen," he called, mindful of his manners, and phrasing the reply in Adult Siblings.

The Right Noble Kareen yos'Phelium allowed herself a second sigh. "What are you doing under there?" she asked again, still in that tone of exasperated scolding.

"Replacing the winder-gasket and repairing the sync-motor," Daav said, carefully using a solvent-soaked towel to clean the gasket seat.

There was a short silence before his sister asked, with lamentable predictability, "And that is a task of such urgency you must attend it before you receive your own kin?"

"Well," Daav allowed judiciously, working the new gasket around to the proper orientation. "There is some urgency attached to it, yes. The final part required for the repair only arrived from Terra last evening and as soon as I have the sync-motor geared, the cycle will be in fine state for racing. I confess I have been wanting to race it anytime this last Standard, but it would not do, you know, to enlist an unsafe machine."

"Race!" Kareen's voice carried a wealth of loathing much more suited to the elder sibling mode she yet insisted upon than the mode he had offered. "One hopes you have more care for your duty than to endanger the person of Korval Himself in a race. Most especially as you have not yet seen fit to provide the clan with your heir."

"Oh, no!" Daav said, as the gasket clicked satisfyingly into place. "Please do not tease yourself on that account one moment longer! Of course I have designated an heir. Only this morning I re-initialed the document pertaining to the matter."

"Only this morning," Kareen repeated, voice suddenly silken with malice. "How very busy you are, younger brother. No doubt this re-initialing has much to do with yos'Galan's latest impropriety."

"yos'Galan's impropriety?" Daav demanded, letting go the gasket and staring wide-eyed at the boots. "Never tell me Aunt Petrella's been brawling in taverns again!"

"Yes, very good. The clan hovering on the brink of ruin and you in one of your distempers!" She stopped herself so sharply Daav fancied he had heard her mouth snap shut.

"On the brink of ruin?" he repeated, in accents of wonder. "Are we impoverished, then? Small wonder you disturb yourself to come to me here! I honor your sense of duty, that you brought the news yourself."

One of the boots lifted. Daav watched it with interest, wondering if he had so easily driven Kareen to the point of stamping her foot at him.

The boot hesitated, then sank, with only the faintest of heel-clicks, to the floor.

"Will it please you to come out?" she asked with astonishing mildness. "It would be best, could we discuss a certain matter face to face."

Beneath the cycle, Daav frowned. Kareen's conversation rarely descended into civility. She must want something from him very badly, indeed.

"Well," he said, by way of seeking a range, "I had hoped to effect the necessary repairs this morning . . ."

"I see." That, at least, was as acerbic as a brother might wish, but the sentence that followed was nothing short of alarming. "If you will name a time when it will be convenient to speak with me regarding a matter of utmost seriousness, I shall endeavor to wait upon you then."

Oh, dear, Daav thought. *If this goes on we'll actually have her calling me by name.*

He toyed with the notion of sending her away until the afternoon, but reluctantly gave it up. The interview with Anne Davis might well prove lengthy and he had no wish to crowd himself on a matter of such importance.

Sighing lightly, he turned onto his back and called out, "A moment! I shall attend you forthwith!"

He then scrambled out from beneath the Hebert, an operation not abundant of grace, and came 'round to lean a hip against the fender, stripping off his oily gloves as he considered his sister's face.

"All right, Kareen. What is it?"

She flinched at the state of his clothes, which was expectable in one who regarded dirt as a personal affront, but forbore from comment.

Instead, she bowed, if not respectfully then at least with that intent, and straightened to look him in the eye.

"It has come to one's attention," she said, mildly, "that the delm has Seen a child called yos'Galan, which yos'Galan has not likewise Seen. Such an irregular circumstance must, alas, awaken the liveliest speculations among those who move in the world. That the child exists outside of any recorded contract thickens the sauce, while the fact of mixed parentage adds piquancy for those whose favorite dish is scandal broth."

Herself chiefest among them, Daav thought uncharitably. He raised his eyebrows.

"I must say, it seems a very bad case, put thus."

"And yet not entirely hopeless," Kareen assured him. "Given one who is known in the world, who possesses the necessary skills, working with the clan's interest at heart—the broth may never gain the dining board." She inclined her head.

"It is thus that I may serve Korval."

"You offer to undertake damage control, do you?" He grit his teeth against a surge of anger at the effrontery of it. Kareen, to wash Er Thom's face for him? More likely the scheme of letting a house in Solcintra would find the delm's favor than—

"How much?" he snapped, barely resisting the temptation to address her in the mercantile mode.

Kareen stared. "I beg your pardon?"

"Oh, come, come!" He moved a hand in a sweeping, deliberately meaningless gesture. "Surely we know each other too well to pretend of coyness! You offer to perform a service. I desire to know your price. I will then decide if the price is fair or dear." He met her eyes, his own hard as black diamond.

"Tell me what you want, Kareen."

She touched her tongue to her lips, though she matched him, stare for stare.

"I want my heir returned me."

Of course. Daav reached up and fingered the silver twist hanging in his ear, souvenir of his Scouting days.

"Your heir," he mused, letting his gaze wander from hers and fix upon a point slightly above her head. He continued to play with the earring. "Enlighten me. Has your heir a name?"

"His name is Pat Rin, as you well know!"

Well, at least they had done with that unnatural civility. Daav very nearly smiled as he let the earring go.

"And have you seen Pat Rin of late?"

"I saw him not twelve-day gone," she answered, somewhat snappishly.

"So nearly as that. Then you will be able to tell me of his latest interest."

"His interest?" Kareen glanced aside. "Why, his studies interest him, naturally, though I must say that Luken bel'Tarda does not insist upon the level of achievement I consider—" She broke off, respiration slightly up, and fingered the brooch at her throat before continuing.

"He is forever rambling about outdoors, so I expect, as all boys, he is fond of falling in streams and—and climbing trees and fetching down bird's nests . . ."

"Guns," Daav said gently. Kareen's head jerked toward him as if he had pulled a wire.

"Guns?" she repeated blankly.

"He bids fair to become an expert on guns," Daav told her. "Everything about them interests him. How they work. Why one sort is superior to another sort. How they are put together. How they are taken apart. Relative benefits of velocities versus projectile size. The theory of marksmanship." He bowed slightly. "When I last visited, I took him a beginner's pistol and we had a bit of target practice. I would say, should his interest continue, that he holds potential as a marksman of some note."

"A *marksman*." Kareen did not even try to mask the loathing in her voice.

Daav raised an eyebrow. "Our mother belonged to Teydor's, did she not? And successfully defended her place as club champion for five years together. Why should Pat Rin not be as good—or better? Or at very least have the chance to explore his interest to its fullest?

"But you are not interested in such matters," he continued after a moment. "You are most naturally interested in knowing whether the service you offer will be accepted." He moved a hand in negation. "Your price is found too high."

"So." It was nearly a hiss. "Er Thom yos'Galan is to be allowed a bastard mongrel and not required to make so much as a bow to society! But I, who have done duty and desire only to serve the clan, must have my son fostered away without my consent, for no reason other than *you* had decided—"

"I will remind you that the delm decided," Daav cut in. "I shall also give you two pieces of advice: The first is to compose yourself. The second is that you drop the words 'bastard' and 'mongrel' from your vocabulary. The child's name is Shan yos'Galan. He is the son of Er Thom yos'Galan and Anne Davis, both of whom acknowledge him as their own, so you see that 'bastard' is inexact."

"'Mongrel' however is no more than plain truth!" Kareen cried, apparently choosing to ignore his first piece of advice.

"I find the word offensive," Daav said evenly, and sighed sharply. "Come, Kareen, have sense! Your concern is that those with nothing better to do than scrounge for trouble will scan back through *The Gazette* and find that there has been no contract between Er Thom yos'Galan and Anne Davis, with the child to come to Korval. Eh?"

"Yes, certainly—"

"And yet you choose to ignore the fact that persons of such mind will without difficulty find listed in that same *Gazette* the information that Pat Rin yos'Phelium has been taken from his fostering and returned to his mother. And that they will think to themselves, *bribe*."

"And you consider yourself equal to the task of cleaning Korval's *melant'i* among the High Houses—"

"I remind you again that I am delm," Daav interrupted with exquisite gentleness. "Should Korval's *melant'i* require repair, it is no less than my duty to see such repair done. However, there is nothing to be mended. The clan accepts who it will, and no explanations due any outside of the clan." He took a careful breath.

"I advise you to leave me, Kareen. Now."

Her lips parted but no words came and in a moment she had made her bow.

"Good-day," she stated, in a tone so absolutely neutral it might be said to be mode-less. She left him then, quickly, heavy steps rattling the paving stones.

Daav stood where he was until he heard a motor start up, far down the hill. Then and only then did he allow his shoulders to lose their level rigidness and, pulling the gloves back over his hands, went to put his tools away.

THEY WOKE EARLY, shared a glass of morning wine and a leisurely, sensual shower. Then, like children sneaking a holiday, they had gone to explore the house.

Anne was soon thoroughly lost, her head a muddle of Parlors, Public Rooms and Receiving Chambers, and at last stopped in the middle of an opulent hall, laughing.

"Don't leave me, love, for if you did I'd never find my rooms again!" She shook her head. "I can see I'll have to carry a sack of bread crumbs with me and remember to scatter them well!"

"Yes, but you know, the servants are very efficient," Er Thom murmured, swaying close and smiling up into her face. "Likely they would have the crumbs swept up far ahead of the time you wished to return."

"Then I'm lost! Unless you'll draw me a map, of course."

"If you wish," he replied and she looked down at him, exotic and achingly beautiful in the embroidered house-robe. He shook the full sleeves back and caught her hands in his.

"Shall I show you one more thing?" he murmured, eyes bright with the remains of his smile. "Then I swear I will allow you to eat breakfast."

"One more thing," she agreed, giving herself a sharp mental rebuke: *Don't gawk at the man, Annie Davis!*

"This way," Er Thom said, holding tight to one hand and keeping so close to her side that his robe bid fair to tangle in her legs.

They walked the hallway without mishap, however, and went midway down one slightly shorter.

"Here," he said, squeezing her hand lightly before he let it go.

Stepping forward, he twisted an edge-gilt china knob and stepped back with a fluid bow. "Enter, please."

Anne hesitated fractionally. The bow had been of honored esteem, but Er Thom's eyes showed an expectation that was nearly hunger. Smiling slightly, she went into the room.

The walls were covered in nubby bronze silk, the floor with a resilient grass-weave the color of *Jelaza Kazone*'s leaves. A buffet along the back wall supported two small lamps and there were bronze sconces set at precise intervals around the walls. Three rows of twelve chairs each were arranged in a precise half-circle before a—

"It's beautiful," she breathed, going across the woven mat as if the omnichora had reached out a hand and pulled her forward. She stroked the satiny wood, pushed back the cover and ran her fingers reverently over the pristine ivory keys.

"It pleases you?" Er Thom asked from her side.

"Pleases me? It overwhelms me—an instrument like this . . ."

"Try it," he said softly and she shot him a quick look, shaking her head as she lifted her hand from the silent keys.

"Don't tempt me," she said, and he heard the longing in her voice. "Or we'll be here all day."

He caught her hand, lay it back on the keyboard, fingertips lazing over her knuckles.

"Turn it on," he murmured. "Play for me, Anne. Please."

It took no more encouragement than that, so hungry was she to hear the 'chora's voice, to test its spirit against her own.

She played him her favorite, *Toccata and Fugue in D Minor*, an ancient piece meant for the omnichora's predecessor, the organ. It was an ambitious choice, without the notation before her, but her fingers remembered everything and threw it into the perfect keyboard.

The music filled the room like an ocean, crashing back at her, bearing her up on a wave of sound and emotion until she thought she would die there, with the music so close there was no saying where it stopped and Anne Davis began.

Eventually, she found an end, let the notes die back, let herself come out of the glory, and looked at Er Thom through a haze of tears. She scraped her sweat-soaked hair back from her face and smiled at him.

"What a glorious instrument."

"You play it well," he said, his soft voice husky. He moved a step closer from his station at her side. It was then that she saw he was shivering.

"Er Thom—" Concern drove all else before it. She spun around on the bench, reaching out for him.

"Hush." He caught her questing hands, allowed himself to be pulled forward. "Anne." He lay his cheek against her hair, gently loosed a hand to stroke her shoulder.

"It is well," he murmured, feeling the way her muscles shivered with strain, in echo of his own. He stepped back and smiled for her, tugging lightly on her hand. "Let us go and eat breakfast. All right?"

"All right," she said after a moment, and turned to power-off the 'chora, and to cover the glistening keys.

THEY WERE IN THE DINING ROOM, rapt in each other, various dishes scattered near them on the table. Er Thom was wearing a house-robe, the Terran scholar a plain shirt and trousers.

Petrella glared at them for several minutes, her fingers gripping Mr. pak'Ora's arm. When she was convinced that neither her son nor the guest would soon turn a head and decently see her, she hit the floor a sturdy thump with her cane.

Both heads turned then, but it was Er Thom's eye she wanted.

"You, sir!" she snapped, "a word, of your goodness." She stumped off with no more than a inclination of the head as good-morning to the guest.

Er Thom sighed lightly and put his napkin aside.

"Excuse me, friend," he said softly, and went off in the wake of his mother.

CHAPTER TWENTY-FOUR

A Dragon will in all things follow its own necessities, and either will or will not make its bow to Society. Nor shall the prudent dispute a Dragon's chosen path or seek to turn it from its course.

—From *The Liaden Book of Dragons*

"YOU WILL HAVE THE goodness to explain," Petrella announced as the patio door closed behind the butler, "why *three* messages to your personal screen have gone unanswered from the time of sending to this moment?"

Er Thom bowed. "Doubtless because I have not gone by my rooms since an hour before last evening's Prime Meal, nor have I collected messages from the house base."

Petrella took a deep breath, fingers tightening ominously around the head of her cane. A breeze played momentary tag with the flowers at the edge of the patio, gave up the sport to tease the sleeves of Er Thom's robe, then veered again, showering Petrella with flower-scent as it chased off.

"Mother, allow me to seat you," he murmured, slipping a solicitous hand beneath her elbow. "You will overtire yourself."

It was just such gentle courtesy as he was wont to offer. Tears filled Petrella's eyes as she accepted it, though she could not have said whether they were tears of rage or of love.

Love or rage, her voice shook when next she spoke.

"If you think that I will close my eyes to any impropriety you and that—*person*—chose to perform in this house—"

"Forgive me." He did not raise his voice, but some slight edge, immediately recognizable to those who were of Korval—and those who dealt with them—warned her to silence.

"Professor Davis is a guest of the House," he continued after a moment, voice unremittingly gentle. "The Code teaches us that the well-being of the guest is sacred. Professor Davis is—accustomed— to depending upon me for certain comforts; she felt herself adrift among strangers, alone on a world far different than her own. Shall I doom her to sleeplessness and worry from a concern for *propriety*? Or shall I offer accustomed and much-needed comfort, that she might rest easy in our House?"

"All from concern for the guest," Petrella said acidly. "I am enlightened! Who would have considered you possessed the genius to twist Code in such a wise, all with an eye to gain your own way! *I* had thought you a person of *melant'i*, but I see now that judgment— and the judgment of your foster mother—was in error. I see that what I have is a clever halfling, strutting his own consequence and flaunting his faulty understanding for all the world to see! Never fear that I am too ill to lesson a disobedient boy. Give me that ring!"

Er Thom froze, eyes wide in a face gone somewhat pale.

"Well, sir? Will you have me ask it twice?"

Slowly, then, he raised his hands; slowly, drew the master trader's amethyst from his finger. He stepped forward and bowed, and lay the ring gently in her palm.

"So. We have at least a base of obedience upon which to build. You relieve me." She clenched her fingers, feeling the edges of the gem cut into her palm. "With this ring you give me your pledge, Er Thom yos'Galan. You pledge you will withhold such—comforts—as you have been accustomed to provide the Terran scholar, beginning immediately. Carry through your pledge and in eleven day's time, when her guesting is done, you may ask me for your ring." She gripped the gem tighter as she spoke, grateful for the slight, simple pain.

"Fail of your pledge and I shall return this ring to the Trade Commission, and ask that your license be withdrawn."

There was little chance that the Trade Commission would revoke the license of Master Trader Er Thom yos'Galan. But a request for revocation would mean a review. And a review would suspend Er Thom's ability to trade for a minimum of two Standard Years.

Er Thom drew a deep breath. Perhaps he meant to speak. If so, he was rescued from that indiscretion by the cheery voice and sudden advent of his *cha'leket*.

"Good-morning, all! What a lovely day, to be sure!" Daav paused beside his foster-brother and made his bow, all grace and easy smiles.

"Aunt Petrella, how delightful to see you looking so rested! I am come to speak with the guest. Is she within?"

"In the dining hall," Petrella told him, with scant courtesy, "when last seen."

"I to the dining hall, then." He turned and caught Er Thom's hand. "Good-morning, darling! Have you been naughty?"

Er Thom laughed.

Daav smiled and raised the hand he held, bending his head to kiss the finger which the master trader's ring had lately adorned.

"Courage, beloved," he said gently. Then he loosed his brother's hand and vanished into the house.

"Another mannerless child!" Petrella snapped peevishly, flicking her hand in dismissal. "Leave me," she commanded her son. "Take care you recall your pledge."

ANNE LOWERED HER COFFEE CUP, glancing up eagerly as a shadow flickered across the dining room door.

Alas, the shadow was not Er Thom, returning from his interview with his mother, but Er Thom's foster-brother. She rose quickly and bowed good-morning, but some of her disappointment must have shown in her face.

"Ah, it is only Daav!" that gentleman cried, striking a pose eloquent of despair in the instant before he swept his own bow of greeting. "Good-day, Scholar."

It was a bit of incidental theater worthy of one of Jerzy's more manic days and she gave it the laughter it deserved.

"But I thought we'd agreed that I was to be Anne, not 'Scholar,'" she protested.

"My dreadful manners," he said mournfully and Anne grinned.

"If you're looking for Er Thom, his mother needed to speak with him for a—"

"Yes, I've seen them," Daav interrupted, leaving Adult-to-Adult and entering Terran. "But it's you I've come to speak with. Have you half-an-hour?" He tipped his head. "There's a room down the hall where we may be private."

"The whole house is full of rooms where people can be private," she told him, coming slowly around the table.

"Have you seen all of Trealla Fantrol? You must be entirely exhausted." He bowed her through the door ahead of him.

"Only a corner of it, I'm afraid." She sighed. "My head's in a muddle. I'm not even sure I can find the 'chora room again."

"So you have seen that," he murmured. "How did you find the omnichora?"

"It's magnificent," she said frankly. "The Academy of Music on Terra has none finer."

He sent her a glance from beneath his lashes, a trick he shared with Er Thom, else she would never have caught it.

"Have you been to the Academy of Music on Terra, I wonder?"

"I was there on scholarship for two years," she said evenly. "Funding slipped in the third year and there was no way my family could—" She shrugged, cutting herself off.

"I went home and finished out college, snared a fellowship and went on to advanced work."

In record time, she added silently. Driven by the grief of losing her first love, determined to make a success of her second, studying to the exclusion of everything, even—especially—friendship . . .

"I see," Daav said, guiding her into a small room and pulling the door closed. He waved toward a pair of overstuffed, almost shabby chairs.

"Please, sit. May I give you wine?"

"Thank you—white, please."

The chair she chose was delightfully comfortable, the seat wide enough for her hips, the tall back sweeping 'round her shoulders, and sufficiently high-set that she barely needed to fold her legs at all.

Daav sat opposite her, placing two glasses on the low table between them.

"So, now." He settled back into his chair. "I have questions which must be answered. Believe that I do not wish to distress you in any way." He smiled. "Er Thom would hand me my ears if I did, you know."

She laughed. "Yes, very likely!"

"Ah, you don't think so? But surely it's no more than duty to protect the peace of a proposed spouse?"

"A proposed—oh." She shook her head. "Er Thom told you that he asked me to sign a marriage contract. I turned him down, and if he didn't tell you that he should have."

"He did," Daav said gently.

"Then what—" She frowned, searching his thin, foxy face. "I don't understand."

"Hah." He tasted his wine, considering her over the edge of the glass.

"May I know," he said eventually, "your intentions toward my brother?"

She barely knew, herself. It was plain she would have to give the man up—soon. Unfortunately, it was equally plain that giving him up was like to rip the living heart out of her.

Anne reached for her glass, buying time with a sip of wine. When she had put the glass aside, she was no closer to an answer.

"Should we," she asked, flicking a glance at Daav's face, "be having this conversation in—the High Tongue?"

"Certainly, if you would feel more comfortable," he said agreeably. "But I find Terran so free, don't you? No need to sift through a dozen modes in search of one particular nuance . . ."

She grinned. "It's only that I thought, since I seem to be speaking with the delm—"

"Ah, my regrettable manners! The delm, stuffy fellow that he is, remains aloof for the moment. You are speaking to Daav yos'Phelium, on behalf of his brother, who asked that I talk with you."

"Regarding my intentions?" Drat the man, why couldn't he ask her himself, then?

"Or your feelings," Daav murmured. He tipped his head. "It's an impertinence, I know. Alas, I've always been a impertinent fellow— and my brother is very dear to me."

She glanced up, charmed by his candor.

"Well," she said wryly, "he's very dear to me, too. How I'm going to give him a tolerable good-bye at the end of semester break is more than I can see." She shook her head.

"I should never have come to Liad—I see that now. It was only that he—he came to find me. *Me.* He was in trouble—" she smiled, recalling Er Thom's way of it—"in *difficulty.* And I thought, foolishly enough, that I could help . . ." She glanced aside.

"Nothing foolish at all," Daav said gently, "in wishing to aid a friend."

"Yes, but I should have thought it through," she said, biting her lip. "Naturally, you, or his mother or—other friends—would be more able to help him than—than a Terran." She raised her eyes to meet Daav's black gaze.

"I'm a handicap to him here, whatever his trouble is. But he wanted the delm to count Shan—it was so important—and then I had word from Scholar yo'Kera's associate and—oh, it all seemed to fall into some sort of pattern! Shan would be counted—that was small enough—my friend's associate would get her assistance, and—" She faltered, swallowing against sudden tears.

"And you would help Er Thom extricate himself from his difficulty," Daav finished for her. There was a slight pause. "You didn't think of parting?"

She laughed ruefully. "At the beginning, I was braced—waiting for him to leave. Of course he would have to leave, I knew that.

But he stayed and he kept insisting that we go to Liad and I kept insisting that Shan and I would stay on University—" She shook her head.

"Quite a donnybrook—and all wasted effort. Er Thom got his way, of course—*that* should teach me not to argue with a master trader! The more we were together, the less I thought of parting. He was with me and I loved him—more now—much more now—than—before." She glanced down, saw her fingers twisted around each other on her lap, sighed and looked up. "Is that what you wanted to know?"

Daav's eyes met hers with a curious intensity.

"You never thought of a lifemating?" he asked.

Anne frowned. "I'm Terran."

"And a Terran wife must necessarily be a burden," he commented dryly. "Yet, if he offered a lifemating—"

"No." She shook her head decisively. "No, I couldn't let him do that. It's not—necessary—that he make such a—I'll be able to—to show him a dry face, when it's time to leave."

"Will you?" His voice was very soft, one eyebrow well up.

Anne looked at him, feeling the tightness in her chest. "Yes, I will," she said with a certainty she was a long way from feeling. "I've done it before, after all."

"I MIGHT INDEED GIVE HIM HIS RING BACK," Petrella informed her nephew tersely. "He knows what he must do to earn it."

"Yes, but only consider the unnecessary speculation awakened in the minds of the idle," Daav urged, "does he but go into Solcintra thus."

"There is no reason for Er Thom to go into the city."

Daav stared. "Why, there is *every* reason for him to do so!" he cried. "The normal demands of his duty take him to Solcintra and the Port many times over a twelve-day." He checked his pacing. "Unless you've relieved him of those, as well?"

"Certainly not," she said, righteously. "Only the Trade Commission may relieve a master trader of his duties."

Daav clamped his jaw against a sharp return to that and mentally reviewed a Scout's relaxation exercise, deliberately bringing his anger under control.

"Aunt Petrella," he said after a moment, with credible, if fragile, calm. "If you believe Er Thom will keep from duty simply because you choose that he not wear mark of rank, you have a very odd view of his character."

"Thank you!" she snapped. "I choose to teach him obedience, sir, as I told you last evening. You will not interfere in this."

"You wish to shame the clan's master trader before the Port entire and claim it's none of mine? Aunt—"

She struck the floor with her cane. "I will not have him interpreting Code for his own benefit!"

Daav froze, staring at her out of wide eyes.

"Isn't that what it's for?"

Petrella glared, thin chest heaving with rage, hands gripped like talons about the head of her cane.

"I may die before your eyes this moment," she said grimly, "and leave you a wrongheaded, disobedient boy as thodelm. It's no less than you deserve."

"I don't *want* a dog broken to heel!" Daav shouted, control and gentle-speaking alike be damned. "I want intelligence, clear sight, strength of duty—as my mother did before me! And I tell you now, Chi's sister, if you break Er Thom yos'Galan, you break Korval!"

She straightened in her chair as if he had struck her, sucked in breath for she barely knew what reply—

Too late. Daav was gone.

CHAPTER TWENTY-FIVE

The dramliz want young Tor An's genes. Farseers predict twins from the match and offer the girl-child to us—to Clan Korval—as settlement.

Jela would say that a wizard on board tips the scale to survival— which remains sound reasoning, though we're planet-bound now and in honorable estate, or so the boy will tell me . . .

As it transpires, Tor An met his proposed wife several days ago, through Dramliza Rool Tiazan's good graces, I make no doubt! The boy's smitten, of course, so the marriage is made.

Perhaps the girl-child will fail of being dramliz . . .

—Excerpted from Cantra yos'Phelium's Log Book

"MASTER MERCHANT BEL'TARDA," Mr. pak'Ora announced from the doorway. "Master Pat Rin yos'Phelium."

Petrella glanced up from her desk with ill-concealed irritation as Luken, looking every inch the rug merchant he was, crossed into the room, holding a dark-haired boy of about six Standard Years by the hand.

The man bowed greeting-between-kin, a certain trepidation marking the gesture. The boy's bow, of Child-to-Clan-Elder, was performed with solemn exactitude. He straightened, shifting the brightly-ribboned box he carried from the left hand to the right, and showed Petrella a sharp-featured face dominated by a pair of wary brown eyes.

"Good-day, Luken," Petrella said, inclining her head. For the boy, she added a smile. "Good-day, Pat Rin."

"Good-day, Grand-Aunt," Pat Rin responded politely, nothing so like a smile in either lips or eyes.

Stifling a sigh, she looked to the man, who gave the impression of fidgeting nervously, though he stood almost painfully still.

"Well, Luken? What circumstance do I praise for this opportunity to behold your face?"

The face in question—blunt, honest, and mostwise good-humored—darkened in embarrassment.

"Boy's come to bring a gift to his new cousin," he said, dropping a light hand to Pat Rin's thin shoulder and flinging Petrella a look of respectful terror. "Just as his mother would wish him to do, all by the Code and kindness to kin."

It was perhaps the piquancy of a point of view that could suppose Kareen yos'Phelium capable of wishing her heir to associate in any way with an irregularly-allied child of lamentable lineage that saved Luken the tongue-flaying he so obviously anticipated. Petrella contented herself with a sigh and the observation that news traveled quickly.

Luken moved his shoulders. "No trick to reading *The Gazette*," he commented. "Do so every morning, with my tea."

Petrella, who had failed of her own custom of *The Gazette* with breakfast only this morning, openly stared.

"You wish me to understand that there is an announcement of Shan yos'Galan's birth in this morning's *Gazette*?" she demanded.

Luken looked alarmed, but stuck to his guns.

"Right on the first page, under 'Accepted.'" He closed his eyes and recited in a slightly sing-song voice: "'Accepted of Korval, Shan yos'Galan, son of Er Thom yos'Galan, Clan Korval, and Anne Davis, University Central.'"

He opened his eyes. "That's all. Simple, I remember thinking."

"Indeed, a masterwork of simplicity," Petrella said through gritted teeth and was prevented of saying more by the unannounced arrival of her son, dressed at last in day-clothes.

"Luken. Well-met, Cousin." Er Thom's voice carried real warmth, as had his bow. He smiled and held out a ringless hand. "Hello, Pat Rin. I'm glad to see you."

The tense face relaxed minutely and Pat Rin left his foster-father's side to take the offered hand. "Hello, Cousin Er Thom." He held up the festive box. "We have a gift for Cousin Shan."

"That's very kind," Er Thom said, matching the child's seriousness. "Shall I take you to him, so that you may give it?"

Pat Rin hesitated, glancing over his shoulder at his foster-father.

"Of course you would welcome the opportunity to meet your new cousin," Luken coached gently and Pat Rin turned his serious eyes back to Er Thom.

"Thank you. I would like to meet my new cousin."

"Good. I will take you to him immediately. With my mother's permission . . ." He bowed respect in her direction, gathered Luken with a flicker of fingers and moved toward the hallway.

Petrella gripped her chair.

"Er Thom!"

He turned his head, violet eyes merely polite in a face still somewhat pale. "Mother?"

"An announcement of your child's acceptance," she said, with forced calm, "appears in this morning's *Gazette*."

"Ah," he said softly, and, seeing that she awaited more, added: "That would be the delm's hand."

"I see," Petrella said, and spun back to her desk, releasing him.

HE HAD JUST REVIEWED the last of the day's pressing business and was considering a climb up the Tree. Seated on the platform he and his brother had built as children, the world below reduced to proper insignificance, surrounded by the benign presence of the Tree—there he might profitably begin to consider Er Thom's tangle.

Indeed, he had pushed away from the desk and was half-way

across the room when he heard his butler's familiar step in the hallway beyond and paused, head tipped to one side, wondering—

In another moment, wonder was rewarded by delight.

Mr. pel'Kana bowed in the doorway, "Scout Lieutenant sel'Iprith," he announced, standing aside to let her pass.

"Olwen."

Smiling, Daav went to meet her. Mr. pel'Kana discreetly withdrew, pulling the door shut behind him.

She was in leathers, as if new-come from space, and carried a small potted plant carefully in both hands. Looking up, she returned his smile, though somewhat less brightly than usual, and went past to put the pot on the desk.

Daav watched her, abruptly cold.

"Olwen?"

She spun away from the desk and flung against him, arms hard around his waist, cheek pressed to his chest.

She was sweet and familiar, warm where he was so suddenly chill. Daav hugged her close, rubbing his face in her hair.

They stood thus some time, neither speaking, then she stirred a little, muscles tensing as if she would move away.

He loosened his embrace, though he did not entirely free her. Olwen sighed and seemed to melt against him.

"Wonderful news, old friend," she said, so softly he could barely make out the words. "I'm recalled to active duty."

"Ah." He closed his eyes, acutely aware of the softness of her hair. He drew a careful breath.

"When do you leave?"

"This afternoon." Her arms tightened bruisingly; she released him and stepped back, one hand rising to brush his cheek. "Be well, Daav."

He caught her hand and kissed the cool fingertips. "Good lift, Olwen. Take care."

"As ever," she returned, which was the old joke between them.

He walked with her to the door, and watched as she went down the path and slipped into her car.

When the sound of the engine had gone beyond his hearing, he returned to his office, taking care that the door was well-closed behind him.

Nubiath'a sat upon the corner of the desk, where she had placed it. He shivered and bent his head, gasping, hands coming up to hide his face, though no one was there to see him cry.

"IT'S NONE OF MY BUSINESS," Luken muttered for Er Thom's ear alone as they strolled along the hall, Pat Rin well ahead, "and you needn't bother snatching my hair off if I'm expected to turn a blind eye. But I wonder what's happened to your ring."

Er Thom lifted an eyebrow. "My thodelm keeps it for me," he said mildly, and smiled. "More than that loses you hair, Cousin."

"Fairly warned," the older man said with the good-humor that won him friends in both the Port and the City.

"Announcement in *The Gazette* took me unaware—" he confided—"felicitations, by the way! But the last I knew of matters, yos'Galan was looking to Nexon to provide your heir—" He threw Er Thom a sudden look. "Not that it concerns me, of course!"

Er Thom laughed. "Poor Luken. Do we abuse you?"

"Well," the other replied candidly, "you and Daav cut up a trifle rash as cubs—and it's a certified wonder you weren't drowned as halflings. Though," he said hastily, as if recollecting himself, "I believe that to be the case with most halflings."

"And as adults we daily snatch you hairless," Er Thom murmured, "and do you no better good than setting Kareen at your throat."

"No," Luken said as they climbed the stairs. "No, I wouldn't have it that way. Daav visits often, you know—he and the boy are quite fond. I find him much easier now he's come back from the Scouts and taken up the Ring. You—you were always the sensible one, cousin, and if you have from time to time been sharp, why, it's doubtless no more than I deserved. I'm not a clever fellow, after all, and it must be a trial to you quick ones to always be bearing with us slow. Kareen, now—" Luken sighed, eyes on the child who went so solemn and un-childlike ahead of them.

"The boy makes gains," he said eventually. "No more nightmares—well, none to speak of." His mouth tightened. "My back's broad. Kareen yos'Phelium may do her worst to me, if it buys the child his peace."

Er Thom lay a hand on the other's arm, squeezing lightly.

"Thank you, Cousin."

"Eh?" Luken gave a startled smile. "No need for that, though you're very welcome, I'm sure." He moved his shoulders. "That's always been the difference between you lot and Kareen. Good-hearted, the both of you, and not dealing hurt for the joy of hurting." He raised his voice.

"Ho, there, boy-dear, you've gone past the door!"

Up ahead, Pat Rin turned and came slowly back, holding the gift between his two hands.

Er Thom lay his palm against the nursery door and bowed his cousins within.

"CATCH!" Anne tossed the bright pink sponge-ball in a lazy arc.

Shrieking with laughter, Shan grabbed, the ball skittered off his fingertips and he flung down the long room after it, giggling.

Anne shook her hair back from her face, clapping as he caught up with the ball and snatched it high.

"Now throw it back!" she called, holding her hands over her head.

"Catch, Ma!" her son cried and threw.

It wasn't too bad an effort, though it was going to fall short. Anne lunged forward on her knees, hand outstretched for the grasp—and turned her head, distracted from the game by the door-chime.

"*Mirada!*" Shan ran and threw himself with abandon into his father's arms, ignoring the other two visitors entirely. Anne came off her knees and went forward, ball forgotten.

Er Thom caught Shan and swung him up into an exuberant hug. "So, then, bold-heart!"

Beside them, the older of the two visitors—a sandy-haired man of perhaps forty-five, with a bluff, good-humored face—pursed his lips and lay a lightly-ringed hand on the thin shoulder of his companion. Anne smiled at the fox-faced little boy and received a solemn stare out of wide brown eyes.

"Play ball, *Mirada!*" Shan commanded as Er Thom set him down.

"Indeed not," he murmured. "You must make your bow to your cousins." He turned his head and caught Anne's eye, giving her a smile that jelled her knee-joints.

"Anne, here are my cousins Luken bel'Tarda and Pat Rin yos'Phelium. Cousins, I make you known to Scholar Anne Davis, mother of my child and guest of the House."

"Scholar." Luken bel'Tarda's bow puzzled for an instant, then she had it: Honor to One Providing a Clan-Child. "I'm glad to meet you."

"I'm glad to meet you also, Luken bel'Tarda." Honor-to-one-providing had no neat corollary, so Anne chose Adult-to-Adult, which was cordial without leaping to any unwarranted conclusions regarding Luken bel'Tarda's *melant'i*.

"Well, that's kind of you to say so," he said, with apparent pleasure. He squeezed the little boy's shoulder lightly. "Make your bow to the guest, child-dear."

Bow to the Guest it was, delivered with adult precision, and a quick, "Be happy in your guesting, Scholar Davis," delivered in a husking little voice, while the brown eyes continued, warily, to weigh her.

Anne bowed Honor to a Child of the House, adding a smile as she straightened. "You must be Daav's little boy," she said gently.

Pat Rin ducked his head.

"Begging the lady's pardon," he said quickly, "I am the heir of Kareen yos'Phelium."

"But he has his uncle's look, certain enough," Luken added, rumpling the boy's dark hair with casual affection and sending Anne a glance from guileless gray eyes. "His mother's dark, as well. I don't doubt you'll be meeting her soon. Never one to allow a duty to languish, Lady Kareen."

"I look forward to the pleasure of meeting her," Anne told him, with was only proper, and wondered why he blinked.

"And here," Er Thom said gently, "is Shan yos'Galan. Shan-son, these are your cousins Luken and Pat Rin. Make your bow, please."

Shan hesitated, frowning after the Liaden words.

"Shannie," Anne prompted in Terran. "Bow to your cousins and tell them hello."

There was another momentary hesitation, followed by a bow of no particular mode. On straightening, he grinned and offered a cheery "Hi!"

Luken bel'Tarda sent a startled glance to Er Thom. "I'm afraid—oversight, of course!—I've never learnt—aah—Terran—"

"Hi!" Shan repeated, advancing on his cousins. Pat Rin tipped his head, brown eyes wide.

"Hel-lo?" he said uncertainly.

Shan nodded energetically. "Hello, yes. Hi!" He thrust out a hand. "Shake!"

Pat Rin flinched and stared. Then, lower lip caught between his teeth, he reached out and brushed Shan's fingers with his.

"Hel-lo," he repeated and snatched his hand back. "I am glad to meet you, Cousin Shan," he said in rapid Liaden and held out the package he carried. "We've brought you a gift."

Shan took the package without a blink. "Thanks. Play ball?"

"My son thanks you for your thoughtfulness," Er Thom said for Luken bel'Tarda's benefit. "He asks if his cousin might play."

"That's very kind." Luken looked gratified. "It happens the boy and I are promised in the City today, but I'd be delighted to bring him to visit again soon. He might spend the day, if you've no objection, cousin."

"Of course Pat Rin is always welcome," Er Thom said and Anne saw the tense little face relax, just a bit.

"That's fixed then," Luken said comfortably. He turned and bowed, giving Anne the full honor-to-one-providing treatment.

"Scholar Davis. A delight to meet you, ma'am."

"Luken bel'Tarda. I hope to meet you again."

Unprompted, Pat Rin made his bow, and then the two of them were ushered out by Er Thom, who turned his head to smile at her as he was departing.

"Well!" Anne sighed gustily and grinned at her son. "Do you want to open your present, Shannie?"

CHAPTER TWENTY-SIX

There is nobody who is not dangerous for someone.

—**Marquise de Sevigne**

THE CHIME RECALLED HIM, blinking, from the world of invoices, profit and cargo-measures. He rose, half-befogged, and keyed the door to open.

"Anne." The fog burned away in the next instant, and he put out a hand to catch hers and urge her within.

"Come in, please," he murmured, seeing his delight reflected in her face. "You must forgive me, you know, for thrusting Luken upon you, all unexpected. I had not known you would be with our son—"

"Nothing to forgive," she said, smiling. "I thought he was delightful." The smile dimmed a fraction. "Though Pat Rin is very—shy . . ."

Trust Anne to see through to the child's hurts, Er Thom thought, leading her past his cluttered worktable, to the double-chair near the fireplace.

"Pat Rin progresses," he murmured, which was only what Luken had told him. "I thought him quite bold in dealing with our rogue."

She laughed a little and allowed him to seat her. He stood before her, availing himself of both her hands, smiling into her face like a mooncalf.

Her fingers exerted pressure on his, and a frown shadowed her bright face. She bent her head; raised it quickly.

"You've taken off your ring." The tone was mild, but the eyes showed concern—perhaps even alarm.

"Well, and so I have," he said, as if it were the merest nothing. He raised the hand that should have borne the ornament, and silked her hair back from her ear, the short strands sliding through his fingers.

"How may I serve you, Anne?"

She moistened her lips, eyes lit with a certain self-mockery. "Keep that up, laddie, and neither of us will get to our work." She turned her head to brush a quick, pulse-stirring kiss along his wrist.

"And that?" he murmured.

She laughed and shook her head so that he reluctantly dropped his hand.

"It happens I'm going to need that car you offered," she said, in a shocking return to practicality; "and probably a driver, too. Drusil tel'Bana can see me this afternoon."

"Ah. Shall I drive you?"

"I'd like that," she said, with a regretful smile. "But I'm liable to be some time. If Doctor yo'Kera's notes are in as bad a way as she's led me to think—" She shook her head. "No use you kicking your heels for hours while a couple of scholars babble nonsense at each other. It's a shame to even force a driver . . ."

"Nonetheless," Er Thom said firmly, laying a daring finger across her lips. "You *will* have a driver. Agreed?"

"Bully." She laughed at him. "I'd like to see what would happen if I *didn't* agree—but as it happens, I do. I'm not at all certain of my directions, and if the work should keep me until after dark . . ."

"It is arranged," he said. "When shall you leave?"

"Is an hour too soon?"

"Not at all," he returned, around a stab of regret. He stepped back, reluctantly releasing her hand.

Anne stood. "Thank you, Er Thom."

"It is no trouble," he murmured and she sighed.

"Yes, you always say that." She touched his cheek lightly and smiled. "But thank you anyway. For everything." She lay a finger against his lips as he had to hers.

"I'll see you later, love," she whispered, then whirled and left him, as if it were too chancy a thing to stay.

"**SCHOLAR DAVIS**, how delightful to meet you at last!" Drusil tel'Bana's greeting was warmth itself, couched in the mode of Comrades.

Anne bowed and smiled. "I regret I was not able to come sooner."

"That you came at all is sufficient to the task," the other scholar assured her. "I had barely dared hope—But, there! When I wrote I had not known you were allied so nearly with Korval. I do not always read *The Gazette*, alas, and with Jin Del's death—" She gestured, sweeping the rest of that sentence away. "At least I did read today's issue! Allow me to offer felicitations."

"Thank you." Anne bowed again. "I will share your felicitations with my son and his father."

Drusil tel'Bana's eyes widened, but she merely murmured, "Yes, certainly," and abruptly turned aside, raising a hand to point.

"Let me show you Jin Del's office. His notes—what are remaining—have been kept just as they were found when—The state of disorder, I confide to you, Scholar, is not at all in his usual way. I thought, at first, you know, that—but it is foolishness, of course! What sense to steal the notes for a work that will perhaps excite the thought of two dozen scholars throughout the galaxy? No. No, it must only have been that he was ill—much more ill, I fear, than any of us had known."

Anne glanced down at the woman beside her, seeing the care-grooved cheeks, the drooping line of her thin shoulders, the jerky walk.

"Doctor yo'Kera's death has affected you deeply," she offered, cautiously feeling her way along the border of what the other would consider proper sympathy and what would be heard as insult. "I understand. When I received your letter, I could barely credit that he was gone—he had seemed so vital, so brilliant. And I had only known him through letters. What one such as yourself, who had the felicity of working with him daily, must feel I may only surmise."

Drusil tel'Bana threw her a look from tear-bright eyes and glanced quickly aside.

"You are kind," she said in a stifled voice. "He was—a jewel. I do not quite see how one shall—but that is for later. For now, there is Jin Del's work to be put into order, his book to be finished. Here—here is his office."

She turned aside, fumbled a moment at the lockplate and stepped back with a bow when the door at last swung open and the interior lights came on.

"Please."

Anne stepped into the room beyond—and smiled.

Overcrowded shelves held tapes, bound books, disks and unbound printouts. Two severe chairs were crowded together at the front of the computer-desk, a battered, rotating work chair sat behind it. A filing cabinet was jammed into one corner, a double row of books at its summit. Next to it was a plain table, bookless, for a wonder, though that lack was more than made up by the profusion of 'scriber sheets, file folders and note cards littering its surface.

The floor sported a dark red rug that had once very possibly been good. The walls were plain, except for a framed certificate which declared Jin Del yo'Kera, Clan Yedon, a Scholar Specialist in the field of Galactic Linguistics, and a flat-pic, also framed, of three tall Terran persons—two women and a man—standing before an island of trees in a sea of grasslands.

"He had gone—outworld—to study, as a young man," Drusil tel'Bana said from the doorway. "Those are Mildred Higgins and Sally Brunner with their husband, Jackson Roy. Terrans of the sort known as 'Aus.' Jin Del had stayed at their—station—one season. They taught him to—to shear sheep." Anne glanced over her shoulder in time to see the other woman give a wavering, unfocused smile.

"He had another picture, of a sheep. He said that they were—not clever."

Anne grinned. "My grandfather kept sheep," she said, "back on New Dublin. He contended that they were smarter than a radish—on a good day."

Drusil tel'Bana smiled and in that instant Anne saw the woman as she had been: Humorous, vivid, intelligent. Then the cloud of grief enfolded her again and she gestured toward the laden table.

"These are his notes. Please, Scholar, of your kindness . . ."

"It's what I came for," Anne said. She spun the desk chair around to the table, reached out a long arm and snagged one of the straight-backed "student's" chairs.

"Do you have time to sit with me?" she asked Drusil tel'Bana. "In case I should have questions as I go through?"

"My time is yours," the other woman said, sitting primly on the edge of the straight chair.

Anne, perforce, sat in the battered, too-small desk chair, and pulled the first stack of folders toward her.

HOURS LATER, she sat back and scraped the hair from her face, staring blankly at the blank wall before her. Her shoulder and back muscles were cramped and she didn't doubt her legs would stiffen up when she finally tried to stand—but none of that mattered.

Disordered as his notes undoubtedly were, it was plain to one who had corresponded with him and who tended in certain directions of thought herself, that Jin Del yo'Kera had found it. He had found what she herself had been looking for—the proof, the empirical, undeniable evidence of a common mother tongue, which had then given birth to its disparate, triplet children: Liaden, Terran, Yxtrang.

Jin Del had found it—his notations, his careful reasoning, his checks and double checks—all here, needing only to be re-ordered, culled and made ready for presentation.

All here, all ready.

All, except the central, conclusive fact.

Anne looked aside, to where Drusil tel'Bana still sat patiently in her hard chair, face grooved with grief, but otherwise composed, calm.

"Is there," Anne asked slowly. "Forgive me! I do not wish to ask—improperly, but I must know."

Drusil tel'Bana inclined her head. "There is no shame in an honest inquiry, Scholar. You know that is true."

Anne sighed. "Then I ask if there are—people—who would feel their—*melant'i* at—risk, should a fact be found that linked Terra to Liad?"

"There are many such," the other woman said, with matter-of-fact dreariness. "Even among your own folk, is there not the Terran Party, which would wish to deny Liad the trade routes?"

The Terran Party was a gaggle of cross-burning crackpots, but it *did* exist. And if the Terran Party existed, Anne thought wildly, why shouldn't there be a Liaden Party?

"You feel," Drusil tel'Bana said hesitantly, "that there is something—missing—from Jin Del's work?"

"Yes," Anne told her. "Something very important—the centerpiece of his proof, in fact. Without it, we merely have speculation. And all his notes lead me to believe that what he had was proof!"

Beside her, the other woman sagged, tears overflowing all at once.

"Scholar!" Anne reached out—was restrained by a lifted hand as Drusil tel'Bana shielded her face.

"Please," she gasped. "I ask that you do not regard—I am not generally thus. I shall—seek the Healers, by and by. Only tell me if you are able, Scholar."

Anne blinked. "Able?"

"Able to take on Jin Del's work, to find his proof and finish his lifepiece. I cannot. I lack the spark. But you—you are like him for brilliance. It was your thought that started him on this path. It is only fitting that you are the one to complete what you caused to begin."

And there was, Anne admitted wryly, a certain justice to it. Jin Del yo'Kera had unstintingly given of his time and his knowledge to the young Terran scholar he had graciously addressed as 'colleague.' Together, the two of them had constructed the quest represented by the notes now spread, helter-skelter, before her. That one of the two was untimely called aside did not mean that the quest was done.

She sighed, trying not to think of the years it might take to recapture that one vital fact.

"I will need to take this away with me," she told Drusil tel'Bana, waving a hand at the littered table. "I will require permission to go through his files—the computer. The books."

"Such permissions are on file from the Scholar Chairman of the University. If you find it necessary to take anything else, only ask me, Scholar, and I shall arrange all." The Liaden scholar rose and went to the desk, pulled open a drawer and extracted a carry-case.

"What you have upon the table should fit in here, I think."

CHAPTER TWENTY-SEVEN

Love: the delusion that one woman differs from another.

—H.L. Mencken

"SACRIFICE?"

Er Thom sagged to the edge of the desk, staring at Daav out of stunned purple eyes.

"Anne said it would be a *sacrifice* for me to become her lifemate?"

"She stopped short of the actual word," Daav acknowledged, "but I believe the sentence was walking in that direction, yes."

"I—" He glanced aside, moved a slender, ringless hand and rubbed Relchin's ears.

"There—must be an error," he said as the big cat began to purr. "She cannot have understood." He looked back to Daav.

"Anne is not always as—certain—of the High Tongue as—"

"We were speaking Terran," Daav interrupted and Er Thom blinked.

"I—do not understand."

"She said that, also." Daav sighed, relenting somewhat in the face of his brother's bewilderment. "She admits to being in love with you, darling—very frank, your Anne! However, she is sensible that a Terran lover makes you vulnerable, as she would have it, and that a Terran wife must make you doubly so." He smiled, wryly. "An astonishingly accurate summation, given that she does not play."

Er Thom chewed his lip.

"She asked me," he said, all his confusion plain for the other to read. "She asked me to guard her *melant'i.*"

"She did?" Daav blinked. "In—traditional—manner?"

"We were speaking Terran," Er Thom said slowly. "Last evening, when I had gone to escort her to Prime. We were about to leave her apartment and she suddenly paused and looked at me with—with all of her heart in her face. And she said, *Don't let me make a mistake . . .*"

"And you accepted this burden on her behalf?"

"With joy. It was the avowal I had longed for, which she had not given, though there was certainly sufficient else between us—" He broke off, eyes wide. "It was plain," he said stubbornly. "There could have been no error."

"And yet," Daav said, "the lady spoke—plainly, I assure you!— of her intention to show you a dry face, when time had come for her to end her guesting and return to University."

"No." Er Thom's voice broke on the denial. He cleared his throat. "No. She cannot—"

Daav frowned. "Would you deny an adult person the right to her own necessities?"

"Certainly not! It is only that there must be some error, some nuance I am too stupid to see. Anne is honorable. To ask for the care of a lifemate and in the next breath speak of giving *nubiath'a*—it is not her way. Something has gone awry. Something—"

"And how," Daav cut in gently, hating what he must put forth. "if the lady asked not for lifemate's care, but for that of kin?"

"Kin?" Er Thom's face showed blank astonishment. "I am no kin of Anne."

"Yet her son is accepted of Korval," Daav murmured, "which might encourage her to believe herself in a manner—kin—to you."

A vivid image of Anne's body moving under him, a recollection of her kiss, her face transcendent with desire—Er Thom glanced up. "I am not persuaded she believes any such thing."

"Hah." Daav's lips twitched, straightened.

"Another way, then. Understand that I honor her abilities in the High Tongue. However, you, yourself, say her proficiency sometime wavers. How if her understanding of custom is likewise uncertain? How if she should consider that a guest of the House might ask this thing of a son of the House?" He moved his shoulders.

"She has already made one error of custom, has she not?" He asked his brother's stubborn eyes. "In the matter of naming the child?"

"Yes," Er Thom admitted after a moment. "But there is no—" He broke off, sighing sharply.

"I shall endeavor to arrive at plain speaking," he said slowly, "and show Anne—" He stopped, wariness showing in his face.

"Is it—possible—that the delm will allow a lifemating between myself and Anne Davis?"

"The delm . . ." Daav moved from his chair, took two steps toward the desk and his brother—and halted, hands flung, palm out, showing all.

"The delm is most likely to ask you to consider what this affair has thus far bought you," he said levelly. "He is likely to ask you to think on the anger of your thodelm, who refuses to See your child, and who is prepared to ring such a peal over you as the world has never witnessed! The delm may ask you to look on the disruption your actions have introduced into the clan entire." He took a gentle breath, meeting his brother's eyes.

"The delm is likely to ask you if another coin might spend to better profit, brother, and the Terran lady released to her necessities."

Er Thom was silent, eyes wide and waiting.

"The delm may well ask," Daav concluded, with utmost gentleness, "that you give this lady up."

"Ah." Er Thom closed his eyes and merely sat, hip on the desk, one foot braced against the carpet, hand quiet along Relchin's back.

"With all respect to the delm," he murmured eventually, and in the Low Tongue, so Daav understood that as yet the delm was safely outside the matter. "Might it be—permitted—to mention that one has striven for several years to put this lady from one's mind?" He opened his eyes, tear-bright as they were.

"Whatever the success of that enterprise, certainly she remained in one's heart." He moved his shoulders, almost a shudder. "The delm needs no reminder of one's—adherence to duty—saving this single thing. To give her up—that is to go now, tonight, to Solcintra, and give myself to the Healers."

And have Anne Davis ripped not only from his memory but from his daily mind, Daav thought, overriding his own shudder. *Which commission the Healers certainly would refuse.*

However, were Anne Davis to depart according to her stated intention, the Healers would very easily agree to assuage what measure of grief Er Thom might experience from the parting.

Daav stared at his brother's face, seeing the pain there, *feeling* his longing, and his need.

It's ill-done, he warned himself, though he already knew he would fail to heed his own warning. *You set him up to fail; you bait the trap that will spring forgetfulness with that which he most desires to recall . . .*

"Daav?"

He started, went forward and enclosed his brother in embrace. Laying his cheek against the warm, bright hair, he closed his eyes, and allowed himself a fantasy: They were boys again, the lie went, and nothing loomed to mar their love. They were one mind with two bodies, neither ascendant over the other. There was no dark power that one held which with a word would change the other, irrevocably and forever . . .

"A wager," Daav whispered, never caring that his voice trembled. It did not matter. Er Thom would take the bait. He must.

Daav stepped back and met his brother's eyes. "A wager, darling," he repeated softly.

"Tell me."

"Why, only this: Woo the lady while she is here. Win her—plainly, mind—and with full understanding between you! Win her aye, and win all. The delm shall overrule yos'Galan, the lady shall stand at your side, the child shall be your acknowledged heir. All." His mouth twisted wryly.

"Does your wooing fail to sway the lady from her necessities, then the day she leaves Liad is the day you make your bow to Master Healer Kestra."

"Hah." Er Thom's lips bent in a pale smile, eyes intent on Daav's face.

"Shall I lose, brother?" he asked softly.

"I will tell you," Daav said with the utter truth one owed to kin, "that I think you shall."

"So little faith!" Er Thom moved his shoulders. "It is only a continue of the throw made three years past. The game continues." He smiled more widely and gave a little half-bow from his perch against the desk. "We play on."

Daav returned the bow, speechless and grief-shot, in a fair way to hating delm and clan and homeworld and the necessities the weaving of all created—

"Never mind." Er Thom came off the desk and moved forward, raising a hand to cup Daav's cheek, to trace the line of a bold black brow.

"Never mind, beloved," he whispered, and touched the barbaric silver earring, sending it to trembling. "I shall not lose."

SOME HOURS LATER, Daav leaned far back in his work chair and stretched mightily, fisted hands high over his head.

"Well," he said, righting himself and glancing over to where Er Thom sat beside him, silently perusing the screen. "Does that cover everything, do you think?"

"I believe it is a solid beginning," Er Thom replied, picking up his glass and sipping. "A contract of formal alliance between Clan Korval and Anne Davis. Free passage on any Korval ship. Right of visit to our son . . ."

"And half your personal fortune," Daav finished, tasting his own wine. "Your mother will dislike that excessively, darling."

Er Thom shrugged, much as he had earlier when this point had been raised.

"Money is easy to come by," he murmured now, dismissing his parent's displeasure as the merest annoyance. "Why should Anne not have comfort in her life?"

"Why, indeed?" Daav sighed. "I do wonder—"

Er Thom flashed him a quick purple glance. "What is it you wonder?"

"Only if the lady's understanding of custom was equal to the knowledge that her child belongs to Korval. I had the distinct impression that she meant to take him away with her when she returned to University." He sipped wine. "Though I could be mistaken."

"I am certain that she understands that Shan is of Korval," Er Thom said. "We had discussed it—several times."

"Quite a *donnybrook*, as the lady described it," Daav agreed. "Still, I wonder if she does know."

"Since I am already embarked upon a mission of clarity, I shall undertake to be certain that she does." Er Thom frowned. "What is a *donnybrook*?"

"An argument," Daav murmured, "named in honor, or so I am told, of a possibly-mythic town on Terra where fisticuffs is the pastime of choice." He grinned. "A language to love, admit it!"

"I fear my proficiency falters daily," Er Thom said mournfully. Far down the hall, a clock could be heard striking the hour.

"Gods, only hear the time! And I expected early at Port tomorrow—"

Daav eyed him doubtfully. "Are you?"

"Yes, certainly. I must tend some matters on the *Passage* first, then there are orders to place, people to see . . ."

"Naturally enough, since you have been away for some time. However," Daav hesitated.

"Your thodelm expects there is no reason for you to go into Port. Or so she said."

Er Thom glanced down at his naked hands; back to Daav's face.

"My thodelm," he said levelly, "is—alas—mistaken."

"Yes," Daav agreed, "I thought that she might be." He waved a hand at the screen. "Get you home, then. I shall send this lot on to Mr. dea'Gauss. He should have the framed contracts to you within a two-day. You and I can then discuss any modifications that may be necessary before the final papers are presented to Anne."

"All right." Er Thom rose and smiled. "Thank you, Daav."

"Thank me, is it? Go home, darling, you're in your cups."

HE LET HIMSELF in through the door off the East Patio and went, surefooted and quiet, through halls illuminated by night-dims.

In the upper hallway, he lay his hand against a door-plate, and stepped gently into the darkened room beyond.

Anne lay in the long, wide bed, fast asleep in the wash of star shine from the open skylight. She looked vulnerable, thus, and incalculably precious: a jewel for which a man must gamble—and never think of losing.

He sighed as he stood over her, for he understood Daav's wager well enough, knew the dangers that dodged his steps and his brother's distress—who could have no less failed to offer the wager than Er Thom declined to take it. To be delm was an awesome and perilous duty. Daav had never wanted the Ring, which was Er Thom's certain knowledge. He had, indeed, begged his delm to pass him by, to place the Ring in abler hands—

In Er Thom's hands.

She had refused, which was wisdom, and Daav was thus Korval, gods pity him. Daav possessed full measure that trait which allowed him to offer such a thing as this twisty wager to his *cha'leket*, expecting him to fail—for the good of the clan.

It is a terrible thing, Er Thom thought, leaning above his sleeping love, *for a delm to have a brother.*

Beneath the star-glown blanket, Anne stirred and lifted a hand.

"Er Thom?" Sleep-drugged and beautiful, her voice. He caught her questing hand and bent to gently kiss the palm.

"Hush, sweeting," he murmured, soothing in the Low Tongue. "I had not meant to wake you. Sleep, now . . ."

"You, too," she insisted in Terran. "It's late."

"Indeed, and I am to go early to Port . . ."

"Tell the computer to wake you up," she mumbled, her hand going slack in his as she slid back toward sleep. "Come to bed . . ."

With exquisite care, he lay her hand back atop the coverlet, then stood still in the starlight, watching her and recalling what his thodelm had ordered.

Thinking on Daav's damned, labyrinthine wager.

Woo the lady. Win her aye and win all . . .

Anne feared that a lifemate's burden of shared *melant'i* put him at risk in the world. Such fear did her only honor, so he considered it, and proved—if it happened he required proof—the depth of her love.

To win her, he must cross custom one final time, show her his heart and his innermost mind—as if they were already lifemated many years.

There was nothing dishonorable in such a path, as he conceived it. Anne was the one his heart had chosen; his lifemate, in truth, whatever a new dawn might bring.

Decided, he crossed the room to the house console and tapped in instructions to wake him at dawn.

Back at the bed, he removed his clothing and slid under the covers, curled against Anne's warmth—and plummeted into sleep.

CHAPTER TWENTY-EIGHT

A person of melant'i *deceives by neither word nor deed and shall have no cause to hide his face from the world.*

—Excerpted from the *Liaden Code of Proper Conduct*

HE ENTERED HIS OFFICE aboard *Dutiful Passage*, jacket collar still turned up against the rain in the port below. One moment he paused as the door shut behind him, eyes closed, breathing in the elusive taste of ship's air, listening to the myriad, usual sounds that meant the *Passage* was alive all around him.

Sighing with something like relief, he opened his eyes and crossed the room to his desk, spinning the screen around to face him.

Twenty minutes later, he was still standing there, quick fingers plying the keypad. He barely registered the whisper of the door opening at his back and very nearly started at his first mate's voice.

"Ah, you are here!" Kayzin Ne'Zame exclaimed in Comrade, the mode in which they usually conversed. "I might have known you'd come up ahead of the early shuttle. Felicitations, old friend, on Korval's acceptance of your child! When shall I be pleased to make his acquain—"

Er Thom took a careful breath and deliberately turned to face her, hands in plain sight.

She chopped off in mid-word, her eyes leaping to his.

"Old friend?" Very careful, that tone, even from Kayzin, who had known him from his twelfth name day. Almost, Er Thom sighed.

Instead, he gave her courtesy, and the gentleness due a friend.

"My rating is intact," he murmured, gesturing toward the computer. "You may call the Guild Hall to be certain, if you wish."

"Yes, naturally." She moved her shoulders. "Ken Rik is concerned of Number Eighteen Pod and requests the captain's earliest attention. The radio-tech sent by the Guild was—unable to meet our standards. I took the liberty of dispatching her Port-side. Shipment from Trellen's World will meet us at Arsdred, something about the trans-ship company's credit record. I will look into that, of course . . ."

Er Thom leaned a hip against the desk and Kayzin drifted over to perch on the edge of a chair, both caught in the business they knew best, no blame nor shadow of doubt between them.

THE AFTERNOON among the warehouses was slightly less felicitous than the morning on his ship. There were none who actually refused to take his requisitions, though there were enough glances askance to leave one's belly full down the length of a long lifetime.

One fellow did demand a cantra to "hold" the order, to the very visible horror of his second. Er Thom gave him a long stare, then flicked the coin from his pocket to land, spinning, on the counter.

"A receipt," he said, entirely bland. The merchantman swallowed.

"Of course, Master Trader," he stammered, fingers jamming at the keys.

Still bland, Er Thom took the offered paper and gave it leisurely perusal before folding it into his pocket and going his way, setting his boot heels deliberately against the worn stone floor.

Some while later, he was in the public room of the Trade Bar, having just concluded a trifle of business with Zar Kin pel'Odma. Wily old trader that he was, Zar Kin had not allowed himself even a glance at Master Trader yos'Galan's hands. Which, Er Thom thought, sipping a glass of cold, sweet wine, told as much about Trader pel'Odma's *melant'i* as it did about the speed at which news traveled, Port-side.

He touched the port-comm's power-off, sipped again at his wine and closed his eyes, wondering if it were worth walking to the Avenue of Jewels on the chance that Master Jeweler Moonel would be disposed to see him.

"Captain yos'Galan, how fortunate to find you here, sir!"

The voice was not immediately familiar, the accent unabashedly Chonselta.

Er Thom opened his eyes and looked up, encountering a pair of hard gray eyes in a determinedly merry face. Her hair was also gray and clipped close to her skull in the manner favored by Terran pilots. It was a style that showed her ears to advantage, and all the dozen earrings piercing each. On her hands she wore, not the expected hodgepodge jewelry of a Port-rat, but a single large amethyst, carved with the symbol of the Trader's Guild.

"Master Trader Jyl ven'Apon." So she introduced herself, clanless, bowing as between equals. She straightened and gave him a knowing look. "Captain."

Er Thom acknowledged her introduction with a bare nod of his head and fixed her with a gaze that would have given anyone of *melant'i* serious doubts regarding the wisdom of imposing further.

Jyl ven'Apon was far from entertaining any such doubts. Uninvited, she pulled out the chair Zar Kin pel'Odma had lately vacated and sat, arms folded on the table before her.

"One hears," she said, leaning forward with a show of candor, "that Er Thom yos'Galan has been seen about the port this day, devoid of his master trader's ring. Of course, this can but pain those of us who wish him well, of whom there are—most naturally!—dozens. It is indeed fortunate that one such well-wisher as myself should have the means to offer—easement in loss."

"Oh, indeed?" Er Thom raised his eyebrows. "You fascinate me. But you merely mean to sell me another ring, of course."

The gray eyes narrowed and the face lost a little of its merriness, though she did bend her lips slightly in the parody of a smile.

"The—captain—will have his joke," she allowed. "But the matter in which I can provide easement is in the area of trade." She sent a sharp glance into his face. "You perhaps did not receive my correspondence regarding a certain extremely lucrative business venture. Several traders have already seen the advantages of this—venture—not merely in terms of the cantra to be earned, but in the sense of winning greater rank. Indeed, I do not think any who assist in bringing the project to fruition can escape the notice of the Trade Commission. In the case of some, the prospect of gaining—or regaining—the rank of master trader must carry all other considerations before it."

So that was the bait that had snared yo'Laney and Ivrex. Er Thom stared at her coldly.

"I recall the correspondence," he said flatly. "I will tell you that I hold severe doubts regarding the viability of your enterprise and am distressed to find you still enjoy hopes of luring others into a scheme that must fail. I suggest—most strongly—that you re-evaluate your plan of business in this instance, else a review before the Guild must be inevitable."

"Oh, must it?" She laughed, and deliberately poured herself a cup of wine from the pitcher.

"Will you call me up for review, *Captain*? I wish you might try!" She drank deeply of her cup and grinned. "But of course if you no longer care for amethyst, there's nothing more to be said."

Er Thom put his wine cup aside, turned the port-comm's screen around and pushed the keyboard across the table.

"You might," he suggested gently. "Call up today's Guild list of master traders in Port." He leaned back in his chair, hands folded before him on the table, face and eyes composed.

Her startlement showed clearly for an instant, then she spared him another hard-edged grin, hit the power-on and typed in the request.

Still grinning, she finished the dregs of her wine, poured more and turned her eyes back to the screen.

The grin faded.

Er Thom inclined his head.

"I had been taught that a master trader was made by skill, and that the ring bestowed upon attaining that level of skill was an acknowledgement, not a license." He lifted an eyebrow. "Doubtless, other clans teach other wisdom."

Jyl ven'Apon touched her tongue to her lips. "As you say."

"Ah. Allow me to offer advice, from one who is master of trade to one who wears the ring. Let the lithium deal go. Return the buy-ins you have collected. This would be equitable and not likely of failure, nor notice to the Guild for review."

"You threaten me, in fact."

"I am of Korval," Er Thom said softly. "I merely tell you what is."

She managed another laugh at that, though not so convincingly as formerly, and threw the rest of the wine down her throat. She then rose to bow a seemly enough farewell—and went away down the room, swaggering like a Low Port bravo.

MOONEL HAD BEEN IN and willing, for a wonder, to talk, by which circumstance he did not arrive home until well after Prime, to find his mother at tea with Lady Kareen.

He made his bows from the doorway and, obedient to his mother's gesture, came forward to sit and take refreshment.

"I ask pardon," he murmured with all propriety, "that I show myself in all my dust. I am only this moment come from the Port."

His mother shot him a sharp glance. Kareen's was more leisurely—and, naturally, thorough.

"Why, Cousin Er Thom," said she, in tones of false concern, "I believe you may have misplaced your ring."

Bland-faced, he met her eyes. "You are mistaken, Cousin. I am well-aware of the location of my ring."

"But to go thus to the Port," Kareen insisted, eyes gleaming with spite, "where the lack of rank-ring must be noted and commented upon, is—surely—foolish?"

"Is adherence to duty foolish?" Er Thom wondered, sipping his tea. "I cannot agree with that."

Kareen's eyes narrowed, but before she could launch another attack, his mother introduced a change of topic and the rest of the visit passed almost agreeably.

He stood and bowed as Kareen took her leave and was on the point of departure himself, when his mother snapped, "Stay."

Eyebrows up, he resumed his seat, folded his naked hands upon his lap and assumed an attitude of dutiful attentiveness.

"To the port, is it?" Petrella snarled after a moment. "I bow to your sense of duty, sir. And where, one wonders, did duty dictate you sleep yestereve?"

Er Thom merely looked at her, eyes wide and guileless.

"I see," his mother said after a long minute. She closed her eyes. "In the time of the first Daav," she said eventually, "a certain Eba yos'Phelium was publicly flogged by her thodelm. The instrument employed was a weighted leather lash, from which Eba received six blows, laid crosswise, along her naked flesh. History tells us she carried the scars for the rest of her life." She opened her eyes and regarded her son's bland face.

"I bore you," she surmised. "Or perhaps you believe me too weak to wield the lash. Never mind—we shall speak of pleasanter things! Delm Nexon's delightful visit of this afternoon, for an instance."

Only silence from Er Thom, who kept his eyes and face turned toward her.

"Delm Nexon," Petrella said, "wonders—most naturally!—what Korval means by the announcement that appeared in yesterday's *Gazette*. She wonders if Korval has been toying with Nexon, by raising hopes of a match advantageous to both sides—*she* says!— and then withdrawing all hope in this churlish manner. Delm Nexon wonders, my son, if she has been insulted, though she does hope—very sincerely—that this will be found not to be the case."

When he still remained silent, she fixed him with a stern eye. "Well, sir? Have you anything to say, or will you sit there like a stump until dawn?"

Er Thom sighed. "Delm Nexon," he said softly, "is entirely aware that no insult has been given. No contract exists. Preliminary negotiations of contract-marriage flounder and fall awry every day. As to what Korval might mean by publishing notice of Shan's acceptance to the clan—that is entirely by the Code, and nothing to do with Nexon at all."

"Bold words," Petrella commented. "Bold words, indeed, A'thodelm. Especially as there is yet the matter of an heir to the Line—which is nothing to do with this *Shan*. I will have a proper heir out of you, sir, and I find in Nexon's daughter your suitable match." She held up a hand, stilling his move of protest.

"You will say that you do not know the lady—that we are no longer in the time of the first Daav. True enough. Nor do I wish to thrust you into the contract-room with a lady whose face you have not seen. You shall meet her beforehand."

"I will not—" Er Thom began and Petrella cut him off with a slash of her hand through the air.

"We have had quite enough of what you will and will not! What you *will* is what you are commanded by your thodelm. And you are commanded to attend the gathering that will be held in this house two evenings hence. At that time you will meet Syntebra el'Kemin, who I suggest you begin to think of as your contracted wife."

Er Thom's eyes were hot, though his voice remained cool. "Scholar Davis will yet be a guest in this house."

Petrella moved her shoulders. "The scholar is welcome to join the party, if she is so inclined. It may prove—instructive—for her."

"*No!*" He snapped to his feet, towering over her, slim and taut as a cutting cord. "Mother, I tell you now, I shall not—"

"Silence!" she shouted, pounding her cane on the floor. She lifted it, agonizingly slow, until the point was on a level with his nose.

"You do not raise your voice to me," she told him, Thodelm to Linemember. "Beg my pardon."

For a long moment he stood there, quivering with the fury that filled his eyes. Then, slowly, he bowed apology.

"I beg your pardon."

Eyes holding his, she lowered the cane-tip to the floor.

"Leave me," she said then. "If you are wise, you will go to your room and meditate upon the path of duty."

He hesitated a fraction of a heartbeat before he bowed Respect-to-the-Thodelm—and obediently quit the room.

CHAPTER TWENTY-NINE

On average contract-marriages last eighteen Standard Months, and are negotiated between clan officials who decide, after painstaking perusal of gene maps, personality charts and intelligence grids, which of several possible nuptial arrangements are most advantageous to both clans.

In contrast, lifemating is a far more serious matter, encompassing the length of the partners' lives, even if one should die. One of the pair must leave his or her clan of origin and join the clan of the lifemate. At that time the adoptive clan pays a "life-price" based on the individual's profession, age and internal value to the former clan.

Tradition has it that lifemates share a "bond of heart and mind." In view of Liaden cultural acceptance of "wizards," some scholars have interpreted this to mean that lifemates are "psychically" connected. Or, alternatively, that the only true lifematings occur between wizards.

There is little to support this theory. True, lifematings among Liadens are rare. But so are life-long marriages among Terrans.

—From "Marriage Customs of Liad"

ANNE SIGHED AND PUSHED back from the computer. Standing, she stretched high on her toes, ceiling tiles an inch beyond her fingertips.

It takes going to Liad and living among folk half your own size to find a ceiling that's tall enough. She grinned and finished her stretch, glancing to Doctor yo'Kera's work table, where Shan sat, silky white head bent over his *Edu-Board.*

The *Edu-Board* was a self-paced, self-programmed wonder, sure enough, and it held Shan's attention like nothing before. Anne tipped her head, watching her son work, feeling a buzz of determined concentration somewhere in the behind of her mind.

Just like his ma, she thought, and felt her mouth twist into a smile. *And his da, too, truth be told.*

The smile grew a bit wistful. She had woken in the gray of dawn, to feel warm lips on her cheek and a light hand caressing her hair.

"Sleep again, darling," Er Thom whispered in the intimate, only-for-kin Low Tongue. "I shall see you this evening."

Drowsily obedient, she had nestled back into the quilt, waking again several hours later to full sunlight and the wonder of having *two* endearments from Er Thom within the space of a single night.

Gods love the man, she thought in exasperation. *How am I ever to leave, if he turns up sweet now?*

"Ma?" Shan looked up from his device. "Says play and rest."

"Module full?" She moved, bending over him to peer at the miniature screen.

EXERCISE TIME! The top line was in Terran, scribed in cheery blue letters. Below, in green letters, was the Liaden approximation: PLAY WITH THE BODY, REST THE MIND.

Anne blinked and looked down at the top of her son's bright head. "What does this say?" she asked, pointing at the Terran letters.

"Time to exercise," Shan said, patient, if inaccurate.

Anne pointed at the Liaden line. "What does this say, Shannie?"

"*I'ganin brath'a, vyan se'untor.*" He craned his head backward to look at her out of wide silver eyes. "Play in body, rest in mind. *Mirada* says. *Mirada* says, pilots run *and* think."

"Well, *Mirada's* certainly right there," Anne said wryly, recalling Er Thom's hair-raising dash between the lumbering big-rig and his son.

Planned that trajectory to a hair, laddie, she thought. *And then called it nevermind.* She sighed and reached down to touch her son's face.

"You like *Mirada* a lot, Shannie?"

"Love *Mirada.*" He blinked solemnly. "Play now, Ma?"

She laughed and rumpled his hair. "Regular con artist." She shook her head ruefully.

"I expect I could use a rest, too. How's this meet your fancy, boy-o? We'll have us a race down to the snack shop at the end of the hall, nibble a bit, then come back for an hour more so I can finish my search line. Okay?"

"Okay!" he said energetically and popped out of his seat. "Last winner's a rotten egg!"

It was Jerzy who had taught Shan first winner and last winner, a philosophical concept that was about as alien to Liaden thought as you could get. Anne hesitated, turning to stare around Doctor yo'Kera's tiny, comforting office.

Liad.

Liadens.

An entire culture that counted coup, that held *melant'i* and the keeping of *melant'i* to be vital work. A culture cutthroat and competitive in every imaginable area, where people were divided into two camps—kin and opponents.

On Liad, there were never first winners and last winners.

On Liad, you won. Or you lost.

Anne shivered, remembering Drusil tel'Bana's grief-filled half-ravings. Had there been some esoteric balancing of social accounts which Doctor yo'Kera had lost, thus forfeiting the central proof of his life-work?

Forfeiting, as well, his life?

"Ma?" Shan tugged at her hand, bringing her out of her morbid dreamings. She smiled down at him.

"Ma's being a rare, foolish gel. Never mind." She opened the door, turned and made certain it was locked before she looked back to her son and dropped his hand with a flourish.

"Last winner's a rotten egg!" she cried and they were off.

✧ ✧ ✧

IT HAD TAKEN MORE THAN AN HOUR—or even two—to finish her systematic search of Doctor yo'Kera's private terminal. Somewhere in the midst of it, she roused herself to call Trealla Fantrol and leave two messages: One for the host, regretting that she would be unable to attend Prime meal.

And one for Er Thom—rather warmer—regretting the same and hoping to see him later in the evening.

You're shameless, she told herself. *Why not practice leaving go of the man now?*

But, after all, there would be plenty of time to practice life without Er Thom—later. Anne sighed and glanced over at Shan, who was curled up atop the work table, fast asleep in the nest of her jacket, white head resting on Mouse.

He woke on his own just as the data-core copy was completed. A disk sighed out of the side slot. She pulled it free and shut down the main system, shaking her head.

Fruitless.

She'd known it would be, of course, but hope had been there. The next task, she supposed, tucking the disk safely away into her case, was a search of the books—a daunting task, and one likely to take more time than remained of semester break.

She wondered if Er Thom might give her a special rate on shipping the things to University.

Books as ballast, she thought with a tired giggle. *Why not?*

"All right, now, laddie, it's home for us!"

Shan yawned and wriggled free of her jacket. She caught him under the arms and swung him to the floor.

"Gather your things and let's be off."

"Okay."

In very short order, the *Edu-Board* was stowed in her carry-all, Shan was in his jacket and Mouse was in his arms. Anne shrugged into her own jacket, glanced once more around the tiny office, got a grip on her case and nodded to her son.

"Stay by me, now."

She made sure of the door, checking the lock twice, turned— and nearly fell over a man hovering at her elbow.

"For goodness'—" She retreated a step, which put her back against the door, her hand rising toward her throat in a gesture of surprise.

The man—perhaps thirty, with a peculiarly blank face and curiously flat brown eyes, neat, forgettable clothing, neat, nondescript hair—also fell back a step, bowing profoundly.

"I beg your pardon," he said in expressionless Trade. "It seemed you were experiencing difficulty with the door and I had thought to offer aid."

Anne looked down at him—rather a way, as he was significantly shorter than Er Thom—and returned his bow of Stranger-to-Outworlder precisely.

"Thank you," she said, choosing the High Tongue mode of Nonkin, which was cool. Very cool. "I am experiencing no difficulty. I had merely wished to be certain the mechanism was engaged."

The man's eyes flickered. He bowed again—Respect-to-Scholarship, this time—and when he answered, it was in the High Tongue, Student to Teacher.

"You must forgive me if my use of Trade offended. I did not at first apprehend that of course you must be the Honored Scholar who shall complete Doctor yo'Kera's work." He lay his hand over his heart in a formal gesture. "I am Fil Tor Kinrae, Linguistic Technician, Student of Advanced Studies."

Anne inclined her head. "I am Anne Davis of University, Linguistics Scholar."

"Of course. But I keep you standing in the hallway! Please, allow me to carry your bag and walk with you to your—"

"Ma!" Shan's voice was sharp. She looked at him in surprise, saw him staring in—fright?—at the man before her.

"Go home, Ma! Go home *now!*"

"Oh, dear." She swooped down and gathered him up, felt him shivering against her, and threw a distracted, apologetic smile at the bland-faced grad student.

"I regret, sir. My child requires attention. Another time and we shall talk."

"Another time." Fil Tor Kinrae bowed precisely. "An honor to meet you, Scholar Davis."

"An honor to meet you, as well." Anne barely knew what she replied. Shan was never—*never*—afraid of strangers. Her stomach cramped in fear as she turned and walked rapidly down the hall, toward the carport.

THE PATIENT DRIVER settled them in the back of the car and wasted no time in putting the campus behind them. Gradually, Shan's shivering stilled. He sighed and snuggled into her arms.

"Okay now, Shannie?"

"Uh-huh."

Anne rubbed her cheek against his hair, feeling decidedly better herself. *Really,* she thought. *Of all the foolish starts, Annie Davis . . .*

"What happened?" she asked her son softly.

He pushed his face against her neck.

"No sparkles," he whispered—and shuddered.

SHE WAS LEAVING THE NURSERY, her thoughts on finding Er Thom, when she was intercepted by no less a personage than the yos'Galan butler.

"Scholar Davis." Stately and austere, he inclined his head. "Thodelm yos'Galan requests the pleasure of your company in the Small Parlor."

Which request, she thought wryly, had the force of command. She stifled a sigh and inclined her head.

"I shall be delighted to bear Thodelm yos'Galan company," she said, glad that the Mode of Acceptance leached any flavor of untruth from her words.

"Follow me, please," the butler replied, and turned briskly on his heel.

"WINE FOR SCHOLAR DAVIS," Petrella yos'Galan directed and wine there was.

Mr. pak'Ora also refreshed the cup on the table at the old woman's side, then left, the door snicking shut behind him.

Petrella took up her wine and sipped, her movements firm and formal. Anne followed suit—a solitary taste of wine, and the glass put gently aside.

"You are comfortable in our house, Scholar?" Petrella's choice of mode this evening was Host to Guest.

Anne inclined her head and responded in like mode. "I am extremely comfortable. Thank you for your care, ma'am."

"Hah." Petrella glanced down, made a minute adjustment to the enameled ring she wore on the second finger of her left hand. Abruptly, she looked up, faded blue eyes intense.

"Your command of the High Tongue is praiseworthy, if I may extend a compliment," she said with formal coolness. "It is perhaps not to be expected that your grasp of custom be so exact." She smiled, slightly, coolly. "Indeed, I know well how slippery custom becomes, world-to-world. One would require Scout's eyes, to never err. Few of us, alas, are able to achieve so wide an understanding."

Anne eyed her dubiously, wondering if the old lady were going to give her a tongue-lashing for missing dinner. She inclined her head carefully.

"One hears that Captain yos'Galan's *cha'leket* had been a Scout."

"So he had. The children of yos'Phelium are often sent to the Scouts; it's found the training tames them." She paused. "The Scouts teach that all custom is equally compelling, which may well be true in the wide galaxy. On Liad, matters are quite otherwise."

Anne kept silent, hands folded tightly in her lap, waiting for her host to come to the point.

A smile ghosted Petrella's pale lips and she inclined her head as if the younger woman had spoken.

"A word in your ear, Scholar Davis?"

"Certainly."

"You have," Petrella said after a moment, "borne my son a child. Understand that we are grateful. At such a time in the clan's history, when the Line Direct is become so few, every child, no matter how irregularly gotten, is a jewel. You must never doubt that the clan's gratitude shall show itself fitly, nor that the child shall receive all care, nuturance and tutelage."

She paused, eyes sharp, and Anne hoped fervently that her face was properly bland, giving away nothing of her bewilderment.

"Necessity, however, exists," Petrella continued slowly. "It existed before the advent of yourself and the child you give to Korval. It exists now, unchanged. As much as your son shall be a treasure to the clan, it cannot be denied that he is but half of the Book of Clans. Such a one cannot be accepted as the heir of he who will soon be Thodelm yos'Galan. The a'thodelm is aware of this. He is also aware that a contract-wife has been chosen for him and that he is required now to wed. Indeed, a gathering in honor of the to-be-signed contract shall be held in this house two evenings hence. You are welcome to attend the gather, should you care to wish the a'thodelm and his bride happy."

Care to wish him happy? Anne thought, around a jag of icy, incredulous grief. *Could ye not have waited until I was gone?* She wanted to scream the question at the woman across from her. Instead, she swallowed and remained silent, hands fisted on her lap, face determinedly smooth.

Once more, Petrella's faded eyes scrutinized. Once more, she inclined her head as if Anne had made some fitting reply.

"My son speaks highly of you, Scholar. I believe that such delight as you shared must long remain in fond memory. However, it is now time for the a'thodelm to do his duty. He will expect you to stand aside." She glanced down, rubbing her ring with an absent forefinger.

"Surely," she murmured, eyes coming back to Anne's face, "even among Terrans a pleasure-love must yield to a wife."

Sleep again, darling, Er Thom murmured tenderly in memory.

Confusion washed through her, threatening to tear away her fragile mask of calm; she thought she must be trembling. Fatal to call Thodelm yos'Galan's word into question. Even to ask for a clarification of Shan's status in Clan Korval would expose weakness, make her vulnerable . . .

Carefully, she inclined her head.

"I am grateful for the care of the House," she said, concentrating on keeping precisely to the mode of Guest-to-Host. "Naturally, one would not wish to be untoward . . ." It was all she could think of, but it seemed it was sufficient.

Petrella smiled her cool, ravaged smile and raised a hand on which the thodelm's enameled band spun loosely.

"Pray do not say more. It is the honor of the House to guide the guest."

"Yes, of course." Anne stood, desperately willing her trembling legs to support her, and made her bow to the host. "I am certain you will forgive me for leaving you so soon," she said, though she was certain of no such thing. "My day was long and somewhat arduous. I feel the need of rest."

"Certainly," Petrella said, moving her hand with a remnant of grace. "Good health to the guest."

"And to the host," Anne responded properly, and forced herself to walk, slow and steady, from the room.

CHAPTER THIRTY

A Healer should be contracted to attend every birth for the purpose of keeping the mother's soul attached to her body and for easing the way through childbirth.

Such attention is doubly necessary in the case of one who has the honor to bear a child for an allied clan. In this instance, the child's clan must instruct the Healer in addition to blur memory and assuage any painful emotions the mother may otherwise experience.

A Healer should also be summoned before the one who gave the child-seed rejoins his own kin.

—From The *Liaden Code of Proper Conduct*

THE CHILD SHALL RECEIVE ALL CARE, *nuturance and tutelage . . .*

Sleep again, darling . . .

Even among Terrans, a pleasure-love must yield to a wife . . .

I am not a thief, to steal our son . . .

No sparkles!

The clan shall show its gratitude—

"Anne?"

Gasping, she spun, hands outflung, half-curled and protective.

Er Thom caught both, his fingers shockingly warm, reassuringly strong. Her friend, her love, her ally against Liad and the terrors of Liaden custom—

Who had lied, after all, and stolen her son; who came to bed with endearments in his mouth even as he planned to wed someone other—

"Anne!" His grip tightened; worried violet eyes looked up at her out of a face that showed clear consternation.

She made a supreme, racking effort. Fatal to antagonize Er Thom. Fatal to assume, to assume—

"You're hurting me." Her voice sounded flat, cold as iron. Cold iron, to bane an elf-prince . . .

His fingers eased, but he did not let her go. Face turned to hers, concern showing plain as if it were real, he bespoke her in the Low Tongue.

"What has happened, beloved? You tremble . . ."

"I've just come from your mother—" She blurted the truth in Terran before she considered what lie would best cover her agitation.

But it seemed the truth served her purpose very well. Anger darkened Er Thom's eyes, his mouth tightened ominously.

"I see. We must speak." He glanced around the hallway. "Here." He tugged on her hands. "Please, Anne. Come and sit with me."

She let him lead her down the unfamiliar hall, into a room shrouded in covers, illuminated by the dusty light from a center-hung chandelier.

Her mind was working now, smoothly and with preternatural efficiency, laying out plans in some place that was beyond pain and bewilderment, that was concerned only with necessity.

"Here," Er Thom said again, his Terran somewhat blurred—a certain sign of his own agitation. He left her to swirl a dust-sheet from the sofa before the dead hearth, rolled the cloth into a hasty bundle and cast it aside.

"Please, Anne. Sit."

She did, curling into the high-swept corner. Er Thom sat next to her, turned sideways, one knee crooked on the faded brocade seat, one elbow propped along the back cushion. He looked elegant, all grace and beauty in his wide-sleeved shirt and soft-napped trousers. Anne looked away.

"My mother has distressed you," Er Thom said gently. "I regret that. Will you tell me what she has said?"

She considered that, deliberately cold. First and foremost, she must have verification of her worst suspicions. Yet she must gain such verification without alerting Er Thom to her plan.

"Your mother—confused me—on a couple things. I thought I understood—" She hesitated, then forced herself to meet his eyes.

"Shan is accepted of Clan Korval, isn't he?"

Something flickered in Er Thom's eyes, gone too quickly for her to read.

"Yes, certainly."

"But your mother said that he wasn't—wasn't good enough to be your heir," Anne pursued, watching him closely.

Anger showed again, though she sensed it was for his mother and not for herself. He extended a slim, ringless hand. "Anne—"

"It's just—" She glanced at the dead hearth, feeling how rapidly her heart beat. *Gods, gods, I'm no good at this . . .*

"It's that—" she told the cold bricks, "if Shannie's going to be a burden on your clan, maybe it would be best if I just took him back to University—"

"Ah." His hand gripped her knee very briefly; her flesh tingled through the cloth of her trousers. "Of course Shan shall not be a burden upon the clan. The clan welcomes children—and doubly welcomes such a child as our son! To snatch him away from kin and homeplace, when the clan has just now embraced him as its own . . ." He smiled at her, tentatively.

"Try to understand, *denubia*. My mother is—old world. She has held always by the Book of Clans, by the Code—by Liad. To change now, when she is ill and has lost so much in service of the clan—" He moved his shoulders. "I do not think that she can. Nor, in respect, must we who hold her closest demand such change of her." He seemed for an instant to hesitate. One hand rose toward her cheek—and fell again to his knee.

"I regret—very much—that she found it necessary to speak to you in such terms of our son. If you will accept it, I ask that you take my apology as hers."

A rock seemed lodged in her throat, blocking words, nearly blocking breath. That he could plead so sweetly for a parent who showed him not an ounce of affection, who ordered him to her side as if he were her slave rather than her son . . . Anne managed at last to get a breath past the blockage in her throat.

Verification, announced the strange new part of her mind that was busily molding its plans. *We proceed.*

"I—of course I forgive her," she told the hearth-stones. "Change is difficult, even for those of us who aren't—old—and—and ill . . ." She cleared her throat sharply and closed her eyes, hearing her heartbeat pounding, crazy, in her ears.

"I find I'm to wish you happy," she whispered, and there was no iron in her voice now at all. "Your mother tells me you're going to be married—"

"No."

His hands were on her shoulders, his breath shivering the tiny hairs at her temple. Anne shrank back into the corner of the sofa, a sob catching her throat.

"Anne—no, *denubia,* hear me . . ." His hands left her shoulders and tenderly cupped her face, turning her, gently, inexorably, toward him. "Please, Anne, you must trust me."

Trust him? When he had just confessed to lying, to kidnapping, to using the trust she had borne him to—no.

On Liad, you won. Or you lost.

It was absolutely imperative that she win.

She allowed him to turn her face. She opened her eyes, looked into his and saw, incredibly, tenderness and care and longing in the purple depths.

Er Thom smiled, very gently, ran his thumbs in double caress along her cheekbones before taking his hands away.

"I love you, Anne. Never forget."

"I love you, too," she heard herself say, and it was true, *true,* gods pity her, and the man had stolen her son.

Never mind, the cold planner in the back of her mind told her. *Disarm him with the truth, so much the better. Put any suspicions he may have fast asleep. Then the plan will work.*

He sat back, reluctantly, to her eye, and folded his hands carefully on his knee. The face he showed her was earnest, his eyes tender and anxious.

"This marriage which my mother desires," he said softly. "It is old world, and as a dutiful son I should accept the match and give the clan my heir, which is duty long past fruition." He tipped his head, anxiety overriding tenderness for the moment. "You understand, this is the—manner in which things are done—and no slight to you is intended."

"I understand," she said, hearing the iron back in her voice.

Er Thom inclined his head. "So. But it happens that there is you and there is our son and we two—love. There is that bond between us which—after even such a time—remains unabated. Unfilled. That is true, Anne, is it not?"

"True." *True . . .*

"I had thought so," he said, very softly, and she saw the shine of tears in his eyes.

"Since we wish not to part—since we wish, indeed, to become lifemates—this marriage that my mother hopes for is—a nothing. I have taken counsel on the matter. A lifemating between us shall be allowed, does the delm hear from your lips that it is your desire as well as my own. Alas, that my mother has sought to—to force the play—striving to divide us and burst asunder the bond we share." He reached out and took her hand; her traitor fingers curled tight around his.

"If we stand together, if we hold now as the lifemates we shall soon become, she cannot win," Er Thom said earnestly. "It will be difficult, perhaps, but we shall carry the day. We need only give her what she desires—in certain measure. She desires to have the lady here to meet me. So we acquiesce, you see? The lady is a child. She does not want me. She wants the consequence of bedding an a'thodelm, of having borne a child to Korval.

"The—infelicity—of the proposed match can easily be shown

her, gently and with all respect, in the course of such an affair as my mother plans." His fingers gripped hers painfully, though Anne made no demur.

"We need only stand together," he repeated earnestly. "You must not allow yourself to be frightened into leaving our house. To do so ensures my mother's victory. You must only attend the gather and show a calm face. Why should you not? When the gather is done, we shall go hand-in-hand before the delm and ask that he acknowledge what already in fact exists."

Lifemates? For a moment it seemed she spun, alone in void, the familiar markers of her life wiped clean away. For a moment, it seemed that here was a better plan, that kept her son at her side, and her lover, too, with no duplicity, no lies, no anguish. For a moment, she hovered on the edge of flinging herself into his arms and sobbing out the whole of her pain and confusion, to put everything into his hands for solving—

The moment passed. Cold reason returned. Er Thom had lied. From the very beginning, he had intended to steal Shan from her, though he swore he would do no such thing. There was no reason to believe this plea for lifemates was any truer than his other lies.

"Anne?"

She stared down at her lap, at her fingers, twisted like snakes each about the other, white-knuckled and cold.

"Your mother," she said, and barely recognized her own voice, "will be just as well served if I shame you."

"It is not possible," Er Thom said quietly, "that you will shame me, Anne."

She had thought herself beyond any greater agony, foolish gel. She stared fixedly down at her hands, jaw clenched until she heard bone crack.

"We may go tomorrow into Solcintra," Er Thom continued after a moment, "and arrange for proper dress."

"I—" *What?* she asked herself wildly. *What will you say to the man, Annie Davis?*

But she had no more to say, after all, than that bare syllable. Er Thom touched her knee lightly.

"Lifemates may offer such things," he murmured, "without insult. Without debt."

Oh, gods... From somewhere, she gleaned the courage to raise her head and meet his eyes levelly.

"Thank you, Er Thom. I—expect I will need a dress for—for the gather."

Joy lit his face, and pride. He smiled, widely, lovingly. "We play on," he said, and laughed lightly. His fingers grazed her cheek. "Courageous Anne."

She swallowed and tried for a smile. It was apparently not an entirely successful effort, for Er Thom rose and offered his arm, all solicitude.

"You are exhausted. Come, let me walk you to your rooms."

In the moment of rising, she froze and stared up into his eyes.

"Anne, what is wrong?"

"I—" Gods, she could *not* sleep with him. She wouldn't last through one kiss, much less through a night—she would tell him everything, lose everything . . .

"I was thinking," she heard her voice say, "that maybe we should—sleep apart—until the gather is over. Your mother—"

"Ah." He inclined his head gravely. "I understand. My mother shall see that all goes her way, eh? That the guest has heeded her word and behaves with honor regarding the House's wayward child." He smiled and it was all she could do not to cry aloud.

Instead, she rose and took his arm and allowed him to guide her through unfamiliar hallways to the door of her room.

Once there, she hesitated, and some demon prompted her to ask one last question.

"Your mother had said that the clan would be—grateful—for Shan's adoption. I didn't quite—"

"That would be the proposal of alliance," Er Thom said gently, "as well as other considerations. Daav and I had drafted the papers yesterday, and a trust fund has been created in your name." He smiled up at her, sweetly. "But these matters are moot, when we are lifemates."

Speechless, she stared down at him, wondering what—*considerations*—what possible sum of money—Clan Korval had thought sufficient to buy a child.

"You are tired," Er Thom murmured. "I say good-night. Sleep well, beloved." He raised one of her hands, kissed the palm lightly and released her.

Tear-blinded, Anne spun and fumbled her hand against the lock-plate, escaping at last into grief-shot solitude.

"WHY NOW?" Daav demanded.

Petrella regarded him calmly from the comm screen. "Why not now? He has been coddled long enough. Nexon calls Korval's *melant'i* into question. What better way to give such question rest than by proceeding as planned?"

"As *you* planned!" Daav snapped and sighed, reaching up to finger his earring.

"Aunt Petrella, be gracious. The guest will still be with you two nights hence. She holds Er Thom precious, whether you will see it or no. What can possibly be gained by wounding her in this manner? Such action does more harm to Korval's *melant'i* than all Nexon's petulance can accomplish!"

Petrella raised her hand. "I hope we are not rag-mannered, nor behind in our duty to the guest," she said austerely. "Certainly, there was instruction given. The guest cannot hope to know our custom. A word in her ear was sufficient, as it happens. I find Scholar Davis a very sensible woman."

"Oh, do you?" Daav closed his eyes briefly, running a Scout's calming exercise, trying not to think of Er Thom's desperate gamble and what must be made of his wooing now.

"Indeed I do," Petrella replied. "Shall I have the honor of seeing you at the gather, my delm?"

"Why certainly," he said, hearing the snap in his voice despite the exercise. "I can always be depended upon to dance for you, Aunt Petrella. Good-night." He swept the board clear with a violent palm and surged to his feet as if he would run immediately out into the night.

Instead, he walked very slowly over to the windowsill and reached down to stroke the leaves and white flowers of the plant Olwen had left with him. *Nubiath'a.*

"Ah, gods, brother," he whispered to the little plant, "what a coil we have knotted between us . . ."

CHAPTER THIRTY-ONE

Accepted of Clan Korval: Identical twins, daughters of Kin Dal yos'Phelium and Larin yos'Galan.

> *Accepted of Line yos'Galan: Petrella, daughter of Larin.*
> *Accepted of Line yos'Phelium: Chi, daughter of Kin Dal.*

—From *The Gazette* for Banim Fourthday
in the Third Relumma of the Year Named Yergin

TWO DAYS AGO she had dreamed of such a visit to the City of Jewels. Then, Solcintra had gone past the car-window in a dazzle of possibility, and she had imagined walking the wide streets safe on Er Thom's arm, enclosed by his *melant'i*, guided by his care.

Today, she stared, sand-eyed, at a city gone gray, and listened to the cold, back-brain planner make its cold and necessary plans.

Tomorrow and today were her last on Liad. On the morning after Er Thom's betrothal party, she and her son would be gone. That was the plan.

The plan called for precise timing. It called for the ingenuity to forestall Er Thom immediately petitioning the delm to acknowledge lifemates. It called for pulling a few strands of wool across the eyes of an unsuspecting yos'Galan driver. It required the fortitude to leave everything—*every*thing—behind, save her son and what could be carried in her briefcase.

Necessity existed. These things could be done.

It required sufficient funds to book passage for herself and her child on the first available ship.

Cash was the sticking point: She had a little, in Terran bits, which enjoyed an—unequal—exchange rate on Liad.

Of course, she would sell her jewelry, paltry stuff that it was. Er Thom's good-bye gift would fetch the most of the lot, but she was not fool enough to suppose it would cover even a tenth of the passage price to New Dublin.

For it was to New Dublin she had determined to go, where laws were sane and where she would have her brother's staunch and stubborn support.

From Liad to New Dublin the price will be dear, she told herself wearily, as she had told herself all last night, pacing, exhausted and shivering, through the luxurious, alien apartment.

She wondered if she dared ask Er Thom how to access the trust fund he had set up for her.

While she was weighing that question, the car pulled into a parking slot and stopped.

"We arrive," Er Thom said softly, and turned to look at her. "Are you well, Anne?"

He had asked her that once already, this morning at breakfast. Anne had a moment of despair, that a whole day in her company would reveal to him that she was sick with fright, bloated with deception. She would lose—

I will not lose, she thought firmly. *Clan Korval does not own Shan. My son is not for sale.*

Resolutely, she summoned the best smile stiff face muscles could provide.

"I'm fine," she lied. "Just—tired. I didn't sleep very well."

"Ah." He touched the back of her hand with light fingertips. "When we are lifemated, perhaps . . . The clan keeps a house by the southern sea. We might go there, if you like it, to rest and—grow closer."

Pain twisted, a mere flicker of agony in the larger pain of his betrayal. Anne smiled again.

"That sounds wonderful," she said, and it was true. "I'd like that very much, Er Thom."

If it all was different. If you hadn't lied. If you hadn't schemed and connived. If I could dare even pretend that this might be true . . .

"Then it is done." He smiled. "Come and let us put you into Eyla's hands."

EYLA DEA'LORN STOOD BACK, gray head cocked to a side, lined face impish.

"So, your lordship brings me a challenge," she said to Er Thom, and rubbed her clever hands together. "Good."

To Anne, she bowed slightly, eyes gleaming.

"Ah, but you will provide such opportunity, Lady—I give you thanks! Nothing usual for you, eh? Nothing the same as so-and-so had it at Lord Whomever's rout. Hah! No, for you, everything must be new, original!" She shot a gleaming glance aside to Er Thom.

"An original. There is no possible comparison between this lady and any other lady in the world. In this, the world has failed us, but the lady shall be accepted on the terms of her own possibility. I accurately reflect Your Lordship's thought?"

"As always," Er Thom told her, lips twitching, "you are a perfect mirror, Eyla."

"Flattery! Recall who made your first cloak, sir, and speak with respect!" She beckoned Anne. "Come with me if you please, Lady. I must have measurements—ah, she walks as a pilot! Good, good. Put yourself entirely in my hands. We shall send you off in a fashion the world has rarely seen! Such proportions! So tall! The bosom, so proud! The neck—Ah, you are a gift from the gods, Lady, and I about to expire of boredom, or strangle the next same-as who walked through my door!"

The little woman's eagerness pierced even the iron-gray dreariness that enclosed Anne. She smiled.

"I fear I may prove a little too far out of the common way for such a debut as that," she murmured as she was led back to the measuring room.

"Never think it!" Eyla told her energetically. "The world is a great coward. Merely keep a level gaze and a courteous face and the world will bow to you. Some will scoff, certainly, but you needn't mind those. An original is a Code unto herself. And you have the advantage of sponsorship by Korval, which has elevated originality to an art form." She rubbed her hands together, looking Anne up and down with eager appraisal.

"And now," she said, going over to a discreet console. "If I may ask you to disrobe . . ."

THE GOWN WOULD BE brought to Trealla Fantrol no later than mid-morning, tomorrow. The color was to be antique gold, to "show that delightful brown skin." Eyla gave Er Thom a patch of fabric, which he solemnly placed in his pocket.

"We shall be going along to Master Moonel presently," he murmured. "When the design is fixed, perhaps you might call and allow him to name a suitable jeweler."

"He'll want the work himself," Eyla predicted with a smile. "Only show her to him. The deadline will mean nothing to Moonel, with such a showcase for his craft." She clasped her hands together and bowed them out with energy.

"And to think that only last evening I was considering retirement!"

"YOU AND EYLA are good friends?" Anne asked, because it was necessary to say something. It was imperative that Er Thom think everything was just the same between them, and to put down any oddness in her behavior to the effects of a restless night.

"dea'Lorn and Korval are old allies," he murmured, guiding her along the flower-scented street with a gentle hand on her elbow. "Eyla will want to make your entire wardrobe."

"Would that be wrong?"

"Not—wrong. Indeed, it might well be prudent. Eyla has the gift of seeing exactly what is before her, rather than what she believes is there." He smiled up at her. "It has in the past been considered—expedient—to engage the services of several tailors, so Korval's patronage may not be used to undue advantage."

"But if your Houses are allied—"

"Not allied. Not—precisely—that. Doubtless my Terran falls short. It is—in the time of my fourth-great-grandfather—the youngest of dea'Lorn, who had just finished his apprenticeship, came with a proposal for trade. The dea'Lorn would undertake to make whatever clothes Korval required at cost, in return for materials at cost."

Anne frowned. "That sounds rather audacious."

"Indeed it was. But audacity amused my grandfather. He inspected those items the dea'Lorn offered as samples of his work, and made a counter-offer. He would provide shop space in one of Korval's Upper Port warehouses and a very favorable discount on materials, as well as options on certain—exotic—fabrics. These things would constitute his buy-in and make him one-half partner in the dea'Lorn's business, which would indeed make Korval's clothes. Free of charge."

"But in return he got free advertising," Anne said, "and the opportunity for his clothes to be seen at society functions . . ."

"And so he prospered," Er Thom concluded. "The dea'Lorn's daughter was able to move the shop to its present location and to retire Korval's partnership. The trade agreements remain in place—and dea'Lorn from time to time makes Korval's clothes. At cost." He sent her a glance from beneath his lashes.

"Anne?"

She drew a careful breath, willing her face to be neutral. "Yes?"

"I wish," Er Thom said, very softly, "that you will tell me what troubles you."

Oh, gods . . . She swallowed, glanced aside, groping for a lie—

"I—it's foolish, I know," she heard herself saying distractedly, "but I can't seem to get it out of my mind."

Annie Davis, she demanded in internal bewilderment, *what are ye nattering about?*

"Ah." The pressure of Er Thom's fingers on her elbow changed, guiding her to the edge of the sidewalk and a bench beneath a flowering tree.

"Tell me," he murmured.

The bench was not particularly roomy. Er Thom's thigh against hers woke a storm of emotion, of which lust and anguish were foremost. Anne bit her lip and almost cried out when he took her hand in his.

"Anne? Perhaps I may aid you, if I can but understand the difficulty."

Well, and what will you tell him? she asked herself with interest. But the back-brain planner had been busy.

"It's probably nothing," she heard her voice say uncertainly. "But—I took Shannie with me yesterday to Doctor yo'Kera's office. I was doing an inventory of his research computer, and it took longer than I had expected—I sent you a note."

"Yes, so you did," Er Thom murmured, apparently not at all put out by this rather rattle-brained narrative.

"Yes. Well, it was late when we finally did leave—the night lamps had come on in the hallway. I made sure the office door was locked, and when I turned around there was—a man. He startled me rather badly, though of course—" She shook her head, half in wonderment at herself, half in remembered consternation.

"A Liaden man?" Er Thom wondered softly.

"Oh. Yes. Very ordinary-looking. He spoke to me in Trade at first—I'm afraid I was pretty sharp in setting him straight. He was polite after that—offered to carry my case—and of course he had a perfect right to be there, since he's a grad student . . ."

"Do you recall his name?"

"Fil Tor Kinrae," she recited out of memory, "Linguistic Technician and Student of Advanced Studies."

"Ah. And his clan?"

Anne frowned. "He didn't say."

"Did he not?" Er Thom's glance was sharp.

"No," she said defensively, "he didn't. Why should he? It was more important for me to know that he was a linguistics student with a perfectly legitimate right to be where he was."

"Yes, certainly." Er Thom squeezed her hand gently. "What disturbed you, then?"

"It was Shan," she said and shivered, recalling her son's fright. "He's never—you know he's never afraid of anyone! But he was afraid of Fil Tor Kinrae. Demanded to go home *now*." She looked down into Er Thom's eyes.

"In the car, I asked him what had happened. And he said—*no sparkles*—and hid his face . . ."

Er Thom's eyes darkened. "*No* sparkles?" He glanced aside, chewing his lip.

"There is—a thought," he said after a moment. "My grandmother had been a Healer, you know. I recall she once said that no one holds the key to all rooms. That those who are locked and dark to one Healer may be open and full of light to another." He looked up into her face.

"Shan is young. If this is the first person he has met who does not—broadcast on the same frequency, Daav would say—he may well have been frightened." His gaze sharpened, a little.

"It might be wise, were we to ask the delm to call a Healer to our child. He is very young to be experiencing these things. There is perhaps something that may be done to alleviate such distress as was occasioned last evening."

And only another Healer would know what to do, she thought, suddenly cold. *Whatever are ye about, Annie Davis, to be taking the laddie away from such aid? How will he learn what to do with his sparkles, when there's no one who's Terran can teach him?*

She snatched at his hand. "Er Thom!"

"Yes, *denubia*." His voice was soothing, his fingers firm. "What else troubles you?"

Almost, she told him. It hovered on the tip of her tongue, the rollygig of loss and love, hope, denial and confusion. She was a heartbeat away from burying her face in his shoulder and sobbing out the whole.

Down the walkway beyond the tree came a couple, very fine in their day-clothes and jewels. The woman turned her head and met Anne's eyes. Disgust washed over her perfect Liaden features; she clutched her companion's arm, leaning close to whisper.

He turned his head, face and eyes cold.

They walked on.

Anne cleared her throat.

"It's nothing," she said, and could not meet Er Thom's eyes. "I—Thank you, Er Thom—for listening."

There was a long silence, and still she could not bring herself to raise her face to his. Finally, she felt him move, coming smoothly to his feet, his hand still firmly holding hers.

"I shall listen whenever you wish," he said gently. "Will you come with me now to port?"

"Yes," she said numbly and stood, and let him lead her back to the car.

MASTER JEWELER MOONEL was as taciturn as Eyla dea'Lorn was voluble. He took the bit of fabric from Er Thom's hand and glared at it as if he suspected it held a flaw.

"Tomorrow?" he snapped and moved his eyes to Anne. "This the lady for whom the items are destined?"

"Scholar Anne Davis," Er Thom murmured, "guest of Korval. Please feel free to give Eyla another name, Master, if the deadline is too near."

"Yes, very likely." Moonel spun on his stool, showing them his back as he reached for his tools. "I'll send them 'round by mid-day. Good morning."

"Good morning, Master Moonel," Er Thom said, bowing to the older man's back. He smiled at Anne and held out his hand.

Hand-in-hand they came out into the narrow Avenue of Jewels.

"Would you care for luncheon?" Er Thom asked as they turned down a slightly wider side street.

"Good-day to you, Captain yos'Galan!" The passerby who gave the greeting had close-cropped gray hair and a multitude of earrings. She raised a hand from across the way and the sunlight gleamed on her master trader's ring.

"I've yet to hear from the Guild, sir!" the little woman added gaily. Her sharp eyes swept once over Anne's face and then she was gone, swallowed in the crowd.

Er Thom's face was stiff with anger, his mouth a tight line. Anne blinked in amazement.

"Who was that?"

He took a deep breath and sighed it out forcefully, then looked up into her face, violet eyes bland.

"No one," he said flatly. "Let us go to Ongit's for luncheon."

CHAPTER THIRTY-TWO

The last of those who had hand in Eba yos'Phelium's capture and shaming seven years ago is dead. Balance achieved.

—Daav yos'Phelium, Sixth Delm of Korval
Entry in the Delm's Diary for Trianna Seconday
in the Fourth Relumma of the Year named Sandir

"MORNING WINE OR RED?"

"Red, if you please," Er Thom answered absently, eyes on the counterchance board sitting ready before the hearth.

Daav filled the glass and put it into his brother's hand, added a splash of morning wine to his own cup and shot a shrewd glance at the other's abstracted face.

"What's amiss?"

"Hmm?" Er Thom had wandered over to the board. He picked up a pair of dice, idly shook and released them: Eighteen.

"Is it true," he murmured, perhaps to the dice, "that Eba yos'Phelium was publicly whipped by her thodelm?"

Daav's eyebrows rose. "Yes," he said matter-of-factly, "but you must understand that it was the means by which her life was preserved."

Violet eyes flashed to his face. "Ah, was it?"

"Certainly. Times were—unsettled. To make a complex tale simple, Eba fell into the hands of those who wished Korval ill. They then showed her, still bleeding from the abduction, knife along her throat, to her thodelm, who was also her *cha'leket*.

"The enemies of Korval were adamant that Eba be punished for some insult they had concocted. The one with the knife claimed the right to her life and professed herself willing to do the thing at once. However, there were cooler heads present, who saw that their ends would be met as well by a public shaming." Daav sipped his wine.

"The young thodelm judged Eba's odds of survival, not to say recovery, significantly better did he wield the lash himself, so he contended for, and won, the right."

Er Thom picked up the dice and made another cast: Six.

"And?"

Daav moved his shoulders. "And he laid the stripes, then ran, weeping, to cut her down, his back guarded by all of the clan who could hold a weapon. Balance commenced immediately she was safe at Jelaza Kazone and her wounds had been treated. Seven years were required for fruition, as there were several Houses involved." He lifted an eyebrow.

"Shall I show you the entries in the Diaries?"

"Thank you," Er Thom murmured, raising his glass and meeting Daav's eyes across the rim, "that will not be necessary."

"Ah." Daav lifted his own glass, but did not drink. "Has your thodelm threatened to flog you, darling?"

Er Thom grinned. "One is amazingly disobedient, after all."

"So I've heard. Does it occur to you to wonder whither Aunt Petrella has purchased these sudden notions of propriety?"

"Perhaps her illness . . ." her son offered, and sighed. "I miss our mother," he said, very softly.

"As I do." Daav drifted over to the table, picked up the dice and threw. Eleven.

"Our mother would have liked your Anne, I think," he murmured. "The devil's in it that I believe Aunt Petrella would like her well enough, were we only able to show her Line and House!"

Across from him, Er Thom shifted. Daav looked up, eyebrows high.

"You wonder that the delm would ask you to give her up, eh? But the lady's summation was unfortunately correct: Accepting a Terran makes the clan vulnerable. It can be managed, if it must be managed. But how very much easier, to go on as always we have. As for Daav—" he moved his shoulders and threw again: Seven.

"Daav likes her very well indeed and thinks it a great pity that Liad must be so overfull with Liadens."

Er Thom laughed. "Spoken like a Scout! But there. When have we ever gone on as proper Liadens? The Diaries tell us that is not our contract. Here are our mothers born aside the Delm's Own Word, simply because Kin Dal and Larin could not keep from each other!"

"And they send us to be Scouts and traders," Daav agreed. "Which makes us even odder." He tipped his head. "How does Anne take news of your betrothal?"

"Unhappily," Er Thom said, frowning. "For one who states she will not be played, my mother throws the dice with energy."

"Will Anne show her face at the gather, I wonder?"

"Certainly. We have settled it between us." He smiled. "I believe I may soon bring you proof of a win, brother, and ask the delm to See my lifemate."

"So? I will wish you joy gladly, darling. Is there reason the win must wait upon the gather?"

"Kindness for Nexon's daughter," Er Thom said softly. "At the gather I shall have opportunity to show her that we would not suit. Also, a matter of Balance, in part. It is ill-done to hold such an event at this moment. Add to that the manner in which my mother chose to speak to Anne regarding our son—I will tell you, brother, it has disturbed Anne greatly! She is distracted—anxious ... It is a shame to the House, that a guest be treated so, never mind what punishment thodelm finds proper for a'thodelm!" He raised his glass and drank, showed a rueful smile.

"Still, she has agreed to attend the gather, bold heart that she has—and show a calm face to Nexon and her daughter, not to speak of Thodelm yos'Galan."

"Honor to the lady," Daav said, with sincerity. "She may yet learn to be a player to fear." He sipped.

"Should you bring a lifemate before the delm," he said after a moment, "certain things shall be required, for the good of the clan. You will be required to provide the clan several more children. Your lifemate shall be required to take pilot's training."

Er Thom inclined his head. "I shall discuss these things with Anne."

Daav eyed him with a touch of wonder. "Oh, and will you?"

"Of course," Er Thom said. "How else?"

"How else, indeed?" his brother replied politely.

"There is a matter which might be brought to the delm's attention, however," Er Thom continued, oblivious to—or ignoring—irony.

"Our son has recently met with one who frightened him—an unusual occurrence. The reason he gave his mother for this fright was that the person in question possessed 'no sparkles.' In view of his extreme youth and the apparent precocity of his talent, it may be wise to call a Healer, before he experiences another—perhaps needless—fright."

"Yes, I see." Daav frowned down at the counterchance board. "He is very young for this, is he not? Mostwise, talent shows when one comes halfling . . ." He shook himself and looked up.

"Certainly, a Healer must be summoned. The delm shall see it done."

Again, Er Thom inclined his head. "I shall inform Anne of the delm's care." He lifted his glass and drained it.

"I shall have to leave you now. Is there a commission I may discharge for you in Port?"

"Thank you, no. My steps are for the City this morning. The delm and Mr. dea'Gauss are called to renegotiate with Vintyr."

"Pah." Er Thom made a face. "Vintyr is never satisfied, brother."

"So I begin to notice. I believe I may mention it to Mr. dea'Gauss, in fact. It seems a change of course is indicated."

"Good lift to the delm, then," Er Thom said, with a lighthearted bow. "I shall see you at the gather, shan't I?"

"Indeed, how could I stay away, when Aunt Petrella was so gracious as to order my appearance?"

Er Thom lifted troubled eyes.

"Her illness weighs more heavily upon her, I think."

"I think so, as well," Daav said, and resolutely shook off his sudden chill. "I shall be there to support you this evening, never fear it. Until soon, darling."

"Until soon, Daav."

WELL, ANNIE DAVIS! *And you preened in the green gown and thought yourself so fine.*

The new gown, like the old, was cut low over her bosom, close in to her waist. There, all similarity was done.

A wide collar swept up to frame her throat, belling, flower-like, to cup her face. Long sleeves fell in graceful pleats, calling attention to her hands, and the floor-length skirt, deceptively slim, was slashed to permit all of her accustomed stride.

Eyla dea'Lorn twitched the skirt into more perfect order and smiled.

"Yes," she said, standing back and clasping her hands before her. "I believe his lordship will be pleased."

Before Anne could make answer to that, the little tailor held up a finger.

"Attend me, now, Lady. The dress is all very well, and Moonel's jewels will shame no one. However, if you are wise, you will take my advice in a few certain matters. First—hair. Sweep yours up—yes, I know it is not long! Up and back, nonetheless. The collar's work is to frame the face—a little daring, I admit, but not wanton. Of a sophistication, perhaps, that a master trader might encounter—and admire—far outside of Liad's orbit." She rubbed her hands together.

"You walk well, with a fine smooth stride. The dress is made to accommodate you. Your hands—so beautiful, your hands! Show them, thus—" She extended an arm and flicked her wrist. "Try."

Anne copied the other woman's gesture; the sleeve flipped smoothly back from her hand, revealing strong, slender fingers.

"Good," Eyla approved. "An original is a Code unto herself.

There is not your like on all of Liad. The rules that bind you are not found within the world, but within yourself. Recall it and carry your head—so! Eh? There are those who must crane to admire you—that is their concern, not yours. There are those who will turn their face away and cry out that you are not as they." She lifted a hand to cover a bogus yawn.

"Boors, alas, are found in even the highest Houses."

Anne smiled, palely, and inclined her head. "You are kind to advise me."

"Bah!" Eyla swept thanks away with an energetic hand. "I will not have my work shamed, that is all." She smiled and bent to gather up her work-kit. "His lordship means to fire you off with flair, which is profit to me, does this gown please." She straightened.

"It will be amusing to see what the world makes of you, Lady. And what you will make of the world."

SHAN WAS FRACTIOUS and weepy. He jittered from one end of the nursery to the other; even the *Edu-Board* failed to hold his attention for more than a few seconds. All Anne's attempts to ease him into a less frenzied state were met with utter failure.

At last, feeling her own frazzled nerves about to go, she gathered him into her lap, thinking that a cuddle might do them both good.

"No!" He jerked back, body stiff, silver eyes wide.

"Shannie!"

"No!" he shouted again and smacked her hand aside, so un-Shan-like that she let him go in astonishment.

"*Mirada!*" He stamped his foot, glaring up at her. "I want *Mirada*! Go away! Go away, bad Ma!"

And with that he was gone, running pell-mell down the long playroom—and into the arms of Mrs. Intassi, who had just stepped through the door that led to the nursery's kitchen.

"Bad Ma!" Shan cried, hurling himself against the nurse's legs and hiding his face in her tunic. "I want *Mirada!*"

"That's all very well," Mrs. Intassi said in firm and unsympathetic Terran. "However, you are not very kind to your mother. You should beg her pardon."

"No," Shan said stubbornly, refusing to raise his head.

Sick to her stomach, shivering and weary, Anne rose, shaking her head at the tiny ex-Scout.

"Never mind," she said, hearing how her voice shook. "If he doesn't want me here, then I'll go." She turned toward the door, missing the concerned glance Mrs. Intassi flung her.

"Good-bye, Shannie," Anne called. "Maybe I'll see you tomorrow."

The nursery door slid closed behind her with a sound like doom.

SHE WAS LYING on her bed some while later, staring blankly through the overhead window. The Liaden sky was brilliant, blue-green and cloudless.

The brilliance pierced her, searing the tumbling thoughts from her mind, scalding emotions to ash.

Seared, scalded and gone to ash, she closed her eyes against the brilliance.

When she opened her eyes again, the brilliance had faded. She turned her head against the pillow. The clock on the bedside table told her there were two hours left to prepare for the gather.

Sighing, feeling not so much exhausted as drained—of thought, of emotion, of any purpose save the plan—she rolled out of the wide bed, glanced at the mirror across the room—and frowned.

On the vanity beneath the mirror, among her familiar belongings, were two unfamiliar boxes.

The large box was covered in lush scarlet velvet. Anne lifted the lid.

A rope braided of three gold strands: Pink, yellow and white, weeping drops of yellow diamond exactly matching her gown. Tiny yellow diamond drops to hug her earlobes, glittering allure. Woven gold combs and pins, dusted with yellow chips, to hold her hair, up and back.

Anne looked down at the velvet box's treasure, at jewels that cost more than she would likely earn in a lifetime, created to grace one dress, created in turn for one gathering . . .

His lordship means to fire you off with flair.

Anne sighed, feeling, perhaps, a distant relief.

Now she would have enough money to buy passage. Home.

The smaller box was wood, carved with vines and flowers, a center medallion inlaid with bits of ivory. She opened it, found a folded square of ivory-colored paper. Her name, written in uncertain Terran characters, adorned the outer fold.

Inside, the words were in Liaden, the letters true and bold.

For my love. To say hello, and never to say good-bye. Er Thom

Nestled in a satin pillow was a band of rosy gold. The gem set flush to the metal, simply cut and pure as pain, was precisely the color of his eyes.

For a long moment she simply stood there, wondering if her heart would take up its next beat, if her lungs would accept another breath.

When it seemed that she would, after all, live, she closed the little box and set it gently aside. The scrap of creamy paper she placed in her briefcase, sealed in the pocket with the disk from Jin Del yo'Kera's computer.

The velvet box she let stand open, giving its expensive glitter to the room while she began at last to ready herself for the gather.

CHAPTER THIRTY-THREE

Here we stand: An old woman, a halfling boy, two babes; a contract, a ship and a Tree.
Clan Korval.
How Jela would laugh.

—Excerpted from Cantra yos'Phelium's Log Book

A'THODELM YOS'GALAN, Syntebra reminded herself forcefully, *is a person of* melant'i, *son of an old and respected House. It is a signal honor to be chosen as his wife.*

To be sure, she thought, cold fingers twisted together beneath her cloak, to marry an a'thodelm of Korval would be a very great thing, indeed.

Except her heart—that traitor which had lifted so quickly upon hearing Korval had Seen a child of A'thodelm yos'Galan—her heart, now an ice-drenched stone pitted in her chest, did not seem to find it a great thing at all. She had said as much, tentatively, to her father.

"Not marry the yos'Galan?" Her father stared, as well he might, Syntebra allowed fairly. "Are you mad?"

Syntebra felt the easy tears rise to her eyes, and her father's face softened.

"Doubtless you're thinking now a child is Seen there's no cause for him to marry. Nothing could be farther from the case, I assure you. Korval is in sorry state of late—wretched luck for them, certainly, but golden fortune for us, do we throw the dice canny!" He leaned forward with the air of one offering a treat.

"Why, if the yos'Galan does not want you, there's Korval Himself still in need of an heir!"

But that was even worse, for Korval was a Scout, all the world knew that! And Syntebra was afraid of Scouts.

Tearfully, she had attempted to explain this to her parent. She met Scouts from time to time at the port, where she went—dutifully— to put in her hours of flying. Scouts possessed the oddest manners imaginable, and a bold, unnerving way of looking directly into one's eyes.

Scouts forever seemed to be enjoying some obscure joke, or secretly laughing at *some*thing. Syntebra rather thought that they were laughing at her.

"Oh, posh!" her father cried, all out of patience. "You'll do as you're told, and none of your vapors! Hearing you, one would think the yos'Galan scar-faced and Korval dissolute! You are very fortunate, my girl. I recommend you seek solitude and consider that aspect of the case."

Which is how Syntebra came to be at her delm's side in Trealla Fantrol's great formal entry hall, handing off her cloak to a servant and dutifully striving to recall that it would be a very great thing indeed, to wed A'thodelm yos'Galan.

"RAKINA LIRGAEL, Delm Nexon," Mr. pak'Ora announced. "Syntebra el'Kemin."

They came slowly down the long room, the elder lady leaning lightly upon the younger's arm. Neither was dressed in the first style of elegance, though the younger lady's gown was slightly more elaborate, designed to show a winsome shape to perfection.

Stationed beside his mother's chair, Er Thom watched their progress. Young Syntebra's plentiful hair had been pinned high, then allowed to tumble with calculated artlessness to kiss her bare shoulders. Here and there a diamond winked among the rioting dark ringlets. Diamonds glittered in each tiny ear and a solitaire suspended from a chain fragile as thought trembled at the base of her throat.

"Delm Nexon," Petrella said from her chair. "Be welcome in our House."

Nexon bowed, the glitter of her dress-jewels all but obscuring sight of the clan Ring.

"Your welcome is gracious," she stated. Straightening, she indicated the younger lady. "Allow me to make you known to Syntebra el'Kemin, a daughter of Nexon's secondary Line. Syntebra, here is Thodelm yos'Galan."

Syntebra's bow was charmingly done, though to Er Thom's eye a trifle ragged at the start.

Petrella inclined her head and raised a hand that trembled visibly. Er Thom felt a stab of concern. His mother was pushing her limit tonight. Gods willing, she would not push it too far.

"My son," his mother was telling the guests, "Er Thom, A'thodelm yos'Galan."

He made his bow to Nexon, receiving in return an inclined head and a civil, "Sir."

To Syntebra then he bowed, which was rather a trickier undertaking, for he must neither appear cool to the careful eye of his parent, nor so warm to the eye of the lady that impossible hopes were nourished.

Thereby: "Syntebra el'Kemin," he murmured, all propriety and very little else. "I am pleased at last to meet you, ma'am."

Wide, opal-blue eyes looked up at him from a tight little face, the luscious red mouth pinched pale.

Gods abound, the child's terrified! Er Thom thought, and felt a spate of anger at their respective parents, for insisting upon this farce.

Syntebra made her bow—not quite as pretty as her first.

"Sir," she returned in a breathless, husky voice. "A'thodelm yos'Galan. I am—very—pleased to make your acquaintance."

Well, Er Thom thought wryly, as he obeyed his mother's

hand-sign and went 'round to pour wine for the guests, *it should be no very great thing to show her that we shall not suit . . .*

IT WAS ALL SYNTEBRA could do to keep the tears at bay. Certainly, she could not bring herself to look up at the tall gentleman beside her, nor could she think of one gay or witty or even *sensible* thing to say.

He would think she was a fool. He would—her delm would—

"Drink your wine, child."

The voice was very soft, the mode Adult-to-Adult. Syntebra looked up in startlement.

Violet eyes met her gaze straightly from beneath winged golden brows.

"You'll feel the better for it," he murmured, raising his own glass for a sip. When he lowered it, she saw he was smiling, just a little. "I won't eat you, you know."

Almost, the ever-ready tears escaped. She had not expected kindness. Indeed, she had expected nothing but scorn from so grand a gentleman. Of course, he was quite old, and it was perhaps not entirely flattering to be addressed as "child," when she had all of twenty Standards . . .

"One is informed," A'thodelm yos'Galan said in his soft voice, "that you have but recently attained your second-class license. Do you plan to pursue first class?"

First class? She wished she had never attained second! The sorriest day of her life thus far had been the day she tested well in the preliminaries. She hated piloting. She hated ships. She hated the port, with all its noise and rabble and bewildering to-and-fros—

But, of course, one could scarcely voice such sentiments to a man who was both master pilot and master trader. Syntebra took a hasty swallow of wine—and was saved from answering by the dismaying call of the butler:

"Daav yos'Phelium, Delm Korval!"

DELM KORVAL was more terrifying than she had anticipated.

He spent some time speaking with Nexon and Thodelm

yos'Galan, as was only proper. However, after the introduction, in quick succession, of Mr. Luken bel'Tarda and Lady Kareen yos'Phelium, he had turned his silent Scout steps toward her *tête-à-tête* with A'thodelm yos'Galan.

Now, Syntebra had long been wishing for something like this to happen. It was only ill-chance that her rescuer should be more dreaded than he from whom she was rescued.

"Ma'am." He gave her the grace of a small bow, and such a look from his bold black eyes that she wished she might sink into the floor.

Happily, the bold eyes moved in the next instant as Korval addressed his kinsman.

"Good evening, darling. Shall the guest be with us, after all?"

"I believe so," A'thodelm yos'Galan said in his soft way. He turned to Syntebra. "Scholar Anne Davis, guest of the House, is to be present this evening, as well."

Syntebra very nearly blinked. Scholar Anne Davis? But surely—She became aware that she was the object of study of two very vivid pairs of eyes, and raised a hand to her throat.

"I—ah—the Terran lady?" she managed, trying to seem as if she were quite in the way of meeting Terrans.

A'thodelm's yos'Galan's golden brows rose slightly. "Indeed," he murmured politely, "the Terran lady."

"You needn't be nervous of her, you know," Korval added in his deep, coarse voice. "She's quite gentle."

She looked up at him, but his face was composed, without a hint of the laughter she suspected he harbored in his heart.

"It is merely that one does not speak Terran," she said, striving to recover her dignity. "And to converse in Trade would seem out of the way."

"Ah, no, acquit her as the cause of such inconvenience, I beg." Korval said. "Her grasp of the High Tongue is entirely adequate."

"Scholar Davis," A'thodelm yos'Galan murmured, "specializes in the study of linguistics."

At that moment Lord and Lady yo'Lana were announced, then Delm Guayar. Syntebra, looking aside from the progress of these luminaries, saw A'thodelm yos'Galan exchange a quick glance with his kinsman.

"Scholar Anne Davis," the butler announced, and Syntebra saw A'thodelm yos'Galan smile.

"Hah." He bowed gracefully to Syntebra, gave his delm a nod. "Pray excuse me."

In the next moment he was gone, crossing the room to meet the lady who had just entered.

Syntebra fairly gaped. She had considered A'thodelm yos'Galan and Delm Korval out-of-reason tall, but Scholar Davis revised that thought.

A'thodelm yos'Galan greeted her with the bow between equals and, looking warmly up into her face, offered his arm. The lady took it and they went down the room, pausing here and there to make proper introductions.

"There," Delm Korval said. "She doesn't look at all savage, does she?"

Undeniably, he was laughing at her. Of course the lady didn't look savage, though how such an immoderately tall, deep-bosomed creature could contrive to seem so regal went beyond Syntebra's understanding. She went 'round the room on A'thodelm yos'Galan's arm as if she were precisely High House, making her bows with grace, her clear voice carrying effortlessly to all corners of the suddenly quiet room.

"She bears an accent," Syntebra said to Delm Korval. The gentleman lifted one eyebrow.

"Well, and so do I," he said equably. "My Terran is quite marred by it, I fear."

She was spared any answer to this by the advent of the guest and A'thodelm yos'Galan.

"Daav." The Terran smiled, making free of Korval's personal name, as if, Syntebra thought, they were kin. She shrank into herself, anticipating the withering set-down to be delivered the lady for her audacity.

On the contrary.

"Anne," Korval returned with a smile that transformed his face into something approaching beauty. He bowed gently. "You look magnificent. Dance with me later, do."

The Terran actually chuckled, mischief lighting her eyes. "Do you only dance with magnificence, sir?"

"Ah, do not tease!" Korval returned in desperate tones. "If you won't have me there's nothing for it save I dance with my sister."

"A fate to be most ardently avoided." She smiled and inclined her head. "Count me your rescue, then." She turned her attention to Syntebra.

"Syntebra el'Kemin, Clan Nexon," A'thodelm yos'Galan said softly, "Scholar Anne Davis, guest of Korval."

Really, Syntebra thought, making her bow, *that dress is entirely wanton.*

However, there was no wantonness in the Terran lady's bow, or in her very correct, "Syntebra el'Kemin, I am pleased to meet you."

"Anne Davis, I am pleased to meet you," Syntebra replied, since she must.

She had to crane her neck to see the Terran's face. It was in no way a beautiful face, further marred by lines around the eyes and mouth. There was the suggestion of a smile in the grave brown eyes, and it was the outside of enough, Syntebra thought pettishly, to be laughed at by a *Terran.*

"Allow me to give you wine," A'thodelm yos'Galan said.

The Terran lady agreed to the suggestion and they went off, leaving Syntebra alone with Delm Korval.

"WILL YOU TELL ME," Er Thom said in soft Terran, "if the ring displeases?"

It was wrong to ask it; twice wrong to ask it here, now. But the sight of her naked hands had hurt—appallingly. It was as if he had leaned to kiss her and she turned her face aside.

"The ring is—lovely," Anne said, keeping her eyes steadfastly from his. "I—I chose not to wear it."

His breath was out of pace and he felt uncannily close to tears. Exercising stern control, he poured her wine and held the glass. She took it, looking down.

"Anne . . ." Gods, he was going to break and shame them both by weeping before all these gathered. He swayed a daring half-step closer, not caring who marked it.

"Anne, I beg you will tell me what is wrong!" The whispered plea came out with the force of a shout, and at last she raised her head.

Her eyes were desolate—determined. He saw the lie form in their depths, felt the price she paid for speaking it as if it were wrung from his own soul.

"There is nothing wrong," she said, and took a breath. "Shouldn't you be attending to that pretty child?"

"That pretty child," he said, hearing the edge on his voice, "is terrified of me. The best I might do for her is to arrange matters so we need never meet again."

Anne glanced around in time to see Luken bel'Tarda approach Syntebra and Daav.

"Then you won't mind if you lose her to Luken," she said, raising her glass to sip.

"If Luken can abide her, he's welcome." He turned away and poured himself a glass of the red.

"At least tell me," he said, looking back to her, "if you yet intend to allow me the honor of becoming your lifemate."

Agony. Boiling lye poured across the open wound of his heart. He gasped, clutching his glass as the room spun dizzily out of control—and steadied. Before him, Anne's face was stark, desolate eyes sparkling tears.

She will lie, he thought around the singing in his ears. *Gods, I cannot bear it, if she lies to me again.*

Anne turned her head sharply, breaking his gaze.

"I must ask Daav to make me known to his sister," she said abruptly, and with no more ceremony than that she left him, walking so smoothly the gown barely rustled.

Er Thom took a sip to calm himself—and another—and moved out into the room, meticulously taking up his duties as host.

CHAPTER THIRTY-FOUR

The lower docks of Solcintra port are the sphere of thieves, murderers, rogues and criminals of every description. Clanless and desperate, they have nothing to lose, and are completely willing to relieve the unwary of their purses and, often enough, their lives.

—From ***A Terran's Guide to Liad***

THE FINAL GUEST at long last bowed out, Er Thom leaned dizzily against the wall and raked his hands through his hair.

He'd lost track of Daav during in the evening; he supposed his *cha'leket* to have simply slipped away when the crush became too wearisome. He remembered that Anne had retired about mid-way through the dancing. Daav, her self-appointed cavalier, would have likely made his escape soon after.

The two dearest to him in someway accounted for, Er Thom closed his eyes, trying to ignore the roaring in his ears and consided what he could recall of the evening.

He had a vague notion that he had performed his hostly duties with competence, if not flair. Daav had attached himself to Anne, for which kindness his brother loved him all the more.

Luken had taken young Syntebra in to dinner, and danced with her several times. Duty had compelled Er Thom to claim the lady's hand for at least one dance, which he had done, and come away wondering how Luken could bear the chit hanging on his sleeve all evening.

But there, he thought, leaning his head back against the wall, Luken was a patient, good-hearted fellow. The child's apparent distress would be sufficient to assure her of his good offices.

Of the rest of the evening, he could recall nothing, save a feeling of bone-deep coldness, nausea, and the desire to break into tears at the most inopportune moments.

Ill, he thought, clawing his hair back from his face. *I must be ill.*

He'd been ill, once or twice, so long ago he could scarcely remember the occasions, much less the symptoms. He tried to recall when he had first felt poorly this evening—and gasped, coming up straight in the hallway.

Anne.

He'd been speaking with Anne. Anne who had not been her accustomed self for several days. Anne who had lied to him and who, reasonless, declined to wear his ring. Anne—

Gods, if Anne is ill—

He was on his way down the hall, half-running, shivering now with fear, lest she be lying in need and he unaware—

The door to the Smaller Salon opened. His mother came one step into the hallway and held up her hand.

"A word with you, sirrah. Now."

"Your pardon," he stammered, barely knowing what he said. "I must go to Anne immediately."

His mother's hand moved, flashing out with all her old speed, fingers locking around his wrist, crushing his lace, biting into his flesh.

"I think not," she said ominously.

For all her sudden strength, he could have easily broken the hold. But she was kin; she had borne him and given him aside, that he might be raised with Daav yos'Phelium, his beloved other self— and for that she was owed.

"Mother," he said gently, standing where she held him. "I have reason to believe the guest is ill."

"I see," she said, remotely polite. "A very grave affair, I agree. Mr. pak'Ora shall be dispatched to inquire into the guest's health. You will come with me."

For a heartbeat he thought he would not; thought he would break with clan entirely, rip away his arm and run abovestairs to his heart's own love.

But he felt the deep tremors in the hand that held him, saw the exhaustion in her face and the half-mad glitter in her eyes that said she kept her feet by will alone.

"Certainly," he murmured and they went together into the Smaller Salon, she leaning heavily on the arm of her supposed captive.

Er Thom seated her in a chair by the busy fire, then stood back, solemnly studying the table at her side.

Petrella's glittering eyes raked his face.

"Think I'm beyond keeping my word, do you?" she snapped and pulled the intercom to her.

The order to inquire into the state of the guest's health was given, brusquely, and the intercom shoved aside.

"Satisfied, A'thodelm?"

Er Thom bowed. "My thanks, Mother."

She made no answer to this, but simply sat for a time, staring into his face, fingers gripping the arms of the chair.

"The Terran scholar looked uncommonly fine this evening," she said at last, and in milder tone than he had anticipated. "Eyla dea'Lorn's work, I think?"

Er Thom said nothing. In spite of the fire he was cold—*cold*. He felt certain his mother could see him shiver.

"And the jewels," she pursued, after a moment. "Who but Moonel would think a yellow diamond rope? Allow me to offer my compliments, A'thodelm: You do handsomely by your light-loves." She paused, eyes burning into his.

"You will now have the goodness to name the day in this *relumma* on which you shall wed Syntebra el'Kemin."

Er Thom inclined his head. "I shall not marry Syntebra el'Kemin," he said steadily. "Not in this *relumma* or in any other."

"Ah, so?" His mother lifted her eyebrows in polite interest, her voice dangerously mild. "Pray, why not?"

"For the first part, because the child is frightened of me."

"A condition," Petrella pointed out, still in that tone of menacing mildness, "you did very little to alleviate this evening. But I interrupt! If there is a first part, then a second must be at hand! Enlighten me, I beg."

His hands were ice; he felt sweat gathering along his hairline; his stomach was cramped and there was a roaring in his ears that overrode the crackling of the fire. Er Thom grit his teeth and bowed.

"Scholar Davis and I are agreed to become lifemates," he said, around a strangling tightness in his throat. "We go to seek the delm tomorrow."

Silence. Petrella was seen to close her eyes—and open them.

"I forbid it."

"You cannot," he answered.

"Ah, can I not?" She leaned forward, fingers clawed into the carven arms of the chair. "I remind you that I am Thodelm yos'Galan. It is I who decides issues of Line and I have decided that it is not necessary to take a Terran into yos'Galan. Why should we do so? We are Liaden!"

"We are Korval!" Er Thom's shout startled him as much as his mother. "There is strength in diversity, weakness in samehood! You have read Cantra's logs—" He flung his hands out, showing her his empty palms.

"Mother, you have not even seen the child we made," he said, voice somewhat calmer. "Bright, bold-hearted and quick—as quick as any in the clan at his age—quicker than many! How is this ill-done? Why, the clan can use a dozen such!"

"And may have them yet, should I decide to breed you thus often!" Petrella pushed to her feet, face nearly white in the fire glow.

"Mother—"

"Silence!" The Command Mode: Thodelm-to-Line-Member. She pinned him with glare.

"You are forbidden," she stated, all in High Command. "You are forbidden from this moment forward to see, touch, speak to or think upon Anne Davis. She is not for you. You are commanded to name a day when you shall wed Syntebra el'Kemin. Now."

"Never!" he cried. "As for denying Anne, I shall not! We are lifemates, in all but word! Tomorrow morning, we shall be lifemates entirely! You cannot stop us from seeking the delm, you cannot—"

"I forbid this lifemating!" Petrella snarled. "Pursue it at your peril, A'thodelm, unless you wish to make a way for yourself and your *lifemate* on the Lower Docks!"

Er Thom froze, jaw tight. He met his mother's eyes straightly.

"There is no need for a master trader to seek the Low Port," he said, and the inflection of his voice was nearer Terran than any proper mode. "And if you will have my license called in question, then I remind you there is yet no reason for a master pilot to go further than the Guild House in the Upper Port." He bowed.

"If you will have it so, ma'am, then you will. I wish—with all my heart—that it were otherwise. As it is not, I shall take myself and mine—"

"Enough!" The Command Mode: Delm to Clanmember. Er Thom bit off his sentence as Daav came, quick and silent, across the room.

"You!" He flung a hand out to Petrella, black eyes bright in a face that might have been carved of gold. "We bar none from the clan tonight! You!" The hand flashed to Er Thom, Korval's Ring snagging the firelight. "We drag none unwilling into the clan. Ever!"

Er Thom started, was stilled by a flare of black eyes. "The lady has told me—tonight!—that she would have none of you. She swore it, and I believe her. The game is done."

"No!" Er Thom shook off his delm's gaze. "I will see her, speak with her! There is something gone ill and she—"

"Silence!" Korval commanded and Er Thom gasped, staring into black, black eyes. In the fireplace, a stick broke noisily, releasing a rain of sparkles.

"You will go to your rooms," Korval commanded then, "and await the Healer. Anne Davis is none of yours. I trust you will not trouble her further."

She had denied him. His mind logged the thought into a loop, that began at once to repeat, over and over: Anne had denied him. Anne had denied him. Anne . . . Anne.

His body moved, graceless and wooden—a bow to the delm's honor, followed by another, to the thodelm. His—legs—moved, carrying him past delm and thodelm, out of the room, into the hall, down corridors pitch black and bitter cold, until at last he came to an end of walking.

He stared around the place where he found himself: Stared at the laden worktable, the mantelpiece cluttered with bric-a-brac from an hundred worlds, the pleasant grouping of chair and doublechair before the laid and unlit hearth.

He walked toward the hearth, eyes caught by a flutter of red and gold among the mantel's clutter. Reaching, he had it down, and stood gazing at the thing.

A scrap of red silk no longer than his hand, that was all. That, and a length of tarnished, gold-colored ribbon, elaborately knotted into a fraying flower, through which the red silk had been lovingly threaded.

"Anne!" Her name was a keen, jagged with agony. He crashed to his knees, clutching the bit of silk as if it were a lifeline, bent his head and wept.

"WELL." Petrella sank into her chair, quivering in every muscle. She looked up into her nephew's set face. "Better late than never arrive, I suppose. It comforts me that at last you perceive the good of the clan."

"The good of the clan," Daav repeated tonelessly. He stared down at her, eyes black and remote. "Is Korval so wealthy, aunt, that we might cast aside a master pilot, and shrug away the cost? Or has your intention always been to end yos'Galan with yourself? Speak plainly, I beg you."

"End yos'Galan—Ah." Petrella closed her eyes and let her head fall against the chair's padding. "You heard me threaten him with the Lower Docks, did you? Then you also heard that he was raving. I spoke to frighten, and to shock him into sanity."

"And failed in both intents," Daav snapped. "He was on the

edge of accepting your terms, ma'am, when the delm ordered him to cease!"

There was a small silence. Petrella opened her eyes.

"I believe you had mistaken the matter, nephew."

"Oh, had I?" Daav returned bitterly. "'I shall take myself and mine—' was what he said! Am I the only one of us who can clearly hear the end of that sentence?" He bowed, deeply and with irony. "My compliments, aunt—In one throw you make your son clanless and a thief."

In the depths of her chair, Petrella shivered, assailed by a pain far different than that which wracked her body.

"He—is ill," she achieved after a moment. "To turn his face from the clan and follow a Terran? It is—"

"Master Healer Kestra will be with him tomorrow. Would that she had been able to come tonight." Daav turned away to stare into the fire. Suddenly, he whirled.

"Damn you for a meddlesome old woman!" he cried. "Why could you not have let it be? The lady had said she would not have him! She loved him too well, for your interest, aunt—too well to allow him the *sacrifice* of aligning himself with a Terran. If only his mother loved him half so well! But you—you must needs demand and shame and assert your dominion, sowing pain with every throw!" He came forward, one step, and stopped himself, staring down at her as if she were prey.

"The lady would have gone!" he shouted. "Of her own will, she would have left us and sought what healing she might. My brother would have likewise sought the Healers, to ease the grief of her going. There would have been honor for both in this, and a minimum of pain." He paused and Petrella found she could breathe again, though she dared not take her eyes from his.

"All thanks to your wisdom," he finished with brutal calm, "we have now two bleeding from wounds which may never heal clean, and a child abovestairs, crying aloud for both."

He swept a low, mocking bow, his lace rustling in the utter silence of the room.

"Sleep well, Aunt Petrella. I shall return tomorrow."

She made him no answer; barely knew that he was gone. She watched the fire—and, later, the embers—letting her mind ride the waves of pain, until she was back in a time when her twin was alive and all of life stretched before them.

CHAPTER THIRTY-FIVE

Er Thom fell from the Tree this morning.

I hasten to add that all is well, though of course he took damage. A matter of broken ribs and dislocated shoulder—that's the worst of it. Nothing beyond the auto-doc's capabilities.

I cannot for certain say how far he fell, for all Daav can tell me is that the pair of them had "never been so high." Er Thom was craning for a better sight of the Port when an end-branch broke under his weight.

He was caught, twig-lashed and unconscious, by the big by-branch about seven meters up—you know the one, sister. The luck is in the business twice: The child doesn't remember falling.

Daav saw the whole, and kept a cool head—far cooler than I should have kept at eight Standards, and so I swear! 'Twas he climbed down, fetched me out of a meeting with dea'Gauss, and showed me where Er Thom lay.

Nor would he be parted from his cha'leket, but kept vigil at 'doc-side and bed. I at last persuaded him to lie down whilst I kept watch, and he fell instantly asleep—to wake a quarter-hour later shrieking for Er Thom to come back, "Come back! The branch is breaking!"

I await the Healer as I write this . . .

**—Excerpted from a private letter to
Petrella yos'Galan from Chi yos'Phelium**

✿ ✿ ✿

SHAN TOOK HER HAND listlessly and went without any of his usual chatter down the long hallway toward Doctor yo'Kera's office, Mouse clutched tight against his chest.

Anne eyed him worriedly. According to Mrs. Intassi, he had passed a restless night, his sleep broken by bad dreams and bouts of crying. It sounded remarkably like Anne's own night and she wondered, half-dazedly, if she had caused her son's unrest or he had caused hers.

She shook her head. *Sure and there's plenty of pain for everyone to have their own share.* Er Thom's night would have surely been no better; she recalled the look in his eyes, as he begged her to tell him what was wrong.

Annie Davis, I hope you know what you're doing.

But after all, she told herself, working the lock on Doctor yo'Kera's door, there was nothing else to do. By now, Daav would have told Er Thom that Anne had lied when she had agreed to be his lifemate. Er Thom could not possibly forgive such a lie, such a strike at his *melant'i*. Of course, he would come after her—but he would do so in any case, once he found Shan was gone. It was her intention to be firmly within Terran jurisdiction by the time Er Thom finally caught up with her.

"Ma?" Shan looked up at her from heavy-lidded silver eyes. "Where's *Mirada*?"

Oh, gods. She dropped her bulging briefcase and went to her knees, gathering her son's small body close.

"*Mirada* can't come, Shannie," she whispered, cheek tight against his hair. "His clan needs him."

He slipped his arms around her neck, she felt him sigh, then: "We stay here? With *Mirada*?"

"No, baby," she whispered and closed her eyes to hold back the tears. "We're going home—to visit Uncle Dickie. A nice, long visit."

She thought briefly of her post on University: Good-bye tenure track. Well, she could get a job on New Dublin, surely. She could be a translator at the port, or a teacher of Standard Terran in the private school.

Or she could raise sheep. Her arms tightened around her son. "I love you, Shannie."

"Love you, Ma." He pushed back against her arms and lifted a hand to her face. His fingertips came away wet. "Sad."

"Sad," she repeated, voice cracking. She tried a smile; it felt wrong on her face. "We'll be happy again. I promise."

She stood and lifted him onto the table; plucked Mouse from the floor and laid it across Shan's knees.

"I'm going to call a cab," she told him. "Then we can go to the port."

It took a few minutes and some ingenuity to thread the university's comm system, but she finally got an outside line and placed her call. The cab was promised in fifteen minutes, at the secondary door, as directed. Anne nodded to herself and cut the connection, glancing around Doctor yo'Kera's cluttered, comfortable office for the last time.

In an ocean of hurt, the pain of leaving his work undone, of walking away from the mystery of missing corroboration, was imbued with special flavor. Jin Del yo'Kera had been her friend, steadfast down a dozen years. In a way, she had loved him. Gods knew, she owed him more than she could ever repay. To leave him this way, with his research in shambles, his brilliance dimmed in the memories of his colleagues . . .

She shook her head, denying the tears that made a glittering riot of the book-crammed shelves. Turning from the shelves, she found herself contemplating the flat-pic of three Aus at their sheep station: Mildred Higgins, Sally Brunner, Jackson Roy. Strong, straightforward people they seemed, smiling out of the battered frame. People who would see nothing odd in teaching a Liaden scholar to shear sheep.

The flat-pic was slightly wrinkled, as if someone had lately had it out of its frame and reseated it imperfectly. Or, Anne thought, perhaps the picture was so old the paper was beginning to dissolve. She had a moment's urge to take the thing off the wall and smooth the pic tidy. Shaking her head at the impulse, she turned back to Shan.

"Time to go, laddie," she said, swinging him to the floor. "Hold tight to Mouse, now."

She picked up her briefcase, took her son's hand and stepped out into the hall.

Shan uttered a sharp squeak and fell silent, his hand gone cold in hers.

Fil Tor Kinrae finished his bow and smiled, coldly, up into her eyes.

"Scholar. How fortunate that I meet you. We have much to speak about."

Anne inclined her head and allowed a note of irritation to be heard. "Alas, sir, I am unable to accommodate you today. I am bound for the port."

"Then I am twice fortunate," he said in his curiously flat voice. "I go to the port, as well. Allow me to drive you."

"Thank you, no. I have transport." She made to go past him down the hall, but he was abruptly before her.

The gun in his hand was quite steady. He was pointing it at Shan.

"You do not seem to grasp the situation, Scholar," he said, and the mode was Superior to Inferior. "You will allow me to drive you to the Port. You will continue to do precisely as I command. Fail, and I shall certainly harm—that." The gun moved minutely, indicating Shan.

"He's only a child," Anne said slowly. Fil Tor Kinrae inclined his head.

"So he is. Walk this way, if you please, and pray do not do anything foolish."

HE CAME TO HIMSELF in the gray of foredawn, face crushed into the hearth rug, one outflung hand clutching a tattered piece of red silk and a tawdry, fraying love knot.

His body ached amazingly, but that was no matter. His mind was clear.

He had dreamed.

Baffling, grief-laden dreams, they were, that robed the veriest commonplace in twisty, alien menace until his stomach churned with the strangeness of it and his head felt likely to burst asunder.

There were tolls demanded, now and again—he gave what was asked: His ring, his fortune, his peace. In return he was promised safe passage through the surrounding menace. He was promised love, *melant'i* and a return of peace.

The toll-man demanded his son.

"He's my son, Er Thom!" he cried out and felt as if his heart were broken anew. "He's a Terran citizen! Your clan doesn't know and your clan doesn't care!" He covered his face and wept aloud.

"I came home," he whispered distractedly, "and you were gone . . ."

Full awake, lucid and calm, he rolled to his back, careless alike of complaining muscles and ruined finery. He stared up at the gray-washed ceiling and considered his own folly.

Of course Anne did not care of Shan's place in Line—that would be to think as a Liaden. To think as a Terran—to think like *Anne*—one would weigh the answers to such questions and find in them proof that the man she had asked to guard her *melant'i*—the man she loved too well to allow his *sacrifice*—had willfully cheated her, stolen her child and placed him beyond her reach—forever.

Comes the same man pursuing his suit and Anne is flung headlong and frightened into a game so complex it might well give a seasoned player pause.

The man cries lifemates—does he lie? He had lied once, had he not? Assume he lies—necessity demands it. Lie to him in return, a little; better, allow him to deceive himself. Play for time, play for the single, slender moment of escape.

She had played well—brilliantly well, for one unused to the game. Yet she had been unable, even for necessity, to lie entirely. Honor would not allow her to wear the ring he had given.

He wondered, lying there, if she had known her confidence to Daav would end thus, with Er Thom safely out of the way, and her path clear from nursery to space port. It seemed likely.

He sighed and moved his head from side to side against the floor.

Anne's window of opportunity was today—this morning. She would take it—she must, or all play was for naught. He rather thought she would try to barter Moonel's jewelry for passage away, an enterprise she might find more difficult than she had supposed.

His course was clear. He spared a thought for his brother—but it seemed he was beyond feeling any new pain. The Healer would soon arrive; she must find an empty room when she did.

He came to his feet, wincing a little at the protest of his muscles, and went along to the shower, stripping off his formal clothes as he walked.

MUSCLES EASED BY A HOT SHOWER, Er Thom dressed in plain, serviceable trousers, plain shirt, comfortable boots. Each of the boots carried a cantra in the heel.

The belt he ran around his waist carried two dozen cantra between the layers of leather; the cunningly-made silver buckle could be traded either for melt-price or as an artwork.

From the lock-box he took other sorts of money: Terran bits, loops of pierced shell and malachite, rough-cut gems. These he disposed in several secret pockets about his person, and closed the safe on a dozen times the amount he had taken.

He shrugged into his leather pilot's jacket, feeling it settle heavily across his shoulders. Coins were sewn between the outer lining and the inner; more coins weighted the waist.

For a moment he fingered his jewel-box, frowning—and decided against. He pulled a second, smaller box toward him, lifted the lid and brought the gun out.

Quickly, he cracked it, checked it, reassembled it and slipped it into a jacket pocket. Extra pellets went into still other pockets. He closed the box and put it meticulously back in its place.

So. He looked around his room, reviewing his plan.

Anne's first object must be to leave Liad. Thus, he would find her at the Port. Necessity might dictate that she bear her son away, but she loved Er Thom yos'Galan. He knew that. She would allow him to come close enough to speak to her—close enough to touch her.

The gun weighed like a stone in his pocket. For a moment he

hated it with an intensity that should have been shocking—then he shook the emotion away. He must make haste. Daav would be here with the Healer very soon.

Pilot quick, he went back to the parlor and opened the window wide. The door was unlocked; he didn't bother locking it or scrambling the access code. Such tactics would scarcely slow Daav. The best plan was to be gone, and quickly.

He spared a glance for *Jelaza Kazone*, stretching tall and true across the valley, visible sign of Cantra yos'Phelium's love for Jela, her partner, and the father of her child. Tears pricked his eyes; he dashed them away, swung over the sill and began the downward climb.

DAAV RAN ACROSS TO THE OPEN WINDOW, heart in his mouth. *Gods, no, he would not—*

But his brother's broken body did not lie on the path so far below. Indeed, a cooler perusal of the vine that grew along the window and below discovered disturbed leaves, torn runners, crushed flowers—damage one would expect a climber to inflict.

Daav swore, though with more relief than anger, for it was an appalling climb down a sheer rock wall and the vine very little aid, in case one should fall.

"However, he did not fall," Master Healer Kestra commented from behind him. "So you may lay that fear aside, if you please."

He turned back to her and bowed fully. "My apologies, Master Healer. It appears my brother had—business elsewhere."

"Urgent business," she agreed in her dry way. She paced to the hearth rug, bent to pick up a scrap of red fabric and a bit of gold ribbon.

"The room," she murmured, her face losing its accustomed sharpness as she reached for nuance beyond the mere physical.

"The room tells me of great distress, of two people—wounded, yet fighting for understanding—of—resolution . . ."

"Two?" Daav demanded, for surely Er Thom would not have been so disobedient as—A breeze from the window mocked the thought.

From the hearth-rug, Master Kestra frowned. "Two? Of course—No. No, I believe you are quite correct. *Three* people. But surely one is—a child? A rather exceptional child. I would be interested in making the child's acquaintance, I think."

"It had been intended," Daav said as his mind raced, placing piece against piece until he had the shape of how it must have been.

The lady would not leave without the child, he thought, with icy calm. *Er Thom would not stay without the lady. The luck send I'm in time to catch them at the port!*

"Master Healer, I am wanted urgently elsewhere."

She turned from her study of the mantelpiece and gave him a look of sleepy amusement, running the red-and-gold ornament absently through her slender fingers.

"Go along, then. I shall await your return."

Without even a bow he was gone, running at the top of his considerable speed.

A few moments later the sound of a landcar's engine came through the open window and faded rapidly into the distance.

The Healer sat cross-legged upon the hearth rug, dreamy-eyed and languorous. She smoothed the tattered little love token flat on her palm, closed her eyes, and prepared herself to listen.

CHAPTER THIRTY-SIX

To be outside of the clan is to be dead to the clan.

—Excerpted from the *Liaden Code of Proper Conduct*

SHE SPOKE ONCE on the ride to Solcintra Port, to offer their captor the jewels in her briefcase, in trade for their freedom.

"I am not a patient man, Scholar," Fil Tor Kinrae replied without sparing a glance at her face.

Anne sat back in the short, cramped seat, shoulder bumping the opaqued window, put her arms around her son and tried to think.

Marksmanship had been part of her required course of study at the Academy of Music. She had never been comfortable carrying a gun, though, and given the habit up on her return to New Dublin.

Of course, she attended the mandatory self-defense practice course for faculty every other semester. But the prospect of taking a gun away from an undoubted professional while ensuring he did not shoot her child iced her blood.

Perhaps a chance would present itself when they left the car. If she could keep between Shan and the gun—in her lap, Shan twisted to push his face against her breast.

He hadn't uttered a sound since his squeak of terror in the hallway, miles and minutes ago. Anne lay her cheek against his hair and stroked him silently, hearing the echo of his fright, feeling her own muscles tense in response.

Don't, she warned herself sharply. *For the gods' sake, gel, don't set up a loop. The laddie's frightened enough—and you need your wits about you.*

She closed her eyes and deliberately thought of Er Thom as he had been back on University, after it was settled that Shan would come to Liad—after they could be easy with each other again. She thought of his understated humor, his care and his thoughtfulness. She thought of him cross-legged on the floor, assisting in the design of a block tower; she thought of him holding Shan in his lap, telling a story in his soft, sweet voice . . .

In her lap, Shan relaxed, the hand that clutched her sleeve loosened. Anne resolutely thought of the good times, and it seemed that she could see him before her, his hair brighter than gold, his eyes purple and compelling beneath winged brows. The mind-image grew sharper until it seemed she need only extend a hand to feel the silked surface of his old leather jacket, to finger the new scar along the shoulder, to touch his cheek—once more . . .

The car stopped.

She sat up, Shan tensing against her. Now, perhaps . . .

The door popped open. Fil Tor Kinrae reached in, grabbed Shan by one arm and dragged him from Anne's lap.

"Ma!" he shouted, then gasped into silence. Anne flung out of the door—and froze, staring at the gun.

"Good," the man said without inflection. "Have the goodness to bring the case, Scholar. If the child makes another sound he will regret it. Impress that upon him, won't you?"

Anne licked her lips and looked down into her son's wide silver eyes. "Shannie," she said, keeping her voice firm and even, "you have to be very quiet, Okay?"

He swallowed and nodded, keeping his face turned away from the man who held him. Anne reached into the car and pulled out her briefcase.

"Good," Fil Tor Kinrae said again and moved the gun. "This way, Scholar."

They were in an alley, thin, dirty and deserted. Anne walked past two empty shop fronts and turned into a third, obeying the movement of the gun. The man pushed ahead and shouldered the door open, dragging Shan into a dank vestibule. He pointed the gun at a set of twisty, ill-set steps.

"Up."

Obediently, she went up, minding the shallow stairs and hearing, in the hidden pocket of her mind, the sound of her son's silent sobbing.

At the top of the flight was another door, this one slightly ajar.

"In."

Anne pushed the door wide and walked in. Behind her the door closed, tumblers falling loudly.

The woman at the console spun in her chair, snapping to her feet in such haste her many earrings jangled.

"Cold space, it's the yos'Galan's Terran!" The hard gray eyes went past Anne. "And the mongrel. Have you gone mad?"

Fil Tor Kinrae sent Shan reeling against Anne's legs with negligent brutality and walked within, moving his shoulders.

"What business of mine, if the yos'Galan keeps cows?"

"And is so very careless as to lose them," the woman agreed, running a hand on which a master trader's amethyst gleamed over her close-cropped head. "Well enough. But that child is Korval, my friend, and if you believe the Dragon will not tear the port to ground to find him, you *have* run mad!"

"But they're not at the port, Master ven'Apon," Kinrae explained in his flat voice. "They're at the university."

"Oh, are they?" The hard eyes flickered over Anne's face.

"That might serve," she allowed. "I trust no one saw you take them." Her face shifted. "And I trust you'll allow them to be found far away from here, as well. I need no trouble with Korval, thank you. The yos'Galan has already done me the favor of calling my name before the Guild, scar his face!"

Kinrae stared at her. "If I chose to leave them here, I hope to hear no word from you, Master."

"Leave your dirty linen to me, will you?" the little woman

demanded hotly, putting her palms flat on the desktop. "Damn you, wash your own laundry."

The gunman looked at her blandly. "I believe you've had handsome payment."

"And worked handsome hard!" the woman retorted. "I've told you I'm called before the Guild! How if I scrub clean and show the gentles the way of buying a master trader's license?"

"Would you sing that song?" he wondered flatly. "But birds have such short lives, Master ven'Apon." He moved his gun, negligently.

"I shall be using the back room and I expect I shall not be disturbed." The gun was on Anne, who was holding Shan against her and stroking his hair.

"Touching. This way, Scholar." He reached out and pulled Shan away, fingers twisted in the back of the child's collar. "Bring the case."

SHE HAD NOT ATTEMPTED to sell the jewels back to Moonel, nor had she been seen in the Gem Exchange. He considered it unlikely that she knew of the less-savory establishments on the border of Mid Port. Besides, they would not give her near the sum she must have.

It could perhaps be judged an error of play, that she had not asked him for money. How simple a matter, after all, to point out that her purse was slimmer than she liked. He would have emptied his pockets at her word. It was thus, between lifemates.

But Anne, Er Thom thought, standing at the curb on Exchange Street—Anne would see such asking to be dishonorable, the coins themselves tainted, devalued by deceit.

Wondering where next to seek her, he stuck his hands into his pockets, shuddering when his fingers touched the gun.

Ah, gods, beloved, must it be this path?

But there: Anne had chosen their course; to unchoose it was not possible. Bound to her as he was, with spider-silk lines of love and lies, it was his part, now, to follow.

He stepped off the curb and crossed the busy street, walking back to his car, puzzling over where she might have gone. Frowning and abstracted, he lay his hand against the door, and spun around, certain he had heard someone call his name.

The street behind him was very nearly empty. No one stood near, hand raised in greeting.

He heard the call again—slightly louder. His name, certainly, the voice seeming to come from—the east. Toward Mid Port.

Holding his breath, he slipped into the car, started the engine— and sat waiting, stretching his ears, though of course that was foolish. When the call came again, he put the car into gear and followed the fading echoes through the noisy chatter of the outside world.

"YOU WILL HAVE THE GOODNESS to produce the piece of bogus evidence linking Liaden language to Terran."

Anne eyed Fil Tor Kinrae carefully. The gun was steady, but at least he had let Shan sit next to her on the hard wooden bench. The crying in the back of her mind had stopped, replaced by a kind of exhausted half-trance.

"If the evidence is bogus, why bother with it?" she asked the gunman.

He returned her scrutiny blandly. "I collect lies, Scholar; it is an avocation. Produce the material or pay the price. Please understand that I am able to extract whatever payment I will. Behold the destruction of the Languages Department on University and believe me." He moved the gun. "The proof, Scholar. Now."

"I don't have it," she said, meeting his disturbingly expressionless eyes and willing him to believe the truth.

"Jin Del yo'Kera had it," he returned.

"So I believe. However, the central argument is missing from his notes. I thought it might be in his research computer, but I was not able to find it." She nodded toward the briefcase leaning against the wall. "I copied the core. The disk is in my case. You're welcomed to take it."

"Am I? But how kind. However, I am not interested in negative results, Scholar. I give you one more opportunity to cooperate: Produce this central argument of Jin Del's, this masterpiece of error that attempts to link Liad and Terra to a common mother tongue."

Her son's body was a torch, scorching her side, his presence in her mind an alert somnolence. She met the gunman's eyes fully, and saw Jin Del yo'Kera's death in their depths.

"I have no such information."

"I see. It is my belief, Scholar, that you are not fully awake to the vulnerability of your position. Perhaps a demonstration is in order."

THE VOICE NO LONGER called his name.

Indeed, Er Thom thought, threading the narrowing streets toward Mid Port with rapid skill, that which guided him was no longer voice, but—compulsion. He followed it and in good time pulled over to the side of an alley, just behind another, nondescript and slightly battered, landcar.

He got out of the car and walked a short distance. It took less than a minute to persuade the street door to admit him, after which he lost no time in going up the rag-tag stairway.

Jyl ven'Apon spun round as he burst through the door, her hand flashing toward the weapon set ready on the desk—too late.

Er Thom's gun was already out and aimed, with regrettable accuracy, at a point in the precise center of her forehead.

ANNE TRIED TO BLOCK THE MAN with her body and earned a fist against her shoulder for her efforts. He grabbed for Shan.

The child flung himself back against the wall, soft-booted feet flailing at the man's face.

"*Mirada!*" he screamed in piercing hysteria. "*Mirada! Mirada!*"

Fil Tor Kinrae swore and snatched again, clawed hand grabbing for fragile throat. Anne twisted, flung the man half backward and used her elbow in the way she had been taught.

One blow to crush a man's windpipe. Kinrae dropped like a stone. Before he hit the floor, Anne had the gun out of his hand and caught Shan to her.

"Hush, baby. Hush, Okay?"

Face against the side of her neck, he nodded. Anne held him, mind working feverishly. The woman in the other room: She would have to be prepared to kill her, as well. Anne swallowed, feeling the gun in her hand, the plastic still warm from Kinrae's grip.

"Shannie, listen to me. You listening?"

"Yes."

"Okay. I'm going out for a minute. You need to stay here (*with a dead man on the floor, Annie Davis?*). I'll be back in a minute and then we'll leave. (*Gods willing.*) Promise me you'll stay here until I come for you."

"Promise, Ma."

"Good." She hugged him tight. "I love you, Shannie."

The warning was little enough—a light step in the hall beyond. Anne came to her feet, thrusting her son behind her, gun held ready.

The door burst open.

"*Mirada!*"

Er Thom's eyes flashed over her face, took in Shan and what was left of Fil Tor Kinrae on the floor. He slipped his gun away and held out a hand.

"Come away now. Quickly."

ER THOM HAD THE BRIEFCASE, Anne was carrying Shan, uncertain if the shaking she felt was his or her own.

They went through the console-room. A glance revealed no body bleeding its life out on floor or desk. Anne swallowed around a mingled sense of nausea and relief, recalling what was left behind on the back room floor.

"How did you get here?" she asked Er Thom, voice sounding thin in her own ears.

He spared her a quick violet glance. "I heard you calling."

"Oh." She gulped, hugging Shan tight. "We're leaving Liad, Er Thom."

"Yes," he said, leading the way down the tricky stairs. "I know." At the bottom of the flight he turned to her.

"You and our child must be attended by a Healer as soon as possible. We should thus book passage on *Chelda*, which leaves this afternoon and has a Healer on-staff. After we are safe away, we may modify direction."

She stopped, blinking into his beautiful, beloved face. "We?"

He met her eyes, his own unguarded, his face fully open to her. "If you will have me."

Have him? Anne drew a careful breath, aware of Shan, trembling in her arms. "We have to talk," she said.

Er Thom bowed slightly. "We do, indeed. Let us board *Chelda*. The Healers shall tend to you and to our son. We shall talk. Fully, I swear it. If you choose then that we must go separate paths, I shall trouble you no further." He held out a tentative hand.

"Can you trust me in these things, Anne?"

She touched his fingertips lightly with her own. "Yes."

"Good," he said gravely. "Let us go away from here."

CHAPTER THIRTY-SEVEN

In the case of a clan's loss of an individual member through the actions of a person unrelated to the clan, Balance-payment is hereby set forth. Such payment weighs equally the occupation, age, and clan-standing of the individual who has been lost. The attached chart shall henceforth be the standard by which all clans shall compute such Balance-payment.

—From the Charter of the Council of Clans,
Fifth Amended Edition

"YES, I SEE." The Healer folded neat hands into his lap. "For the child, forgetfulness. And for yourself as well, if you wish it, Lady."

Anne found herself looking into a pair of bright brown eyes.

She frowned, fighting to think with a mind that seemed frozen and unwieldy. Er Thom had handled the arrangements at the reservation office, slicing through what Anne dimly perceived as a daunting mountain of red tape. He had bespoken them a suite aboard *Chelda*, she remembered that he had said so. But what else he might have told her, she could not presently call to mind.

On consideration, they might very well be on *Chelda* now, in the very suite Er Thom had rented, though the shuttle trip seemed likewise lost to recollection. The only thing she clearly remembered was the scene in the Mid Port back room, where she had killed a man and left him lying on the floor . . .

The Healer was looking at her, head tipped to one side, face alert and friendly.

"Forgetfulness," she managed. Her voice was shaking badly, she noted with detachment. "You can make Shan forget what happened?"

The Healer inclined his head. "Very easily, Lady. Shall I?"

"It would be best," she heard Er Thom murmur beside her.

She hugged Shan tight against her chest. "Yes," she said awkwardly, the dead man looming before her mind's eye. "If you please."

"Very well." He stood, a diminutive man with a quantity of curly gray-shot hair, and held out a hand. "We shall have to be alone, Shan and I. It will not take long."

On her lap, Shan stirred, looking up at the tiny man out of dull silver eyes. Abruptly, he wriggled upright and leaned forward in Anne's hold.

"Beautiful sparkles," he announced, and raised a hand toward the Healer. "Show me."

The Healer smiled. "Certainly."

Shan wriggled again, and Anne took her arms away. Her son slid from her lap and clasped the Healer's hand. Together they disappeared into an anteroom.

"Anne?" Er Thom's voice was worried. She turned to look at him. "Shall you take forgetfulness, as well?"

Forget . . . She wanted, desperately, to forget. Especially, she wanted to forget that last moment, when her body had taken over from her mind and—She had killed a man. She had *intended* to kill him. He had threatened her child, herself. He had murdered Jin Del yo'Kera, by his own word, he had destroyed the Language Arts building and only pure luck that no one had died of it—

"Anne!" Er Thom's hands were on her shoulders.

She realized she was trembling, looked wildly into his face.

"What happened—happened to the—master trader?"

His fingers were kneading her shoulders, setting up a rhythm in counter to her trembling. "She need not concern you."

"You killed her."

"No." He lifted a hand and tenderly cupped her cheek. "There was no need. She ran away." Gently, he bent and lay his lips against hers, whisper-light and warm.

Tears spilled over. She lurched forward, face buried in his shoulder, arms tight around his waist. The trembling turned to violent shaking, the tears to half-cries, gritted out past locked teeth.

Er Thom held her, one hand stroking her hair, the vulnerable back of her neck. He spoke in the Low Tongue, honoring her, loving her. Indeed, he barely knew what he said, except it came full from the heart. It seemed the sound of his voice soothed her.

The storm passed, quickly for all its passion. She lay shivering in his arms, her cheek pillowed against his shoulder.

"Remember something for me," she said huskily, her breath warm against the side of his neck.

He stroked her hair. "What shall I recall?"

"That—Fil Tor Kinrae. He wanted the central argument—the material that was missing from Doctor yo'Kera's proof. I know—I think I know where it is." She drew a shuddering breath. "It's behind the flat pic of—of the Aus sheep farmers. In his office. Remember that, Er Thom." Her arms tightened around him. "It's important."

"I will remember," he promised.

"Thank you." She sighed and nestled her cheek against him, seeming more peaceful, though she trembled still.

The door to the anteroom opened and the Healer spoke with the ease of one for whom there are few surprises in life.

"The child is asleep. If the lady will come with me, I shall see what might be wrought."

She stirred and moved her arms from his waist. Er Thom stepped back, took her hand and helped her to rise. Slipping her arm through his, he guided her to the doorway and gave her over to the Healer.

"I will be with you," he said, smiling up into her beloved and careworn face, "when you wake."

She gave him an uncertain smile in return. "All right," she mumbled, and allowed the Healer to lead her away.

✧ ✧ ✧

THE HEALER'S EXHAUSTION showed clearly in his face. He accepted a glass of wine with unfeigned gratitude and slumped into the offered chair with a sigh.

Er Thom sat in the chair opposite, sipped his wine and put it aside.

"It is fortunate," the Healer said after a sip or two of his own, "that they were able to be seen so quickly after the event. I anticipate no complications for the child: The dream will be hazy when he wakes from trance and will continue to fade over the next two or three days.

"The lady I believe capable of recapturing the entire experience, did necessity exist. She has a disciplined mind and a very strong will. If she should find it difficult to concentrate, if her sleep is disturbed, if she is troubled in any way—only call. I shall be honored to assist her."

Er Thom inclined his head. "I thank you."

"It is joy to serve," the Healer replied formally. He had recourse once more to his glass.

"The child," he said then and met Er Thom's gaze. "Your lordship is perhaps not aware that the child is something out of the common way. It would be wisdom, were he to be shown—soon—to a Master Healer, or brought to a Hall."

Again, Er Thom inclined his head. "I shall discuss the matter with my lady."

"Certainly." The Healer finished his wine and rose to make his bow.

Er Thom rose, returned the man's salute with gravity, straightened and held out a hand in which a six-cantra gleamed.

"Please accept tangible evidence of my gratitude for the service you render my lady and our son."

"Your lordship is gracious." The coin disappeared. The Healer inclined his head.

"Good day, sir. Fair fortune to you and yours."

"And to you, Healer."

Er Thom walked the smaller man to the door and let him out

into the wide, cruise-ship hallway. He closed the door and locked it—and went back through the parlor to the bedroom, there to keep watch at Anne's bedside until such time as she should wake.

COMING OUT OF SLEEP was like coming out of heavy cloud, into lighter cloud, to dense fog, to mist—to bright, unencumbered sun.

Anne stretched luxuriously. She felt wonderfully well, without care or grief; lucid and joyful for the first time in days.

She stretched again, knowing that they were booked on the cruise ship *Chelda*, bound for Lytaxin and points outward, scheduled to leave Liad orbit this very afternoon. Her son was safe and happy— deeply asleep at the moment, she knew. Er Thom was traveling with them—she forgot precisely how that had come about, for surely—

The thought slid away, vanishing into a warm glow of happiness.

"Hello, Anne." His voice, in gentle Terran. "Are you well?"

"Well?" She opened her eyes and smiled up into his, extended a languid hand and brushed his cheek with her fingertips, relishing the slow stir of passion. "I'm wonderful. I guess I needed a nap."

"I—guess," Er Thom agreed softly. He traced her eyebrows with a light fingertip. "You are beautiful."

She laughed. "No, laddie, there you're out. I am *not* beautiful."

"You really must allow me to disagree with you," he murmured, fingertips like moon-moths against her lips. He smiled, eyes smoky, fingers running the line of her jaw. "Beautiful Anne. Dar-ling Anne. Sweetheart."

She gasped, as much from surprise as from the tingle of pleasure his caresses evoked.

"You don't—You never say—things . . ." His fingers were tracing a line of fire along the curve of her throat.

"My dreadful manners," he murmured, bending his bright head as his clever fingers worked lose the fastening of her shirt. "Forgive me."

His mouth was hot over the pulse at the base of her throat. His fingers were teasing a nipple to erection.

"Teach me," he whispered, raising his head and kissing her cheek, her eyelids, her chin. "What else should I say, Anne?"

She laughed breathlessly, cupping his face in her two hands and holding him still.

"I don't think you need to say anything more at the moment," she murmured, and kissed him, very thoroughly, indeed.

SHE WOKE AGAIN, sated and a-tingle in every nerve, opened her eyes and saw him leaning above her, face suffused with tenderness. She shivered and reached for him.

"Er Thom, what's wrong?"

"Ah." He stroked her hair softly back from her forehead. "I shall—miss—my clan."

Coldness leached into her, riding confusion. Why was he here? The plan—hadn't the plan been to take Shan and herself away to New Dublin? Er Thom was to have stayed with his clan, wasn't that the plan? How—She groped after the precise memory. It eluded her, leaving her blinking up into his eyes, feeling half-ill with loneliness, vulnerable as she had never been vulnerable.

"You could—" Gods, she could scarcely breathe. She pushed her voice past the tight spot in her throat. "The ship's still in orbit, isn't it? You could—go home . . ."

"No, how could I?" He smiled gently and lay his finger along her lips. "You and our son are leaving Liad. How can I stay?" He kissed her cheek. "I shall learn, sweetheart. I depend upon you to teach me."

She stared at him, speechless—then blinked, attention diverted. "Shan's waking up."

"I shall go to him," Er Thom said, slipping out of the wide bed and bending to retrieve his clothes. He smiled at her. "If you like, we three may go up to the observation deck and watch the ship break orbit."

He was going to stay with them, loneliness and vulnerability be damned. She felt his determination echo at the core of her. He was turning his back on his clan, on wealth and position; throwing his lot in with Linguistics Professor Anne Davis, untenured.

"Er Thom—"

"Hush." He bent quickly over her, stopping her protests with his lips. "I love you, Anne Davis, with all of my heart. If you will not have Liad, then you must lead me to another place, and teach me new customs. Only do not put me aside . . ." His voice broke, eyes bright. "Anne?"

"You lied," she said uncertainly, for that had suddenly come crystal clear. "You said you weren't a thief—"

"Nor am I." He sat on the edge of the bed and caught her hands in his. "Anne, listen. If there were a child who was Davis, and I caused him to brought into Korval, that is thievery. But a child named yos'Galan, brought into Korval—how may yos'Galan steal a yos'Galan?" His fingers were tight on hers; she felt the truth in him, like a flame, melting away old fears.

"I erred. That, yes. I mistook local custom and thought I had explained enough. I thought, having done honor in name, you now passed the full joy of another yos'Galan to the clan, as was right and proper. Liaden. I plead stupidity. I plead pride. But you must acquit me of lying to you, Anne. That, I never undertook."

"You'll come with us?" she said, wonderingly. "To New Dublin?"

"Is that where you are bound?" Er Thom moved his shoulders. "I shall stand at your side. It is what I wish." He tipped his head. "We may need to tarry upon Lytaxin. Our son should be seen in the Healer's Hall—unless there is such on New Dublin?"

She shook her head. "We'll need to talk," she said, and heard a vague, fog-shrouded echo. She let it fade away, uncurious.

Er Thom inclined his head. "So we shall. I will go to our son now."

"I'll sort out my clothes," Anne said, with wry humor, "and meet the two of you in the parlor very soon."

SHAN PRONOUNCED HIMSELF both hungry and thirsty. He submitted with a certain ill-grace to having his hair combed and a wet cloth passed over his face, but took Er Thom's hand willingly enough and went with him into the parlor.

One step into the room, Er Thom froze, staring at the man in the black leather jacket who lounged at his ease on the low-slung sofa, long legs thrust out before him and crossed neatly at the ankle. He lifted a glass of blood-red wine in salute and sipped, room lights running liquid off the enamel-work of his single ring.

"Daav!" Shan cried joyously.

"Hello, nephew," the man replied gently. His black eyes went to Er Thom. "Brother. I perceive I am in time."

CHAPTER THIRTY-EIGHT

Take the course opposite to custom and you will almost always do well.

—Jean Jacques Rousseau

SHAN WAS SETTLED at a low table in the corner, a crystal glass of juice and some tidbits of cheese to hand. Er Thom came back to the center of the room and stood staring down at the man on the sofa.

"My family and I," he said eventually, and in Terran, "are bound for New Dublin."

Daav raised his glass, lips pursed in consideration.

"A pastoral location," he allowed in the same language. "Do you plan a long stay?"

"I believe Anne means us to settle there."

"Really?" Daav lifted an eyebrow. "I don't see you as a farmer, *denubia*."

"That has very little to say to the matter," Er Thom informed him flatly.

"Ah. Well, that is lowering, to be sure." He flourished the glass, switching to Low Liaden. "Drink with me, brother."

"I regret to inform you," Er Thom said, keeping stubbornly to Terran, "that your brother is dead."

"Oh, dear. But you are misinformed, you know," Daav said kindly, pursuing his end of the conversation now in Low Liaden. "My brother was seen not very many hours ago, booking passage for three upon *Chelda*. Unless the line's service has gone entirely awry, I believe we may assume he is enjoying his customary robust health."

"*Mirada!*" Shan called from across the room. "More juice. Please!"

"You will have to teach him to call you otherwise," Daav murmured, and lifted an eyebrow at Er Thom's start.

"Father," he suggested in soft Terran, meeting the determined violet eyes. "Papa. Da. Something of that nature."

"*Mirada*?" Shan called.

Er Thom went to him, refilled the glass and ruffled his frost-colored hair. Then he came back to stand and stare. Daav sipped wine, unperturbed.

"I repudiate the clan," Er Thom said, the High Tongue cold as hyperspace.

"Yes, but you see," Daav returned earnestly in the Low Tongue, "the clan doesn't repudiate you. If things were otherwise, I might very well wave you away. An off-shoot of the clan on New Dublin might be amusing. But things are not otherwise, darling. The clan needs you—you, yourself, not simply your genes. I cannot allow you to leave us. Necessity." He used his chin to point at Shan, engrossed in his snack.

"And if you think I shall allow that child beyond range of a Healer Hall any time before he has completed formal training, I beg that you think again." He cocked a whimsical eyebrow. "Come home, darling, do."

Er Thom's mouth tightened, his eyes wounded.

"My family and I," he repeated steadfastly, though his Terran had gone rather blurry, "are bound for New Dublin. The ship leaves within the hour."

Daav sighed. "No," he corrected gently. "It does not."

Er Thom drew a careful breath. "The schedule—"

"I see I have failed of making myself plain." He swirled what was left of his wine and glanced up, black eyes glinting.

"This ship goes nowhere until I leave it. And I shall not leave it without yourself and your son in my company." He raised his glass and finished the last of the wine.

"There is an important package due from Korval," he said, somewhat more gently. "The ship is being held for its arrival. It will make rather a hash out of traffic, of course, but that's the port master's problem, not mine." He put the glass aside.

"When I leave the ship, the package will be delivered and *Chelda* may be on its way." He moved his hand as if he cast dice. "It is now your throw, brother. How long shall we hang in orbit?"

There was a long silence.

"Anne and I are—tied together," Er Thom said eventually, and in, his brother heard with relief, the Low Tongue. "Understand me. I heard her call—from across the Port. I followed her thought to a place—" He moved his shoulders. "There is a dead man named Fil Tor Kinrae in the back room of a warehouse in Mid-Port."

"How delightful. Your work?"

"Anne's. In rescue of our son." He lifted a hand and ran it through his hair. "The Healer has been to both."

"Very good. I hesitate to mention that Master Healer Kestra awaits you at Trealla Fantrol."

Er Thom stiffened. "Anne and I are tied. I had just told you."

"My dreadful memory," Daav murmured. "I do however seem to recall that the lady swore she would have none of you. This leads me to the unfortunate conclusion that any—bonding—that exists is on your side alone."

Er Thom bowed with exquisite irony. "As you will. One-sided or not, it exists. I go with Anne, since choice is necessary. I cannot do otherwise."

"Ah, can you not?" Daav frowned; turned his head.

The door to the bedroom slid open and Anne came into the room. She advanced to Er Thom's side and looked down, her face tranquil, as the faces of those newly Healed tended to be. Daav inclined his head.

"Good-day, Anne."

"Daav," she returned gravely. "Have you come to take Shan away?"

"Worse than that," he said, watching her face with all a Scout's care. "I've come to take your son and your lover away."

Something moved in her eyes; he read it as anger.

"Er Thom makes his own choices," she said flatly. "My son comes with me."

"To New Dublin?" Daav asked, keeping his voice gentle, his posture unthreatening. "Anne, your child bodes to be a Healer of some note, if he does not come to halfling as one of *dramliz*. How shall New Dublin train him to use these abilities? Will you wait until he harms someone through ignorance—or until he begins to go mad—before you send him back to Liad to be taught?" He showed her his empty palms.

"How do I serve my *cha'leket* by denying his son the training he must have to survive? How does flinging talent into exile serve Korval?" He lowered his hands and gave her a rueful smile.

"For good or ill, Shan is of Korval. We are in Liaden space, subject to the law and customs of Liad. Shan's delm commands him to bide at home. The law will find no different."

She licked her lips. "Terran law—"

Daav inclined his head. "You are free to chart that course. However, for the years such litigation will doubtless encompass, the child bides with Clan Korval, his family of record." He shifted; came to his feet in one fluid move, hand out in a gesture of supplication.

"Anne, hear me. The luck was in it, that you brought your child to Liad. There is nowhere else in the galaxy where his talents are understood so well. I am not your enemy in this, but your friend. Only think and you will see that it is so!"

Her mouth was tight, fine eyes flashing. "You seem to have me over a barrel," she commented. "What do you propose I do, hang on as Clan Korval's guest until my son is come of age?"

Daav tipped his head, watching Er Thom's face out of the side of an eye.

"Why, as to that," he said calmly, "here is my brother says he can do nothing other than stand at your side, whatever ground you choose. He makes a rather compelling case for himself, casting aside his delm's word and escaping from his rooms down a vine. If things were otherwise, I might well give such devotion its just reward. But the devil's in it, you see—I need him. Korval needs him. He comes with me, if I must have him off this ship in chains."

"So the great House of Korval holds hostages, does it?" Anne flashed. "Is this honor?"

"We had been—wishing—to talk," Er Thom said, very softly, from her side. "Perhaps—we might find the proper compromise—on Liad."

Anne spun to look at him, eyes wide.

Er Thom met her gaze. "Is the intent of the trade to keep we three together?" he asked. "Or is it to keep us forever at—at—"

"Loggerheads," she supplied, almost absently. "You would burden yourself with a Terran on Liad?" There was a note of wistfulness beneath the disbelief. Daav relaxed, carefully. Er Thom took her hand and smiled up into her eyes.

"You would have burdened yourself with a Liaden," he murmured, "on New Dublin."

Daav felt a small hand slip into his and looked down into Shan's bright silver eyes.

"Hi, Daav," that young gentleman said comfortably. He smiled impartially at all three adults. "We go home now?"

"MAY I OFFER YOU more fruit, Master Healer?" Petrella yos'Galan asked from the head of the table, "Cheese?"

"Thank you, my needs have been well provided for." Master Healer Kestra inclined her head.

Thodelm yos'Galan's displeasure with her son was entirely audible to the Healer's inner ears. It was, of course, bad form to broach the subject of emotional turmoil with one who had not specifically requested aid, and Kestra had scrupulously kept to good form. Thus far. She could not help but admit, however, that her sympathies lay on the side of the abruptly absent a'thodelm and the lady his heart would not relinquish.

The shabby little love-knot had been compelling, as had the struggle she had perceived in the room's echoes. Two people who loved each other, each striving for right conduct. More the pity that the two were persons of *melant'i* and that right conduct shifted like moon shadow, world to world.

"I must offer apology," Petrella yos'Galan said ill-temperedly, "for my son's lack of manner. Of late he has come unruly, to the clan's distress."

"No need of apology," Kestra returned mildly. "Those of Korval are understood to be unruly." She smiled.

"I recall when the delm—Scout Cadet yos'Phelium he was at the time—applied for Healing, after his ship was disabled. Four Healers were required for the task of smoothing the memory—myself and another of Master rank, with two high adepts—and he wished to forget!" She sipped tepid tea and set the cup down with a tiny click.

"For all of that, we did not entirely accomplish our goal. We succeeded in blurring the experience, but he recalls it. I am certain that he does. I believe it to be a distant recollection, devoid of emotion, as if he had read of the incident in a book. But I am entirely certain he could tap the memory in all its horror, did he become convinced of necessity."

Her host said nothing to this and after a moment the Healer continued, in not so *very* good form:

"It has perhaps—forgive me!—escaped notice that your son's love for this lady and their child goes very deep."

"So?" Petrella said harshly. "We have all lost that which we loved, Healer. It is the nature of the game."

"True," Kestra allowed. "But it is not the purpose of the game."

"Enlighten me," the thodelm requested, with acid courtesy, "is it myself you have been requested to Heal?"

Kestra inclined her head. "Ma'am, it is not. You must forgive me and lay fault with my years. I find that old women are often impertinent."

"Not to say incorrigible," Petrella remarked, and Kestra smiled, feeling the tingle of the other's amusement.

"I had told Korval I should await his return," Kestra said. "If it does not inconvenience the House—"

But she got no further. There was a subdued clatter in the hallway, the door to the dining room swung open and Delm Korval entered with his long, silent stride, accompanied by a very tall lady and a fair-haired man carrying a child. The Healer came to her feet, inner eyes a-dazzle.

Fumbling like a novice, she Sorted the images. Thodelm yos'Galan she could now ignore; likewise Korval's vivid emotive pattern. The others . . .

The strongest was a dazzle of tumbling color and untamed light—rather as if one had fallen head-first into a kaleidoscope. With difficulty, the Healer traced the tumbling images to their source, bringing the pattern to overlay what was perceived by the outer eyes—gasped and automatically damped her own output.

"I am—honored—to meet Shan yos'Galan," she said, perhaps to the room at large. "I would welcome—indeed, require!—opportunity to spend more time with him. But if my primary concern is to be A'thodelm yos'Galan, I must ask that the child be removed. He is— enormously bright."

Korval was already at the wall-mounted intercom. A'thodelm yos'Galan also moved, leaving the tall lady standing alone near the door.

"Mother," he said, going gracefully to one knee by Petrella yos'Galan's chair. "I bring your grandson, Shan, to meet you."

The old lady's pattern, seen dimly through the rioting light show that was the child, registered yearning, even affection. However, the face she showed the one who knelt before her was bitterly hard. She did not so much as lift her eyes to the child.

"Sad sparkles," the child said suddenly and wriggled in the a'thodelm's grasp. Set upon his feet, he reached out and took one of Petrella's withered hands in his.

"Hi," he said in Terran, and then, in Low Liaden, "*Tra'sia volecta, thawlana.*"

"Grandmother, is it?" Petrella glared into the small face, then sighed, suddenly and sharply. "Good-day to you as well, child. Go with your nurse now, before you blind the Healer."

"Come along, Shan-son," the a'thodelm said softly. He took the child's hand and led him to the nurse hovering at the door.

"Mrs. Intassi," Shan cried, flinging himself against her, "we went to the port!"

"Well, what an adventure, to be sure!" Mrs. Intassi returned and led him out, carefully closing the door behind her.

Master Healer Kestra let out a sigh of heartfelt relief, ran an exercise to calm her jangled nerves, and trained her inner sight on the a'thodelm.

It was a pleasing pattern: Sharp-edged and cunning; subtly humorous, with a deep, well-guarded core of passion. The Master Healer nearly sighed again: Here was one who loved deeply—or not at all. There were signs of stress on the overlay, which was expectable, and a tenuous, almost airy construct that—

The Healer frowned, focusing on that anomaly. There, yes, feeding straight to that core place where he kept himself so aloof. And it fed from—where?

Laboriously, she traced the airy little bridge—and encountered another pattern entirely.

This one was also orderly, well-shaped and passionate, overlain with the fragile skin of a recent Healing. The humor was broader, the heart-web less guarded, more expansive. The Healer lost the bridge in a twisting interjoin of passion and affection.

"Oh." Master Healer Kestra opened her outer eyes, seeking Korval's sparkling black gaze. "They're lifemates."

CHAPTER THIRTY-NINE

There are those Scouts—and other misinformed persons—who urge that the Book of Clans be expanded to include certain non-Liaden persons.

I say to the Council now, the day the Book of Clans includes a Terran among its pages is the day Liad begins to fall!

—Excerpted from remarks made before the Council of Clans by the chairperson of the Coalition to Abolish the Liaden Scouts

"I BEG YOUR PARDON," Petrella said acidly, "they are certainly not lifemates."

The Master Healer turned to her. "Indeed they are," she said, striving for gentleness. "It is very nearly a textbook case—a shade tenuous, perhaps, but beyond mistake."

Petrella turned her head and glared at the tall a'thodelm and his taller lady, standing side-by-side at the door.

"I forbid it," she said, the Command mode crackling minor lightnings.

Kestra saw the flicker in the a'thodelm's pattern and acted to prevent a response which could only pain all.

"Forgive me," she said firmly to Petrella. "It is plain you have failed of grasping the fullness of the situation. I am not speaking of pleasant signatures on a contract and a formal announcement in *The Gazette*. I speak of a verifiable, physical *fact* which is not in any way subject to your commands."

"Lifemates?" Petrella flung back with pain-wracked scorn. "Which of them is a wizard, pray?"

"Well, now, the gaffer, he was a water-witch," the tall lady said in a peculiar, lilting voice, a glimmer of half-wild humor lighting her pattern.

The Healer frowned after the sense of the words, feeling a similarity to Terran, but unable to quite—

"A water-witch," Korval murmured in Adult-to-Adult, "is one who has the ability to locate water below ground without use of instrumentation." He flicked a glance at the Terran lady. "Correct?"

She moved her head up and down—Terran affirmative. "He found other things, too," she said in accented, though clear, Liaden. "Lost sheep. Jewelry, once or twice. A missing child. But mostly he stuck to water." She shrugged. "If you listen to the talk on New Dublin, all the ancestors were—*fey*, we say. It adds color to the family tree."

"You are yourself a wizard, then?" Petrella's voice was sharp.

The Terran lady shook her head. "No, a language professor."

"You know when the child wakes," the a'thodelm murmured from her side. "You know when I am troubled. I heard you calling me, from many miles away, and followed your voice."

"And yet neither are of the *dramliz*," the Master Healer said, firmly. "I recall when the a'thodelm was tested at Healer Hall as a child. We tested twice, for, after all, he *is* of Korval." She moved her shoulders and caught Korval's attentive eye.

"Plain meat and no sauce, the a'thodelm. Yourself—you have *some*thing, my Lord. If we are ever able to quantify it, I shall tell you."

He inclined his dark head. "You are gracious."

"*You* are dangerous—but, there. It is what one expects of Korval." She turned her attention once more to Petrella.

"Neither pretends to wizardhood, Thodelm. I suspect the only talent either ever held was the ability to recognize and meld with the other. That work has proceeded as it must—hindered, alas, by the demands of custom, *melant'i*—and kin. It may not be stopped, nor may it be undone." She showed her empty hands, palm up.

"You speak of wrapping the a'thodelm in forgetfulness, of sending the lady far away. To speak of these things is to be ill-informed. If they are separated by the length and breadth of the galaxy, still they will find each other. They are lifemates, Thodelm. If your pride cannot be thwarted, you must have the lady killed—and the child, as well. Then, the a'thodelm will be free of her."

"Yet history tells us that Master Wizard Rool Tiazan's lady lived in him after the death of her body," Korval commented from across the room.

Kestra hid her smile with a bow. "Indeed. You understand that the tie between these two may not be so potent—or it may well be potent enough. Certainly they are both strong-willed. Certainly they both love. It may be that the areas where the match is not entirely perfect are those which are not so—very—important. Who can say?"

There was a silence in the room. Korval shifted slightly, drawing all eyes to himself.

"Cry grace, Aunt Petrella," he said gently. "The game has gone to chance."

"Chance," the Terran lady murmured, a flutter of panic through her steady, beautiful pattern. "Chance without choice."

"Choice was made," A'thodelm yos'Galan said, "several times over." He took her hand, looking earnestly up into her face. "I love you, Anne Davis."

It thrilled along all the matrices of her pattern, resonating within his. She smiled. "I love you, Er Thom yos'Galan." The smile faded, and she spoke again with a certain sternness. "But we still have to talk."

"Certainly," he returned, smiling as if they were quite alone in the room. "Shall I show you the maze? We may be private there."

"All right . . ."

He turned back to the room, making his bows, pattern a dazzling, sensuous clatter.

"Master Healer," he murmured, with a propriety that belied the joy ringing through him. "Mother." He turned to face Korval and checked, the clamoring joy within him stuttering.

Carefully, silently, he bowed respect for the delm.

Straightening, he stepped back, opened the door and allowed his lady to proceed him into the hall.

"MASTER MERCHANT BEL'TARDA," Mr. pel'Kana announced from the doorway.

Daav looked wearily up from his work screen.

Luken had got a new jacket—an astonishing affair in bright blue with belled sleeves and citron buttons. The buttons flashed irritatingly when he made his bow.

"Wine for Master bel'Tarda," Daav instructed Mr. pel'Kana and waved a hand. "Sit, cousin, do, and tell me what brings you so far from the City."

"Well, it's not as far as that," Luken said seriously, disposing himself with unusual care in the leather chair across the desk. "Matter of an hour's travel, if you're unlucky in the route." He received his glass from Mr. pel'Kana and took the required sip, watching Daav trepidatiously over the rim.

Daav smiled, picked up his near-empty cup and also drank, setting the thing aside as Mr. pel'Kana closed the door.

"Well, Luken, you might as well make a clean breast, you know. I can hardly be expected to go before the Council of Clans on your behalf unless I know the awful whole."

"Council of Clans! Here now, it's nothing—" Luken sputtered, caught himself and sighed.

"It's no wonder the world finds us odd," he said severely, "when you go on giving rein to that sense of humor of yours."

"Horrid, isn't it?" Daav agreed. "Now you've vented your feelings, shall you tell me what is wrong? Pat Rin?"

"Eh? Oh, no—no. Ease your heart there—the boy's fine, though we had his mother yesterday. Why that woman insists on—Well."

He glanced down and brushed an imaginary fleck of dust from one of his improbable sleeves.

"It's about young Syntebra," he said, and raised a hurried hand. "Now, I know she's intended for Er Thom, but the thing is—well, damn it, it just won't do!"

Daav lifted an eyebrow, momentarily diverted. "No, won't it?"

"Terrified of him," Luken said warmly. "Of you, too, if it comes to that. Nothing against her. But she's only a child, you see—and mid-House, beside. Hardly knows how to go on in that world, much less rubbing High House shoulders. I'm not saying she can't make a success of things—but she needs more work than Er Thom's likely to have time to give. He's a busy one, and he stands too close to the delm."

Daav looked sharply away, picked up his glass and drained it. "Does he?"

"Well, he's your heir, isn't he? And the pair of you as cutting quick and twisty bright as any would wish—I'll tell you what, it's *tiring* trying to keep abreast! The girl would be miserable, lost and uncertain of herself." He eyed Daav consideringly.

"You alarm me, cousin. I certainly would not wish one of Korval to be the agent of such distress. However, I feel sure you are about to offer me a solution to young Syntebra's troubles."

Luken grinned, rather shamefacedly. "See through me like glass, can you? Well, it's no matter—I know I'm not a clever fellow. Here it is: I'll engage to marry Syntebra. Another child is no hardship on me—the eldest is away at school more often than she's home now-days, and Pat Rin's no trouble at all. Nexon will be put to rest and a more equitable wife can be found for Er Thom."

"Undoubtedly, a more equitable wife can be found for Er Thom," Daav murmured, possibly to himself. He looked at Luken with a grin.

"I take it the lady does not find yourself—aah—*terrifying*, cousin?"

"Not a bit of it," Luken said comfortably and smiled. "I get on with most, after all."

"So you do." Daav closed his eyes and resisted rubbing his aching forehead. He opened his eyes.

"I shall speak with Thodelm yos'Galan tomorrow," he told Luken. "However, I feel certain that your solution will be adopted. Now there is an active nursery at Trealla Fantrol, Pat Rin may be relocated for the duration of your marriage." He cocked an eyebrow. "Unless you think that unwise?"

Luken pursed his lips. "I'll speak with the boy," he said eventually, "and let you know his wishes." He sent a sharp look at Daav. "Not that he isn't fond of his cousin Er Thom, nor that young Shan doesn't look a likely child. But I would dislike going against the boy's strong inclination, if he has one."

"Certainly." Daav inclined his head. "You do well by us, cousin," he said in sudden and sincere gratitude. "I find you honor and ornament the clan."

Luken blushed, dark gold spreading across his cheeks. He glanced aside and picked up his glass.

"Kind of you," he muttered, and drank.

It took two rather hefty swallows to recover his address. He glanced at Daav.

"I'll hear from you, then?" he said hopefully.

Daav inclined his head. "I expect you may hear from me as soon as tomorrow."

"Good," said Luken. "Good." He rose. "You're a busy man, so I'll be taking my leave. Thank you."

"No trouble," Daav said, rising also and coming 'round the desk. He forestalled Luken's bow by the simple maneuver of taking him by the arm and turning him toward the door.

"Allow me to see you to your car, cousin . . ."

IT WAS RATHER LATE.

Daav had no clear notion of precisely how late. He had put the lights out some time back, preferring the room in firelight while he drank a glass or two in solitude.

Firelight had become emberlight and the glass or two had become a bottle. Daav leaned his head against the back of his chair and thought of his brother's cold face and unwarm bow.

Gods, what have I done?

He closed his eyes against the emberlight and strove not to think at all.

"You're going to have a dreadful headache tomorrow," the sweet, beloved voice commented.

With exquisite care, Daav opened his eyes and lifted his head. Er Thom was perched on the arm of the chair across the counterchance board. Someone had thrown a fresh log on the fire. His hair gleamed in the renewed brightness like a heart's ransom.

"I have," Daav said with a certain finicking precision, "a dreadful headache *now*."

"Ah." Er Thom smiled. "I rather thought you might."

"Have you come to cut my gizzard out?" Daav asked, dropping his head back against the chair. "I believe there's an appropriately dull knife in the wine table."

"I don't know that I'm particularly skilled at gizzard-cutting," Er Thom said after a moment. "Shall you like some tea?"

"Gods, at this hour? Whichever it is—" He moved a hand in negation. "No, don't disturb the servants."

"All right," Er Thom said softly. He rose and vanished into the fringes of the firelight. A minor clatter was heard from the direction of the wine table. Daav wondered somewhat blearily if the other had decided upon the knife after all.

"Drink with me, brother."

Daav opened his eyes. Er Thom was before him, limned in the firelight, holding two cups.

"Thank you," Daav said around a sudden start of tears. He accepted a cup and drank—a full mouthful—swallowed—and laughed. "Water?"

"If you drink any more wine you're likely to fall into a snore," Er Thom commented, lifting his own glass. There was a gleam of purple on his hand.

"Reinstated, darling?"

"My mother attempts to accept the outcome equitably." He smiled. "She speaks of—perhaps—accepting the child."

"Gracious of her." Daav sighed. "Will your Anne be happy with us, do you think?"

The smile grew slightly wider. "I believe it may be contrived."

"Hah. So long as my work as delm is not entirely confined to scrambling planetary traffic and threatening my kin with chains—" He shuddered and looked up into bright violet eyes.

"The window was—distressing."

Er Thom inclined his head. "I apologize for the window," he murmured. "But there is no way to close it, you see, once you are climbed through."

Daav grinned. "I suppose that's true."

Er Thom tipped his head. "May I know what Balance the delm may require of me?"

"Balance." Daav closed his eyes; opened them. "How shall the delm require Balance, when it was he did not listen to what you would tell him?"

Er Thom frowned. "I do not believe that to be the case," he said in his soft, serious way. "How should any of us have expected such an extraordinary occurrence? Recall that I gave *nubiath'a*! Indeed, it may be that such—adversity—as we met with enlivened and strengthened our bond." He bowed, slightly and with whimsy.

"Delm's Wisdom."

"Amuse yourself, do." Daav tried for a look of severity, but his mouth would keep twitching in a most undignified manner. He gave it up and grinned openly.

"*All's well that ends well,*" he quoted in Terran, "as your lady might agree. Tell her: *Be fruitful and multiply.*"

Er Thom laughed. "Tell her yourself. We shall want the delm to See us tomorrow, after all."

"Whatever for? I distinctly recall Master Healer Kestra informing us that your arrangement is beyond the ken of command or Code."

"Ah, but, you see," Er Thom said earnestly. "There is local custom to be satisfied. I would not wish to be backward in any attention the world might deem necessary."

"Certainly not. Korval has its standards, after all."

Er Thom laughed.

CHAPTER FORTY

The first attack was a hammer-blow at the Ringstars. A dozen worlds were lost at once, including that which was home to the dramliz and the place the Soldiers call Headquarters. There was rumor of a seed-ship—as high as a hundred seed-ships—sent out from Antori in the moment before it died. Much good it may do them.

Jela says The Enemy means to smash communications, then gobble up each isolated world in its own good time.

Jela says anyone with a ship is a smuggler, now. And every smuggler is a soldier.

I've never seen anything like this . . .

—Excerpted from Cantra yos'Phelium's Log Book

IT WAS EARLY, the halls yet empty of scholars, save the one who walked at Er Thom's side. When they came to a certain door, he stood away, and watched her bend over the lock, quick brown fingers making short work of the coding.

Straightening from her task, she flung him a smile and caught his hand, pulling him with her into a tiny, cluttered office smelling of book-dust and disuse.

Just within, he paused, holding her to his side while he scanned

317

the shabby and book-crammed interior. Satisfied that they were alone, he allowed them another step into the room, then turned to lock the door.

Anne laughed.

"As if we were in any danger among a crowd of fusty professors!"

Er Thom bit his lip. Of course, she did not recall. He had not doubted the wisdom of immediately summoning a Healer to ease Anne's distress. To be abducted at gunpoint, to have one's child and one's own life threatened, to make one's bow to necessity and take a life—these things were certainly best quickly smoothed from memory and peace restored to a mind unsettled by violence.

Yet now it seemed that in doing her the best service he might, he had placed her in the way of future peril. One madman with a gun did not necessarily argue another, but it was only wise to be wary.

And difficult to be wary when the memory of past danger was washed clean away.

"Er Thom?" She was frowning down at him, concern showing in her eyes. "What is it?"

He caught her other hand in his and looked seriously into her face.

"Anne, I wish you will recall—I am in very earnest, *denubia*! I wish you will recall that Liad is not a—safe place. There are those who love Terrans not at all. There are those who actively hate—who may seek to do you harm for merely being Terran, or for the direction your work takes you . . . Liadens—there is pride, you understand. It pleases many to think Liad the center of the universe and all others— lower. With some, this pleasure becomes obsession. Korval's wing is broad, but it is far better to be vigilant, and avoid rousing the delm to Balance."

"Better to be safe than sorry," Anne murmured and inclined her head. "I understand, Er Thom. Thank you." She hesitated; met his eyes once more.

"I knew how to use a pistol, once. I'm willing to brush up and carry a gun."

He smiled in relief. "That would be wise. I shall teach you, if you like it."

"I like it." She grinned, squeezed his hands and let them go, crossing the room in three of her long strides and taking a framed flat-pic down from the wall between two reverent palms.

"Er Thom," she said, as she lay the frame face down and began to ease the back away. "Aren't *you* Liaden?"

He drifted over to the desk, watching her face, downturned and intent upon her task.

"We are Korval," he said, softly. "You understand, we are not originally from the Old World—Solcintra, it was called. Cantra came from the Rim, so it states in the logs, and her co-pilot in the endeavor which raised Liad—young Tor An had been from one of the Ringstars, sent to Solcintra for schooling. Poor child, by the time his schooling was done, the Ringstars were no fit place for return."

Anne had raised her head and was watching him intently. "Every other clan on Liad can trace its origins to—Solcintra?"

"Yes, certainly. But Solcintra was only one world in what had been a vast empire." He smiled into her eyes. "And not a particularly— forward—world, at that."

"You know this," she said, very carefully, "*historically*?"

He bowed. "It is of course necessary for one who will be Korval Himself—and for one who may be delm—to have studied the log books of Cantra yos'Phelium, as well as the diaries of the delms who had come before."

She bit her lip. He had a sense of—hunger?—and a realization that, for one who studied as Anne did, such information as he had just shared might be pearls of very great price.

"One empire," she murmured. "One—language?"

"An official tongue, and world-dialects. Or so the logs lead one to surmise." He showed her his empty palms. "The logs themselves are written in a language somewhat akin to Yxtrang—so you see they are not for everyone. Korval is counted odd enough, without the world deciding that we are spawn of the enemy."

"May I see them?" Anne's voice was restrained, intense. "The logs."

Er Thom smiled. "It is entirely likely that you will be *required* to see them, beloved."

Her face eased with humor. "Home study for the new Dragon," she quipped, and turned her attention once more to the task of easing the back from the rickety old frame.

This went slowly, for Anne seemed as intent on keeping the frame in one piece as the frame itself seemed determined to fail. Her patience won in the end, however, and the frayed backing was set aside.

Atop the pic-back lay one thin square of gray paper.

Anne picked it up, frowning at the single row of letters.

"What is it?" Er Thom wondered, softly, so not to shatter her concentration.

"A notation," she murmured. "I don't quite—" She handed him the paper, shaking her head in perplexity.

A notation, indeed, and one as familiar to him as his brother's face.

"Lower half of the second quadrant, tending toward eighty degrees." He read off the piloting symbols with ease and raised his eyes to Anne. "Alas, I lack board and screens."

She stared at him. He saw the idea bloom in her eyes in the instant before she caught his arm and turned him with her toward the overfull bookshelves.

"Lower half," she murmured, moving toward the shelves, her eyes on the books as if they might up and bolt if she shifted her gaze for a moment. " . . . of the second quadrant . . ." She knelt and lay her hand along a section of spines, eyes daring to flash a question to him.

He inclined his head. "Just so."

"Tending," Anne ran her fingers lightly, caressingly, down the spines. "Tending. Toward eighty de—Dear gods."

It was a small, slim volume her forefinger teased from between two of its hulking kinsmen, bound in scuffed and grit-dyed leather, looking for all the worlds like someone's personal debt-book that had been left out in the rain.

Anne opened it reverently, long fingers exquisitely gentle among the densely-noted leaves, her face rapt as she bent over this page and that.

Er Thom moved to kneel beside her. "Is this the thing you were seeking?"

"I think . . ." She closed it softly and held it cupped in her hand as if it were a live thing and likely to escape. "I'll have to study it—get an accurate dating. It looks—it looks . . ." Her voice died away and she bent her head sharply over the little book with a gasp.

"Anne?"

She shook her head, by which he understood he was to be still and allow her time for thought.

"Er Thom?" Very unsteady, her voice, and she did not raise her face to his.

"Yes."

"There was a man—a man with a gun. I—the grad student. He killed Doctor yo'Kera. For this. To suppress this." At last she raised her head, showing him a face drawn with sorrow and eyes that sparkled tears.

"He wanted the information from me—threatened Shan." She swallowed. "I killed him. Fil Tor Kinrae."

"Yes." He reached out and stroked her cheek, lay his fingers lightly along her brow. "I know."

She bit her lip and looked deep into his eyes, her own showing desperation. "They're going to come and demand balance," she said. "His clan."

Er Thom lifted an eyebrow. "More likely they will come and most abjectly beg Korval's pardon for the error of owning a child who would abduct and threaten yourself and our son." He moved his shoulders. "In any wise, it is a case for the delm."

"Is it?"

"Indeed it is," he returned firmly. "Shall I fetch you a Healer now, Anne?"

"You did that before." She bent her head and reached out to take his hand, weaving their fingers together with concentration, the ring he had given her scintillant against her skin.

"I think," she said softly. "I think I'll try it without—forgetting. It's not—it seems very—misty. As if it happened a long time ago . . ." She looked up with a smile. "If things start to slip, I'll let you know. Okay?"

"A bargain. And in the meanwhile you shall practice with your pistol, eh?"

"I'll practice with my pistol," she promised, and glanced down at the little book she held so protectively. She looked back to Er Thom's face. "Will—the delm—want to suppress—assuming it's real!—this information?"

"The last I had heard, the delm was advised by his grandmother in matters such as these," Er Thom said carefully. "That being, you understand, Grandmother Cantra. Her philosophy, as seen through the logs, leads me to believe that the delm will not wish to suppress anything of the sort, though he may very well have certain necessities with regard to the *manner* in which it is made available to the world." He inclined his head. "For the good of the clan."

"I—see." One more glance at the book, a brilliant look into his eyes and a warm squeeze of her hand. "Well, it's too valuable to stay here, so I guess I'll just drop it in the delm's lap before we go on our honey-trip." She grinned. "Which reminds me, if we don't move soon, we're going to be late for our own wedding."

"Now that," Er Thom said, "would be very improper. I suggest we leave immediately."

"I suggest," Anne murmured, swaying lightly toward him, "that we leave in just a minute."

"Much more appropriate," he agreed, and raised his face for her kiss.

SCOUT'S PROGRESS

For the binjali crew:
past, present and future

CHAPTER ONE

Typically, the clan which gains the child of a contract-marriage pays a marriage fee to the mating clan, as well as other material considerations. Upon consummation of contract, the departing spouse is often paid a bonus.

Contract-marriage is thus not merely a matter of obeying the Law, but an economic necessity to some of the Lower Houses, where a clanmember might be serially married for most of his or her adult life.

—From "Marriage Customs of Liad"

"SINIT, *MUST* YOU READ AT TABLE?"

Voni's voice was clear and carrying. It was counted a good feature, Aelliana had heard, though not so pleasing as her face.

At the moment, face and voice held a hint of boredom, as befitted an elder sister confronted with the wearisome necessity of disciplining a younger.

"No, I'm just at a good part," Sinit returned without lifting her head from over the page. She put out a hand and groped for her teacup.

"Really," Voni drawled as Aelliana chose a muffin from the center platter and broke it open. "Even Aelliana knows better than to bring a book to table!"

"It's for anthropology," Sinit mumbled, fingers still seeking her cup. "Truly, I am nearly done, if only you'll stop plaguing me—"

"If you keep on like that," Aelliana murmured, eyes on her plate, "your teacup will be overset, and Ran Eld will ring down a terrific scold. Put the book aside, Sinit, do. If you hurry your breakfast you can still finish reading before your tutor comes."

The youngest of them sighed gustily, and closed the book with rather more force than necessary.

"I suppose," she said reluctantly. "It is the sort of thing Ran Eld likes to go on about, isn't it? And all the worse if I had spilt my tea. Still, it's a monstrous interesting book—I had no idea what queer folk Terrans are! Well," she amended, prudently sliding the book onto her lap, "I knew they were queer, of course—but only imagine marrying who you like, without even a word from your delm and—and kissing those who are not kin! And—"

"*Sinit!*" Voni put a half-eaten slice of toast hastily back onto her plate, her pretty face pale. She swallowed. "That's disgusting."

"No," Sinit said eagerly, leaning over her plate, to the imminent peril of her shirt-ribbons. "No, it's not disgusting at all, Voni. It's only that they're Terran and don't know any better. How can they behave properly when there are no delms to discipline and no Council of Clans to keep order? And as for marrying whomever one pleases—why that's exactly the same, isn't it? If one lives clanless, with each individual needing to make whatever alliance seems best for oneself—without Code or Book of Clans to guide them, how else—"

"Sinit." Aelliana thought it best to stem this impassioned explanation before Voni's sensibilities moved her to banish their younger sister from the dining hall altogether. "You were going to eat quickly—were you not?—and go into the parlor to finish reading."

"Oh." Recalled to the plan, she picked up a muffin-half and coated it liberally with jam. "I think it would be very interesting to be married," she said, which for Sinit passed as a change of topic.

"Well, I hardly think you shall find out soon," Voni said, with a return of her usual asperity. "Especially if you persist in discussing such—perverse—subjects at table."

"Oh, pooh," Sinit replied elegantly, cramming jam-smeared muffin into her mouth. "It's only that you've been married an hundred times, and so find the whole matter a dead bore."

Voni's eyes glittered dangerously. "Not—quite—an hundred, dear sister. I flatter myself that the profit the clan has made from my contract-marriages is not despicable."

Nor was it, Aelliana acknowledged, worrying her muffin into shreds. At thirty-one, Voni had been married five times—each to Mizel's clear benefit. She was pretty, nice-mannered in company and knew her Code to a full-stop—a valuable daughter of the clan. Just yesterday, she had let drop that there was a sixth marriage in the delm's eye, to young Lord pel'Rula—and that would be a coup, indeed, and send Voni's quarter-share to dizzying height.

"Aelliana's been married," Sinit announced somewhat stickily. "Was it interesting and delightful?"

Aelliana stared fixedly at her plate, grateful for the shielding curtain of her hair. "No," she whispered.

Voni laughed. "Aelliana," she said, reaching into the High Tongue for the Mode of Instruction, "was pleased to allow the delm to know that she would never again accept contract."

Round-eyed, Sinit turned to Aelliana, sitting still and stricken over her shredded breakfast. "But the—the parties, and all the new clothes, and—"

"Good-morning, daughters!" Birin Caylon, Delm Mizel, swept into the dining room on the regal arm of her son Ran Eld, the nadelm. She allowed him to seat her and fetch her a cup of tea as she surveyed the table.

"Sinit, you have jam on your face. Aelliana, I wish you will either eat or not, and in anywise leave over torturing your food. Voni, my dear, Lady pel'Rula calls tomorrow midday. I shall wish to have you by me."

Voni simpered. "Yes, Mother."

Mizel turned to her son, who had taken his accustomed place beside her. "You and I are to meet in an hour, are we not? Be on your mettle, sir: I expect to be shown the benefits of keeping the bulk of our capital in Yerlind Shares."

"There are none," Aelliana told her plate, very quietly.

Alas, not quietly enough. Ran Eld paused with a glass of morning-wine half-way to his lips, eyebrows high in disbelief.

"I beg your pardon?"

I've gone mad, Aelliana thought, staring at the crumbled ruin of her untasted breakfast. Only a madwoman would call Ran Eld's judgment thus into question, the nadelm being—disinclined—to support insolence from any of the long list of his inferiors. Woe for Aelliana that her name was written at the top of that list.

Beg his pardon, she told herself urgently, cold hands fisted on her lap. *Bend the neck, take the jibe, be meek, be too poor a thing to provoke attack.*

It was a strategy that had served a thousand times in the past. Yet this morning her head remained in its usual half-bowed attitude, face hidden by the silken shield of her hair, eyes fixed to her plate as if she intended to memorize the detail of each painted flower fading into the yellowing china.

"Aelliana." Ran Eld's voice was a purr of pure malice. Too late for begging pardons now, she thought, and clenched her hands the tighter.

"I believe you had an—opinion," Ran Eld murmured, "in the matter of the clan's investments. Come, I beg you not be backward in hinting us toward the proper mode. The good of the clan must carry all before it."

Yes, certainly. Excepting only that the good of the clan had long ago come to mean the enlargement of Ran Eld Caylon's hoard of power. Aelliana touched her tongue to her lips, unsurprised to find that she was trembling.

"Yerlind Shares," she said, quite calmly, and in the mode of Instruction, as if he were a recalcitrant student she was bound to put right, "pay two percent, which must be acknowledged a paltry return, when the other funds offer from three to four-point-one. Neither is its liquidity superior, since Yerlind requires three full days to forward cantra equal to shares. Several of the other, higher-yield options require as little as twenty-eight hours for conversion."

There was a small pause, then her mother's voice, shockingly matter-of-fact: "I wish you will raise your head when you speak, Aelliana, and show attention to the person with whom you are conversing. One would suppose you to have less *melant'i* than a Terran, the way you are forever hiding your face. I can't think how you came to be so rag-mannered."

Voni tittered, which was expectable. From Ran Eld came only stony silence, in which Aelliana heard her ruin. Nothing would save her now—neither meekness nor apology would buy Ran Eld's mercy when she had shamed him before his delm and his juniors.

Aelliana brought her head up with a smooth toss that cast her hair behind her shoulders and met her brother's eyes.

Brilliantly blue, bright as first-water sapphires, they considered her blandly from beneath arched golden brows. Ran Eld Caylon was a pretty man. Alas, he was also vain, and dressed more splendidly than his station, using a heavy hand in the matter of jewels.

Now, he set his wine glass aside and took a moment to adjust one of his many finger-rings.

"Naturally," he murmured to the room at large, "Aelliana's discourse holds me fascinated. I am astonished to find her so diligent a scholar of economics."

"And yet," Mizel Herself countered unexpectedly, "she makes a valid point. Why should we keep our capital at two percent when we might place it at four?"

"The Yerlind Shares are tested by time and found to be sound," Ran Eld replied. "These—other options—my honored sister displays have been less rigorously tested."

"Ormit is the youngest of the funds I consider," Aelliana heard herself state, still in the mode of Instruction. "Surely fifty years is time enough to prove a flaw, should it exist?"

"And what do I know of the Ormit Fund?" Ran Eld actually frowned and there was a look at the back of his eyes that boded not so well for one Aelliana, once the delm was out of hearing.

She met his glare with a little thrill of terror, but answered calmly, nonetheless.

"A study of the Exchange for as little as a twelve-day will show you Ormit's mettle upon the trading floor," she replied,

"Information on their investments and holdings can be had anytime through the data-net."

The frown deepened, but his voice remained dulcet, as ever. "Enlighten me, sister—do you aspire to become the clan's financial advisor?"

"She might do better," Mizel commented, sipping her tea, "than the present one."

Ran Eld turned his head so sharply his earrings jangled. "Mother—"

She held up a hand. "Peace. It seems Aelliana has given the subject thought. A test of her consideration against your own may be in order." She looked across the table.

"What say you, daughter, to taking charge of your own quarter-share and seeing what you can make of it?"

Take charge of her own quarter-share? Four entire cantra to invest as she would? Aelliana clenched her fists until the nails scored her palms.

"Turn Aelliana loose upon the world with four cantra in her hand?" Ran Eld lifted an elegant shoulder. "And when the quarter is done and she has lost it?"

"I scarcely think she will be so inept as to lose her seed," Mizel said with some asperity. "The worst that may happen, in my view, is that she will return us four cantra—at the end of a year."

"A year?" That was Voni, as ever Ran Eld's confederate. "To allow Aelliana such liberty for an entire year may not be to the best good, ma'am."

"Oh?" Mizel put her cup down with a clatter, eyes seeking the face of her middle daughter. "Well, girl? Have you an opinion regarding the length of time the experiment shall encompass?"

"A quarter is too short," Aelliana said composedly. "Two quarters might begin to show a significant deviation. However, it is my understanding that the delm desires proof of a trend to set against facts established and in-house. A year is not too long for such a proof."

"A year it is then," the delm announced and flicked a glance to her heir. "You will advance your sister her quarter-share no later than this evening. We shall see this tested on the floor of the exchange itself."

Sinit laughed at that, and Ran Eld looked black. Voni poured herself a fresh cup of tea.

Aelliana pushed carefully back from the table, rose and bowed to the delm.

"If I may be excused," she murmured, scarcely attending what she said; "I must prepare for a class."

Mizel waved a careless hand and Aelliana made her escape.

"But this is precisely the manner in which Terrans handle affairs of investment!" Sinit said excitedly. "Each person is responsible for his or her own fortune. I think such a system is very exciting, don't you?"

"I think," Voni's clear voice followed Aelliana into the hallway, "that anthropology is not at all good for you, sister."

CHAPTER TWO

Each person shall provide his clan of origin with a child of his blood, who will be raised by the clan and belong to the clan, despite whatever may later occur to place the parent beyond the clan's authority. And this shall be Law for every person of every clan.

—From the Charter of the Council of Clans
Made in the Sixth Year After Planetfall
City of Solcintra, Liad

"LADY YOS'GALAN," the butler announced from the doorway.

The man at the desk looked up from his screen, rose and came forward, hands outstretched in welcome.

"Anne. You're up early." His Terran bore a Liaden accent, lighter than a year ago, and he smiled with genuine pleasure. "Are you well? My brother, your lifemate—and my most excellent nephew!—they enjoy their usual robust health?"

Tall Anne Davis grinned down at him, squeezing his hands affectionately before releasing him.

"You only saw us two days ago," she said. "What could go wrong so quickly?"

"Any number of things!" he assured her, striking a tragic pose that won a ripple of her ready laughter. "Only see how it comes about: This morning I am a free man—this evening, I am affianced!"

Trouble crossed her mobile face, as well it might, she being Terran and holding little patience with contract-marriage. Intellectually, she allowed the efficiency of custom; emotionally, she turned her face aside and would far rather speak of other matters.

"Is it going to be very dreadful for you, Daav?" There was sisterly sympathy in her voice, acceptable from the lifemate of his foster-brother. And indeed, Daav thought wryly, rather more than he had received from his own sister, who, upon hearing the news of his impending contract, had allowed herself an ironic congratulation on duty embraced—at long last.

"Ah, well. One must obey the law, after all." He moved his shoulders, dismissing the subject, and moved toward the wine table.

"What may I give you to drink?"

"Is there tea?"

"As a matter of fact, there is," he said, and drew a cup for each from the silver urn. He carried both to the desk and resumed his seat, waving her to the chair at the corner.

"Now, tell me what takes you abroad so early in the day."

Anne sipped and set her cup aside with a tiny click, leveling a pair of very serious brown eyes.

"I am in need of Delm's Instruction," she stated in the High Tongue, in the very proper mode of Respect to the Delm.

Daav blinked. "Dear me."

Anne's mouth twitched along one corner, but she otherwise preserved her countenance.

Sighing lightly, he glanced down at his hands—long, clever hands, blunt-nailed, calloused along palms and fingertips. He did not care overmuch for ornamentation and wore but a single ring: A band that covered the third finger of his left hand from knuckle to knuckle, the lush enamel work depicting a tree in full leaf over which a dragon hovered on half-furled wings. Clan Korval's Ring, which marked him delm.

"Daav?" Anne's voice was carefully neutral.

He shook himself and looked back to her face, one eyebrow quirking in self-mockery.

"Perhaps you had best make me acquainted with the details of your requirement," he said, in the blessed casualness of Terran. "The delm may not be necessary, tiresome fellow that he is."

Once again, the mere twitch of a smile.

"All right," she said, following him obligingly into her own tongue.

Daav relaxed. It was not entirely clear how much this very unLiaden member of his clan understood of *melant'i*. He had never known her to make a blunder in society, but that might well be put to the account of her lifemate, who would certainly never allow her to place herself in a position of jeopardy. Whether now moved by understanding or intuition, she was willing to allow him to put off for the moment the burden of his delmhood, and that suited Daav very well.

"In obedience to the Delm's Word," Anne said, after another sip of tea, "I've been studying the diaries of the past delms of Korval, as well as the log books kept by Cantra yos'Phelium, the—inceptor— of the clan."

Daav inclined his head. It was necessary for every member of the Line Direct to master the knowledge contained in Diaries and Log. Terran though she was, Anne stood but two lives from the Ring herself—another subject of which she held shy. Much of the Diaries had to do with politics—doubtless she had come across the record of an ancient Balancing and found herself—understandably!— fuddled.

Daav smiled, for here was no case for Delm's Instruction, but only that teaching which elder kin might gladly offer junior.

"There is a passage in the Diaries which is not perfectly plain?" He grinned. "You amaze me."

She returned the grin full measure, then sobered, eyes darkening, though she did not speak.

"So tell me," Daav invited, since it became clear that such prompting was required, "what have you found in Korval's lamentable history to disturb you?"

"Hardly—entirely—lamentable," Anne said softly, then, firmer: "The Contract."

"So?" He allowed both brows to rise. "You doubt the authenticity of Cantra's Contract with the Houses of Solcintra?"

"Oh, no," she said, with the blitheness of the scholar-expert she was, "it's authentic enough. What I doubt is Korval's assumption of continuance."

"Assumption. And it seems to me so plain-written a document! Quite refreshingly stark, in fact. But I must ask why my *cha'leket* has not been able to resolve this difficulty for you. We have had much the same instruction in these matters, as he stands the delm's heir."

She looked at him solemnly. "I didn't ask him. He's got quite enough to explain about the Tree."

"You question *Jelaza Kazone*? That is bold." He waved toward the windowed wall behind him, where the Tree's monumental trunk could be glimpsed through a tangle of flowers and shrubbery. "I would have been tempted to begin with something a bit less definite, I confess."

Anne chuckled. "Pig-headed," she agreed and moved on immediately, leaving him no time to contemplate the startling picture conjured by this metaphor. "Er Thom says the Tree—talks."

Well, and it did, Daav acknowledged, though he would not perhaps have phrased it so—or even yet—to her. However, the Tree *did*—communicate—to those of the Line Direct. Er Thom, that most unfanciful of men, knew this for fact and had thus informed his lifemate, against whom his heart held no secret.

"I see that he has his work cut out for him," Daav said gravely. "Balance therefore dictates my defense of the Contract. It is fitting. I make a clean breast at once: The Contract does not speak, other than what sense the written words convey."

"Entirely sufficient to the discussion," Anne returned. "The written words convey, in paragraph eight, that—" She paused, flashing him a conscious look. "Maybe you'd like to call a copy up on the screen, so you can see what I'm talking about?"

"No need; the Contract is one of—several—documents my delm required I commit to memory during training." He sipped tea, set the cup aside and raised his eyes to hers. "I understand your trouble has root in the provision regarding the continuing duties of the Captain and her heirs. That seems the plainest-writ of all. Show me where I am wrong."

"It's very plainly written," Anne said calmly. "Of course it would be—they were making such a desperate gamble. The Captain's responsibilities are very carefully delineated, as is the chain of command. In a situation where assumption might kill people, nothing is assumed. I have no problem with the *original* intent of the document. My problem stems from the assumption held by Clan Korval that the Contract is still in force."

Oh, dear. But how delightfully Terran, after all. Daav inclined his head.

"There is no period of expiration put forth," he pointed out calmly. "Nor has the Council of Clans yet relieved Korval of its contractual duty. The delm of Korval is, by the precise wording of that eighth paragraph, acknowledged to be Captain and sworn to act for the best benefit of the passengers." He smiled.

"Which has come to mean all Liadens—and I do acknowledge the elasticity of that interpretation. However, one could hardly limit oneself to merely overlooking the well-being of the descendants of the original Houses of Solcintra. Entirely aside from the fact that Grandmother Cantra would never have accepted a contract that delineated a lower class of passenger and a higher, the Council of Clans has become the administering body. And the Council of Clans, so it states in the Charter, speaks for all clans." He moved his shoulders, offering another smile.

"Thus, the Captain's duty increases."

"Daav, that Contract is a thousand years old!"

"Near enough," he allowed, nodding in the Terran way.

She closed her eyes and took a deep breath, perhaps to calm herself. Eyes still closed, she said, flatly, "Paragraph eight makes you the king of the world."

"No, only recall those very painstaking lists of duty! I'm very little more than a tightly-channeled—what is the phrase?—feral trump?"

"Wild card." She opened her eyes. "You do acknowledge the—

the Captain's *melant'i*? You consider yourself the overseer of the whole world—of all the passengers?"

"I must," he said quietly. "The Contract is in force."

She expelled air in a *pouf*, half laugh, half exasperation. "A completely Liaden point of view!"

Daav lifted a brow. "My dear child, I'm no more Liaden than you are."

Her eyes came swiftly up, face tensing—and relaxing into a smile. "You mean that you've been a Scout. I grant you have more experience of the universe than I ever will. Which is why I find it so particularly odd—the Council of Clans must have forgotten the Contract even exists! A thousand years? Surely you're putting yourself—the clan—at risk by taking on such a duty now?"

"Argued very like a Liaden," Daav said with a grin, and raised a hand to touch the rough twist of silver hanging in his right ear. "It does not fall within the scope of Korval's *melant'i* to suppose what the Council may or may not have forgotten. The second copy of the Contract was seen in open Council three hundred years ago—at the time of the last call upon Captain's Justice."

"Three hundred years?"

He nodded, offering her the slip of a smile. "Not a very arduous duty, you see. I oversee the passengers' well-being as I was taught by my delm, guided by Diaries and Log—and anticipate no opportunity to take on the *melant'i* of *king*."

Silence. Anne's eyes were fixed on a point somewhat beyond his shoulder. A frown marred the smoothness of her brow.

"I have not satisfied you," Daav said gently. "And the pity is, you know, that the delm can do no better."

She fixed on his face, mouth curving ruefully. "I'll work on it," she said, sounding somewhat wistful. "Though I'm not sure I'm cut out for talking Trees and thousand-year Captains."

"It's an odd clan," Daav conceded with mock gravity. "Mad as moonbeams. Anyone will say so."

"Misspeak the High House of Korval? I think not." Anne grinned and stood, holding out her hand. "Thank you for your time. I'm sorry to be such a poor student."

"Nothing poor at all, in the scholar who asks why." He rose and took her hand. "Allow me to walk you to your car. Your lifemate still intends to bear me company tonight, does he not? I won't know how to go on if he denies me his support."

"As if he would," Anne said with a shake of her head. "And you'd go on exactly as you always do, whether he's with you or not."

"Ah, no, you wrong me! Er Thom is my entree into the High Houses. His manners open all doors."

"Whereas Korval Himself finds all doors barred against him," she said ironically.

"That must be the case, if there were more students of history among us. But, there, scholarship is a dying art! No one memorizes the great events anymore—gossip and triviality are all."

Halfway across the sun-washed patio, Anne paused, looking down at him from abruptly serious brown eyes.

"How many is 'several'?"

He lifted a brow. "I beg your pardon?"

"You said you'd had to memorize 'several' documents, besides the Contract. I wondered—"

"Ah." He bowed slightly. "I once calculated—in an idle moment, you know!—that it would require three-point-three *relumma* to transcribe the material I have memorized. You must understand that I have committed to memory only the most vital information, in case the resources of *Jelaza Kazone*'s library be—unavailable—to me."

"Three-point-three. . ." Anne shook her head sharply. "Are you—all right?"

"I am Korval," Daav said, with an austerity that surprised him quite as much as her. "Sanity is a secondary consideration."

"And Er Thom—Er Thom has had the same training."

So that was what distressed her of a sudden. Daav smiled. "Much of the same training, yes. But you must remember that Er Thom memorizes entire manifests for the pleasure of it."

She laughed. "Too true!" She bent in a swoop and kissed his cheek—a gesture of sisterly affection that warmed him profoundly. "Take care, Daav."

"Take care, Anne. Until soon."

She crossed the patio with her long stride and slipped into the waiting car. Daav watched until the car went 'round the first curve in the drive, then reluctantly went back into the house, to his desk and the delm's work.

CHAPTER THREE

Those who enter Scout Academy emerge after rigorous training capable of treating equitably with societies unimaginably alien, some savage beyond belief

Scouts are by definition courageous, brilliant, supremely adaptable and endlessly resourceful.

—Excerpted from "All About the Liaden Scouts"

"THE QUESTION we address in this scenario," Aelliana replied sharply, "is not, 'am I able to perform this level of math without a computer lab to back me up?' but, 'shall I acknowledge the effort to be impossible, and give myself up to die'?"

The six students—five Scouts and a field engineer—exchanged glances, doubtless startled by her vehemence. So be it. If startlement bought them life, their instructor had served them well. She inclined her head and continued.

"I consider that any student still enrolled at this point in the course will possess sufficient memory and strength of will to win through to life, provided they also possess a ship with a functioning Jump unit."

Her students looked at her expectantly.

"Availability of the ven'Tura Tables is useful, but the full tables are not required if the following can be determined: Your initial mass within three percent. Your initial Jump charge to within twenty percent as long as it falls within the pel'Endra Ratio—which, as you know by now, may be derived using the local intrinsic electron counterspin and approximate mass-curve of the nearest large mass. If you are outside a major gravity well you may ignore the Ratio and proceed." She paused to consider six rapt faces, six pairs of avid eyes, before concluding the list of necessaries.

"You must, finally and most importantly, have lines one through twenty and one-ninety through one-ninety-nine of the basic table memorized."

Someone groaned. Aelliana suspected Var Mon, youngest and least repressible of the six, and fixed him with a stern eye.

"Recall the problem: You are stranded in an unexplored sector, coordinates lost, main comp and navigation computer destroyed or useless. Your goal must be to arrive within hailing distance of one or more space-going worlds. You will break many regulations by applying the approach I outline, but you will adhere to the highest regulation: Survive."

She paused.

"This approach requires thought before implementation: You must know the system-energy coordinates of the location you will be Jumping to before you arrive. There is opportunity for error here, as the Jump equation requires you to transform your current mass-energy ratio into one exactly equivalent to that of the rescue destination. Therefore, the initial definition, including the first assumption, must be exact to within several decimal places, to assure a match of both magnetic and temporal magnitudes."

Once more Aelliana surveyed their faces; saw several pair of doubtful eyes. Well for them to doubt. The danger was real: A mismatched equation meant implosion, translation into a mass, explosion—death, in a word. It was hers to demonstrate that such a situation as the problem described—all too common in the duty the Scouts took for themselves—was survivable. She raised a hand.

"A demonstration," she said. "Please provide the following: Rema—an existing system equation."

It came, a shade too glib. Aelliana 'scribed it to the autoboard behind her via the desk-remote, sparing a mental smile for Scout mischief. Every class thought they would catch her out with a bit of clever foolery. Every class learned its error—eventually.

"Var Mon—a reasonable mass and charge for your ship—" He supplied it and she called on the others, bringing the portions of the equation together and transcribing them to the autoboard. Now.

"Overlooking for the present that one marooned in Solcintra Port might just as easily call a taxi—this is a survivable situation. One could indeed Jump from Solcintra to the outer fringe of Terra system by deriving the spin rates from the tables—note line fourteen and its match in line one-ninety-seven, part three for the proof."

There was sheepish titter from the class, which Aelliana affected not to hear. Really, to assume she would fail of knowing the coords for the largest spaceport on the planet! She raised her hand, demanding serious attention.

"To our next meeting you will bring the proof just mentioned, with an illustration of derived figures. Also, an explanation of the most dangerous assumption made by the student supplying the Terran system equations."

She looked around the half-circle. Several students were still 'scribing into their notetakers. Scout Corporal Rema ven'Deelin, who had an eidetic memory, was staring with haze-eyed intensity at the autoboard.

"Questions?" Aelliana murmured as the chittering of note-keys faded into silence.

"Scholar Caylon, will you partner with me?" That was Var Mon, irrepressible as always.

"I fear you would find me entirely craven in the matter of fighting off savage beasts or in conversing with primitive peoples," she said, bending her head in bogus scrutiny of the desk-remote.

"Never should I risk losing such a piloting resource to savage beasts! You should stay snug in the ship, on my honor!"

Rema laughed. "Don't let him cozen you, Scholar—he only wants someone to do the brain work while he sleeps. Though it is true," she added thoughtfully, "that Var Mon is uniquely suited to—ahh—*grunt-work*—eh, Baan?"

Scout Pilot Baan yo'Nelon moved his shoulders expressively as Var Mon slid down in his chair, the picture of mortification.

"Never, never, never shall I overlive the tale," he groaned. "Scholar Caylon, have pity! Rescue me from these brutes who call themselves comrades!"

But this was only more of Var Mon's foolery, entirely safe to ignore. Aelliana did so, rising to signal the end of the session.

Her class rose as one student and bowed respect.

"Thanks to you, Scholar, for an astonishing lesson," said Field Technician Qiarta tel'Ozan, who, as eldest, was often spokesperson for the class. "It is, as always, a delight to behold the process of your thought."

Prettily enough said, but inaccurate—deadly inaccurate for any of these, whose lives depended upon the precision of their calculations. Aelliana brought her hand up sharply, commanding the group's attention.

"Beholding the process of my thought may delight," she said, shaking her hair away from her face and looking at them as they stood before her, one by solemn one. "But you must never forget that mathematics is *reality*, describing relationships of space, time, distance, velocity. Mathematics can keep you alive, or it can kill you. It is not for the weak-willed, or—" she glanced at Var Mon, to Rema's not-so-secret delight—"for the lazy. The equations elucidate *what is*. Knowing what is, you must act, quickly and without hesitation." Her hand had begun to shake. She lowered it to her side, surreptitiously curling cold fingers into a fist.

"I do not wish to hear that one of my students has died stupidly, for want of the boldness to grasp and use what the calculations have clearly shown."

There was a moment's silence before the field tech bowed again: Honor-to-the-Master. "We shall not shame you, Scholar."

Aelliana inclined her head; her hair slipped forward, curtaining her face. "I expect not. Good-day. We meet again Trilsday-noon."

"Good-day, Scholar," her students murmured respectfully

and filed out, Rema and Var Mon already involved in some half-whispered debate.

Aelliana sank back into the instructor's slot, dawdling over the simple task of clearing the autoboard and forwarding copies of the lecture to her office comp and to Director Barq.

Chonselta Technical College employed Scholar of Subrational Mathematics Aelliana Caylon with pride, so the director often said. Certainly, it prided itself on her seminar in practical mathematics. What a coup for the college's *melant'i*, after all, that Scout Academy sent its most able cadets to Chonselta Tech for honing.

Such reputation for excellence earned her a bonus, most semesters, a fact she had never seen fit to mention to her brother. Ran Eld liked it best when she bowed low and gave him "sir" as she surrendered her wages. Indeed, he had once struck her for her infernal chattering, which action had, remarkably, earned him the delm's frown. But Aelliana took good care never to chatter to her brother again.

The copies were made and sent, the autoboard was clear. The hall beyond the open door was empty; she sensed no patient, silent Scout awaiting her. They learned quickly enough that she was tongue-tied and graceless outside of class. This far into the semester no one was likely to disturb her uneasy peace with an offer of escort.

Yet she sat there, head bent, eyes on her hands, folded into quiet on the desk. She bore no rank within Mizel; her single ring was a death-gift from her grandmother. Aelliana stared at the ancient weavings and interlockings until the scarred silver blurred into a smear of gray.

How could she have been so foolish? Her mind, released from the discipline of instruction, returned to its earlier worries. Whatever was she thinking, to challenge Ran Eld's authority, to call his judgment into question and shame him before the delm? The last half year had seen a decrease in her brother's vigilance over herself. She had dared to believe—and now this. A slight that held no hope of passing unavenged, born of three words, whispered in a lapse of that essential wariness . . . Aelliana bit her lip.

Peace lay in meekness, safety in invisibility. To care—about anything!—to lift up her face and challenge the dreary, daily what-is—that was to become visible. And in exposure to Ran Eld's eye lay an end to both safety and peace.

In the warm classroom, Aelliana shivered. Resolutely, she unfolded her hands, placed the remote precisely into its place and rose, going down the hall silent and unnoticed, head bowed and eyes fixed on the floor directly before her.

CRAVEN, she had tarried long in her office and returned home in the cool evening, ghosted across the dim foyer and up the front stairway, toward her rooms.

He burst from the shadows on the second floor landing, catching her hard around the wrist.

Aelliana froze, wordlessly enduring the touch. His fingers tightened, ring-bands cutting into her flesh.

"We missed you at Prime Meal, sister," he murmured and she could not quite damp her shudder. Ran Eld laughed.

"How you hate me, Aelliana. Eh?" He shook her wrist, rings biting deeper. "You were bold enough at breakfast, were you not? Raised your head and stared me in the eye. I fancied I saw a bit of the old wildness there, but mayhap it was a trick of the light. Best to be certain, however, so one knows how to proceed."

That quickly he moved, knotting her hair in his free hand and wrenching her head up.

She gasped—a whispered scream—and closed her eyes against a surge of sick panic. Thus had her husband handled her, time and again, until her body grew to loathe the touch of any hand, kindly or severe.

"Look at me!" Ran Eld snapped. Precisely thus had *he* commanded her. Twice, perhaps, in the very beginning, she had willfully kept her eyes closed. He very soon broke her of such nonsense.

Half-strangled with fright, she forced her eyes open.

For an age she hung suspended in the malice of her brother's glare, the mauling of her wrist and the misuse of scalp and neck muscles reduced by terror to the veriest nothings.

"So." He twisted her knotted hair more tightly, perhaps hoping for another outcry. When none came forth, he brought his face close to hers, eyes glittering in the dimness of the landing.

"It occurs to me, *sister*," he purred, breath breaking hot against her cheek, "that you give very little toward the upkeep of this clan. Such paltry wages as you bring me from your teaching are hardly more than might be made by one or two well-considered contracts."

Her heart lurched. She forced herself to swallow, to hang limp in his grasp and keep her eyes open against the sear of his anger.

"The delm," she whispered, voice trembling, "the delm gave me her Word. I am acquitted of more marriages."

"So you are," Ran Eld murmured, eyes glinting. "However, a new delm may very well hold a new understanding of the clan's necessities and the duty owed by—some." He smiled suddenly, eyes raking her face.

"Why, I do believe you had not thought of that! Poor Aelliana, did no one tell you that nadelms become delms?"

Her face must have shown the full measure of her dismay for he laughed then and released her with a shove that sent her reeling against the landing-rail.

"I am delighted we have had this opportunity for discussion," Ran Eld said, bowing with broad irony. "It would have been a dreadful thing, indeed, to allow you to continue on with no anticipation of the pleasant future to sustain you."

He laughed once more and shook his lace into order. Aelliana huddled where she had been flung, hands gripping the rail so tightly her fingers cramped.

Her brother turned to go; turned back.

"Ah, yes, there was something else," he said with studied negligence. One hand moved; four coins flashed in the dimness, falling. "Your quarter-share."

He smiled.

"Invest wisely, sister. And do remember to give me a written report on the progress of your portfolio every twelve-day. I would be behindhand in my duty if I did not closely oversee so chancy a venture." He bowed. "Good-night, Aelliana. Dream well."

He was gone. At last she shut her dry eyes, listening as his footsteps faded down the stairs and crossed the stone-floored foyer. A moment later she heard the door to the parlor creak on its ancient hinges, hesitate, and fall closed.

Aelliana sank to her knees on the thin carpet. Gods, how could she have been so stupid? How could she have forgotten, when from that single irrefutable fact came all that she was today: Nadelms became delms.

Of course they did.

And she, blind fool, to think Delm's Word would shield her forever; to believe that she had only to appease Ran Eld sufficiently, to show that she did not—had never—wanted it. To think that, eventually, matters would mend.

Ran Eld would be delm someday; gods willing, not soon.

But when he finally came into his rightful estate there was one task he would immediately set himself to accomplish: The annihilation of Aelliana Caylon, his old and bitter enemy.

He would kill her, she thought, shuddering. He would breed her until her body broke, choosing such husbands as would discover the first to be a paragon of gentle virtue. He would invite her to beg his mercy and glory in refusing it; he would slap her face in company and fling her into walls for the pleasure of hearing her cry.

Gods, why had she never seen that every time the current delm stayed Ran Eld's hand, two blows were banked for later delivery?

I must leave.

The thought was so shocking, so perfect, that she raised her head, shaking tangled hair away from her face, the better to stare into the dim air. Terrans lived clanless, did they not? And by all accounts prospered—or the clever ones did. One needed only be canny in one's investments, and—

Investments.

She flung forward, scrabbling among the frayed rug-loops. Her frantic fingers found them quickly; she cradled their coolness in her hot palm, breathing fast and hard.

Four cantra.

Not a fortune, certainly, though she approached seven, counting her hoarded bonuses. It might well be enough to buy her free of a future where Ran Eld was delm.

Clutching her meager treasure, she lurched to her feet. She would leave the clan, leave Liad, start anew among the free-living Terrans. She would go now. Tonight.

She stowed the four cantra in her right sleeve-pocket, sealing the opening with care.

Then she went, silent and breath-caught, down the stairs. She crossed the foyer like a waft of breeze and let herself out the front door and into the mist-laced night.

CHAPTER FOUR

As each individual strives to serve the clan, so shall the clan provide what is necessary for the best welfare of each. Within the clan shall be found, truth, kinship, affection and care. Outside of the clan shall be found danger and despite.

Those whom the clan, in sorrow, rejects, shall be Accepted of no other clan. They shall neither seek to return to their former kin nor shall they demand quarter-share, food or succor.

To be outside of the clan is to be dead to the clan.

—**Excerpted from the** *Liaden Code of Proper Conduct*

DAAV CAME INTO THE SMALL PARLOR, eyebrows up.

"Good evening, brother. Am I late?"

"Not at all," Er Thom yos'Galan replied, turning from the window with a smile. "I came before time, so that we might talk, if you would."

"Why would I not? Wine?"

"Thank you."

Er Thom preferred the red. Daav splashed a portion into a crystal cup and handed it aside, surveying his *cha'leket*'s evening clothes with a smile.

"You look extremely, darling. Bindan shall have no hesitation in opening the door this evening."

"As they would certainly hesitate to admit Korval Himself," Er Thom said, in echo of his lifemate.

Daav grinned and poured himself a cup of pale blue *misravot*. "No, you are the beauty, after all. What could Bindan find for pleasure in such a fox-faced fellow as myself?" He sipped. "Discounting, of course, an alliance such as no one of sense will turn aside."

"So bitter, brother?" Er Thom's soft voice carried a note of sorrow.

Daav moved his shoulders. "Bitter? Say jaded, rather, and then pardon—as you always do!—my damnable moods." He raised his cup. "What had you wished to speak of?"

"We are on my subject," his brother said gently. "It had been in my mind that you did not—like—the match."

"Like the match," Daav repeated, staring in surprise. For Anne to question the validity of a contract-marriage was expectable. To hear such a query from Er Thom, who was Liaden to the core of him—that must give one pause.

"Have you information," he asked carefully, "which might—alter—the delm's decision in this?"

"I have nothing to bring before the delm. Indeed, lady and clan appear perfectly unexceptional, in terms of alliance and of genes. My concern is all for my *cha'leket*, who I—feel—may not be entirely reconciled to marriage."

"I am reconciled to necessity," Daav said, which did not answer his brother's concern, and held as its only virtue the fact that it was true.

Worry showed plain in Er Thom's eyes.

"Daav, if you do not like it, stand aside."

Plain speaking, indeed! Daav allowed astonishment to show.

"Darling, what would you have me do? The law is clear. Necessity is clearer. I must provide the clan with the heir of my body. Indeed, full nurseries at *Jelaza Kazone and* Trealla Fantrol must be the delm's goal, for we are grown thin—dangerously so."

He saw that point strike home, for it was true that the Line Direct had suffered severe losses in recent years. And yet—

"If you cannot like the lady," Er Thom insisted, with all the tenacity a master trader might bring to bear, "stand aside. Bid Mr. dea'Gauss find another—"

"As to that," Daav interrupted, with some asperity, "I like her as well as any other lady who has been thrown at my head these past six years."

"You have grown bitter. I had feared it." He turned aside; put his glass away from him. "I shall not accompany you this evening, I think."

Shock sent a tingle of ice down Daav's spine. In the aftermath of disbelief, he heard his own voice, dangerously mild.

"You refuse to assist your delm in a matter of such import to the clan?"

Er Thom's shoulders stiffened, his face yet turned aside.

"Will the delm order me to accompany him?" he inquired softly.

Yes, very likely! Daav thought, with a wry twist of humor. Order Er Thom to any thing like and Daav would gain as his evening's companion an exquisitely mannered mannequin in place of a willing, intelligent ally. It was no more Balance than he would himself exact, were their places changed.

Er Thom being quite as much Korval as Daav, persuasion alone was left open. He extended a hand and lay it gently upon his brother's arm.

"Come, why shall we disagree over what cannot be escaped? If not this lady, it must be some other. I am of a mind to have the matter done with, and the best course toward finish lies through begun."

Er Thom turned his head, raised troubled violet eyes. "Yet it is not—meet, when you do not care for her, when any is the same as one—"

"No," Daav interrupted gently. "No, darling, you have lost sight of custom. The Code tells us that a contract-spouse is chosen for lineage and such benefits of alliance and funding as must be found desirable by one's delm. It notes that resolution may be brought about more speedily, if both spouses are of generally like mind and neither is entirely repulsed by the other. You know your Code, own that I am correct."

"You are correct," Er Thom acknowledged, with an inclination of the head. "However, I submit that the Code is not—"

"I submit," Daav interrupted again, even more gently, "that you have been taught by a Terran wife."

A flash of violet eyes. "And that is an ill, I understand?"

"Not at all. Scouts learn that all custom is equally compelling, upon its own world. I point out that Korval is based—however regretfully—upon Liad."

Er Thom's eyes widened slightly. "So we are," he murmured after a moment. He grinned suddenly. "We might relocate."

"To New Dublin, I suppose," Daav said, naming Anne's homeworld with a smile. "The Contract is still in force."

"Alas." Er Thom recovered his wine glass and sipped, eyes roving the room.

The point was his, Daav considered with relief, and had recourse to his own glass.

"I do wish," Er Thom murmured, "that you might find one to care for—as Anne and I . . ."

Daav raised a brow. "I shall advertise in *The Gazette*," he said, meaning to offer an absurdity: "'Daav yos'Phelium seeks one who might love him for himself alone. Those qualified apply to *Jelaza Kazone*, Solcintra, Liad.'"

Er Thom frowned. "You do not believe such a one exists."

"I have met a great many people in the six years I have worn the Ring," Daav said with matching gravity. "If such a one exists, she has been—reticent."

Er Thom glanced away then, but not before Daav had seen the quick shine of tears in his eyes.

They finished their wine in a silence not so easy as usual.

"It is time, brother," Daav said at last. "Do you come with me?"

"Yes, certainly," Er Thom replied. "I had left my cloak in the hall."

"Mine is with it," Daav said, and arm-in-arm, they quit the room.

IT WAS LATE.

Aelliana had no very clear notion of precisely how late; her thoughts, fears, and discoveries muddled time past counting.

Less hasty consideration showed that her initial plan—to leave Clan Mizel and Liad immediately—required modification. She walked the misty streets for unheeded hours, working and reworking the steps, weighing necessity against certitude, honor against fear.

Fact: In due time, and barring unfortunate accidents, nadelms did, indeed, become delms.

Fact: Learned Scholar of Subrational Mathematics Aelliana Caylon, lately resolved to flee her homeworld for the comforts of a Terran settlement, spoke not one word of Standard Terran, nor any of the numerous Terran dialects. She did, of course, speak Trade, and understand somewhat of the Scout's finger-talk, but she could not, upon sober reflection, suppose this knowledge to balance her ignorance.

She might take sleep-learning to remedy her deficiency of language. But even sleep-learning takes time; and the skills thus gained must be exercised in waking mind, or else be lost like any other dream.

There were, of course, luxury liners which made such things as Learning Modules available to their passengers, but to book such passage was—

Fact: Beyond her meager means.

A visit to the ticketing office in mid-city had revealed that seven cantra would indeed buy passage to a Terran world, via tramp trader. If she wished to crew as part of her fare—and if the captain of the vessel agreed—she might reduce her cost to four cantra.

In either wise, she arrived at her destination—one *Desolate*—clanless, bankrupt; ignorant of language, custom and local conditions.

A badly flawed equation, in any light. She leaned against a damp pillar and closed her eyes, sickened by the magnitude of the things she did not know.

Ran Eld was right, she thought drearily: She was a fool. How could she have considered leaving Liad? She was no Scout, trained in the ways of countless odd customs, able to learn foreign tongues simply by hearing them said . . .

"Scholar Caylon?" The voice was familiar, light and young, the mode, of all things, Comrade, though she took pains to be no one's friend.

"Scholar Caylon?" the voice persisted, somewhat more urgently. She had the sense that there was a body very close to her own, though her interlocutor did not venture a touch. "It is Rema, Scholar. Do you require aid?"

Rema, Scout Corporal ven'Deelin. She of the eidetic memory. Aelliana pried open her eyes.

"I beg your pardon," she whispered, answering the warmth of Comrade mode with the coolth of Nonkin. Her glance skated past the Scout's face.

"Indeed, it is nothing. I had only stopped to rest for a—" Her gaze wandered beyond the Scout's shoulder and for the first time in many hours Aelliana's brain attended to the information her eyes reported.

"What place is this?" she demanded, staring at a wholly unfamiliar plaza, at a double rainbow of lights that blazed and flashed along a sidewalk like a ribbon of gold. Folk were about in distressing number, most in cloaks and evening dress, small constellations of jewels glittering about their elegant persons. Others were dressed more plainly, with here and there a glimpse of Scout leather, such as the girl before her wore.

"Chonselta Port," Rema said patiently, yet insisting upon Comrade. "It is the new gaming hall—Quenpalt's Casino. We've all come down to see it—and half Solcintra, as well, by the look of the crowd!"

Chonselta Port. Gods, she had walked the long angle through the city, entirely through the warehouse district, passed all unknowing between the gates and then walked half her original distance again. It must be . . . must be . . .

"The time," she said, suddenly urgent. "What is the time?"

"Local midnight, or close enough," Rema replied. She swayed half-a-step closer. "Forgive me, Scholar. It is plain that you are not well. Allow me to call your kin."

"No!" Her hand snapped up, imperative. Rema's eyes followed the motion, snagged—and slid away.

Startled, Aelliana glanced down. The bracelet of bruises circling her wrist was green and yellow, distressingly obvious in the extravagant light.

"Perhaps," the Scout suggested softly, "there is a place where you would prefer to spend the night. Perhaps there is a—friend—in whose care you might rest easy. I am your willing escort, Scholar, only tell me your destination."

She felt tears prick the back of her eyes, who had long ago learned not to weep.

"You are kind," she murmured, and meant it, though she dared not allow herself the mode of comrades. "There is no need for you to trouble yourself on my behalf. I have only walked further than I had supposed and the hour escaped my notice."

"I see," Rema said gravely. She hesitated and seemed about to say more.

"Well, for space sake," commented an irritated voice only too plainly belonging to Var Mon, "if your object was to stand out in the damned mist all night—" He blinked, coming up short just beyond Rema's shoulder.

"Scholar Caylon! Good evening, ma'am. Have you come to beat the house?"

"Beat the house?" she repeated stupidly, wondering how she might explain her late homecoming, when Ran Eld was already watching, eager for a chance to pain her.

"Certainly! Have you not taught us that there is no such thing as a game of chance? For every mode of play there is a pattern which, once recognized, may be manipulated according to the rules of mathematics. You recall the lecture, Rema, I know you do!"

"I do," his friend said shortly, and without sparing him a glance. "Scholar, please. You are plainly far from well. Allow one who holds you in highest respect to offer aid."

"Not well?" Var Mon sent a brilliant glance into Aelliana's face, then tapped Rema's shoulder with an authoritative forefinger. "She's wet, is all. Anyone would be, standing around in this stupid mist. I'm getting wet myself, if it comes to that. Glass of brandy will set her right." He pointed down the length of golden sidewalk to a cascade of gem-lit stairs crowned by wide ebon doors.

"Nearest source of brandy's right there—not to mention shelter from the weather. There's room at our table for the Scholar. After she's warmed herself she can give us some advice on winning against the random and we'll see her into a cab before we start back to Academy. Everything's *binjali*, hey?"

Binjali—a not-Liaden word enjoying currency only among Scouts, so far as Aelliana knew—meant "excellent" or "high-grade. " She forced her fuddled brain to work. Something must be done to disarm Rema's all-too-apparent concern. Scouts were observant, many were empathic, as well, though of a different skill level than an interactive empath, or Healer. Perhaps a glass or two of wine, and a lecture on practical math in relation to games of chance. . .

"That sounds a good plan," she said, looking past Rema's grave eyes to Var Mon's mischievous face. "I am damp and would welcome a chance to dry."

"Good enough," the boy returned with a grin. Without more discussion, he spun on his heel and moved away down the crowded sidewalk, obviously expecting that they would follow.

"Scholar?" murmured Rema, but Aelliana pretended not to hear and pushed away from the friendly wall, following Var Mon's leather-clad back through the glittering crowd.

CHAPTER FIVE

Remember who we are.
We are not Solcintran.
We are not derived from the Old Houses.
We are Korval
Keep the Contract, protect the Tree, gather ships, survive.
But never, never, never let them make you forget who you are.

—Val Con yos'Phelium,
Second Delm of Korval,
Entry in the Delm's Diary for Jeelum Twelfthday
in the Fourth *Relumma* of the Year Named Qin

THE LADY HAD EXPECTED a more costly jewel.

Not that she was so ill-bred as to actually say it, but Scouts are skilled in reading the language of muscle and posture: To Daav, her disappointment could scarcely have been plainer had she cried it aloud.

He was stung at first, for it was a pretty piece, and he had expended time and care in its choosing. However, his innate sense of the ridiculous soon laid salve upon injured feelings.

Come, Daav, he chided himself, *where is the profit in contracting*

Korval, if not in having extravagant jewelry to flaunt in the face of the world? Being so little fond of jewels yourself, this aspect of the case doubtless escaped you.

He had a sip of tolerable red. *No matter,* he thought. *The marriage-jewels shall be more fitly chosen, now her preference is known.*

Beside him, Samiv tel'Izak gently replaced the troth-gift in its carved wooden box and set it on the table. Daav felt another twinge of regret. He had carved the little box himself—not, it must be admitted, with the lady at all in his thoughts, but rather as a means of calming mind and heart on a day some years past. Still, the feel of hand-carving must be unmistakable against her fingertips, odd enough to earn at least a second glance.

Samiv tel'Izak took up her glass and lifted grave eyes to his face.

"I thank your lordship for the grace of your gift."

It was said with complete propriety in the mode of Addressing-a-Delm-Not-One's-Own. There were several other modes she might have chosen with equal propriety—and greater warmth: Addressing-a-Guest-of-the-House, Adult-to-Adult, or even Pilot-to-Pilot, though that approached the Low Tongue, and might be considered forward-coming.

Samiv tel'Izak was not forward-coming. A solid daughter of a solid mid-level House, Daav suspected that her delm's instruction held her to a loftier mode than she might have chosen on her own: Addressing a Delm Not One's Own was taking the High Tongue high, indeed.

In balance, Daav should make answer in Addressing One Not of His Clan, which came uncomfortably close to Nonkin. He chose instead to set an example of good fellowship in this, their first meeting alone, and hope well-bred manners would force her to follow his lead.

"To give the gift is joy," he told her in Adult-to-Adult, then offered a branch of active friendship: "Joy would be made greater, did you consider yourself free of my personal name."

Long, mahogany-colored lashes swept coyly down, while shoulder muscles shrieked aloud of triumph and some daring.

"Your lordship is gracious."

Daav's eyebrow twitched, which warning sign she did not see. He sipped his wine, blandly considering the studied curve of her neck.

So I'm to be smitten, am I? he thought sardonically—and then thought again. Perhaps, instead, he was punished for giving so paltry a gift? He wondered which would become annoying soonest, gloating or greed.

"One learns that your contract with *Luda Soldare* commences somewhat sooner than expected," he murmured, keeping stubbornly to Adult-to-Adult. "When do you lift?"

"The master trader was pleased to amend the route," she replied, keeping just as stubbornly to her own choice of mode. "We break orbit tomorrow, Solcintra dawn."

First Class Pilot tel'Izak had signed an employment contract with the captain of the newly commissioned trade ship *Luda Soldare* just prior to her delm's receiving notification of Korval's interest. This previous commitment was the reason that this evening Samiv and Daav signed a letter of intent rather than a contract of marriage.

Once signed, they were bound to each other by the terms of the letter, which further stipulated that the actual marriage commence not more than three full days after *Luda Soldare* released Pilot tel'Izak from her duty. There were the usual buy-out clauses on the side of Bindan. As the clan seeking the marriage, Korval waived right of termination.

"And has the master trader also been pleased to alter the tour?" Daav wondered, watching his soon-to-be-betrothed closely.

Her face remained properly grave, though the breath on which she answered was slightly deeper than the one before it.

"On the contrary, the master trader counseled one to plan the signing of one's marriage lines on the third day of the coming Standard Year."

Three Standard Months—a very prudent time for a new vessel's shakedown voyage. Daav inclined his head and, obedient to the promptings of his lamentable sense of humor, offered the lady a sardonic compliment:

"I shall count each day as three, until you are returned."

"Your Lordship is gracious," she murmured, and he detected neither irony nor pleasure in her voice.

He was saved the necessity of forming a reply to this rather uncommunicative statement by the entrance of the butler, come to summon them to the signing room, where Delm Bindan and Er Thom had been arranging things this age.

Samiv tel'Izak rose immediately and bowed, allowing him to precede her, which was the privilege of his rank. He stifled a sigh as he followed the butler down the hallway and decided that, before either greed or gloating did their work, propriety would drive him mad.

THE TABLE WAS LARGE, crowded and boisterous. A place was made for Aelliana between Rema and Var Mon, the shortage of chairs being remedied by a bit of deft piracy from neighboring tables.

Brandy was called for—"A double for the Scholar!" Var Mon ordered—and arrived amid a chef's ransom of food platters. At once, Rema snatched up a filigreed plate and began loading it with exotic savories.

Aelliana had a cautious sip of brandy and watched the Scout in awe. Her own appetite was never robust and it seemed such an amount of food would serve her needs for a week. Yet Rema clearly intended this laden plate to be a mere snack or late-night luncheon.

She assayed another sip of brandy, relishing the resulting sensation of warmth. Brandy was not her usual beverage—indeed, she rarely drank even wine—but she found it pleasing. She had a third sip, somewhat deeper than the first two.

"Of your grace, Scholar." Rema again. Aelliana lowered her glass and regarded the plate the Scout set firmly before her with a mixture of astonishment and dismay.

"The house brandy is potent," Rema murmured. "You will wish to eat something, and minimize the effects."

Having thus issued her instruction, the Scout turned away and leapt willy-nilly into a spirited discussion taking place at the opposite end of the table. As less than half the comments were rendered in Liaden—and none in Trade—Aelliana was very soon adrift and perforce turned her attention to that dismayingly over-full plate.

Mizel laid a simple table and Aelliana was not such a pretender to elegance as her elder brother, to be always dining at the first restaurants. Of the foodstuffs chosen for her, she could reliably identify cheese, fresh vegetables and a thin slice of fruit-bread. All else was mystery.

Well, she thought, brief moments ago brandy had likewise been a mystery, and only see how pleasant that encounter had been.

Indeed, the brandy was displaying ever more beguiling charms. She not only felt warmed, but rather delightfully—unconnected, as if the terrors that had driven her from Mizel's clanhouse only hours ago had someway ceased to exist. She sighed and reached for a flagrantly unfamiliar morsel, biting into it with a will.

It took very little time, really, to empty the plate of all its delightful mysteries. Sated, Aelliana leaned back in her chair, now and then sipping brandy, and drowsily watching her tablemates, paying no heed to their conversation, even when they happened to be speaking a language she understood.

It occurred to her that she felt *relaxed*, a state she dimly recalled from girlhood, when her grandmother had been alive, before Ran Eld Caylon had discovered the way to bring down the most dangerous of his siblings.

I believe, Aelliana thought, assaying another sip, *that I could come to be quite fond of brandy.*

"Warm now, Scholar?" That was Var Mon. She turned to look at him, shaking her hair back from her face and squarely meeting his eyes.

"Quite warm, I thank you," she said courteously, and saw his wide brown eyes go somewhat wider.

Before she had opportunity to wonder over that, he rose and stepped back with a light bow.

"Will you walk with me? A tour of a gaming house on your arm can only be instructive."

Well, and why not? Such opportunity to observe the laws of

her study area operating under field conditions was not to be lightly set aside.

"Certainly."

Putting away her glass, she came easily to her feet, muscles moving sweetly, unencumbered by fear. Some unfamiliar, brandy-created sense told her that Rema had also risen, and she nearly smiled at the Scout's continuing concern.

She wondered if Rema knew about the healing effects of brandy. It seemed likely, Scouts being privy to just such odd knowledge. That being the case, Rema's continued vigilance suggested there was something in the nature of brandy-healing that was perhaps not entirely salubrious.

The thought should have disturbed, but Aelliana allowed it to flow away as she followed Var Mon through the restaurant and into the first of the playing rooms.

THE MOON WAS FULL, shedding more than enough silvery light for a Scout with excellent night vision to find his way through the familiar branches of the Tree.

A steady ten-minute climb brought him to a wooden platform firmly wedged between three great branches.

Daav sat with his back against one of the branchings, carefully folding his legs. Er Thom and he had built this sanctuary as children, a double-dozen years before—it had seemed a vast space indeed, then.

He leaned his head against the warm wood and sighed. As if in echo, a breeze stirred the branches around him. Something fell with a sharp thunk to the board by his hand. He picked it up: A seed-pod.

"Thank you," he said softly to the Tree and opened the pod, cracking the nuts in his fingers and solemnly eating the minty-sweet kernels.

"Oh, gods." He closed his eyes, allowing the tears to rise. Here, there was no one—no thing—save the Tree to know, if he wept.

His coming marriage—that was the smallest source of pain. If the lady were greedy and venal and held him no more than his rank, it was nothing other than he had expected. It was only required that she provide him a healthy child. Did she perform that one service, she might gladly have from him all the jewels and expensive gidgets her heart wished for.

His own child, held warm and safe in his arms—that image filled him with a longing so intense he felt nearly ill with wanting. His own child, upon whom he might lavish the love that threatened to sour, locked up as it was in the depth of his heart. His own child, who might replace the love Er Thom's lifemating had stolen away—

No.

Er Thom loved him no less, and to that mainstay of his life was added Anne's true affection, as well as the rambunctious regard of young Shan, Er Thom's heir. It was no drawing back on Er Thom's part—no slighting on the side of his lifemate—that fed Daav's loneliness. Truth was far more melancholy.

There, with his back against the Tree, Daav owned himself jealous of his brother's joy, and wept somewhat, that he should not be a better man and receive his beloved's joy as his own.

The tears soon spent themselves, for he was not a man who wept often, and he remained leaning against the Tree, his mind open and unfocused.

It was not meet that the new child bear the burden of all Daav's love. Did he discover himself so ill a parent, the child would be fostered into Er Thom's care immediately, there to be loved and disciplined in moderation.

Nor was it reasonable to expect Er Thom—with a lifemate, an heir, and the duties of master trader and thodelm to absorb him— to provide everything his more volatile *cha'leket* required of human contact. Another solution must be found, else Daav would grow bitter, indeed.

For the good of the clan, he thought, yawning suddenly in the cool, mint-tanged air.

He might have dozed—a few minutes, no more—and woke with the shape of an answer in his mind.

He smiled as he considered it, for, after all, it was an obvious step, and one he should have undertaken for himself ere this.

"Thank you," he said once more to the Tree and fancied the leaves moved in slight, ironic bow.

Then, he let himself over the platform's edge and began the climb down.

CHAPTER SIX

Your ship is your life. Stake your air before you stake your ship—and your soul before you stake either.

—Excerpted from Cantra yos'Phelium's Log Book

PLAY WAS DEEP and as usual Vin Sin chel'Mara was in the deepest of it, pulling cantra from the pockets of the young fancies-about-town like a magnet pulling iron filings to itself.

He was a wizard with cards, was the chel'Mara, any of his cronies would say so. And it took either a god-kissed or an innocent to sit across from him at the pikit table and lay hand on deck to deal.

The universe being itself, there was no shortage of god-kissed for chel'Mara to fleece, innocents being something rare in the neighborhoods he frequented. Yet it seemed that tonight one had muddled into the depths of Quenpalt's Casino, and stood watching the play with wide, misty eyes.

She was utterly out of place in the jewel-glitter, silk-whisper crowd of players. Her quilted shirt was large and shapeless, fastened tight around her fragile throat. Her only adornment was an antique silver puzzle-ring.

Her hair, dark blonde or light brown, draggled too close around her face, and her eyes, thought yo'Vaade, who saw her first, were grey, or possibly a foggy green.

She stood quiet as a mouse at the side of the table, flanked by two halflings in Scout leather, foggy eyes intent in the thin, hair-shrouded face.

At first he thought it was chel'Mara she was after, so raptly did she watch his play. And why not? He was a well-looking man, and of good Line, though that would matter less to her than the cantra piled before him. The chel'Mara would never consider something so dowdy, yo'Vaade knew, but what harm to let the mouse dream?

Then he saw that it was the *cards* she was watching and frowned to himself. Fastidious as he was in bedmates, chel'Mara would play against any who sat to table. But surely, thought yo'Vaade, a ragged girl, with scarcely a cantra for her quarter-share, if he was any judge—

"You find the game amusing?"

chel'Mara's query hovered on the edge of Superior to Inferior—proper enough for a High House lordling out of Solcintra when addressing a mouse of unexalted birth. It would have been more gentle to bespeak her otherwise, he being a guest in her city, but the chel'Mara was not a gentle man. He gathered in his latest winnings and stacked the coins before him in careful towers of twelve, hardly sparing a glance at the mouse's thin face.

"I find the game interesting," she returned in an unexpectedly strong voice, and in the mode of Adult-to-Adult. "And I cannot for the life of me, sir, understand why you continue to win."

chel'Mara raised his eyebrows in elegant amusement. "I continue to win because my line of play is superior."

"Not so," she returned with such surety that yo'Vaade openly stared. "It is a badly flawed line, sir. Indeed, a solid loser, over time."

chel'Mara leaned back in his chair and gazed blandly up into her face.

"How very—interesting," he purred and moved a languid hand, showing table, cards and cantra. "We have before us the means to test your theory. "

She hesitated not at all, but came forward and sat in the chair sig'Andir had just vacated. Her guardian Scouts came forward, as well, and stood, one behind each shoulder. "Certainly, sir."

"Certainly," chel'Mara repeated. "But it's a valiant mouse, to sit with the cats!" He bowed, seated as he was, the gesture full with mockery. "What shall you stake, Lady Mouse?"

"My quarter-share," she stated, and produced it—four cantra, which was better than yo'Vaade had thought, but nothing near chel'Mara's more usual stake.

"Four cantra it is," he agreed, plucking a matching amount from his treasury—

"Oh, yes, very handsome!" cried sig'Andir, who was a bitter loser. "The poor lady stakes her entire quarter-share and you match it with four from your hoard! Where's honor in that? Stake something that will pain you as much, should you lose it, and make the play worth her while!"

chel'Mara raised his eyebrows. "I cannot imagine," he drawled, "what could possibly mean as much to me as four cantra does to this—lady."

sig'Andir grinned tightly. "Why not your ship, then?"

"My ship?" chel'Mara turned wondering eyes upon him as a crowd began to gather, drawn by the ruckle.

"It would be done thus," the male Scout said unexpectedly, "in Solcintra." He grinned, fresh-faced, and bowed to chel'Mara's rank. "My Lord need have no concern of pursuing a *melant'i* stake here. I am assured that Quenpalt's aspires to be the equal of any casino in Solcintra." He raised his voice. "The Stakes Book, if you please!"

There was a shifting of the crowd as the floor-master came panting up with Book and pens.

"A *melant'i* stake," someone of the crowding spectators whispered loudly. "Value for equal value, absolute. Ship against quarter-share."

"Ship against quarter-share!" The information ran the casino. Play stopped at other tables and in the main room, the wheel was seen to pause. yo'Vaade held his breath.

For a long moment, chel'Mara stared at the book the floor-master held ready. Then one elegant hand moved, fingers closing around the offered pen. He signed his name with a flourish.

The book was presented to the mouse, who took the pen and wrote, briefly. The floor-master made the House's notation and stepped back, reverently closing the gilded covers.

Lazily, almost lovingly, chel'Mara replaced his four coins on the proper stack. Likewise, he produced a set of ship keys strung together on a short jeweled chain and lay it gently beside the mouse's quarter-share in the center of the table.

"Ship against quarter-share," he murmured and inclined his head. "Your deal, Lady Mouse."

IT WAS A LONG GAME, and the mouse a better player than yo'Vaade would have guessed. Indeed, she won at first, made her four cantra into six—seven. Then chel'Mara found his stride and the mouse's cantra went back across the line, until only one remained her.

yo'Vaade thought it was ended then, but he had reckoned without the Scouts.

Indeed, he had quite forgotten about the Scouts, who had remained standing, silent and patient as leather-clad statues, behind the mouse's chair. It was doubly startling, then, to see the boy lean across the mouse's shoulder, ringless hand descending briefly to tabletop.

He straightened and yo'Vaade looked to the mouse's bank, richer now by three cantra.

chel'Mara frowned into the Scout's face.

"Do you buy in, sir? I had understood this a test of theory between the—lady—and myself."

"Payment of a long-standing debt, Your Lordship," the Scout returned blandly. A murmur ran the crowd.

There was no comment from the mouse. Indeed, there had been no comment from her since play began, she apparently being one who concentrated wholly upon her cards.

A moment longer the chel'Mara stared into the Scout's face.

"I have seen you," he remarked, in such a tone that said, *Having seen you twice, I shall remember you long.*

The Scout bowed. "Indeed. your lordship saw me but three nights ago, at the Stardust in Solcintra Port, where your lordship was pleased to win the quarter-share of Lyn Den Kochi and certain payments from three future quarter-shares."

chel'Mara lifted an ironic hand. "There are those who are not friends of the luck."

"As your lordship says." The Scout returned to stillness and chel'Mara went back to his cards.

"ARE YOU MAD?" Rema hissed into Var Mon's ear. "To set her against Vin Sin chel'Mara—"

"My dear comrade, *I* didn't set her against my lord, she set herself. Where's the harm?"

"You ask that, when you saw him ruin Lyn Den? What if she should lose, tipsy as she is?"

"She's winning and you know it. I can almost see where that line of play is going, and you're quicker than I am. Where is she going, Rema?"

"I—am not certain."

"But she's winning."

"Perhaps."

"No perhaps about it," Var Mon asserted, eyes on the fall of the cards. "You don't see it and I don't see it, but Scholar Caylon sees it—and it's her board." He paused as Aelliana took a trick, then continued, softly.

"As for being tipsy—look at her! She looks as she does when she lectures—I should be so cool when I sit to Jump!"

"If he should take exception . . ."

"The cameras are on it," Var Mon told her. "The Scholar's line is fair—she's got the pattern and she's got the break-key, even if her students are too stupid to see it. How can he take exception to a fair line? Stop fretting."

THE TEMPO CHANGED shortly after the Scout's three cantra entered the game.

It was as if, yo'Vaade thought, the mouse had at last found the path she had been seeking, though her previous play had in no way been marred by hesitation.

Now she played with a surety that was awesome to behold, calling the cards to her hand like kin. It took less than an hour for all the coins to cross back over the line, until it was seven on her side and the keys alone, and chel'Mara bidding a Clan Royale.

It was what all the rest had been building toward—this last hand, this locking of wills. The crowd held its breath, and yo'Vaade held his. chel'Mara's face was seen to be damp. The mouse sat cool as water ice, cards a smooth fan between quiet fingers, and called for her seconds.

"Scout's Progress," she announced in that surprisingly clear voice, which was esoteric enough, surely, but no match for a Clan Royale. One by one, she lay the cards out, face up for all to see, and looked over to chel'Mara.

"Ah." He sighed, and a great tension seemed to go out of him all at once, so that yo'Vaade began to feel sorry for the poor, valiant mouse.

chel'Mara's cards came down in a practiced sweep, face up for all to see: Delm, Nadelm, Thodelm, A'thodelm, Master Trader. . .

"Ship," the crowd whispered among itself. "He's missing the Ship. A broken run . . . The lady wins . . ."

"The lady wins," Vin Sin chel'Mara announced, loud enough to be heard in the far corners of the room. He snapped his fingers. "Bring a port-comm!"

"A port-comm!" the crowd babbled. "A port-comm for Lord chel'Mara!"

It came and he tapped in one sequence, then another, and looked over to his erstwhile opponent, who was staring down at her run as if she had never seen cards before.

"Your name?" he inquired neutrally and when she looked up with a start, explained with overdone patience: "In order to change the registration of the ship, I will need to file your name as new owner."

"Oh," she said, and picked up the keys to frown at before replying. "Aelliana Caylon Clan Mizel."

There was a flutter of something through the crowd at that, and yo'Vaade considered the taste of the name. It meant nothing to him:

it obviously meant nothing to chel'Mara. Behind the mouse's chair, the Scouts preserved attitudes of silent attention.

chel'Mara had recourse to the port-comm's keyboard, finished his entry, tapped the send key and lay the comm aside. He came to his feet and stood gazing down at the mouse. The look in his eyes, thought yo'Vaade, was not good. Not at all good.

"The ship is called *Ride the Luck,*" he said. "It is kept at Binjali Repair Shop, Solcintra Port. Ownership entire remits to you at Solcintra dawn. I shall require the hours between to remove my personal effects." He bowed, low and mocking. "I wish you joy of your winnings, Lady Mouse," he said softly.

He turned to go, his eye falling on sig'Andir, who was openly smiling. "Satisfied, sir?" he purred and waited until the smile died and all color drained from the boy's face before he swept away through the crowd, toward the lounge-room and the bar.

"GOOD EVENING, JON."

The man at the desk finished writing out his line before glancing up. As it happened, he needed to glance up quite a way, he being seated and his visitor being somewhat above the average height, for a Liaden male.

He was also dressed in work leathers, his hands innocent of rank ring, which meant High House gossip was not the purpose of this visit. The spirited dark hair was neatly confined in a tail that hung below his shoulders; from his right ear dangled the twisted silver loop he had earned from the headwoman of the Mun.

He bowed, Student to Master, and straightened; the glow off the desk lamp underlit his sharp-featured face, throwing the black eyes into shadow.

"I need work," he said, speaking in Comrade mode, which was how they always spoke at Binjali's.

"Hah." Jon rubbed his nose. "Happens we have work." He jerked his head at the window and the repair bays beyond. "Go on out and call yourself to Trilla's attention."

"Thank you."

Another bow and he was gone, walking with a Scout's silent

stride, melting out of the light as if he had never been. A moment later, Jon saw him crossing the bay, lifting a hand toward Trilla on the platform. The office noise-proofing was top-grade, so he missed the shout that must have accompanied the gesture. But he saw Trilla wave back and the flicker of hand talk: *come on up*.

Needed work, did he? Jon thought, between a grin and a worry. He sighed and returned to his papers.

"MAY I WORK AGAIN TOMORROW?"

Jon deliberately finished cleaning his hands, shook the rag and hung it back on its nail.

"We're open to casual labor. You know that."

"Yes. I only wanted to be certain I would not be—inconvenient."

"Inconvenient." Jon grinned, reached out and caught the younger man's elbow, turning him toward the so-called crew's lounge. "Let's have a cup of tea. I'll ask some nosy questions, you'll snatch what remains of my hair from over my ears and we'll part friends, eh?"

The other laughed, a rich, full sound that had pulled Jon dea'Cort's mouth into a grin from the very first time he'd heard it.

"A bargain," he cried and appeared to sober abruptly, glancing sideways from glinting black eyes. "How old is the tea, I wonder?"

"Must be six, seven hours old by now," Jon admitted without shame.

"Perfect."

A few moments later they were both seated on rickety stools. In addition to tea, Jon had helped himself to the last of the stale pastries and was busily dunking it into the depths of his mug.

"How is it, Master Jon, that the mugs never melt?"

"Had 'em made special out of blast glass," Jon returned and disposed of his soggy sweet in two bites. He took a scalding swallow of bad tea and threw his former student a stern look.

"They don't keep you busy enough out in Dragon's Valley, Captain?"

"Alas, they keep me out of reason busy," came the reply. "I swear to you, Master Jon, if I am required to speak to one more Liaden I shall either go mad or strangle him."

Jon laughed. "Spoken like a true Scout! But the fact of the matter is that you're too important a man to either go mad or take it upon yourself to strangle the bulk of the population. Not," he admitted around another gulp of tea, "that most of 'em wouldn't be better for a throttling. But it's out of Code, child: the natives are likely to take issue."

"Understood. And so I ask for work."

"I can give you work. But I'd like to know you're not turning your face from matters needing your attention. There are those things, as we all learn in Basic, that only you can do, Captain. Leave them aside and the world could be a lot worse."

"You terrify me."

"Some respect for your elder, if you please. I can give you work, but is work what you need?"

The other man sipped gingerly at his mug, screwing up his face in comic distaste. "Magnificent," he pronounced, and gave Jon dea'Cort all his black eyes.

"My brother," he murmured, "falls just short of suggesting we remove to New Dublin."

"It delights me to hear your honored kin has, however late in life, come into his heritage," Jon returned with a touch of acid. "Had he anything useful to suggest?"

"You are severe. Yes, something useful."

"But you'll see me damned before you tell me what it was," Jon said comfortably. He finished his tea and rose to transfer the dregs from the pot to his mug.

"All right," he said, resettling on his stool. "You need work, I've got work. Casual schedule; call if you're expected and something forestalls you. But if your self-healing hasn't earned out in a *relumma*, I will cease to have work, young Captain, and I would then strongly suggest—as a comrade—that you visit the Healers."

"A *relumma* should be more than sufficient to relocate center. I thank you." The younger man stood, poured his tea down the sink, washed out the mug and put it to drain.

"Until tomorrow, Master Jon."

"Until tomorrow, child. Be well."

CHAPTER SEVEN

The number of High Houses is precisely fifty. And then there is Korval.

—From the Annual Census of Clans

"*WHAT* LONG-STANDING DEBT?" Aelliana demanded of a grinning Var Mon as they left the card room.

"Why, only the honor of being allowed to sit at the feet of Aelliana Caylon for an entire semester and catch the jewels as they fell from her lips!" He stopped to bow, coincidentally disrupting the flow of traffic between the card room and the music lounge.

Aelliana frowned. "You are absurd."

"Not to say impertinent," Rema put in, adding a rider to her comrade in a flutter of finger-talk. To Aelliana's eyes, it seemed a list: Twelve variations on the sign for *idiot*. Var Mon laughed.

"You will be very well served if Scholar Caylon pockets your three cantra and says no more," Rema scolded audibly. "How will you come about then?"

"Indeed, no," Aelliana said hastily; "I do not wish to keep Var Mon's money. But it is ill-done to say you are repaying a debt when it is no such thing!"

There was a moment of complete silence, her companions staring at her from rounded eyes.

"Chastised," Var Mon murmured.

"Justly," returned his partner. "Local custom."

"Exactly so." He bowed once more, taking care not to discommode others nearby. "I ask your forgiveness, Scholar," he said in the mode of Lesser-to-Greater, which was the High Tongue and not a quiver of merriment to be heard. "You are gracious to illuminate my error."

Aelliana considered him, suspecting a joke. The boy's face showed nothing but serious courtesy, and perhaps a touch of anxiety. His three cantra were safe in her right hand, mingling with the jeweled chain and the keys to—the keys to *her* ship.

"You knew that lordship," she said abruptly.

Surprise showed at the corners of his face. "I know his name," he allowed, still in Lesser-to-Greater, "and his reputation."

"Vin Sin chel'Mara," Rema murmured, "Clan Aragon."

Aelliana sighed. She had learned, as any child, the rhymes for Clans and Sigils, Houses and Tasks. But childhood was many years gone and her general grasp of such matters fell far short of the knowledge held by one who moved in the world.

"High House?" was the best she could hazard now, looking at Rema.

The Scout blinked. "Not so high as Korval," she said slowly.

But this was merely a quibble. Who in all the world outranked the Dragon? Even Aelliana knew the answer was, none.

"I—see," she said, the keys hot in her hand.

"The play was clean." That was Var Mon. "We were surrounded by those who know their cards, and the house camera, beside." He grinned, irrepressible boy bursting free of the solemn gentleman he had been a moment before.

"Scholar Caylon, *you* don't say the game was false?"

"The game was entirely true," she said tartly. "Nor was it at all necessary for you to offer your cantra. His lordship's line was irretrievably flawed." She held out the coins in question. "I thank you for your aid, though it was in no way required."

"Ouch," said Var Mon mildly, and took his money with a bow.

❈ ❈ ❈

AELLIANA SHIFTED IN THE PULLDOWN tucked between the pilots' stations and inner hatch, and considered her circumstances.

It would appear that she was, in unlikely truth, the owner of a spaceship, which she was even now on her way to inspect.

She closed her eyes, feeling how quick her heart beat. She owned a spaceship; possibilities proliferated.

If it was, as she suspected, a rich man's toy, she would contrive, discreetly, to sell, thus ensuring outpassage and a stake upon which to build her new life.

If, against all expectation, *Ride the Luck* was a working class ship, she would—

She would keep it.

A pilot-owner might find work anywhere, she was tied to no single world. A pilot-owner need owe none, was owned by no one.

A pilot-owner was—free. Alone, independent, autonomous, sovereign . . . Aelliana leaned back in the pulldown chair, stomach cramped with longing.

If *Ride the Luck* was a working ship . . .

Of course, pilot-owners held piloting licenses, which Aelliana Caylon did not. The life she so avidly envisioned required she be nothing less than a Jump pilot.

"Asleep, Scholar?" Var Mon's voice broke in upon these rather lowering considerations.

"Not entirely," she replied, and heard Rema, at first board, chuckle.

"Good," Var Mon said, unruffled. "We set down in three minutes, unless Rema forgets her protocols. I'll conduct you to Binjali's, if you wish, and make you known to Master dea'Cort."

Aelliana opened her eyes. "Thank you," she said, as a flutter of her stomach reported the ship was losing altitude. "I would welcome the introduction."

"MASTER JON! Joy to you, sir!" Var Mon strode into the center of the repair bay, head up and voice exuberant.

Aelliana, trailing by several steps, saw a stocky figure come to the edge of shadow cast by a work-lift, casually wiping its hands on a faded red rag.

"I'm not lending you another cantra, you scoundrel," the figure said sourly, for all the mode was Comrade. "What's more, you're due in Comparative Cultures in twenty minutes and I'll not have it said I was responsible for keeping you beyond time."

"Not a bit of it," Var Mon cried, apparently not at all put out by this rather surly welcome. He reached into his pouch and danced into the shadow. Grasping a newly-cleaned hand, he deposited two gleaming coins on the broad palm and closed the fingers tight.

"Debt paid!" he said gaily and spun, bowing with a flourish that called attention to Aelliana, hesitating yet between light and shadow.

"Master Jon, I bring you Aelliana Caylon, owner of *Ride the Luck*. Scholar Caylon, Master Jon dea'Cort, owner of Binjali Repair Shop."

"Caylon?" Master dea'Cort at last stepped forward into the light, revealing a man well past middle years, sturdy rather than stout, his hair a close-clipped strip of rusty gray about four of her slender fingers wide. Eyes the color of old amber looked into her face with the directness of a Scout.

"Scholar Aelliana Caylon," he asked, big voice pitched gently, though he still spoke in Comrade mode, "revisor of the ven'Tura Tables?"

She inclined her head, and answered in Adult-to-Adult. "It is kind of you to recall."

"Recall! How might I—or any pilot!—forget?" He bowed then, distressingly low—the bow of Esteem for a Master—and straightened with his hand over his heart.

"Scholar, you honor my establishment. How I may be allowed to serve you?"

Aelliana raised her hand to ward the reverence in the old man's voice. To know her as the revisor of one of the most important of a pilot's many tools—that was grace, though not entirely unexpected. Jon dea'Cort had undoubtedly been a Scout in former years and Aelliana strongly suspected his "master" derived from "master pilot."

"Please, sir," she said, hearing how breathless her voice sounded.

"You do me overmuch honor. Indeed, it is not at all—" Here she hesitated, uncertain how she might proceed with her disclaimer, without calling the master's *melant'i* into question.

"Var Mon, are you here, you young rakehell?" the old man snarled over his shoulder.

"Aye, Master Jon!"

"Then jet, damn you—and mind you're on time for class!"

"Aye, Master Jon! Good-day to you, Scholar. Until Trilsday-noon!"

Var Mon was gone, running silently past Aelliana's shoulder. She heard nothing, then a whine and sigh as the crew door cycled.

"So." Jon dea'Cort smiled, waking wrinkles at eye-corners and mouth. "You were about to tell me that I do you too much honor. How much honor should I lay at the feet of the scholar responsible for preserving the lives of half-a-thousand pilots?"

"Half-a—oh, but that's averaged over the years since publication, of course." Aelliana looked down, tongue-tied and graceless as ever when dealing outside the familiar role of teacher-to-student.

"You must understand," she told her boot-toes. She cleared her throat. "The tables were in need of revision and I was able to under-take the project. To recall my name as the one who did the work—that is kind. But, you must understand, to offer such honor to one who merely—" She faltered, hands twisting about each other.

"I teach math," she finished, lamely.

There was a short silence, before Jon dea'Cort spoke, voice matter-of-fact in Comrade mode.

"Well, nothing wrong with that, is there? I taught piloting, myself, and to such a thankless pack of puppies as I hope you'll never see!"

Aelliana glanced up, hair swinging around her face. "You are a master pilot."

"Right enough. Most of us are, hereabout." He tipped his balding head to one side, offering another smile. "What might I do for you, math teacher?"

She lowered her eyes, refusing the smile as she refused Comrade mode.

"I had come to inspect *Ride the Luck*, of which I am owner."

"So my problem-child said," Jon dea'Cort said placidly. "I hadn't known *Ride the Luck* was for sale."

"I—it wasn't." She moved her shoulders. "I won it last evening from Lord Vin Sin chel'Mara—in a round of pikit."

"Beat him at his own game!" Jubilation was plain in Master dea'Cort's voice, from which Aelliana deduced that his lordship was not a favored patron. "Well done, math teacher! Here, let me fetch the jitney and I'll take you out myself. Beat the chel'Mara at pikit, by gods! I won't be a moment . . ."

"SHE'S A SWEET SHIP," Jon dea'Cort was saying some minutes later, sending the jitney full-speed down the yard's central avenue. "She's seen some hard times of late, but she's sound. Show her kindness and she'll do very well . . . Here we are."

The jitney shivered to a stop; Master dea'Cort slid out of the driver's slot and walked toward the ramp.

In the passenger's seat, Aelliana sat and stared, her hands cold and slick with sweat.

"Scholar Caylon?" There was worry in the big voice.

With an effort, Aelliana moved her eyes from the ship—hers, *hers*—to the face of the man standing beside her.

"It's a Jumpship," she told him, as if such a vital point of information could have someway escaped a master pilot's expert notice.

He glanced over his shoulder and up the ramp, then returned his amber gaze to her face. "Class A," he agreed gravely, and held out a companionable hand. "Care to see inside?"

She could remember wanting nothing else so much.

"Yes," she said hungrily and slipped out of the jitney, deftly avoiding Jon dea'Cort's touch.

AELLIANA BROUGHT THE BOARD UP and watched, rapt, as the ship ran its self-check. Each green go-light added to her wracking store of joy until she found herself clutching the back of the pilot's chair, wet fingers smearing the ivory leather.

The check ended on three chimed notes and she reluctantly

touched the off-switch before allowing Jon dea'Cort to lead her further into the ship.

There was a dining alcove containing a gourmet automat, as well as a tiny dispensary housing a premium autodoc.

"Likes everything binjali, the chel'Mara," Master dea'Cort murmured and led her down a short companionway.

Aelliana followed him over the threshold of what should have been the pilot's quarters and stopped short, blinking at mountains of silks, sleeping furs, pillows of every hue and size. The floor was covered in a rug so fine she felt a pang of sorrow for having set her boots upon it. Tapestry gardens burgeoning with ripe fruits made the walls an oasis.

The illumination in the chamber was unusually firm and Aelliana glanced up, expecting to see a light fixture in keeping with the rest.

Instead, she looked up into the room she was standing in, Jon dea'Cort at the door, lined face carefully bland, while her own, reflected without distortion, showed slightly pale, with lips half-parted.

She glanced down, not quite able to stifle the sigh, and spoke over her shoulder.

"Everything *binjali*?"

"Understand," Master dea'Cort said earnestly, "the chel'Mara's no pilot. Happens he had other uses for a ship. And yon mirrors are top-grade."

"I see." She walked past him and into the room across the hall, which would have been the co-pilot's quarters in any other ship. In this ship, it was the twin of the orgy room. Aelliana sighed again and turned down the light.

"Guess you're ready to see the hold," Master dea'Cort said then, and showed her the way to the access door and how to punch in her code.

The door slid back and the lights came up and the first things she saw again were the damned mirrors. She had just enough time to wonder how anyone could be such a popinjay, when she saw the rest.

Some items she could name—silken cords and leather lashes, a few of the less arcane articles laid neatly in their cases, the swing suspended from the ceiling, the post with its built-in manacles.

Most, however, were unfamiliar: What, for instance, was the purpose of that oddly-shaped table, or the counterbalanced bench or—

Aelliana took a deep breath, turned carefully and lifted her face. Resolutely, she met Jon dea'Cort's eyes, and saw sympathy there.

"Master dea'Cort, I need your advice," she said, yet keeping to adult-to-adult.

"Math teacher, ask me."

With an effort, she kept her face up, her eyes steady; her hands were behind her back, twisting themselves into sweat-slicked knots.

"I had—thought," she said, "that I had acquired a working ship. It seems instead that I have acquired a—a bordello. What is your estimate of the time and expense required to restore this ship to its—original specifications?"

"Not a cantra," he said promptly, "and about a three-day— maybe four, depending on the crew I get." He grinned.

"No need to look like I'm pulling teeth," he told her. "I told you the chel'Mara liked everything *binjali*, eh? The toys are worth something, sold to the right party, and the mirrors—Math teacher, you could refit to spec on the profit from the mirrors alone! Had 'em set on gimbals, so they'd always be oriented, whatever G or spin the ship took on—made out of scanner-glass to withstand take-off stress and not flow—a rare wonder, these mirrors, and there are those who appreciate wonder."

Aelliana closed her eyes, trying to think, to work the steps.

"Do you know the proper—the proper buyers? I confess that I am not—"

"I can act as broker," he said easily. "My fee's ten percent off the top. We'll bring her back up to working weight, deduct labor and parts from what remains and put the profit into your ship's account. Deal?"

She opened her eyes. "Profit?"

"Bound to be a cantra or two left over," he said, looking around the gleaming playground. "Some of the toys are speciality items, and those mirrors haven't gotten any cheaper."

"Oh," Aelliana said, feeling rather adrift. She inclined her head formally. "Thank you, sir. I accept your deal."

"Well enough, then." He waved her out ahead of him.

"Will you be starting to work her at once?" he asked as they went back down the companionway.

"At once? I—I must take the piloting exam," Aelliana said, slowly. "And—flight time . . ."

There was a slight sound from behind her, as if Master dea'Cort had sneezed.

"You haven't—forgive me. I understand you to say that you have no piloting license."

"Not at the moment," she said, "but I shall be taking the exam— I have classes tomorrow . . . I shall take the exam on Banim. Second class is required to lift Class A locally, sir, is that correct?"

"Correct."

They had reached the dispensary. Aelliana paused, staring down into the 'doc's opaque hood.

"I shall acquire a second class, then," she said, feeling necessity like a stone in her gut. "I *will* work this ship."

"I don't doubt it," Jon dea'Cort said from beside her. "If you wish, I can test you, or one of my crew. We're all of us master class, as I said. Or you can call ahead to the Pilot's Guild in Chonselta and be sure they can accommodate you on Banim."

"I believe that will be best," she said, still staring down into the darkness.

"I'll call them now," he said, "while you use the unit here."

She turned sharply. "Use the unit?"

"No sense leaving that untreated when you've the means to mend it," he said, tapping his own wrist. "It's a rare wonder how those little things can eat away at your concentration." He moved down the hall. "I'll just get Chonselta Guild on the line . . ."

He was gone. Aelliana looked down at the bruises circling her wrist. They seemed more vivid now than they had, hours earlier, outside of Quenpalt's Casino. And, now that she was reminded of them, they did ache.

Well, she thought, with a flash of amused irritation, she was here and the autodoc was here. At the very least, mending the hurt would put a stop to all this rather embarrassing solicitude.

So thinking, she tapped the proper code into the 'doc, rolled back her sleeve and slid the wrist through the open hood.

CHAPTER EIGHT

ⓍⓍⓍⓍⓍⓍⓍⓍⓍⓍⓍⓍⓍⓍⓍⓍⓍⓍⓍⓍⓍⓍⓍⓍⓍⓍⓍⓍⓍⓍ

What's in a name? That which we call a rose
By any other name would smell as sweet.

—From *Romeo and Juliet*, Act ii,
Scene 2, William Shakespeare

VIN SIN CHEL'MARA was not a man accustomed to his delm's close attention. Most especially, he was unaccustomed to the felicity of receiving such attention during his rather belated breakfast.

"How pleasant it must be," Aragon murmured politely, as tea was poured and set before him, "to sleep so far into the day that one may dispose of noon meal and waking meal in one repast. I quite admire the efficiency of such an arrangement."

Since this particular arrangement had been in force for a number of years without awaking the delm's displeasure, his comment now was doubtless prologue to some other, less amiable, subject. chel'Mara inclined his head, as one acknowledging a pleasantry, and poured himself a second glass of wine.

"The single difficulty I detect in such a system," Aragon pursued, "is that it opens one to disadvantage in the matter of collecting rumor and anecdote—vital work, as I am certain you will agree. For an instance, I had today from Delm Guayar an entirely amusing anecdote out of Chonselta, of all places. Had I adopted your strategy of late sleeping, rather than rising early to attend Lady yo'Lanna's breakfast gather, I should have failed of harvesting this amusing— and instructive—tit-bit."

The chel'Mara schooled his face to calmness; deliberately raised his glass and sipped.

"You are behindhand, Vin Sin," his delm chided softly. "Good manners dictate you allow me the pleasure of imparting my news."

Vin Sin chel'Mara did not reign over Solcintra's deepest tables because he was a fool. Still, there was nothing for it but to allow this trick to fall to Aragon and accept whatever chastisement became his due. He was not in the habit of falling under his delm's displeasure, and he considered the odds favorable for a quick recover.

He inclined his head. "Forgive me, sir. I fear I am dreadfully stupid so early in the day. Whatever came out of Chonselta to amuse you?"

"Why, the drollest tale I've heard in many a breakfast gather," Aragon said composedly. "It seems a certain Quenpalt's Casino has opened in Chonselta Port and it is rumored to stand with the best Solcintra has to offer. Last evening, indeed, much of Solcintra undertook the journey to the far side of the world in order to see this wonder for themselves."

"And was reality as pleasing as rumor?"

Aragon pursed his lips in consideration.

"Rumor and reality appear to have agreed splendidly," he said after a moment. "Quenpalt's is, by all accounts, a casino in which one such as yourself, let us say, may be perfectly at ease."

He paused to sip tea. chel'Mara refrained from his wine.

"To make a long tale short," Aragon resumed gently, "it transpires that—again—one such as yourself was present at Quenpalt's last evening, and, having availed himself of certain monies thrown in his direction by a gentleman who has regrettably never mastered the art of pikit, set himself to contend against a walk-in." Aragon gazed pensively into chel'Mara's face.

"There were some oddities attending this walk-in. She was

shabby-dressed, according to report, and plain-spoken, when she spoke at all; she did not offer her name, nor was she asked to give it. She was accompanied by two Scouts—one male, one female, both young.

"The shabby lady declared she would stake her quarter-share, some four cantra, according to my information. The gentleman so like yourself plucked four cantra from his bank—and was forestalled by the person he had just bested, who called to mind—quite properly!—certain delicate points of *melant'i*, in which he was seconded by the male Scout. The Stakes Book was called for and the wager recorded thus: Quarter-share against ship. It was the very first entry, you will be interested to learn, in Quenpalt's Stakes Book." He had recourse to his tea once more. chel'Mara sat like a stone, his hands quite cold.

"So. The shabby lady won her venture—aided once more by the male Scout, who chose, I am a told, an interesting point in the play to settle a debt he had long owed her. The ship of the gentleman so very like yourself changed hands. In the course of recording the win, the shabby lady at last gave her name: Aelliana Caylon."

It was time to have done with this charade. chel'Mara inclined his head with exquisite courtesy.

"So she did."

"So she did," his delm echoed gently. "And, having now heard it twice, the name yet awakes no interest. I fear, Vin Sin, that you have not been as close a student of the world as I had always supposed."

chel'Mara swallowed a sharp return, preserving a courteous countenance with—some—effort.

"Aelliana Caylon," Aragon continued, after a moment spent savoring the last of his tea, "is the third child of the four borne by Birin Caylon, who has the honor to be Mizel." He moved his shoulders. "Mizel totters on the edge of mid-House. It is my notion that it will tumble into Low House, when the present nadelm comes to his own. But that is not the card we must trump."

"Aelliana Caylon," the chel'Mara suggested, with delicate irony, "supports the tottering fortunes of her clan by performing—card tricks, shall we say?"

Aragon raised a considering brow. "It might do," he allowed gently, "although I believe the lady's range to be somewhat wider than mere—card tricks." His eyes sharpened. "Do the ven'Tura Tables wake recollection, Vin Sin?"

"Certainly."

"Ah, delightful. You will then be able to tell me the name of the author of the revision, dated, I believe, eight years ago?"

chel'Mara frowned. "The name? Truly, sir, it was merely this scholar or that. No one I've met."

"Until last evening. How unfortunate, that you were not able to give Honored Scholar of Subrational Mathematics Aelliana Caylon her full bow, upon introduction." Aragon leaned forward, hands flat on the pale cloth.

"The foremost mathematical mind on the planet," he said, very softly, indeed, "who makes the study of random event her *speciality*. Her thesis—a classic in the field, so Guayar assures me—was entitled, *Chaotic Patterning in Pseudorandom Events*. In it, the scholar demonstrates the manner in which one may predict card-fall, based upon an ordered diminishment of pooled possibility, as one might find when playing pikit." He leaned back, with a soft sigh.

"By happenstance—I place it no higher!—the pattern which gains the final prize in Scholar Caylon's illustration is *Scout's Progress*. This is the woman you thought to best at pikit, Vin Sin. Are you not diverted? I assure you that Guayar, who made it his business to be at my side throughout the gather, found the tale amusing in the extreme. Indeed, he repeated it to everyone."

The chel'Mara grit his teeth and met his delm's eye steadily.

"But you do not smile!" Aragon said, sitting back in sudden ease. "My tit-bit has not amused. Never mind, I have an addendum calculated to please. You recall the Scouts?"

"Indeed, sir, I recall them—specifically."

"Ah, then you will certainly know their names."

chel'Mara raised a brow. "Whatever for?"

His delm lifted an admonitory finger. "Now that was careless. One should always know the names of those with whom one is engaged in an affair of Balance. How fortunate it is that I am able to supply you with this vital information. The name of the female Scout is Rema ven'Deelin, Clan Ixin—High House, you perceive. The male is Var Mon pin'Aker, Clan Midys—solidly Mid-House. He and Corporal ven'Deelin are partnered. He likewise has the honor of standing *cha'leket* to one Lyn Den Kochi, whose quarter-share was tragically left behind at Sunrise House three—possibly four—nights ago."

There was silence. chel'Mara stared down into the dark depths of his wine, considering the trap and the skill with which it had been sprung.

Certainly, a *cha'leket* might undertake Balance on behalf of his foster-kin. That the trap had been set with skill and something of wit made it no easier to bear.

"A nameless lady attended by Scouts approaches your table and calls your play into question before all the world," Aragon said pensively. "Did it not occur to you, Vin Sin, that you might—just possibly—have been set up?"

"Alas, sir, it did not. An error, I admit."

"Do you? But how gracious you are!" The bite of irony in his delm's voice brought chel'Mara's eyes up.

Aragon held his gaze, allowing him to see anger.

"I shall say no more of your carelessness in this matter of last evening," Aragon said in clipped tones, "except that I find you well-rewarded in the loss of your vessel—and that I see no necessity for Aragon to Balance the Caylon's most valuable lesson to yourself. Of this other, however—you will tell me, Vin Sin, if you habitually prey upon halflings and innocents."

chel'Mara felt a flicker of his own anger and lowered his eyes, lest it be seen.

"As you say, sir, the lady was no innocent. For Master Kochi—I fear he forced the matter and then did not know when to bow away."

"And you, most naturally, gave him no hint, but continued to play until he had lost not merely this quarter's share but significant amounts from future shares. You waited, in fact, for his *cha'leket* to comprehend the situation and act to end it. After all, Master Kochi has the accumulated wisdom of seventeen entire Standards to support him. His *cha'leket*, I believe, is every day of eighteen."

"He was cleared to play," chel'Mara said flatly. "Am I to be held as nanny for every babe with the means to buy a deck?"

"I see. You consider that fleecing children adds to your *melant'i*. I am desolate to inform you that your delm considers otherwise. You will restore Master Kochi to his quarter-share and relieve him of the burden of future debt. You will accomplish these things before Prime Meal this evening. I do expect you to dine at home this evening, Vin Sin."

chel'Mara allowed surprise to show. "Certainly I shall undertake your orders regarding Master Kochi, sir. However, I am engaged to dine with—"

"Cancel it." Aragon held out his empty cup and chel'Mara, perforce, poured tea. His delm sipped. "Excellent. Yes." He set the cup aside and met chel'Mara's eyes with a cool smile.

"You think me harsh, but indeed my concern is solely for yourself, that you have opportunity to take proper leave of your close-kin."

"Leave-taking?" The chel'Mara fairly gaped. "I have no plans to travel, sir."

"Ah, I have been maladroit! Your delm, Vin Sin, requires you to travel on business of the clan. A bunk has been reserved in your name aboard *Randall's Renegade*, which breaks orbit an hour before Solcintra midnight. Prime has been set up an hour, to accommodate the necessity of your early departure."

chel'Mara sat still, the chill having moved from his hands to his belly.

"If I have indeed purchased so large a share of my delm's displeasure in the matters of Master Kochi and Scholar Caylon, I am of course desolate," he said, speaking gently, indeed. "But—sent off-world on a Terran trampship? Surely, sir—"

Aragon held up a hand. "You are about to say that such a measure is over-Balance, are you not? I repeat that the Caylon's instruction on her own behalf surpasses anything I might undertake for her. As for Master Kochi, I believe a return of his losses and relief from the specter of indebtedness shall settle his account fairly, with additional benefit accruing him through the vehicle of a very stern fright." He sipped tea. "Yes, I think we emerge a little to the good from your encounter with Master Kochi."

"Then this travel, this—ship . . ."

"Ah, yes." He leaned back in his chair, hands cradling his cup. "Guayar and I are well-known to each other," he said, at what one who did not know him might consider a tangent. "We are not *comrades*, you understand—the interests of our Houses but rarely intersect. And yet, I have known Guayar many years, since before ever the Ring was set upon his finger. His is a stringent *melant'i*, I do allow you that. But I have never known him *spiteful*, Vin Sin, nor inclined to go beyond verifiable certainties in discussion."

chel'Mara reached for his glass, downed the half of it in one swallow. It met the roil in his belly like oil poured on live flame.

"So," Aragon said softly. "I offered Guayar a ride to his next appointment as we left yo'Lanna's, which he was gracious enough to accept. His grace extended to a recitation of some of your past activities, and a candid avowal of concern."

chel'Mara cleared his throat. "Surely, sir, rumor and—"

"I spent the remainder of my morning verifying Guayar's information," Aragon continued, "which was—illuminating." He raised his eyes and chel'Mara could not look away.

"You may not be aware of certain inclinations of Aragon's fortunes—indeed, you concern yourself so little with the business of the House, that I am persuaded you cannot know!—but for the past several years we have been in a state of—mild, but worrisome—disadvantage. Interest rates rise by a point. Warranty periods are made shorter. Surcharges are added to the most commonplace of orders. Contract renewals are written so tightly one might almost suppose dea'Gauss himself had put his hand upon each. And I wondered, Vin Sin. I wondered, why. Guayar has shown me the answer, and I count myself in his debt."

"Sir—"

"No less than *three* delms of clans with which we do business regularly lost—catastrophically lost—to you at play—two of them when they were no older than Master Kochi. Four thodelms, an equal number of nadelms—and this does not begin to account for the favored youngers and *cha'leket*s who have been dealt public humiliation at your table since you reached your majority." He sighed, abruptly.

"I had known you were expensive. It is my error, that I failed to know *how* expensive. Now that I am informed, my duty is plain. It may be that the clan can yet recover something of value from you. The attempt must be made, else I am remiss in my duty to those others I hold in care."

The chel'Mara sat with his hands in his lap, thinking, *this cannot be happening.* And yet, incredibly, his delm continued, as if he were in verymost earnest.

"You will be aboard *Randall's Renegade* this evening, Vin Sin. My own car will bear you to the shuttle. In due time, you will be set down upon Aedryr, where you will be met by your aunt my sister Sofi pel'Tegin, who will conduct you to the family holding and instruct you in your responsibilities. I will tell you that I believe those responsibilities will at first have to do with mastering the recipes of various soil mixtures required to sustain the plants grown at the holding. The major portion of the holding's income derives from these same plants, so you will readily understand that a thorough knowledge of soil is of utmost importance."

chel'Mara licked his lips. "Uncle . . ."

Aragon reached into his sleeve and produced a card.

"Your identification card. I counsel you to guard it closely, as it is necessary to present it whenever you wish to travel beyond the land to which you are registered."

The card was extended toward him. chel'Mara raised an arm grown heavy with dread and forced nerveless fingers to grip the slick plastic. He took a rather ragged breath and looked into his delm's face.

"How long?"

Aragon sipped the last of his tea and put the cup down. "Your aunt appears confident that you will be able to master the intricacies of the House's business on Aedryr in five Standard Years. I leave it to her judgment, if you require a longer curriculum."

"Five Standards." On a *farm*? Mastering the mixtures of *soils*? It was a jest. It must be a—

Aragon rose. chel'Mara rose as well and made his bow, barely attending what he did.

"Until Prime, then," Aragon said, and turned. Halfway down the room, he checked, as if he had bethought himself of something else. chel'Mara sighed, feeling his heart lift, for now, surely, his delm would reveal the jest and—

"I had almost forgot, Vin Sin, the most diverting thing imaginable! Do you care to hear?"

He forced his lips into a smile and bowed lightly. "Why, certainly, sir."

"Ah, good. This planet—Aedryr. Gaming is unlawful by order of the planetary government. Anyone found with so little as a deck of cards in his possession is favored with a Standard of government labor, no appeal. Is it not amusing? Good day to you."

Aragon was gone.

chel'Mara sank down into his chair and closed his eyes, the thin plastic card gripped tight between his fingers.

He had never felt less like laughing.

IT WAS EARLY AFTERNOON IN CHONSELTA.

Aelliana began the walk from the train station to Mizel's Clanhouse with an absurdly light heart. The keys to her ship hung about her neck on a chain provided by Jon dea'Cort.

Using Binjali's comm, she had verified the transfer of owner-ship, opened a ship's account with the Port Master's Office and transferred her hoarded bonus money from Chonselta Tech's in-house bank.

She had perused *Ride the Luck's* regular maintenance records, finding also that the ship's berthing at Binjali Repair Shop was paid a full year ahead.

"Shall I refund that amount to Lord chel'Mara?" she had asked Jon dea'Cort doubtfully.

The old Scout snorted. "Ship paid the berthing fee out of its former account. The chel'Mara's arrangement was that he paid in advance without benefit of refund, should he decide to berth elsewhere. Your luck, math teacher."

"I suppose . . ."

She had been introduced to Master dea'Cort's apprentice, a compact and cheerful person who spoke with a marked Outworld accent.

"Trilla, give greeting to Aelliana Caylon, math teacher and owner of *Ride the Luck*."

"Aelliana Caylon." The bow was crisp and matter-of-fact, augmented by a smile and a flash of bright eyes. "Good lifting."

"Thank you," Aelliana said, returning the bow with relief. No embarrassing respect from Trilla, thank gods; merely a very Scout-like acceptance of what was.

Departing Binjali's, she had not forgotten to stop at the Ormit Fund's Office to make disposition of her quarter-share before catching the ferry to Chonselta.

Now, heading home lighthearted and not a bit weary, she re-assessed her position.

By her reckoning, she had one year to achieve a first class piloting license, learn Terran and garner what money she might. The delm had given her a year, after all, to prove her point regarding the investment of funds. Ran Eld would be held in check for precisely that long, saving Aelliana did nothing to provoke him or to arouse his suspicions.

So be it. She had ten years' practice of appeasing Ran Eld. For *Ride the Luck*—for freedom—she could endure one year more.

She walked up Raingleam Street, rapt and unseeing, so that her sister's voice gave her a severe start.

"Aelliana!" Sinit caught her sleeve and tugged her hurriedly up-street. "Come in the back way, do. Ran Eld's got his eye on the front door." She giggled. "Primed to ring down a terrifying scold!"

She turned stricken eyes to her sister's face. "What have I done now?"

"Well, you didn't come down to breakfast," Sinit said, turning into the back courtway, Aelliana firmly in tow. "That annoyed him. He sent Voni up to rouse you, but you weren't in your room. That annoyed him even more—you know what Ran Eld is. Then it transpired you weren't in the house at all!" She grinned and paused to work the latch on Mizel's gateway.

"Voni says your bed hadn't been slept in. *She* says you have a lover." She looked up, eyes brimming laughter. "Ran Eld's not about to stand for that!"

"A lover?" Aelliana stared, stone-still. "Voni thinks I have a lover?"

"Why not?" Sinit asked matter-of-factly. "Go in—quickly! Up the serving stairs and into your room—and mind you remember to come down to Prime!" She gave Aelliana a firm push and turned back to latch the gate.

For one long moment, Aelliana hesitated, heart pounding.

Then she turned and flew into the house, taking the thin back stairs two at a time.

Silent as a Scout, she negotiated the short hallway leading to her rooms, slipped inside and—futile gesture!—locked the door behind her.

She affected not to see the house comm's blinking message-waiting light, opaqued the windows and crossed to the narrow bed.

Fully clothed, she lay upon the coverlet, closed her eyes—and slept.

CHAPTER NINE

. . . by this note convey said land and building to the Liaden Scouts for the purpose of establishing an academy and training center for future Scouts and those whom the Scouts deem it wise to train . . .

**—Excerpted from a Contract of Gift
signed by Jeni yos'Phelium,
Ninth Delm of Korval**

"WE MISSED YOU AT BREAKFAST, sister." Ran Eld's voice was sweet and mild—a bad sign.

Aelliana set her teacup down and kept her eyes on her plate. They were four at table, the delm having sent word that she would join them later.

"Such an unusual happenstance," Ran Eld pursued. "Our sister was concerned for your health. Imagine her surprise when she entered your room and found you absent, the coverlet smooth atop the bed."

"I am grateful to my sister for her care," Aelliana told her plate, though the words felt like to choke her.

"Very proper, I am sure," Voni snapped from her place up-table. "But that does not address where you were all the night, Aelliana."

"Where would I be?" Aelliana wondered softly.

"Exactly what I wish to know!" her sister said sharply. "Really, Aelliana, I suppose you will deny that your bed had not been slept in!"

"Not at all. I—" she focused on a grayish square of vegetable pudding. "I was up much of the night, considering the wisest investment of my quarter-share. This morning I placed the funds as seemed best." She cleared her throat and reached for the teacup. "I did not wish to be behindhand in obeying the Delm's Word."

There was a charged pause, before Ran Eld's voice, very dry: "Commendable."

"Well, I think it is commendable," Sinit announced from her seat at the foot of the board. "Truly, Ran Eld, you make it seem a crime to heed the delm's wishes! The Code tells us plainly—"

"Thank you, little sister. I believe my comprehension of Code may be—somewhat—superior to your own."

"Oh, then you know you're making a stupid twitter over none of your concern," Sinit cried in a tone of broad enlightenment. "I, for one, am greatly relieved. You mustn't mind them, Aelliana—Ran Eld's in a temper and Voni's snipe-ish because Lady pel'Rula found fault with her dress."

"You were listening at the door!" Voni's voice shook in outrage. "I shall tell mother. Of all—"

Through the shield of her hair, Aelliana saw Sinit smile.

"Lady pel'Rula said Voni's dress was immodest, and not at all what one looked for in a lady of impeccable manner." The smile broadened to a grin. "It was, too."

"What do you know of the matter?" Voni snarled. "That design was copied from a gown created for yos'Galan! If Lady pel'Rula is so provincial that she turns her face from a look sanctioned by Korval—"

"Then she's well-rid of," Sinit suggested, eyes wide.

Voni frowned and extended a graceful hand for her wine glass. "Naturally not. Mother and I are to call upon her ladyship tomorrow after luncheon."

"And you'll wear a less dashing dress, won't you, Voni?"

Aelliana saw Voni's fingers tighten on the stem of her glass, knuckles paling. She answered in a voice rigid with fury.

"You need not concern yourself with my wardrobe, Sinit. I shall consider it an impertinence if you continue."

"Sinit, let be," Aelliana whispered urgently.

"Excellent advice." Ran Eld said, voice cloying as sugared tea. "How good of you to overwatch your sister, Aelliana, and drop these little hints in her ear. Allow me to perform the same service on behalf of yourself."

Aelliana reached for her teacup. It was empty. She swallowed hard in a dry throat and folded her hands onto her lap, eyes on her untasted dinner.

"Certainly," she said, hearing her voice tremble. "I welcome instruction from one so much my elder, and who is accustomed to going about in the world."

"Yes, you're not much used to the world, are you?" Ran Eld murmured, swirling his wine. "One tends to forget just how ill-suited you are to caring for even so small a portion of the clan's *melant'i*. But, there. If those who are wiser do not pause to instruct their inferiors, the wiser must share in the fault, when the inevitable disgrace occurs." He sipped, waiting.

Aelliana clenched her hands about each other. "As you say," she whispered.

Voni giggled and helped herself to another spoonful of baked melon.

"Precisely," Ran Eld said, lazily. "No, Sinit, *don't* speak, I pray you. Aelliana and I have quite agreed that she welcomes my tuition." He finished off his wine and set the glass aside, pushed plates, bowls and sauce-thimbles back and folded his arms atop the cloth.

"Look at me," he murmured, leaning forward.

Teeth-grit, she raised her head, met his eyes with a flinch.

"So." He smiled, not pleasantly. "Scouts, Aelliana."

She stared at him, speechless, saw his mouth tighten with impatience and blurted, "I teach Scouts."

"Precisely," he purred, mouth easing with satisfaction. "You teach Scouts, for which you receive a wage. A regrettable necessity.

However, necessity ends with the ending of the school-day. There is no need for—and, indeed, very good reason to refrain from—association—with Scouts."

"Scouts are not our kind," Voni elucidated, perhaps for Sinit's benefit. "Scouts, pilots, mechanics—it all comes down to bad manners, oily fingers and dirty faces. I hope no one of Mizel is so foolish as to credit such disreputable persons with heroism and vast knowledge. Heroism is a great piece of nonsense. I infinitely prefer good manners."

A flicker of mind pictures: Jon dea'Cort tidily wiping his broad hands on a red rag; Rema's spotless leathers and courteous concern; Var Mon's scrubbed-til-it-shone, mischievous boy-face . . .

"I—"

Ran Eld raised a hand and leaned closer across the table, eyes leveled like lasers.

"Scouts are not fit companions for one of Mizel. For *anyone* of Mizel," he said, spacing his words as if her ears were defective—or her wits. "Do you understand me, Aelliana?"

Bow the head, she told herself, desperately. *Be meek. Remember. Remember your ship.*

"I understand you," she whispered, heartbeat pounding in her temples.

"Well, what have we here, a tableau?" Birin Caylon stood in the doorway. She raised a hand on which Mizel's Clan Ring gleamed and stabbed a finger toward her son.

"Ran Eld is the insatiable cat about to eat the unfortunate mouse, portrayed by Aelliana—so!" She dropped her hand and came into the room. "Did I guess correctly?"

Ran Eld laughed and eased back into his chair. "Correct as always, Mother!"

"Indeed, ma'am," Voni ventured, rising to hold the delm's chair, "we were merely striving to show Aelliana and Sinit the unsuitability of associating with Scouts and other such persons."

"A cup of wine, Ran Eld, if you please—and a saucer of soup, if any remains."

Provided with these, she tasted her wine before turning her attention to her middle daughter, who sat yet in her pose of mouse-about-to-be-devoured. Birin Caylon felt a stir of compassion. The child looked unwell, her thin face was pinched and there were great bruised circles under her misty eyes.

Abruptly, Birin wondered if a particular Scout might be the subject of this lesson in appropriate behavior. She had a spoonful of soup. *Really*, she thought, *Ran Eld is too hard on the girl*.

"No doubt but that Scouts are odd-tempered," she said, after another spoon of soup. "I recall your father, Aelliana. What that man was for questions! He would babble on concerning a certain mix of tea, or the practice of drinking morning-wine only in the morning, or whether cats told jokes. He found the most mundane affairs cause for high amusement. Very nearly he drove me to distraction—and he merely trained at Academy and not a true Scout at all!" She sighed.

"Your grandmother, who was of course delm at that time, found him unexceptional. For his part, he showed her great deference and spoke highly in her praise, so he was not lost to proper feeling at all, as some claim of Scouts."

"And yet you do not deny that he, as all Scouts, was odd in his manner," Ran Eld said.

"No," said Birin, frowning after her thoughts. "No, my son, I cannot deny that he was considerably out of the common way. At the time, I suspected him of laughing at me. However, I have come to see that much of his oddness must be laid to his training." She paused.

"It is necessary for those who would take up the chancy duties Scouts claim for themselves to undergo rigorous and specialized education, the better to survive in the wide universe. It is to be regretted that an effect of attaining excellence in this curriculum must also make one—different.

"I have heard it said that Scouts are other than Liaden—that of course is nonsense. What I believe is that Scouts are burdened with an understanding that takes into account not only Liad, but the universe entire." She reached for her wine. "I believe such understanding sets them apart forever from those who look no further than Liad."

"Then you credit Scouts with heroism, do you, ma'am?" Sinit's voice carried clear amusement and Birin turned to frown at her.

"I credit Scouts with other-ness," she said sternly, "and perhaps with loneliness. It is possible that there is something to be learned from them, should one have the ability to grasp it. Not all do—which is no shame. Nor is there shame in finding that one has that certain ability." She moved her gaze to Ran Eld, sitting attentive beside her.

"I find no disgrace in the companionship of Scouts."

He inclined his head politely. Satisfied, Birin returned to her soup.

The silence was broken by the scrape of a chair. Aelliana rose and made her bow.

"If you please, ma'am. I have student work to review."

Birin waved a hand. "Certainly. Good evening, daughter."

"Good evening," the girl whispered and pushed her chair to, leaving a full plate of food and an empty teacup behind.

At the door of the dining hall, she paused and spun, one hand outflung. The silver ring that had belonged to her grandmother caught the light; lost it.

"Please, ma'am," she said breathlessly. "What came of him?"

Birin glanced up with a frown. "Of whom?"

"My—my father."

"Child, however should I know what came of him? I last saw him twenty-seven years ago, when we signed the completion of contract."

"Oh." Her shoulders drooped inside the cocoon of her shirt. "Of course. Good evening, ma'am."

"Good evening, Aelliana," Ran Eld called dulcetly, but the doorway was empty.

"HE DID WHAT?" Var Mon stared at his *cha'leket* in patent disbelief. "Have you gone mad?"

"No, but my lord chel'Mara doubtless has!" Lyn Den crowed. He flung himself into his *cha'leket*'s arms and kissed his cheek. "Come and rejoice, darling, I needn't join the Terran mercenaries, after all!"

"As if they'd have you," Var Mon retorted grumpily, "or as if you'd live a day in battle, if they did. And the office of informing your father doubtless falling to myself. Lyn Den, are you certain it was Vin Sin chel'Mara?"

"Am I likely to forget his face?" the other asked, spinning about in sheer exuberance. "Hello, Rema."

"Lyn Den." She inclined her head and came to stand at Var Mon's side, her face serious. "How do you go on?"

"Delightfully. Deliriously. I have had the best fortune imaginable, could I but convince this brute of a *cha'leket* that my mind is firm."

"Or as firm as ever it has been," Var Mon muttered. Rema smiled, briefly.

"What's come about? Has your father redeemed your debt?"

"Better—a dozen times better! Vin Sin chel'Mara himself met me after my early class—only imagine His Lordship cooling his heels in a university hallway! He met me, I say, and returned my entire loss, with a paper stating I owed him nothing in the future; that anything I might have come to owe him in the past is forgiven. Here—" He pulled a much-folded piece of vellum from his sleeve— "read it for yourself."

Var Mon snatched the paper free and unfolded it. Rema put her head against his and together they scanned the brief document.

"His signature, certain enough," she murmured, fingering the drop of orange wax and pendant silver ribbon. "Sealed up proper as you please."

"Well." Var Mon re-folded the page and thrust it back to his foster-brother, setting his face into a most un-Var Mon-like frown.

"I judge you've encountered an unreasonable bit of good luck. One only hopes that the fright you've had will be sufficient to keep you out of gaming-houses for the rest of your days."

"Oh, indeed. I intend to live retired and entertain but rarely, and that at home."

"Laugh do," Var Mon said, serverly. Rema and I are twelve day away from our solo examinations. Have the grace to grant me ease of mind where you are concerned. Or must I leave Academy and appoint myself your keeper?"

"There, old thing, don't take on!" Once more, Lyn Den flung

into Var Mon's arms. He lay his cheek against the leather-clad shoulder. "I'll be good, darling, never fear it. Truly, I've learnt my lesson—if I never see a deck of cards again it will be some days too soon for my taste!"

"Well." Var Mon allowed himself a tender smile as he set his *cha'leket* back. "Mind you stay wary. You'd best get on, now. We're bound for piloting practice—and you have your afternoon classes to consider."

"Monster." Lyn Den grinned, sobered. "Shall I see you again, before you leave for your solo?"

"Of course," Var Mon said. "You know I daren't leave planet without making my bow to my mother your aunt."

"True enough," Lyn Den laughed and swept a bow. "Pilots. Good lifting."

"Take care, Lyn Den," Rema called, as he ran lightly down the Academy's front ramp. She glanced aside and met Var Mon's puzzled eyes.

"A peculiar course for His Lordship to plot," she commented.

Var Mon sighed. "Do you know, I was only just now thinking that exact thought."

CHAPTER TEN

&c&c&c&c&c&c&c&c&c&c&c&c&c&c&c&c&c&c&c&c&c&c

There shall be four levels of pilot acknowledged by the Guild. The base level, or Third Class, shall be qualified for work within system and orbit, operating ships not above Class B.

Mid-level, or Second Class, shall be qualified to lift any ship to Class AA within system and orbit.

A pilot holding a First Class license shall be competent in accomplishing the Jump into and out of hyperspace.

Master Pilot is one able to perform all aspects of piloting with excellence. This grade may undertake to train and test any of the lower three levels.

For the purposes of these by-laws, Scout-trained pilots shall be understood to hold a license equal to Master Pilot.

—Excerpted from the By-laws of the Pilots Guild

THE TESTING CHAMBER was familiar, even comforting. In just such a cubicle had she taken her university placement tests, winning a full mathematics scholarship to the University of Liad.

Even the problems that flashed so quickly across the screen were comforting. There were no mysteries here; no danger. No doubt.

Aelliana's fingers flew across the keyboard, structuring and restructuring the piloting equations as required. She hesitated when the focus of testing shifted from practical application to law and regulation, blinked, shifted thought-mode and went on, speed building toward a crescendo.

The screen went blank. A chime sounded, startling in the sudden absence of key-clicks.

"Part One of your examination is completed," a mechanical voice announced from the general area of the cubicle's ceiling. "Please await your examiner with the results."

Aelliana sat back in the squeaky chair, hands folded sternly in her lap, head slightly bent, eyes on the quiet keys.

She felt no anxiety regarding this initial phase of testing. The piloting problems had been quite ordinary, almost bland. The abrupt change from math systems to regulatory language had startled her, but the questions themselves had been entirely straightforward.

She was less sanguine regarding her ability to perform satisfactorily at a live board. It was true that she had lifted and landed a Jump-ship. It was equally true that she had done so exactly thrice, each time monitored closely by Scout Lieutenant Lys Fidin, one of her most brilliant—and outrageous—students.

Within the shelter of her hair, Aelliana smiled. Lys had taken advanced training, gaining for herself the ultimate prize. When she left Liad it had been as a First-In, among the best the Scouts possessed, trained to go alone into uncharted space, to make initial contact with unknown cultures, to map unexplored worlds and star systems.

It had been Lys who attempted to convince her teacher to "go for Scout," and would hear nothing like 'no' when it came to Aelliana's lifting a live ship.

"Theory's all very well," the Scout insisted. "But, damn it, Aelli, you can't teach pilots survival math without ever having a ship in your hands!"

Lys won that effort, and lift a ship Aelliana did.

The next campaign had been for Aelliana's enlistment in a piloting course, which came to a draw: Ran Eld would certainly have denied such an expenditure from his sister's wages and might well have felt moved to make a retaliatory strike to remind her of his authority.

So, Aelliana audited Primary Piloting at Chonselta Tech, read the manuals from basic to expert, worked with the sim-boards in the piloting lab—and with that Lys had to be satisfied.

"Scholar Caylon." The door to the cubicle slid back with a rush, revealing Examination Officer Jarl. He bowed.

"I am pleased to report that you have flawlessly completed the initial testing. If you will accompany me to the simulation room, you may commence the second segment of the examination."

ONCE AGAIN SCENE and task were familiar, clear and comforting. Indeed, Aelliana found the sim sluggish, less sprightly than the board she still worked from time to time in the piloting lab.

The slow response threw her off-balance during the systems check and clearance operations. By the time it became necessary to engage the gyros and lift, she had largely adjusted to the slower pace, though the sluggard navcomp irritated. In the end, she simply ran the equations herself, feeding the numbers into the board and executing required maneuvers without bothering to wait for the comp's tardy verification.

She attained the prescribed orbit and, as before, the screen went abruptly blank. A chime sounded, the webbing retracted and the hood lifted. Aelliana stepped out into the larger room.

Examination Officer Jarl, who had been monitoring her progress in the master-sim, cleared his throat.

"Very quick—ah—Scholar. I note you were routinely ahead of the navcomp."

"The comp was slow," Aelliana said, hanging her head. "It was much more efficient to simply do the calculations myself and feed them in manually." She paused, gnawing her lip. "Shall I be penalized, sir?"

"Eh?" He coughed. "Oh, no. No, I don't believe so, Scholar. Though I must remind you that Port regs insist a ship's navcomp be engaged and online during lift and orbiting."

"Yes, sir," Aelliana whispered. "I will remember."

"Good," he said, rising and rubbing his hands together. He looked at her askance, as if she had suddenly grown a second head, then made his bow.

"As before, Scholar, a flawless—if slightly irregular—performance. I believe it is time for you and I to walk out to the field and see what you might make of the test-ship."

"Yes," Aelliana said and followed him out of the sim-room, head down and stomach churning.

AELLIANA INITIATED THE SYSTEM CHECKS and webbed into the pilot's chair, nervously double-checking the calibrations in her head. She brought the navcomp online and ran a test sequence, comparing the computer's results against her own.

Satisfied to six decimal places, and relieved to find this board more lightsome than the sim, she glanced over to the examination officer, who was webbed into the copilot's station.

"I am here as an observer, Scholar," he said, folding his hands deliberately onto his knee. "If difficulties ensue, or if it becomes obvious that ship's control is not firm, I shall override your board. If that should occur, it will be understood that you have failed the third phase of testing and may retest in twelve days. In the meanwhile, I am barred from answering any questions you may ask, or from offering any aid save override and return to berth. Is this clear?"

"Sir, it is."

"Good. Then I will tell you that I expect to arrive in Protocol Orbit Thirteen within the next local hour. Once stable orbit has been achieved, you will receive instruction for return to planet surface. You are cleared to proceed."

Aelliana took a deep breath, shook her hair back and opened a line to Chonselta Tower.

STABLE P-13 ORBIT was achieved in just under one local hour. The lift was without incident. Aelliana paid scrupulous attention to her navcomp and charted a course remarkable for its dignity.

It must be said that several times during this stately and

undemanding progress Aelliana found herself computing quicker, less grandmotherly approaches. Once, indeed, her hand crept several finger-lengths in the direction of the communications toggle, while her mind was busy formulating the change of course she would file with the Tower.

She pulled back with a gasp and continued the course as filed.

"Protocol Orbit Thirteen achieved, Master Pilot," she murmured, tapping in the last sequence and relaxing against the webbing. "Locked and stable."

"So I see." Examination Officer Jarl spun his chair to face her. "You disappoint me, Scholar. After such a run at the simulation, I had expected a lift like no other."

She swallowed, forcing herself to meet his eyes. "This navcomp is more able, sir."

"That would account for it, naturally," he said with a certain dryness. He glanced at his board, then sent a sharp gaze into her face. "Tell me, Scholar, how much time could have been saved, had you filed that change of course mid-lift?"

"I—As much as five-point-five minutes, sir. Perhaps six, depending upon precise orientation with regard to orbit approach."

"I see," he said again. "Yet you chose to continue the course first filed, despite significant time variation. I wonder why."

Aelliana inclined her head. "The safety factor was slightly higher," she murmured, "as well as the chance of absolute success. It is— important—that I gain my license, sir. I dared risk nothing that might endanger a positive outcome."

"Dared not put your license on the line, eh? Forgive me, Scholar, but this is not promising news. Surely you know that a pilot's first concern is for passengers and for ship. If he loses his license preserving either, that is regrettable, but necessary."

Aelliana bit her lip, feeling sweat between her breasts, where *The Luck's* keys hung. Surely—surely he would not fail her because she had chosen a less-chancy approach. The regulations—

"I shall give you an opportunity to redeem yourself, Scholar, and to show me your mettle."

She caught her breath, hardly believing she heard the words.

"Sir?"

He inclined his head, lips curved slightly upward.

"I wish you to return us to our original location. I expect you to halve your lift time—or better."

IT WAS FRIGHTENING, exhilarating. It demanded every bit of her attention, so that she forgot to sweat or worry or take precious seconds to calculate some alternate, less rambunctious descent.

She abandoned the navcomp early on, letting it babble gently to itself while she ran and modified the necessary equations and plugged them into the board.

Local traffic presented no difficulty, though she caught an edge of chatter from a slow-moving barge: At least one pilot thought she was pushing the luck. She forgot it as soon as she heard it.

Numbers flickered, equations balanced, altered, formed and re-balanced; Aelliana dropped the test-ship through eleven protocols, skimmed along the twelfth and fell like a stone into atmosphere.

Lys had taught her to extend the wings and wait on the jets. It was a Scout trick, designed to conserve fuel in circumstances where fuel might very well be scarce.

"Fly her as long as you can," the Scout had told her. "You don't have to kick in those retros until you can see the street where you live."

Flying was somewhat more difficult than mere lifting or jet-aided descent. Flying meant manual defeat of local weather conditions. Local weather conditions had been milk-mild on Aelliana's three previous ventures.

They were not so today.

The ship bucked and twisted, nose going down despite her efforts at stabilization. Scan reported precipitation, turbulent winds. Maincomp reported hazard.

Aelliana hit the jets.

One short blast, as Lys would have done it—just enough to get the nose up and calm the bucking. They flew smoothly for a minute, two.

Aelliana hit the jets again.

And again.

And one more time, as she took up the approach to the Guild's field. This time she kept them on, letting them eat the remaining velocity, until the ship hesitated and touched down, light as a mote of dust, on the designated pad.

The jets killed themselves. Aelliana drew in the wings, ran the mandated systems check, reported her safe condition to Tower and began the shutdown. Beside her, Examination Officer Jarl was silent.

Check completed, Aelliana shut down the board, retracted the webbing and spun her chair, lifting her head and meeting the man's eyes.

"Arrived, sir. I believe the time is somewhat less than half the ascent time."

"Yes." He closed his eyes, sighed deeply, opened his eyes and retracted the webbing. "I apprehend you have trained with a Scout." He stood and looked down at her, his face damp with sweat.

"Such an approach is very effective—and entirely acceptable, should you be carrying Scouts or—inanimate cargo. For your general run of passenger, however, you will wish to go more gently."

Aelliana inclined her head. "Yes, Master Pilot."

Once again, he closed his eyes and sighed, somewhat less deeply. Apparently recovered by this exercise, he bowed as to a fellow Guild-member.

"If you will accompany me to the registry office, Pilot, I shall be pleased to issue a provisional second class license in your name."

Aelliana stared at him, gulped air and managed to stand on legs suddenly gone to rubber. She returned the bow, augmenting it with a hand-gesture conveying gratitude to the instructor.

"Yes, well." He cleared his throat. "You are required to complete certain hours of flight-time in order to gain regular status. Flight-time requirements must be met within a *relumma* of this date and certified by a master pilot. I note you are acquainted with Jon dea'Cort. He or any of his crew are qualified—I would say, peculiarly qualified—to assist you and in providing any further training you may wish to undertake."

Aelliana bowed her head. "Yes, Master Pilot. Thank you, sir."

"I believe there are no thanks due, Pilot. You have earned this prize with your own hands. Follow me, if you please."

Shivering with reaction, heart pounding in terror—or jubilation—Aelliana followed.

CHAPTER ELEVEN

I have today received Korval's Ring from the hand of Petrella, Thodelm yos'Galan, who had it from the hand of Korval Herself as she lay dying.

My first duty as Korval must be Balance with those who have deprived the clan of Chi yos'Phelium, beloved parent and delm; as well as Sae Zar yos'Galan, gentle cousin, a'thodelm, master trader. There is also Petrella yos'Galan, who I fear has taken her death-wound.

Sae Zar fell defending his delm. All honor to him.

Chi yos'Phelium died of a second treachery and in dying gave nourishment to her sister, my aunt, who alone of the three was able to win back to home.

The name of the world which has fashioned these losses for Korval is Ganjir, RP-7026-541-773, Tipra Sector, First Quadrant.

This shall be Korval's Balance: As of this hour, the ships of Korval and of Korval's allies do not stop at Ganjir. Korval goods do not go there; Korval cantra finds no investment there. And these conditions shall remain in force, though Ganjir starves for want of us.

. . . I note that my mother is still dead.

**—Daav yos'Phelium Eighty-Fifth Delm of Korval
Entry in the Delm's Diary for Finyal Eighthday in the
First *Relumma* of the Year Named Saro**

✧ ✧ ✧

DAAV FINGER-TIGHTENED THE LAST SCREW, reached over and swung the powertorque into position.

The repair had been tedious, badly located and generally ill-wished. His back ached from bending, his wrists tingled from the torque's vibration, his left leg had gone numb some minutes ago and sensation was now returning in a flood tide of needles.

He aligned the torque with the first screw, steadied it with his left hand and hit the go-stud with his right. Vibration rattled his hands, screamed through his head. He welcomed these minor pains as he had welcomed the others.

He hit the second, third and fourth screws, killed the power and allowed the torque rise to the height of its tether. Cautiously, he straightened.

Abused back muscles sued urgently for their guild rep. Daav raised his arms shoulder-high, then over his head, stretching high on his toes, pulling his entire body taut.

At the height of the stretch, muscles quivering and tense, he closed his eyes and ran a mental sequence he'd been taught as a Scout cadet. Colors whirled before his mind's eye, there was an abrupt *click*, loud in the inner ears. Daav brought his arms down to shoulder-height, then the rest of the way, tension and minor aches receding in a wave of delicious warmth.

By the time he had settled flat on his feet, he felt as if he'd had, if not quite an entire night's sleep, a very substantial nap.

"Well," he said to himself, or possibly to Patch, Binjali's resident cat, who had watched the repair from atop the tool cart. "That would seem to be that."

Patch yawned.

"Yes, very good. Denigrate my efforts. It won't do for me to go above myself. I do remind you, however, that I am merely casual labor, which must account for my clumsiness and ill-use of time. I make no doubt that Master dea'Cort—or, indeed, yourself!—would have managed the thing in high style and half the time. Perhaps someday very soon now I shall be privileged to see Master dea'Cort work."

That he had not lately been so privileged was not Jon's fault, but Daav's, as he would have been first to admit. Indeed, after pleading so urgently for access to Binjali's particular grace, he found the necessities of Clan Korval conspired to keep him away for four days together. He had returned only this morning, to be greeted with precious off-handedness by Jon, who had set him to the repair of the back-up jitney.

An hour or so later, Jon called that he was going over to Apel's for a glass, which Daav knew to be an undertaking of some hours. Trilla was due in the afternoon, Clonak, Syri, Al Bred and perhaps a few others would appear when they were seen. If trouble arose which Daav couldn't handle, Jon desired to be called from his wine so that he might marvel at it.

Now, the repair at last done, there was no sign of Trilla, Clonak or the other possibles. Daav moved Patch from the cart to his shoulder and stowed the tools. The cat arranged himself, stole-like, about the man's shoulders and stuck his nose into a vulnerable ear, purring.

"I suppose it's nothing to you that your nose is cold and damp? I thought not. Contrive to leave my hair rooted to my head, if you please. And if I detect so much as a paw-flick toward that earring, you, my fine sir, are mouse meat."

Tools neatly hung away, Daav closed the cart and moved silently toward the front of the garage, stripping off his work gloves as he walked. The sight of his naked hands gave him a momentary shock, and he lifted a finger to touch the chain about his neck. Korval's Ring hung, secret and safe, hidden below the lacing of his shirt.

"Do you know," he said to the cat riding his shoulders, "I believe I shall see if I can repair the tea-maker. It's my belief Jon has recalibrated the brewing sensor in order to save money on leaf."

Patch yawned. This was an old line of chat, after all. Dozens of Scout fingers had been inside the tea-maker over the years, seeking to correct its tragic fault—all, thus far, in vain.

"I might just buy a new unit," Daav mused, rounding the ladder that led to the cat-walk. "And install it one day while he's out courting Mistress Apel."

That idea appealed. Daav ducked under a guy-rope and came

out into the minor open space of the crew's lounge. Sitting before the tea-maker on the scarred counter—indeed, entirely concealing that rather bulky object—was a box. Attached to the box was a paper, 'scribed in garish orange ink. Daav plucked the paper free.

Leave my teapot alone, you assassin. Jon dea'Cort's perpendicular hand was unmistakable. *When you've done with that minor five-minute repair job up-bay, lift this to Outyard Eight. Gat expects delivery before Solcintra midnight.*

Daav grinned. "Horrid old man," he said affectionately, reaching up to rub Patch's ear. The purring intensified, setting up a very pleasant vibration across his shoulders.

"So, my friend, shall you watch the shop until Trilla arrives? Or shall we go back to the office and see what sense can be made from the roster-sheet? There's a—" Patch shifted abruptly on his shoulder, claws skritching across the leather vest.

Daav turned as the crew door cycled, admitting a wedge of mid-morning sun and a bulky, hesitant shadow.

The shadow came two steps into the garage, walking with something near Scout silence, then paused, head moving from side to side while the door cycled closed behind.

Patch twisted to his feet and jumped from Daav's shoulder, landing noisily atop one of the ancient stools.

"Hello?" The voice was strong and even, an odd partner for that uncertain manner. She came forward, soft-footed on the hard floor.

"Master—oh." A tensing of her entire body, as if for a blow, and a jerky inclination of the head. "I—beg your pardon," she stammered in Adult-to-Adult. "I was—Is Master dea'Cort about?"

"Not just at the moment," Daav said, deliberately relaxing his muscles and letting his mouth curl slightly upward. "May I assist you? I am Daav—one of the crew here, you see." He used his chin to point at the black-and-white cat now perched, erect and dignified, atop a stool cushioned in dull green leather.

"Patch will vouch for me."

She turned her head, furtively, as if expecting a reprimand, and drifted forward another few steps, pausing with her hip against the farthest of the disordered semi-circle of stools.

"Patch?"

"Half-owner and resident cat," Daav returned, pitching his voice for foolery. "We've been known to each other any time these eight years. His word is quite as good as Jon's."

She turned back, head lifting sharply, giving him sight of a tense, fine-featured face dominated by a pair of shadowed green eyes.

"You—are—a Scout."

"Retired, alas," he replied, hoping serious gentleness might fare better than comradely joking. "Is there some way in which I might serve you?"

"I had come," she began, and then cut off with a gasp, not recoiling so much as freezing in place, head bent to stare—

At Patch, who was twisting this way and that, stropping himself against her hip and purring outrageously.

"What—" Her voice died as if breath had failed her. Daav stepped gently forward.

"He wants his chin rubbed, spoiled creature. Like this." He reached down, carefully unthreatening, and demonstrated. The purring reached an alarming level.

"I—see." She extended a thin hand adorned by an antique puzzle-ring and used two tentative fingers on the black-splotched chin.

"A bit more forcefully," Daav coached gently. "It's a hedonist, I fear."

Once again, that quick lift of the head and startled flash of eyes. Then her attention was back on the cat, her face hidden by a rippling fall of tawny hair.

Daav made himself restful, as Rockflower had labored to teach him, cleared his mind of judging thoughts and allowed the woman before him to elucidate herself.

Observed thus, she was not bulky, but desperately thin, disguised and armored in layers of overlarge clothing. Likewise, the feral tension and the quiet, uncertain movements were two wedges of the same shield, meant to hold the world away.

Look away, her tense shoulders seem to say. *Look at anyone—at anything—else, but at me.*

She was misused, whoever she was—a person urgently in need of the benediction of friendship.

One of Jon's stray kittens, Daav thought, but the notion sat not entirely balanced. He watched her fingers on the cat, more certain now, having moved from chin to ear in response to Patch's explicit direction.

Comrades she might need, and someone to ensure she was fed, yet he felt she was not entirely a stray. About the rigid shoulders sat a mantle of purpose and from beneath the imperfect, ill-confining armor roiled such a potent brew of energy that Daav shivered.

The woman's thin body registered his movement, countered it with an abrupt cessation of her own motion. He received the impression that green eyes had read his face through the curtain of her hair.

"I had come," she said, and the burr of a Chonselta accent tickled his ear, "to find if my ship was ready to lift. Master dea'Cort had said—perhaps it might be—today. Depending upon the crew."

"Ah. I am able to assist you, then. If you will walk with me to the office, we may check the roster."

"I am grateful," she said formally, and kept a wary step behind him down to Jon's office at the back of the bay, Patch walking, high-tailed, at her side.

Daav tipped the screen up and tapped the on-switch.

"May I know the name of your ship?" he murmured as she came forward, stopping with the solid mass of the desk between them. Patch jumped nimbly to the cluttered surface and leaned companionably against her side.

"*Ride the Luck.*"

In the act of calling up the roster, he froze, and shot a glance at her shrouded face. Daav knew Vin Sin chel'Mara, as well as mutual dislike allowed, and knew somewhat of His Lordship's habits. He cleared his throat.

"Ma'am . . ."

"It is not complete," she interrupted, shoulders sagging within her large, shabby shirt. "I had hoped—but of course there was a great deal of work to be done. Might—might the roster indicate, sir, when she will be ready to lift?"

"Well," Daav murmured, "let us see." He tapped in the required information, then stood, blinking like an idiot, reading the name on the work order, over and over.

"Up to spec and ready to lift," he said after a moment, eyes yet stuck to the screen. A moment more and he managed to move, transferring his stare to the person before him.

"Forgive me. You are Aelliana Caylon?"

Green eyes met his amid a silken ripple of hair. "Yes, I—Of course, you will want identification! I do beg—" Her head was bent once more. She produced a thin metal card from a sleeve pocket and held it out, face averted.

He took it, automatically, noting the blurry likeness, and the date—two days gone. Provisional Second Class.

"Thank you," he murmured and gave himself a sharp mental shake, trying to align this tentative individual with the extraordinary mind that had reconstructed the ven'Tura Piloting Tables, the brilliant scholar who taught Practical Mathematics, or, as it was called in Scout Academy, Math for Survival.

"You are the revisor of the—"

"Of the ven'Tura Tables," she said breathlessly, all but snatching her license back from his hand. "I am. Please do not bow. I—I have explained to Master dea'Cort."

"Which is certainly enough for both of us," Daav said, grabbing for equilibrium. He smiled. "Your ship is ready and able to lift. You have, as I see, the skills necessary to the task. Good lift, pilot."

"I—That is." She floundered to a halt, took a shuddering breath and raised her head to squarely meet his eyes. "The fact is, I am in need of flight time. I've never lifted—you understand, I've never actually *gone* anywhere. And the regs—I had thought Master dea'Cort . . ."

"I see." Daav tipped his head, considering. "It happens there is a small errand left me by Jon. If you like it, I can serve as your second, and you may actually go somewhere. Outyard Eight to be precise."

The misty eyes took fire. "I would like that—extremely, sir."

"Then that is what we shall do. However, I must insist upon a condition."

Wariness cooled the fire, leaching color from her eyes. "Condition?"

"It is relatively painless," he said, offering her a smile. "The custom at Binjali's is to speak in Comrade. No one demands it, it is merely custom. In no case, however, am I 'sir.' I prefer to be addressed as Daav. If you find that too intimate, then 'pilot' is acceptable." He tipped his head. "Are you able to meet this condition?"

She inclined her head, very solemn. "I am—Pilot."

"Good," he said, and shut down Jon's computer. "Let us see if Trilla has come on-shift."

CHAPTER TWELVE

❧❧❧❧❧❧❧❧❧❧❧❧❧❧❧❧❧❧❧❧❧❧❧❧❧❧❧❧❧❧❧❧

The delm must be a smuggler-class pilot—take from yos'Galan if yos'Phelium fails, as it likely will. I'm a sport, child of a long line of random elements, and Jela—

Young Tor An's folk have been pilots since the first ships lifted beyond atmosphere, back among the dead Ringstars. yos'Galan will breed true.

The best pilot the clan possesses must be delm, regardless of bloodline. This will be taken as a clan law.

The delm's heir must be a pilot—of like class to the delm—and as many others of the clan as genes and the luck allow.

There must be ships, spaceworthy and ready to fly: As many ships as it is possible to acquire. Such a number will necessarily require funds for maintenance—whole yards devoted to their readiness. Therefore, Clan Korval must become wealthy as Jela and me only dreamed of wealth.

Serve the contract, as long as it's in force. The boy don't hold with oath-breaking.

—Excerpted from Cantra yos'Phelium's Log Book

"LIFTING TO OUTEIGHT?" Trilla grinned. "Convey my undying affection to Gat."

"Yes, very likely," Pilot Daav returned, shrugging into a worn leather jacket.

Aelliana looked at that battered item hungrily. "Pilot's jacket" most would say, because of the cut, and as if any third-class barge runner might have one. In truth, only those who mastered Jump held the right to wear a pilot's jacket.

Trilla laughed and winked at Aelliana. "Scholar, good day to you. What luck at Chonselta Guild Hall?"

"Second class provisional," she said, pulling her eyes away from Pilot Daav's jacket, and warily meeting the other woman's merry glance.

"Everything fulfilled but the flight time! *Ge'shada*, Pilot." Surprisingly, the Outworlder swept a bow of congratulation. When she straightened, her face was somewhat more serious.

"Daav's among the best you can have next to you at board, don't fret yourself there. Very good with ships—eh, Master Daav?"

"It humbles me to hear you say it, Master Trilla."

She laughed again, fingers shaping the sign for *rogue*. "Get your box, then, and haul out. I've work to do. Where's the Master?"

"Apel's."

"Think they'd just set up house—be cheaper, which ought to compel Jon."

"Yes, but Apel's not such a fool," the man said earnestly. "Besides, I expect she likes drinkable tea."

"Much more compelling, I allow. Heard news of crew?"

"Clonak, perhaps, and Syri. Al Bred this evening, if at all. The back-up jitney's on-line."

"Put you on that, did he?" She grinned and lifted a hand, turning toward the office with Patch at her heels. "Good lift, pilots."

"Thank you," Aelliana whispered, watching the man raise the bulky cargo box easily to his shoulder.

"After you, Pilot," he said courteously, black eyes level and calm. Scout's eyes, that saw everything, gave back little, and judged nothing.

"Of course," she stammered, and turned to lead the way to the crew door, feeling him, silent and solid, behind her.

Outside, he stowed the box in the jitney's boot, straightened and stood looking down at her from his height, head tipped to one side.

"Shall you drive, or shall I?"

Aelliana swallowed, trying without success to calm nerves set all a-jangle by the last few harrowing days. The acquisition of the precious piloting license had not eased her position within Mizel, but rather increased the necessity for Ran Eld's unquestioning acceptance of her subservience. It had been necessary to placate her brother not once but several times, each time bowing lower, until she could taste carpet dust on her tongue, mixed with the bile of impotent fury.

It had been a risk to steal away today, she thought with a heart-wrench of panic. In general her days off were spent in the tiny office at Chonselta Tech. Ran Eld knew that. What if he were to seek her there and find the door bearing her name locked? He would want to know where she had been—would demand to know—and what might she tell him, that would buy his belief, while preserving her limited independence? She had been mad—she *was* mad, gods help her. How could she have thought—

"Scholar Caylon." Calm, deep voice, warm sense of a body near—too near!—something, feather-light, against her sleeve—

She gasped, cringing back, shoulders jamming up around her ears. Through her hair, she saw alarm cross the tall Scout's face, replaced instantly with careful neutrality. His hand, for it was his hand, dropped from her sleeve and he stepped back, beyond the boundaries of isolation she had woven for herself.

If he had simply turned and gone, she would certainly have fled to the ferry, and spent the return trip to Chonselta pleading with a pantheon of uncaring godlings for the grace of undiscovery.

He did not leave. He spoke, in Adult-to-Adult mode, very precisely, so the accent of Solcintra rang sharp against her ear.

"I regret that my presence troubles you, Scholar. Allow me to bring Trilla, so that she may sit second board for you."

His presence *did* trouble her: Tall, slim and graceful, with his odd, twisty earring and neat, overlong hair, the black eyes bold in a sharp, compelling face—He troubled her as the cat had troubled her, and for the same reason.

The cat—so soft, so *comforting*. Once she had started to stroke it, she could not stop; the joy the creature received from her caresses had awakened some dangerous nameless need—

The cat had *seen* her.

Tall Daav, with his bright black eyes, had *seen* her as well and knew her to be—real.

"Scholar?"

"I—" She shook her hair away from her face, forcing herself to meet those sightful eyes. "I beg your pardon yet again, sir—Pilot. The last few days have been—uneasy. It would be best, I think, not to lift today."

"Hah." His mouth curved slightly—a gentle smile—though his eyes remained neutral. "Sky-nerves, we had used to call it at Academy," he said, in Comrade once again. "The best cure is to lift as planned."

Lift as planned. Aelliana felt the words strike somewhere at the nearly-forgotten core of her.

She took a deep, trembling breath and inclined her head.

"That is doubtless excellent advice," she said evenly and saw something move in the depths of the Scout's dark eyes. "I will ask that you pilot the jitney, however. It seems the surest course for arrival."

The smile became more pronounced. "I drive with delight," he said, and moved 'round the jitney to the driver's slot.

AELLIANA FILED A COURSE on the challenging side of the equation, scrupulously remembering to bring the navcomp on-line, and took the opportunity of the quarter-hour wait to tour *Ride the Luck*.

The refurbished hold was eminently satisfying, though the pilots' quarters remained in their previous state of lavish comfort, lacking only the ceiling mirrors.

Aelliana looked about the chamber, feeling the slight vibration of the ship's gyros, hearing the hum of the support system, the muted clamor of Port chatter feeding in over the mandatory open line, and sagged against the wall, the room blurring through a rush of unaccustomed tears.

Hers.

The fierceness of possession warmed her, terrified her. It was dangerous to want something this much. So many things might go wrong—and the clan . . . Until the day she cleared Liad orbit, heading for her Jump-point, she was an asset of Clan Mizel; her possessions no more her own than the clan's. Mizel could as easily dispose of Aelliana Caylon's ship as it was legally able to dispose of Aelliana.

"Pilot?" Daav's voice came quietly from the wall speaker at her shoulder. "We are cleared to lift in two minutes."

"Thank you," she said, pushing shakily away from the wall. *Sky-nerves* . . . "I am on my way."

THE LIFT TO OUTYARD EIGHT was almost—restful. Master pilot that he was, Daav kept a serene second board. He took communications to his side with a murmured, "By your leave, Pilot," and offered neither chatter nor any other assault upon her privacy.

Not so Yardkeeper Gat.

"What ship?" It was not so much query as demand, loud enough to pierce Aelliana's concentration on the approach path, so she shot a glance full of startlement to her co-pilot.

A wiry golden hand moved to flick the proper toggle. There was a band of lighter gold about the third finger, Aelliana noted, and a faint indentation, as if Pilot Daav had left off an accustomed ring.

"*Ride the Luck*," he answered the abrupt query. "Pilot Aelliana Caylon at first board. Daav from Binjali's on second. Yard comp downloaded ship's particulars two-point-four minutes gone, Keeper, and cleared us for Bay Thirty-Two."

"I don't care what her name is or how good she can add! I've got a second class provisional on a non-standard approach to my Yard. What does she know about docking? How do I know she won't hole the ring?"

Daav grinned, which did unexpectedly pleasant things to his foxy face. "Ah, the sweet anticipation!" he said gaily. "Never fear, sir, all shall be resolved in a very few minutes. Unless you would rather we simply jettison the cargo and leave?"

"All a good joke, is it?" the Yardkeeper snarled. "Bay Thirty-Two ready to accept *Ride the Luck*. You've got eight minutes to get in, unload that cargo and dump out."

"Unless, of course, we hole the ring," Daav murmured politely. The in-line hummed empty.

Daav laughed, sending a bright glance toward Aelliana. She ducked her head, but did not entirely turn away.

"Non-standard approach?" she asked, voice breathless in her own ears.

"Dear Gat. He only means to say that, measured against other first approaches to ring-docking by provisional second class pilots he has seen in the past, this one is a bit too quick, a bit too flat—very nearly Scout-like, in fact." His fingers moved, swift and certain among the instruments. "Two-thirds local velocity must be dumped within forty-three seconds, Pilot, else we buy a bumpy docking and Gat's disapprobation."

"Good gods." Aelliana spun back to her board.

SEVEN-POINT-NINE MINUTES LATER, *Ride the Luck* tumbled out of Bay Thirty-Two, oriented, and commenced descent.

The boards worked sweetly under Daav's fingers; he was agreeably surprised in *Ride the Luck*, which seemed to sing with joy around them.

He was likewise surprised in Aelliana Caylon, who, for all her skittish, wary ways, knew what to do with a ship in her hands. From power-up to dump-out, there had been not one false move. The minor flutter of hesitation upon approach he assigned to Gat's account, for breaking the web of her concentration and recalling her to the chancy world of human interaction.

The course she had chosen to OutEight had been ambitious for a second class provisional, though well within her abilities. Daav had several times noted her pushing the navcomp, as if she found its entirely respectable response time almost too slow to bear. The filed descent was worthy of a Scout and Daav had no doubt she would execute it with aplomb.

Aelliana Caylon, he thought, watching her fragile hands

flickering over prime board, might very well be that rarest of precious things: a natural pilot.

Guild law required a master pilot engaged in evaluating a junior to judge and implement appropriate training. Aelliana Caylon, in the judgment of Scout pilot/Master Daav yos'Phelium, was easily capable of achieving first class. It was likely that master pilot was within her grasp, did she care to leave her own work for a *relumma* or two and devote herself to study.

Thus, a variation from the simple meeting of second class flight-time requirements was mandated. Daav ran an experienced eye over his scans, double-checked the filed approach and addressed the pilot, pitching his voice soft out of care for her concentration.

"I wonder," he murmured, keeping his eyes scrupulously on his board, "if you might wish to attempt a sling landing."

"Now?" she asked, voice sharp with surprise.

"You will have to master the skill, soon or late," he said, all gentle reason. "Why not begin today?"

"To refile the course, to tie up the port's emergency sling . . ."

"The most minor readjustment of course," Daav soothed, "and no need to discommode port at all. Binjali's has a sling."

Hesitation. Daav consulted his scans and dared push his point a bit, before time became too short.

"I can call Jon, if you like it, and see if we have clearance. We will come in on automatic first time, of course." He paused. "Unless you have already trained on sling-shots?"

"No . . ."

"I'll call now," Daav said, flicking the line open.

"Good-noon, Captain darling!" Clonak ter'Meulen's voice filled the tiny cabin a moment later. "What service shall my humble self be delighted to perform for you?"

Daav's lips twitched. "Where's Jon?"

"Up to his neck in a gyro-fix. Service?"

"Sling-shot, automatics, current coords—" he reeled them off, confident of Clonak's abilities as of his own. "Flight plan down-loaded—*now*. Cleared?"

"Cleared, oh Captain. You and the pilot can take a nap. Until soon."

"Until soon, Clonak." He cut the connection and turned his head to glance at Aelliana Caylon.

She was looking directly at him, green eyes wide, less misty than he recalled, and holding something akin to—amusement.

"It seems a sling-shot is mandated," she observed, and there was the barest thread of laughter, too, in the weave of the fine, strong voice. Daav grinned.

"Your pardon, Pilot. Of all people, you must know what Scouts are!"

"Bent on mischief," she agreed, astonishingly tranquil, "and decided entirely upon their own course." She turned back to her board and her hair shifted to conceal her. "I shall file an amended descent."

THEY WERE WELL INTO THE AMENDED DESCENT when a certain subtle lack called Daav's attention to the upper left quadrant of his board. Apparently the navcomp's inefficiencies had become too burdensome to tolerate, for it was shut entirely down. He reached for the reset.

"That's wrong," Aelliana Caylon told him sharply.

"Wrong?"

"Off by two places." Her fingers were flying over the board, as well they should, he thought abruptly, with her running such a course on manual. He punched navcomp up.

Wrong, indeed, and off by nearly three places. Swearing silently, he called for the back-up. It came on-line with a suspicious stutter, accepted its office—and failed.

CHAPTER THIRTEEN

In the absence of clan, a partner, comrade or co-pilot may be permitted the burdens and joys of kin-duty. In the presence of kin, duty to partner, comrade or co-pilot must stand an honorable second.

—From the *Liaden Code of Proper Conduct*

"COMP TWO DOWN," Daav said, eyes raking the scans. It was too late by several minutes to change course now.

"We're committed to the sling. I'll call Jon and file the change. Begin sending your numbers to me for verification."

"Yes," she said, never looking away from her board. Daav hit the comm.

"Navcomp suspect," he told Clonak a heartbeat later, "back-up's dead."

"How lovely for you, darling."

Daav grinned. "Pilot Caylon will be bringing her to the sling on manual."

A short pause, then a cheery, "Right-o!" in what Clonak fondly considered an Aus accent.

"*Ride the Luck* out."

"Ta-ta."

Daav slapped the line off, dumped his holding bank and leapt into a river of numbers.

Ordered and swift, the equations flowed, through his bank, into the board and out, a continuous perfect stream of checkpoint and balance. He forgot about the navcomp, which should have been tested and cleared as standard procedure. He forgot the oddities of the woman beside him. He forgot Delm Korval.

There were the equations flowing to him, cold and pure, to be verified and fed in. There were the scans. There was the sense of the ship around him. There was the background chatter along the open line.

"When you feel the sling lock," he said, hardly hearing his own voice through the wall of his concentration, "you will cut the gyros. Immediately."

The small portion of his mind not urgently concerned with equations, scan and ship expected an outcry, for to cut the gyros was to be immediately and irrefutably within the talons of gravity. Cutting the gyros meant the ship would *fall* . . .

"Yes," said Aelliana Caylon and said no more.

He picked up the next sequence, noting that it was the set-up— the final equation. He scrutinized, verified and locked it, leaning back slightly in the web of safety straps.

"Twelve seconds. Mind the sling-lock, Pilot . . ."

It came, a distinct sensation of ship's progress halted, of plate metal and blast glass grasped tightly in the jaws of an inconceivable monster . . .

Aelliana cut the gyros.

The stomach twisted, the inner ear protested, the heart clutched as for an instant it seemed that the monster's jaw had slackened, and the ship sliding free to—

"Caught," Daav announced quietly. "And retained. A difficult task, executed well. *Ge'shada*, pilot."

"No need for congratulation," she said. "You were correct, after all. I shall need this skill." She threw him a glance, eyes brilliantly green in a pale golden face. "What is the procedure for clearing the sling?"

"Jon sends a workhorse and hauls the ship to its berthing—heading out now, your two-screen."

"I see. And the pilots?"

"In this case, I believe the pilots should make haste to Master dea'Cort. The luck was in it, you caught that error in time."

Once again, that brilliant green glance. "I know regs demand the navcomp be running—but I find it distracting. Doubtless it is my inexperience and I do expect to learn better, s—" She paused, lips tightening. "I cannot help but keep checking the equations, and when it started giving me bad numbers . . ."

"It was even more distracting," Daav concluded amiably. "Perfectly understandable. Point of information: Normal procedure in such circumstance includes engaging the secondary comp."

She looked abashed, the brilliancy of her eyes dimming a fraction. "I had no notion there was a back-up navcomp, sir."

"Daav. Ships of this class carry a primary navcomp and one back-up as standard. Most pilots will install a second back-up. Some prefer more. It is wise to check before dropping to manual, especially if you are running solo."

She bowed her head. "I will remember."

"Good," he said and retracted the webbing. "Lessons being done for the moment, I suggest we wait upon Jon."

"A BEAUTIFUL LANDING!" Jon dea'Cort announced, raising a large, heavy-looking tea mug. "Not at all like some I've seen, where the ship comes in upside down and backward, eh, Daav?"

Clonak, the pudgy Scout with hair on his face—"A *mustache*," Pilot Daav had murmured in Aelliana's ear, at her initial start of surprise—laughed aloud and made an ironic, seated bow. "You shall never outlive it, Captain."

"So it seems," Pilot Daav returned placidly and looked back to Master dea'Cort. "What about that navcomp, Jon?"

The older man took a hearty swig from his mug. "I'd say replace it."

"Replace—Oh. Oh, no." Aelliana slid off the stool Jon had insisted she take and stood, hands knotted before her. "Navcomps are—Master dea'Cort, *Ride the Luck* is not a wealthy ship. I intend to work her, but until work can be found, expenses must be held to a minimum. You have been very helpful—indeed, generous, in the refitting, but I—" She stumbled to a halt.

A pair of humorous amber eyes considered her. "Spit it out, math teacher. We're all comrades here."

She drew in a breath, trembling as she met that gaze. "I cannot afford to replace the navcomp."

"Well." Master dea'Cort took counsel of the ceiling.

"Regs are pretty clear," he said eventually. "Navcomp's got to be online while the ship is in use within Port-controlled space. Unless you can afford fines and temporary suspension easier than a replacement comp?"

"It—it needn't be off-line for an instant!" Aelliana cried, the plan taking shape even as she spoke. She leaned forward, cold hands twisted into a cramped knot, eyes on Jon dea'Cort's face.

"I'll engage the navcomp, sir, I swear it! It will be—I can learn to ignore it, use override and merely run manual, as I did today. Then, when there has been sufficient work—" Something moved in the man's face and she stopped, gulping.

Clonak broke the small silence, voice hushed.

"Daav, I'm in love."

"What, again?"

The sound of his calm, deep voice recalled her to a sense of duty left undone and she spun, not quite meeting his eyes.

"I am remiss. You did very well, Pilot, to keep the pace. I am—I am grateful for your assistance and the gift of your expertise."

Trilla, seated beside Clonak, gave a shout of laughter. Jon grinned. Clonak popped off his stool and bowed full honor.

"We shall make a pilot of you yet, oh Captain!"

Aelliana gasped in dismay. She had not meant to hold him up to ridicule before his comrades, but to thank him sincerely for his aid. She felt her cheeks heat.

"No, I—"

But Daav was already making an answering bow toward Clonak.

It was a pure marvel, this bow, swept as if the work leathers were the most costly of High House evening dress. One long arm curved aside and up, holding the imaginary cloak gracefully away as the sleek dark head brushed one elegant, out-thrust leg.

"You do me too much honor."

"Well, that's certainly likely," Jon declared, and shot a glance aside. "Clonak, sit down or go away. In either case, be quiet. Daav, descend from the high branches, if you please. Math teacher, pay attention."

She turned to face him, hands clasped tightly before her.

"Yes, sir," she said humbly.

"Huh." He glanced to the ceiling once more, then back, eyes and face serious.

"Nobody here says you can't run the board by hand forever without a mistake. But there's nobody here who hasn't at least once made a mistake, and been glad there was a double-check to save 'em. We're master class, each one of us." He used his chin to point: Trilla, Clonak, Daav, and tapped himself on the chest with a broad forefinger.

"Master class. The ship don't fly us, which is the case with the chel'Mara. We fly the ship. But blood and bone gets tired, math teacher—even Scouts have to sleep. Say you were hurt and needed time in the 'doc—do you leave the ship to a glitched comp, or do you sit that board and hope you don't pass out?"

She licked her lips. "Surely, in Solcintra. In local space—"

"The luck is everywhere—for good or for ill—and it's best not to spit in its face." Jon leaned forward on his stool, one arm across a powerful thigh.

"We're not talking regs, child. We all agree the regs are expendable—given sufficient cause. What we're talking is common sense. Survival. You understand survival."

"Yes," she whispered and swallowed hard in a tight throat. "Master dea'Cort, I cannot afford a replacement navcomp. I cannot afford to be grounded. *Ride the Luck* is a working ship and I intend that we—that we earn our way."

"That being the case," Daav said from behind her, "commission

Binjali Repair Shop to replace the navcomp and drop in two back-ups. Jon holds the note and you pay as work becomes profit."

Jon looked at her seriously. "That's sound advice, math teacher."

"Daav has very sound judgment," Clonak chimed in, irrepressible as Var Mon, "though I grant you wouldn't think so, to look at him."

"I—I can't ask—hold a note for a replacement—for *three* replacements? Master—"

"No choice in the matter," Trilla said in her blunt, Outworld way. "Need a working comp to lift. Need work to finance the comp." She grinned. "You might take a loan against the ship, of—"

"No!"

"Huh." Jon again. "Sounds settled to me. I'll hold the note for my cost, plus labor. You'll pay me as able. In the meantime, if I have something to lift, you take it at your cost and we'll call that the interest. Agreed?"

There was, as Trilla said, no choice. Still, Aelliana struggled with necessity a moment longer. A debt of such magnitude would surely increase the time she must stay upon Liad, thus increasing the chance of discovery. And yet, it was required that the ship be able, if work was to be gained.

She inclined her head, vowing to pay this debt as quickly as she might.

"Agreed, Master dea'Cort."

"Good enough. When's your shift end, Daav?"

"Midnight."

"Glutton. Take Clonak and go pull that comp. I'll find the replacements." He smiled at Aelliana. "We'll have you up to spec by tomorrow mid-day, math teacher. I'll leave a complete accounting in your ship's in-bank."

"Thank you," she said, feeling tears prick her eyes. She ducked her head. "I am grateful."

Jon slid off his stool and stretched. "Same as we'd do for any of our own—no gratitude demanded."

"Clonak, old friend, your skills are in demand!" Daav had a tool belt over one shoulder and was holding out another.

"And I with a thought to dinner," the pudgy Scout sighed.

He turned as he passed Aelliana and performed an absurdly ornate bow.

"For you, Goddess, I forgo even food!"

"Nor like to starve of it," Daav commented.

"Cruel, Captain."

"Merely honest. Come along, dear." Black eyes found hers, though she made an effort to avoid the glance.

"Pilot Caylon, it was a rare lift. I hope to sit second for you again."

"Thank you," she stammered and felt she should say more.

But Daav was gone.

"NAVCOMP PULLED, sealed and dispatched to the port master via Pilot ter'Meulen, who swears he's for a sup and a glass, lest he die of starvation."

"Well enough," Jon allowed, pouring the dregs from the pot to his mug. He glanced over his shoulder at the slender man perched on the green stool, Patch sitting tall on his knee.

"Pastry?"

"Thank you, no."

"Not stale enough for you?" Jon speared a iced dough-ring for himself and carried tea and snack over to his accustomed stool.

"Too stale, alas. My *cha'leket* insists upon fresh pastries for his table, and you see how his decadence affects me."

Jon snorted and had a bite, followed by a swallow of tea.

"I wonder," Daav said pensively, rubbing the cat's ears. "Who certified that navcomp at refitting?"

"Checked it myself," Jon said, somewhat indistinctly. "Sang sweet and true." He paused for more tea, and pointed a finger.

"Occur to you to wonder how it is the chel'Mara, who never piloted anything other than a groundcar on manual in all his life, isn't splattered from here to the inland sea, running automatic with an insane navcomp?"

"It did." Daav sighed. "I spent an hour looking for a meddle, but if it was there, it was very cleverly tucked away."

"Don't have to be there now," Jon pointed out. "I checked the log—suspicious old man that I am—and you looking to become another such, if I may say so." He finished off the dough-ring in two bites.

"Log says that on the night he played pikit with our math teacher and lost his ship by way of it, Vin Sin chel'Mara—that's *Lord* chel'Mara to you—stopped by the shop and entered his once-was ship, to clear out his personal effects. Didn't take him long. In fact, turns out he left quite a number of very expensive—and portable— items behind."

Daav said something impolite in a language native to a certain savage tribe some fourteen zig-zagged light-years out from Liad. Jon grinned.

"No proof. Not that I don't favor it myself, for personal reasons. The chel'Mara's very careful of his *melant'i*. Doesn't do a man's *melant'i* any good to lose his ship, true enough. But you might be able to recoup something from the debacle, if she were straightaway seen to crash it."

"Which she might have done," Daav said, so heatedly Patch jumped to the floor. "If she had been *any* second class provisional, making her first sling-shot when that comp went bad—" He took a hard breath. "Your pardon."

"Nothing to it." Jon grinned. "A rare wonder, our math teacher, eh?"

Daav moved his shoulders. "I'd like to know who beats her."

"I'd welcome news of that, myself. At least they didn't send her here battered and bruised-up today, small grace." He finished his tea and looked up into the younger man's eyes.

"Good idea of yours, me holding the note."

"I can guarantee the loan, if you like it," Daav returned quietly. "Or tell me the account and the price and I'll make the transfer now."

"Don't be an idiot. She intends to work that ship, and I'll tell you what I think. I think what our math teacher puts her mind to do is good as done. I'll hold her note."

"If it becomes a burden, old friend, only tell me. There's the Pilots Fund, after all."

"So there is. Well." He bounced to his feet and stretched with a mighty groan. Daav slid lightly from the stool and stood looking down at him, affection plain in his sharp, clever face.

"Hah." Jon smiled up at him. "You coming in tomorrow?"

"Perhaps the day after."

"All right, then. Glad you were to hand today. Matters could have gone ill, even if she is a wizard at the board."

"She wouldn't have attempted the sling if I hadn't suggested—demanded—it." He hesitated. "She's a natural, Jon."

"Is she?" the older man said, with vast unsurprise.

Daav laughed and bowed. "Good-night, Master."

"Good-night, lad. Convey my highest regards to your *cha'leket*."

CHAPTER FOURTEEN

A Dragon does not forget. Nor does it remember wrongly.

—From **The Liaden Book of Dragons**

"**MASTER DEA'CORT** sends you his best regards, brother." Daav and his *cha'leket* were strolling arm-in-arm across Trealla Fantrol's wide lawn, angling more-or-less toward the wild garden and the river.

Er Thom sighed sharply. "Whatever have I done, to earn Jon dea'Cort's notice? We have scarcely exchanged a greeting in twelve years, so seldom do our paths cross, yet I cannot be abroad these last few *relumma* without hearing news of his regard! Only yesterday, Clonak ter'Meulen crossed Exchange Street at the Port's busiest hour to bring me Master dea'Cort's wish for my good health!"

Daav laughed. "Why, I suppose you've won his admiration, darling. Is it burdensome?"

"Merely bewildering, since I go on quite as usual, with the exception of succeeding to yos'Galan's ring, and I cannot for my life see what that should have to do with Jon dea'Cort!"

"Nothing at all—and you are correct in supposing a man's coming into his intended estate would utterly fail to win Jon's interest, much less his admiration. No," Daav murmured, "I believe it is your lifemating which has bought his heart."

Er Thom stiffened and shot a brilliant violet glance into Daav's face. "My lifemating, is it? A subject which falls well outside his reasonable area of concern."

"You are severe," Daav said, stroking the stiff arm soothingly. "Recall that Jon is a Scout. He expresses the greatest admiration for Anne's work. For yourself, he admires your—moxie, as he would have it."

"Moxie?" Er Thom frowned after the Terran word.

"Courage," Daav translated, rather freely. "It is not every Liaden, after all, who might lifemate a Terran, flying in the face of custom and—some would say—good sense."

Er Thom laughed softly. "Indeed, there was hardly a choice!"

"Yes, but you mustn't let Jon know that!" Daav said earnestly. "Allow him, I beg, to continue believing you and Anne lifemated because love was stronger than custom!"

"Of course—" He caught himself with another slight laugh. "Let Jon dea'Cort believe what he likes, then! I only wish he will give over such lavish regard."

"You might send him a token in Balance, if you find his esteem a burden." Daav grinned. "In fact, I believe I know just the thing! Have you a tin of that particular morning tea Anne favors?"

"'Joyful Sunrise'? Certainly. I can easily part with a dozen, if you feel it might answer."

"One tin should suffice, I think, and a card inscribed by your lady, desiring Master dea'Cort to enjoy the beverage as she does."

"Hah. It shall be done this evening!" Er Thom smiled, then sobered. "What word from Pilot tel'Izak?"

Daav lifted an eyebrow. "Word? No, no, darling—you mistake the matter entirely! It is I who ought to be about sending word. The lady believes me at her feet." He sighed lightly as they passed through the gap in the hedge. "And means, I fear, to have me remain there."

On the other side of the hedge, Er Thom stopped, rounding with such a look of outrage that it was all Daav could do not to laugh aloud.

"*You* at Samiv tel'Izak's feet? She has audacity, I see."

"Merely self-consequence." He slanted a glance into Er Thom's indignant eyes and fetched up a doleful sigh. "You have taken her in dislike."

"Indeed, how might I take her in anything at all, when she kept High Mode the evening through and refused to give one sight into —" Er Thom's mouth tightened. "This is a joke."

"Ah." Daav caught the other's arm and turned him gently toward the wild garden. "Alas, it is not a joke, but plain observation. The pilot considers that Korval's solicitation of herself exposes vulnerability." He paused. Er Thom's eyes were still stormy; he stood on the knife's edge of taking the lady in extreme dislike, on Daav's account.

And that, Daav thought suddenly, was neither seemly nor kind. For a time Samiv tel'Izak would be his wife, bound by the terms of the contract to live apart from the comforts of clan and kin, surrounded by strangers upon whom she must depend for what day-to-day gentleness one human being might have from another. To enter thus unprotected into a House where so substantial a person as her husband's *cha'leket* held her in despite—no, it would not do.

"The assumption is doubtless original with the lady's delm, and is not altogether shatterbrained," he said, looking gravely into Er Thom's eyes. "Only think: All the world wishes to marry Korval— and Korval chooses Samiv tel'Izak. Those of Korval wed pilots—and she is a pilot. But there are other pilots, who are not Samiv tel'Izak, and who remain unchosen."

Er Thom's eyes were somewhat less stormy. "True enough," he allowed, though brusquely.

"True enough," Daav murmured and shaped his lips into a gentle smile. "Think again, brother. It was you urged me stand away, if I did not like the match. We are Scouts and traders—odd folk by any count. We might think of turning our face from custom—even at the risk of our delm's displeasure, eh?"

Er Thom laughed quietly.

"Yes." Daav allowed his smile to grow to a grin. "But consider one who is without our resources—to whom custom bears the weight of law—desired by her delm to come forth and take up duty.

She must accept her delm's elucidation of circumstance: The Dragon offers for Samiv tel'Izak because none but herself will do." He moved his shoulders. "Shall we deny such a small comfort to one who will be so short a time among us?"

There was a pause.

"Certainly the lady is welcome to what comfort she may make for herself," Er Thom said softly. "I had been angered because it seemed she held you cheap."

"My lamentable sense of humor," Daav said ruefully and offered his arm. Er Thom took it and they continued their walk along the artful wilderness, talking of this and that, until Daav turned them, regretfully, back toward the house.

"The Council of Clans devours the remainder of my day," he said.

"Another meeting?" Er Thom frowned. "They proliferate."

"Geometrically," Daav agreed. "A land dispute has arisen between Mandor and Pyx. I think it a matter requiring the skills of two or three *qe'andra*, rather than a full Council."

"Why not offer Mr. dea'Gauss as arbiter?" Er Thom murmured, naming Korval's own man of business.

"Pyx has already taken up the *melant'i* of victim," Daav said, "and chose the Council as offering the widest scope for spite." He sighed sharply as they passed through the hedge.

"Had you heard that Vin Sin chel'Mara lost his ship in a game of pikit?"

"The port speaks of nothing else," Er Thom replied. "The detail that remains unclear in the reports I have heard is the name of the winner. Some say a pair of Scoutlings, some others say a professional sharp-player from Chonselta City."

"Ah? I had heard Aelliana Caylon."

Er Thom's winged brows pulled together. "The mathematician? Who had that tale?"

"Clonak. His father was present during the play."

"Well, then, there can hardly be doubt," Er Thom said, who knew Delm Guayar for a person of quite savage accuracy. "Good lift and safe landing to the scholar." He paused, his fingers exerting a mild pressure on Daav's arm.

"Do you know," he said softly, "I had heard something else. Talk is that the chel'Mara is sent off-world by his delm, in Balance for losing his ship." He flicked a quick violet glance to his brother's face. "Which is no more than he bargained for, no matter the winner. What fool stakes his ship at chance?"

"The chel'Mara's sort of fool, apparently," said Daav. "Well, and if Aragon is at last moved to apply discipline, then the world is twice indebted to Scholar Caylon."

Er Thom laughed lightly. "Thrice, you must mean, brother, else you cannot have ever seen the chel'Mara fly."

"Well," said Daav with a smile, "perhaps I do." And the talk turned to other things.

"THAT WAS A *BINJALI* sling-shot, Scholar Caylon!" Var Mon hit his seat with a grin. "We scanned the tape, then rode the sims 'til dawn, but no one came close to your run—not even Rema."

"Hardly until dawn," Rema said, entering the room with rather less energy and giving Aelliana a proper bow of greeting. "Good-day, Scholar Caylon."

"Good-day, Rema." Aelliana returned the bow with an inclination of the head, then shook her hair back to consider Var Mon.

"I thank you for your praise. However, it must be remembered that my co-pilot was most able. I doubt the landing would have been so adroit, had I made the attempt solo."

Var Mon's face went abruptly and entirely blank. He lowered his eyes and bustled noisily with his notetaker.

"No doubt but your co-pilot was exemplary," Rema murmured, over her comrade's sudden clatter. "However, the tape clearly shows it was your hand brought the ship in, Scholar. An astonishing run, our piloting instructor declared it."

"And you never saw one so tightfisted of praise!" Var Mon finished, returning to his usual mode as abruptly as he had departed. "Scholar Caylon, you must go for Scout!"

"Indeed, I must not," she replied firmly as Baan, Qiarta and Nerin arrived, made their bows and took their seats.

"Good-day. This is, as you all know, our last session together. I have given you everything that I know how to give, to insure you each hold the best possibility for survival. In spite of my best effort, it is conceivable that I have failed of being as clear as I might have been upon this point or that. This last session is yours. What is less than glass-clear and utterly certain in your minds? Review now what we have covered throughout the semester. No point is too insignificant to ask upon. I shall take the first question in six minutes."

That quick, notetakers were out and fingers were flying. Rema leaned back in her chair, eyes unfocused on a corner of the ceiling.

Aelliana bent her head over her console and felt her lips curve in the rarity of her smile.

A beautiful landing! Jon dea'Cort applauded from memory, while Daav's deep voice gave quieter praise: *A difficult task, executed well.* And now: *A binjali sling-shot, Scholar! . . . An astonishing run . . .*

Aelliana closed her eyes and felt something loosen, down close in her chest, so the next breath she took was a shade deeper, a fraction less hurried, as if she had taken one single sip of brandy.

The timer rang, and Aelliana raised her head, smiled at her class and lifted a hand, inviting the first question.

THE DISPUTE BETWEEN PYX AND MANDOR was resolved with gratifying speediness. No more than six additional delms had found it necessary to rise and speak of matters in tenuous relationship to the subject and the vote, when taken, showed a clear majority in favor of Mandor's claim.

Daav shut down his tally screen, almost smiling with a surge of sheer exuberance. An entire afternoon open to his own expenditure, with no meetings and no duty pressing upon him. He considered going down to Binjali's, but that would mean returning home, to exchange his delm's finery for the comfort of his leathers. Perhaps—

"Hedrede is seen. Rise and state your business." Speaker for Council's voice contained a note of dryness that Daav registered as out of place even as he re-activated his tally screen.

Hedrede was old: The name was to be found on the passenger list of *Quick Passage,* 'scribed in Cantra yos'Phelium's strong, sharp hand. Indeed, one Vel Ter jo'Bern of House Hedrede had been co-signer of the contract between Cantra and the Solcintran Houses.

For all of these years and past glories, however, Hedrede was not High House. It stood for centuries within the top five percent of Mid Houses, and there it seemed content to remain, neither speaking out in Council nor concerning itself with matters outside of Liad's orbit.

There was a faint shuffle, then a figure rose along the tables of the fifth hub and made a perfunctory bow toward the Speaker.

"Hedrede calls upon Korval." The voice was strong, not young, female.

Swallowing surprise, Daav came to his feet, bowing toward the fifth hub. "Korval is here."

There was a slight pause to accommodate the rustling of amaze from among those gathered. Hedrede calls upon Korval before full Council? Two clans less likely to have aught to do with each other could scarce be found.

What could it be? the rustling delms asked each other, by eye and by whisper. Indeed, conjecture stretched so wide that Speaker for Council was moved to touch her chime and command them all to silence.

"Korval rises at Hedrede's word. Hedrede may speak."

"No one here," Hedrede announced to a chamber grown suddenly still, "need be reminded of the place Korval holds in history. More, perhaps, than any clan here-gathered may it be said of Korval, 'This clan is kin to Liad.'"

This, thought Daav, standing in the formal attitude of attention which custom demanded of him, *is going to be bad*.

"Having so illustrious an history," Hedrede continued, "and standing so close to Liad and Liadens, it must surely be mere— oversight—that a certain item which wrongs both homeworld and history has been lately published by Korval." She bowed, with lavish respect. "I call upon Korval to riddle this paradox."

Oh, thought Daav, as the chamber again erupted into murmuring speculation. *Oh, damn*.

Speaker for Council touched her chime, forcefully, and raised her voice to ride the hubbub.

"Korval may reply to Hedrede's query."

He bowed—to Speaker for Council, and to Hedrede. He turned slightly in his place, opening his hands in a gesture of gentle astonishment.

"It is assumed that honored Hedrede refers to a certain scholarly work compiled by one of Korval and recently published through University Press." He paused and bowed again, careful to avoid irony. "One wonders in what way this work is found to wrong the homeworld."

"The work in question," Hedrede replied, for the benefit of those observing this unexpected and delightful diversion, "purports to establish a link between Terra and Liad by demonstrating an ancient, common tongue." She bowed. "Korval will, naturally, correct any error in this summation."

"The summation is entirely accurate. One is yet unenlightened as to the wrong thus visited upon Liad."

There was a short pause, which carried the vinegar bite of irritation to Daav's sensitivities.

"The work," Hedrede continued, after a moment, "has been written by one of Korval who is by birth, Terran. To the untutored eye, this combination of fact would seem to spell one who has seen the value of a wide and varied *melant'i* and has determined to spend that value, for the betterment of her own kind."

Anger rocked him. *How dare*—

He closed his eyes, ran the calming sequence of the Scout's Rainbow; remembered to breathe. This was a direct attack upon Korval. To answer in anger would be to answer in error. Anne's *melant'i* was staked here—and Er Thom's—and his own. Kin to Liad, was he? He'd bloody well—

He snatched the thought, turned, searched—found the face he wished to find, high up in the ninth tier, and bowed.

"Korval calls upon Yedon."

She rose with an alacrity that led him to think she had been expecting the call.

"Yedon is here."

"Verification is sought of the initial scholarship of the work under discussion," Daav said, forcing his voice to calmness, though he could feel anger shivering in elbows and knees. "One recalls that the first discovery of a common tongue from which proceeded both Terran and Liaden was made by Learned Scholar Jin Del yo'Kera Clan Yedon."

"Korval's memory," said Yedon solemnly, "is accurate—and long."

A slight murmur stirred the chamber at that. Daav bowed.

"One also recalls that before his death Scholar yo'Kera had completed much of the work toward eventual publication."

"Correct," Yedon replied and turned to Hedrede in explanation. "Jin Del had considered this work to be the crown of his life. It was his intention to publish the results. That Scholar Davis was available to compile his notes and see them published in accordance with his express wish could only give joy to kin and colleagues."

Hedrede inclined her head. "You tell me that a Liaden had formulated this theory and had intended to publish it abroad?" She raised a hand. "But perhaps the theory which is published is not that which the Learned Scholar had at first put forth?"

The anger was less jarring this time; colder, more dangerous. Daav allowed himself a small sigh as Yedon made answer.

"Indeed, I had seen the work directly before publication, as had several of Jin Del's colleagues. It matches his intention in every particular. Scholar Davis was generous with the gift of her genius."

There was silence in the chamber. Eventually, Speaker for Council touched her chime.

"Has Hedrede further call upon Korval in this matter?"

Hedrede started, visibly collected herself, and bowed.

"Hedrede has no further call upon Korval within Council," she said formally and resumed her seat.

Daav bowed, in his turn releasing Yedon, and sat with exquisite care.

Soon after, Speaker for Council ended the session and touched the chime to release them. Daav fussed over gathering and regathering papers and by such schoolboy stratagems eventually left the chamber alone, and last.

CHAPTER FIFTEEN

"Liaden Scout" must now be seen as a misnomer, for to become a Scout is to become other than Liaden. It is to turn one's face from the homeworld and enter a state of philosophy where all custom, however alien, is accepted as equally just and fitting.

We are told by certain instructors that not everyone may aspire to—nor all who aspire, attain—that particular degree of philosophical contrariness required of those who are said to have "Scout's eyes."

For this we must rejoice, and allow the Scouts full honor for having in the past provided refuge for the disenfranchised, the adventurous and the odd.

—Excerpted from remarks made before the Council of Clans by the chairperson of the Coalition to Abolish the Liaden Scouts

THE WOMAN BEHIND THE COUNTER wore an embroidered badge on the shoulder of her leather jacket: A bronze-winged, green-eyed dragon hovering protectively over a tree in full, luxuriant leaf. Beneath the graphic was written, not the "I Dare" which would have completed the seal and identified the wearer as one of Clan Korval's Line Direct, but "Jazla pen'Edrik, Dispatcher."

She heard Aelliana out with grave courtesy, hands folded upon the counter.

"As it happens, we do from time to time require the services of freelance pilots," she said at the conclusion of Aelliana's rather breathless presentation. "May I see your license, please?"

She held it out, wishing bitterly that her hand did not tremble so, then folded both hands before her as the dispatcher turned and fed the card into the reader.

Korval was ships, everyone knew that. No clan owned so many; no other clan or company employed so many pilots. It had always been so—stretching back to the very ship, the very pilots, who had brought Liadens safely out of the horror of the Migration.

Clan Korval took pilots and piloting very seriously, indeed. Thus Aelliana had gone first to Korval's Solcintra Dispatch Office to request that her name be added to the list of pilots available to fly.

"Aelliana Caylon," the dispatcher said, eyes intent on the reader's screen. "Provisional second class—quite recent. One assignment completed on behalf of Binjali Repair Shop. Master Pilot dea'Cort lists himself as reference. So." She tapped a sequence into her keyboard, retrieved Aelliana's card and held it out with a grave smile.

"I shall be very pleased to add your name to our roster, Pilot Caylon. May I know the best means of contacting you?"

"Chonselta Technical College," Aelliana recited the number of her private office line, "or a message might be left at Binjali's—" She repeated the code Jon dea'Cort had given her. "You may wish to note that I am owner of a Class-A single-hold."

"So," the dispatcher said again, fingers dancing briefly across the keys. "Please contact this office immediately your certification changes, pilot." She glanced up. "I advise that the possibility of a second-class provisional attaining work from this office is not high. That you own a ship is of value; that you have already successfully completed one assignment is likewise of value," she smiled. "As is, of course, Master dea'Cort's word."

Aelliana swallowed, face stiff.

The dispatcher inclined her head. "If it is not amiss, Pilot, I offer advice."

"I should be grateful for advice," Aelliana returned sincerely, clutching her license in cold fingers.

"Register with the Guild Office on Navigation Street. Tell them that you fly your own ship and are willing to carry a hold-full or a courier pack. Ask to be placed on the Port Master's Roster." She tipped her head, birdlike. "They may not wish to do so until you have achieved solid second-class. But ask. And when you lose provisional, go back and ask again."

Aelliana bowed. "That seems sound advice. I thank you."

"No thanks due," the dispatcher assured her. "Good lift, Pilot."

"Safe landing," Aelliana returned, which proper response tasted oddly sweet along her tongue. She made her bow and exited Korval's office, making for the next dispatching station on her carefully-researched list.

"IS THIS YOUR IDEA OF A JOKE?" Jon demanded, holding a gaily-painted tin high on one broad palm.

Daav gave the tin a moment of earnest perusal before turning a grave face to the older man.

"Alas, Master Jon, try as I will, I find nothing amusing within the object. It seems quite an ordinary tea-tin."

"Ordinary!" Jon roared, at such volume that Trilla leaned over the edge of the catwalk and Syri came out from behind the toolbox, head cocked inquisitively.

Jon thrust the tin in her direction. "Identify this."

"Joyful Sunrise morning blend," she returned promptly.

"In a stasis-sealed tin," Jon amended, and fixed Daav in an awful glare. "Do you know the price of this tin on the port?"

Daav opened his black eyes wide. "No, how could I?"

"Puppy. A cantra on a glut-day, for your interest."

"Ah, then I appreciate your concern!" Daav cried, much enlightened. "Such a leaf will do no justice to your teapot, Master! Best return it to the merchant who sold it you, and ask for less of something more noble."

High on the catwalk, Trilla laughed. Syri raised a hand to hide her smile and Patch the cat wandered over to strop against Daav's legs.

Jon's lips were seen to twitch. "I suppose it's nothing to do with you, that the yos'Galan chooses to send this particular gift?"

"The yos'Galan?" Daav repeated, with a fine show of bewilderment.

"Oho, you wish me to believe that the yos'Galan's *lady* conceived this, do you? It may be her hand, young Captain, but I know better than to suppose it her thought." Jon raised his face to shout.

"Trilla, bring your hammer!"

"Aye, Master Jon!" She snagged a guy-rope and rode it briskly down, alighting with a snappy salute.

"Come along," Jon directed, and turned toward the crew lounge, Trilla at his heels.

Syri sent Daav a wide stare. "He never means to break the seal with a hammer!"

"Perhaps he merely intends to deliver the coup to the teapot," Daav said, bending to scoop Patch to his shoulder before moving off in Jon's wake.

"Never," Syri returned, falling in beside him. "That teapot's like a child to him. He'd sooner use a hammer on Patch."

"Hah. In that wise, we had best put speculation aside, and consider the evidence of our senses."

She laughed, that being one of the basic precepts of Scouthood, and they continued like two shadows down the bay, Patch riding tall on the man's leather-clad shoulder.

"We'll have a shelf here," Jon was telling Trilla, tapping his finger on the wall next to the teapot. "Good, sturdy work, mind. We'll need a locking case, and a place to display the lady's card. You," he turned to glare at Daav. "Get 'round to Min Del's and tell him I need a case, so—" he shaped it roughly in the air, one hand still holding the tin— "quicktime. Mind you tell him it's to lock to my print and none other! I'm damned if I'll have you bunch of hooligans breaking into my tin and replacing this leaf with sage!"

"But, Master Jon," Syri protested, "don't you mean to drink it?"

"Drink it?" Jon stared. "Have you run mad? Drink Joyful Sunrise? Why, I'd as soon—"

The crew door cycled noisily and Patch leapt from Daav's shoulder, running tail-high and spring-footed to greet the new entry.

Aelliana Caylon bent and stroked the cat's back where it curved against her knee in exuberant hello. Straightening, she tried to walk on, but found herself forthwith entangled in cat. She paused once more, bent and stroked; straightened—and nearly fell as her feline admirer wove joyfully between her legs.

She hesitated a heartbeat—two—before bending again and inexpertly gathering the cat into her arms. Patch settled against her shapeless chest, eyes slitted in ecstasy, front paws kneading the sleeve of the thick shirt. Aelliana came forward.

"Afternoon, math teacher!" Jon called, raising the tin in salutation.

"Good afternoon, Master dea'Cort," she replied solemnly. She paused, Patch purring like a cat besotted in the basket of her arms. One-by-one she surveyed Trilla, busy with her measurements, Syri's open-faced concern, Jon's hand and the tea-tin. The question, when it came, was addressed to Daav.

"Forgive me. I wonder if there is something—gone awry."

"Not a bit of it," he returned cheerfully. "Jon is only building a shelf to house a newly-acquired treasure."

Aelliana's head turned back toward Jon, hair shimmering. "A tea-tin?" she asked, bemusement sounding clearly. Daav grinned.

"Damn me if you're not as bad as he is!" Jon cried, sweeping his unencumbered hand toward the taller man. "This isn't just any tea-tin, math teacher, this is a gift from Master Trader Er Thom yos'Galan, honored son of the exalted House of Korval! What've you to say now, eh?"

Aelliana cuddled Patch absently against her. "It's a very pretty tea-tin," she offered after a moment.

Trilla choked and nearly dropped her measuring-wand. Syri gulped and walked rather unsteadily over to inspect the contents of the pastry carton.

"Pretty," Jon repeated tonelessly. He reached into his vest pocket and reverently produced a folded card of the sort used to write notes of invitation. Gravely, he showed the front of the card—the Tree-and-Dragon, complete with the boldly embossed "Flaran Cha'menthi"—and thrust it at Aelliana.

"Read it, then."

Smoothly, she readjusted Patch's weight, took the card and opened it, one-handed. She frowned for a moment at the message within, then raised her head, hair falling away from her face as she offered the card back to Jon.

"I am ashamed to admit that I neither read nor speak Terran," she said quietly. "It is a deficiency I intend soon to remedy. For today, however, I am ignorant."

"Hah." Jon fingered the card open. "It says—this is from Lady yos'Galan, understand, Learned Scholar of Language Anne Davis, out of the Terran Community. It says: 'To Master Pilot Jon dea'Cort. Please accept this token of . . . regard . . . from myself and my—lord, would you say that rendered, Daav?"

Daav lifted an eyebrow. "How can I know?"

"Uncommonly awake," Jon commented and went back to his note. "' . . . lord. It is our . . . wish that you will . . . delight in . . . the gift, as we delight in the giving.' Then it is signed, you see, 'Anne Davis, Lady yos'Galan.'"

Aelliana's head was bent above Patch, her hair obscuring all of the cat but the blissfully kneading toes. "She sounds a—most gracious lady," she said after a moment. "Though I cannot help but wonder, sir, if she might have wished you to drink the tea."

"Truly, Jon," Syri said, turning from her study of petrifying pastries, "Lady yos'Galan cannot have meant you to imprison the gift in a lock-box. Where is joy in that?"

"Joy a-plenty," he returned promptly. "How many other garages have a gift from Korval to display, eh, Daav?"

"I have no notion, Master Jon. Shall I mount a survey?"

Jon grinned. "I thought you were sent to Min Del's on an errand."

"I can take that one," Syri offered. "My shift is done and it is a simple matter to chart a course past Min Del's on my way down-port."

"Simple enough," Jon agreed. "Are you here tomorrow?"

"Dawn to luncheon," Syri returned, "then I'm wanted back with my team." She bowed. "Pilot Caylon. Good health and fair flying."

"Fair flying." Aelliana tried to return the courtesy, but Patch took exception and the bow turned into a scramble to set him safely down. When she looked up again, Syri was gone and Trilla was walking toward the back of the bay.

"What've you been up to today, math teacher?"

Aelliana sighed and looked to Jon dea'Cort, who was carefully returning Korval's note to his vest pocket.

"I've been to the dispatch offices, and to the guild hall, requesting my name be added to the freelance rosters," she said. "The dispatcher at Korval's office advised me to put my name on the Port Master's list, but the guild rep ruled I must lose provisional status first."

"So you did go to Korval's offices." That was Daav, moving silently over to perch on a stool.

"Of course," she said, with a flicker of green eyes. "Korval is ships, after all."

"So it is," he agreed gravely. "Were you accepted for the roster there?"

"Readily—and asked to update my information, when I came full second-class." She turned to Jon dea'Cort.

"Your word of reference was in my favor, sir. I—am grateful— for your kindness."

"No kindness about it," he said gruffly. "If you'd done a bad job, there would have been no reference. Happens you did a binjali job and earned every word. How are you going about learning Terran?"

She sagged onto the edge of a stool, blinking at him. "I—hardly know," she said, somewhat abashed. "I had—thought—sleep tapes, you know. Chonselta Tech's library is not so well supplied . . ."

"Hah. No surprise. You might be able to get tapes copied from Scout Academy—your name's cantra there. Problem with tapes is you need to practice or the data just fades out again."

"Most of us are fluent," Daav said, offering her a smile. "What sort of Terran do you wish to learn?"

She blinked. "What—sort?"

"Indeed. You teach practical mathematics, do you not? So—do you wish to learn practical Terran, or theoretical?"

"Oh. Of course. I—I wish to understand and be understood under—under field conditions."

"Easy enough," Jon said, moving over to the teapot and pouring himself a mug full. "You get around all right in Trade?"

"I am comfortable conversing in Trade," Aelliana assured him in the mode-less monotone of that language.

"Even easier, then. We teach you from Trade, eh, Daav?"

"It would seem best," he replied. "Shall you arrange for the tapes?"

"Might be better for her to learn it in waking mind." Jon chose a pastry and ambled back to the stools. "You have a timetable?"

She swallowed, took a breath, and raised her eyes to his. "As soon as possible," she said, voice gone raspy and tight. "It would be—good—if I were—fluent—within the year."

The amber eyes held hers for a long moment, then Jon looked away and hoisted himself atop the green stool. "All right. We'll lay the basics, then supplement with tape as necessary. Daav's most fluent among the current crew. Trilla's good. Clonak's good, if he can be prevailed upon to speak something other than Aus-dialect. My ear is better than my accent, I fear, though I read well enough. Syri's about at my level—no, Syri's back to her team tomorrow . . ." He paused for a sip of tea. "This course of study suit you?"

"I—" She cleared her throat, looking from the old man to the young one. "Thank you—extremely. Balance must be—owing, however. I cannot—"

Jon sighed gustily. "First lesson in Terran, math teacher—pay attention."

She swallowed. "Yes, sir."

"Stop thinking like a Liaden." He grinned. "Thought it was going to be easy, did you? I told you we're all comrades here, eh? Happens that's true. What's owing is what's received: Comfort, safety and succor. Balance, right?"

The words vibrated in the air. She sat on the edge of the stool, listening to them, feeling them strike, one by one, at the core of her.

What they offered was—clan. What they asked in return was that she strive for her most perfect self—to the betterment of them all.

And I tell you, Birin Caylon, it's Aelliana should be set upon the delm's road, and none of that vain, precious boy of yours! Hanelur Caylon's voice was as strong in memory as it had been a dozen Standards ago, when carelessness had left a study door ajar and two pair of ears heard what had far better been left unsaid.

Aelliana raised her head and met Jon dea'Cort's knowing amber gaze. "Balance," she said, solemnly. "I shall do my best."

CHAPTER SIXTEEN

The thing to recall about Dragons is that it takes a special person to deal with them at all. If you lie to them they will steal from you. If you attack them without cause they will dismember you. If you run from them they will laugh at you.

It is thus best to deal calmly, openly and fairly with Dragons: Give them all they buy and no more or less, and they will do the same by you. Stand at their back and they will stand at yours. Always remember that a Dragon is first a Dragon and only then a friend, a partner, a lover.

Never assume that you have discovered a Dragon's weak point until it is dead and forgotten, for joy is fleeting and a Dragon's revenge is forever.

—From *The Liaden Book of Dragons*

IT WAS WARM in this corner of the garden—warm and blessedly quiet. So quiet, indeed, that orange-and-white Relchin had given over birding to lounge in the shade of the old stone wall and watch Daav grub about in the dirt.

Korval employed several very able gardeners, whose task it was to tend the formal gardens and lawns. The most senior of these formidable individuals walked the Inner Court once each *relumma*, offering suggestions and advice—only that. The care of the Inner Court, from the moss garden to the Tree itself, was Daav's self-appointed and jealously-held privilege.

This morning, he was engaged in digging and dividing gladoli bulbs. Much of this bounty would be ceded to his gardeners, but he wished to hold out a dozen to present to Lady yo'Lanna, who had been his mother's stalwart friend, and would know how to value a gift of Chi yos'Phelium's favorite flowers.

He was roused from this agreeable work by the step, and then the person, of his butler.

"Delm Bindan is come, sir, on the matter of your lordship's pending nuptials."

Daav sat back on his heels, bulb in one hand, trowel in the other.

"Bindan is here?" he repeated stupidly.

Mr. pel'Kana inclined his head. "I have put her in the Small Parlor, sir."

Daav closed his eyes, swallowing a regrettable reply.

"Provide Delm Bindan with refreshment," he said instead. "I shall be with her, say, before next hour strikes."

Mr. pel'Kana bowed and departed, leaving Daav to stare down at his crusted gloves and grubby coveralls. For one mad instant he considered rising and going directly to the Small Parlor in all his dirt, which was surely no more than she had purchased by appearing thus, dispatching neither card nor call to warn him.

The instant passed. He sighed and lay aside his trowel, made certain the bulbs were damp in their nest of moss, and rose, stripping off his gloves.

"On the matter of your lordship's pending nuptials," he told Relchin, in wickedly accurate imitation of Mr. pel'Kana's stately tones. The big cat smiled up at him through slitted green eyes. Daav dropped his gloves beside the trowel and went, reluctantly, away.

IT LACKED A FEW MINUTES of the new hour when he arrived in the Small Parlor, freshly showered and dressed in a comfortable white shirt and soft blue trousers.

He bowed, Delm to Delm, and Bindan rose to do likewise, muscles stiff with outrage.

"I regret you were obliged to wait," he said, in response to that outrage. "Had word been sent ahead, I should have been immediately accessible."

Her eyes narrowed, though she otherwise preserved her countenance. "I shall bear the lesson in mind," she said, inclining her head. "In the meanwhile, Korval, there is a matter touching upon our contract which must be discussed."

"Ah. Then you must allow me first to refresh your wine, and provide myself with a glass."

She did allow it, though he had the impression she would have rather not, and took a single ritual sip before setting the cup aside.

In his turn, Daav drank and set aside, then leaned back in his chair.

"How may Korval serve Bindan?"

She considered him for a long moment before inclining her head. "It is known," she said, very carefully, "that Korval charts its own course and cares little for scandal. It is perhaps lesser known that Bindan holds itself aside from such matters as may lead to the shouting of its name in open council."

Daav lifted an eyebrow. "And yet the matter upon which Korval was called in yesterday's council was found to be no scandal at all."

"It was found," Bindan said tartly, "that Korval had sidestepped the question in favor of showing that initial discovery was made by a Liaden scholar from a clan of scholars, all of whom are quite mad enough to wish such a thing introduced to the world." She inclined her head, ironically. "Korval's greatness is no matter of luck."

He grit his teeth against irritation and inclined his head in calm acceptance of the jibe.

"I ask you plain, my lord: Shall you keep your Terran within propriety?"

There was a charged silence, long enough for Bindan to feel the full force of her error.

"Thodelmae yos'Galan," Daav said deliberately, "is an honored member of Korval. She has done nothing to incur her delm's censure and much to excite his pride. I remind you that a contract of alliance does not in any way surrender Korval's authority to Bindan."

Her mouth tightened, but, to her credit, her gaze did not falter. "I say again, we are a House unused to scandal. Korval shall soon have the care of one of Bindan's dearest treasures. If Korval cannot hold itself aloof from scandal for the duration of its alignment with Bindan, Korval might best seek contract elsewhere."

For a heartbeat, he thought he would accept the trade she offered and count himself well-rid of Clan Bindan and Samiv tel'Izak.

Then he recalled the weary round of searching to be undertaken once again—the grids to be scanned, the gene-maps to weigh, and there were none of them different at core from Samiv tel'Izak, and none of them less respectable and solid than Bindan. Korval was trouble and scandal and oddity. It had always been so: Descendants of a pirate, a soldier and a Houseless schoolboy, had could it be otherwise?

Gods, he thought, *only let me soon hold my child.*

He inclined his head into Bindan's glare.

"Korval shall make every effort to avoid scandal from this hour and until the conclusion of our association with Bindan," he said formally, and glanced up.

"Bindan must understand that Korval's necessities are—unique."

"Necessity does not trouble me," she replied. "Scandal is my concern."

She rose and made her bow, and Daav likewise. He touched the bell and Mr. pel'Kana came and escorted Delm Bindan out.

"CORRECT TO FIVE PLACES," Aelliana announced, leaning back in the pilot's chair with a sigh.

"At least while we're sitting safe and cold," Daav amended, concluding his own checks and releasing the second backup comp to slumber.

Aelliana turned to look at him, hair a silken shimmer in the glow of the board lights.

"You suspect a main system error?"

"Ah, no, nothing on that line!" He raised a quick hand, smile tinged with irony. "It is merely that Jon certified the former comp while the ship was quiet—and see what nearly came of us while we flew!" He moved his shoulders, sending a bright black glance sideways into her face.

"Jon predicts I shall grow into a suspicious old man."

"Better than to die a naive young man," she replied, tawny brows drawn above frowning green eyes. "You are correct. In light of previous failure, a prudent check must include lift and land."

"Hah." He grinned. "Shall you request clearance, pilot?"

She hesitated on the edge of an eager affirmative, looking away from his face to scan the board. The clock's message killed the *yes* before it passed her lips, and she glanced back to him with a sigh.

"I haven't time left me today for a proper test. What is your shift tomorrow?" She bit her lip, then, the darker gold of a blush kissing her cheeks as she looked aside. "Forgive me," she said, voice tight. "I meant no offense, Pilot."

"Nor was offense taken," Daav answered, still in the warmth of Comrade mode. "I had said it was an honor to sit board with you and wished to do so again. Gods know, it's an ill enough face, but does it seem to you deceitful?"

Her eyes flew up, startle-wide and brilliantly green. And then was Daav forced to sit quite still, face and eyes plain as for any comrade or clanmate, while she subjected each feature to minute study.

"Indeed," she said, eventually and quite seriously, "I find it neither ill nor dishonest. As for the other matter—It is my understanding that you are a master pilot employed by Master dea'Cort. Surely it is out of my place to order you?"

"But you had not ordered me," he pointed out. "You had merely asked my shift. To which the answer must be, as I am casual labor and Jon allows me woeful license—When shall you be ready to lift?"

"I—" Her eyes moved, taking in the board, lit and waiting to receive its office. Hunger, and a dizzying desire to spin her chair now, open the line to Solcintra Tower and file a course up—out and away . . .

"Tomorrow," she said to the man at her side and looked into his calm eyes. "I can be here in the first hour after Solcintra dawn." Better—much better—to be gone from Mizel's clanhouse before anyone was about to ask questions, or to forbid her going at all.

Daav inclined his head. "I shall meet you at the foot of the ramp," he said, "in the first hour after dawn, tomorrow." He grinned. "And then we shall give her a proper testing, eh?"

In the depths of her chest it seemed as if another knot loosened and relaxed toward uncoiling. Aelliana felt her lips curve upward as she met the sparkling black gaze.

"Indeed we will."

"Hah." Daav tipped his head slightly to one side. "I wonder, must you leave at once?"

She flicked another glance at the clock, wariness awake once more. "There are nearly three hours," she said slowly, "before the twilight ferry leaves."

"Plenty of time to inventory your emergency equipment," he returned briskly, "and to be certain your suits are functional."

She looked at him in patent dismay. "I—forgive me. I am afraid I don't even know where the suits are."

"I thought as much," Daav said, with an odd side-to-side movement of his head. He rose and beckoned with one long-fingered hand. "Come along, Pilot."

MASTER DAAV pronounced the emergency equipment adequate, though he frowned a long moment over the neat rack of four oxy-tanks, forefinger tapping the status dials.

"Keep close watch on these," he said, and Aelliana heard a tremor of something chill down near the root of his warm deep voice. "You don't want to run out of air. It might be wise to add another can or two, in case of malfunction."

"Is it likely," Aelliana wondered, "that life support will malfunction?"

"I had been on a ship that lost life support," he said, frowning down at the canisters. "While such a failure does not often occur, I submit that once is more than sufficient, should you carry inadequate air, an inferior emergency kit or a defective suit." He took a deep breath then and seemed to shake himself—flashed her a brief smile.

"There, I don't mean to alarm you. Merely be vigilant and watchful of your equipment, as any good captain must be. Extra cans will come a necessity, should you add a copilot. For the moment—" He turned a hand palm up. "Pilot's choice."

She blinked, inclined her head. "Thank you. I shall recall your advice."

"Well enough," he said briskly and turned to lay a hand on the suit rack. "Tell me, have you ever worn one of these?"

"GOOD EVENING, CAPTAIN, DARLING!" Clonak moved his arm sharply as Daav walked by, releasing a red ball about the size of Aelliana's two fists together.

The ball zagged a crazy course, dipping and wobbling until the eyes ached trying to track it.

Daav extended a negligent hand, barely checking his stride, snagged the ball and skated it back in one smooth, unhurried motion.

"Hello, Clonak."

The pudgy Scout skipped one step forward and two aside, captured the ball and threw again.

"Your servant, Goddess."

Aelliana blinked, panic rising—and saw her hand flick and snatch, felt the weird weight of the thing and threw, instinctively calculating a trajectory that would take it—

Clonak leapt up with a laugh, cradling the ball against his chest. His boot-toes barely brushed the floor before he threw again.

"Well tossed! I hereby issue challenge, the loser to drink a mug of Jon's tea!"

"Challenge?" Aelliana choked. "I can't—" But there was the ball hurtling not exactly toward her and before she had properly attended her body's doings she had danced into the place where it *would be*, scooped it out of the air and hurled it back with a will.

"Aha, she means to hurt me, Daav!" Clonak dove, rolled and tossed from the floor.

"No more than you've asked for," Daav returned, hoisting himself atop a tool-chest and crossing his long legs under him.

The ball's erratic course took it floorward and into an unlikely arc. Aelliana spun to catch it as it swerved behind her, reached—and stumbled, blinded by the swirl of hair across her eyes.

"A clear miss!" Clonak cried, bounding down-bay after the escaped toy. "I claim the win!"

On one knee, half-blinded by hair, Aelliana felt a bite of fury at her own incompetence, an acid wash of failure in the base of her gut. Slowly, she climbed to her feet, shoulders sagging even as she scraped the clinging strands out of her eyes.

"A win by default," Daav was saying in his deep voice; "Pilot Caylon was disadvantaged."

"A win, nonetheless," Clonak argued, coming back, tossing the ball from hand to hand.

"Always the lazy course," Daav said, then, slightly sharper. "Pilot."

Aelliana glanced up, eyes pulled by his tone. He smiled and reached behind his head, twisted—and threw.

"Don't let him win," he said. "Make him fight for it."

Aelliana's hand flashed out, snatching a plain silver hair-ring out of the air. She glanced back at Daav, sitting crosslegged atop the tool cart, his hair falling loose along his shoulder, one eyebrow up and his smile with an edge of—challenge?

Once again, her hands moved of their own will, sweeping her mass of hair back, twisting and clipping it tight. She turned to face Clonak and inclined her head. "I am ready to accept your challenge, sir."

"Right-o," he said. And threw.

It was more difficult this time. The universe narrowed to the ball and its antics, to the absolute necessity of catching and throwing and catching and—

There was no ball.

Disoriented, Aelliana spun, found Clonak, his hands hanging empty and a sheepish look on his round, mustached face. To the right Daav still sat atop the tool cart, his hair neatly braided. To the left was Jon dea'Cort, red ball held high in a hand.

"*I* win," Jon announced, fixing Clonak in his eye. "How long has this been going on?"

"About half-an-hour," Daav spoke up. "Indeed, Master Jon, I was about to call time, as Pilot Caylon must make the twilight ferry."

Jon moved his glare to Aelliana, who became aware that her heart was pumping hurriedly and she was warm and rather damp.

"If you have to catch the ferry, math teacher, now's the time to jet. Good evening."

She bowed, trying to bring her rapid breathing under control. "Good evening, Master dea'Cort. Clonak—"

"I'll deal with Clonak," Jon said awfully. "Move."

Aelliana blinked and flicked a glance to Daav. His fingers moved atop one knee, shaping a word in Scout finger-talk: *jet.*

In the back of the bay, the clock that kept official Port time sang the quarter hour.

Aelliana ran.

It wasn't until she left the ferry in Chonselta Port and was walking quickly toward the train station that she recalled the hair-ring and reached up to pull it free.

Her hair flowed forward, shielding her from the world. Slowly, almost reluctantly, she slipped the ring into her pocket.

Tomorrow, in the first hour after dawn, she thought and smiled within the fortress of her hair. Whatever pain Ran Eld might mete this evening, tomorrow she would fly.

CHAPTER SEVENTEEN

Preserve your life, preserve your folk, preserve the Tree, no matter what the means. Grovel, if your enemy demands it; beg; swallow any insult. Stay alive, preserve you and yours.

Watch close, stay alert. And when your enemy turns his back, kill him and run free.

—Excerpted from Cantra yos'Phelium's Log Book

THE CREW DOOR CLOSED and Jon spun back to Clonak, red ball held out like a judgment.

"I shall be very interested to hear," he stated in a height of tone one very rarely had from Jon, "your reasons for engaging in a round of bowli ball with Pilot Caylon."

Clonak very nearly gaped. He did shoot a glance over his shoulder at Daav, but gained nothing from that quarter save a grave inclination of the head.

"Why not?" he asked, returning his full attention to Jon. "She gave good game."

"Good game!" Jon's glare grew blacker. He took a step forward, shaking the bowli ball until its internal gyro squealed. "Good game! Do you have any notion how long I stood there, watching you?"

"Well," Clonak allowed, leaning slightly back from the older man's approach, "there was the game to be concerned with, Master Jon, and my goddess out to knock my head off, if she could but manage it." He grinned. "I'm fond of my head, after all, so it seemed prudent to keep both eyes on the ball."

"You never had a prudent thought in your life, you heedless—" Jon cut himself off abruptly. "Fifteen minutes I stood there, watching as you—you, who visit the gym every day and follow a full exercise routine!—barely held your own against a desk-bound, half-starved scholar with her second-class license shiny-new in her hand! I've a good notion to tell your trainer that—"

"Second class!" Clonak yelped, going back a step and flinging a look of wild amazement over his shoulder. "Daav!"

"Second class provisional," that gentleman said calmly, "awarded barely ten days gone."

"What meat-brain granted her a provisional? She's as fast as any first class I've ever seen—faster than most!"

"Flight time, Master Clonak," Daav chided gently. "The regs are quite clear."

Clonak said something rude regarding the regs.

"Yes, dear. I showed her where her suits were stowed today, and helped her inventory the emergency kit."

"She's never so green as that!"

"She's every bit as green as that!" Jon shouted. "And if she had succeeded in knocking your useless block into the center of next twelve-day—which I swear is no more than she should have!—she'd have stuttered and stammered and blamed herself and we'd have never seen Aelliana Caylon at this yard again!" He took a mighty breath, and released it in a roar.

"Gods abound, I *will* tell your trainer!"

"It never happened!" Clonak cried. "Jon, for pity's—"

"And you!" Jon hurled the ball forcefully to the right and down. It twisted, hummed, skated and charted a rising course for the tool chest, speed increasing. Daav put out a long arm, captured the thing in a swoop and set it upon his knee, stroking it with firm fingers, as if it were a particularly frolicsome kitten.

"I?" He lifted an elegant eyebrow.

"Don't you come all High House with me! What the devil did you mean by letting that go on? Timing it, were you? I suppose it never occurred to you to interfere? It was easier to sit up there like a *melant'i*-choked dirt-scruffer—"

"Certainly not," Daav said, his calm voice cutting effortlessly across the other's tirade. "I hope I know my obligations, as trainer, as comrade and as copilot. In any of those faces I'd be blind not to see she needs to learn how to fight—quickly."

It could not be said that Jon's mouth actually hung open. However, there was a long moment of silence before a grudging, "Well, that's the first sensible thing I've heard said in the last ten minutes, all considered. Still, lad, she might have took damage. Clonak's got the edge."

"It's what I've been telling you!" Clonak cried plaintively. "My so-called edge was enough to keep the pace." He moved his shoulders. "I don't say I couldn't have worn her down, if it came to an endurance test. But the unvarnished truth is, Master Jon, she might very well have pegged me before it came to stamina—and I'd be in the 'doc even now, growing me a new head!" He set his hands on his hips and gave Jon back his glare. "Tell my trainer, then!"

"Hah." Jon flicked his glance aside. "Daav?"

"Not entirely unlike my own judgment, though I believe Clonak over-tender in regard to his head. I rather thought she was homing in on his nose."

"Smashed to a purple pulp," Clonak mourned. "Blood all sticky in my mustache."

"Brace up, darling, the 'doc would have put everything right."

"Yes, but you know," Clonak said earnestly, "it still hurts."

"One of life's inequities," Jon said, and sighed. "Why I ever let the pair of you pass piloting is a puzzle for my old age. How came you to be our math teacher's copilot, young Captain?"

"She asked me to accompany her on a thorough testing of the new navcomp and backups," Daav said, sliding silently to his feet. He tossed the bowli ball lightly to Clonak, who scooped it up in the instant before it touched his belt buckle.

"We're to lift in the first hour after dawn, tomorrow."

"If she keeps this pace, she'll lose provisional well ahead of spec," Jon said. "Good lift to you, then." He turned back toward his office.

"Fair flying, Master Jon," Daav returned softly, and cocked a meaningful eyebrow at Clonak.

"End of shift, old friend?"

The pudgy Scout sighed and used the tips of three fingers to smooth his mustache. "I suppose you're right," he said, walking at Daav's side toward the crew door. "Why are you always right, Captain?"

"Now, do you know, my perspective is that I'm often wrong."

"A terrifying statement! Do not, I pray, say it to anyone else! As for myself, consider my lips sealed—I shall carry your secret to the grave."

The crew door cycled and they stepped out into the twilight. Clonak drew in a noisy lungful of free air and grinned up at Daav. "Come 'round to Apel's and let me buy you a glass of wine."

A glass of wine with Clonak had a woeful tendency to become many glasses of wine, and a night so late it might just as easily be called tomorrow. Daav moved his shoulders and returned his friend's grin.

"Another time. I've an early lift."

"So you do! I'm reminded that I'm jealous." Clonak lifted a hand and moved away. "Until soon, darling."

"Take good care, Clonak." Daav stretched, drinking in the evening air, then turned toward Mechanic Street and his landcar. *An early lift*, he thought, and smiled.

RAN ELD STROLLED INTO HER ROOM without the courtesy of a ring to announce his presence. He had long ago possessed himself of an override to Aelliana's door-code and used it as his right. She suspected that he also kept an ear on her so-called private comm line, and thus routed all calls to her office at the college.

Aelliana blanked the reader and spun, coming quickly to her feet. She had as little desire for Ran Eld to discover her perusing a volume on Terran culture as she had for being trapped in her chair against the desk, her brother looming close above her.

As it was, her position was less than perfect, with her back to the L-shaped desk and a bookshelf cutting off escape to the right. Still, she was on her feet and that was something, she told herself as her brother came close—and then closer—a sheaf of printout in his ring-heavy hand.

"Good evening, Aelliana, how delightful to find you yet awake." His voice held its usual note of sweet malice, though with a certain undertone that said he would have been better pleased, if it been necessary for him to roust her from bed.

He moved the sheaf of papers carelessly, fanning her face with a cold, tiny breeze. Aelliana shivered.

Ran Eld smiled. "I have the report on the progress of your investment, sister. Allow me to congratulate you on the timeliness of your delivery. Alas, I find I am not entirely convinced of the superiority of your Fund; it seemed to run neck-and-neck with my own."

"A twelve-day is not sufficient time to test out," Aelliana said, hating the quaver in her voice. "You know that."

"Do I? But perhaps I had forgotten. Stupid of me." He moved the papers closer, laying the sharp edges against her cheek. Aelliana shrank back, the papers followed, edges beginning to bite. She froze.

"I hear," Ran Eld said conversationally, "that you have taken to frequenting gaming places. That you tend—after receiving tuition on the subject from your elders—toward the company of Scouts. Is what I hear true, sister?"

The paper edges burned against her skin. One quick move of her brother's hand and her cheek would be sliced, eye-edge to jaw. Aelliana took a deep breath and forced herself to meet his eyes.

"How could I frequent gaming houses?" she asked, keeping her voice humble, welcoming now the despicable, cowardly quaver. It sometimes happened that Ran Eld gave over punishment, if her groveling proved sufficiently amusing. "My wages are given entirely to yourself, brother—and you even now hold the proof of what befell my quarter-share."

There was a long pause, long enough for Aelliana to feel the breath begin to thicken in her throat.

"So I do." He lifted the papers away, glanced at them—and glanced up.

"I note a copy forwarded to the delm. Why is that?"

"I—Merely I had thought it proper," she gasped. "It was Delm's Word began the venture and I—I meant no offense, only right action."

Another pause, excruciating to her quivering nerves.

"Better to err on the part of right action than to fail of giving full honor," Ran Eld allowed at last, though not as if this judgment pleased him. "I advise that there is no need to send future reports to the delm. Do you understand me?"

She bowed her head cravenly, blessing the forward-falling shroud of hair. "I understand you, brother."

"Good. Of this other matter—you will look at me, Aelliana."

Swallowing against terror, she raised her head. Gods, what if one of Ran Eld's cronies had seen her in Quenpalt's Casino? What if the tale of her win had come after all to his ears? Her ship—Ran Eld must not, *must* not, be allowed—

"I ask you again, sister, if you have not been gambling in casinos. If perhaps you had not acquired—a spaceship—through playing a game of chance with a High House lord out of Solcintra?"

"A spaceship?" She stared at him, striving for a look of rankest stupidity. "What should I do with a spaceship?"

Ran Eld's eyes bored into hers. Somehow, she endured it, feeling the weight of *Ride the Luck's* keys, hanging cold between sweat-slicked breasts.

"I thought it a wine-tale," he said at last, moving his eyes from hers. It took every erg of will not to sag against the desk and sob aloud with relief, though she did dare bow her head, and draw the curtain of her hair once again across her face.

Above her, Ran Eld sighed. "Do you recall, Aelliana, your instruction regarding Scouts?"

"I am—am only to teach those Scouts registered to my courses," she said hoarsely, "and shun their company at all other times."

"Precisely. I warn you now, sister, that it will go extremely ill with you, do I find you have disregarded this instruction. Scouts are not fit company for one of Mizel—even if that one is only yourself. Do you understand?"

"I understand," she whispered around a sudden surging desire to behold at this moment any of Binjali's crew, with a special thanks to the gods if that any should chance to be Daav or burly Jon dea'Cort.

"Very good," Ran Eld said, out of the real and dismal present. "I give you good-night, sister. Sleep well."

She raised her head sufficiently to watch him cross the room and pass through the door. The closing of that portal was like a knife against the wires of fright that held her upright.

With a dry sob, she crashed to her knees, hands flying up to cover her face as she huddled against the desk-legs and shivered.

CHAPTER EIGHTEEN

We signed the final draft of the contract tonight. Thought they'd choke on Captain's Justice. Stupid groundlings. How do we know the length of voyage, assuming we even break out? How do we know there's any worlds left to run to? Situation like this, there has to be one voice that's law, not some damn committee. And that law has got to be in favor of the ship, and the greatest good. There can only be one captain. One voice. One law. For the best survival of the ship.

—Excerpted from Cantra yos'Phelium's Log Book

IT WAS RAINING in Solcintra Port.

Aelliana ran through the downpour, less conscious of the wet than the joy that heated her blood, reducing Clan Mizel to a speck and Ran Eld Caylon to an infelicity born of a bad night's dreaming.

Here in the wakeful world, she would soon meet her co-pilot at the foot of her ship's ramp, and Liad itself would be left behind, reduced to a mathematical necessity, one of many factors supporting an equation of flight.

She reached *The Luck's* pad, raced 'round the curve to the end of the ramp—and all but cried aloud, her run shattered by dismay.

There was no tall graceful figure awaiting her at the base of the ramp, rain-jewels glittering along leathered shoulders. The gantry was empty, from tarmac to hatch. Aelliana swallowed, shivering in the dismal downpour, and walked the rest of the way forward on joy-dead feet.

To the left, a flicker of noiseless movement. Aelliana spun as Daav ducked out from beneath the ramp, leather collar turned up against the wet, long fingers dancing cheerfully.

Relief hit in a giddy wave, rocking her into laughter as she shook sodden hair away from her face.

"A very fine morning, to be sure!" She answered the silent greeting aloud. "I thought you had forgotten me!"

"No, but I have an excellent memory," he said earnestly. "Even Jon allows me that much." He sighed heavily, shoulders slumping in an attitude of exaggerated remorse. "My woeful decadence is to blame for your distress and I humbly ask pardon."

Giddy yet with the return of joy, Aelliana smiled and tipped her head, trying to read beyond the mischief in the black eyes and into the heart of the joke.

In a moment she had given it up, glancing away from a gaze that seemed to read her all too easily, while remaining a cipher to her closest study.

"Decadence?" she asked.

"Well, you see," he said, slipping past her and ghosting up the ramp, "I would much rather be dry than wet."

She choked on another laugh and followed him, pulling the keys up on their neck-chain and slipping it over her head. "I wonder that Master dea'Cort allows one so in love with comfort to work for him."

"How could you not, when Master dea'Cort wonders as much himself? Often. And loudly."

Almost she laughed again, but lost it in a tiny shiver of alarm. The landing was very thin and Daav, slim as he was, filled a significant percentage of the available space. She would need to practically lean against his chest to access the hatch panel.

As if he felt her hesitation in his own muscles, Daav pivoted sideways on the ramp, arms outstretched, one hand gripping the rail, the other resting against the hull. He grinned and inclined his head.

"Your shelter from the storm, pilot. Be quick, I beg you, else I will be wet!"

She slid by, feeling his nearness like sunlight on her back, raised the shield and fingered the first key into place. The ID board came alive. She fed in her code and seated the second key. There was a muted click and the hatch began to rise.

Aelliana pulled the keys free and turned carefully on the landing, inclining her head with a forced smile. "Quickly, before you are soaked."

"Pilot first." Daav stayed where he was, one eyebrow askance. "I've been well drilled in protocol."

Pilot first. Aelliana blinked as the words found home, then drew a deep breath and stepped into her ship, deliberately squaring her shoulders as she did.

DAAV ENTERED THE SHIP; the outer hatch cycled and locked behind him.

Before him, Aelliana hesitated on the edge of the inner hatch. He read in the set of her body an awareness that had nothing to do with wariness and saw, in one of the flashes of instinctive understanding characteristic of him, that Aelliana was poised on a precipice of change. Here and now, she was engaged in letting go of something past and potent and simultaneously reaching forth to grasp something other and infinitely precious.

He took a careful breath, and remanded himself to utter stillness, that he not distract her in the midst of this chanciest of undertakings.

That she reached toward claiming her own skills, her ship, her comrades, seemed likely. That his taking shelter beneath the ramp had precipitated this moment of change also seemed likely. Her dismay at discovering an empty ramp, and the giddy relief she showed at his appearance told the tale plainly. He wondered if she yet realized that she was speaking to him in Comrade.

Within the frame of the inner hatchway, Aelliana shifted—turned.

"Will you check the board while I go and dry myself?" she

asked, as a comrade might well ask. She held out the ship keys on a link of short chain and long. Daav stepped forward and received them with a smile.

"Indeed I will."

"Thank you." She crossed the threshold into the pilot's chamber, moving left toward the companionway, wet garments clinging heavily, hinting at the shape they were meant to conceal. Daav went right, sorting the keys for the board—

"Daav?"

For the first time, his name: Intuition had not failed him. He turned, taking care to move gentle, and smiled.

"Aelliana?"

She came forward a few steps, hand outstretched, a silver gleam between the fingers.

"I had—taken your hair-ring—last evening . . ."

"Ah." He lifted a hand to touch his queue. "I have another, you see, and it seems you might put that one to good use. Keep it, of your kindness." He offered a grin. "Clonak may demand a rematch, you know."

Her eyes took fire and her mouth curved, fingers closing tight around the paltry gift.

"Thank you," she said again, and hesitated, head tipped to one side. "Clonak. Did Jon—"

"No mortal wounds," he said cheerfully. "Clonak has a gift for irritation against which even Jon is not immune."

Laughter sparkled across her face, gone in the next instant. She turned without another word and went down the companionway. After a moment, Daav went to the board and slid into the copilot's chair.

THE THICK OVERSHIRT refused to give up its moisture.

Aelliana, who had been simultaneously warmed and dried by the 'fresher in the pilot's cabin, fingered the sodden beige item uncertainly.

The valet had done admirably by the rest of her clothing, depositing them in the out-bin pressed and smelling softly of *jazmin*.

Liked everything binjali, the chel'Mara, she thought with a grudge of admiration as she pulled on black trousers, plain singlet and a white silk day-shirt trimmed with faded green ribbon. None of these garments was new, nor did they fit her well. Indeed, in the absence of the overshirt, the trousers required severe belt-pleating to keep them even indifferently moored by her waist. The shirt—a gift from Sinit on a name day long past—had wide sleeves pulled tight into green-trimmed cuffs, and a loose cut, though the silk would cling, here and there.

But the overshirt, that was the thing. It was her custom always to wear this article of clothing; it was her armor, her huddling place, her quilted coat of invisibility.

And it hung, like a dozen or so freshly caught fish, chilling her fingertips.

Aelliana bit her lip. Even her boots had dried under the valet's persuasion, and been returned to her gleaming with polish, worn heels evened. That the one most necessary item should—

"Tower gives us grace to lift, Pilot." Daav's voice flowed out of the wallspeaker. "Pending receipt of course."

Aelliana gasped and spun toward the speaker, her eye catching a flash of movement to her right.

"I shall be—another moment," she managed and barely waited to hear his "Right" before spinning back to the valet, snatching open the hatch and stuffing the soggy shirt within.

She chose "ultra-dry" from the option list, slammed the hatch, and turned again, confronting the mirror.

No lift-proof wonder, this, but a simple rectangle of polished metal, showing, at the moment, a painfully thin woman in baggy trousers and a shabby silk shirt, blast-dried hair snarled across her face.

Aelliana snatched at her pocket, finger-combed the static-charged mass back from her face and clipped it firmly with Daav's hair-ring.

The woman in the mirror hesitated a heartbeat longer, poised on the balls of her feet, thin body quivering, eyes wide and green in a gaunt, pale face.

She inclined her head. "Pilot," she said quietly, and was gone.

✧ ✧ ✧

A MUG OF TEA STEAMED gently on the arm of her chair, keeping company with a cheese muffin. Daav, reclining in the copilot's place with his long legs thrust out before him, glanced up from finishing his own muffin, earring swinging.

"I hope you don't mind cheese," he said apologetically. "I meant only to order my own, you know, and what must my fingers do but stutter on the key and the automat give out two!"

Aelliana considered him thoughtfully.

"I should like to see your fingers stutter," she decided after a moment.

Daav grinned. "Alas, it happens all too often. Dreadfully clumsy."

"No doubt even Jon will say so," she agreed gravely, slipping into her place. She picked up the cup and frowned into the reddish depths.

"What is it about Scouts," she wondered, "that makes them so eager to feed one?"

"Well, you see, we're trained to respect efficiency and to mend those things which hinder efficient work. Observation has shown that a person carrying significantly less than optimum body-weight functions at lowered efficiency. Such persons are subject to exhaustion, muddled thinking, and bouts of terror, which are not merely inefficient, but active threats to survival."

Startled, she looked up and met a pair of sober black eyes.

"A pilot keeps herself fit," she said, quoting from the guild-book.

Daav inclined his head. "That," he agreed quietly. "Also it is the duty of the copilot to ensure the pilot's health—and the care of a comrade to answer need with aid."

"I see." She put the teacup back on the broad arm of the chair and reached for the muffin. "I have been—long aside—from the world," she said, breaking the cake open and breathing in the cheesy aroma. "While I eat, will you tell me if you have formed any notion of how best to test the navcomp?"

"Several," he said readily, "but you must tell me how much time you may spend."

Aelliana glanced at the board clock and back to her copilot. "Twelve hours."

"Ah," he said with a smile, "in that wise . . ."

CHAPTER NINETEEN

~~~~~~

A statistically significant number of Scouts are reported eklykt'i—*unreturned—every Standard Year. While some undoubtedly fall prey to the omnipresent dangers of their duty, there is reason to believe that most have simply found a world that suits them better than the homeworld and have decided to stay.*

There are those who argue that Scouts who are eklykt'i *are the most successful Scouts of all.*

—Excerpted from "All About the Liaden Scouts"

LIAD HUNG IN HER THIRD SCREEN, a glowing wizard's-ball caught fast in a thick net of traffic. Outyards Four, Five and Three, moored to the edge of the net, also showed, gratifyingly distant. All that remained between *Ride the Luck* and the beginning of Jump space was the hailing beacon—and Scout Station.

Aelliana sighed.

"Tired, pilot?"

"Not at all," she returned, spinning in her chair to meet her copilot's smile. "I was merely thinking how—satisfying—it would be to continue our route out."

"Eminently satisfying," Daav said, his smile going a little

crooked, "and very tempting. Liad does grate upon one, from time to time." He extended the hand which bore the mark of the ring he did not wear and locked his board.

Aelliana bit her lip, leaning over to lock her own board. "Have you been—retired—very long?" she asked, which was none of her concern at all.

"Six years," Daav answered, as if it had been an entirely appropriate question. "I had been active for ten."

"Clonak—Clonak calls you captain," she told him, as if this might have someway escaped his notice.

Daav laughed. "Well, and Clonak's an odd creature, as even those who love him must own. It happens I had been his team leader, though I barely had such courtesy from him then. And," he added kindly, "before you sprain your tongue in an attempt not to ask the next perfectly logical question: Scout Captain, with a specialty in Cultural Genetics."

Swiftly, she lifted her eyes to his. "I beg your pardon," she said, feeling heat wash along her cheeks. "I had been taught it impolite to inquire of—of—" She staggered to a halt, for "stranger," the word she had been about to utter, did not fit the cipher; nor did "non-kin," her other choice, strike closer. Indeed, she was more likely to receive care and accurate data from stranger-Daav than ever she might of Ran Eld.

"All by the Code and very proper in its place," Daav said, coming smoothly to his feet. "The so-called polite world being its place. You have every right to ask of me, Aelliana. I am your copilot and your comrade. It is imperative that you trust me, as I might well be required to make a decision in your name. If you cannot trust me to act as you would, you had best know it quickly."

She stared up at him for a long moment before rising with a sigh. "I venture to say that you would not in any case act as I would," she said slowly. "I would far rather trust your judgment than my own."

"Then you are no pilot."

She flinched, snapped straight, hands fisted at her sides. "I am a pilot!" she cried, as if it were wrenched from the core of her. "I will master Jump within the year!"

Daav lifted an eyebrow. "If you will," he said with a cool and distant courtesy that put her forcefully in mind of Lady pel'Rula. "I must allow, however, that I have never known a Jump pilot who would place another's judgment above her own in any matter of her ship."

She glared, her own voice echoing in memory's ear: *I do not wish to hear that any of my students has died stupidly . . .*

She drew a careful breath.

"Master Pilot," she said. Daav inclined his head.

"Pilot?"

"I strive to be an apt pupil," Aelliana said formally, and bowed as one of her students might bow to her: Respect and honor to the instructor. "I have been many years aside the world. This information is not offered to excuse ineptitude, but to aid the instructor's judgment. It may be I am unworthy of the instructor's notice. Certainly, I have much to learn."

"Though nothing to learn at all in the science of delivering a devastating setdown!" Both of Daav's eyebrows were up. He flung out that curiously unringed hand, fingers slightly curled. "Cry friends, Aelliana, do! I swear not to come the lordling."

She blinked at him, baffled. "But—you are entirely correct," she stammered. "I must learn all a pilot's *melant'i*, and that quickly. Else how shall it be when I am beyond Liaden space and none but myself to consult? I read of all manner of strange custom in out-space. When my ship and myself are ranged against such and the decision must always be first to preserve the ship—" She slammed to a stop, heart pounding.

"Your ship is your life," Daav said softly, and with the air of quoting someone.

"Yes." She let out a shaky breath. "Yes, exactly so."

"Which is why the chel'Mara is a fool." He smiled, tipping his head so the silver earring spun sparkling in the cabin's light. "Shall you cry friends, Aelliana, or am I in blackest disgrace?" The long fingers beckoned gently.

She hesitated, feeling the familiar clutch of fear in the pit of her belly. A test . . . And once again, she thought, clammy fingers twisting together as she stared at that beckoning hand, Daav was right. Who was she to claim for herself the courage necessary to leave clan, kin and homeworld—the boldness to survive among strange custom—when she dared not even reach out her hand to touch the hand of her comrade?

It was difficult. To her screaming, hard-won instincts, it required an entire day to step closer, a twelveday to raise her hand, another to hold it forth, a entire *relumma* to close her fingers around his and feel the warm, answering pressure, by the end of which quarter-year she was trembling in every muscle and her legs barely firm enough to hold her.

"Reprieved!" Daav's voice sounded gaily. He pivoted smoothly, drawing her with him as he moved across the chamber. "I expect you'd like some lunch before we proceed."

"Lunch?" Aelliana repeated. She shook herself and drew a ragged breath, noting with something like panic that she was clutching Daav's hand with a force that hurt her own. "Thank you, but I—don't believe I am hungry."

"Yes," he said placidly, "I know."

It was not until he had seated her in the tiny canteen and gently reclaimed his hand in order to ply the menuboard that a certain ominous thought struck her.

"Daav?"

He turned his head. "Yes."

"I—" she stared down at her tightly-folded hands, her eyes following the intricacies of the puzzle ring, round and round. She bit her lip. "Are you a Healer?"

"Ah." He left the board and leaned across the little table, laying one hand over both of hers. He smiled as her eyes leapt to meet his.

"My empathy rating is—high," he said softly, "but I am not a Healer." He looked closely into her eyes, his own serious. "Shall I fetch you a Healer, Aelliana?"

It was an appropriate offer, from a comrade. Aelliana blinked against tears, tore her gaze away.

"Thank you, no. It is—I believe it is—too late—by many—years. I had only wondered—it seemed you are so—"

"Meddlesome," Daav said lightly, standing away with a smile. "It's a sad case, but—Scouts, you know. Shall you have soup with your salad or merely a roll?"

She stared at his back, torn between frustration and laughter. "Only a roll, of your goodness."

There was, of course, no hope that she would merely receive a roll and a cup of tea, and it was with no real surprise that Aelliana sat some moments later considering a rather large salad, augmented by cheese and breadstick.

Daav, who was having soup with his own salad, dug in with a will. Aelliana picked up her tongs.

"How did you learn the silent tongue?"

Aelliana glanced up from her all-but-empty plate with a blink.

"I teach Scouts," she said, with a slight smile, "and Scout minds—as you must know!—are very often bent on mischief. I learned it for survival, through observation." She moved her shoulders, denying his look of admiration. "When I finally came to realize that the finger-flickers among the class must be a language of some kind, it was only a short step to reading it—which is the extent of my skill."

"You've never tried to speak so yourself?"

"Oh, no," she said, glancing down at her plate and fingering her tongs. "I would be hopelessly clumsy, you know."

"Having observed you at a piloting board, not to mention deep in a game of bowli ball," Daav said somewhat dryly, "I know nothing of the kind. It's a useful language—and staggeringly simple to learn. Much easier than Terran."

"Which I must also master." Aelliana sighed, shoulders slumping. To capture first class, to become proficient in Terran, to acquire tolerance of exotic custom, to earn both funds and recommendations, all the while keeping ship and comrades hidden safe from Ran Eld's eye—

"Have you only a year?" Daav asked and she started, so closely did he echo her thoughts, then relaxed, lips curving upward.

"Very high," she commented, and moved her shoulders. "A year it must be. It may be necessary to give over the seminar."

"Ah, no, that would be cruelty. If Liad is to lose you altogether, at least allow another class of Scouts the benefit of your knowledge."

Extremely high in the empathy range, Aelliana thought, with sudden understanding. *And augmented by all a Scout's observational skills. Small wonder he finds the polite world grates on him.* She raised her eyes.

"Do you know anything of a world called Desolate?"

"Yes, and none of it good," Daav said bluntly. "If that is your destination, and the hope of your study, you would do far better to remain on Liad."

"I had thought—some time ago—that I might go there," she said. "Before *Ride the Luck*. Plans have—altered. But I had wondered."

"Hah." Daav finished off his tea and set the cup aside. "The World Room at Scout Academy is what you want. Apply to the commander for use-time."

She hesitated. "Do you think—"

"Your name is cantra at Academy, Aelliana," Daav said, pushing back his chair and gathering up the remains of his meal. "Jon had told you so."

"So he had." She rose, gathered up her leavings and fed them to the disposer before turning back to her tall copilot.

"I wonder," that gentleman said with the easy air she was beginning to recognize with trepidation, "if you might wish to have a taste of Jump."

Her heart leaped, the calculations running, quicksilver, in her head. "The gravity well . . ."

"A serious problem, were we to attempt full Jump. I'm suggesting Little Jump, or Smuggler's Ace, as my piloting instructor was used to call it. We barely phase out, skim atop hyperspace and return. In such a venture, the gravity well—"

"The gravity well acts as anchor and catalyst—I see!" Aelliana interrupted, the figures flowing, bright and perfect, before her mind's eye. She looked hungrily into Daav's face.

"Can we . . ."

"Let us call Scout Station and clear it with them. However—no disgrace of your skill!—I will run first board."

"Yes, of course," said Aelliana, and almost ran back to the pilot's chamber.

SCOUT STATION GAVE ITS AYE with cheery unsurprise, recommending them to "enjoy the bounce". Daav grinned and closed the outline—and then the mandatory open line.

"No open lines in Jump", he murmured, fingers dancing along his instruments. "Your board to me, if you please."

She assigned it with a pang, sighing as her screens went dark.

"Patience, child," he chided, and before Aelliana could protest such address, her screens were live again, board-lights winking bright.

"Your board is slaved to mine. Every toggle I trip, every bit of data I feed in—everything will be reflected there, for your interest. Well enough?"

For her most intense interest! "Well enough," she agreed, eyes hungry on the tell-tales.

Daav laughed. Across Aelliana's board lights brightened, darkened, flared, flicked; data strings like a river at thaw stormed across the pilot's net; navcomp held steady, steady, perfect to five digits. Scout Station passed from screen three to four to five, outline stretched by velocity, until it shot off the edge of screen seven and vanished as the warning beacon flowed into screen one, heading for two—

The ship flinched, the screens went gray. Navcomp beeped and took itself off-line.

"Jump achieved." Daav's voice was calm as always, but Aelliana thought she detected a thread of sheer, savage joy in that smooth weaving.

At the bottom right corner of prime screen, red digits ticked time. One-minute-six, one-minute-nine, one-minute-twelve— The lights jigged manic across the board, data hurtled—one-minute-fifteen—

Navcomp sang and came alive; ship's eyes opened, showing the diminished, ensnared globe of the homeworld. Aelliana bit back something woefully near a curse, hand moving to demand elucidation from maincomp. Nothing happened, of course, she was still slaved to the master board.

"But—"

"Smuggler's Ace, recall it?" He wasn't even trying to hide his exuberance. He grinned like a boy and opened the mandatory line with a flourish, letting in all the babble of the workaday universe.

"How can we be—be—" She slammed to a halt, aware that she was not entirely certain where they were, excepting beyond range of Port and Tower, beyond Scout Station, beyond the beacon—

"Ah, hyperspace!" Daav said gaily. "We don't go through, we go between. The gravity well gives a pretty boost, though brief."

She glared at him, suspicion gathering, now that it was too late. "Where are we?" she demanded awfully.

"My dreadful manners." His hands moved across his board, reassigning control to her.

She blinked, snatched at the board, read the numbers and found herself not much enlightened. Irritably, she slapped maincomp up, demanding the filed record of their outward course—

"I fear that won't be there," Daav said apologetically. "My cursed clumsiness."

"You wiped the comp?" She stared at him in patent disbelief, while she recalled his fingers moving across the board. So swift, so—very—certain.

He sighed dolefully. "Alas."

"Another lesson, Master Pilot?"

"You had," he pointed out, "indicated a need for accelerated study. Only consider, Aelliana, how rich this situation is in practical application."

"Is it indeed?"

"Oh, amazingly," he assured her, ignoring irony. "Why, by the time you've discovered where we are, calculated a return, and taken us home, you will be well on the way to losing provisional entirely."

She eyed him, suspicion flowering into dread—or perhaps, anticipation. "I'm to take us home? Unaided?"

Daav folded his arms elaborately across his chest. "Well, you don't think I'm taking us home, do you? I did my part. I got us here." He closed his eyes.

Aelliana took a breath. "You are—" Words deserted her.

"Despicable," Daav offered obligingly, not bothering to open his eyes.

She let her breath out in a puff that might have been exasperation or laughter. Sharply, she cycled her chair, opened the board and set about the task of discovering just where, precisely, they were.

CHAPTER TWENTY

It must be the ambition of every person of melant'i *to mold individual character to the clan's necessity. The person of impeccable* melant'i *will have no goal, nor undertake any task, upon which the clan might have reason to frown.*

—Excerpted from the *Liaden Code of Proper Conduct*

"**YOUR LORDSHIP IS ALL GRACE,** to bestir yourself to meet me at this hour." The red-haired man bowed profoundly.

Ran Eld Caylon inclined his head haughtily and sat first, as befitted his rank. The red-haired man took the chair across.

"Wine, Your Lordship?"

"I thank you," Ran Eld said and took the glass of canary as it was poured, tasted it and sighed.

Ran Eld Caylon was fond of fine things: Fine wine, fine jewelry, fine comrades. The man across the table was one of the latter class—or had been. Recently, however, San bel'Fasin had become a dead bore.

"I trust Your Lordship enjoys his usual robust health?"

Once again, Ran Eld inclined his head. "I am quite fit."

"And Your Lordship's delightful sisters are likewise well?"

The red-haired man had never met Ran Eld's sisters, though it had been his policy from the first to find them delightful.

"My sisters are well," Ran Eld admitted, and assayed another sip.

"And your honored mother, the delm—she is—of course!—in the best of good health?"

"My mother blooms, I thank you."

"Excellent, excellent! Then there will be no difficulty in calling upon her with my little matter."

Ran Eld froze, wine glass halfway to his lips.

"I beg your pardon."

bel'Fasin moved his hands in gently. "Why, the insignificant matter of twenty cantra forwarded to your lordship last *relumma*. Certainly you recall it?"

"*Twenty* cantra?" Ran Eld treated the red-haired man to his coldest stare. "You are mistaken. The amount owed is four."

"Four cantra were originally lent," San bel'Fasin agreed urbanely. "At interest of twenty percent per twelve-day, plus penalties."

"Penalties? What penalties?"

"One hundred percent rolled over at the conclusion of each twelve-day unpaid," bel'Fasin said promptly, and met Ran Eld's glare with a glance so deathly chill the nadelm shivered. "Your Lordship signed a paper."

So he had, and Aelliana's quarter-share had been destined to retire this particular debt of honor. But what must occur, Ran Eld thought furiously, except the Delm's Own Word had forced him to hand the sum to *Aelliana* and no way to lose another four cantra from the House's meager funds. . .

"When might it be convenient for me to call upon your delm?" bel'Fasin asked courteously.

Ran Eld set aside his glass, of a sudden sick of wine. *Twenty cantra, gods . . .*

"There is no reason for you to call upon Mizel, friend bel'Fasin."

"Alas, your lordship, there is every reason. Unless . . ."

Ran Eld looked up, hope a painful crush of heart and lungs.

"Unless?"

"Perhaps Your Lordship would be willing to represent another case to your honored delm?"

"What case?"

bel'Fasin smiled and sipped his wine. Ran Eld grit his teeth and let the moment stretch, though it was torture to his screaming nerves.

"Mizel owns a certain—leather manufactory, I believe?"

Sood'ae Leather Works was the most profitable of Mizel's three manufactories. Alas, it was also the eldest of the clan's holdings and certain updates were sorely needed.

Ran Eld inclined his head. "True."

"Ah. Then I wonder if you might not be able to—bring your delm to see the—benefit—of a partner in that business."

Sood'ae was freeheld, Ran Eld thought. The delm would never . . . He caught San bel'Fasin's cold eyes on him and took a deep breath.

Twenty cantra, at twenty percent and one hundred percent penalty every . . .

"I shall speak to Mizel," Ran Eld told the red-haired man with formal coolness. He picked up his glass and threw the rest of his wine down his throat.

THEY WERE IN MID PORT, between Virtual Arcade and the zoological museum. It was mid-evening and the byways were crowded with jostling strangers—Liadens, mostly, but with a mixing of Terrans, tall and loud in their clusters of comrades. Aelliana and Daav were holding hands, that they should not lose each other in the press.

The problem set her up-space had, indeed, been rife with opportunity. Aelliana bested the problem, eventually, and earned not only her tutor's quiet praise, but a warm glow of pride in her own accomplishment. They were in Mid Port by way of celebration.

To Aelliana, whose knowledge of Solcintra Port encompassed the ferry station, the monorail and Mechanic Street to the door of Binjali's, mid-Port was an unrelieved marvel. She craned into shop windows, marveled at street-corner playlets, and stared at passersby, the jangle of a dozen languages like wine for her ears.

"Here." Daav tugged on her hand, charting a slantwise course from the edge of the walk inward, toward the shops lining the right. Perforce, Aelliana followed, trusting him to bring them to safe docking, then paused on the threshold of the shop he chose, her nose telling tales of exotic spices, hot bread and other delights.

"More food?" she cried, hauling back on his hand.

"Food!" His eyes sparkled like black diamonds, in-lit with delight. "You wrong me, Pilot, and so I swear. As if I would guide you here for mere food!"

It was so easy to laugh. Laughing, she let him tug her inside, to stand beside him in a long line until it was at last their turn at the counter.

Daav saluted the grizzled counterman with a grin. "Pecha, of your goodness, old friend—and a pitcher of the house's best! This my comrade has never partaken of your specialty."

The counterman grinned and rang in the order, though Aelliana saw no coin change hands.

"Enjoy!" he recommended in badly-accented Liaden and waved a big hand, giving Aelliana a wink before he turned to the customer behind.

"He's—" Aelliana began, as Daav guided across the crowded floor to a table against the rear wall.

"Paol Goyemon," Daav said. He slid onto the bench seat at her right and gave her a lifted eyebrow. "You find him repulsive?"

"Not at all. I hadn't known Terrans held shop in port."

"A cantra is a cantra, no matter who makes it—or pays it." He grinned. "A principle of economics that does much to sustain my faith in humankind."

She chuckled, then sobered, slanting a look into his face. "Is it burdensome, being—world-bound?"

Something flickered across his face, touched his eyes.

"It is," he said slowly, "somewhat of a burden. It is the training, you understand. In making us fit for the universe, we are made unfit for Liad." He smiled, wryly. "It does not help, of course, that the polite world labels Scouts odd and holds us in mingled trepidation and dismay. 'Scout's eyes' they say, as if it were something of magic, rather than merely learning to see what stands before one."

She frowned, groping after a certain thought . . . "There is Clonak, growing hair on his face—like a Terran. Liadens don't grow beards. Surely those who have never left Liad cannot be expected—"

"Liadens," Daav broke in, "live in danger of losing the game to complacency. They think themselves the ultimate in civilization and scorn what is not written in the Code. The Code is all very well, but courtesy to difference has not been named a virtue. If—" He caught himself on a half-laugh and raised his hand, gesturing apology.

"There, I promise not to rant."

Before she could assure him that he was not even approaching one of Ran Eld's lectures, let alone a rant, the pecha and pitcher arrived.

Pecha was flat round dough, spiced red sauce, vegetables, and cheese, baked until cheese and sauce bubbled, served on a hot stone. The dough was cut into six fat slices. One detached a slice from the circle of its fellows, balanced the treacherous wedge atop one's fingers—and ate.

Aelliana followed Daav's example, imperfectly at first, gaining confidence with each bite. The flavor was strong, spicy enough to raise tears—delicious. The wine—sweet, red, glacier-cold, with citrus smiles floating in it—cooled the mouth and sharpened the appetite.

"This is wonderful," Aelliana said, liberating her second slice. Daav smiled and raised his glass in silent salute.

Too quickly, it was done. They lingered over the wine, side by side and backs comfortably braced against the wall, watching the crowd of diners ebb and change.

"How did Clonak come to have a—*mustache*?" Aelliana wondered lazily.

"We all have our souvenirs." Daav's voice was equally lazy. He lifted a hand and touched his earring. "The tale of how Clonak came by his mustache is—alas!—not to be told for forty years, by order of the Scout Commander. What I can tell you is that he very badly wished to speak to someone who would not treat with a 'beardless boy,' as the phrase went. Clonak thus sought permission of his team-leader and then commended himself to the autodoc, rising much as you see him today." He paused, considering.

"Slightly more demented," he said at last, sipping his wine. "I do believe age has mellowed him."

"And yourself?" Aelliana wondered softly. Daav looked up, one brow askance.

"Ah, but I have always been precisely as demented as you see me today!"

She laughed and moved her head in the Terran negative he had taught her. "But I meant your earring," she said. "Surely that is a—a *souvenir?*"

"So it is." He touched it once again, smile going slightly askew.

"This certifies my place as a son in the tent of the Grandmother of the Tribe of Mun, whose name, we would say, is 'Rains-in-the-Desert,' though I rather think 'Rockflower' a closer fit." He paused for a sip of wine; reached 'round to finger his tail of hair.

"This signifies that I am unmarried."

Aelliana stirred, looking up into black eyes gone misty with remembering.

"And when you marry?" she asked, meaning it for lighthearted, though it sounded utterly serious to her own ears.

Daav smiled, wistfully, she thought. "A married hunter will wear his hair clipped close to his skull, of course. And he will have a second earring, that names his wife's tent. But until one has been chosen from among those who stand around the marriage fire and enters the tent of one's wife, the hair is worn thus."

"Marriage fire . . ." Aelliana sighed and sipped at the last of her wine. "Did you—But you said you were unmarried."

"Rockflower had determined I should stand around the fire at the next gathering of the tribes," he said, very softly. "My team came back for me before then."

She looked up into his face. "You're—sorry?" she asked, tentatively, because it did seem there was sorrow shadowing his bright eyes.

"Sorry?" He moved his shoulders. "I should have been a poor choice, for a woman of the Mun. Undergrown—and not—terribly— skilled with my spear. To choose such a one to provide for a new-made tent, where there likely would soon be children—" He shook his head, Terran-wise, drank off his wine and turned a full grin upon her.

"But, who can say? I might have been chosen by a woman of an established tent, secure enough to please herself, and then I might have had a life of ease!"

His grin was infectious. Aelliana smiled back and thought she had never felt so happy.

"Shall we walk?" Daav asked, and Aelliana put her hand unhesitatingly into his and allowed him to lead her once more into the bustling, exhilarating, magical evening.

THE VIRTUAL ARCADE WAS FULL OF BODIES and light in motion, and sound that ranged from racket to roar.

Aelliana and Daav waded through the uproar, stopping here and again to watch the play at the games. Aelliana, Daav noted, seemed particularly interested in the more sophisticated games of chance, and as they went further into the Arcade, her tendency was to stop for longer intervals, lips moving silently, as if forming the boundaries of an equation.

Another might have felt pique at this apparent desertion. But Daav neither hurried nor chivied her, finding himself well-content with watching the changes in her eyes and face as this thought or that caught at her. He did keep a firm hold on her hand, for in her present tranced state he considered it possible that she might wander away and lose herself, and used his body to shield her from the worst of the crowd's jostlings.

So it was, traveling in this stop-and-go, eventual way, that they came to *Pilot to Prince*. Aelliana watched the computer replay a space battle of epic proportions from memory: Battle gave way to an emergency docking, which evaporated into a trading session, which segued into—

Daav smiled at the attention she gave the game. It was popular among the shuttle-toughs and Port-crawlers and usually, he thought, had lively play. This evening, it stood empty.

Not quite empty, he amended, as two figures stirred in the dimness of the back corner and walked toward them: A girl and a boy—halflings, no more—identically dressed in tight clothing a parody of genuine spaceleathers, faces hard, hungry—desperate.

Daav tightened his hold on Aelliana, meaning to draw her away, but before he could do so, the boy raised his hand and the girl called out:

"Game, gentles? Sed Ric and me will stand the fee, if you care to play for something more tangible than fun."

Aelliana frowned. "You mean play for money?" she demanded, with very real sternness. "That would be terribly foolish of you, ma'am."

The girl smiled humorlessly. "Ah, the challenge is too heady for the lady! Let us play three-way with your partner, then—he looks a man game for—"

"Wait," said Aelliana, looking about her for the twelve-sided die in a wheel that was the symbol of a sanctioned betting station. "This game doesn't pay off," she told the girl seriously. "You would be risking your funds against strangers. That hardly seems fair."

The boy—Sed Ric—laughed this time. "So what is fair, ma'am? We all risk our money with every purchase. We'll pay the game fee—dex a player at hazard—if you care to see what kind of pilot you might be."

Aelliana glanced at the replay in progress beyond the boy's shoulder: A holed ship careered about the screen until a barrage of rockets sent it slamming into a nearby asteroid.

"You will lose your money," she said flatly. The boy jerked a shoulder.

"Maybe so," the girl said. "*We're* not afraid to bet."

Aelliana hesitated, her hand tightening—indeed, Daav thought she would turn and walk off . . .

Her eyes wandered back to the screen, flicked to the posted game-regs.

"We can win," she murmured, perhaps to herself.

"Can we?" Daav asked, just as softly, and with one eye on the halflings. Tension whined off the pair of them; Daav's teeth ached with the intensity of their desperation.

They bore themselves as if they knew kin and clan—not

ordinary Port rats. Though marred by fear, there was a certain smooth efficiency in their movements which spoke of potential pilots—*If they don't skid off the edge of Mid Port,* Daav amended silently, *and land themselves in a Low Port bordello.*

"Daav?" Aelliana murmured. He glanced down into shadowed green eyes. "Tell me what is wrong," she whispered.

"Wrong . . ." He sent one more glance at the halflings: Hungry, afraid and too proud to ask aid. Too young to be here, hustling strangers for two dex the game . . . He sighed sharply and smiled into Aelliana's eyes.

"I think we should play," he said softly, "since these young gentles ask so nicely."

She hesitated, her eyes scanning his. He saw the decision cross her face, then she turned away, fingers dipping into a pocket. Two coins flashed toward two halflings.

"Done," she said with professorial sternness. "We shall take the merchanter."

The start of joy from their opponents was regrettably obvious.

"After you, Pilot," Daav said, and followed her to their station.

CHAPTER TWENTY-ONE

After the safety of the ship, the well-being of the passengers is the captain's greatest care.

—Excerpted from Cantra yos'Phelium's Log Book

THE SITUATION WAS NOT QUITE UNTENABLE, but it was far from good. They were down on fuel, having chosen to run from the last attack rather than pit the merchanter's light weapons against the pirates' superior firepower.

The pirates had followed, of course, and were now lurking just off-station, waiting for the hapless merchanter to set forth.

Daav's suggestion—faking a refuel and coming around the planet to attack—was refuted by Aelliana: "Suppose they go for a LaGrange Point rather than a simple orbit? They'd have all the advantage and we would be in a difficult orbit."

Her suggestion of dropping all cargo pods but one in favor of a high-value freight and top acceleration had merit, though it relied heavily on the skill of the pilots in eluding the pirates and gaining the Jump point first. Meanwhile, the longer they sat at station, the more points they lost.

Instinctively, Daav glanced over the instruments, checking ship's stats. The board was authentic, the image surrounding them utterly convincing. The bits of station-chatter filtering across the open line had apparently been lifted from tapes of the real thing.

The station master's messages had been rather too courteous to a ship which had come in trailing pirates and debris, but there were limitations, Daav thought wryly, to even the best of games. He sighed and put his attention back on the cargo board.

"How if we drop five pods," he suggested softly. "We trade in the cargo with known destinations for cargo the pirates can't suspect."

"It would give us an edge in gaining a Jump point," Aelliana agreed, fingers flying across the board. "Carador," she said, echoing his thought as if they were partners of many years. "We'd have close to a stern chase to Jump. If the timing favors us, and if we buy all the Greenable listed, we should turn a profit."

"Agreed. What of the synthfish—high intrinsic value and rare on Carador, according to the chart."

"But badly affected by high acceleration. We'd need an eighty-nine percent survival rate to make our margin and we could hit—" She paused, briefly. "Six gee is not out of reach—"

Not quite out of reach, Daav thought with a mixture of amusement and respect. Aelliana Caylon expected a great deal of her ship—and of herself.

"All right," he said, watching her fingers work the keypad to prove the results her head had already produced. "We load Greenable. But I want to buy pod-lot 47—distress merchandise listing. It won't slow us too much and it's cheap."

"Surplus material from Losiar's Survey? But—"

"Trust me," he murmured, and her fingers danced, approving the purchase while she sang out orbit and range figures for him to check.

Daav felt better now, though the run was still risky. The creator of this game had a wonderful mind for trivia, and with a very small corner of luck he hadn't just bought fifteen thousand Terran tons of survey rods. The density levels on that pod were extremely close to something his lamentable pack-rat of a memory thought it recalled . . .

The ship readied: He pulled in the fuel figures, calculating times in his head and running trajectories as if they really were about to launch.

"They'll fire to capture, won't they, Daav?" Aelliana's voice was serious.

"Or at least to get the goods. Likely a capture, though, since they score extra for that."

"Yes. I'm arming the long-range weapons as soon as we break seal, and hit the meteor shield to full—"

Her face was earnest, snared in the seeming reality of the game. Daav lifted an eyebrow. "Station will scream—not to mention the fine."

"Only if we come back," she returned and Daav nearly laughed with joy of her, speaking as bold as if she broke a dozen rules every morning, and he—what was he but the grandchild of a pirate, himself?

The sequence ran down to go. The ship tumbled away from its dock and Aelliana slapped up weapons and shield.

In the real universe, taking arms off safety so close to a station would cost the pilot her license. In this universe, station, as predicted, screamed, though with nothing approaching the verve of any actual station master of Daav's acquaintance.

"They see us," Daav said as the pirate ship hove into view around the curve of the nearer moon. "I'll take the guns, you fly her."

The virtual ship shuddered and acceleration pressed him into his seat as the couches tilted to simulate motion. He watched the cross-hairs converge, his hands moving toward the fire button—

"*Fancy-Freight* we've got a fine on you unless you cut those weapons now! You have your warning—cut those weapons—" The simulated station master blared his accusations.

"Trap!" Aelliana cried. "They broadcast everything we do to the pirates!"

"Hah. So that's why the children think they have a fixed game."

His hands moved, slapping fire buttons. Virtual rockets crossed virtual space, arcing away toward the suddenly retreating pirates.

The explosion was a bright flare across his screen. It drew howls of protest from the station master and unsubtle curses from the pirates, who immediately returned fire.

A waste of energy, Daav thought, holding his own meager

weapons in reserve: *Fancy Freight* was still in the shadow of the station, protected by its defenses.

That situation changed as Aelliana kicked the ship into a lurching high-gee skid toward the proper Jump point. Even on game time they'd need all of the luck to make the distance and score.

Daav watched his boards carefully, saw the pirate ship taking a leisurely tumble toward—

"They're targeting the wrong Jump point," he said quietly. "They thought we were heading out with the flegetets on board for Terra."

Aelliana sighed. "I regret those—But the math didn't work. Four hundred percent profit and three hundred percent dead . . ." Her eyes narrowed.

"They aren't coming on with as much acceleration as they did before, Daav."

He looked to his screens, touched a knob to increase magnification.

"Took some damage, poor children—running on eight tubes instead of ten. Pegged to the intercept course, though—you have that stern chase you wanted—"

"I didn't *want* a stern—Ah, *no* . . ."

The distress in her voice caught him. He looked up sharply, saw real pain in her face.

"Aelliana! What has happened?"

"I—" She looked over to him, eyes wide and stunned. "I— miscalculated. The fuel reserves on the pirate ship—they have the edge. I forgot—Forgot! They'll catch us before Jump."

Daav blinked, recalled the reserves the pirates had taken on from a peripheral kill early in the game. Something moved in the corner of his eye; he turned to track it—and saw six missiles drop out and leave the pirate's ship.

"Recalculate," he said, automatically calling up interceptors, slapping dead plastic where the defense beam toggle would be on a real ship—"based on losing the lot of non-Greenable."

The screen flared as one of Daav's interceptors took out a missile; half a second later another did the same.

"Aelliana?" he asked gravely, glancing up at her again.

"Yes. I had forgotten that you are a Scout. That was a difficult interception there . . ." She lapsed into silence, flying and calculating at once, then shook herself.

"We may win, but the margin is small—one percent, perhaps one-point-five, depending on when and how we lose that pod." Her voice was somber.

"Shall we surrender, then?" Daav asked quietly.

There was a moment's hesitation, too short for him to be certain that the struggle he sensed was anything other than his imagination. Her eyes lifted to his, green and wide.

"No."

"Good," he said, letting her see the pride he felt in her, and turned back to his board.

The play got tighter as the pirate ship's greater power-to-mass ratio began to tell. The pattern of attack changed though: Now the goal was interception. No fancy flying for extra points, no capture option, just interception.

"Daav. We have one hundred seventy-six seconds until Jump. They'll intercept in one hundred forty."

"I see. When they're thirty seconds behind, jettison Lot 47. That should give us—"

"The added acceleration will help, but they'll still catch us by fourteen seconds—"

"But we'll be throwing things at them. They'll have to avoid."

"That's random—I can't calculate—".

"No surrender," Daav said earnestly.

"No surrender."

They were quiet then, each watching their screens. Daav fended off several more missile attacks. The pirates were being more careful with their weapons now, and so was Daav. By his count they had thirteen to launch and he had three . . .

"On my mark," Aelliana said calmly, "it's five. Mark. Four, three, two, one . . ."

The ship lurched as the pod fell away, looming huge in the simulated view screen. It tumbled behind them, directly into the path of the oncoming pirates.

Daav counted to three and launched his last missiles.

"Oh," said Aelliana, "that's more mass away . . . I still don't think it's going to be—Daav, a bad trajectory. You've targeted the—"

Two missiles skimmed the edge of the tumbling pod, dodged by and went on toward the pirate ship, which was beginning evasion. The missiles followed, and the pirate launched four interceptors.

Daav's third missile hit the tumbling pod full center. The flare of explosion grew, brightened, grew still more, expanding into a glowing rainbow cloud.

The Jump warning went off: twelve seconds.

"What was it?" cried Aelliana.

"In a moment. They'll be firing the last of their—yes. Avoidance pattern, please."

Through the glowing cloud came two missiles, though only one was on course for them. Aelliana used the maneuvering rockets to spin the ship, hit acceleration, kept accelerating until the red warning light came on.

They saw the simulated explosion fade into green nothingness behind them in the instant before the virtual ship Jumped away.

Aelliana cheered.

The piloting chamber melted, the shock webbing retracted. Daav rose, looked about—and sighed.

The pirates were gone.

"THIS WAY, SED RIC," Yolan hissed, groping ahead in the thick darkness of the service corridor.

There! Her questing hand found the emptiness that meant the cross-hall. Another few minutes in this stifling darkness and they would be free of the Virtual Arcade and the two undoubtedly angry marks they had deserted at *Pilot to Prince*.

Yolan sighed. She hated the service corridors; the hot dark gave her horrors, calling forth ghosts and hobgoblins from childhood stories. There were no ghosts or goblins, of course. She knew that. The world held far more terrible things than mere monsters. Cops, for instance. Port proctors, for another. Not to mention angry marks who had won a game they had no business to win and were now cheated of their cash.

"Here." Sed Ric's voice rasped in her ear.

"Right. Stay close." She found his hand and held it—to lead him, she told herself fiercely—and groped her way toward the cross-hall.

Slowly, she moved forward, free hand extended, fingers touching the wall. The wall ended, her fingers stroked emptiness—

Something grabbed her hand.

Yolan screamed.

"Well," an amused masculine voice said. "What a noise." Light snapped on and Yolan blinked, gasping into silence.

Before them stood the very marks she and Sed Ric had just rooked of their rightful winnings. The man, with his sharp, foxy face and his worn leathers, looked infuriatingly amused, though his fingers, now around Yolan's arm, were surprisingly strong.

The pale-haired woman held a portable light, and she looked angry, her eyes cat-green in the sudden brightness.

"What clans own you?" she demanded as Sed Ric stepped up to Yolan's side.

Yolan moved her shoulders. "We own ourselves."

The green eyes widened. *Shocked her*, Yolan thought, with a twist of bitter satisfaction.

"You're clanless?" the woman asked, casting a look at her tall friend.

"More profit to ourselves," Sed Ric said, "than the clan ever showed."

"Playing tourists for two dex a round?" the man drawled, dark eyes showing something Yolan thought uneasily was not amusement. "And running when it's time to pay?"

"We usually play for higher stakes," Sed Ric said, as Yolan snapped, "We don't often lose!"

"Hah." The man looked from one to the other, moved his shoulders and glanced at his partner. "Well, Pilot? You had wanted them."

"If you want your four dex," Sed Ric, with a calm Yolan knew he was a long way from feeling, "we'll pay now."

"After we've chased you and shaken it out of you," the pale-haired woman said ironically. "How kind." Her bright eyes moved from Yolan's face to Sed Ric's. "In truth, you are clanless?"

"*Yes*," Yolan hissed, and felt the man's fingers tighten around her arm.

"Grace to the pilot, Clanless," he said softly, and Yolan swallowed, abruptly cold.

"Where do you live, then?" the pale-haired pilot demanded.

Yolan clenched her jaw.

"I expect that they had been sleeping in a wayroom," the fox-faced man said. "I also expect the rent on the cot came due today, and that the money they stole from you, Pilot, was meant to buy it tonight." He sounded bored.

"Is that true?" the woman asked.

It was Sed Ric who answered. "True," he said, trying to sound as bored as the man. He didn't quite succeed.

There was silence, stretching long. Yolan tensed against the man's hand; froze at his lifted brow.

"What shall you do, if we let you go?" the woman asked quietly.

Yolan looked away. *On the Port tonight*, she thought dismally, clenching her jaw tight. No place to sleep and nothing to eat, unless the luck smiled. They could always walk a bit further south, slip over the line into the Low Port. There might be something to gain there. But Low Port was dangerous . . .

"Low Port, is it, Clanless?" If anything, the man sounded more bored than previously. He looked at Sed Ric. "Will you sell your lady here to the first bidder, or were you planning to sell yourself and leave her without a partner?"

Sed Ric's jaw tightened. "We don't have to cross the line."

"No? Well, it's your life, free as you are of the restrictions of House and, apparently, honor." He said carelessly, though his grip on Yolan's arm never slackened.

The pilot stirred. "Will you play an honest game?" she demanded, her eyes wide and half-wild in the glow of her torch. "Or are you thieves, and craven?"

"We'll play," Yolan snarled and Sed Ric said, "What's the game?"

"Take the four dex and buy a bed," the pilot said sharply. "Tomorrow dawn show yourselves to Master dea'Cort at Binjali Repair Shop in Mechanic Street, Upper Port. Tell him that Aelliana Caylon thought you might be of use. You tell him, too, to keep four dex out of whatever wages he might care to grant you and put it aside, to repay a debt of honor." She fixed them both with a stern eye. "You're still game?"

Yolan hesitated, looking for the trap; it was Sed Ric who said, "Still game."

"Good." The pilot stepped back, dimming the torch. Her mate released Yolan's arm and likewise went back, clearing the way to the exit hatch.

"That's it?" demanded Sed Ric. "That's the whole game?"

"Something more," the man said, taking the pilot's hand and flicking a quick smile down into her thin face. "Over on Scorn Street there's a grab-a-bite called Varl's. You know it?"

"Yes," said Yolan.

"Go over now and order yourselves a meal—high-quality protein, and solid carbohydrate, mind me! Tell the counter help to add it to Daav's chit."

"But, why?" demanded Yolan, horrified to find herself close to tears. She hadn't cried in—in—Sed Ric's hand came up to grip her shoulder; she bit her lip and blinked.

"Why not?" returned the man, amusement back in the foxy face.

"At least work long enough to pay back what you owe," the woman said. "If you've no delm to look to, how much more closely must you mind your own *melant'i*?"

Yolan stared at her, torn between a desire to laugh and to fling herself into the thin arms and wail.

In the end, she did neither, merely took Sed Ric's hand and inclined her head gravely.

"Good evening, gentles."

"Good evening," the man returned, and "Take good care," said the woman.

They walked away, scarcely comprehending what had happened,

triggered the hatch at the end of the hallway and slipped out into the night.

After a moment, Daav and Aelliana followed.

SHE SHIVERED as they came out into the street and Daav looked at her in concern. "You're cold."

"A little," she admitted, handing him the torch and watching him stow it in his belt pouch. She shivered again. "I left my overshirt on the—Dear gods."

He turned, following the direction of her eyes, seeing the crowd, the clutter of kiosks, the ship-board, the clock—

"The time," she whispered urgently. "Daav, I *must* go home."

He flicked another look at the clock and did a rapid calculation. "We can make the next ferry. Can you run?"

"Yes!" she answered and they wasted no more words. Hand in hand they crossed the plaza, running quick and pilot smooth, and hurtled down a side street.

CHAPTER TWENTY-TWO

Each clan is independent and each delm law within his House. Thus, one goes gently into the House of another clan. One speaks soft and bows low. It is not amiss to bear a gift.

—Excerpted from the *Liaden Code of Proper Conduct*

"**DAAV,** there is not the slightest necessity for you to escort me. I am quite accustomed to riding the ferry."

"Ah," he said, neither perturbed nor persuaded by this argument. He maintained his position at her side, fingers laced in hers, waiting for the gate to slide away and admit them into the Chonselta Ferry.

The holding platform was crowded, nor were all who waited perfectly sober. Daav had detected at least two pickpockets, discreetly working the edge of the crowd. He nudged Aelliana closer to the gate, deliberately adopting the stance of a man prepared to argue right of place with his fists. The crowd shifted, grumbled—and let them by.

Beside him, she shivered. He glanced down, frowning at the thin silk shirt.

"Let me give you my jacket, Aelliana, you're cold." He moved— stopped in something very near awe when she lay a quick hand against his chest, looking up at him with a laugh, her eyes out-dazzling the platform's spotlight.

"I'll soon be in the ferry, and warm. My friend, you cannot have considered. To give me escort to Chonselta means four hours gone from a night already far advanced. I shall be perfectly fine."

Behind them, a mutter of conversation, the ugly edge of drunkenness clear to a trained ear.

"My company wearies you?" he asked, meaning it for a joke. Aelliana-like, however, she chose to hear it as serious and honor him with an answer.

"Your company is—a joy," she said, with her nearly Scout-like frankness. "I—Daav, I—cannot—offer you hospitality of the house. To have you journey so far in my behalf and be constrained to return without even a cup of tea—It shows poorly on the clan, yet I dare not—"

She was beginning to tense, the foggy misery moving into the edges of her eyes. *Damn them,* he thought, with concise, futile fury. Aelliana shrank back as if she had heard the thought, hand falling from his chest, eyes widening in alarm.

Gods, he must be sliding into idiot ineptitude, that his anger at her clan showed plain enough to frighten her! He conjured a smile, quirked an eyebrow.

"And an ill-mannered fellow I'd look, indeed, rousing the house to do the pretty at this hour of the day! My desire to escort you is utterly selfish, Aelliana—I could not sleep a moment, without knowing you were safe at home." He let the smile widen to a grin. "Indulge me."

Her alarm faded in a sigh that was also a laugh; her fingers tightening, unconsciously, he thought, about his.

"Indeed, I am—glad—of your escort," she said, tipping her head toward the rising discussion behind.

"Then the matter is settled," he said, at which moment the gate slid wide and all his thought went to shielding her from rude jostlings and locating well-placed seats.

"DO YOU THINK they're really clanless?"

Daav retracted the shock webbing and turned in his seat. Aelliana looked up at him from her place against the bulkhead, worry plain in her face.

"Something is certainly—wrong," he said carefully, wishing neither to influence her to a chancy course, now she had time for cooler reflection, nor lose the children her friendship, was she yet disposed to grant it.

"Possibly something is very wrong. Whether they are in fact clanless . . ." He moved his shoulders. "I had been trying to recall. It seems to me that there have not been any casting-outs listed in *The Gazette* this *relumma*, and I don't think they can have been on the port longer—even granting them extraordinary luck."

She sighed, settling her shoulders against the metal wall. "They're no older than Sinit," she murmured. "And to be without kin on Liad, and no hope of going elsewhere . . ." Her mouth tightened. "Will Jon be angry? I hardly know how I dared, except that Binjali's is so—safe—and I had thought . . . But to put Jon's *melant'i* at peril—that was ill-done."

"If Jon considers you've put his *melant'i* at peril, he shall not be shy of explaining the matter to you. In the meanwhile, if they go to him and present you as their patron, he's certain to keep them by until you can explain the matter to him."

"If they go," she repeated. "You think they will not?"

"They may," Daav said gently. "Or they may not. That rides upon their *melant'i*."

She was silent for a moment, her eyes on his, before reaching out and taking his hand.

"It is the custom," she said, as much perhaps for her own benefit as for his, "to shun the clanless and withhold any aid."

"Merely custom and not law," he returned calmly. "The Code, not the Council."

"Ah," she smiled, very slightly. "Yet another concept to master." She squeezed his fingers. "It was kind in you to feed them."

He returned both her smile and the pressure of her fingers. "Little enough to do—and not the first time Varl has had the feeding of my stray puppies. Scouts, you know . . ."

Aelliana chuckled; raised her free hand to cover a sudden yawn.

"Your pardon," she murmured, and then, more strongly: "Now, tell me what was in that pod, if you please!"

He laughed softly and settled back in his seat. "Why, only a comet."

"A comet!"

He smiled at her disbelief. "You've heard of Losiar's Survey? Not many have—it's ancient history, and Terran history, at that." He shook his head.

"Mr. Losiar, you see, was wealthy, of scientific bent, and quite, quite mad. Over time, he became convinced that the—how did he have it?—that the 'building blocks of the universe' might be discovered in the hearts of comets. Convinced, he acted, and outfitted hundreds of drone ships to go forth and capture all the comets in the galaxy, or near enough, and bring them back for study." He sighed.

"Alas, Mr. Losiar died testing an anti-gravity machine he had invented soon after the last drone left Terran space. His ships full of comets are still found, now and again. Most use them for target practice."

"So there was ice and particles in that pod," Aelliana said slowly, "and when you blew it open—"

"The children found themselves flying through the center of a comet. Disconcerting."

Her laugh turned into a second yawn, and that yawn became a third, belatedly covered with a languid hand.

"I do beg your pardon. I cannot think why I should be so tired."

"After all," Daav said ironically, "you have only been flying since Solcintra dawn, not to mention a port walk and an engagement with pirates."

She grinned, eyelids heavy. "True. I had—" another yawn interrupted her.

"Sleep, if you like," Daav said, knowing it was scandalous and out-of-Code. Yet why should she struggle to stay awake when she was so tired and there was her copilot at hand to guard her?

"I think I shall," said Aelliana, rather muzzily, and without further ado released his hand and settled herself closer into the chair.

✵ ✵ ✵

SNUG AGAINST THE BULKHEAD, with himself between her and the aisle, Aelliana slept.

Seen thus, without the great green eyes sparking fire, she seemed astonishingly frail—a mere bundle of bone shrouded in the golden velvet of her skin, carelessly wrapped in rusty black and shabby silk. Daav knew a desire to gather her up and hold her against him, head tucked under his chin, as if she were one of his small nephews. He shook the feeling aside: Aelliana was no child, but a woman grown, and none of Korval, beside.

He wondered anew at her clan, who seemingly placed her value so low it cared nothing if she ate or starved, went clothed or naked.

Not permitted to grant a comrade courtesy of the house, is it? he thought with a recurrence of anger, and sighed. Well, and perhaps her kin misliked Scouts. There were those, in sufficient plenitude, though his darker side noted sardonically that Delm Korval would likely command slavish welcome, whatever hour he might call.

In her sleep, Aelliana stirred, shivered, nestled deeper into the cool plastic seat.

Daav sat up, moving with exquisite care. He slipped off his jacket and tucked it around her, turning the soft leather collar up to shield her face from the eyes of the curious.

Settling back, he thrust his legs out before him and folded his hands over his belt buckle. Eyes half-closed, he reviewed a linked series of exercises, assigning one segment of his mind to keep watch while the most of him dozed.

SHE TRIED TO LEAVE HIM IN CHONSELTA PORT, arguing that there was no call for him to endure a train ride halfway across the city only to be obliged to return immediately to the port.

"No, but I shan't be returning *immediately* to Port," Daav said, sliding his coin into the box and requesting two tickets. "Unless you live in the station?" He handed her a ticket.

Aelliana stared up into his face, trying valiantly for a glare. "You are quite stubborn enough!"

He sighed, taking her elbow and guiding her toward the platform.

"My *cha'leket* tells me exactly the same. It's a burdensome nature, I agree, and far too late to correct it. I am on my knees before the gift of your forbearance."

"Yes, very likely. Daav, nothing ill is going to befall me between here and Raingleam Street."

He looked down at her, eyes wide. "A foretelling, *dramliza*?"

"I am not a wizard! You, however, are entirely ridiculous!"

"Yes, yes, as much as you like," he assured her over the hiss of the train's stopping. "Is this our shuttle?"

She gave it over then with a laugh and marched before him into the compartment.

That was the last laugh he had from her—and very nearly the last word. The closer the train brought them to her clanhouse, the quieter she became, sitting stiffly beside him on the bench, steadfastly staring at nothing.

The train stopped four times to discharge and admit passengers. As it slowed for the fifth time, Aelliana raised her face. Daav bit back a cry of protest: The bright green eyes were shrouded in fog, wary and chill in a face etched with tension.

"Aelliana—"

She raised a hand, forestalling he hardly knew what mad speech.

"This is my stop," she said, and the warmth was at least still in her voice. "I suppose it's useless to ask that you spare yourself a walk and a return alone through an unknown city?"

He smiled for her, keeping his voice light. "I'm a Scout, my friend. Unknown cities are something of a specialty with me."

Her lips quirked a smile. "I suppose they are," she said and stood, moving toward the door.

She made no protest when he took her hand, though the station was hardly crowded. Indeed, her fingers tightened about his as she guided him out to the street.

As urgently as she had cried her need to go home, it seemed that now, with home near to hand, her urgency had deserted her. She led him sedately down thin streets lined with yard-enclosed houses. The further they walked, the smaller the yards became, the more closely the houses crouched, shoulders all but rubbing their neighbors.

Raingleam Street was meager, the public walk crumbling and weed-pocked, the houses brooding over scanty squares of grass held captive by rusting, lance-tipped fences.

"Here." Aelliana stopped before a fence near the top of the way. The grass beyond the lances looked unkempt in the light from the street lamp, a flowering vine softened the brooding facade of the house.

In the puddle of lamplight, Aelliana spun to face him, catching up his other hand in hers.

"Daav—thank you, my friend. For the escort, for the lessons, for—for your care. I cannot—I don't believe I recall when last I spent a pleasanter day."

"Well, as to that," he said gently, feeling her hands trembling in his, "the pleasure has been mutual." He hesitated, glanced over her head to the forbidding house, looked down into a face from which all joy had retreated.

"Aelliana?"

"Yes?"

"I—may I give you my comm number, Aelliana? Call me, if there is need."

She did not laugh, nor ask what need she could possibly have of him, now she was delivered safe back to her kin.

She sighed, seemed to sag—and caught herself, looking up.

"Thank you. You're very kind."

"Not at all." He recited the code for his private line, saw her memorize the digits as she heard them. "There is an answering machine," he told her softly, "if I am not—immediately—to hand."

"Thank you," she said again and stepped back, her hands slipping away with a reluctance he could taste.

"Good lift, pilot," she said from the shadow aside the lamplight. "Have a care, going home."

"Safe docking, Aelliana."

He tarried in the light-splash, watched her cross the walk and open the sagging gate. Her footsteps were light on the flagstones, her figure no more than a thin shadow. The footsteps changed, climbed three wooden stairs; he lost her shape in the larger shadow of the vine.

The porch creaked, a door opened on faintly whining hinges, hesitated, soundless—and shut with a clatter of tumblers falling home.

Abruptly, Daav shivered, though the night was barely cool and his jacket very warm. Almost, he went forward, through the gate and down the path—*Some pretext—some bit of piloting lore you forgot 'til now to tell her . . .*

"Do be sensible, Daav," he chided himself, voice loud in the still street. He turned his back on his inner urgings, on the gate to Mizel's Clanhouse, and retraced the route to the station, walking with determined speed.

"GOOD MORNING, AELLIANA, how pleasant to have you thus returned to us."

Two steps into the foyer, Aelliana froze, staring into her brother's eyes, recalling all at once the overshirt left behind on *The Luck*, and her hair, drawn back and caught with the ring Daav had given her. Voni erupted from the parlor to her right—where the large window enjoyed an unimpaired view of the street.

"I saw him!" she squealed. "Great, lank-limbed creature flaunting his leather in a respectable street! A Scout or a grease-ape, brother, and Aelliana with no more shame than to be clutching his filthy hands!"

"Gently, sister." Ran Eld was gliding closer, savoring his moment. "I feel certain Aelliana will tell us everything we wish to know about the fellow." He raised a hand heavy with rings and smiled lazily at her. "Won't you, Aelliana?"

She swallowed, mind gone to putty. He meant to strike her, she read that plain in his eyes: He meant to hurt her . . .

"Whatever is the reason for so early a racket?" Birin Caylon peered over the rail, blinking sleepily down at the three in the foyer.

"Ran Eld? Voni? Aelliana, then! *Some*one explain this untimely commotion!"

It was Voni who recovered her wits first. She bowed and flirted her eyes as their mother came stubbornly down the stairs.

"Aelliana was so late coming home, ma'am, we had quite despaired of her!"

"I see," the delm said in a dry tone that indicated she found this explanation wanting. She reached the foyer floor and paused, subjecting first her son and then her eldest daughter to an uncharacteristically penetrating stare. This done, she continued forward and took Aelliana's arm.

"Just come home, have you?" she said pleasantly, turning back toward the stairs, middle daughter in tow. "How delightful it is to be young and able to roister with friends until dawn! I recall my own youth—why, there were twelve-days together when I was scarcely home at all! I was a sad scamp in those days, though I daresay you would hardly credit it—" Talking thus, she mounted the stairs, and Aelliana with her, barely able to believe in her rescue.

At the top of the stairs, Mizel changed her subject, lowering her voice to a level not meant to reach the two left below.

"So, had you a fine, bold day, Daughter?"

"In—Indeed I did, ma'am," Aelliana took a hard breath. "I had meant to be home for Prime, but the time—the time quite got away from us."

"And your friend, I apprehend, was good enough to escort you to our gate. Could you not have offered the house's hospitality, child?"

"Ran Eld—" she swallowed. "Ran Eld has no liking for Scouts, ma'am. And, indeed, my—friend said himself he would seem a rag-mannered fellow, rousing the house at such an hour."

"Very nice of him," Birin Caylon said approvingly. "You must, however, invite him to tea soon so that I may thank him for his care of you." She frowned at Aelliana's start. "It need not trouble you— or your friend—what private opinion Ran Eld chooses to hold of Scouts."

Oh, gods, and if Mizel rebukes Ran Eld for this evening's work— She swallowed and inclined her head. "Thank you, ma'am."

They had reached Aelliana's door. Birin Caylon smiled and patted her daughter's arm before relinquishing it. "Never mind, child. What is your friend's name, I wonder?"

"Daav," Aelliana whispered, voice catching. She cleared her throat and looked straight into her mother's eyes. "His name is Daav."

If Mizel found anything odd in the lack of surname or clan, she chose not to mention it.

"I see. A well-enough name. Gentle dreams, daughter." She turned and went back up the hall, toward her own apartments.

Trembling in every muscle, Aelliana escaped into her room.

CHAPTER TWENTY-THREE

Feed a cat, gain a cat.

—**Proverb**

"WELL, AND WHERE HAVE YOU BEEN?" Jon's voice carried an edge of amused irritation.

Daav continued to the counter and poured himself a cup of pitiless black tea.

"Chonselta," he said and threw the murderous brew down his throat with a shudder.

"Chonselta, is it? I suppose that answers for the whereabouts of Pilot Caylon." Jon came forward to perch on the green stool. "I reviewed that tape."

Daav manfully swallowed the rest of his tea and set the mug in the sink. "Did you? And your recommendation?"

"She pilots solid second class—which we'd all known. On the basis of yesterday's adventure—setting aside that I believe the master in charge to be moving matters along rather swiftly—I'd be tempted to write a provisional first."

"If it were board-skill alone, I would agree with you," Daav said, sitting down and bracing a heel on a stool-rung. "However, there are those things of which she knows very little."

"And of which she ought to know much, bound as she is for the wide universe." Jon sighed. "All too true. Second class it is, then. Will you sign it?"

"Yourself, if you will."

"Hah. She know who you are yet?"

Daav lifted an eyebrow. "She does not know my surname, or my clan."

"Quibbled like a Liaden! I'll play that game to the extent it does her no harm."

"And how shall I harm her, I wonder?" Dangerously soft, that question.

"Gently." Jon raised both hands in the age-old gesture of surrender. "Gently, child—I meant no disrespect. Forgive an old man his meddlesome ways."

Abruptly, Daav became aware of tense muscles, of a hand curled closed along his thigh. He shut his eyes, ran the Scout's Rainbow, and felt the tension flow away. Opening his eyes, he offered Jon a smile.

"It is you, rather, who must forgive a young man his equally meddlesome ways—and his weariness." He showed an empty palm. "I mean her only well. If she learns the workings of comradeship through Daav, who flies out of Binjali's, where's harm in that?"

"Well enough," Jon said, lowering his hands. "Seek your bed and we'll say no more about it."

"In a moment." Daav shifted on the stool, sent a quick glance into Jon's face. "Dawn-time brings you rare joy, Master."

Jon sighed. "Now what?"

"A brace of halflings, boy and girl. They claim to be clanless."

"Sending me your lame kittens, Captain?"

"Not at all," Daav said austerely. "They belong to Pilot Caylon."

"Oh, do they? And what does Pilot Caylon want me to do with them?"

"Put them to work, if you think they might be useful."

Jon considered him blandly. "Are they likely to be useful?"

"Possibly. I believe them to be pilot-grade; the girl at least has had some training. They're able-bodied and quick, though not as quick as they think themselves. Cocky, but well-spoken enough when forced to the point."

"A pair of delightful children, I see. All right. I'll hold them, pending Pilot Caylon's pleasure."

"Thank you," said Daav and came to his feet. He tipped his head, looking down into Jon's seamed face. "Find out who they are, if you can manage it."

Grizzled brows rose over amused amber eyes. "I thought they belonged to Pilot Caylon."

"My lamentable curiosity," Daav murmured, moving a languid hand.

Jon laughed. "Sleep well, lad."

"Good evening, Master. I have no shift this three-day."

"All right," Jon said and watched him walk, graceful and tall, across the bay and out the door.

SHE WOKE FROM A DREAM of rich, easy safety, her mouth still curved with pleasure.

Sunlight bleached the thin blue curtains to gray; the clock on her desk told of an hour approaching mid-day.

The first thought that occurred was tinged with wonder: Ran Eld had allowed her to sleep through breakfast.

Her second thought was that it was late, and she would be wanted in Solcintra.

She flung the blanket back with energy, came to her feet and slipped on her ragged robe. The house beyond her door was quiet, the hall empty; there was no Voni barricaded in the bathroom they shared. More and more curious. Aelliana locked the door behind her and took a rapid shower.

Back in her own room, she stared into her tiny closet with dismay, seeing the meager rack of shabby shirts and shapeless trousers as if for the first time. Exploration did uncover an orange day shirt laced with black cord, of a slightly more recent vintage than the rest, and a pair of tough indigo trousers that required only minimal pleating with a wide black belt. In the very back of the closet, she found the blue jacket her grandmother had given her on the occasion of her fifteenth name day.

The bold blue had faded somewhat, but the lining was whole, the outer shell water-resistant. She shrugged it on.

That she not outgrow so expensive an item before she had used it fully, the jacket had been bought too large. It settled over her shoulders now as if it had been made for her. Aelliana smiled.

Then it was time to leave.

Cautiously, she stepped out into the empty hall. From below, she heard the sound of a door opening, and the waspish echo of Ran Eld's voice.

There was no time to be lost. Heart in mouth, she ghosted down the hall to the back stairs, thence out into the world.

"MORNING, MATH TEACHER."

"Good morning, Jon," Aelliana said, stopping to stroke Patch. She straightened and looked around her. The garage was unusually quiet; neither Trilla nor any other of Binjali's changeable crew in sight. She turned back to Jon.

"I wonder—did—did the pirates come to you?"

He raised his eyebrows. "Pirates? I wouldn't rate 'em much higher than Port rats, myself." He used his chin to point at the crew door. "They're here. Trilla's got them doing clean-up on Number Six Pad."

"Oh." Tension eased out of her, though a wrinkle of worry remained around the bright green eyes.

She was in looks today, Jon thought with approval, and dressed like she'd paid some attention to the matter instead just draping herself in whatever outsized bits of clothing came to hand. The tawny hair was combed neatly back over her ears and caught into a tail, showing the world a face at once ethereal and intelligent.

Some fitting clothes and a sprinkle of jewels and no one in the room would deny her a beauty, Jon thought, and said aloud, "Well?"

The worry intensified. "I was afraid you would care, though Daav—" She cleared her throat. "I meant no assault upon your *melant'i*, Jon."

"Take more than a gaggle of halflings to do that," he said gruffly. "You sent them to work off a debt, according to their tale. I've enough unskilled labor to keep them a day or two, and welcome they are to all of it. But what will you do with them after that? Turn them back onto the Port?"

She stared at him, eyes wide. "They're clanless."

"So they said."

"To turn them back onto the Port, after having taught them to hope—" She caught herself, teeth indenting her lower lip.

"I do not consider," she began anew, after a moment. "I do not consider that they are stupid, or even without honor. They were frightened and in despair, which condition might make a thief of anyone. They are very quick, and—and pilot-like. Surely, they can be trained—"

"Might be," Jon agreed, "if they had clan. Them claiming no one, that gets tricky. Though," he amended, seeing she was disposed to take it hard, "if they're real good, or found a patron, they might gain the Academy. The Scouts don't care who's clanless."

Hope showed in her thin face, tempered with wariness. "Are they—real good?"

"Too soon to tell. They're sharp enough—and quick, as you say. Whether they're quick enough, or sharp—that wants testing. Also—" He eyed her consideringly. "Might be only one will make it. I think the girl's some faster."

"And the boy seems somewhat sharper," Aelliana returned, chewing on her lower lip. "And the Scouts do train others, who are never meant to be fully Scouts." She raised her eyes. "My name was cantra, you said, at Academy."

"That's right."

"Then there may be a way, though I doubt two days is long enough to find who they are themselves. Perhaps—"

"I'll find work," Jon interrupted. "We'll keep them by long enough to test them fairly."

She smiled, and there was no need for jewels or fine clothes to make her beautiful, Jon thought.

"Thank you," she said. "You are very kind."

"I'm an interfering old man," he corrected her, and swept a hand toward the back and his office. "Daav left you a thing, if you'd care to claim it."

Eagerness made the bright eyes brighter. "Yes."

They went side-by-side, Aelliana carrying Patch.

"You'll spoil him so he'll always want a ride," Jon grumbled and almost gasped to hear her laugh.

"I must carry him or I cannot walk," she said. "Which is worse: To stand for hours stroking him, or to carry him where I wish to go?"

"I'll put a team on it," he said and bowed her into the office ahead of him.

She paused at the near side of his desk to put Patch down; Jon went 'round to the terminal side and fingered a stack of hardcopy.

"Here we are." He held it out; watched her take the thin metal card, disbelief warring with joy across her face.

"Second class." Wonder gleamed along her voice.

"Daav left me a tape of yesterday's little adventure, along with his recommendation that you be relieved of provisional. Asked me to get the card to you, if I agreed." He grinned then, in simple pride of her. "If I agreed! How I could do other than agree is what I'd like to know!" He held out his hand. "*Binjali* flying, pilot."

She blinked at the outstretched hand, extended her own and met his firmly.

Jon grinned again, gave her fingers a little squeeze and released her.

"I'll have to speak to Master Daav about his methods," he said. "To expose a new pilot to that level of stress—"

"Indeed," Aelliana said earnestly, clutching the precious card tightly. "Indeed, I had asked him to—to try me fully. My need is for working first class in no more than a year."

"If he keeps you at this pace, you'll be working master in two *relumma*," Jon told her, with very little exaggeration.

She smiled briefly. "I shall need to update my registration with the guild," she said. "And with Korval." She looked up, suddenly hesitant.

"Is Daav working today? Or—possibly—tomorrow?"

"Left word not to expect him for a day or three," Jon said, and marked how her shoulders drooped inside the blue jacket.

"I—see." Another hesitation, then a deliberate squaring of those thin shoulders. "I wonder—is there someone willing to sit second for me tomorrow? I wish to lift—early."

A second class pilot lifting in local space did not require a copilot, according to regs. However, Daav, damn him for a pirate, had shown her Little Jump and Jon dea'Cort was too wily an old piloting instructor to think that one brief taste of hyperspace would suffice her. Indeed, it was to her honor, that she asked for second board.

"Clonak's due early tomorrow," he said. "Or I could spare Trilla, if you'd rather. You'd best chose who, otherwise you'll have them fighting for the honor."

She smiled and moved her shoulders, disbelieving him. "Is Clonak never serious?"

"Clonak's a damn' fine pilot," Jon said soberly. "Daav came up drinking coil fluid instead of tea—they haven't built the ship he can't fly. Got the master's easy as breathing. It wasn't that way with Clonak. He sweated for every equation, bled for every coord. He learned his piloting piece by piece and he earned that license. You can learn from him, if you care to."

Aelliana inclined her head. "I care to learn all I can about piloting," she said. "If Clonak will fly with me, I will have him with joy."

"I'll tell him," Jon said. "When do you lift?"

Something flickered over her face: Jon read it as mingled exhilaration and terror.

"An hour after Solcintra dawn," she said firmly.

"I'll tell him," Jon repeated and she inclined her head.

From the main garage came the sound of exuberant voices.

"Trilla's back," Jon said, moving around the desk. "Care to have a word with your rescues?"

Aelliana hung back a instant after Jon left, looking quickly down at the card in her hand: Second class, dated this very day. Fingers none too steady, she turned it over, found the name of the master pilot certifying grade . . .

Jon dea'Cort.

She sighed, then, and put the card safely into her pocket before going to make the re-acquaintance of the pirates.

"PARDON US, PILOT, but are you Aelliana-Caylon-who-rewrote-the-ven'Tura Tables?" The boy's face was earnest.

She inclined her head. "I am."

"I told you so!" he rounded on his mate, who had the grace to look abashed. He turned back to Aelliana. "Yolan thought you weren't old enough. In fact," he added, flicking another glance at the girl, "she thought the tables had been revised fifty or sixty years ago!"

"Well, what does it matter when they were revised," the girl snapped, "as long as they're correct?"

"Very true," Aelliana said gravely and Yolan sent her a quick glance before ducking her head.

"Indeed, Pilot, Sed Ric and me are grateful for your—patronage—to Master dea'Cort. We'd looked for work, but no one would have us . . ." She looked to her partner, who promptly took up his part.

"We're also grateful to the fox-face—to your partner—for putting us in the way of a meal. We don't intend that he be out of pocket for . . ."

Aelliana frowned and the boy stumbled to a halt, stricken. She sighed, releasing the irritation she felt on Daav's account—fox-face, indeed!—and moved her hands in the gesture for peace.

"You may give him his rank, which is captain," she said, with a measure of austerity she had not intended.

Yolan flicked a mischievous look aside. "*Captain* Fox," she told her partner, soto voce.

Aelliana turned toward her, but before she could deliver the blistering set-down rising to her tongue, Jon dea'Cort spoke up.

"In point of fact," he said, considering the pirates impartially over the rim of his mug, "Scout Captain Fox."

"Scout!" The boy sagged—laughed, short and sharp. "Of all the marks to pick up—a Scout and the Caylon! Our luck, Yolan!"

"Seems exactly like," she agreed wryly and looked back to Aelliana.

"We meant no disrespect to the captain, Pilot. It's only we didn't know what to call him, isn't it Sed Ric?"

"That's right," he said eagerly. "We'll speak him fair, Pilot—you needn't blush that you know us!"

"Very well," Aelliana said, after a short silence. "Master dea'Cort has said that you may work for him until—until such work as he has is complete. I expect you will comport yourselves honorably and give honest work for honest wages. If Master dea'Cort should find it necessary to turn you off, you needn't look for grace a second time."

"No, Pilot," the boy said, bowing low; and: "Yes, Pilot," said the girl, bowing equally low.

Aelliana looked over their bent heads to where Jon leaned against the counter, sipping his tea. He grinned at her and one hand came up to shape the word, *binjali*.

CHAPTER TWENTY-FOUR

Be aware of those actions undertaken in your name. . .

—From the *Liaden Code of Proper Conduct*

FOUR HOURS' SLEEP and a shower did much toward restoring one's perspective. Robed, damp hair loose along his shoulders, Daav poured himself a glass of morning wine and padded out to his private study.

He had barely crossed the threshold into this rather cluttered chamber when the comm chimed.

Six people had the number to Daav's private line: Er Thom; Clonak ter'Meulen; Scout Lieutenant Olwen sel'Iprith, former lover, former team-mate, currently off-planet; Frad Jinmaer, another team-mate; Fer Gun pen'Uldra, his father, also off-planet—and Aelliana Caylon.

The chime sounded again; Daav had crossed the room and struck the connect key before the note was done.

"Yes."

Er Thom's image was serious, even for Er Thom; the inclination of the head stiffly formal.

"The delm is hereby made aware of yos'Galan's Balance to an insult received of Clan Sykun."

Balance . . . Daav sank to the arm of his desk chair, staring into Er Thom's eyes. He read anger; he read resolution; worry—and an utter absence of grief. Anne and the child were safe, then.

"The delm hears," he said, the High Tongue chill along his tongue. He moved a hand in query and dropped into the Low Tongue.

"What's amiss, darling?"

Er Thom took a hard breath. "Delm Sykun found it fitting to turn her back upon Thodelmae yos'Galan at a public gather this morning." He paused. "You haven't heard?"

"I've just risen," Daav said, reaching for the keypad. "You know how slugabed I am." Three keystrokes accessed the house computer and his mail.

"My, my. A letter of apology from Ixin. An apology from Asta. A letter from Lady yo'Lanna, promising to strike Sykun from her guest list—" He glanced over to Er Thom, still and solemn in the comm screen.

"There's a good come out of whatever it is. Lady yo'Lanna does so love to strike people from her guest list."

Er Thom did not smile. "As you say. Mr. dea'Gauss has been instructed to sell any stock yos'Galan may hold in Sykun's concerns— at a loss, if necessary, and noisily. Letters of cancellation have been issued on all contracts yos'Galan holds with Sykun. Mr. dea'Gauss has advised that he will also be selling his private holdings of Sykun business."

"Hah." Daav tapped more keys, mind racing. A public cut was a serious matter, demanding swift and unhesitant answer. Such a cut to Anne Davis, Lady yos'Galan, author of a text which linked Terra to Liad in a manner not likely to find acceptance among many Liadens—It could not be said that Er Thom's answer was too harsh.

That Korval's man of business also chose to enter Balance was eloquent of the magnitude of the insult. In Mr. dea'Gauss were mated pure *melant'i* and an exacting sense of honor.

"Aha. I have Mr. dea'Gauss' analysis," he said to Er Thom. "The Pilots Fund holds four hundred of Sykun's shares." He touched a key, scanning the file rapidly, and grinned.

"Mr. dea'Gauss indicates that the Fund shall realize sufficient cash from the sale of these four hundred shares to buy a block of stock in Vonlet's instrumentation venture." He flicked another glance to Er Thom's face, finding it marginally less angry.

"In fact, Mr. dea'Gauss is in a fair way to considering the incident fortuitous."

A smile showed unwillingly at the corner of Er Thom's mouth. "Hardly that, though one readily comprehends Mr. dea'Gauss' thoughts upon the subject."

"Just so," Daav agreed, keying in instructions for his man of business to sell any and all Sykun shares held by Korval or, privately, by Daav yos'Phelium.

"Shall the delm take further action?" Er Thom asked, very softly.

Daav shook his head. "Korval takes no public action, other than divesting itself entirely of Sykun stocks. Of course, the delm shall not find it possible to attend any function where Sykun is also a guest, but I rather think the world will have decided that already. I fancy I hear the match programs running as we speak."

Still Er Thom would not be tempted to a laugh, nor even to the fullness of his smile.

"I wish you will come to us," he said suddenly. "Anne—She is not in agreement with Balance. She feels—she says that it is—a joy— to have found Sykun so rude, for now she is relieved of the necessity of courtesy when they meet."

"Which is true enough," Daav pointed out. "Excepting that they shall—very likely!—not meet again."

"Yes, but—" Er Thom bit his lip, looked away. "She says," he continued, very low, "that to answer insult with Balance is to bring all eyes upon it—upon her—us. She—I feel she—is angry." He looked up. "She is gone to play the 'chora."

"Hah." Daav stood, shaking his hair back. He smiled into his *cha'leket*'s worried face. "I'll come. Until very soon."

"Until soon, Daav."

"WHAT DO YOU THINK of these oxy tanks?"

Clonak gave them consideration, fingering his mustache with absent affection.

"They're very nice oxy tanks," he offered after a minute's critical study. "Symmetrical—and of a pleasing color. Full, too. I like that in an oxy tank."

Aelliana sighed. "Forgive me. I had meant to ask if you thought four sufficient, or if these four should be replaced with four of larger capacity."

"Four's the regulation number, Beautiful Goddess, but no one's going to howl if you want to carry more. If the hold's empty you can indulge your whim to the limit."

"Yes, but it's not my whim," she said with a fair semblance of patience. "Daav had seemed to think that four was not enough, and I—"

Clonak's face changed, and she suddenly knew she had his serious and entire attention.

"What precisely did Daav say, Goddess?" Very careful, that tone, with the taffy eyes gone solemn as stone.

Aelliana blinked. "Why, that he had been on a ship which had lost life support, and that one need only be in such a situation once, with a too-short supply."

"So-ho. I shouldn't have thought he remembered that." His voice was quiet, as if he spoke to himself. He made no other comment.

"Why shouldn't he remember?" Aelliana demanded and almost flinched at the sharpness of her own voice.

"Because he had the Healers," Clonak said, and grinned his crazy grin. "And the Healers had the devil's own time, as I heard it. They swore he'd forgot. Gods know, he wanted to forget."

"He—ran out of air?" *But that's absurd*, she thought distractedly. People who ran out of air were far beyond giving advice of any kind . . .

"Not quite," Clonak assured her. "Not—entirely—quite." He shifted, opened the suit closet, slid the rack free.

"You understand, his ship was holed—comps blown to bits, shielding in rags. He kept patching the hole, the patching kept cracking—an outside job, but he'd had the bad luck to Jump into the middle of a rock storm—a matter of a place error in the unrevised Tables, as it happens.

"However that was, it was certainly suicide to go out. Daav's no suicide—he stayed in. Loosed his beacons. Blew what was left of the coils trying to send Mayday along the pin-beam. Did what he could, you see? Then all there was to do was wait—and use up oxy."

"But you came—" Aelliana said, without knowing how she knew it.

"I came," the pudgy Scout agreed, bending to check the seams on suit number one. "I came in thirty-six Standard Days." He looked up, showing her eyes bleak as rain.

"I Jumped in, caught the beacons, hit the comm—" He took a hard breath. "He didn't answer—for a—a long time." He moved his shoulders.

"Took some talk before he'd believe I was there—he's always been stubborn. I finally latched on and crossed. He was on his last canister—three-quarters down, I guess. Maybe more. He was building a gadget—planned to separate the hydrogen atom and the oxy atoms in the reservoir—make his own air. Last I heard, they were still studying that one, down Academy lab . . ." He glanced aside, mouth twisting.

"Convinced him to come over to my ship. Convinced him to leave the gadget behind. Even convinced him to crack the suit—to conserve the air in the canister, you see. But damn me if he didn't sit there in the copilot's slot and keep turning the air down from the board! Had to threaten to sprain his head for him and stuff him in the 'doc before he stopped." He fingered his mustache. "Wouldn't have liked to try that. Daav's strong—and scary quick. Even then. Especially then." He shook his head, Terran-wise.

"He started to shake when we hit Headquarters. Olwen and Frad got their arms around him and just hung on 'til the Healers came through."

"And the Healers made him forget," Aelliana whispered.

"That's what I've always thought." Clonak frowned.

"I'll tell you what," he burst out suddenly. "I was ready for the Healers myself. Daav—Daav's the best pilot you're going to find—and one idiot math error left him hanging in a holed tin can, waiting to die! I thought I was too late, when it took him so long to open his line. Then I knew he was alive and I thought everything was *binjali*—until I saw him sitting his board calm as you like, turning the air down and talking in that reasonable way of his—And if that could happen to Daav, who's the best there is, then what might happen to clumsy Clonak? It scared me. I thought about quitting Academy. I talked to Jon. I talked to the commander—to Olwen—Frad. The more I talked, the more I determined to quit. Had my kit packed, in fact." He shook his head, hard.

Aelliana licked her lips, forced herself to extend a hand. "But you didn't quit."

Clonak stared, stepped forward and took her hand gently between his palms.

"I didn't quit," he said, "because I stopped to say good-bye to Daav. He asked why I was leaving and I told him, 'Because it's dangerous. Because people die, doing what we're trained to do.' And he said . . ." He grinned, lopsided.

"He said, 'That's life, you know.'" Clonak moved his shoulders. "So, I stayed."

"Are you glad?" Aelliana asked. Clonak snorted.

"Glad? I'm doing the only work worth doing. Does that make me glad? Or mad as any other Scout?" He stepped back, releasing her hand, and gestured toward the suits. "Have you done any practice with these?"

"I've had one on and tested the circuits."

"Well, I see we've got our work cut out for us! Why don't you file for something upper-level and out of the way? Outyard One has a nice quiet little lagoon where we can park us and do a bit of walkabout outside."

"All right," Aelliana said, pushing away from the wall and heading for the companionway. She paused. "What is *walkabout*?" she asked, pronouncing the non-Liaden word with care.

"Aha!" Clonak said with a laugh. "Odd that you should ask . . ."

"IT'S THAT DAMN BOOK!" Anne snapped. "Of all the foolishness I never heard—it was meant for scholars! Who else minds about the dead, dusty past?"

The dialect was the one she had spoken in her childhood, which was, Daav thought, indication enough of her upset. He perched on the arm of a parlor chair and lifted an eyebrow.

"Very true," he said, calm in Standard Terran. "What would you have had us do instead of what has been done?"

"Ignore it," Anne cried, rounding on him swiftly. "Let it go. Turn the other cheek. Act as if the great House of Korval were above children's games and found such goings-ons just—faintly—ridiculous."

"Ah. And what would that accomplish, I wonder?"

She glared as if she suspected him of laughing at her. He showed her his palms, fingers spread wide and empty.

"Anne, I ask because I don't know. You say there is a better way to answer Sykun's insolence. Teach it to me."

"You're not a fool."

A complimentary manner, indeed, in which to address one's delm. Daav grinned. "I have my moments. As do we all. What is gained by allowing Sykun license to abuse you?"

She sank to the edge of the chair opposite his, fingers tightly gripped together. "Forgetfulness."

He waited, head tipped and face attentive.

"She—cut me—because she wanted to show that the book—the proof of the common back-tongue—was a lie. She wanted to make a stir, don't you see? And by rising to the bait, you've given force to her argument. You've said, in effect, that Korval has something to apologize for. People will notice. People will talk. Instead of the whole thing dying down, like an eight-day wonder . . ." She shook her head.

"If you had just ignored it, then people would have shrugged and said that Sykun was making a mountain out of a molehill—She would have looked ridiculous—and people would have talked about something else."

"Ah." He closed his eyes, weighing it, tasting it, feeling the shape of it and the outline of the culture which would make such action sensible.

"I see," he said eventually, "that this might, indeed, be the appropriate response." He opened his eyes to Anne's hopeful face. "Elsewhere."

Hope died. "Daav—"

He raised a hand. "Given a society based upon the communal effort of unallied individuals, each of whom cooperates with the others solely for individual gain, this response has obvious merit. To shake off an insult is to conserve energy for the more important work of individual advancement. However, such a society does not exist upon Liad and the answer you suggest will not work. Worse," he said, deliberately softening his voice, "it may do active harm."

"I don't—"

"Recall that we are predators, enclosed in kin-groups, held in check by the laws of Clan and Council. Precedence is guarded as jealously as children. *Melant'i* opens more doors than cantra, as a rich man who has sullied his name may tell you. Insult must be Balanced, immediately and stringently, else the other predators see that you are weak."

"But—"

"Hear me out. I do not say that your answer is wrong. I merely say that Er Thom's is better. On Liad. To preserve our *melant'i*, our precedence—and our right to peace—Sykun must be lessoned. Did we ignore this morning's insult, the world would talk, and wonder— and plan. The next insult must in such a case be more daring—and we reach a point very soon where we play with lives."

Anne stared.

"This way," Daav said gently, "Sykun looses a few cantra and the pleasure of a few parties. Korval must make some adaptation of trade and contract. It is done. The world is satisfied and the matter falls away, as you wish it to do, in a twelve-day or so. To follow your plan—" He leaned forward and took her hands in his.

"We are too few. I cannot risk one life on the chance of a Balance done badly. It is Korval's duty to protect its own. Which duty I take most seriously."

She was silent a moment or two, eyes searching his face.

"What are the odds," she asked then, "of this getting— dangerous?"

Sharon Lee & Steve Miller

Dangerous. He paused a moment, considering what that might mean to her. Surely, he decided, in this case her danger and his were the same—physical harm befalling lifemate, child, herself, or other kin.

"Less this afternoon than this morning," he told her, with the utter truth one owed to kin. "Two moves have so far been made upon the theme and we have answered appropriately. It may be some shall try a third time. Vigilant response to that must establish our position without doubt."

She sighed, and took her hands away, though pensively, and not in anger.

"Your lifemate," he said softly, "will protect you with all of his skill. And your delm shall protect you, with all of his."

"Yes." She sighed, then, and rose, tall and graceful and Terran. "Thank you," she said, which—Liaden—kin should have no cause to say, one to another. "I'll speak to Er Thom."

He smiled and rose also. "Rest easy," he told her. "All will be well."

CHAPTER TWENTY-FIVE

In an ally, considerations of house, clan, planet, race are insignificant beside two prime questions, which are:
1. Can he shoot?
2. Will he aim at your enemy?

—From Cantra yos'Phelium's Log Book

"YOUR ANALYSIS IS ELOQUENT, my son. Allow me to hold it for a day or three, that I may give it the study it merits."

Ran Eld bowed, fighting to conceal his dismay. He had sweated over that analysis, striving to illuminate every benefit to be gained by adopting San bel'Fasin as a partner in Sood'ae Leather Works. Indeed, he had written so compellingly of the advantages of upgraded facilities and increased production he had quite convinced himself that selling bel'Fasin as much as half the enterprise would be all Mizel's gain. Surely even cursory study must make these advantages plain to the delm's eye?

And the twelve-day was winding to a close.

"The gentleman who makes the offer of partnership," he said, careful to keep his voice even, his face calm, "did seem desirous of a speedy resolution."

"Ah, did he?" Mizel glanced up. "It is well to recall that the gentleman approached us, we did not seek him. If he cannot wait upon rational consideration, he is free to offer his partnership elsewhere."

Ran Eld went cold. "Mother, perhaps—"

She raised a hand. "My son, I see that you are convinced of the benefits of the scheme. You are perhaps too young to understand that no scheme brings unalloyed profit. I must consider what it is this San bel'Fasin thinks he will gain in the venture, and whether Mizel can afford to indulge him." She smiled. "We learn something of value, should it transpire that San bel'Fasin cannot afford to wait. Nor do I think a man who is unable to adopt a temperate course will be a suitable partner for Mizel. Slow, steady and careful are the cards to play, when we decide for the clan's future. I shall give your analysis due thought, never doubt it."

There was finality in her voice and, perforce, Ran Eld bowed.

"Good-day, Mother."

"Go in joy, my child."

He gained the safety of his rooms and shut the door firmly behind him. Gods, what should he do, if the delm refused the scheme? Twenty cantra—soon to be doubled! But there, he assured himself, splashing brandy into a cup, she would not refuse. Further study could only show the plan's excellencies to fuller advantage. His mother was not stupid, merely conservative. Caution must bow to good sense.

Soon.

IT WAS A SMALL, neat house on a small, neat street handy to Solcintra's business district. Daav worked the gate-latch and followed the stone path through the meticulously-kept front-garden, mounted six shallow stairs to the porch and pulled the bell.

He had not sent ahead, nor was he dressed in the formal style mandated by the Code, when a delm went calling upon a delm. Indeed, he might almost be a solicitor who had wandered a few blocks north of his usual preserve, excepting, of course, that not many solicitors were adopted of the Mun.

The plain blue door opened wide and Daav found himself looking down into the serious face of a boy no older than eight Standards.

"Good-day," the child said, eyeing the leather jacket with interest even as he lisped the doorman's traditional challenge. "Who calls and upon what business?"

"Daav yos'Phelium calls," he returned, in Visitor-to-Child-of-the-House, "upon business of the House."

The child frowned. Line yos'Phelium belonged to Korval, as he assuredly knew. The precise place held by Daav of Line yos'Phelium was likely at the root of the frown, as the personal names of delms tended to become lost outside the circle of their own kin.

"Line yos'Phelium does not belong to Reptor," the boy said, with certainty. "I shall need to know your business, sir."

"Very proper," Daav murmured, bringing his hand slightly forward, so that Korval's Ring glinted in the afternoon sun. "My business is with Delm Reptor."

The boy's eyes moved, tracking the glint—widened and came up.

"Sir," he said and stepped back from the door, bowing as Child-of-the-House-to-Honored-Guest. "Be welcome in our House."

"Thank you," Daav said gently and stepped into the dim entrance hall.

He stood aside while the child shoved the door to and engaged the lock, then followed him down a short hall to a room overlooking the back garden.

"Refreshment will be brought," the boy said, with all the gravity due his House's honor. "I go to fetch the delm, sir."

"Thank you," Daav said again, and the boy ducked back into the hall, leaving the door open.

Daav glanced around at the book-lined walls and comfortably shabby chairs. This was no state chamber, as called for by the Code, preserved in soulless perfection for the edification of formal visitors. This was a room lived in, enjoyed and enjoyable. Daav moved toward those temptingly overfull shelves.

A step in the hall beyond brought him around in time to see

a girl perhaps a year the doorman's senior cross the threshold, bearing a tray.

This she carried to the stone table before the window; rapidly set out a sweat-studded carafe, two plain crystal cups and a painted plate piled high with cookies. Turning, she made a hasty bow, "Sir," and was gone, all but running out into the hall. The door swung gently on its hinges as she passed.

Refreshment, as promised, and which courtesy required that he sample. Daav poured clear liquid from the carafe to the cup and sipped: Simmin wine, icy cold and tart enough to take one's breath. He looked wryly at the hopeful plate of sweet things and carried his cup with him to the shelves.

He had barely grazed the contents of the first shelf when a new tread was heard down the hall. Daav turned and moved to the center of the room, wine cup in one hand, Korval's Ring in plain view.

The man who stepped firmly into the chamber was soft-bodied and sandy-haired, not old, though some years older, Daav thought, than himself. He was dressed in rumpled day-clothes and scuffed houseboots, and had extraordinarily quick brown eyes, set wide in a weary, clever face.

Those quick eyes flicked to Daav's hand and back to his face, betraying puzzlement without alarm. He raised his own hand to show Reptor's Ring and bowed, Delm-to-Delm.

"How may Reptor serve Korval?"

"By forgiving this disruption of your peace," Daav said in Adult-to-Adult. "And by granting Daav yos'Phelium the gift of a few minutes of your time."

"Well." Reptor took a moment to consider Daav's face, eyes bright with intelligence. He moved a hand, as if he threw dice, and inclined his head.

"Daav yos'Phelium is welcome to my time," he said at last, and in Adult-to-Adult. He went to the stone table, poured wine into the remaining cup, sighed lightly at the plate of cookies and turned back to Daav.

"I am Zan Der pel'Kirmin." He waved at the two comfortable chairs. "Sit, do."

"I thank you." Daav sank into the nearer of the two, sipped his wine and set the cup on the elbow table. Zan Der pel'Kirmin followed suit and sat back, eyes showing curiosity, now, and somewhat of speculation.

"What brings Daav yos'Phelium to my house?"

"A rumor," Daav said gently. "I am fairly confident of my information, but I ask, for certainty's sake: Has Reptor lately— mislain—two of its own?"

The clever face went still, brown eyes glancing aside. "Mislain," he murmured, as if to himself. "Gently phrased." He looked back to Daav's face.

"Their names are Yolan pel'Kirmin and Sed Ric bin'Ala," he said, and his voice was not entirely steady. Pain and hope warred in the quick eyes. "Have you—you do have—news?"

"They are safe," Daav told him, and saw relief leach some of the pain. "Just now, they are under the protection of Pilot Aelliana Caylon, who flies out of Binjali's Yard in Upper Port." He paused, looked square into the other man's eyes. "They claim to be clanless."

Color drained from the round face; the brown eyes shone tears.

"Clanless." He might have said *dead* with the same inflection. "I—" He turned his head away, biting his lip. "Forgive me," he managed after a moment. He groped for his cup, lifted it, drank.

"I had inquired," he said, low and rapid, eyes yet averted. "I made certain they would seek the Port, ship-mad as they both are—" He glanced to Daav, pale lips tight. "Your pardon."

"No need. I believe many halflings are so."

"As you say. Be it so, my inquiries came to dust. They—I recruited myself to wait, but they did not return home, and I began to fear—offworld . . ." He sighed. "Clanless. Gods." He sagged back into his chair, showing Daav a face at once bewildered and relieved. "They are not clanless."

"And yet they have said that they are. Several times."

"A word, spoken in anger and no more meant than—" He closed his eyes, took a deep breath and opened his eyes.

"Their—patron. Aelliana Caylon, I believe you had said. That is the same Caylon? Of the ven'Tura Revision?"

"It is."

"I am in her debt. To extend her *melant'i* in such a wise, and care for those who claim no kin—that is—extraordinary. I am in her debt," he repeated and moved a hand. "And in your own."

Daav smiled, deliberately rueful. "No debt on my account, if you please. I am meddling, if you will have the truth, and must ask you to fail of mentioning this visit to Pilot Caylon, should you speak to her."

"Of course I shall speak to her!" Zan Der pel'Kirmin cried, eyes opening wide. "I must speak to her—and at once! They cannot be left a burden upon her grace, when they have kin eager to welcome them home . . ." He paused, brows drawing together.

"What had the pilot—I mean no disrespect!—I only wonder what Pilot Caylon had thought she might do for them, crying clanless and so little trained . . ."

"Ah." Daav reached to his glass and sipped the cool, tart wine. "I believe she had meant to sponsor them into Scout Academy."

"Scout Academy," the other repeated blankly.

"Pilot Caylon's name is cantra, among Scouts," Daav explained gently. "As she has very little, herself, in the way of other currency, and as your pair seemed quick enough, and clever. . ."

"Gods smile upon her, a great and wide-hearted lady," Reptor said reverently. "They—Yolan and Sed Ric have had some small training on the boards; their piloting instructors do not despair of first class. If it had not been for this other matter—but I shall go to her, to Pilot Caylon, immediately, and relieve her of Reptor's troubles."

"Immediately," Daav said delicately, "may not be possible, as Pilot Caylon resides in Chonselta. She does, however, fly—"

"Out of Binjali's Yard," the other interrupted, with a pale smile. "I understand. You are very good."

"No, only meddlesome, as I've said." Daav stood and made his bow to the host. "Having meddled sufficiently for one day, I shall restore you to your peace. Be well, and thank you for the gift of your time."

"The gift was well-given." Zan Der pel'Kirmin said, standing and bowing in reply. "My name is yours, to use in need."

Daav smiled, profoundly warmed, for it was no light thing given, but a man's whole *melant'i*, for Daav to use as he would.

"You do me too much honor," he said, and meant it.

"Not at all," the other man said firmly and offered his arm. "Allow me to guide you to our door."

"FIGHT?" Aelliana looked from Jon to Trilla to Clonak. "Why shall I need to know how to fight?"

"Because ports and docks and Outworlds in general are chancy places, Beautiful Goddess."

"Because a captain must protect herself, her ship, her cargo," said Jon, "and her partner, should she take one."

"All true," Trilla finished in her casual, Outworld way. "Ability to frame a clear 'no' never stood a pilot ill."

Aelliana stared at the three of them and hoisted herself to a stool. Patch immediately jumped from the floor to her lap.

"I don't know the first thing about fighting," she said, as the cat rammed his head into her shoulder, rumbling like an infant earthquake.

"That's why you have to learn," Clonak said patiently. "If you already knew, it would be a waste of our time to teach you."

"We learned self-defense as part of pilot training," Yolan observed, looking up from the parts bin she and her mate were sorting.

"It wasn't enough, though," Sed Ric added. "We had to make adjustments." He stood and Yolan with him, and they stepped toward the stools in their usual formation: Yolan on Sed Ric's right.

"See?" the boy said and his right hand moved, jerking something bright and lethal from his belt. It jingled, hissed and fell still as Clonak came forward, hand outstretched.

"Jang-wire," he said, holding it up for the rest to see. Aelliana blinked.

It looked like nothing more than a length of thin chain, looped and hooked into a leather grip.

"Illegal, of course," Clonak finished and tossed the loop back to Sed Ric, who snagged it out of mid-air and hung back on his belt.

"Works," he said, and Yolan added. "We keep it on the right because I'm left-handed. I walk at Sed Ric's right. If he goes down—"

"There's one of you still weaponed and able," Jon concluded. "Partner-work, right enough." He turned to Aelliana. "Those who don't fight die, math teacher."

She met his eyes squarely. "I am craven, Master Jon. Only raise a hand and see me cringe."

"All the more reason to learn, fast and well," Trilla said. "If you get real good, no one'll touch you." She slid off her stool, shaking a shower of finger-talk at Clonak.

"Couple different styles of fighting," she said, pointing out a spot for him to stand. "Clonak here likes Port rules, which is to say, no rules."

"See a head," Clonak said gleefully, "punch it."

"This way," said Trilla and moved.

Aelliana leapt from her stool, dumping Patch floorward. Jon caught her wrist and she cried out sharply, then stood, aghast and enthralled, watching as Clonak countered Trilla's attack with a kick toward the Outworld woman's midsection, except Trilla had sidestepped and aimed her own kick at Clonak's knee and he went down, rolling, and she jumped forward, kicking at his head, except Clonak had jackknifed and it was Trilla down, one arm bent high behind her back and her cheek against the concrete floor.

"Yield!"

Clonak was up before the word's echo died, bending and offering a hand for her to rise.

"Well played, old friend."

She grinned and moved her shoulders, looking over to Aelliana. "So, I'm not real good."

"Trilla likes the dance," Clonak said, reaching into his belt and withdrawing a wickedly curved finger.

"Pretend a knife!" he shouted, and lunged.

Trilla melted away from the attack, spun, kicked, wove. The knife followed, desperate for a hit, growing increasingly heedless— and Trilla swept forward with no more force than a dance move, her hand connected sharply with Clonak's wrist, his hand snapped upward—

"Disarmed!" he cried, and collapsed cross-legged to the floor, grinning up at Aelliana. "Bow to necessity, divine. The universe is dangerous."

"First lesson tomorrow," Jon decreed, at last loosing her wrist. "Trilla will teach you to dance."

CHAPTER TWENTY-SIX

Jela spent his whole off-shift rigging guy-wires and safety nets to hold his tree in what it thinks is proper position. He was going to run an orientation plate off the main engine, but I canceled that project.

If that tree's got to be in the pilot's tower, it can damn' well take the same risks the pilots take.

—Excerpted from Cantra yos'Phelium's Log Book

DAAV KNOTTED THE SILVER RIBBON and let the beaded ends fall. Glancing into the mirror, he straightened his lace and pulled his collar into more perfect order. The beaded ribbon trailed an elegant tendril across a shoulder, counterpoint to the rough twist swinging in his ear.

He paused in his toilette, hand rising to touch the earring, seeing again the morning Rockflower had led him out of the tent; dew soaking his boots, on the edge of the plain, on the edge of the dawn.

She faced him to the rising sun and shouted his name—Estrelin—Starchild—which was not the most fortunate the Mun might bestow, who considered the stars brought madness—and bade him stand fearless. He saw the knife flash in the corner of his eye, felt it bite his earlobe, heard Rockflower grunt with approval.

"Blood and blade, Estrelin, child of the grandmother's tent."

It was back to the autumn camp then, and the silver worker's tent. Rockflower herself twisted the heated metal into the proper design, the hot wire went through the gash in his ear, cauterizing the minor wound, and the ends sealed into a continuous loop. As nothing could break the silver loop, she told him, so nothing would break his bond to her tent.

At *Jelaza Kazone*, in the hour before a formal meal, Daav smiled wryly at his own reflection. The silver loop could, of course, be broken all too easily: A snip of wire cutters, a careful withdrawal, a minute or two in the autodoc to erase the tiny scar . . . He had not done it. He would not do it. Captive among Liadens, there yet remained a fragment of Estrelin, child of the grandmother's tent.

He broke his own reflected gaze, looked down and opened his ornament case. Among the guests tonight would be his betrothed, home between test-Jumps, and who would expect to see him jeweled as befit his station. He chose a sapphire-headed pin and seated it carefully in the lace at his throat, wondering idly if Estrelin of the grandmother's tent would follow custom and cut his hair when he was wed.

Actually, he thought, slipping a sapphire ring onto the first finger of his right hand, Mun custom dictated that one's wife perform this service on the morning following the consummation of their vow. He tried to imagine dainty Samiv tel'Izak bowing to such a custom, but very soon abandoned the effort. A Mun marriage was a lifemating, within its peculiar laws; and, come to consideration, it was much easier to picture Anne cutting Er Thom's hair. Not, he assured himself, with an amused glance at his reflection, that one's *cha'leket* was ever less than impeccably barbered.

"Very fine, your lordship," he told himself, gesturing fluidly with a hand that glittered silver-and-blue. He moved his head, sending the earring swinging and felt the weight of his hair slide across his shoulder.

"I don't think I shall cut it," he said, giving his reflection serious attention. He shook the lace cuffs out, brushed a possibly imaginary speck of dust from the soft black trousers and stepped back, making his bow with a bite of irony.

"Have a pleasant evening, sir. And do try to value Pilot tel'Izak as you ought."

MASTER DEA'CORT had said they might sleep in the pilot's dorm off the aux supply room. Accordingly, they had pushed two cots together, arranged blankets and pillows—and discovered that they were neither sleepy nor in the mood for sport.

"Walk?" Yolan asked, running her hands through her hair and standing it all on end, so she looked like a Yolan-sized dandyweed. "I'm all over twitches."

"Me, too," Sed Ric admitted. He dug around in his pouch and brought out their carefully hoarded wages. Master dea'Cort paid generous for grunt-work, though not quite enough to make a four-dex loss into a nothing. Sed Ric counted the ready and looked up with a sidewise grin.

"Buy us an ice?"

Yolan laughed. "Why not?"

They went out through the main garage, cutting past Master dea'Cort's office.

The old Scout was sitting at his desk, head bent over a bound book, seemingly oblivious to his surroundings. Sed Ric looked at Yolan. Yolan cleared her throat.

"Out Port-running, is it?" Jon asked, without bothering to lift his head. "Give Pilot Caylon joy, to find the two of you turned up dead."

Yolan bit her lip. "We're only gone for an ice, Master. If you think the pilot won't like it—"

He did lift his head, then, and considered them out of bland amber eyes. "Young things," he said after a moment, and waved a broad hand. "Go on and have your sweet. Watch yourselves, that's all. I don't want to be the one to explain a tragedy to the pilot."

"No, Master," Sed Ric said, jerking his head at Yolan. "We just thought to step around to the East Selling."

"We'll be careful," Yolan put in. "Of course we will."

"All right," said Jon, and went back to his book.

Yolan and Sed Ric faded back out of the office and made their way across the garage, through the crew door. Outside, they went left, aiming to cut a diagonal course across Binjali's Yard and use the utility gate at the eastern corner. From the gate to the East Selling was a matter of two short blocks, and an ice vendor was among the first of the kiosks encountered.

"Think the pilot will be needing crew, when she takes herself off-world?" Yolan voice was too casual, as it was when she wanted to pretend that a burning question was of no moment.

Sed Ric sighed. "Not much crew room on a Class A Jump," he commented. "Her and the captain'll run things snug between 'em."

"Likely," Yolan allowed and they walked silent awhile, down the long corridor of ships asleep on their cold-pads in the Port's early evening.

"Maybe they'll take us," Yolan said and it was desperation in her voice.

Sed Ric stopped and looked at her. "Take us where?"

"Offworld," she said and reached for his hand. "Someplace where they don't mind what's our family—or how close we stand cousins. They might take us—the pilot would, I'll wager."

"Yes, and her partner's cut from whip-leather."

"Maybe not," she said, clutching his hand feverishly. "Maybe not—so much. Who fed us, after all? And the counter help never blinked, did they, Sed Ric? Runs a chit there, does Captain Daav—for all we know, he feeds the port."

"All of which argues him stupid enough to lift dead weight when cargo is what keeps his ship able. Air dreams, Yolan. You know it."

Her shoulders sagged. "What will we do, then? Master dea'Cort won't keep us forever—he paid us for make-work today! Who else will have us? Walking the dim side, that's not—you heard him: Who will we sell first, you or me? If it comes to that—"

"It won't," Sed Ric said firmly. He chewed his lip, looking into her face. "I've been thinking," he said, slow and careful, because he had been thinking—and because she wasn't going to like hearing what his thoughts had taught him.

"I've been thinking," he said again, "that we might go and—talk—to Uncle Zan Der."

"Talk to Father? We talked to Father—and more use talking to hullplate! We showed him the chart and how the genes scanned—did he even look? Did he even *care* that it's only been us for each other since we were in nursery together? Did he even—"

She was working herself into a state, which he might have known she would. He gathered her close, pushing her head down to his shoulder and rubbing his cheek against her hair. "Easy. Easy. I was just thinking, that's all."

And thought still showed that port-running was increasingly risky. Yolan was in peril, whether she would face it or no. Uncle Zan Der would see she got the rest of her training—went for Jump-pilot. He thought—he thought he could make a case for himself being 'prenticed to Cousin Peri, who kept warehouse on Mordra. They would be separated and the reason they had left clan was that they *would not* be separated.

But he couldn't keep her safe.

"Let's get that ice," he said, husky into her hair.

She stirred, lifted her head and stepped back. "Sure."

Hand-in-hand they walked on, down the row and across, nearing *Ride the Luck*, snug on her ready-pad.

Yolan froze, her hand tensing in his. "What's that?"

"What's—" He saw it, a shadow, moving stealthy near the bottom of *The Luck's* ramp.

"Maybe Captain Fox?" Yolan sounded uncertain.

"Why would he sneak around in the dark?" The figure moved and he frowned. "Not tall enough."

The figure set foot on the ramp, boot heel hitting metal with a sharp clang.

"Let's go!" Yolan urged and was gone, running full tilt toward the ramp.

Heart in mouth, Sed Ric ran after.

DAAV HAD EXERTED SOME CARE in the matter of the guest list. It would not, on one hand, be considerate of Bindan's rank among the mid-level clans to invite exclusively from the Fifty, however much it might gratify Delm Bindan's ambition. And to have only Er Thom, Anne and cousin Luken bel'Tarda in addition to his affianced wife and her delm—the scheme he favored most— would surely be seen as an insult by Bindan, and justly so. Such intimate gatherings belonged to the days preceding a formal offer of contract.

The number of guests for a gathering such as this, falling between offer and final signing, might with perfect propriety be kept to a dozen, but very few of those dozen had best be Korval's kin or Bindan's.

Korval's allies, that was something else.

In the end, he had Er Thom and Anne, for his own comfort; Guayar and Lady yo'Lanna, for the comfort of Bindan's ambition. To leaven the loaf, he called upon Thodelms Hae Den pen'Evrit Clan Yron and Dema Wespail Clan Chad, pilots both, and keepers of secondary lines in mid-level Houses long tied to Korval with the threads of trade and ships.

Dutiful Passage being at the moment in port, he invited sensible Kayzin ne'Zame—Er Thom's first mate, and another with long ties to Korval—finishing the list with two representatives of port merchant families—Gus Tav bel'Urik and Len Sar Anaba, clans Shelart and Gabrian, respectively.

The gather had begun well. The guests had arrived and been made known to each other. Wine had been served, conversations had begun and then Guayar had prettily—not to say, audibly— complimented Anne on the process of her thought and begged that she do him the favor of endorsing his copy of her book.

"I should certainly be delighted to do so, sir," Anne said properly, and Guayar bowed, hand over heart.

"I am in your debt." He turned to Bindan. "Have you yet had the opportunity to read Lady yos'Galan's work?" he inquired, which was, Daav thought, really too bad of him. He had put his coin on Lady yo'Lanna, Guayar's sister, that she would be equal to stemming just such a start, but she was across the room, speaking with Kayzin ne'Zame and Merchant bel'Urik.

Bindan bowed with only a trace of stiffness. "Alas, sir, circumstance has not yet permitted me this pleasure."

"It is an excellent work," Guayar said. "I cannot praise it too highly. You must assuredly obtain a copy and read it."

"Indeed, ma'am, you must not encourage him to prate on about books!" Lady yo'Lanna reproved with mock severity, swooping into the conversation amid an aggression of scented draperies. "He will have you here all night and well past tomorrow morning's meal if you give him the least excuse! Do you admire flowers at all? I confess to a passion. Walk with me to the window, do. There is the most exquisite bank of gloan-roses! I was only just now saying to Master pel'Urik . . ."

Chattering, she bore Bindan off. Er Thom moved over to engage Guayar's attention and Daav allowed himself an internal sigh of relief before returning his attention to the discussion nearer at hand.

The topic was the most efficient coil-to-mass configuration in Class C Jump ships and his conversational partners—pilots tel'Izak and pen'Evrit—were so absorbed by it that neither had noted his momentary lapse of attention, or, he fervently hoped, Guayar's bit of mischief.

"And I tell you, sirs," Samiv tel'Izak was saying, with rather more spirit than Daav had heretofore observed in her, "had we not that autonomous tertiary system, we might yet be in Jump this evening. The matter ran that near the edge of irrecoverable."

"Yes, but, ma'am, you speak only to one case," pen'Evrit objected. "How often, in truth, is the third—never say the fourth!—system called into use? Certainly, in the case of a liner, where the mass to be translated is already vast, dropping a redundant and statistically underused system can only—"

"Endanger the passengers," Daav said, reentering the lists with a vengeance.

"Precisely!" Samiv tel'Izak flashed him a look of approval. pen'Evrit raised his eyebrows.

"Yes, but it is Korval, ma'am, and he is bound to say so. Are you not, Pilot?"

"Not at all," Daav said courteously. "I would merely point out that a line which is forever losing passengers and ships will likely be ruined in a very short time. How much better to err on the side of a tertiary safeguard—the translation mass of which is already figured into the cost of the voyage—and continue to reap profit?"

pen'Evrit inclined his head. "Indeed, who among us can argue against profit?"

"And cantra is so much more compelling than lives," Daav returned, smoothly deflecting what was surely a thrust devised to test the strength of Samiv tel'Izak's armor.

pen'Evrit's mouth quirked and he inclined his head just slightly, conceding the point, and was prevented from making another foray by the chime of the hour bell.

Er Thom offered his arm to his lifemate and flicked a quick violet glance over one shoulder. Daav lifted an eyebrow and his *cha'leket*, thus instructed, led the company from the formal parlor, down the hall to the dining room. From the edge of his eye, Daav saw Guayar accept Kayzin ne'Zame's arm, a meal-pairing that would, he thought, serve very well indeed.

pen'Evrit made his bow, "Your pardons, Korval—ma'am," and escaped precisely three steps before his right arm was commandeered by Lady yo'Lanna on behalf of Delm Bindan, the Lady herself having appropriated the corresponding limb attached to Len Sar Anaba, who was one of her particular favorites.

Daav turned to his betrothed—and paused in the midst of his bow, arrested by the tension of the muscles around her eyes.

"Have I offended you?" He asked impulsively, before weighing the question's propriety, which was certainly wanting. Worse, he asked in the mode between pilots, which they had been speaking with pen'Evrit, which was as close to Comrade as the High Tongue allowed, when she had not given him use of her name . . .

She drew a breath and it was puzzlement he saw in her face, more than anger.

"No offense," she answered, at least allowing him Pilot-to-Pilot. "Surely you knew that stroke was meant for me. I wonder why you took it to yourself."

Daav lifted an eyebrow. "Should I allow my proposed wife to be abused?"

Her face cleared, as if, disturbingly, his answer had verified some opinion about himself that she held close. "I am instructed," she murmured, still in the mode between pilots. "One currently holds place among the Dragon's possessions."

He had thought himself as well-armored as any other player on the fields of Liaden society, but the cut was cunning and actually struck flesh. Daav drew a breath, and saw Samiv tel'Izak raise a quick hand, her eyes wide with something very like fear.

"Forgive me. I meant no disrespect, merely an understanding of motive and what shall be required of me, beyond the lines of contract."

They were alone in the parlor. If they did not gain the dining room soon, the timing of the evening would be cast into disarray and the guests would be supping scandal stew.

"My motive," he said, speaking as gently as he was able, "was to keep you from distress. You are a guest in my house and it was in my power to shield you from pen'Evrit's boorishness. As for what may be required of you—only the contract lines, if you will, Lady. But I should be honored, if we were to be friends."

"Friends." He might have been speaking the tongue of the Grandmother's tent for all the comprehension he saw in her eyes. She glanced about her, apparently only just now aware that they were alone. "We are behind."

"So we are." He drew a careful breath. "Samiv."

She looked up at him, startled.

"My name is Daav," he told her, and offered his arm. After a moment, head slightly bent, she lay her hand on his sleeve.

"One is not—accustomed," she murmured, "to considering *friendship* a factor of marriage. Friendship is for—crewmates, Pilot. You understand me, I am certain."

"Indeed I do," he assured her, moving them toward the door. "But perhaps we might consider ourselves crewmates, even—copilots."

She was silent as they went down the hall. On the edge of the dining room, she raised her head and gave him a straight glance.

"It seems the sort of thing a Scout might perfectly well

consider," she said slowly, "but which comes—uneasy—into less—encompassing—minds."

She did not say she would attempt it, which of course she would not, having survived thus long in a society where the slightest weakness invited attack.

Still, she sat next to him at table and conversed easily during the meal, with much less than her previous restraint, and Daav was encouraged to believe that she might, after all, try to consider him more pilot and less Dragon.

THERE REMAINED ONE MORE TRADITION to satisfy, and Samiv had not been adverse to a suggestion of a walk in Korval's famous garden.

So, while the other guests retired to the card tables in the parlor, Daav led his betrothed down a side hall and let them both through a door, into the Inner Court.

The path grew dim as they strolled away from the house, and he offered an arm. She lay her hand atop his sleeve, allowing him to guide her down the old stone path.

"What a delightful spot, to be sure," she murmured. "Our gardens are not a half so—full."

The Inner Court did tend toward profusion, as even Daav would admit. He loved the wild, half-magical feel of the place, with its riots of flowers and congregations of shrubs, its unexpected glades and secret pools. The hours he spent caring for it were among the happiest of his present wing-clipped life.

"I would like to show you to *Jelaza Kazone*, if you will walk just a bit further," he murmured.

It was Korval's custom to present proposed spouses to the Tree—a courtesy, so Daav considered it, though his mother had taught such presentation was made to gain the Tree's approval.

"I shall be honored to see Korval's tree," Samiv tel'Izak said courteously.

"I warn you that it is rather large," he said, negotiating the path's penultimate and largely overgrown twist. "And somewhat—unexpected."

The path twisted once more, and ended in a smooth carpet of silvery grass.

The Tree gleamed in the clearing, casting the pale blue phosphorescence of moonvines into banks of fog. Daav paused at the edge of the glade and looked down into Samiv's face.

"Of your kindness—it is our custom to ask spouses-to-be to come forth and lay a hand against the Tree and speak their name. It would gladden my heart, if you consented to do this."

She hesitated a heartbeat, but what, after all, was the harm in touching a plant, no matter how large, and speaking one's name in the moonlit quiet of a garden?

"I am honored," she said once more and walked by his side across the grass to the Tree. A low wind rustled the moonvines and Samiv shivered in the sudden chill.

"A moment only," Daav said, slipping his arm free. "In this manner, you see, Pilot." He placed his hand, palm flat against the massive trunk, feeling it warm immediately with the Tree's accustomed greeting. "Daav yos'Phelium."

Samiv stepped forward, placed her right hand against the trunk and said, very plain, "Samiv tel'Izak."

It happened in a heartbeat. Daav's hand went ice-cold. The wind, which had been playing among the moonvines, roared, rushed across the clearing and hurtled into to the branches above their heads, showering them with leaves, twiglets and bark.

Samiv tel'Izak cried out, wordless and high, and raised both arms to shield her head. Daav flung forward, caught her up amid a hail of twigs and urged her toward the entrance of the clearing.

The wind stopped the moment Samiv's feet touched the pathway.

"How can you abide it?" she demanded, whirling to face him in the dimness, left hand cradling right. "Cold, horrid, *looming* thing—how can you live here, knowing it might fall at any time and crush the house entire!"

He stared at her, his own hand just beginning to warm into flesh.

"The Tree is Korval's charge," he managed, keeping his voice level in the mode between pilots, while his mind replayed the wind, the chill, the rain of arboreal trash. "As best we know, it is in the prime of its life, pilot, and not likely to fall for many, many years."

Samiv tel'Izak drew herself up, face stiff.

"If that is all which is *required*, my lord," she said, and it was all the way back to Addressing-a-Delm-Not-One's-Own, "I wish to be returned indoors."

"Certainly," Daav said, and offered his arm, hardly noticing that the touch of her fingers on his sleeve was slight and shrinking. He guided her down the pathway absently, remembering the hail of Tree-bits shaken loose by that puppyish wind—leaves, wood bits, twists of ancient birds nests.

But not one seedpod.

They reached an overgrown portion of the path and he stood back to allow Samiv tel'Izak to precede him. That she did so without demur, though his rank gave him precedence, spoke eloquently of her distress. Daav shook himself, for it was no more than his duty to soothe her fear.

"Samiv," he began and felt her fingers twitch.

"Please," she said, her voice tight, "I do not wish to speak."

"Very well," he said and guided her silently back down the Inner Court, all the while wracking his memory to recall if the Diaries told of any previous time when a spouse was spurned by the Tree.

CHAPTER TWENTY-SEVEN

Pen vel'Kazik comes into the Pilot's Tower only when forced by her fellow Counselors, and stands as near the ladder as she may, sweating and wringing her foolish hands until the others declare their business done. The boy swears it's Jela's tree that frightens her. I say, if it is, may the gods soon afflict them all likewise.

—Excerpted from Cantra yos'Phelium's Log Book

"MORNING, MATH TEACHER." Jon was leaning against the counter, tea mug in one hand, attention centered on a bound book held precariously open in the other.

"Good morning, Jon. Is Trilla on-shift?"

"Haven't seen her yet," he answered, trying to turn a page with his thumb. The book wavered and slipped, leaves fluttering helplessly.

Aelliana swept forward, captured the slim volume in the instant before it hit cement and straightened, holding it out.

Amused amber eyes met hers. "Quick," Jon commented and turned to set his mug aside.

A test, Aelliana thought, feeling the weight of the book in her hand. Of course it had been a test. Master Pilot Jon dea'Cort would never be so clumsy as to drop—She glanced down, frowning at the silver-gilt lettering.

In Support of the Commonality of Language, the glittery title read. *The Lifework of Learned Scholar Jin Del yo'Kera Clan Yedon, Compiled by Learned Scholar Anne Davis Clan Korval.*

"Book worthy of study," Jon said as Aelliana glanced up. "You can have the loan of it when I'm done, if you like."

"Thank you, I would like it, very much," she said, surrendering the book. "The last issue of *Scholarship Review* was given to discussion of this work."

"Ah? And what did the host of learned Liadens think of the proof of a common back-tongue linking Terra and Liad?"

"That I cannot tell you," she answered seriously. "Most wished only to say that such a notion was entirely ridiculous, without addressing the proofs at all. The single reviewer attempting to face the work on its own merit was Scout Linguist pel'Odyare. In her estimation the scholarship had been impeccable throughout and the conclusion logically drawn. She wrote that she would implement a search of certain Scout records, to find if independent corroboration of the conclusion could be established."

"Master pel'Odyare does *binjali* work," Jon said, smoothing the gilt letters with absent fingers. "If proof is there, she'll find it." He sighed, and slid the book away next to the tea-tin trophy box. "Bold heart, Scholar," he said softly.

He looked back to Aelliana with a wry smile.

"Your pirates came in last evening with a tale of someone hanging about your ship," he said. "Gave chase, but lost the quarry—which is a smile from the luck, though they won't see it. Seem to think they're quick enough to dodge a pellet, if the sneaker had held a gun. Anywise, I did a check and nothing seemed amiss. You might want to do the same, for certainty's sake."

"Yes, of course . . ." She blinked. Someone had been hanging about *The Luck*? Her heart stuttered, animal instinct shrieking that it had been Ran Eld, that she was discovered, hovering on the brink of lost . . . She took a hard breath and met Jon's eyes.

"I shall do an inspection immediately. Are the pirates—Sed Ric and Yolan—available to attend me?"

"Hah." Jon grinned. "They're here." He raised his voice to a bellow. "Pirates!"

There was a clatter and two rapid shadows flung into the lounge.

"Aye, Master Jon!"

They spied Aelliana then and made their bows, low and respectful. "Pilot."

"I am told that you surprised a lurker about my ship last evening. Your assistance is required now on a cold-inspection, during which you will give me the round tale."

"Yes, Pilot." More bows, and attentive waiting, Yolan at Sed Ric's right hand.

Aelliana inclined her head and looked to Jon. "If Trilla should arrive, sir, will you assure her that I am eager to learn the dance and shall engage to do so, directly I return?"

Jon grinned. "I'll do that, never fear."

Her lips twitched, but she otherwise preserved her countenance. "I thank you."

She gathered the pirates with a gesture, turned and marched them out. Jon watched until the crew door cycled, then reached up and pulled down his book.

"SHE IS AFRAID OF the Tree?" Er Thom sank to the stone wall enclosing Trealla Fantrol's patio and stared at Daav out of wide purple eyes.

"Worse," Daav said ruefully. "I apprehend that the Tree holds her in severe dislike."

Er Thom digested this in silence as Daav paced from the wall to the ornamental falls and stood looking down into the tiny, frothing torrent.

His search through Korval's Diaries had been fruitless. None of the delms before him had discovered the Tree in disliking anyone, much less an all-but-signed spouse. The single hint toward the possibility of such a thing came from Grandmother Cantra's log, and even there it was writ so vague. . .

"What will you do?" Er Thom asked quietly from the wall.

Daav sighed.

"I thought," he said, coming back to sit next his brother on the warm stones. "I thought perhaps—my wife—and I—might live at the ocean house. If the ocean pales before the matter is done, there is the chalet, or even—"

"Daav."

He stopped. It took an active application of will to raise his eyes to Er Thom's.

"Hear yourself," his brother said. "Will you actually get a child upon a woman whom the Tree dislikes? What then? Shall you live at the ocean house for the rest of your days? Or only until the child is of an age to be sent off-world? How can you—"

"How can you assume that the Tree will likewise disdain the child?" Daav demanded, voice rising above Er Thom's arguments— true, just and sane, gods—" The child will be yos'Phelium, and yos'Phelium guards the Tree! There is no proof—" His voice squeezed out and he remembered, all too vividly, his hand, held there against the Tree, and how cold, how inhumanly cold . . .

"You chart a chancy course, darling," he said, sounding sullen as a halfling in his own ears. "Whenever did you ask the Tree's aye of Anne?"

"And yet we both know," Er Thom said after a moment, "that the Tree approves Anne. Your point is moot."

Daav closed his eyes; opened them and held out a hand. "It is, and ill-natured, besides. I—"

"What's wrong?" Anne was halfway across the patio, and moving fast, her face etched in worry, her eyes on Er Thom.

Her lifemate came to his feet in a fluid rush, went forward and caught her hands in his. "Anne—"

She allowed herself to be stopped, though the look she threw Daav was anything but calm.

"What's *wrong*?" she demanded once more, staring down into Er Thom's face.

"It is—" But here Er Thom faltered and flung a helpless glance to Daav, who slid to his feet, showing empty palms.

"It is nothing," he said, pitching his voice for gentleness.

"My brother and I have had one of our rare disagreements. There is no cause—"

"Don't lie to me." Standard Terran, her voice absolutely flat.

He drew a deep breath and bowed, very slightly. "And yet there is nothing you can do, should I tell you the truth."

"Then there's no harm in my hearing it," she returned, "and knowing what frightens Er Thom."

Frightens. Daav looked to his brother. Purple eyes met his unflinchingly, showing all.

"Hah." He resumed his seat upon the wall and in a moment Er Thom did likewise, leaving Anne standing alone, hands on hips and her face filled with waiting.

"Well?"

"Well," Daav replied, looking up. He sighed. "Are you able to believe that the Tree can—make its wishes known—to those of the Line Direct?"

She stood quiet for a long moment, then went to sit beside her lifemate and placed her hand upon his knee.

"For the purposes of this discussion," she said, like the scholar she was, "it is stipulated that *Jelaza Kazone* the Tree is able to communicate with those of Korval's Line Direct."

"Then you may know that my brother's trouble springs from the knowledge that *Jelaza Kazone* the Tree has expressed a—distaste—for Samiv tel'Izak. A distaste of which she is—alas—very aware."

"Oh." She blinked, turned her head to gaze across the valley, where *Jelaza Kazone* could be plainly seen, stretching high into the morning sky. "That wouldn't be good, would it?"

"Not—very—good," murmured Er Thom. "No."

"Well," she said, turning back to Daav. "You have other houses. There's no need to make her uncom—"

"There must not be a child born unsanctioned by the Tree!" Er Thom cried.

"Yes, but, love, Shan wasn't sanctioned by the Tree," Anne pointed out with shocking calm. "I don't—" She stopped abruptly, staring from one pair of serious eyes to the other.

"I think," she said finally, and a bit breath-short, "that I have to draw the line at a galaxy-wide telepathy."

Daav inclined his head. "Say then that Er Thom, who as a child was used to climb all over the Tree, had been far too well-trained to choose other than one who would meet approval."

"Then," Anne asked reasonably, "what happened to you?"

Daav lifted a brow. "I beg your pardon?"

"What happened to you?" She repeated, and used a long fore-finger to point, one to the other. "You were raised side-by-side, learned the same things, ate the same things, *memorized* the same things. Interchangeable parts, made by the delm's wisdom, so Korval could go on, if one of you happened to die!" Her voice was keying upward. Er Thom stirred, raising a hand toward her cheek.

"Interchangeable," Daav said. "Not exact."

She glared, though it seemed to him her eyes were not—precisely—focused. "Call it off."

So simple. It struck at the core of him and he came upright before he knew what he did, shaking with—with—"I must have a child!" He heard raw anguish in his voice and swallowed, closing his eyes and seeking after the Rainbow.

"But not *this* child," Anne pursued relentlessly. "You and Er Thom are the sons of identical twins, so close there's no choosing between you. Er Thom and I are lifemates, hooked by the soul, so I can feel his touch halfway across the house—and more!" She paused and Daav opened his eyes, meeting her fey gaze with fascination.

"Where is your lifemate, Daav yos'Phelium?"

"Anne!" Er Thom snapped to his feet, his hands on her shoulders, his body between her and his delm. "Have done."

"I repeat." He was breathless, voice squeezed out of a chest gone achy and cramped. "We may be interchangeable. We are certainly not identical. And even if what you suggest is true—that we were both formed for lifematings—there is yet no guarantee that—my—lifemate has been born." He took a hard breath. "Or that she has survived."

"Oh," she said, and of a sudden sighed, reaching up to rub at her eyes like a child. "Well," she murmured, almost too softly for him to hear, "I guess you'd better ask the Tree."

"I guess I had better," he returned, just as softly, and smiled sadly into Er Thom's eyes.

RIDE THE LUCK tested clean.

Aelliana heard Sed Ric and Yolan's account of their adventure and read them a stern lecture on the stupidity of charging unknown and potentially deadly lurkers. They both looked rather sheepish and assured her most earnestly that they would never again undertake so shatterbrained an enterprise.

All thus in accord, they exited *The Luck* and walked back toward the garage, Yolan speculating on this ship and that, with Sed Ric occasionally amending her IDs.

They turned out of the avenue of sleeping ships just as a landcar pulled up before Binjali's and a light-haired man got out, heading for the crew door.

"Father!" Yolan hissed, braking hard and flinging an arm across her partner's chest.

"Uncle Zan Der!" Sed Ric gulped at the same moment—and in the next, they were gone, flying back down the row of cold pads, heading for the eastern gate.

Aelliana had gone three steps after them before common sense reasserted itself. It was useless for her to chase them, port-wise as they were. They knew the way back—and the odds were they would return, once they reckoned "Uncle Zan Der" gone.

So thinking, Aelliana turned back to discover what it was about a mere light-haired man that sent two Port-runners to flight.

"... PILOT CAYLON?" the stranger was asking as Aelliana stepped through the door.

Jon used his chin to point over the man's shoulder. "There she comes now."

He turned, brown eyes flicking across her face in the moment before he bowed respect.

"Pilot Caylon, I am Zan Der pel'Kirmin Clan Reptor," he said, as if he were but a clansman, and the delm's Ring he wore merely an ornament. "I ask pardon for this disruption of your peace. My excuse can only be that I have had news of two over whom you have spread your protection."

She considered him, and he bore it, patient as if he treated with Scouts every hour. Besides patience, she saw worry, and weariness and a wary sort of hope. Behind those cares, she saw also humor and a glimmer of indefinable something that reminded her, forcibly, of Yolan.

"I have recently—commended—two halflings to Master dea'Cort's attention," Aelliana said carefully, watching the man's weary, wary eyes. "He is kind enough to provide them day-work. But I must tell you, sir, that this pair of children claim—most strongly—to have no kin."

Hope flared beyond wariness for an instant; the mouth bent into a tired smile. "I had heard that they claimed themselves clanless. To you, I take oath that this is not so, though they may themselves believe otherwise. If I might be granted an opportunity to speak with them—" He raised a quick hand, Ring glinting. "They are under your protection. I honor that. There is nothing I wish to say to them that I would be ashamed to have you hear as well."

And that, Aelliana thought, was extraordinarily courageous, for a man who had all but lost two of his clan through what he represented as a misunderstanding. She had thought Yolan and Sed Ric might have had reason, such as she had, to embrace the clanless state. Indeed, it might be that their reasons were just. Yet this man here seemed no one like Ran Eld, only exhausted with worry and eager to amend a wrong.

"If you might—produce them . . . ?" he said, delicately.

Aelliana smiled wryly, thinking of two swift figures, racing down the row of cold pads. "I think it unlikely—" she began—and heard the crew door cycle behind her.

DAAV SET HIS HANDS ALONG THE TRUNK, took a breath and swung up into the branches. At the first major cross-branch, he ended his climb, sitting astride the big limb, feet swinging in air, leaves rustling and whispering around him.

"If you have anything to say," he stated, rather crossly, "you might as well say it to me."

There was neither a cessation nor an increase of leaf-rustle. Not, Daav thought, that he had expected it.

"I hope you're proud of yourself," he continued aloud. "Terrifying a guest of the House—and one's wife-elect. I should think an ancient hulking brute like yourself might find more seemly amusements. Forgive me if I speak too plainly."

The leaves directly above him flittered. Daav frowned.

"Laugh, by all means. I suppose it's nothing to you if yos'Phelium dies with me? No, I do an injustice. yos'Phelium shall die with Pat Rin—but before that, young Shan will be delm."

A breeze kissed his cheek, and the smaller branches nearby danced. Daav closed his eyes, feeling the warm bark beneath his fingers, the age-old solidity of wood between his thighs. "I shall marry Samiv tel'Izak," he said, forming each word with precision, "and the child of that union shall come to Korval."

The wood beneath his hands cooled. Perceptibly. Daav sighed.

"May I then solicit your further guidance? Or do we return to placing an advertisement in *The Gazette*? Notice, I do not ask how I shall extricate Korval solvent from a contract most binding. I am fully alive to the fact that details do not interest you."

The leaves had stilled all about. The branch he straddled became neither warmer or cooler. Deliberately, Daav emptied his mind of all conscious thoughts, treading a path Rockflower had once shown him, past need and want and everyday busy-ness to a place where there was only—peace.

He sat there, tranced, until the late noon sun lanced a ray through the leaves and dazzled him awake. *Jelaza Kazone* had not spoken and he wished, with everything in him, to be at Binjali's.

"UNCLE ZAN DER." He came forward, alone, which made him seem half, for Aelliana had never yet seen one pirate without the other—and made his bow to his elder.

"Sed Ric." The man put out his hands, eyes afire with longing. "Are you well, child?"

"Well . . ." He went another jerky step forward, and stopped, face twisting. "I think—we should come—home, Uncle . . ." His voice choked out and he threw a glance to Aelliana, eloquent of she knew not what.

"Where is Yolan?" she asked him, thinking, of a sudden, of lurkers, and guns and the girl's bright, brash courage.

"Here." The single word was flat with despair. Stiff-legged, Yolan came forward, to her place at Sed Ric's right. The look she gave him might have frozen iron.

"Now what?" she rasped—and began, quite suddenly, to cry.

CHAPTER TWENTY-EIGHT

Delm's Discretionary Account Three, The Pilots Fund. Established for the aid and succor of pilots and former pilots, regardless of clan, race or lineage. Profit margin of funding stocks no less than forty percent.

—From Korval's Account Ledgers, Discretionary Monies

THIS TIME SHE WOULD NOT ELUDE HIM.

Ran Eld waited in the shadow of the main staircase, ears straining for the sound of stealthy footsteps.

He had determined to follow her yesterday and the day before yesterday, only to find upon arising that she had quit the house hours before, leaving behind insolent messages about engagements to dine elsewhere. Very well.

Today, she would not elude him.

He would follow her to the Scout and deal with that. Then, he would escort her home, and deal with *that*.

In the shadow of the staircase, Ran Eld smiled.

It was plain that Aelliana wanted disciplining—oh, badly. She so far forgot herself as to disobey a direct order from one who was both her elder and her superior—then flaunted her disobedience, daring him to do what was no more than his duty. For the good of the clan.

The fact that disciplining this most dangerous of siblings would give him positive delight was to Ran Eld's way of thinking no more than just. Aelliana should not be delm. It was a sad pity that the old delm, their grandmother, had put such a notion into the girl's head. The idea was ludicrous on the face of it. He was nadelm, in every way his sister's superior.

Which he would prove, as often as necessary.

He considered that his first attempt at bringing this point home had been successful. One year of marriage to Ran Eld's friend had produced ten years of quite satisfactory behavior in Ran Eld's sister. To be sure, it had occasionally been necessary to administer cer-tain—remedial—lessons, but that was expectable, even—enjoyable. Ten years for one was a good investment of time and funds, so he flattered himself.

From the landing above came the lightest of footsteps.

Ran Eld half-crouched in his dim niche, eagerness shortening his breath. The footsteps continued their light path, across the landing, down the remaining stairs. He smiled and dared to lean just slightly out of his hiding place, to better see—

His delm.

He shifted sharply in disappointment, boot heel scraping against marble floor.

Birin Caylon turned. Seething, Ran Eld slipped out of the niche and made his bow.

"Mother."

"My son." She inclined her head, appearing to find nothing unusual in either the time or the place of their meeting. Indeed, she smiled. "I am fortunate to find you about so early. Break your fast with me, if you have not already eaten. I have completed my study of your analysis regarding San bel'Fasin's offer of partnership and I believe you may be interested in the decision."

So. Ran Eld bowed once more to hide his smile of triumph. "I am, as always, at your service, ma'am," he said and followed her into the dining hall, leaving the door slightly ajar.

Tea had barely been poured when he heard footsteps on the stair, and saw a slim shadow flicker across the half-open doorway. Half a heartbeat later, the front door moaned on its hinges, and snapped softly shut.

AELLIANA STRODE DOWN MECHANIC STREET, head high and face glowing. She was to train with Trilla this morning, after which she was to lift with Jon himself, who had sworn to put her through an emergency drill like no other.

The door cycled and she stepped into the huge dim cavern of Binjali Repair Shop.

Around the teapot was a cluster of leather-clad figures: Jon, Trilla, Clonak—and a tall man, dark hair clipped neatly back, silver twist swinging in one ear, cat sitting tall on his opposite shoulder.

Aelliana felt her heart lift; she very nearly laughed for the sheer joy of beholding him.

As if he heard her unvoiced joy, he turned, a smile lighting his eyes.

"Hello, Aelliana."

"Daav." Her own smile felt wide enough to split her face. "It's good to see you."

"It's good to be seen," he returned gravely and she did laugh then, standing before him with her face tipped up to his.

"Good comes in odd packages," Jon commented from his stool.

"Jon scolds me for carrying Patch," Aelliana told Daav, reaching up to offer the cat a finger. "He says I'll spoil him."

"The damage has long been done, I fear," he replied as Patch bent his head and allowed her to rub his ears.

"Spoil a cat when there are the rest of us, hungering for a smile!" That was Clonak.

Aelliana finished the cat's ear and stepped forward. "Good morning, Clonak."

"Good-morning, Goddess Fair! Will you rub my ears?"

She made a show of giving it consideration, head cocked to one side. "No."

"Heart-torn again! Hold me, Daav, I'm bereft!"

"Perhaps if you grew fur on them?" Daav suggested, not noticeably moved by this plea for comradeship.

Clonak glared. "Mock me, oh Captain."

"If you insist."

"The pirates' delm came," Aelliana said, turning back to Daav, "and fetched them home." She grinned, throwing a glance over her shoulder to Jon. "Or mostly."

He snorted. "Ring-and-monkey show."

Daav smiled down at her, one eyebrow slightly askew. "I surmise that they were not clanless, after all?"

"Not—entirely," she said, slowly. "It did seem to be all in a muddle. But the end of it is that they shall come here to work off—work off a debt Delm Reptor feels most strongly is owing, for Jon having given good wages for grunt-work. In the meanwhile, they—the pirates—shall live under Reptor's roof and—and—strive to—amend their difference." She looked up at him. "Or so he said."

"Ah. And do you believe what he has said, I wonder?"

She frowned, chewing her lip. "Yes," she said finally, "I do. He seemed an honest man—and honestly joyed to find them." She lay her hand on his sleeve and smiled. "It was good of you to send him."

Both brows shot up. "I?"

"Well, it must have been you," she said reasonably. "He knew exactly where to come, and asked for me by name. Jon didn't tell him, nor Trilla nor Clonak. I certainly didn't—I hadn't the least idea of how to go about finding their clan! So—"

"When you have eliminated the impossible," Daav murmured, in Terran, "whatever remains, however improbable, must be the truth."

Aelliana blinked at him. "I beg your pardon?"

He grinned. "An observation by a Mr. Holmes, I believe, on the nature of solutions."

"The game is afoot!" Clonak shouted, clattering off his stool with a flourish. He looked to Jon. "I'll get on that maintenance update, if you like."

"Always after the sit-down job," the old Scout grumbled.

Clonak laughed and headed toward the office, flipping a casual hand at the rest. Patch jumped from Daav's shoulder and followed.

Across the half-circle, Trilla slid to her feet and tossed Aelliana a grin. "Set for a bit of dancing, Pilot?"

"If you have the patience for me," she said. "I am aware I cannot give the challenge you might like."

The other woman laughed as she unbuckled her tool belt. "Oh, and can you not?" She turned to the dark haired man as if she'd heard him speak. "Just a bit of menfri'at, Master Daav. No harm in it. Quite of a bit of good."

He inclined his head. "As you say."

He watched them walk away, noting the set of Aelliana's shoulders, the light, confident walk.

"Hard to believe that's the same woman slunk in here half-a-quarter ago and whispered for her ship," Jon commented from his side. Daav looked down into a pair of speculative amber eyes.

"We'll have her brawling in taverns before the year is done," he agreed, watching Aelliana shed her jacket and face Trilla across sub-bay one. "Fine work, Master Jon."

"Now, now, I can't take all the credit. It was a certain young captain set her feet on the path by handing her a bowli ball and telling her to fight."

Daav laughed. "Cow-handed as that? Poor captain."

"Well, as I say, he's young, but his ideas aren't too bad. Usually."

Trilla's first pass was fast and low—rather faster and lower than he would have expected. He felt his own muscles tense as Aelliana slipped gently to the left, sidestepping the attack and spinning, establishing her rhythm and the range of her dance.

"How long has this been going on?" he asked Jon.

"Matter of two days."

"She's good."

"Not bad. The fast stuff don't bother her, but come at her hard, like you're going to do damage and damn me if she won't back down every time." Jon sighed. "Never did hear who beats her."

The crew door cycled and Daav looked around in time to see Sed Ric bin'Ala and Yolan pel'Kirmin step through. They came forward, the girl to the boy's right, stopped and made their bows.

"Captain."

"Children. Pilot Caylon tells me you are joyfully re-clanned."

Yolan made no answer to that, though the look she flung him held no amazing charge of joy. The boy was likewise somber, but replied courteously enough, "Yes, sir. Thank you, sir."

"Show the captain here your toy, young Sed Ric," Jon directed, pointing at the boy's belt. "Look at this, Daav."

The jang-wire came out with a flash and a snap, held in the down position, limp and almost pretty.

"Hah." Daav extended a hand. "May I?"

Sed Ric offered the leather handle and Daav slid his fingers into the loop.

"I believe this may be original," he said and went back a sudden, silent step, snapping the wire up and flicking his wrist, *so*.

The limp wire went stiff, becoming an arm's length of double-edged blade, Daav grinned, shook the blade carefully and handed the quiescent weapon back to its owner.

"Very nice, indeed. Where did you come by it?"

"Uncle Lip Ten left it to us," Yolan said, "in a crate of things he'd gathered, star-hopping. Aunt Fris said it was junk and wished us joy of it."

"Doubtless Aunt Fris has other virtues," Daav murmured and Yolan laughed, short and bitter. Over in sub-bay one, Aelliana spun and kicked, dancing neatly away from Trilla's snaking grab.

"What—" Daav began, but the question was never finished.

"Aelliana!" Clonak was on a dead run from the office, face, for once, entirely serious. "Aelliana!"

In the circle of the dance, she spun, dropped her stance and came forward.

"What is it?"

"Tower on the line. Fellow on Outyard Five toppled into the mechanics. Autodoc mended the worst, but his heart failed him. Can you lift the spare and the health tech—"

"Yes!" She snatched up her jacket. Clonak was already on his way back to the office.

"Daav." She paused before him, hand on his sleeve, green eyes bright as she looked into his face. "Ride second board for me?"

Adrenaline surged. He grinned. "Yes."

"Thank you," she said, and was gone, running at the top of her speed.

In the next instant, Daav was likewise gone, his shadow merging with hers as the crew door closed.

THE DELM HAD DECIDED against a partnership with bel'Fasin.

Oh, she had reasons, and gave them in-depth, her wish, she said, was to instruct him, so that when he was come delm . . .

He scarcely attended her; sat, cold and disbelieving, while she spoke—rambling, meaningless sentences that meant, in final cipher, one thing:

He was ruined.

In his apartment abovestairs, Ran Eld riffled accounts that had been squeezed dry years ago, called up balance sheets and dismissed them, his hands shaking so badly he must make two and three attempts to strike the proper key.

At length, he rose from his desk, poured himself a brandy and wandered the room, wracking his brain for something—for any-thing—he might sell or take loan against, that would keep San bel'Fasin at bay.

CHAPTER TWENTY-NINE

Emergency repairs at Tinsori Light. Left my ring in earnest. The keeper's a cantra-grubbing pirate, but the ship should hold air to Lytaxin. Send one of ours and eight cantra to redeem my pledge. Send them armed. In fact send two. . . .

**—Excerpted from a beam letter from
Jen Sin yos'Phelium Clan Korval to his delm,
written in the first *relumma* of the year named Dalenart**

THE TECH WENT INTO THE HOLD with his life unit, strapped into the rumble-seat and reported himself ready.

Daav checked the webbing, made certain the unit was properly dogged, advised the tech to take a nap and walked back to his station.

"End," Aelliana said into the comm as he slid into the copilot's slot and pulled the shock-straps tight.

"Confirmed," Tower announced half-a-heartbeat later. "Lift at will, *Ride the Luck.*"

She shot him a look from eyes more brilliant than emeralds. "Ready?"

"Ready."

"Engage gyros."

✿ ✿ ✿

JON DEA'CORT STOOD before the command wall in the side bay, working the dials, swearing ferociously at a shower of static. The band caught suddenly, delivering the curt tones of Port Control.

". . . shift lanes immediately. We have an emergency. Freighter X38519, slipshift to alternate path R9. *Tansberg's Folly* on approach, divert to Binjali's sling—"

"Trilla!" Jon shouted.

"On it," came the laconic response as the alert sounded overhead.

"Allow me to provide visuals, Master dea'Cort." Clonak stepped to Jon's side, his hands dancing over the screen-controls, bringing the four most pertinent to sharp life.

"This is Pilot Aelliana Caylon, *Ride the Luck.*" Calm as if she were discussing the likelihood of rain. "We have our package and are ready to lift at pilot's two minutes. Mark. Request clearance, Tower. Route computed, checks in line, transmitted . . . End."

"*Markham's Mistress,* change lanes now!" Tower snarled. "Lift at will, *Ride the Luck.* All ships, priority clearance to *Ride the Luck.* We have an emergency . . ."

There was a roar and a shifting whine, which was the gyros spinning to full, and then the muted, held-out throb of power that was lift-off, close by. On the visuals, *Ride the Luck* cleared Solcintra Port and hurtled upward. The radio had a moment free of chatter, into which Trilla's exuberant, "Caught her!" sang savage with delight.

The chatter took up again, grousing about skewed schedules, hovering deadlines, pile ups, back ups and—

"At nearest convenience, will *Ride the Luck* put navcomp on line?" Tower requested with unusual politeness. Clonak gave a shout of laughter and Jon grinned. The pirates, hovering at wall-edge, looked at each other with wide-stretched eyes.

"At nearest convenience," Tower repeated—"Thank you, Pilot Caylon."

There was a gabble of chatter—wonderment, such like:

"Caylon? The Tables? *That* Caylon? . . . chel'Mara's ship . . . Flies her like a Scout!"—and then another voice, overriding all the others.

"Aelliana Caylon, *Ride the Luck*, amending filed course. Projected time savings seven-point-three minutes."

"Continue," Tower directed, while the rest of near space held its collective breath.

"We'll be adding a delta vee of 23.8 percent at 14:01.33; and we'll be crossing shipping intersections 14, 15, 16 and 23. At 14:08.14 we will change attitude to 170 degrees exactly and add a delta vee of 33.6 percent plus or minus a tenth. As we hit the tidal effect zone we'll pick up an additional delta vee of 17.04 percent and also be south of the main equatorial shipping lanes so we'll have no clearance problems. My window is 13:59 to 14:03, which at my mark begins in three minutes. May I have confirmation?"

Silence hummed through the lines for a full thirty seconds, broken, at last, by Daav: "Verified."

"In her head!" a Terran-tinged voice whooped from close in. "Working it in her head, damn me for a mudhog! Who's running second—"

"*Ride the Luck*, we have a confirm on that." Tower sounded just the tiniest bit rattled. "You're all go."

The chatter broke over the comm in waves: "Tower fifty-eight seconds behind, running a comp as big as your homeworld!" "I'll drink for free tonight! Caylon at the board, is it?"

There was more of approximately the same, which Jon ignored, glancing instead to the wall of screens.

"What's she got in—"

"The tide!" Trilla cried, leaning over his shoulder to point as Sed Ric and Yolan crowded closer. "She's going to catch the tidal effect at the juncture with planetary grav—"

"She's what?" Clonak cleared a screen and flung the equation into it, fingers blurring as he built the schematic. "I'm damned," he said suddenly. "Jon, look at this."

"I see it. A rare wonder, our math teacher."

It was pretty much textbook then, with one more small adjustment, as Daav kicked them onto an auxiliary approach that put them practically in the yard's back door. It shaved another minute and would have been counted very pretty, had it not been overshadowed by Aelliana's stunning bit of work. Jon backed the chatter down and shook his head, Terran-wise, in admiration.

"The woman's unbelievable," Clonak murmured, keying up the replay. "On the run, in her head . . . I'm in love, Master-mine."

"For the fifth time since yesterday," Jon snorted, elbowing himself a spot at the board. He watched the replay in reverent silence, lost in the beauty of the maneuver. To shave seven minutes—*seven minutes*—off a lift measured and calibrated and understood to the nanosecond, while she was running board, close in traffic, with the possibility of someone breaking out—in her head, as Clonak said . . .

"I'd sign her first class this minute," Jon murmured, "and a blight on the regs. Anyone who can fly like that—"

"A goddess," Clonak sighed, sounding more than half-serious. "I claim the privilege of naming her first class, sir, and I am prepared to duel for the honor."

"Yes, but she'll never believe she earned it that way," Jon said, keying the replay to storage. "The book is the path and the math teacher aims to follow it through every twist and cranny."

"We've been avoiding the tidal effect ever since the first ship shed atmosphere," Clonak was almost singing. "Avoiding it! *Compensating* for it! Aelliana Caylon *uses* it and speeds her package on its way! Poor Daav."

"His trick lost in shadow, eh?" Jon grinned. "He won't mind."

"No, I suppose he won't. Anything that improves the lift is joy to Daav, no matter if your grandmother conned it."

Jon started, eyes widening, then going narrow. "There's a notion, though." He turned from the screens and strode down-bay, snagging his jacket from the hook as he went by.

"I'll be back!" he called and vanished through the door, as Trilla, Clonak and the pirates exchanged puzzled stares.

TECH AND PACKAGE off-loaded, *Ride the Luck* rode a holding pattern, waiting for Port Control to sort the scrambled traffic and give them clearance to land.

The pilot had gone to fetch tea from the pantry, leaving the board in charge of her copilot, who had reclined his long self at his station, watching the go-lights through half-closed eyes.

Brief as it was, Daav thought, one ear cocked toward the radio, this lift had thus far been among the most remarkable of his career. Who but Aelliana Caylon could have conceived the notion of using the tidal influence every other pilot in the universe so busily avoided? Who but that same amazing mind could have framed, checked and executed so exciting a new maneuver in the time—

"Daav? You did want tea?"

He opened his eyes with a grin and extended a languid hand for the mug. "It's a lazy second you're burdened with, Pilot."

"Yes, certainly." She laughed softly and perched on the edge of her own chair, eyes flicking over screens, lights, readouts.

"It was fortunate you had known of that auxiliary route," she said. "I should have lost us three minutes at the last, lining up the primary approach."

"No more than one-point-five," Daav corrected. "And you had already gained us seven that were utterly unlooked-for."

She moved her shoulders and glanced down into her mug. "I had been working on a notion about the tidals about a year ago," she said. "It wouldn't come together, so I put it aside. Something— shifted—when you showed me Little Jump the other day. And then today, when I saw the numbers and the relationships—" She looked up, pride apparent, though she fought to keep her features composed. "It all just tumbled into place." Abruptly she gave up the struggle for dignity and allowed the grin its freedom. "Pretty, isn't it?"

"A thing of astonishing beauty," Daav agreed, smiling into sparkling green eyes. Those same eyes widened, then moved aside, flashing over the stat-lights.

"You did send Delm Reptor to find the pirates, didn't you?" The look she gave him was quizzical. Daav sighed.

"I suppose I will have to own the act, though I refuse to bear all the blame." He raised his mug to her in light salute. "Jon found who they were."

"Oh." She sipped tea, frowning slightly at the floor-plates.

"That was clever of him," she said eventually. "I had tried, you know, to find their surnames, but I don't expect I was very subtle." Her frown deepened and she raised doubtful eyes to his.

"Do you think we—do you think we did well?" she asked, leaning forward.

Daav raised an eyebrow, caught by her intensity. "Do you think we did not?"

"I—am not certain," she said hesitantly, frowning once more at the flooring. "It had seemed—they were hungry and—and compelled toward thievery—and so young." She glanced up, tawny brows drawn. "I do not—you spoke as if it—the Low Port—as if it were dreadfully dangerous . . ."

"It is," he assured her, with utter sincerity, "dreadfully dangerous."

"Yes! And so it seems that we must have done well, to have caught them away from danger and returned them to safety—and— to kin. Yet . . ."

"Yet?" he prompted softly, when a minute had passed and she said nothing more.

She came to her feet all at once, leaving her mug behind in the arm-slot, and paced to the center of the cabin. There, she spun to face him, fingers twisting and twining 'til he thought she might never unknot them.

"They left," she said. "They said that they had left because the time was coming when they might be eligible for—for marriage. Neither wished to be married to any other. They spoke to their delm of their desire to be always together, but he was not—not disposed to hear them as more than children. They spoke to him again on the matter, and he was abrupt, saying consanguinity was too near. They went a third time, bearing gene-charts which showed them unlikely of producing a defective . . ." She faltered.

Daav set his cup aside and straightened in his chair. "Their delm spoke of separating them so they might learn to deal with other folk."

"Yes." She bit her lip. "Yes, of course he did. How could he not? To lose the possibility of liaison marriage from two of the younger—he must look to his clan's whole good. I do not fault him—he spoke as he must. But—" She paused; plunged ahead.

"I—I don't pretend to know a great deal about—and of course marriage is—extremely—distasteful—"

"Is it?"

"Yes—and only think how much more distasteful when there is one you—prefer—above all others—I pity them from my heart and wish—I wish we had not stopped to play!"

"For that I shall bear the blame. They looked in desperate case and unlikely to ask for aid. My whole thought had been to force aid upon them—at least as little as a meal." He paused. "Does their delm still speak of separation?"

She sighed. "It is—under negotiation. A trial separation, to determine the—the depth of their devotion. Sed Ric—Sed Ric speaks of being apprenticed to a cousin on an Outworld, so that Yolan may finish her pilot's study at home."

"Ah. And Yolan?"

"She cries," Aelliana said, shoulders slumping. "Cries and looks at him—I cannot tell you how she looks at him." She frowned at the floor.

"What else may their delm do? They are assets of the clan, to be used, as all are used, for the good of all."

"So the Code teaches us," Daav said rather dryly. He tipped his head, considering her downturned face.

"Is marriage—of course—so very distasteful?" he wondered softly.

She glanced up, mouth hard. "I do not know that it must be," she said with precision. "My own—but that was many years ago."

"From the distance of your exalted age," he said lightly, misliking the tightness of her muscles and the way she stood there, tensed for a blow.

She drew herself up, eyes wide. "Next *relumma*, I shall have twenty-seven Standard Years," she said sharply. "I was married the day after my sixteenth name day."

Too young. Far too young, Daav thought, for one such as

Aelliana. Quivering with something between pity and outrage, he began a seated bow of apology—was arrested by her raised hand.

"I had not meant to snap at you, Daav. It is true that I have—limited—knowledge. Voni—my eldest sister—marries often and seems quite content."

Marries often, he thought wryly, recalling the drab street and moldering clanhouse in which she lived. Contract marriage was an economic necessity for some clans, true enough. Though in a house with several children of marriageable age—

"You have only married once?"

She inclined her head with brittle care. "It was sufficient." She sighed then, and showed him a palm, as if she wished somehow to make amends for his rudeness. "The clan has the care of my daughter."

She spoke with neither warmth nor interest of her child, as if—

"*Ride the Luck!*" The radio blared and they both jumped. Aelliana flashed forward and slapped the toggle.

"Caylon here."

"Acknowledge filed plan and begin descent," Tower directed. "There is traffic waiting behind you."

"Yes," said Aelliana, glancing at the screen and verifying the equations in her head. "Flight plan acknowledged, descent begins on my mark." She turned her head. Daav was strapped in at his station, fingers dancing over the board. He glanced up, dark eyes bright, and gave her the Scout's go-sign.

"Mark."

IT WAS A SOLEMN CREW congregated before the teapot. Jon sat astride his usual stool, Trilla on his right hand, Clonak on his left, Patch lying alert before all.

The door cycled and a tall shadow followed a shorter into the bay. They came forward a few steps, then Aelliana faltered—stopped, face showing pale and wary. Daav paused just behind her left shoulder, eyebrows well up.

"The pair of you," Jon said with a sigh. "Come here, math teacher."

She glanced over her shoulder, up into Daav's face, tension showing in all her muscles. He touched her arm, smiled; she took a deep, shaky breath and went forward.

Directly before Jon's stool, she stopped, hands folded before her, her tall copilot at her side.

"Master dea'Cort."

"Hah. I suppose you know what you did today, with that display around the tidal effect?"

She licked her lips, but kept her eyes steady on his. The pulse at the base of her throat trembled like a bird.

"Yes, sir."

"Yes sir, is it? Well, then, tell me."

"Yes, sir." She gulped air. "We framed and tried a piloting addendum under stringent field conditions. The maneuver has tested successfully and I suspect subsequent testings and refinements as the equation is understood and tuned."

"Invented a whole new sentence in the language of local lift," Clonak intoned.

Her chin came up. "If you like."

"Oh, I do like," he assured her, with a flash of his usual deviltry. "Very, very much."

"Pipe down," Jon directed, and lifted a hand, beckoning. "Closer, please, math teacher. I'm too old a dog to bite you."

Doubt showed at that, but she came forward, Daav still at her side, his hand near her elbow, should she have need of support.

Jon turned his palm up. "Right hand, please."

She lay her palm lightly against his. The ancient silver puzzle-ring flashed, as if with defiance. Jon touched it with a reverent fingertip. "Where did you get this?" he asked gently.

"My grandmother left it me," she answered in the same tone, "when she died."

"So. This is fitting, then, since I have it from my grandmother." He reached into his belt and brought it forth.

It sparkled like a nebula: Big, gaudy, garish bit of trumpery. Sapphires, rubies, emeralds, diamond—every one first cut—set in a platinum band meant to cover a finger knuckle-to-knuckle. Jon held it up, let them all see the flash and the wonder of it. Three of them knew what it was. He heard Daav draw a breath.

"This," Jon said, bringing the ring before Aelliana's wide eyes, "is what pilots wore in the long-ago when they took their Jumpships out to the edge. It was used as a bond of word, as collateral for cargo, as earnest for repairs. A pilot always came back for her ring, that was the wisdom, and most often it was true." He smiled.

"I had this from my mother, who had it from hers, who had it from her father—back more generations than even you can count. It returned to me with my son's body. It's always been worn by a *binjali* pilot. Favor me, by wearing it now."

For a moment, he thought even so little was too much. Her face blanched to beige, but the eyes—the eyes were beyond brilliant.

She inclined her head, with full respect.

"You do me great honor," she said, voice husking and solemn. "I shall wear it—with joy."

"So." He felt a sweep of pride in her—in the person she allowed herself to become. Tears pricked at his eyes and he slid the old ring onto second finger of her right hand. It seated as if it had been made for her and Jon smiled. He had guessed well, he congratulated himself, in telling the jeweler the new size.

He took his hand from under hers, leaned back on his stool.

From his right, Trilla cheered, joined a moment later by Clonak. Daav lay a quiet hand on her shoulder and smiled when she turned her face up to his. Patch rose and stretched and stropped once against her legs before moving off on more urgent business.

"And now," Clonak announced, leaping to his feet and stretching his hands high over his head, "we celebrate!"

CHAPTER THIRTY

A Healer is one who may look into the heart and mind of one who is in pain, soothe the pain and restore the sufferer to joy.

—From the Preamble to the Healer's Guide

PILOTS LINED UP to meet her; Daav murmured their names in her ear as they bowed: "Hela. Kad Vyr. Mordrid. Nasi."

Aelliana returned every bow, repeating each name in an effort to fix it in memory with the appropriate face.

"Illiopa, Pet Ram, Abi Tod—" The line was coming to an end at last, but Aelliana greatly feared that she had lost some names entirely, and muddled others.

"Frad," Daav murmured on a rather different note. Aelliana shook herself and applied special attention to Pilot Frad.

A bland-faced man nearly as tall as Daav, he bowed respect, coupled with a hand-spelt *binjali*. Straightening, he reached out to grip Daav's shoulder and grinned.

"Old friend."

Daav returned grip and grin. "When did you get in?"

"Just in time to catch the most amazing lift I've seen in my poor career, from the vantage of Scout Station."

"Always in the luck."

"Hah!" Frad turned to Aelliana. "Take advice, pilot, and demand the Port Master give you a tenth of the profit she'll realize from selling that tape."

She blinked at him. "Tape?"

"Tried to get a copy myself, but the lines were backed up to next Trilsday. Couple of bars ago I heard a Terran captain offering twenty cantra hard for the first copy reaches his hands before local midnight—" He grinned. "Wants to use it for crew training!"

Aelliana looked to Daav, eyes wide. "He's joking," she suggested, uncertainly.

Daav's lips quirked. "Yes, but it doesn't at all seem like Frad's sort of joke."

"Not a bit of it," that gentleman assured her with utmost gravity. "Given to making pies into the beds of my comrades." He sighed, bland face suffused with sorrow. "Very low sense of humor."

Aelliana chuckled, Frad's name was called by someone across the room and he moved off, raising light fingertips to Daav's cheek in the moment before he was gone.

The small gesture of tenderness awoke an appalling twist of emotion in Aelliana's chest. By custom and by Code, she should have felt shock. That two who were not kin should share such intimacy—to show their depravity in so public a place—It was beyond the pale. If she were Voni, she might well have fainted.

By Code, she should now distance herself from Daav, her surname-less copilot, that his corruption not sully her *melant'i.*

Failing of the Code, she lifted her eyes to find his waiting, quizzical and—wary.

Wary—awaiting her censure. It hurt—astonishingly—that he should think her capable—and it was not shock she felt, Aelliana owned in a rush of self-truth, but jealousy, that Frad should be so dear to him.

She smiled and saw the wariness melt.

"Frad was a member of my team," he told her. "The four of us went through Academy together—Frad, Olwen, Clonak and I."

"There you are!" That was Clonak, wading through the crush of

Scouts, pilots and hanger-ons that clogged Apel's tiny wine-room. "Jon says it's time to move and let this rabble celebrate on their own. They've made their bows, now they want to talk board."

"True enough," Daav allowed. "Where does Jon want us to go, I wonder?"

"Kinchail's," Clonak said. "Meet us. I'll get Frad." He was gone, melting effortlessly into the crowd.

Daav look down at her from dancing dark eyes.

"Hungry, Pilot?"

"Yes!" Aelliana said in surprise and reached out to take his hand.

THEY SAT SEVEN TO DINNER in the comfort of comrades: Jon, Apel, Frad, Trilla, Clonak, Daav, and Aelliana, with Jon at the top of the table and Aelliana between him and Daav.

It was a merry meal, replete with wine and chatter and dish after dish of delicious things, all ordered by Mistress Apel and shared 'round the table.

The last platter having been taken away, Clonak and Frad embarked on a risque joke contest, into which Trilla occasionally threw a laconic one-liner. Apel sat quietly between Jon and Frad, sipping her wine and dividing her attention between the band, setting up in the corner opposite, and the entrance way. Jon and Daav were talking quietly.

"A grand, dangerous work, young captain. Happens Liad isn't ripe for hearing it."

"Liad is not altogether happy," Daav admitted, twirling his glass between long, clever fingers. Fascinated, Aelliana watched his hand, struck once more by the ring-marked, empty finger. It occurred to her to wonder if Daav himself had not fallen aside trouble within his own clan, that stripped him of rank-ring and made him eager to aid a pair of clanless pirates.

"Still," Daav said, "Liad must have heard it, soon or late. Truth will be told, sink it as deep as you may."

"We're for company," Apel commented as a drift of leather jackets came through the door. Across the room, the band struck its first notes.

"Music!" Clonak exclaimed, cutting himself off in mid-joke. He bounced to his feet and made one of his extravagant bows.

"Dance with me, Peerless Goddess."

She stared up at him, feeling Daav's warmth beside her, and the weight of his sudden attention.

"I don't know how to dance," she told Clonak as the band swung into its first number.

"Of course you know how to dance! What has Trilla been teaching you this age?"

"I—"

"We'll show you," Trilla said, pushing back her chair and jerking her head at Frad. "Drafted, mapman."

"Not bad," Frad commented, coming to his feet. "A trifle obvious, but not bad."

Trilla laughed and marched ahead. Aelliana looked up into Clonak's taffy eyes and sighed.

"All right—but no nonsense!"

"Nonsense?" He opened his eyes wide. "When have I ever done less than cherish you?"

"Oh . . ." Aelliana stood, shaking her head at him in Terran fashion. "You are quite ridiculous," she said severely.

"But sincere," Clonak replied, with an evil grin. Taking her arm, he led her out onto the floor.

Learning to dance required as much concentration as learning *menfri'at*. As with the defense system, it was crucial to be aware of the movements and potential movements of one's opponent and to respond correctly. It was made more difficult than *menfri'at*, in Aelliana's opinion, by there being only one correct response—which must be made within the arbitrary rhythm of the music.

Her field of concentration was narrowed to Clonak's body, her own, the music, and the absolute necessity of performing perfectly. She was beginning to sweat with the strain of it, when an unexpected element entered the dance.

"My turn," Daav said calmly and Clonak released her with a preposterous sigh.

Aelliana stood staring up at him, abruptly aware of the others all about—there, Jon and Apel; Frad and a redhead in Scout leather; Trilla with *two* partners, an arm around the waist of each . . .

"Will you dance with me, Aelliana? Or shall I take you back to the table and give you some wine?"

"Dancing is—rather—difficult," she managed, moving closer to him and laying a hand along his sleeve.

"It needn't be," he returned and placed his free hand at her waist, as Clonak had done. "Indeed, dancing can be rather fun— believe me or don't." He grinned. "The first thing you must recall is that the one you dance with is your partner, not your opponent."

She laughed up at him and stepped closer, into the imaginary box Trilla had said she must stay within when dancing. Carefully, she put her right hand on his left shoulder, slid her left hand down to engage his free hand.

"Dance with me, then," she said. "Partner."

He smiled at that, pleasure showing plain. The fingers at her waist tightened; Daav swayed—and they were dancing.

It was absurdly easy. Her body moved without her conscious plan, indeed, it hardly seemed as if she moved at all, but that they did, with no separation so gross as *he* and *she*.

The music ended. Aelliana was still, her hand on his shoulder, his at her waist, and they were two now, with she reluctant to stand away.

"The musicians rest, Aelliana."

Daav's voice sounded—odd. The dark eyes that looked down into hers seemed dazzled. Indeed, she felt herself dazzled, wanting only to stand there, touched and touching, and gazing into his eyes, until it was time to dance again.

Abruptly, Daav cleared his throat, swayed back a step, breaking their gaze as his hand fell from her waist.

"Let us return to the others."

There were new faces around the table, and a shortage of chairs. Clonak came to his feet on the bounce. "We contrive," he announced, gesturing toward his empty place.

"My captain to sit here."

Daav lifted an eyebrow, but sat as he was bade.

"So. And my goddess to sit *here.*" A hand in the middle of her back propelled her forward, to land with surprised grace on Daav's knee.

"Temporary quarters only," Clonak assured her, and struck a pose. "Chairs or death!" He bustled away, to general laughter.

Aelliana bit her lip. "I—beg your pardon," she stammered, looking down into Daav's eyes. "I shall stand."

"What? Forgo the best seat in the house?" Frad demanded, turning from his redhead with a grin. "Besides, Daav wants sitting on, now and then."

The others laughed. Trilla was between her two former dance partners, an arm around one's shoulders, a hand on the other's knee. The first dancer sipped from a glass, then held it to Trilla's lips. After Trilla had drunk, the first dancer held the glass for the second.

Apel, who was leaning on Jon's shoulder, her cheek perilously close to his, frowned down-table.

"Daav, your partner has no wine."

"Wine for Pilot Caylon!" Frad cried, snatching an empty glass from the table's center. He flourished it at the redhead, who captured a neighboring bottle and poured. Frad leaned over and placed the glass with an authoritative thump. "Good lift, Pilot."

His attention was back with the redhead before Aelliana's "Safe landing" was complete.

"Do you wish the chair, Aelliana?" Daav's voice was soft, for her ears alone.

She turned her head, again looking down into his eyes. "I am— afraid—I have never sat on anyone's knee."

"Nor is there reason for you to do so now, if you don't wish it," he said earnestly. "Stand a moment and allow me to rise."

"I—" She bit her lip, then gave him the truth, as a partner ought. "I think I should like to learn, Daav."

Laughter sparked across his face. "Ah, would you? Then allow me to be your teacher." There was a light touch at her waist—his hand, warm and firm, easing her back until she was sitting sidewise against him, her legs across his.

"Your near arm along my shoulders, if you will," he murmured and she complied; her breast pressed gently against his chest.

She stilled. Daav was warm against her, pleasing in a way that seemed related to the dance, his arm supporting her back, his hand curved over her hip.

"Aelliana?"

Deliberately, she drew a breath, and relaxed into him. Dance-like, indeed, she thought, catching an edge of that same subtle dazzlement. She bent her head, saw the shine of silver along his neck, where the collar gaped loose.

She touched it with a forefinger.

"What is this?" she whispered, her mouth near his ear.

"A chain," he whispered back. She laughed softly and felt him shiver.

"Would you like some wine?" he murmured and with her assent leaned forward. She closed her eyes, savoring the feel of him, the muscles shifting as he bent and her body bending with his—within his.

"Wine," he said. She opened her eyes to take the glass and sip, then offered it to him.

"Wine?" she asked softly, as Trilla's friend had done.

His eyes took fire. She felt—something—quiver through him; felt her heart begin an odd, thick pounding . . .

"Heads up!" That was Jon.

Aelliana felt Daav shift under her as the others leapt to their feet, bowing low to the three who approached the table.

Two men, one woman; one of the men in Scout leather; all bearing themselves as persons of authority. Aelliana gasped, suddenly knowing who they must be. Belatedly, she began to rise.

The man in Scout leather raised a hand. "Never mind, Pilot," he said in Comrade. "I'd say you'd earned a comfortable seat and that one—" a casual finger-flip toward Daav—"owes me so many bows he might as well be your chair."

"Commander," Daav said gravely.

The older man inclined his head. "Captain."

"Ah, is this Pilot Aelliana Caylon?" the woman asked, coming forward to stand by Scout Commander. She bowed respect. "I am Narna vin'Tayla, Solcintra Port Master." She reached out and captured the remaining man, who had been speaking strenuously with Jon.

"Pilot Guild Master Per Sea ren'Gelder," she said and the man bowed, quickly.

"We are not here to disturb your celebration," Scout Commander said, with a glimmer of humor. "Master ren'Gelder has an item belonging to Pilot Caylon."

"Yes." Master ren'Gelder made another quick bow, leaned forward and placed a metal card on the table before Aelliana.

"This," he said briskly, "is the license for First Class Pilot Aelliana Caylon. This," he reached inside his jacket and withdrew a data-disk, "is the list of pilots endorsing Pilot Caylon's first class status—" he glanced at his wrist—"as of two hours ago." He inclined his head. "We shall, of course, forward an updated list to *Ride the Luck* maincomp."

Aelliana stared, then bent swiftly forward, reaching for that flat rectangle. Daav's hand shifted to her waist, lending her balance.

First Class: The words leapt out at her, the date of today—or, rather, yesterday—the endorsing pilot—she flipped the card over—

"Acclaim?"

Port Master smiled. "Thus the data-disk. It seems every Scout and master pilot on and around Liad has called to endorse your ascension, Pilot." Her smile widened. "There are several Terran masters in that list, as well."

"I—" It was on the edge of her tongue to protest that she had done nothing, that it had been a mere exercise in—She swallowed, inclined her head, feeling Daav's body solid and sure against hers.

"I thank you," she said formally.

"Custom has now been satisfied," Scout Commander announced, and turned with a sweep of his hand. "dea'Cort, you old ship-jockey, where's my wine?"

SHE HAD ASKED HIM to escort her to her ship, which was nothing more than a pilot might ask of her copilot—or of her partner. He accepted the duty gladly, though he might have served her better by placing her into Clonak's care. His emotions were—not quiescent.

Even now, walking sedately hand-in-hand, he felt her presence as an intoxicant, so that he fought a mad desire to pull her close, to bury his face in her hair, run his hands over her strong, fragile body, to taste the honey of her skin. . .

Shuddering, he drew in a deep lungful of dew-early air.

He must not, he told himself, allow this sudden passion rein. A brief night of shared pleasure and a return to easy comradeship on the morrow—that was for some, and no harm in it. But not for Aelliana. For Aelliana, there must be gentleness and a skillful awakening, and night after night of joy—

He gasped, staggered.

"Daav?" Her voice carried concern.

"A trifle too much wine," he said, charging his voice with rue. "No cause for alarm."

Really, Daav, he scolded himself silently, *such unseemly display.*

Beside him, Aelliana drew an audible breath. "Is there anything I must hold from, when I speak with Scout Commander on Trilsday? I would not wish to make—to make an error."

"Even if you were likely to make an error," Daav said, glad of the diversion of conversation, "Jon will be with you, will he not? You may rely entirely upon him."

"Yes, of course. It is only . . ." her voice faded.

He smiled, which she would not see in the darkness. "Be easy, Aelliana. The commander only wishes to increase the honor of Scout Headquarters by allowing you free run of the World Room."

"And it is very kind in him," she said warmly. "I only wonder how—it is—that people go on in the—in Outspace, when there is no one but one's self to rely upon and the care of strangers must be suspect. Who will I—who insures that error does not occur?"

She begins to understand what the license in her pocket may purchase, Daav thought, *and to see that some of those goods may well be—dangerous.*

"The universe is imperfect, " he said, speaking plain truth, which a copilot must, in matters of the pilot's safety. "Error occurs.

On Liad, the correction of error is social art. In Outspace, it is—a natural force. Those who exercise faulty judgment, die. Those who pilot badly, die. Those who watch, and learn, and have a certain measure of the luck, prosper." He paused, then added, earnestly, "It is possible to be happy, Aelliana. Only be careful, do."

She stopped, her fingers hard around his, and turned to face him in the dark.

"Some pilots take partners," she said, and her voice was not steady.

"Yes."

"Yes," she repeated and after a moment began to walk again, he, hand-linked, beside her.

They came without further talk or incident to *The Luck*. Daav released her hand with a pang and stepped aside so that she might proceed him up the long ramp. At the top, she worked keys and code and the hatch slid open, adding ship's illumination to the dim gantry-light.

In the wash of ship-light she turned to him, close on the narrow landing. Deliberately, she moved closer. Her hand rose to his shoulder, as if they were about to dance.

"Daav?" Her eyes were green, brilliant in the yellow light; her face at once hesitant and resolved.

"Aelliana—" Breath failed him. He stood, quivering, beneath her hand, lost in the brilliance of her eyes.

She bit her lip. "I do not have the pretty words, but I ask you with all—all honor and—care. I feel that Liad chafes—that you would rather be away. I—I will not be able, I think, to return, once I have gone." Anxiety fogged her eyes for a moment. "No dishonor, not—as Scouts understand honor. Merely, a life that is not—world-bound." She drew a ragged breath, her fingers gripping his shoulder tight. "Will you partner with me, *van'chela*, when I go outworld?"

Almost, he shouted *yes*, and threw everything to the stars: tore Korval's Ring from around his neck and hurled it to the stones below, gathered Aelliana into his arms and bore her within.

Almost.

"I—cannot." He heard his own voice quaver. Aelliana's face went still.

"Cannot?"

"I am promised to wed," his voice—his *sense*—made answer. "My clan has—use—for me." He swallowed, hard in a sand-dry throat, extended one shaking finger and touched her cheek. "You offer—my heart's desire, Aelliana. Believe me."

He did not know if she did. Pain tightened her face and she stepped back, her hand falling from his shoulder. She bent her head quickly, but not before he saw the glitter of tears.

"Aelliana—"

She raised a hand, forestalling him. "It is—I regret," she achieved, with a formal intonation that tore at his heart. She cleared her throat and dared lift her face to his.

"Good lift, Daav."

"Safe landing, Aelliana."

She turned and went into her ship. The hatch cycled, shutting him out of the light.

CHAPTER THIRTY-ONE

A lifemating is a far more serious matter than a mere contract-marriage, encompassing the length of the partner's lives, even if one should die. One of the pair must leave his or her clan of origin to join the clan of the lifemate. At that time the adoptive clan pays a "life-price" based on the individual's profession, age and internal value to the former clan.

Tradition has it that lifemates share a "bond of heart and mind." In view of Liaden cultural acceptance of "wizards," some scholars have interpreted this to mean that lifemates are "psychically" connected. Or, alternatively, that the only true lifematings occur between wizards.

There is little to support this theory. True, lifematings among Liadens are rare. But so are life-long marriages among Terrans.

—From "Marriage Customs of Liad"

SHE RAN, for there was no place to hide.

Sick with terror, she hurtled through mazy back streets, across broad plazas, down endless ship-halls—and still—and still—It followed.

Its Shadow fell behind her, annihilating the street she had just traversed. Panting, she skidded around a corner, sprinted across a wide thoroughfare and ducked into the gateway of a private courtyard. She dared not rest long, yet rest she must, for her heart was near to bursting, and her sobbing gasps scarcely brought sufficient air to lungs afire with exertion.

She leaned into the warm friendly shadow of the gateway, muscles trembling. Dimly, she wondered how long she could stay this brutal pace and where in the confusion of port-ways and corridor she might locate a weapon.

Even in the exultation of her terror, she knew that a weapon would not halt the Shadow. It was that which *cast* the Shadow against which she wished, most fervently, to be armed. A being capable of generating so horrifying an adumbration—*that* she would not face unarmed.

Her breath shuddered through her, echoing weirdly off the close walls of her huddling place. She detected a movement at the edge of the street and pushed away from the wall, steeling herself to run again.

Exhausted muscles betrayed her. She moved one step, two, and folded to her knees at the entrance of the gateway, teeth locked to hold in the shout of despair.

The corner she had turned only moments ago—vanished, eaten by a blackness so absolute that the eyes rebelled and insisted on multi-colored lights in the Shadow's depth—a road upon which it was cast.

It hesitated, the Shadow did, and seemed to look about Itself. On her knees atop the paving stones, Samiv tel'Izak held still as might be, hoping against horrified certainty that It would—this once—miss the way.

Half a mile high, It loomed, Its head a twisting mass of black limbs, Its trunk as wide as a warehouse and the wind that proceeded It was cold, carrying the stink of rotting leaves.

The Shadow turned and half the thoroughfare between It and her huddling place was eclipsed. Wind skirled around her, rank with rot, and overhead she heard a steady, ominous beat, as if enormous wings worked the sky. Samiv raised her arms above her head, pitiful shield though they made, and stared down the diminished street, into the blackness of her Enemy.

But the Shadow did not advance. Above, the beat of wings grew stronger, nearer, until at last it was thunder, driving a dust-laden wind into her inadequate shelter, so that she bent, bringing her arms down to protect her face.

The thunder of wings ceased. She straightened into shadow, blinked to clear her dust-grimed eyes.

A hand gripped her shoulder.

Samiv tel'Izak screamed.

THE HATCH CAME DOWN, sealing him out.

Numbly, Aelliana crossed to her station, sat, reached out and triggered initial board check.

Lights flickered, screens glowed: Her ship, coming to life.

Her ship.

She could lift now, this minute; the first class license rode, safe, in her sleeve. There was nothing to tie her here, not clan, nor kin, nor—

"Daav?"

No deep, calm voice answered her whisper; no tall, silent-moving form tickled the edge of her vision. She was alone.

Odd, how badly that hurt. For so many years, *alone* had been everything she wished for.

The board chimed readiness; the screens showed ships, sleeping all around. In screen number six a slim figure walked, shoulders stooped in an attitude so alien it was not until a random light snagged along the silver earring that she knew him.

"Daav!" She snapped forward, palm slapping screen, as if she would reach through plastic, chip and ether—

He reached the top of the row and turned left, vanishing toward . . .

She didn't even know where he lived.

"Oh, gods."

The board lights blurred out of sense. She wiped at her eyes with impatient fingers, mildly surprised when they came away wet. Tears. Her husband had enjoyed tears; had found a thousand ways to wring them from her, until she refused to weep, no matter how he hurt her.

He had been a master of pain, her husband. But no effort of his genius had produced such agony as this.

The comm light glowed in the corner of her eye. She turned toward it, hope igniting its own agony.

She had his comm number.

Call me, his voice murmured from memory, *if there is need . . .*

Her hand flicked forward. She snatched it back, brought it, fisted, against her lips and merely sat there, crying in earnest now, for he was lost, sworn to wed and be of use to his clan, whatever and wherever it was. Bound, as even a Scout may be bound, by the knots of kin and duty. To call him now would surely do harm. To beg him for—

What?

A return to the ensorcellment of the dance, when they had moved and thought as one being? To feel his body, strong and lithe, against hers? The gift of his humor and hard common sense? The certain knowledge that, whenever in her life she looked to the copilot's station, he would be there, keeping his serene, impeccable board?

She scrubbed at drenched cheeks, pressed the heels of both hands against her eyes in an effort to dam the tears that had become a torrent.

The tears would not be stopped. She leaned forward until her cheek was against first board and there she lay, sobbing into the chill plastic, until, at last, she fell into a gray, uneasy sleep.

IT COULD NOT BE SAID that Ran Eld Caylon was a man addicted to news. Where current events touched upon Ran Eld Caylon, there his interest was avid. For events centered in other spheres, his interest was—minimal.

Let Sinit ride the news-wire, exclaiming over Council *on-dits,* the publication of tedious professorial tomes or the undignified stunts of pilots. Enough time for Ran Eld to notice the Council of Clans when he was himself a participant in history. As for the work of professors and pilots—it was difficult to say which bored him more.

So it was by an enormous bit of very bad luck that Ran Eld

Caylon on this particular morning, smarting still under his middle sister's continued elusiveness, came face-to-face with The Net.

The Net was Sinit's preferred news service. He had told her time and time over to use the house screen in the library for her viewing, but such was her passion for news that she would use Ran Eld's, in case Voni had prior claim on the communal screen. Mostwise, she remembered to return the setting to Ran Eld's fund reporter. This morning, she had forgotten.

Ran Eld touched the on-switch and "Caylon" immediately caught his eye, as one's own name is apt to do. Frowning, he perused the story sufficiently to discover that the Caylon found thus newsworthy was one Aelliana, pilot-owner of Class A Jumpship *Ride the Luck*.

Ran Eld—carefully—sat down.

He then read the newsbit thoroughly, learning such items of interest regarding the pilot as her work upon the ven'Tura Piloting Tables at the tender age of eighteen, which revision was hailed as a boon to pilots everywhere. He learned that Pilot Caylon had owned her ship a bare *relumma*, having won it in a game of pikit; that her second class license, awarded a few days after her win, had been upgraded by popular acclaim and on the basis of yesterday's amazing rescue, to full first.

He learned that Pilot Caylon flew out of Binjali Repair Shop, Mechanic Street, Solcintra Port.

HIS HAIR AND FACE were soaked with dew by the time he reached the platform, high inside the Tree. At least, his hair was.

Daav reached behind his head, snatched the silver ring free and slid it into a pocket. Released, his hair hung in a snarled, sullen twist, trailing spiteful tendrils inside his jacket collar.

He sighed sharply and used rather too much force to shake his head. Thick, wet stuff lashed his cheeks before spreading into a fan across his shoulders.

All around, the Tree was quiet.

Before him, through a tunnel of leaf and branch, he could see the lights of Solcintra Spaceport, dim against the lightening sky.

"She has her first class now," he said aloud, his eyes on the distant port. "There's nothing holds her but gravity."

Everywhere the leaves hung still, disturbed by not a breath of breeze.

"Er Thom," Daav continued, watching the distant lights grow dimmer. "My brother tells me that when first he saw his Anne—a Terran woman, you know, in a room full with Terrans—that when he first saw her, it was as if there were two women standing there, one within the other. The first—the outside woman, if you like— was well enough—pretty hair and happy eyes . . . beautiful hands. A bit large, of course, and shaped just—Anne-like. But Anne-like was pleasing and Er Thom was pleased."

The red beacon came on at the Port Authority's pinnacle, signaling the change from Night Port to Day. Daav blinked and raised a hand to wipe at the—dew—drying along his cheeks.

"The second woman—he glimpsed her for a heartbeat, understand! The second woman was hardly woman at all, but music, or light, or a rhapsody of both—at once so intricate and so indescribably *correct* that my brother says he felt he could observe it for the rest of his days and neither tire of it nor find it to contain one note—one light-mote—that was not precisely as it should be." Daav sighed.

"The second woman faded in that heartbeat, leaving Anne, to whom he made his bow, and who, in Er Thom's way, he came to love." He turned, facing the Tree's center down the length of the platform.

"My brother tells me that now—now he hears that perfect music all the time—in his heart, so he has it. And when he closes his eyes, he can see that flawless, intricate, maze of brightness that is Anne—that is Anne's inner self. It comforts him, he tells me, in those times when they must be apart, to feel—to know—that he never is alone."

Silence, dead air; a faint, far sense of something—waiting.

"Anne," said Daav, moving one bare step forward. "Anne tells a like tale. Wherever she is, wherever he is, she feels Er Thom's presence, his passions—the universe is not wide enough to dim her perception. He's like music, she says, being a musician. Like a work in progress and a revered masterwork being played both at once. Powerful, she says. Like a heartbeat. She gives me permission to say that Er Thom is become part of her heartbeat—part of her lifeforce, I suppose she means. But it doesn't seem to frighten her. It's joy, she says—they both say. And Er Thom says, 'I wish . . .'"

Absolute stillness. A silence into which no bird song dared intrude.

Daav took another step forward; stood at the platform's center, hands fisted at his side, trembling badly at the knees.

"At least tell me if it is true," he said, and his voice was trembling, too, "that I am formed as one-half of a wizard's match."

Above, a sharp rustle of leaf, as if a flying mouse had landed. A seed-pod plummeted, striking the planks between his boots with peevish precision. Daav took a breath.

"We danced and it was as if we had been born dancing in each other's arms. I held her and it was sweet—past sweet! And she was caught as tightly as I! *Van'chela*, so she said to me—beloved friend." He went forward another step; another would bring him to the trunk.

"In all of this there was nothing such as my kin describe me—no beautiful mazes, no soul-songs. Even now, she may have lifted— have Jumped!—and I never the wiser, til Clonak called to tell me." He took the last step, raised his fists and lay them, palm-flat, against the trunk.

"Aelliana Caylon," he said. "Clan Mizel."

The bark was rough against his palms, grainy and a little damp. Somewhere in the branches below, a dawn-swallow began to sing.

Daav sagged forward, pressing his cheek against the Tree.

"Samiv tel'Izak does not please you," he whispered. "Aelliana excites no interest. Must I be alone, because Er Thom is not? Shall I tell Bindan that the marriage is canceled, because I have chanced upon one I might love? What shall I do when they cry breach of contract and demand ships and stocks and payments? How shall we keep Cantra's Law, when our ships are gone and we are turned out of our valley? How shall we stay vigilant for the passengers? How will we protect the Tree?"

Nothing, save bark and damp and bird song.

"I should have stayed with Aelliana," Daav whispered, and for an instant it was so: They had the day before them to lay plans and hustle cargo; a course laid Out, and far away . . .

Madness.

He pushed away from the Tree, walked back and picked up the seed-pod. He stood for a moment, holding it in his hand, then went to the edge of the platform and threw it, as hard and as far as he could.

CHAPTER THIRTY-TWO

The pilot's care shall be ship and passengers.
The copilot's care shall be pilot and ship.

—From the Duties Roster of the Pilots Guild

A TALL SHADOW crossed Clonak's light. He lay down his wrench and looked up.

"Master Frad! I hardly expected to see you about so early after such a round of merrymaking!"

The lanky cartographer grinned. "Snatched the words from the tip of my tongue, rascal! What's this you're about? Work? Never say so!"

"I'm a changed man, since my goddess touched my life," Clonak told him piously. Frad laughed.

"Then you're out, Comrade. Or wasn't it Daav who escorted the Caylon to her bed last evening? I admit to being a glass or two over-limit, but hardly giddy enough to mistake length for girth."

"Some of us," Clonak said with great seriousness, "worship from afar."

"All of us, unless I misread the matter badly. I've rarely seen Daav so conformable. One might almost think him tame. And the pilot wears her heart on her face."

"Yes, well." Clonak picked up his wrench. "The devil's in the brew, there, old friend. Daav's betrothed."

"No, is he?" Frad stared, then moved his shoulders, answering himself. "Well, but he must be, mustn't he? Korval is none too plentiful, despite the yos'Galan's contribution. Daav's a sensible fellow—full nurseries are certain to be a priority with him. Merely, he had held himself aloof such a time . . . Well. Who is the intended?"

"Samiv tel'Izak Clan Bindan, as my father has it."

"So? I've flown with the lady, as it happens. Piece of roster work for the Port. *She* unbends, eventually, but her delm's ambitious."

Clonak sighed. "My father said that, too."

"Hah." Frad glanced about. "Are we the only two about? Surely Jon hasn't left the care of the Yard to yourself?"

"Jon's presence was required at the Port Directors meeting. Trilla called in a few minutes ago to say she'd be . . . late."

Frad grinned. "Well, and it was a pretty pair she had with her last night."

"Pretty enough," his friend agreed. "And willing. I have not yet seen my captain or my goddess, but, then, I hadn't expected them."

"So, it is you alone! Well I happened by."

"Why, so it is," Clonak returned with an evil grin. "You might actually be of use, you know, instead of nattering about and holding me from my appointed task. But you never were much of a hand at repair."

"Ho, a challenge! What have you here, a vector engine? Stand aside, sirrah, and give a master room to work!"

SLEEP EBBED, leaving a headache behind. Aelliana sat up creakily in the pilot's chair, and rubbed her gritty eyes. The message-waiting light was on and she touched the amber stud, her heart lifting in hope. Had Daav—?

The communcation was from the Port Master's office, verifying completion of roster-work for the Port, and recording a transfer of three cantra paid into the account of *Ride The Luck*, Aelliana Caylon, Pilot.

She sat back, tears rising, then took a breath, saved the message to ship's log and opened a line to the Pilot Guild's bank. Three cantra earned by ship and pilots, ciphered thus: one share to the ship, one share to the pilot, one share to the copilot. She would transfer Daav's share at—

Hands on the keys, she froze. Transfer his cantra? Yes, surely. And what was his surname—his clan? What, indeed, was the number on his pilot's license?

Aelliana sighed, shut down the connection and stood. Very well. First, a shower. The rest of the day, with its various necessities and pains, would proceed from there.

AS IT HAPPENED, the repair required a team. They barely had the casing open when the crew door cycled. Frad looked round in time to see a nattily-dressed man of about his own age step cautiously within.

For a long moment he stood on the threshold, holding the door back on the tips of his violet-gloved fingers. Then, warily, he came into the bay, mincing lightly, as if he feared soiling the soles of his exquisitely tooled boots.

"Oh, la!" Clonak murmured, catching sight of the stranger. "A bird of paradise!"

"Perhaps he is a buyer," Frad suggested.

"Much more likely a seller," returned Clonak. "His gloves match his lace."

Frad sighed.

Twelve paces into the shop, the stranger paused, his sleek, well-kept head tipped to one side, gloved hands clasped loosely before him, as if expecting at any moment to see an abject lackey hurrying up to beg his pardon. Indeed, for three heartbeats, by Frad's count, he tarried, apparently awaiting this phenomenon. At last, disappointed in his patience, he turned his head and spied the two at work on the vector-engine.

One glove rose with studied elegance. One finger pointed."You there," he stated. "Fellow."

Above the engine, Clonak snorted. "I haven't been 'fellow' to some dog wearing lace in the daytime since I was twelve years old."

"Well, then," said Frad, putting down his probe and reaching for a rag. "I suppose he means me."

Wiping his hands, he walked silently toward the dandy. At precisely the proper distance for speaking with strangers, he stopped and bowed, Adult-to-Adult.

"Good day, sir," he said, also in the mode of Adult-to-Adult. "How may I serve you?"

The dandy had eyes of purest cerulean, large and spaced appealingly, one on either side of his pert little nose. The eyes widened now, with, Frad supposed, insult, and the rather thin-lipped mouth turned down.

"I will speak with the owner of this establishment," he announced, with no "if you please" about it. Frad moved his shoulders.

"Alas, the owner is away."

The frown became definite and a gleam of displeasure was seen in the pretty eyes.

"When," he demanded, "will the owner return?"

"He did not say," Frad returned, unremittingly courteous. "Is there some way in which I might assist you?"

"Perhaps," the dandy allowed and drew himself up, fixing Frad with a very stern stare, indeed. "I," he announced, "am Ran Eld Caylon, Nadelm Mizel!"

"Aha!" Clonak said soto voce from just beyond Frad's shoulder. "That explains the matter perfectly!"

Nadelm Mizel directed what he doubtless wished to be a quelling glance at the source of this lamentable frivolity. However, the glance disintegrated even as it arrowed toward the miscreant. The thin mouth tightened convulsively, as if the nadelm might be ill, and the blue eyes skittered back to Frad.

"You will produce Aelliana Caylon," he ordered. "At once."

Frad raised his eyebrows, face displaying earnest, if laborious, intelligence.

The nadelm frowned heavily. In a mode perilously close to Superior-to-Inferior, he stated: "You will cause Aelliana Caylon to come before me, instantly. I have good reason to believe she is here."

"Aelliana Caylon," Frad repeated, in a tone of wonderment. He glanced to Clonak, who stood lovingly stroking his mustache. "Aelliana Caylon?"

"The ven'Tura Tables," Clonak told him kindly, and looked to the nadelm. "He's a bit of a block, you know, but a very good fellow, nonetheless. He would have remembered, in an hour or three. But, there, it's our turn, and we are wasting your time!" He struck a pose. "Cantra yos'Phelium!"

The nadelm glared at a point just short of Clonak's chin. "I am not here to play Biographies!"

"You're not?" Clonak demanded in fair imitation of idiot bemusement. "Well, whatever are you here for? I must say, Buttercup, it is not at all the thing to be drawing people away from their work to answer your tease, and then refuse to take your turn! Too shabby!"

"*I beg*—" Ran Eld Caylon raised angry eyes to Clonak's face and hastily averted them. "Master Binjali will hear of your insolence, my man!"

Clonak clapped his hands. "Now, that I should like to see!" he cried. "Indeed, sir, you must stay and await Master Binjali. I insist upon it! Come, let me give you some tea—and perhaps a day-old bun, if the cat has left any whole—to ease your wait!"

The dandy drew himself up, splendid in violet lace and tight black coat. "Sir, I see that you must be drunk."

"Oh, no," Frad said soothingly, feeling matters had gone far enough. "Indeed, sir, he's hardly ever drunk this early in the day. Unless, of course," he added fairly, "he's still in his cups from last night."

The nadelm fixed a stare fraught with awful menace on Frad's face. "Do you refuse to bring Aelliana Caylon or Master Binjali to me at once?"

He gave it consideration, taking lengthy counsel of the ceiling. "Yes," he said finally, meeting the angry blue eyes blandly, "I do."

"Very well." Ran Eld Caylon inclined his head. "I then instruct you, as the owner's nadelm, to seal *Ride the Luck* and bring the keys to me."

Frad merely stood there, face bland, posture conveying polite attention.

"I had said," Pilot Caylon's nadelm snapped, "you will seal *Ride the Luck* immediately and fetch the keys to me!"

"I had heard you the first time," Frad said calmly. "I am of course desolate to find myself unable to accommodate you, sir, but I am not authorized to seal an owner's ship."

"So. I shall then await the proprietor of this establishment." *And it will*, his tone stated, *go ill for you then, fellow!*

"Proprietor can't seal a patron's ship, either," Clonak said cheerfully. "Port proctor's what you want, Buttercup—but I'd advise against it."

"I do not recall soliciting your advice," the nadelm informed him icily.

"Yes, but it happens to be excellent advice," Frad said. "Matters such as sealing a ship fall firmly within the Port Master's honor and it is to her that you must apply."

The blue eyes raked his face with a look meant to inspire terror. Frad lifted an eyebrow, face showing no sign of the fury leaping within. Really! This—*popinjay*—held rank over Aelliana Caylon? Liad grew less sensible each time he returned.

"Very well," Ran Eld Caylon said at last. With neither bow nor courtesy, he turned and stamped toward the door, to the detriment, as Frad could not help believing, of his boot-soles. Fingers on the push-plate, he turned to glare.

"Ship and owner had best be in this Yard when I return with the proctors!" With which awful threat he exited.

Clonak collapsed against Frad's chest, wailing with delight.

"Why, why, oh *why* would you not let him stop for Master Binjali?" He gasped, clutching the taller man's shoulder for support. "Only think how lovely it would have been to dust him and water him and turn him to face the sun—" He subsided into howls of merriment.

Frad patted his head absentmindedly and set him straight on his feet. "All right, darling. Get a grip, do, and think why Pilot Caylon's nadelm wants to seal her ship."

"Random act of cruelty," Clonak said promptly. "Did you see that mouth? Spoilt. Ill-tempered, too. And those shoulders, all held thus!" He demonstrated the rigidly level shoulders, screwing his face up in a very passable imitation of the nadelm's look of outrage.

"Yes." Frad stared at the floor, thinking. The nadelm had been *angry*. One would almost suppose him to have not the least understanding of yesterday's flight. And yet, it *was* Liad and local custom was plain: A nadelm had the right to order a lower-ranked clanmember—unless the delm intervened.

"She probably forgot to give him his proper grace at breakfast," Clonak commented, moving back toward the vector-engine, "and he's taken a pet. You know the sort. Something else will annoy him between here and Port Authority and he'll forget all about the proctors."

"Yes," said Frad again, and sighed lightly. The Port Master would make very short work of Ran Eld Caylon's pretensions—which was no guarantee that the nadelm would not return to Binjali's. He was, in Frad's opinion, already on the outer edge of sensible and a scold received of the Port Master would not likely return him to reasoned judgment.

"Did Jon say when we might expect to have the joy of beholding his face?" he asked, shaking off a sudden chill and walking back toward Clonak and the repair.

Behind him, the crew door cycled wide.

"FOUR MINUTES SOONER and you'd have met the personage!" Clonak shouted gleefully.

Aelliana frowned, looking from him to—Frad, Daav's especial friend, who had been at their table last evening. "Personage?" she asked.

Clonak thinned his mouth, scrunched up his shoulders, and announced, in haughty accent: "Nadelm Mizel!"

She felt her knees go to rubber, staggered and snatched herself upright.

"Ran Eld, here!" she stared at Clonak, who had let his caricature fade into a look of genuine dismay. "Why?"

"He wished to see you," Frad said calmly.

"Wanted to seal your ship," Clonak added. "Told him he needed the proctors for that. Last seen, he was on his way to Port Master, where it's my belief he'll take delivery of one of her thundering scolds."

"He wanted to seal my ship," Aelliana repeated, blankly. "Ran Eld knows nothing about my ship! I—" She swallowed, looked up into Frad's face. "It was on the news wires," she whispered. Her heartbeat was a hollow roaring in her ears. "Yesterday's lift."

"I expect it was," he said, voice neutral. "You seem unwell, Pilot, is there—"

"It's nothing . . ." She gasped, pressing damp palms together. "I—forgive me. I must think."

The two Scouts exchanged glances.

"Pull up a stool and think away," Clonak said, almost serious. "Shall I bring you a mug of tea, Goddess?"

"Thank you, no," she managed and went numbly toward the clustered stools. She hoisted herself up on the first she came to and closed her eyes, hands gripped along the edge of the seat. After a moment, and another mute exchange of worry, the Scouts drifted back toward their work.

Ran Eld. Aelliana ground her teeth to keep them from chattering. Ran Eld, *here*—demanding her presence, demanding her ship be sealed. Her heart wanted to scream that it could not be so. Her mind was made of sterner stuff.

Fact: She was discovered.

Fact: Ran Eld would exact his price. Perhaps he would even beat her, as he had in the days just after her marriage, to reinforce her subservience.

Aelliana shuddered. She had no illusions regarding her ability to withstand such treatment: She would surrender *The Luck's* keys willingly, if they were the coin that bought an end to her punishment.

Options. One: Run. Leave now, lifting for the Liaden Outworlds, and hope the luck smiled sufficiently for her to find cargo and contract before her outlawed condition became known.

Objections: She would be leaving Jon dea'Cort and all his shifting crew open to Mizel's Balance. A very creditable case of kin-stealing could be shown to the Council of Clans, in settlement of which Jon might easily lose his yard, while Daav, Trilla, Clonak and Frad might find themselves called clanless . . .

No. She would not call disaster down upon her comrades.

Option Two: Submit to Ran Eld's wishes and hope, in time, to appease him sufficiently that she might live in tolerable peace.

Objections: Prior testing proved this application failed of success.

Option Three: Go home and put her case before the delm.

This was risky. Historically, Mizel championed her heir in any dispute. On several occasions, such as the matter of Aelliana's marriage to Ran Eld's friend, Mizel had allowed herself to be guided entirely by her son's advice and refused to hear any other.

Balancing history was an indication that of late the delm had softened toward her middle daughter. If she were clever enough to show the profit a working ship might bring to the clan—many times over the single gain of a sale . . .

An imperfect solution, but the best she could fashion, for the best good of herself and her comrades. The clan's fortune had not been—robust—of late, despite Voni's marriages. Mizel might very well be receptive to the addition of a new source of funding.

Aelliana opened her eyes, slid off the stool and crossed to the busy Scouts.

Two pair of eyes immediately lifted to her face.

"I am going home," she said, and wished her voice sounded steadier; that she felt more certain of a happy outcome. "You may tell my brother so, if he should come again. I—he will not trouble you further."

Clonak cleared his throat. "Trust me, Goddess, he was no trouble to us at all, despite that Frad would not allow him to await Master Binjali."

"You might stay an hour or two," Frad put in. "It seemed to me that your nadelm was—very angry. Perhaps it would be best to allow him time to cool."

She looked at him straightly. "Ran Eld does not cool, thank you, Pilot. If he has—if he has reached so high a pitch as you say, it is—best—that I return home and put the matter before the delm."

"Hah." Frad looked at Clonak. "Local custom."

"Local custom," the pudgy Scout repeated, but there was a frown between his taffy eyes. "Still it might be better, Aelliana, to stop until Jon returns. Or Daav does."

"That's the card you want!" Frad said, leaning forward. "Call on Daav's assistance, Pilot. Surely, he—"

"No!" she said sharply. Frad blinked and flicked a look to Clonak, who nodded and reached for a rag.

"Then I will come with you," he said, with unClonak-like firmness, "and see you safe before your delm."

"No, you shall not." She drew herself up and mustered a glare. "You do not understand how spiteful—should my brother consider you have thwarted him, he will do his utmost to ruin you." He continued to wipe his hands, entirely uncowed by the prospect of ruin. Aelliana bit her lip.

"Indeed, Clonak, you must not come with me. I—my nadelm several times has ordered me to—to absent myself from the company of Scouts. I have not obeyed and it would . . ." She faltered.

"It would," Frad took up, "make matters immeasurably worse, were you seen to be championed by a Scout." He shook his head, mournfully. "Pilot, take advice. You want Daav for this. He can mend the thing in a thrice."

"No," she said again, and reached into her pocket, pulling out the bank envelope and thrusting it into Clonak's hand. "If you would, however, see that Daav receives this, when he does arrive for his shift? It is his share of yesterday's lift-wage. And . . ." She yanked the chain over her head, ship keys jangling as she pressed those, too, on Clonak.

"Please, ask Jon to hold these for me. I will—say that I will come for them—myself, or. . ." She drew a hard breath. "Or my copilot may claim them, should he have need."

Clonak stared at the items in his hand. "Aelliana . . ."

"No," she said for a third time. "Truly, friends, it is better so. I will—Good lift, pilots." She turned and ran, not waiting for their well-wishing in return.

CHAPTER THIRTY-THREE

Kin and love
Comfort
Home.

> —**From *Collected Poems***
> **Elabet pel'Ongin Clan Diot**

SHE SOUGHT THE SHIP'S HEALER, who listened, probed, and laid salve upon her pain, so that all was well. Until she slept again.

Twice more, Samiv tel'Izak sought the Healer. The third time, he denied her.

"I eradicate the memory of the dream, Pilot, but, when you sleep, you dream again. To eradicate the memory which *causes* the dream—that I might do. But in a situation such as yours, where the pain-matrix or referents to the matrix will be shortly re-encountered, eradicating the older memory—and what defenses you have thus far built—serves you ill, and the Guild counsels against it."

"And what cure does the Guild counsel?" she inquired, voice grating in weariness.

"An old cure," the Healer said softly, "and a harsh one. Confront that which gnaws at your soul, stare into its face and achieve what Balance you may."

Harsh, indeed. She left the Healer and sought her immediate

611

superior. She informed that serious and ship-wise pilot that lack of sleep and stress of spirit made her an active danger to ship and crew; that the Healer had no succor.

Her superior did duty, cancelling what remained of her contract, which was required, as a matter of ship's safety, and would show in her permanent Guild record. He also commended her for exemplary service and expressed willingness to see her under his command at any time in the future, which would also find a place in her record, and fell on the full side of Balance.

Samiv signed the separation paper, removed her effects from quarters and twelve hours later was walking out of Solcintra Guildhall, pack slung over a shoulder, and her heart cold with dread. Confront her fear, indeed.

And then there was one's delm to consider.

STEP BY STEP, Aelliana forced herself home, hands fisted in the pockets of her old blue jacket.

Her feet faltered at the corner of Raingleam Street. She drove herself onward, shaking.

The delm. It was her right, as one of Mizel, to ask a hearing and justice of the delm. She could not be refused this.

Her hand touched the gate and her knees locked, so that she stood for an entire minute, unable to go on.

The delm, she told herself. *Lay all before the delm . . .*

Her hand moved, the gate swung open. She entered Mizel's front garden, closed the gate behind her and walked, step-by-step, to the door.

Three wooden steps to the porch; a touch of her hand to the lock pad.

"Good afternoon, Aelliana." The luck was out. And yet it was her right, to ask, to be heard, by her delm.

She bowed, so low that her forehead touched her knees, and straightened only somewhat, eyes fixed humbly on the faded pink stone of the foyer floor.

"Good afternoon, brother," she murmured, though the words seemed like to choke her.

"So respectful," he commented, rising from his chair in the stair-niche. "Indeed, the very portrait of subservience, drawn with rare skill. I confess myself charmed—but no longer deceived."

She did not raise her head. She did not move. Barely did she breathe. Ran Eld's boots came into her range of vision: They were dusty and scuffed; the right bore a stain of oil along the instep.

"You keep to your character?" he inquired, voice poisonously sweet. "But perhaps you are correct! We are so open here that anyone might chance to see, should you choose to fly your true colors! I suggest we adjourn to the parlor. After you. Sister."

"I have—urgent—need to see the delm," Aelliana said, staring, staring, at that scuffed, stained leather. "Pray conduct me to Mizel at once."

"The delm is from house," Ran Eld purred. "She returns tomorrow, midday." There was a pause, in which she felt his gloating like rancid grease across her skin. "The parlor, sister. Of your kindness."

There was no help for it. Shoulders slumped, eyes lowered, steps mouse-light across the old stone floor, Aelliana entered the parlor. Ran Eld's footsteps gritted noisily behind her. He crossed the threshold and closed the door with a bang, striding to where she waited in the center of the room, eyes on the nap-worn carpet.

"Look at me!" he shouted, augmenting the order with a savage yank of her hair.

She ground her teeth, imprisoning the cry, and met his eyes.

"So . . ." Satisfaction settled in her brother's face. "Have you truly forgotten the old lesson, Aelliana? Do you no longer recall what I had done to you, the last time you challenged me?"

"I remember."

"Ah, she remembers! But where is the failing note in the voice— the twisting together of the fingers? She remembers, but appears to discount the memory. Perhaps she takes comfort in the Delm's Word! What was that promise, Aelliana?"

She stared at him, recalling all of what he had caused to be done to her. He had boasted of it, after, and spoken of such things as made it certain that he and the contract-husband had spent many delicious hours, planning how best to harm her.

"You know well what the Delm's Word was," she told him, and heard the acid in her voice with dismay.

"Ah, but of course I know!" Ran Eld returned, in high good humor. "But you will tell me, Aelliana, because I have commanded it. As nadelm, it is my right—indeed, my duty!—to command you. Surely, you cannot have forgotten that."

She took a careful breath, trying to still her body's shaking, which was all of long-pent fury and hatred, and nothing whatsoever of fear.

"The Delm's Word," she said, neutralizing the acid note with an effort, "was that I had fulfilled my duty to the clan and need never marry again."

"Yes, that is what I thought," her brother said, with a smile. "Never *marry* again. I may be able to keep to that, when I am delm." His face hardened. "In the meanwhile, I learn from the news wires that you are a holder of real property which you have neglected to report to the clan." He moved an elegant, heavily-ringed hand. "Step to the desk, if you please."

She went forward to the tiny letter-desk, stood blinking down at the paper laid there, at the pens, bare-tipped and ready.

Bill of Transfer, the words shouted from the page. *I, Aelliana Caylon Clan Mizel, hereby transfer all right, profit and holding in the starship Ride the Luck to Ran Eld Caylon, Nadelm Mizel, to be his personal property to dispose of or profit by . . .*

"No."

"No?" Incredibly, Ran Eld sounded merely amused. "But you are grown bold!" He smiled viciously into her eyes as she looked up. "You will sign this paper, Aelliana, and this . . ." He pulled a second from the pile on the letter-desk and thrust at her face.

She danced aside, flicking the paper from between his fingers. Another transfer, this one of her Ormit Shares. She dropped the paper onto the desk.

"Not that one either," she said, her voice shaking. "I sign nothing until I have spoken with the delm. If she is from House, I ask that you put me in contact with her. If she is not to be disturbed, I will wait upon her arrival."

Ran Eld's eye had snagged on the glitter of Jon's ring.

"What's this?" he asked, snatching her wrist. "A love-token? Relinquish it."

Her throat closed with outrage. She forced herself to stand quiet in his grip, as Trilla had taught her, waiting for her moment.

"Come along, Aelliana! Have it off!" His fingers tightened. "Or shall I take it off myself?"

"You may not have it," she said, striving for Daav's tone of calm reason. "I earned it and it is mine."

"You *earned* it?" her brother jeered. "In that wise, it is wages, and we had long ago decided what was best done with your wages, hadn't we?"

So they had, and her wages had bought her nothing. Aelliana looked into her brother's eyes and saw that he would never be placated, that no harm he visited upon her would ever be enough to Balance his own fears and failings.

Fool, she told herself. *Why did you not listen to your comrades and stay away?*

Ran Eld jerked her hand forward and reached for the ring. She clenched her fist, braced and twisted free, all as Trilla had taught her.

"I will return when the delm is at home," she said, backing toward the door.

Ran Eld lunged, fist raised, which would have been enough, at some forgotten, rageless point in the past, to have her on her knees, begging his forgiveness.

Aelliana swept sideways, coming 'round in a deceptively graceful spin, her right hand, weighted with Jon's ring, rising, to whip, pilot-quick and anger-hard, across her nadelm's face.

THE BLOW KICKED HIM BACKWARD, dazzled by pain. His hand went up, came down—there was blood—blood! And Aelliana was at the door—through it—hair streaming behind her.

Ran Eld leapt, snatched—caught not hair, but jacket, yanked—

She came around fast, landed a blow to the side of his head, twisted free of his staggered grip and flung into the foyer.

Ears ringing, he hurtled after, grabbing for an arm.

She eluded his fingers like mist, one foot flashing out to touch his knee.

Pain.

He screamed, lurched and went down, flinging out a hand too late to break his fall—

But soon enough to catch her ankle, destroying her balance, and sending her crashing beside him on the gritty marble floor.

He rolled, using his weight to hold her, cuffing her face a time or two, while beneath him she fought with silent ferocity—teeth, fists and feet. His cheek was clawed from eye to chin while he struggled to pin her arms, and when finally he accomplished that— she kneed him.

He grunted, gasped—and she twisted, pitching him aside, flashing to her feet, turning—

There was a sound, as of a particularly sturdy vase being forcibly broken. Aelliana swayed—and crumpled to the floor, left cheek rubbing grit.

"Ran Eld!" Voni's voice quavered. "Brother, can you speak?"

Cautiously, he rolled to his back and blinked up into her horrified face.

"I can speak," he managed, somewhat breathlessly.

She swallowed. "Your face . . ."

"Yes, I don't doubt she marked me well. She certainly meant to do so." He sat up, then wished he hadn't. Blearily, he considered Aelliana's still shape.

"She went mad," he said, for Voni's benefit. "I gave nadelm's instruction and she—struck me." He took a breath, wincing at the pain.

"She ran for the door," he continued. "To have her show such a face to the world—I tried to hold her. She—"

"I saw," Voni said hoarsely. "She was—an animal. I have never—" She gulped. "She must have gone mad. I—Shall I call a Healer?"

A Healer? Ran Eld's stomach turned to ice. A Healer would immediately perceive the cause of Aelliana's revolt—and report it to Delm Mizel. Who would doubtless have many difficult questions to lay before her son and heir.

He licked his lips.

"No," he whispered, then, more strongly, "No. We shall—we shall put her in the sleep learner."

Voni blinked. "The sleep learner, brother? But—"

"The sleep learner," he said firmly, while the idea took root and grew before his mind's eye. An overlay of intensive direct-learning might very well befuddle Aelliana's remembrance of this confrontation. Perhaps, were the session long enough, she would forget the matter altogether.

"She has broken with the Code," he told Voni. "It is our duty to reinitiate her to proper behavior—and that before the delm returns. Only think of our mother's distress, to find Aelliana as you saw her just now—a beast, raising fists against her kin."

Voni looked to Aelliana, lying like a broken doll, her cheek pillowed on stone. "How—"

"The two of us can drag her to the study," he said. "Give me your arm and help me to rise."

She did, flinchingly, and refusing to look at his face. He shambled over to Aelliana and used his foot, none too gently, to roll her over.

"Take her right arm," he directed Voni, bending for the left. Bruises were rising amid the cuts on Aelliana's face, he saw with satisfaction, and the left cheek was badly scored. She would be well-served if he denied her use of the 'doc when she emerged from the sleep learner.

"Pull," he told Voni.

Squeamishly, she did.

HE PUSHED THE TIMER TO THE TOP, selected maximum intensity and yanked the abort button from its socket. In the act of closing the lid he paused, reached down and snatched up his sister's limp hand.

The heavy ring sparkled in the dim light as Ran Eld twisted it brutally free. *Earned* it, had she?

He let her hand fall and slammed the lid home.

"The *Code of Proper Conduct*," he typed into the program

queue. "Volume One, Number One, Page One, Word One. Continue sequentially until timer disengages function."

"Accepted," the sleep learner signaled. "Touch the blue button to initiate the Learning session."

Ran Eld touched the blue button.

"Shouldn't—we—have put her in the 'doc, first?" Voni asked uncertainly. "Her face was—was swollen, brother, and—and raw, where she—"

"Mere bruises," he said airily. "There will be time to tend them when she's schooled. Besides, I have need of the 'doc."

Voni gulped and inclined her head. "Of course."

CHAPTER THIRTY-FOUR

The Learning Module is intended for use as a supplement to conventional learning. It is not intended to replace conventional learning, nor should it be utilized in this manner.

The best use of the Learning Module is in review of old material, in order to sharpen details in the Learner's mind. The Module also has value in laying baseline information, upon which the Learner will then build.

IMPORTANT INFORMATION: The Learning Module utilizes intense, direct-brain stimulation to impart pre-programmed information. Direct-brain stimulation is painful, even dangerous, to some individuals. Always run a compatibility test before logging into a full Learning session.

In no case should a Learner undertake more than one six-hour session of moderate intensity within one twenty-eight-hour period. Cerebral vesication may result from overuse of a Learning Module.

—From the manual for Learning Module No. X5783

"DAAV."

He started, wine splashing in his glass, and guiltily looked up.

"Your pardon, *denubia*. I—fear my thoughts were elsewhere."

"As they have been," Er Thom said, with some asperity. "Perhaps I am inconvenient. I can easily go and come again, after you have rested."

"No, there, don't take a pet—There's a good-natured, biddable fellow!"

Only Daav knew the effort it cost Er Thom to keep the smile from his lips and continue to stare sternly.

"Well, and what am I to think, when I have your person, but neither your eyes nor your thoughts?" His face softened. "What troubles you, brother?"

Daav glanced down, put the glass away and looked back to his brother's eyes.

"Well, if you will have it, Aelliana Caylon desired me to partner with her, when she is ready to forsake Liad forever. And I was tempted, brother. Indeed, I was only now striving to recall why it was I denied her—I should say, denied myself."

"Hah." Er Thom set his glass aside. "I had thought you Pilot Caylon's copilot and comrade. Do you tell me your feeling goes more deeply than that?"

"Well," he moved his shoulders, still unwilling to meet his brother's eye, "we both know me for a volatile brute. Likely I should have grown bored in a *relumma* or two and wished for the comforts of home."

There was a small silence, before Er Thom said dryly, "Very likely."

Daav looked up, extended a rueful hand. "Now, darling, don't, I beg, tell me to stand away! You know I cannot do so, without ruining Korval."

"But I was not going to tell you any such thing," Er Thom said softly. "I only wondered why you had not at least spoken to Pilot Caylon before settling upon the tel'Izak."

Daav closed his eyes. "Because she was not then a pilot," he said, imposing calm upon his voice. "The first parameter in a spousal search is *pilot*, as you well know. She had never even been tested." He opened his eyes and reached for his glass.

"The initial winnowing gained us the names of several promising thirteen-year-olds—yet *Aelliana Caylon* had never been tested!" He took a hard breath and made an effort to soften his voice.

"Had Vin Sin chel'Mara been less a fool, she would be untested at this hour. Fortune smiled, brother, that she held a problem to which the ship provided a solution—could she but achieve Jump pilot."

"And has she?" Er Thom wondered.

Daav moved his shoulders. "This afternoon, should she have the inclination." He smiled wryly into his brother's skeptical face. "Never bet against the Caylon."

"I will remember," Er Thom said. Then, very gently indeed, "*Shall* you stand away from the tel'Izak, Daav?"

He shook his head wearily. "For what gain? Aelliana is for Outspace, as soon as she finds her courage. She sees me as partner, darling, not husband. Indeed, she speaks of the married state in the most—abhorrent—terms possible. Her own mating was too early and—ill-made, as I hear it." He sipped his wine, and added, quietly. "Damn them for clumsy fools."

"Ah," Er Thom said, and said nothing else.

Daav sat with his legs thrust out before him, apparently studying the tips of his boots, now and then sipping wine. Abruptly, he straightened, put his glass aside and looked up, black eyes bright.

"I love you, brother."

Er Thom blinked, for this was a thing little said between them. As well say, "We breathe the air, brother." Still—

"I love you, Daav."

"Yes, with all my faults! I shall strive not to shame you." He smiled, wanly, but with good intent, and pointed at the sheaf of papers Er Thom had brought with him.

"Let us assay your difficulty again, eh? I promise to give you my eyes and my thoughts."

"Fair enough," Er Thom replied and picked up the first.

"**. . . THREE HUNDRED AND FIFTY-EIGHTH EDITION** of the *Code of Proper Conduct*, published under the aegis of the League for the Purity of the Language, Kareen yos'Phelium Clan Korval, editor and chair.

"The first edition of the *Code of Proper Conduct* was compiled during the Exodus by a committee made up in equal part of the Solcintran Houses, the *dramliz*, and the pilots. Transcribed in the margins of expired trade manifests, the document ran approximately 85 pages and was little more than a protocol for shipboard life.

"The second edition, circulated twelve years after planetfall . . ."

Sleep learning is a peculiar undertaking. Neither asleep nor awake, one drifts in and out of phase, sometimes "hearing" the instruction; other times upheld by a wave of image, emotion and language; still other times, simply—elsewhere.

There are periods of lucidness within this shifting trance. One can, for greater or lesser periods of time, think, independent of the program. One can take stock, analyze—react.

So it was that Aelliana drifted out of elsewhere and into a discourse on the history of the Code. She was aware, also, of pain, but it was a thin sensation, all but lost in the thunder of instruction.

Learning Module, she thought, eyes open against the blackness within the unit. *But, why am I Learning the preface to the Code?*

She moved her right hand along the wall of the unit—and found the hole where the end-session toggle should have been.

Ran Eld, she thought, experiencing a rather unnerving desire to laugh. *Does he think being Code-wise will make me less insistent upon seeing the delm?*

Any desire to laugh faded, then, as memory provided the instant; the feel of her hand cracking across her brother's face.

Oh, gods.

Ran Eld had put her in the Learning Module and taken away the deadman switch. He meant her stay until he let her out. And he meant her to have Learned proper respect by the time she was allowed to emerge.

Or he meant her to be dead.

People could die of brain-burn. There had been a student—not, mercifully, one of hers—who had tried to use a Learning Module to cram for a critical test. Six hours in the Module, the needle set at maximum intensity . . .

The thought jellied and slid away, lost in momentary thunder: ". . . newly-formed Council of Clans . . ."

Aelliana went—elsewhere.

ONE'S DELM WAS NOT AMUSED.

"You are plagued by ill dreams," she repeated. "And the Healers are unable to succor you."

Samiv bowed. "In essence, ma'am. The Master at the Solcintra Hall had nothing better than the cure given by the Healer on *Luda Soldare*: look upon the face of that which frightens me and make— a peace." She drew a careful breath, aware that Bindan had very little tolerance for weakness even when an alliance with Korval Itself was not at risk.

"The Healers inform me, ma'am, that this is an old, ungentle cure, but efficacious."

"I see." Bindan's frown had not eased. "One is unaccustomed to counting you timid, and so naturally the question arises: what has birthed this enormous fear? Korval? I did not hide from you that he is odd. His entire clan is thus and has been, clear back to Pilot Cantra.

"Korval's *melant'i* is impeccable—they have sworn to insure your health and comfort and to return you safely to your kin at contract's end. If it is himself. . ." She lifted a shoulder. "I grant he is no beauty, but I had always thought you too intelligent to let a pretty face matter more than honor and obedience to your delm."

"It is not," Samiv said, trying to think clearly through the haze of weariness, "that one wishes to cry off the marriage. Only that one desires the delm's permission to—to call upon Korval beforehand, that the cure may begin with all speed."

Bindan moved a hand in negation. "In three days' time, you shall be his wife. Enough time to roust your terrors after the contract is in force."

She had expected nothing else, yet she was so *very* tired, more than half-ill with fatigue . . .

"If the delm pleases. Korval had said he—wished to stand my friend. I do not think he would hold it a miss-throw, did I take the matter to him and . . ."

Bindan's palm hit her desk with a sound like a whip crack. She surged to her feet and Samiv effaced herself, bowing low, but it was too late to redeem the error.

"You *dare*! Upon what date was tel'Izak given into Korval's care? I remind you that tel'Izak belongs to Clan Bindan and that Bindan solves for you!"

"Yes, ma'am," Samiv murmured, head bent to her knees. "Forgive me."

There was silence. Samiv held the bow a heartbeat longer, then straightened, slowly, head pounding. Her delm sighed.

"You are tired," she said. "Go to your room and rest."

Rest. Samiv folded her lips firmly over a wild desire to laugh.

Rather, she bowed respect for the delm, "Ma'am" and retired, as ordered, to her room.

DAAV ATE SPARINGLY of a meal composed chiefly of gall and wormwood, accompanied by fine vintage vinegar.

At the conclusion of this solitary feast, he rose and rang for Mr. pel'Kana, and instructed that august person that he was not at home to callers.

He then retired to his private apartment abovestairs, where he fussed about for some little time, pretending to put things in order, before finally sitting down at his work table.

Lovingly, he fingered over bits of wood and odd pieces of ivory, choosing at last a rough round of bronwood. Carving would reveal soft black and bronze swirls that would show well, so he thought, against her hair. It would also emit a subtle scent that he was certain must please her.

She might wear it, when she went Outworld.

He held the wood in his hand, feeling the weight and the shape of it, considering how best to carve the comb he saw so clearly in his mind's eye. He pulled a paper pad forward, picked up a pen and sketched quickly. Laying the wood aside the sketch, he felt a stir of pleasure.

"Yes," he said, and reached for the roughing blade.

He had been some time at this project when a muted chime

sounded. Glancing up, he saw it was his private line thus demanding his attention.

He lay the wood and knife aside, his heart inexplicably beginning to pound, for surely it was only Er Thom, calling to ask if he would care to eat Prime at Trealla Fantrol.

Yes?" he inquired, touching the stud. Frad looked at him with unwonted seriousness.

"Hullo, darling. I'm afraid we've made a muddle of things."

THE DOME WOULD NOT OPEN.

Aelliana fought down the urge to beat at it with her fists—a waste of her strength—and of time.

Time was her enemy. The longer she stayed locked into the program, the more certain the chance of damage or death. She could not know that Ran Eld meant her to die—his intent was meaningless to the equation of destruction she saw looming before her. Unless—

Her thoughts staggered; reformed beneath the voice of the program:

". . . heir or assignee of Captain Cantra yos'Phelium shall be acknowledged to hold the rank of Captain and bear the burden of the passengers' well-being . . .

". . . shall continue until such time as the Houses of Solcintra or that ruling body which may succeed it revoke, cancel or otherwise make null and void this . . ."

The thunder began to fizz; she felt her bruised attention slip and thankfully crossed over to that other place which was neither sleep nor waking.

". . . IT NEVER OCCURRED TO ME that she *didn't* know who you were," Frad said. "We tried to get her to rouse you, but she'd have none of it, and—forgive me—it began to seem like bed-sport gone awry. In any wise, darling, here's Jon telling us she came to him the first time fresh from rough usage, and if you're looking for the villain, I'd advise you to lay money on the nadelm." He made a wry face.

"As it happens, you have money to lay. The pilot left a cantra for you here."

Daav remembered to breathe. "A cantra?"

"Your share, so she tells it, of yesterday's work-fee."

He closed his eyes. "Gods."

"Just so. Now you see what comes of mumming innocents. Do you go?"

"At once." He shook himself and looked into Frad's bland, efficient face. "A car, at the main gate of Korval's Chonselta Yard, in an hour."

Frad inclined his head. "Done."

*... **DIRECT STIMULATION.** The Learning Module utilizes direct-brain stimulation ...*

Conceive the brain as a series of relay stations, engaged or not engaged by thought. The Learning Module targets those stations currently disengaged, fills them sequentially and moves on, in theory allowing each station sufficient opportunity to recover from this assault upon its sensibilities. The Learning Module does not approach those stations engaged in cognition, or those concerned with life support.

Within the darkness of the void, Aelliana reached forth her thought and created a star.

And around this star, she placed a world which ran in elliptical orbit, its rotation rate once in eighteen hours, time of orbit transit, four hundred and eighty-five Standard Days.

To the world, she gave a moon, and to the moon a spin three hundred and four days in duration, while it circled its principal once every twenty-two hours.

She held the little system in her mind, painstakingly calculating each orbit, weighing each relationship, adjusting mass and pull and finally, the spin-rate of the little moon.

When all was stable, balanced and beautiful, she added a second world.

Somewhere, there was thunder. Her concentration wavered, the worlds faltered in their carefully-calculated courses. She caught them, replaced them, checked—rechecked—the relational equations; reconsidered certain mathematical alliances and necessities.

The thunder receded.

In time, she added a third world.

Then a fourth.

She populated the second world, strung space stations like Festival lights, ringed the system with beacons and waystations, created satellites and traffic patterns.

In her head, the numbers danced, the equations pure as poetry.

She spun an asteroid pod, skated it 'round the sun, calculating trajectories, stress breakage, possible strikes upon populated areas.

There was no thunder. There was no Code. There was her creation and the vital necessity to keep all in balance—to calculate and continue to calculate, each nuance and effect.

Aelliana—was.

TEN MINUTES TO CHANGE from house clothes to the formal costume appropriate for one delm's official call upon another. Daav knotted the silver ribbon in his hair, caught up his cloak and was gone, the door to his apartment snapping closed behind him.

Dragon's Cub was free-berthed beyond the formal gardens. It was barely more than a Jump-buggy, but it would do very well for this particular mission. He would worry about assuaging his gardener's injured feelings once he knew Aelliana was well.

He was moving down the main hallway at just under a run, when Mr. pel'Kana stepped out of the smaller receiving parlor.

"If your lordship pleases."

Daav shook his head. "I am in great haste. Pray make my excuses to whomever has called."

But Mr. pel'Kana did not bow obedience. Rather, he extended a hand, fingers curled in supplication.

"Please, Master Daav," he said, softly. "I think you will want to speak to the lady."

He blinked, catching himself in mid-stride. "Lady?"

Aelliana? Had she discovered him after all and come to ask his aid, while Jon and Frad and Clonak fretted for her safety? He changed course and swept into the parlor.

Samiv tel'Izak spun away from her contemplation of the mantle—or possibly of Korval's shield, hung above it—and came three steps toward him, one hand outflung.

"Please," she said, voice none too steady in the mode of Comrades. "Please, I—you must help me."

CHAPTER THIRTY-FIVE

The cops called young Tor An to bail me out, which he did, right enough, and all according to copilot's duty. When we were free of the place, he read me such a scold as I haven't heard since nursery. Puppy.

He was right, too.

—Excerpted from Cantra yos'Phelium's Log Book

HE CHECKED, and in that moment took note of her face, which was strained, pale, with black circles under her eyes, her muscles etched in exhaustion.

"Samiv, what has happened?" He hardly thought, answering Comrade with Comrade.

"I . . ." Her eyes filled and she glanced aside, blinking. "Forgive me."

"Freely—and you must return the grace at once. I am in desperate haste. Word has come that—one to whom I sit copilot may be in peril. I must be gone in moments."

She was a pilot: Guild rule was as natural to her as breath. Her eyes leapt to his.

"Of course, you must go at once! I will—" She gasped, eyes widening.

629

"Hold, you say *the Caylon* is in peril?"

Daav lifted an eyebrow. "And who told you, I wonder, that I am the Caylon's copilot?"

She moved a hand. "The tape was on in the Guildroom when I came through. In what way is she imperilled?"

Daav felt his face tighten. "An illegal attempt was made to seal her ship. Last report was that she had gone to treat with the party involved. Who is known to have beaten her in the past."

He had not thought it possible for Samiv to pale further.

"I see," she said, flatly. "Who flies with you?"

"There is only myself here, and to tarry even for my *cha'leket* seemed wasteful of minutes."

"Which I have now wasted for you." She moved forward, resolute. "By your leave, I will sit your second. If the peril is extreme, I may be of use."

And so she might be, he allowed, *if Aelliana* . . .

"Quickly, then," he said, and spun toward the door.

RAN ELD DID NOT COME DOWN TO PRIME, but was served in his apartment, as was his custom when the delm was from home. Voni sat at the head of the table, as was *her* custom when the delm was from home, though she displayed appetite for neither her dinner nor the game of correcting her junior's manners. But, thought Sinit, it might be that she pined for her favorite target of ridicule.

Sinit considered asking after news of Aelliana's return. Indeed, she spent some minutes as she drank her soup, examining phrasing appropriate to the task. In the end, however, nothing seemed quite safe enough to venture. She did not think either Voni or Ran Eld knew of the amazing and adventurous life Aelliana lived, over on the other side of the world, as neither was an aficionado of the news wires, and they would not, Sinit vowed, hear of it from her.

It was of course, terribly exciting to learn that Aelliana *regularly* flew with Daav yos'Phelium, as reported on the pilot's wire. Sinit had taken advantage of her trip the library that afternoon to look Daav yos'Phelium up in the newest edition of the Book of Clans.

Korval Himself sat copilot to Aelliana, which was honor to

Mizel, but Voni would only see that Korval's attention belonged to her and Aelliana had stolen her rights. Ran Eld would say something vile and perhaps slap Aelliana for rising above her place. Ran Eld *did* strike Aelliana, Sinit had seen him do so, twice, no matter if the delm chose to hear of it.

"This dinner is vile!" Voni snapped from the head of the table. "Really, the cook takes liberties with my good nature when the delm is from home!" She rose, flinging her napkin into her soup bowl.

"*You* may continue, if you can stomach such swill!" she told Sinit. "I shall retire to my room. I have a headache. Pray, disturb me for no one!"

Sinit looked up at her. "All right. May I have your popover, then? Mine was excellent."

"Repellant brat," Voni uttered, and swept tragically from the room.

STRAIGHT FROM THE LAWN THEY LIFTED, the little craft hurtling upward with no such niceties as gradual acceleration. Korval flew a brutal course, at a trajectory only a Scout would think sane. Samiv kept her board, exhaustion dissolved by adrenaline.

"Can you tell me now," he said softly, hands quick and certain on his controls, "what it is I must help you resolve?"

She swallowed, eyes on the readouts, and it helped, someway, not to have to meet his gaze as she said it.

"I . . . dream. Frightening dreams. The Healers—send me to face my terror."

There was a small pause. "Which is myself?"

"No." She licked her lips. "I—believe—it is your Tree." She took a breath, fighting tears that came all too easily, these last days. "I resigned my contract on *Luda Soldare*—I could not sleep, my reactions are—in question. I could not endanger the ship . . ."

"Of course not," he agreed and it was uncannily comforting, hearing that said in his deep, rough voice. Samiv closed her eyes briefly, opened them again to the necessity of her board.

"One's delm desires the alliance, of course. I—I would ask your leave to—before the lines are signed—to approach the Tree and— and assure myself that it is—only—a tree."

"Ah. But it is not, you know, *only* a tree." He was silent for a moment, then, "Is your delm aware that you have brought this to me?"

She looked over to him; saw only the side of his face, and the quick, sure hands on the board.

"My delm is—certain—the dreams will abate, once the contract is signed."

"I see." He sighed, and flicked her another of his bold, uninforming looks. "Your board to me, if you will. Thank you. In regard to our present mission—there is a firearm in the pocket beside you. It would be best to check it now, so there are no surprises, if you must use it."

She stared at him, at the eyes that told her nothing. "You think—"

He moved his head from side to side. "We may find that all is well, in which case we will merely be called upon to drink tea and display our manners."

Samiv pulled the gun from its nest. "But you do not expect that."

"I don't," he said gently. "All my life, I've been plagued by hunches. From time to time, one does prove to be merely indigestion." He cast her a glance that seemed rather too full of amusement. "Korval *is* mad, you know."

Samiv looked down and cracked the gun.

SOMEWHERE IN THE BEATITUDE OF EQUATIONS, a chime sounded. Sometime later, there was light.

Aelliana detached a portion of her attention from the problem of the retrograde planet and raised heavy arms, stiff fingers groping against—nothing.

The dome of the Learning Module was open. It took a moment to understand the significance of that.

She was free.

Free belonged to the subset of things which are precious beyond rubies.

Aelliana flung herself up, crying out as her body simultaneously reported every bruise she had gained from her encounter with her brother, and the additional information that she was hideously thirsty.

The room reeled. She clawed the staggered data into sense, lurched toward a low table, hefted a heavy vase full of wilting flowers and lurched back to the Learning Module.

Flowers and solution went into the program box, which fizzed, smoked and popped. She raised the vase in both hands, swung it at the control dials. Her first attempt failed to connect; the force of the missed blow kicked her legs out from under her and she went face-first into the carpet.

Gagging, she clawed her way to her knees, got her hands around the vase once more and smashed at the controls.

The blow connected, hard enough to dent the faceplate. Aelliana whimpered, the controls twisting in and out of perspective. She raised the vase, staring at the main dial, forcing herself to see it through the images that flickered and flashed before her mind's eye. The dial steadied and she swung with all her might.

Glass broke, instrumentation screamed, shrilly, and went silent.

Aelliana dropped the vase, hung onto the edge of the Learning Module and lurched to her feet, staring round at a room that spun out of sense, objects pulsating, edges attenuating into nothingness, the image of a star system she had never seen superimposed over everything and she struggled—struggled to recall. Something. Something—important.

It was dim in the room . . . dark outside the gaping window. Something. Numbers, strung together in the shape of a personal comm code, and a deep, beloved voice, whispering from memory, "Call me, Aelliana, should you have need . . ."

There was a comm in the study. She knew that. Over—over by the window. Yes. She could see the window, through the pulsating stars. First one foot . . .

She fell over a table, lost her balance and hit the floor amid an avalanche of bric-a-brac. Panting, she got to her knees, oriented herself and crawled the rest of the way to the window. Once there, she pulled herself upright with the aid of a built-in bookcase, put her hand flat on its top surface and inched forward, feeling for the comm.

Her fingers touched cool plastic. She bit her lip. Numbers. Daav's comm code. All she need do was code the number into the comm, here beneath her hand. Daav would help her.

Thought formed. There was danger. Danger in using the house comm. Scouts. Ran Eld. Ran Eld would harm Daav.

She must not call.

CHAPTER THIRTY-SIX

I ran copilot for Garen 'til she broke her skull, and the ship came to me, complete with a full load of trouble. I was young enough then to believe my skull was too hard to break—opted to run solo, and take care of the troubles as I met them.

I wasn't looking for a copilot the night I found Jela, though I was old enough by then to know I could die. What I wanted was a glass and a roll in the blankets—one glass, one roll and an early lift out, headed for the Rim with a load of don't-you-care.

Funny, how even simple plans so often fail to work.

—Excerpted from Cantra yos'Phelium's Log Book

SINIT WAS CURLED IN THE ROUND CHAIR in the front parlor, reading. Chonselta City Library had only today placed on its shelves *In Support of the Commonality of Language* by Learned Scholar Anne Davis and Sinit had been fortunate enough to engage it.

Language and the roots of language had their places in the larger art of anthropology and she read with absorption. Indeed, she read with so much attention to the work that it was not the first, but the second sounding of the doorchime that roused her.

Blinking, she uncurled, taking care to mark her place, and pull on her houseboots. She straightened her tunic on the way to the entry hall and tucked her hair behind her ears.

The bell sounded once more.

From above-stairs came the noise of a door opening, feet thumping along thin carpeting, and Voni's voice, wondering: "Whoever could be calling this late in the day?"

Sinit opened the front door.

The taller of the two visitors bowed as the porch light came up, cloak shimmering around him: Visitor to the House, Sinit read, and inclined her head.

"Speak."

Black eyes looked down at her from a stark, clever face; his dark hair was pulled back and secured with a silver ribbon, an end of which lay across his shoulder. A twist of silver was in the right ear; there a flash of slick enameled colors as he brought his left hand up in the age-old gesture and showed her.

Tree-and-Dragon.

"I have the honor to be Korval," he said in the mode of Announcement. He gestured toward his companion. "Pilot Samiv tel'Izak."

Sinit barely attended. Korval. Korval *here*, in the company of a second pilot, who must surely be another of Aelliana's comrades. Yet, if they were come here—

"But," she blurted, looking from his eyes to the smooth, careful face of his companion. "Aelliana is not to House, sir—Pilot. I had thought—*surely*—she is at—at Solcintra?"

They exchanged a glance, the two on the porch, and Sinit caught her breath, afraid suddenly, though not of them.

"Please," she said, backing away and pulling the door wide. "Please, come in. I—"

"Sinit, whatever are you doing?" Voni demanded peevishly from above. Sinit spun, squinting through the dimness toward the landing.

"These gentles are here to speak with Aelliana, sister. Pray, ask her to come down."

There was a moment of shocked silence, then the sound of

footsteps, going swiftly back up the stairs. Sinit felt her knees go weak.

"She must have come in while I was reading," she said, shakily, and pushed the door closed. "Doubtless, she will be here in a moment to greet you. Would you care to step into the parlor, gentles? Refreshment . . ."

Upstairs, a door slammed and the footsteps that pounded hastily down were not Aelliana's. Sinit saw the man know that; saw him convey the knowledge to his comrade with the twitch of a well-marked black brow.

"Callers for Aelliana?" Ran Eld's voice was breathless, but, then, Ran Eld was very little used to running. Sinit went two steps back and to the side, instinctively seeking the shadow of the back hallway. She looked up and directly into the eyes of Pilot tel'Izak. The pilot held her gaze a moment, then turned her head away.

"Who is—ah." The questioner had gained the foyer—a slender and be-ringed young man in a houserobe much too ornate for his surroundings. Samiv frowned as he came into the light. There were marks of paler gold on the man's face, as if he had been scratched and had recent recourse to an autodoc. From the edge of her eye, she saw the halfling doorkeeper fade one more step toward the safety of the hall-shadows.

"I am Nadelm Mizel," the gaudy young man said, inclining his head slightly. "May I know your business, sir, ma'am?"

Korval silently extended his left hand. The Tree-and-Dragon flashed. The nadelm froze, as well he might, then bowed again, ornately.

"The House is honored to receive Korval. How may I serve you?"

Korval did not deign even to incline his head. "I would speak to the House's daughter Aelliana, sir."

"I regret that is not possible," Nadelm Mizel said.

"Ah, I see." Korval said quietly. "In that wise, I will speak with Mizel Herself."

The nadelm spread his hands, rings glittering. "It is my misfortune to disappoint you twice, sir. Mizel is from House."

"That is unfortunate," Korval agreed gravely. "When will she return?"

Relief loosened the haughty shoulders. "Tomorrow midday, by my best information. Shall you call then? Or perhaps Mizel may call upon you?"

"Perhaps we need not embrace either alternative," Korval said, as the elder sister—she who had skittered from the landing—came carefully down the stairs to stand at her nadelm's side. He ignored her.

"When," Korval inquired, "will it be possible to speak with Pilot Scholar Aelliana Caylon?"

The nadelm's lips thinned. "Indeed, sir, Aelliana is the veriest fluttercap! One never knows when she might appear."

In the shadow at the edge of the hallway, the halfling girl jerked—and was still.

Samiv flicked a glance at Korval, but his eyes where all for the nadelm.

"I have never found her thus," he said, meditatively, and the black eyes moved, pinning the elder sister.

"Of your kindness, ma'am, bring me Aelliana, or tell me where I might find her."

The woman fluttered, foolish blue eyes darting this way and that. "Truly, sir, I don't—but it is as Ran Eld says! Aelliana is—she is—" She faltered, staring wildly at her nadelm. "She is—"

"At study," the nadelm said forcefully. "It would be perfectly useless to try and rouse her, sir. Leave your card, and I will see she receives it, when she is sensible again."

Fool, thought Samiv and looked again to the hallway.

The halfling was gone.

"I AM PREPARED TO WAIT," Korval said, fixing the nadelm in his eye, "until Scholar Caylon has completed her study."

The other man's eyes slid aside. "It may be—some time."

"I understand," said Korval. He laced his hands together and moved his eyes to the hall table, his face composed into an expression of gentle meditation.

"See here," Nadelm Mizel said sharply, "you can't just stand in our entrance hall all night—"

The black eyes moved. Gravely, Korval inclined his head.

"Your concern does you credit. I hasten to assure you that it is entirely within my scope to stand in your entrance hall all night— and all of tomorrow, if necessary. However, Pilot tel'Izak would perhaps welcome the use of a chair."

"Thank you," she said, with a composure she was far from feeling. "I am perfectly at my ease."

The nadelm's face tightened in anger. "I do not think you have entirely understood that you are standing within Mizel's own House. I do not—"

"Delm Korval!"

He turned. The halfling who had admitted them to the house skittered to a halt at the mouth of a sidehall, brown eyes wide with terror.

"The Learning Module," she gasped and Daav felt ice down his spine.

"Show me," he said.

She turned and fled back down the hall, he striding after her.

"Halt!" shouted Nadelm Mizel, face suddenly gone pale. "I forbid you to enter any further into Mizel's house!" He flung after Korval and Samiv spun into his path, hand up.

"Hold!"

Snarling, he pushed her aside. She staggered, caught herself and swung before him once more.

"Hold!" she ordered again, gun out and quite steady on his belly. "Proceed at your peril."

THE LEARNING MODULE was empty, the brain-box shorted, the timer shattered, the master controller smashed. The session dial had stopped at five hours. The concentration slide was pushed to the top.

"It makes no sense," the halfling stuttered. "Why would Aelliana wish a maximum intensity review of the Code?"

Excellent question. And he was very sure that the answer

was—*Aelliana* had not. Daav took a deep breath and ran the Scout's Rainbow quickly, bringing both terror and fury down to manageable levels.

"We will be certain to ask her that," he said to Sinit Caylon's frantic face, "when we find her. Have you looked anywhere else? Her rooms?"

"No, sir."

"Do so," he instructed her. "I will see what else may be found here. Quickly. If she has indeed been in the sleep learner for so long a time, she will be—disoriented."

Brain-burned, he amended to himself as Sinit ran from the room. He swallowed against resurgence of terror and began methodically to search the room.

He lingered for a moment by an overturned gidget table, frowning at the trinkets scattered across the rug, then passed on, satisfying himself that delirium had not moved Aelliana to shelter beneath the furniture.

Eventually, he came to the end of the room. There was a comm on the floor beneath the closed window. He bent to pick the unit up and felt a cool breeze kiss his cheek. Straightening, he moved to the window, put his hand flat on the tall center pane and pushed.

The window swung open, soundless on well-oiled hinges. Daav leaned over the sill, a Scout's trained eye picking out the route she had taken through the meager garden, the marks at one consistent height along the length of the worn wooden fence, where she had likely set her shoulder, for balance, and for orientation. The gate at the bottom of the yard stood open, rocking slightly in the night-breeze.

"PIRATE!" NADELM MIZEL SHRIEKED, his face flushed and twisted in rage. "I will see you ruined, outcast and ridiculed! I will—"

Rapid footsteps sounded in the hallway and the halfling flashed by, raced across the foyer without a sideward glance and flung up the stairway, two steps at a time.

"Sinit!" howled the nadelm, but Sinit did not answer.

"Voni!" the nadelm shouted then. "Call the Peacekeepers."

But Voni was sitting on the lower step, head resting on her knees.

Furious, he raised a ring-crusted hand, as if he would strike her. Samiv called his attention to the gun, and he froze, rings glittering—tawdry things for the most part, she saw, all sharp edges and shine.

Except for one. And how had such a tasteless dirt-stomper as Nadelm Mizel come by a Jump-pilot's cluster? she wondered. Such things were priceless—clan treasures, to be locked safe away and brought forth once a twelve-year to marvel upon.

"Samiv." Korval's voice was in her ear. "I have found her trail. She does not appear—well," he said, and she felt a thrill of horror run her spine. "We must overtake her before she comes to more harm."

"Yes," she said. "Go you first while I keep this one—"

The front door clanked and swung ponderously open. A round-faced woman in a travel cloak stepped into the foyer—and froze, as she took in the scene before her.

She swept forward then, raising her hand, so that the Clan Ring was plain to see.

"I have the honor," she said icily, fixing Samiv in her eye, "to be Mizel. You will explain yourselves."

IT WAS DIFFICULT TO TALK; words she did not mean to say fell in abundance from her lips while words she desperately wished to say failed to form themselves.

Still, she had made the taxi driver understand—at least, he drove her to the Pilot's Guildhall in Chonselta Port. She did not think she had precisely asked him to do so, but it was—enough.

"The orbit of the retrograde planet will develop a wobble in approximately ten thousand years," she told him as she fumbled the cantra-piece out of her pocket, "and will fail entirely in eleven thousand."

"Then it's nothing either of us need be concerned of," he replied, pressing the coin firmly back into her palm, and bending her fingers over it, one by one. "Plot a straight course for the dorm, now, Pilot. Time to sleep it off."

"If you are outside a major gravity well you may ignore the pel'Endra Ratio and proceed," Aelliana said gratefully, fingers locked around the cantra.

"I fully intend to proceed, and as quickly as may be," he said. "Hull's cool, Pilot. Out you go."

She managed to disembark and stood trembling on the walkway. The taxi's door began to descend and she said, "Don't tell him you saw me."

The door sealed and the taxi moved slowly away.

Aelliana turned carefully, there being nothing to hold onto here on the walk. She focussed on the doorway, ignoring the random flashes and flarings that had nothing to do with the street before her. Focus established, she moved forward, sliding her feet along the sidewalk, to maintain what balance she might.

She only fell twice before she gained the door.

CHAPTER THIRTY-SEVEN

Duty is not indulgent, nor does it seek vengence.

—Proverb

"SHE'S NOT HERE, SIR!" Sinit's voice came down from the upper floor, closely followed by Sinit herself.

"Mother?" She reached the foyer and made her bow. "Good evening, ma'am. Ran Eld had said you were not expected until tomorrow."

"Well I came tonight," Mizel said coldly. "Are you in a league, Sinit, with pirates who come armed into a clanhouse?"

"Pirates?" Sinit frowned. "Truly, ma'am, Delm Korval and Pilot tel'Izak have called for Aelliana, but she is—she is not to House."

"Learning so, they hold the nadelm at gunpoint. Entirely understandable." Mizel extended her hand. "You will relinquish that weapon to me."

"Forgive me," Samiv said firmly, "but I will not. This person shoved me and then threatened to strike me. I fear for my safety in his presence. More, I fear for Pilot Caylon's safety." She looked up, and Daav saw fury in her eyes. "Did the Caylon wear a Jump-pilot's ring?"

"Yes."

643

Nadelm Mizel took a step back, hand creeping toward his pocket.

"Show it!" Samiv cried. "Show your delm what you wear on your hand!"

"I do not take orders from you!" snarled the nadelm.

"But you do take orders from me," Mizel said, and extended her hand once more. "Let me see this ring, Ran Eld."

Reluctantly, he pulled the cluster from his hand, and laid it in her palm.

"It is a foolishness, ma'am—a bit of paste. I—"

Mizel stared at her palm. "How came you by this?"

The nadelm stood speechless.

"Ran Eld! I ask how you came to have this ring. An answer, if you please."

"It was Aelliana's," the elder sister moaned from her crouch on the bottom stair. She looked up, showing a wet and ravaged face. "He took it off her hand. I saw him. Just before he sealed the lid on the Learner."

IT WAS A SLOW NIGHT at Chonselta Guildhall. Rab Orn and Nil Ten were playing pikit in the common room and Keyn was over in the corner, reading. Beside the occasional hand-bid from the card players, the only noise came from the port comm, a continuous babble so familiar to the three pilots that none consciously heard it.

Nil Ten sighed. "Fold," he muttered, throwing his cards down in a heap. "Glad we're not playing this for cantra."

"We're not?" asked his partner, wide-eyed and the first pilot laughed, looked up and gasped.

Her face was a mottle of cuts and bruises, so swollen the pupil-big eyes could scarcely open. Her hair was snarled in a hopeless knot. She was trembling, visibly and continuously.

"What—" Rab Orn turned in his chair to see, and froze.

"Daav's the card I want to play," the apparition stated, her voice like sand being ground into stone.

"Merciful gods," that was Keyn. She got up out of her chair and came forward, peering into the newcomer's battered face.

"It's the Caylon," she breathed. "I saw her last evening, at

Solcintra, when the Guildmaster gave over her license. Sitting on Korval's lap she was and happy as you please."

"It is the duty of the pilot to protect ship and passengers," Aelliana Caylon said gravely. "It is the duty of the copilot to protect pilot and ship."

The three exchanged glances, then Keyn reached out and touched the other woman's shoulder. "That's right, pilot. Guild rule, plain as plain." She took a deep breath. "Come along with me, and let's get you to a 'doc, eh? Everything's going to be *binjali* . . ."

"*Binjali*." The slitted black eyes locked onto Keyn's face, one trembling hand rose, fumbled and fastened 'round the pilot's wrist.

"Jon dea'Cort." Keyn stared and the Caylon said again, voice rising. "Jon dea'Cort. The retrograde planet will release a hysteresis energy effect proportional to the velocity and spin of Smuggler's Ace, cheese muffins, Daav, efficient function! Call, call if you need me, Aelliana!"

"That's plain." Nil Ten jumped up, oversetting his chair, walked over to the comm and punched in a rapid code. The screen blanked as the unit on the other end chimed, three times, four, five . . .

"Binjali's."

Nil Ten inclined his head to the old pilot in the viewer. "Master dea'Cort. Nil Ten pel'Quida, Chonselta Guildhall, sir. We have one of your crew here, in distress."

MIZEL RAISED HER HEAD, lines showing hard about her mouth and she looked to her son.

"Aelliana's father," she said, speaking in the mode of Instruction, "wore one of these. Other than himself, it was his clan's whole treasure. This ring will ransom a Jump-ship, will it not, Korval?"

"Indeed," Daav said gravely, "that was the purpose behind its making. Ma'am, I beg your pardon. The timer and intensity meter on the Learning Module are frozen at such levels as must cause me extreme alarm. I have found the course Aelliana charted, out the window and through the back gate. She—she is very likely brain-burned, ma'am, and I fear for her life if we do not go after her at once."

"Yes." Mizel looked up at him. "I am correct in thinking that your personal name is Daav?"

"It is."

"So." She held out the Pilot's Cluster. "You will safeguard this and return it to my daughter when you find her. I will do—what is discovered to be necessary—here. Pray inform me of—your progress. Should she return here—" Her mouth tightened. "But you will know where she is most likely to go."

Daav inclined his head, slipping the ring into the inner pocket of his cloak. "If she should return here, ma'am, leave word with Master dea'Cort at Binjali Repair Shop, Solcintra Port." He glanced over to Samiv, who slipped her gun away.

"Will you help me search?"

"I demand the honor," she replied, and followed him down the hallway.

HE TRACKED HER DOWN THE ALLEY, following the path her shoulder had smoothed against splintered fencing. He found the places where she had fallen, the places where she had crawled until she found a fence post, an arbor or a tree to cling to and drag herself up to her feet.

The alley was intersected by a street; on the other side there was no sign of her passage. He and Samiv recrossed the street, she went right and he to the left, looking for a hint, a footprint, a thread.

A thread.

A snag of bold blue, caught in the rust of a sign pole. He cast out, moving in a gradually widening circle around that whisper of hope, but found nothing else. Defeated, he returned to the pole.

Had the Peacekeepers seen her, ill-balanced as she was, and born her away to their Guildhall? But, surely, she would told them her name, her clan?

Or, he thought with a shiver, perhaps not. Brain-burned, she might not recall such things.

Where would she go, if she were able to recall herself?

Binjali's, no doubt.

But in such a condition as he had seen, falling flat when there was no wall to support her? She might, he supposed, flag a taxi, but Aelliana rarely had more than a few dex in her pocket . . .

The hum of a motor brought him to a sense of his surroundings and he turned to see a cab moving slowly up the street. Apparently the cabbie noted his interest, for the vehicle pulled to the curb and the passenger door rose.

"Service, your Lordship?"

"Information," he said, bending down to look at the driver. He pulled a cantra out of his pocket. "I am in search of a friend—a fair-haired lady, very slender. Green eyes. She would have perhaps been confused in her direction and—unsteady on her feet—" The cabbie stiffened, but said nothing. After a moment, Daav murmured.

"You have seen her."

The man moved his shoulders, leaned forward to make an adjustment on his board. "I saw her," he said, and the look he gave Daav was hard and straight. "Took her up-city. Set her down at Commerce Square."

Commerce Square? The opposite direction of the Port. Daav frowned, considering the man's face, almost tasting the lie. And yet . . .

"You must forgive me if I ask again," he murmured, hearing Samiv coming down the walkway from his right. "I am the lady's copilot and I fear she is—very ill. Perhaps she was not—precisely as I had said. Perhaps she had been hurt, eh? And you think you are looking at the cause. I beg you tell me if you took her to Port. I tell you plainly that I fear for her life, should she board ferry for Solcintra."

The cabbie hesitated, then. "I'll see your hands."

Wondering, Daav held them out. Korval's Ring gleamed in the cabin light. The cabbie stared a long moment, then raised his eyes.

"That wouldn't have done the damage I saw. You want stones for that kind of work." He sighed and looked away. "I took her down to the Pilot's Guild, and I'll tell you right now she wasn't making no sense."

✧ ✧ ✧

MIZEL LOOKED AT THE DEEDS of transfers in her hands. Two deeds of transfers, each from Aelliana Caylon to Ran Eld Caylon: one for an Ormit Shares account, one for a spaceship named *Ride the Luck*. Both were signed.

Neither signature was Aelliana's.

"Voni has already confessed to signing these in her sister's stead," Mizel said, her eyes still on those damning papers. "I have seen, I think, enough. While it is possible that your sister Aelliana has survived your use of her—while it is possible, though not probable, that she has survived *intact*—the delm cannot but see that your actions are consistent with a deliberate and knowing desire to take what was not rightfully yours, counting no cost too high. Not even your sister's death."

Mizel raised her head and stared at the man standing before her desk. A man dressed for traveling and not in the first style of elegance. The cloak was serviceable but shabby. The shirt and trousers had been made for him, but some time ago. The boots—would be a difficulty for him. He wore no jewelry. His face was pale.

"Mizel does not sanction kinslaying. Having shown yourself capable of such horror, the delm is unable to do otherwise than declare you dead. You will leave this house now. At once. You will never return. You have no call upon Mizel. You are clanless and outcast."

The man before her bowed his head.

"Because you were once my son, I give you somewhat to take away with you. The clothes you stand in. A cantra-piece." She reached into the desk drawer, removed the keepsafe that had belonged to her mother and the half-gone box of pellets. "A weapon."

Ran Eld looked up, face wet with tears. She put gun and ammunition on the desk. After a moment, he picked them up. Mizel inclined her head and stood.

"I will escort you to the door."

He walked silent beside her down the hall, silent across the foyer. When she opened the door, he turned, but she averted her face and in a moment heard him walk down the steps, whereupon she closed the door and locked it.

Duty done, Mizel gave way to Birin Caylon, whose son had just now died, she lay her cheek against the inner door—and mourned his passing.

CHAPTER THIRTY-EIGHT

He found it in a desert, so he told me—the only living thing in two days' walk. A skinny stick with a couple leaves near the top, that's all it was then.

I don't remember the name of the world it came from. He might not have told me. Wherever it was, when his Troop finally picked him up, Jela wouldn't leave 'til he'd dug up that damned skinny stick of a tree and planted it real careful in an old ration tin. Carried it in his arms onto transport. And nobody dared to laugh.

—Excerpted from Cantra yos'Phelium's Log Book

"YES," the doorkeeper at Chonselta Healer Hall sighed, stepping back to allow them inside. "Jon dea'Cort had said you would be here and that it was out of his power to prevent you." He closed the door and beckoned. Silent, they followed him down a short hallway and into a small parlor.

"There is wine on the sideboard, and filled bread. Hall Master will be down to speak to you very soon. In the meanwhile, I am asked to convey to Pilot yos'Phelium the Master's most urgent plea for serenity. We have novices in-Hall." He bowed and left them, the door swinging shut on his heels.

In the center of the room, Korval sighed, then turned, looking down at her from eyes as giving as obsidian.

"Shall you wish refreshment, Pilot?" he asked, with a gentleness she would not have expected, from such eyes. "Seat yourself, I beg. I have used you cruelly this evening, when you are already in pain through my ineptitude. At least, let me bring you a cup of wine."

"Thank you," Samiv said, moving to a doublechair and sinking into the soft cushions with bleary gratitude. "I believe I will sit, but I do not think wine . . ."

The door swung open and a white-haired woman in plain shirt and trousers stepped into the chamber. She bowed, briefly.

"Chonselta Hall Master Ethilen. Pray, Pilot tel'Izak, do not trouble yourself to rise. Recruit your strength." She turned her face toward the man in the center of the room.

"Well, Korval?"

"Not well, Master Ethilen," he replied. "You have Aelliana Caylon in keeping here. The report I have of her condition from the pilots at Chonselta Guild is—terrifying. I will see her, of your kindness."

"Alas."

Samiv saw Korval's shoulders tense, though his voice was as calm as always.

"She had wanted me, said the pilots at Guildhall. I would show her she is not abandoned by one in whom she placed trust. I am her copilot. I have this right."

"Masters Kestra and Tom Sen are with Pilot Caylon. I cannot allow interference of their work at this juncture. The report you have from the pilot's guild-fellows appears overstated. It is in her best interest that her copilot allow himself to be satisfied with this preliminary information and retire to Solcintra."

"I—"

"Korval, you are blinding the House," the old woman said sternly, and held up a hand. "Yes, I See that you are attempting to control yourself, and I thank you most sincerely for the effort. Without it, my shielding would not be sufficient to allow me to stand in the same room with you and converse. However, no amount of converse will deliver you to Pilot Caylon's side this evening. Believe me in verymost earnest." She sighed and lowered her hand.

"Daav, go home. Come again tomorrow. She will love you no less then."

There was a moment of silence charged so strongly Samiv felt the hairs rise on her arm. Then, Korval swept a bow to the old Healer.

"Tomorrow, Master Ethilen, I am not denied."

She inclined her head.

Samiv got her feet under her and rose, muzzy-headed and aching.

"Pilot."

She looked up into a face utterly without expression. Korval offered his arm.

"Allow me to take you to your delm."

SHE SAT IN THE COPILOT'S CHAIR, but her board was dark. Korval flew, silent, as he had been since leaving Healer Hall.

"Samiv," he said, and she started, though he spoke gently.

She straightened against the webbing and looked to him, seeing the side of his face, the quick, clever fingers, moving among his instruments.

"Yes, Pilot?"

He glanced over to her—lightless eyes in a hewn-gold face—then went back to his board. "I wish you will tell me true. May you?"

She licked her lips. "Yes."

"Good," he murmured. "I wish to know if you, of your own will and heart, desire this marriage which is promised to your delm."

Of her own will and heart. A Scout's question, phrased as if one's own will and heart had place within the weavings of kin and duty. And yet . . .

"If I were—my own delm—I would not seek the marriage," she said slowly, feeling along those unaccustomed threads of personal desire. "I—forgive me . . ."

"I had asked," he said softly. "There is no need to ask forgiveness for truth, among comrades, eh?"

"Just so." She took a breath, hands fisted on her lap. "Truly, Korval, I find I—like—you much more than ever I—But I do not think that we should—that we should—*suit*," she finished, somewhat helplessly.

"Ah." More silence, and she sat back into the chair. It came to her to wonder what her delm might think, could she hear Samiv in such a conversation with her affianced husband, and hiccuped a laugh.

"Are you able to bear some little of your delm's displeasure?" he asked abruptly. "I swear that I will take all that I might to myself. But she is bound to be displeased with you."

"She is displeased with me now," Samiv said blearily. "I was never to have come to ask your aid, you know."

"I see. In that wise, I believe we may win you free of the Tree's attentions, Pilot. You need only stand firm and quiet. And swear me one thing."

She blinked. "What shall I swear?"

He looked at her, one dark brow up. "Come to me, when your delm's anger has cooled, and let us finish Balance between us."

"Korval, there is nothing owing. I—"

"I must beg you to allow me to know the extent of my own debt," he interrupted, all stern-voiced and by-the-Code. Samiv strangled a rising giggle and managed to incline her head.

"As you will, sir. When I may, I will come to you, in order to complete Balance. My word upon it."

"Thank you," said Korval, and flicked up the comm toggle.

"*THIS* IS YOUR NOTION OF PROPRIETY?" Delm Bindan demanded. "Of withholding from scandal? Of safety and respect for Bindan's treasure? I suppose it a mere trifle for you, Korval, nothing higher than a lark! Certainly, go to the opposite end of the world for your mischief, force yourself into a clanhouse, hold a nadelm at gunpoint, subvert the youth and steal away the second daughter! Amusing in the extreme, I make no doubt! Certainly, Delm Guayar thought the news delicious. He called while I was yet at breakfast to share it with me. I could have hidden my face!

"And *you*—" She turned her eyes to Samiv.

"I have only respect," Daav murmured, "for the honor and the fortitude of Samiv tel'Izak, who stood staunch, as a troth-wife must and—"

"Troth-wife!" Bindan spun. "If you dare believe, after last evening's escapade, that I will allow one of Bindan to risk herself and her honor in support of your mad whim—Good-day, sir! Your man of business will hear from mine."

Had he not been frantic to return to Chonselta, he would have laughed aloud. Clonak's father had done his work with admirable thoroughness. And, doubtless, he thought wryly, enjoyed every moment of it.

He bowed to Bindan's outraged face. "Good-day, ma'am. Pilot. Sleep well."

"If your lordship," Bindan's butler murmured from the doorway, "will attend me. I will escort you to the door."

CHARGED WITH UNEXPENDED ADRENALINE, Daav strode across the glade, laid both palms against the trunk and glared up into the branches.

"You may give over terrorizing Samiv tel'Izak," he said, voice shaking. "She and I will not wed."

The bark beneath his hands warmed. "Yes, very good!" he snarled, snatching his hands away. "Approve me, do! What shall it mean to you, that a fine pilot was all but destroyed for your whim? What shall any of us mean to you, who has seen us all die—from Jela to Chi! Breed-stock, are we? Then hear me well!"

He was in the center of the glade now, with no clear notion of how he had gotten there, hands fisted at his sides, shouting up into the branches as if the ancient, alien sentience cared—had ever cared—for his puny, human anguish.

"I shall lifemate Aelliana Caylon, if she will have me, and if you dare—dare!—frighten or in any way discontent her, I will chop you down with my own hands!"

His words hung for a moment, and were gone, swallowed by the still, warm air. Daav took a breath—another—deliberately relaxed his fists . . .

In the height of the branches, something moved.

He tensed, recalling the torrent of trash that had greeted Samiv tel'Izak, thinking that the Tree could easily and with no harm to itself loose a branch onto his unprotected head, thus disposing of a breed-line that had failed of its promise.

The noise grew louder. Daav crouched, ready to leap in any direction.

And fell to his knees as dozens of seed-pods cascaded around him.

CHAPTER THIRTY-NINE

The heart keeps its own Code.

—**Anonymous**

THE DOORKEEPER showed him to a private parlor, served him wine and left him alone, murmuring that the Master would be with him soon.

The wine was sweet and sat ill on a stomach roiled with fear. He set it aside after a single sip and paced the length of the room, unable to sit decently and await his host.

Behind him, the door opened, and he spun, too quickly. Master Healer Kestra paused on the threshold and showed her hands, palms up and empty, eyebrows lifted ironically.

Ignoring irony, Daav bowed greeting, counting time as he had not done since he was a halfling, throttling pilot speed down to normality, though his nerves screamed for speed.

The Healer returned his bow with an inclination of her head and walked over to the clustered chairs. She arranged herself comfortably in one and looked up at him, face neutral.

"Well, Korval."

He drifted a few paces forward. "Truly, Master Kestra?"

She waved impatiently at the chair opposite her. "I will not be stalked, sir! Sit, sit! And be *still*, for love of the gods! You're loud enough to give an old woman a headache—and to no purpose. She's fine."

His knees gave way and, perforce, he sat. "Fine."

"Oh, a little burn—nothing worrisome, I assure you! For the most part, the Learner never touched her. She knew her danger quickly and crafted her protection well. She created herself an obsession: an entire star system, which required her constant and total concentration—I should say, calculation!—to remain viable." She smiled, fondly, so it seemed to Daav. "Brilliant! The Learning Module will not disturb rational cognition." She moved her shoulders.

"Tom Sen and I removed the obsession, and placed the sleep upon her. We did not consider, under the circumstances, that it was wise to erase painful memory, though we did put—say, we caused those memories to feel *distant* to her. Thus she remains wary, yet unimpeded by immediate fear." Another ripple of her shoulders.

"For the rest, she passed a few hours in the 'doc for the cuts and bruises. I spoke with her not an hour ago and I am well-satisfied with our work."

Daav closed his eyes. She was *well*. He was trembling, he noted distantly, and his chest burned.

"Korval?"

He cleared his throat, opened his eyes and inclined his head. "Accept my thanks," he said, voice steady in the formal phrasing.

"Certainly," Kestra murmured, and paused, the line of a frown between her brows.

"You should be informed," she said, abruptly, and Daav felt a chill run his spine.

"Informed?" he repeated, when several seconds had passed and the Healer had said no more. "Is she then not—entirely—well, Master Kestra?"

She moved a hand—half-negation. "Of this most recent injury, you need have no further concern. However, there was another matter—a trauma left untended. Scar tissue, you would say."

"Yes," he murmured, recalling. "She had said she thought it— too late—to seek a Healer."

"In some ways, she was correct," Kestra admitted. "Much of the damage has been integrated into the personality grid. On the whole, good use has been made of a bad start—she's strong, never doubt it. I did what I could, where the scars hindered growth." She sighed lightly and sat back in her chair.

"The reason I mention the matter to you is that I find—an anomaly—within Scholar Caylon's pattern."

Daav frowned. "Anomaly?"

The Healer sighed. "Call it a—seed pattern. It's set off in a—oh, a *cul-de-sac!*—by itself and it bears no resemblance whatsoever to the remainder of her pattern. Although I have seen a pattern remarkably like it, elsewhere."

"Have you?" Daav looked at her. "Where?"

Master Healer Kestra smiled wearily, raised a finger and pointed at the vacant air just above his head.

"There."

It took a moment to assimilate, wracked as he was. "You say," he said slowly, "that Aelliana and I are—true lifemates."

Kestra sighed. "Now, of that, there is some doubt. The seed-pattern was found in the area of densest scarring." She looked at him closely, her eyes grave.

"You understand, the damage in that area of her pattern was—enormous. Had a Healer been summoned at the time of trauma—however, we shall not weep over spilt wine! I have—pruned away what I could of the scar tissue. At the least, she will be easier for it—more open to joy. That the seed will grow now, after these years without nurture—I cannot say that it will happen."

He stared at her, seeing pity in her eyes. His mind would not quite hold the information—Aelliana. She *was* his destined lifemate—the other half of a wizard's match. He was to have shared with Aelliana what Er Thom shared with his Anne . . . She had been hurt—several times hurt—grievously hurt and no one called to tend her, may Clan Mizel dwindle to dust in his lifetime!

He drew a deep breath, closed his eyes, reached through the anger and the anguish, found the method he required and spun it into place.

He was standing in a circle of pure and utter peace, safe within that secret soul-place where anger never came, and sorrow shifted away like sand.

"And who," Kestra demanded, "taught you that?"

He opened his eyes, hand rising to touch his earring. "The grandmother of a tribe of hunter-gatherers, on a world whose name I may not give you." He peered through the bright still peace; located another scrap of information: "She said that I was always—busy— and so she taught me to—be still."

"All honor to her," Kestra murmured.

"All honor to her," Daav agreed and rose on legs that trembled very little, really. "May I see Aelliana now?"

THE ROOM WAS SUN-FILLED and fragrant, with wide windows giving onto the Healers' extensive gardens. She stood in the open window, looking out on the rows of flowers—a slender woman in a long green robe, her tawny hair caught back with a plain silver hair-ring.

He made no noise when he entered, but she turned as if she had heard him, a smile on her face and her eyes gloriously green.

"Daav," she said, and walked into his arms.

CONFLICT OF HONORS

Maidenstairs Plaza
Local Year 1002
Standard 1375

EIGHT CHANTS PAST MIDSONG: TWILIGHT.

In the plaza around Maidenstairs a crowd began to gather: men and women in brightly colored work clothes; here and there the sapphire or silver flutter of Circle robes.

The last echo of Eighthchant faded from the blank walls of Circle House, and the crowd quieted expectantly.

In a thin pass-street halfway down the plaza, a slim figure stirred. She adjusted the cord of the bag over her shoulder, but her eyes were fixed on Maidenstairs, where two of the Inmost Circle stood.

The shorter of the two raised her arms, calling for silence. The crowd held its breath, while across the plaza a dust devil swirled to life. The watcher in the by-street shivered, hunching closer to the wall.

"We are gathered," cried the larger of the two upon the stairs, "to commend to the Mother the spirit of our sister, our daughter, our friend. For there is gone from us this day the one called Moonhawk." He raised his arms as the other lowered hers to intone the second part of the ritual.

"Do not grieve, for Moonhawk is gathered into the care of She who is Mother of us all, who will instruct and make her ready for her next stay among us. Rejoice, indeed, and be made glad by the fortune of our sister Moonhawk, called so soon to the Mother's side."

The crowd spoke a faint "Ollee," and the shorter Witch continued, her voice taking on the mesmerizing quality appropriate to the speaking of strong magic.

"Gone to the Mother, to learn and to grow, Moonhawk walks among us no more. For the span of a full lifetime shall she sit at the feet of the Mother, absorbing the glory, seen by us no more. In this Wheel-turn none shall see Moonhawk again. She is gone. So mote it be."

"So mote it be," echoed the larger speaker.

"So mote it be," the crowd cried, full-voiced and on familiar ground.

The slim watcher said nothing at all, though she ducked a little farther back into the byway. The dust devil found her there and made momentary sport of her newly shorn hair before going in search of other amusements.

A tall woman at the edge of the crowd made a sharp movement, quickly arrested. The watcher leaned forward, lips shaping a word: *Mother*. She dropped back, the word unspoken.

It was useless. Moonhawk was dead, by order of she who was Moonhawk's mother during this turn of the Wheel. The funeral pyre of her possessions had been ignited at Midsong while the mother looked on with icy face and sand-dry eyes. The watcher had been there, too. She had cried—perhaps enough for the mother, as well. But there were no tears now.

In the bag over her shoulder were such belongings as she had been able to bring away from her cell in the Maidens' wing of Circle House. The clothes she wore were bought in a secondhand store near the river: a dark, soft shirt with too-long sleeves that chafed nipples unused to confinement; skintight leggings, also dark, except for the light patch at the right knee; and outworlder boots with worn heels. The earrings were her own, set in place years ago by old hands trembling with pride of her. The seven silver bracelets in the pack were not hers. In the shirt's sleeve pocket was a single coin: a Terran tenbit.

The two of the Inmost Circle left the stairs; the crowd fragmented and grew louder. The watcher quietly faded down the skinny by-street, trying to form some less desperate plan for the future.

Moonhawk is dead. So mote it be.

At the end of the by-street the watcher turned left, toward a distant reddish glow.

You might, she thought to herself diffidently, go to the Silent Sisters at Caleitha. They won't ask your name, or where you're from, or why you've come. You can stay with them, never speaking, never leaving the Sisterhouse, never touching another human being. . . .

"I'd rather be dead!" she snapped at the night, at herself—and began to laugh.

The sound was horrible in her ears: jagged, unnatural. She knotted her fingers in the ridiculous mop of curls, yanking until tears came to replace the awful laughter. Then she continued on her way, the rosy glow ever brighter before her.

Shipyear 32
Tripday 148
Second Shift
10.30 Hours

"LIADENS! GODS-BENIGHTED, smooth-faced lying sons and daughters of *curs!"*

A crumpled wad of clothing was thrown toward the gapemouthed duffel with more passion than accuracy. From her station by the cot, Priscilla fielded it and gently dropped it in the bag. This act failed to draw Shelly's usual comments about Priscilla's wasted speed and talent.

"Miserable, stinking half bit of a ship!" Shelly continued at the top of her range, which was considerable. "One shift on, one shift off; Terrans to the back, *please,* and mind your words when you're speaking to a Liaden! Fines for this, fines for that . . . no damn shore leave, no damn privacy, nothing to do but work your shift, sleep your shift, work your shift . . . *hell!"*

She shoved the last of her clothing ruthlessly into the duffel, slammed a box of booktapes on top, and sealed the carryall with a violence that made Priscilla wince.

"First mate's a crook; second mate's a rounder . . . here!" She slapped a thick buff envelope into Priscilla's hand.

The younger woman blinked. "What's this?"

"Copy of my contract and the buy-out fee—in cantra, as

666

specified. Think I'm gonna let either the first or the second get their paws on it? Cleaned me out good and proper, it has. But no savings and no job is better than one more port o' call on this tub, and that I'll swear to!" She paused and leaned toward the other woman, punctuating her points with stabs of a long forefinger. "You give that envelope to the Trader, girl-o, and let 'im know I'm gone. You got the sense I think you got, you'll hand in your own with it."

Priscilla shook her head. "I don't have the buy-out, Shelly."

"But you'd go if you did, eh?" The big woman sighed. "Well, you're forewarned, at least. Can you last 'til the run's over, girl?"

"It's only another six months, Standard." She touched the other woman's arm. "I'll be fine."

"Hmmph." Shelly shouldered her bag and took the two strides necessary to get her from cot to door. In the hall, she turned again. "Take care of yourself, then, girl-o. Sorry we didn't meet in better times."

"Take care, Shelly," Priscilla responded. It seemed that she was hovering on the edge of something else, but the other woman had turned and was stomping off, shoulders rounded and head bent in mute protest of the short ceiling.

Priscilla turned in the opposite direction—toward the Trader's room—her own head slightly bent. She was not tall as Terrans went, and the ceiling was a good three inches above her curls; there just seemed something about *Daxflan* that demanded bowed heads.

Nonsense, she told herself firmly, rounding the corner by the shuttlebay.

But it wasn't nonsense. All that Shelly had said was true—and more. To be Terran was to be a second-class citizen on *Daxflan*, with quarters beyond the cargo holds and meals served half-cold in a cafeteria rigged out of what had once been a storage pod. The Trader didn't speak Terran at all, though the captain had a few words, and issued his orders in abrupt Trade unburdened with such niceties as "please" and "thank you."

Priscilla sighed. She had served with Liadens on other trade ships, though never on a Liaden ship. She wondered if conditions were the same on all of them. Her thoughts went back to Shelly, who had sworn she would never serve on another Liaden ship; though Shelly had done okay until the Healer had left two ports ago, to be replaced by a simple robotic medkit. That move had been called temporary. "More Liaden lies!" she had said. "They're liars. *All* liars!"

The first mate was a crook and the second a rounder—whatever, Priscilla amended, a rounder was. Liaden and Terran, respectively, and as alike as if the same mother had borne them.

Perhaps, Priscilla thought, the Trader only hired a certain type of person to serve him. She wondered what that said about Priscilla Mendoza, so eager for a berth as cargo master that she had not stopped first to look about her. Yet she *had* been eager. In a mere ten years she had gone from Food Service Technician—which meant little more than scullery maid—to General Crew, and then into cargo handling. Among her goals was a pilot's certificate, though certainly there was no hope for furthering *that* aim while on *Daxflan*.

The Trader's room was locked; no voice bade her enter when she laid her hand against the plate. So, then. She shook her head as the 1100 bell rang. She would be short of sleep *this* shift.

The captain, she decided, would do as well. She continued down the hall toward the bridge, then paused, hearing voices to her right—a man's, raised in outrage; a woman's, soothing.

Priscilla turned her steps in that direction, Shelly's envelope heavy in her hand.

The door to the Liaden lounge was open. Heedless, Sav Rid Olanek flung the paper at his cousin, Captain Chelsa yo'Vaade.

"Denied!" he cried, the High Tongue crackling with rage. "They dare! When all my life I have left this finger free to bear only the ring of a Master of Trade!" He waved gem-laden fingers also at Chelsa, who blinked, automatically cataloging Line-gem, school-gems, Clan-gem among the glittering array of others less important to Sav Rid's *melant'i*.

"They say you might reapply, cousin," she offered hesitantly. "You need only wait a Standard."

"Bah!" Sav Rid cried, as she might have known he would. "Reapply? *That* for their reapplication!" He snatched the letter back and rent it twice before flinging the pieces away. "They think me unworthy? They shall be schooled. We shall show them, *Daxflan* and I, how it is a *true* master of the craft goes about his business!" He turned then, eyes catching on the shadow at the door.

"You, there!" he snapped in Trade, crossing the room in four of his short strides. "What is it, Mendoza?"

Priscilla bowed, offering the envelope. "I did not wish to disturb you, sir," she replied in Trade, "but Shelly van Whitkin bade me give you this."

"So." He tore the envelope open, glanced at the paper with no great interest, and fingered the coin idly before slipping it into his belt.

One cantra, Priscilla saw, her stomach sinking. A sum so far beyond her resources that it was absurd to consider following Shelly's example. She might, she supposed, jump ship, but the thought of the dishonor attached to such an action cramped her stomach further.

"You may go, Mendoza," the Trader told her, and she bowed again before turning away. As she stepped into the hallway, she heard him address another comment in High Liaden to Captain yo'Vaade, something about having made a cantra and lost a big mouth to feed.

DAXFLAN WAS TWO DAYS OUT OF ALCYONE, and dinner looked terrible. Cargo Master Mendoza meekly accepted her tray and carried it into the crowded, steamy Terran mess hall. Peripheral vision showed Second Mate Dagmar Collier waving to her from a table near the door. Face averted, Priscilla moved to a newly vacated corner table. Self-preservation would not allow her to sit with her back to the noisy room, but the temptation was strong.

She frowned at the greasy soup and put her spoon down, then picked up the chipped plastic mug. Grinning, she sipped the tepid coffeetoot, recalling that Shelly had never sat down to a meal on *Daxflan* without indulging in a rant, the salient point of which was always the economic infeasibility of a tradeship serving 'toot instead of the real bean.

It had been Shelly's belief that serving 'toot to the Terrans was another deliberate snipe from the Trader. However, Priscilla had overheard Liaden crew members complaining that the beverage called tea aboard *Daxflan* had never seen Solcintra. Shelly had only a spacer's handful of Liaden, High or Low, and had just shaken her head at Priscilla's theory that perhaps *none* of the crew was treated very well.

Resolutely, the cargo master put the 'toot from her and picked up her spoon. Horrible as it looked, the soup was dinner and she would get no better; the alternative was the sodden breadroll and the sticky lump of cheese she knew from experience to be inedible to the point of nausea. It would have to be the soup.

Taking a gelid spoonful, Priscilla found her mind turning, as it had these last two shifts, back to the containers they had taken on at Alcyone Prime. Sealed cargo. Nothing unusual in that; she had the manifests listing the items the sealed hold contained, their weights and distributions. All according to book. And yet there was something. . . .

With a scrape and a *thump!* the second mate was with her. Priscilla jumped, splashing greasy soup on her sleeve. Clamping her teeth, she patiently daubed at the spot, avoiding Dagmar's eyes. The second grinned and leaned back in the chair, flinging her legs out before her.

"Scare you, Prissy?"

Priscilla's slim shoulders stiffened. Dagmar's grin widened.

"I was thinking." There was no emotion in the cargo master's soft, level voice.

"That's our Prissy," Dagmar said indulgently. "Always thinking." She leaned across the tiny table and touched the back of a slender hand, delighting in the slight withdrawal. "What about after dinner, though? What say I bring along something to keep you from thinking, and we have fun?"

"I'm sorry," Priscilla said, hoping she sounded like it, "but the distribution charts are behind. I'm going to have to spend some of this off-shift getting caught up."

Dagmar shook her head, secretly pleased at Prissy's seemingly endless supply of excuses. The game had run three months now. Dagmar considered the quarry worthy of an extended pursuit. It might be easier if the girl weren't so serious about her work—and so popular with the crew. The younger woman wasn't much on getting high or sleeping around. But Dagmar knew that Priscilla would have to relax and reveal a weak point one day—and when she finally did catch Prissy out, the spoils would be that much sweeter.

"That's all right," she said consolingly. "You work as hard as you want. Good to see that in a new hire. And at the end of the run—if you do *real* good—I'll give you a reward." She narrowed her eyes a bit, looking for signs of distress on the other woman's face. She detected none and played her ace.

"A reward," she repeated, and reached across the table to take one cool, slim hand in hers. "How 'bout . . . at the end of the run you and me go off—just us two—and have a Hundred Hours together? Huh? A hundred hours of loving and cuddling and fancy food and drink. Don't that sound nice?"

It did, Priscilla admitted to herself. Present company excluded.

She withdrew her hand carefully. "You're very generous," she murmured, "but I'm not—"

The second recaptured her hand. "Think it over. Got plenty of time." She squeezed the hand until she heard knuckles crack and then released it. "Nice, long fingers. You ought to wear rings." She smiled again, tipping her own hand so that light glittered sullenly across the dirty gems worn three deep on each fat finger. "I'll buy you a ring," she finished softly, "after our Hundred Hours."

Priscilla drew a deep breath, trying to drown a sudden, flaring urge to mayhem. She stood.

"Going so soon?"

The cargo master nodded. "Those calculations are going to take awhile." She fled the mess hall.

A *ring!* Holy Mother! Priscilla became aware that she was breathing hard, nearly running down the lowering corridor. She slowed, willed her hands to unclench at her side, and continued with outward serenity toward her quarters.

Inwardly she still raged. Day after day of the second's pursuit was bad enough, though at least *she* could be put off with excuses, but only this past shift had First Mate Pimm tel'Jadis come to her in the master's cubicle, and the less thought of *that* encounter the better.

Caught between the two of them, powerful as they were, with neither the Trader nor the captain willing to take the part of a Terran against a Liaden, or of one Terran against another . . . Priscilla slapped the palmplate and thumbed the light switch to HIGH before entering her tiny cabin.

The room was empty.

Of course, she jeered at herself, stepping in and locking the door. She leaned her head against the door frame and closed her eyes briefly. Stress, poor food, little sleep—she was getting nervous, fanciful. Surely the first mate would not secret himself in her cabin and wait to surprise her.

Not yet.

"Damn!" she said violently. She moved to the cramped 'fresher cubicle. Stripping off her clothes, she shoved them into the cleanbot and twisted the dial to SUPERCLEAN. More carefully, she removed the silver and opal drops from her ears and put them on the shelf under the short mirror. Then she dialed the unit temp to HOT, the intensity to NEEDLE, and stepped under the deluge.

Shipyear 32
Tripday 152
Third Shift
19.45 Hours

PRISCILLA RUBBED DRY EYES and sat back, frowning at the screen. She was right. At first, she had mistrusted her equations and so rechecked everything a second time, and a third. There was no doubt. She wondered what she was going to do now. Contraband drugs were certainly nothing she wanted to be involved with—and as cargo master, she had signed for them!

Shaking her head, she leaned over the keyboard again.

First, she told herself, you're going to seal this data under the cargo master's "Confidential" code. Then you're going to take a cold needle shower and hope it'll make up for a sleepless night—you're on duty in an hour! She rose and stretched.

She would make no decisions until she had had at least a shift's sleep. It was important not to make a mistake.

"The following personnel," blared the speaker over the door, "will report to Shuttlebay Two at 20.00 hours: Second Mate Dagmar Collier, Pilot Bern dea'Maan, Cargo Master Priscilla Mendoza, Cargo-hand Tailly Zeld, Cargo-hand Nik Laz Galradin."

"What?" Priscilla demanded, spinning to stare at the speaker. Bay 2 at 20.00 hours? That was less than ten minutes from now!

She spun back to the desk and cleared the screen, then spun again to rake her gaze around the closet-sized room, tallying her meager possessions. There was nothing she would need on Jankalim here. Smoothing her hands over her hair, she left the room.

It was only as she was striding toward Bay 2 that it occurred to her to wonder why she was needed at all. Jankalim was a drop-only, the sort of thing most commonly handled by the first or second and a couple of hands.

Maybe there had been a mistake? There had been no trip world-side listed on her schedule last shift, of that she was certain. Come to think of it, it was *silly* to send the cargo master on a trip like this one. Almost as silly as sending the Trader.

She rounded the corner into the bay corridor at a spanking pace and brought herself up sharply to avoid walking over the small man just ahead.

Trader Olanek turned his head and inclined it in unsmiling recognition. "Mendoza. Punctual, as always." The words were in Trade and heavily accented.

"Thank you, sir," she said, politely shortening her stride to match his. Somehow, she had never managed to inform the Trader that she had limited fluency in his language. She glanced at his profile and shrugged mentally. The Trader's temper was legend on *Daxflan,* but he seemed to be in as amiable mood as she had ever seen him.

"Are *you* going worldside, sir?" she ventured respectfully.

"Of course I am going worldside, Mendoza. Why else should I be here?"

Priscilla ignored the irritation in his voice and plunged on. "Has there been a change in schedule, then? My last information was that Jankalim is only a drop point. If we're going to take cargo on—"

"I must therefore assume, Mendoza," the Trader cut in, clearly irritated, "that your information is not complete."

Priscilla bit her lip. It was folly to goad him further. She inclined her head and dropped back to allow him to precede her into the shuttle. Then, sighing, she slipped into the first unoccupied seat, eyelids dropping. Half an hour, ship to world. At least she would get a nap.

"Hi there, Prissy," an unwelcome voice said in her ear. "You're not asleep, are you?" A hand was placed high on her thigh.

Gritting her teeth, Priscilla opened her eyes and sat up straight.

JANKALIM POSSESSED ONE SPACEPORT, situated on the easternmost tip of the southernmost continent, within a stone's throw of the planetary sea and the edge of the world's second city.

As spaceports went, this one was subaverage, Priscilla decided, watching Tailly and Nik Laz unload the few containers and pallets that represented their reason for stopping here at all. The spaceport boasted three hot-pads for in-system ships, four shuttle cradles, and a double-dozen steel warehouses. All the pads were empty, though there was a surprisingly well-kept shuttle in the end cradle.

She glanced at the corrugated metal building to her right. A lopsided sign proclaimed it to be the port master's office. Trader Olanek had disappeared within it immediately upon setdown, Dagmar trailing behind like a double-sized shadow.

As if summoned by the thought, the second appeared in the doorway, jerking her head as she crossed the yard. "Gimme a hand, willya, Prissy? Trader wants a couple boxes from that end house. Ought to be able to get 'em fine between us."

Raising her eyebrows, Priscilla looked back at burly Tailly and miniature Nik Laz, who were just setting the last pallet in place.

"Aah, give 'em a break, Prissy," Dagmar growled. "They worked plenty hard already."

Kindness was uncharacteristic of the second mate. Probably the woman wanted a little privacy to press her suit further. Trapped without a reasonable excuse, Priscilla nodded and fell into step beside her, keeping a cautious distance between them.

The lights came up as they entered the first warehouse. Dagmar turned confidently to the right; Priscilla, a few steps behind, let her lead the way. Several more turns led them to a musty-smelling hall, somewhat dimmer than the previous corridors, flanked with blank metal doors.

Priscilla wondered what the Trader could possibly want from a section of warehouse that was clearly abandoned, then she shrugged. She was cargo master. It was her job to stow what the Trader contracted for.

It just would have been nice, she stormed to herself, if the Trader had seen fit to inform his cargo master that he expected to take on goods at Jankalim.

Dagmar moved slowly down the hallway—counting doors, Priscilla thought—then stopped and slid a card into a doorslot.

The light in the frame lit, but nothing else happened. Dagmar grunted. "You're real good with computers. You try it."

The tone of voice made Priscilla uneasy. She took the card, inserted it, and was rewarded with both a light and a clicking noise from within.

Dagmar pushed at the door, then grunted again. "Damn thing's stuck. Come 'round here, Prissy—that's right. Now, I'm gonna pull back on the door an' get it started in the track. When it starts to slide, you get yourself between an' *push*, okay?"

"Okay."

Dagmar laid her hands against the door and exerted force. For a moment it looked as if the mechanism would resist. Then Priscilla saw a crack appear. She slipped her fingers into the slender opening as the crack began to widen, adding her own pressure to the enterprise. The gap widened farther. She slid her body into the opening and shoved.

As she pushed, there was a shadowy movement behind her, and she heard Dagmar say, "Can't be all that smart now, can ya, Prissy?" Then something clipped her behind the ear, and she crumpled sideways, tasting salt.

Jankalim Spaceport
Local Year 209

~~~~~~

THERE WAS A WINDOW high in the sidewall, and that was good. The door was locked from the outside, and that was bad. Her head ached, and that, she decided, was worst of all. Neither the soreness of her face nor the pain in her shoulder came near it, though the throb of her ribs ran a close second.

Moving with extreme care, Priscilla went to the window and stood on tiptoe, craning. No way out there: the pane was solid blast-glass, and even had she the means to break it, the opening itself was too small even for her lanky frame.

Outside, the well-kept shuttle was still in its ratty cradle.

Daxflan's shuttle was gone.

Left me, she thought through the fog of dizziness and pain. And then, with a gasp that sent knifing fire down her side, the reality hit her. *Left me! Here,* with the door locked and no way out and *how* could they have left me? Surely the Trader would have missed me . . . or if not me—but how could they *not* have missed me! Tailly, Nik Laz, Bern . . . how could they have *left* . . .

She took a deep, deliberate breath, ignoring the pain.

"I will not," she informed the room austerely, "sanction hysterics."

Her voice came back to her from the empty walls, deep and oddly comforting. Priscilla closed her eyes and concentrated on breathing until the panic stilled.

I have to get out, she told herself, forming the thought carefully.

She surveyed her prison. Empty. Dustless. Dim. What light there was came from the window. She would have to do whatever she did before day failed.

Leaning against the wall, she went through her pockets: stylus, pad of paper, ID, strapping tape, comb, two Terran wholebits, magnetic ruler, penknife, calculator—nothing heavy enough to break a triple-thick window or strong enough to jimmy the door.

She took another look outside. The yard was as empty as the room she stood in. She settled her shoulders against the wall and considered her resources.

Stylus. Not too likely. It went back into her pocket. Likewise the paper; also comb, ID, and money.

Tape? She kept it out for the time being. Penknife? Why not? Ruler? No— Yes. Yes, wait a minute—magnets . . . lock . . . jimmy the *lock!*

She knelt at the door to get the cardslot at eye level, then peered cautiously within. It just might be possible. . . .

Sitting back on her heels, she unrolled the ruler and tried unsuccessfully to pry the thin rectangular magnets off with her fingers. The penknife did the trick—fifteen minutes later she had four flat magnets, each with its own long tail of tape, lined up on the door next to the cardslot.

With the tip of the knife she inserted them, one at a time, thanking the Goddess that there were only four contacts within the mechanism and that no one had expected the place to be used as a jail.

The last magnet was affixed. She withdrew the knife, holding her breath . . . but nothing happened.

Wrong combination, she told herself, and patiently inserted the knife point again, reversing the polarity of the magnet on the extreme left.

She had worked through twelve combinations, and multicolored spots were shimmering before her eyes, when there was a soft click. Hardly daring to breathe, she looked up.

The light over the door frame was lit.

She scrambled to her feet, folding the knife automatically and dropping it into her pocket. Leaning forward, she put her hands against the panel and prepared to push—but suddenly the door slid open.

Priscilla twisted, gasping, and regained her balance before the man on the other side extended a hand to grab her.

"Hold there, now." The grip on her arm changed. "Who by hell are *you?*"

"Priscilla Mendoza—cargo master on *Daxflan.*"

"That's so, is it?" He eyed her. "Bit beyond yer territory, would say?"

"Without a doubt." She gritted her teeth against the pain and fought to keep the edge out of her voice. "There's been a— misunderstanding. I'm sure Trader Olanek will vouch for me. He was with the port master. . . ."

"That be so," the man agreed. "Then he an' his went off. Nothin' was said about a missin' mate. Happen a Trader would notice his cargo master wasn't to hand, would say?"

She sighed. "I don't really think I'm prepared to say any such thing. Are you going to let me out of here, or aren't you?"

"Now there, mistress, don't be chivin' me. Happen you'll have a better tale for Master Farley." He stepped back, keeping a firm hold on her arm. "We'll be walking this way now."

Priscilla clamped her jaw and matched his stride firmly.

The glare of sunshine made her gasp with quadrupled pain. She was abruptly thankful for the man's bruising hold—without his support she would have fallen.

Sunlight gave way to shadow. Her captor paused and laid his hand against a plate, and a door slid open. Obedient to his tug, Priscilla stepped into an echoing cavern of a room. Four dark terminals sat at intervals on the empty counter; the ship-board suspended above displayed one row of tired amber letters, brilliant in the gloom: DUTIFUL PASSAGE SOLCINTRA LIAD.

She stopped, staring at the board. A Liaden ship, surely, but . . . dear Goddess, they *had* gone! They had left orbit, left the sector, without her. She had been abandoned deliberately on this quarter-bit world!

"Come along, mistress, we've not got all the day." The man jerked hard on her arm, and Priscilla went with him, blankly.

She should be angry, she knew, but the various pains and shocks seemed to cancel emotion. Her overwhelming desire was for sleep—but no. There was the port master to see, and an explanation to be made. She would need money—a job. Two Terran wholebits was hardly a fortune, no matter how backward the world.

"In here, mistress." He gave another tug. Priscilla ground her teeth against a snapped retort and obeyed.

Port Master Farley was a plump man with a dejected yellow mustache and apologetic blue eyes. He blinked at Priscilla and turned toward her captor. "Well, now, Liam. What have you here?"

The man holding her renewed his grip and straightened, giving the impression of having brought his heels smartly together. "Computer reported some tamperin' with the lock on door triple-ay, corridor seven, house one—one o' the empty sections, Master Farley."

The port master nodded.

"Went to check things out—thinkin' it'll be a malfunction, you understand." He yanked Priscilla forward. "Found this one on the *inside*. Tells the tale o' bein' Priscilla Mendoza, cargo master on *Daxflan* as just left us."

The port master blinked again. "But what were you doing in the warehouse, lass? Especially along that way—it's been empty for years."

Priscilla took a deep breath. The pain in her side was less, she noted, down to a persistent dull ache.

"Trader Olanek and Second Mate Collier came into this building to speak with you, sir," she said. "I was outside, supervising the unloading. After a time, the second mate came out and asked me to go with her to the warehouse. She said the Trader wanted something out of one of the rooms. When we arrived, she put a card in the lock and asked me to help her push the door open, since it was stuck—"

"Like as not," Liam muttered. "Damn thing hasn't been opened this tenyear."

"And then," Priscilla concluded, "she hit me over the head and left me there. When I came to, I tried to gimmick the lock with a couple magnets off my ruler."

Master Farley was staring. "Hit you over the head and left you? And you her mate? Why would she do such a thing?"

"How do *I* know?" Priscilla snapped, then dredged up a painful smile. "Look, do you mind if I sit down? My head *does* hurt."

"Surely, surely." He looked a little flustered. "Liam . . . ."

The warehouseman loosed her with reluctance and placed the chair close to the desk before taking up a position directly behind it. She sat carefully, hands curled around the plastic armrests.

"Thank you."

"You're welcome." Master Farley sighed, drummed his fingers on the rubbed steel top of his desk, screwed his eyes shut, and opened them again. "You'll be having some ID on you, of course."

She nodded, earning a flash of pain and a renewed flurry of dots. The hand that held her identification out trembled, she noted, and she was aware of a flicker of anger.

Master Farley took the packet and fed the cards one by one into the unit beside his desk. He studied the screen carefully, sighed, and turned back to her.

"Well, your papers are in order. Cargo master for *Daxflan,* out of Chonselta City, Liad—plain as rain." He shook his head. "I'll be right out with you, lass. I can't see the why of leaving you like this. A cargo master is an important part of a trade vessel. All this about being hit on the head and left—it don't add up. And I'll tell you what else: Trader Olanek was here, and we had a very pleasant chat. But I never saw this second mate you be speaking of. Nor I never saw you."

"You don't believe me, in fact."

He waved his hands soothingly. "Now, lass. Admit it don't seem so likely."

"I *do* admit it," Priscilla told him. "I don't know why it was done any more than you do. Perhaps the second felt she had a grudge— but nothing to warrant cracking my skull." Which means the Trader ordered it, she thought suddenly, crystally. Dagmar wouldn't have mugged her and left her—not without orders. It was more in her style to try rape, if she had thought Priscilla had insulted her. And if the Trader had ordered it, that meant . . .

Master Farley's chair creaked as he changed position. "Well, then, lass, I'm just bound to say that done's done. There doesn't seem to be any harm you've done—is that so, Liam?"

"Yessir," the warehouseman said regretfully. "Happens that's so."

The port master nodded. "Then the wisest thing to do is give you back your ID and send you on your way." He pushed her cards across the desk.

Priscilla stared at him. "Send me on my way," she repeated blankly. "I'm *stranded*. I don't have any money. I don't know anybody here." The Trader had ordered it. Which meant that her deduction was correct: *Daxflan* had been carrying illegal drugs in enormous quantity. Never mind how he had gotten at her data, locked under her personal code. He had found it, given her credit for being able to make the deduction—and acted to remove a known danger.

"Best you go to the embassy," Master Farley was saying with apologetic kindness. "Likely they'll send you home."

Home? "No," she said, suddenly breathless. "I want to go—I must get to Arsdred." That was *Daxflan's* next port of call. And then? she asked herself, wondering at her own urgency. She shoved the question away for the present. She would take one thing at a time.

"Arsdred," she repeated firmly.

He looked doubtful. "Well, if you must, lass, you must. But I'm not the one to know how you'll go about it. You said you'd no money . . . ."

"The ship in orbit now—*Dutiful Passage*? Is she a trader?"

He nodded, blinking in confusion.

"Good." She took a deep breath and forced her aching head to work. "Master Farley, you owe me no favors, I know. But I want to apply for work on *Dutiful Passage*. Will you help me?"

"It's not me you need to speak to about that, lass. It'll be Mr. Saunderson, who's the agent." He puffed his chest out a little. "*Dutiful Passage* stops here every three years, regular."

A ship that listed Jankalim among its regular ports of call? And a Liaden ship, too. Priscilla paused, trying to picture conditions less appealing than *Daxflan's*. Imagination failed her, and she smiled tightly at the port master.

"How do I get in touch with Mr. Saunderson?"

"His office is just in the city," Liam said from behind her. "Anyone can tell you the way."

"That's so," Master Farley agreed slowly. Then he squared his shoulders and stiffened his mustache. "You can use the comm to call him from here, if you like to."

Her smile was genuine this time, if no less painful. "Thank you so much."

"That's all right, lass. Pleased to be of help," he muttered, cheeks going pink. "Liam here will show you to the comm room." He made a show of turning back to the unit beside his desk, and Priscilla stood.

Liam looked as if he would have liked to grab her arm again, but satisfied himself with walking close behind her down the short hall to the communication room. He showed her the local screen and, after a moment's hesitation, punched up Mr. Saunderson's code. Priscilla smiled at him, and he flushed dull red.

Mr. Saunderson was old, his face a translucent network of wrinkles from which a pair of obsidian eyes glittered. He listened to her name and the statement that she had been employed until recently on *Daxflan* and heard her say that she was interested in employment on the orbiting ship.

"It is my understanding, Ms. Mendoza, that *Dutiful Passage* is fully staffed. However, if you would care to hold on for a few moments, I will ascertain whether this understanding is correct."

"Thank you, sir. I appreciate your trouble."

"Not at all. One moment, please." The elderly face was replaced with an image of an unlikely landscape, portrayed in various shades of tangerine and aqua. The picture had not been calculated to soothe raging headaches, and Priscilla closed her eyes against it.

"Ms. Mendoza?"

Priscilla snapped her eyes open, cheeks flaming.

Mr. Saunderson smiled at her. "The captain professes himself interested in an interview, Ms. Mendoza, and wonders if you would honor him by a visit." He cleared his throat with the utmost gentility. "He does indicate that *Dutiful Passage* employs a very able cargo master. He does not wish you to visit under a misapprehension, or if you cannot accept any position except that of cargo master."

Priscilla hesitated, wondering what positions the captain had in mind. But she was determined to get to Arsdred.

She looked at Mr. Saunderson, who was patiently waiting in the screen, and tried to visualize him whetting the captain's supposed appetite with a glowing description of her, bruised face and all. The vision brought forth a grin.

"You're very kind," she told the old gentleman carefully. "I am willing to accept any crewing work that might be available on *Dutiful Passage*. When and where may I visit the captain?"

"I shall send 'round Ms. Dyson, our pilot. Is twenty minutes convenient? Good. She will convey you to *Dutiful Passage*. I will inform Captain yos'Galan of your coming."

"You're very kind," she said again.

"Not at all." Mr. Saunderson smiled. "Good luck, Ms. Mendoza." He cut the connection.

Priscilla sighed and leaned back in her chair. She had twenty minutes until Pilot Dyson came to collect her. She looked at Liam. "Is there someplace where I can wash my face and hands?"

He snorted and jerked his head. "Down the hall, first door on the left. Nothin' fancy, it isn't."

"As long as it's functional." She levered herself up and went past him into the hall. He followed and leaned against the wall, arms crossed over his chest, watching as she opened the door and entered the 'fresher.

There was no shower, which was a shame. She had rather hoped for a hot deluge to ease some of the crankiness from her bruises. There was a sink, water, and soap. She would make do.

Automatically, she reached up to remove her earrings, then froze in disbelief when her fingers encountered only naked earlobes. Slowly, she went over to the tiny square of mirror on the far wall.

Reflected back at her was a creamy oval face surmounted by a tangled cloud of ebony curls, black eyes very wide under slim brows, and nostrils distended with anger. The fragile ridge of the right cheek was already purpling. There was a small hole in each perfect earlobe; the left one showed a thin line of blood, as if it was torn just a little.

How dare she? she thought furiously. My earrings, given to me on my Womanday, that were my grandmother's! How dare— Rage, sudden and shocking, drove out pain and fears. Priscilla was abruptly trembling, wishing fiercely to have Dagmar's neck between her hands.

Arsdred, she told herself, trying to still the fury. I'll have them both. Just let me get to Arsdred.

Slowly the rage became manageable; she enclosed it, as she had been taught, banked and ready for the proper moment.

Woodenly she went to the sink, turned on the cold water, bent, and began to splash her face.

Shipyear 65
Tripday 130
Fourth Shift
18.00 Hours

"ASLEEP, MENDOZA?" Dyson inquired from the pilot's chair.

Priscilla opened her eyes and sat up straighter. "Just resting."

"Okay by me. End of the line in about five minutes. Word is you'll be met and escorted to the captain's office. Got it?"

"Yes. Thank you."

Dyson snorted. "Don't thank me, Mendoza; I'm just passing on the facts." She thumbed the comm, reeled off her numbers, and grunted at the acknowledgment before turning her full attention to the board.

Orbit and velocity were matched with an offhanded exactitude that earned Priscilla's silent praise even as she regretted her own uncompleted certificate.

There came assorted mechanical clankings and ringings before a final authoritative *thump*. Dyson locked the board with a sweep of her hand. "Okay, Mendoza. Roll on out."

"Okay." She unstrapped and stood. "Thanks."

"What they pay me for, Mendoza. Beat it, all right?"

Priscilla grinned. "See you around."

She went out the hatch and through the door—then stopped, blinking.

Carpet was beneath her feet; she was struck by the vaulting, the well-lit spaciousness . . . She was in a state reception room.

The identification was hard to refute. To her left and some twelve feet downroom was a grouping of chairs and loungers—Terran and Liaden-sized in equal proportion. Farther on, a podium was shoved against the wall, directly beneath the mural of an enormous tree in full, green leaf. Hovering behind and a little above, nearly dwarfed by the tree it guarded, was a winged dragon, bronze and fierce, emerald eyes looking directly at her. There were words in Liaden characters beneath the roots of the tree.

Priscilla sighed slightly, recalling little Fin Ton, who had taught her Liaden in an even exchange for games of go. But his lessons had not extended to reading. Priscilla turned her head carefully to the right wall, which held what appeared to be a collage of photographs and drawings.

Obviously she was in the wrong place. She had better return to the docking pod and see if there was another door that led onto a more reasonable area—one containing her escort to the captain.

Half a second later she had abandoned that plan. Over the door by which she had entered, the atmosphere lamp glowed clear ruby, indicating vacuum in the pod beyond.

Priscilla turned. The door directly across from her, then? Or a ship's intercom? Surely, in a room as spacious as this one she could find an intercom.

That thought brought to mind all kinds of interesting questions about the room itself. Tradeships did not, in her experience, devote space to ballrooms or auditoriums. Three of *Daxflan's* holds would have fit comfortably into this area.

Priscilla put speculation from her mind. First, she had to find an intercom.

The door across from her opened, and a rather breathless small person erupted into the room. He skidded to a stop about two feet away and executed an awkward bow.

Not Liaden, she noted with relief. But—a child?

"Are you Ms. Mendoza?" he asked, then swept on without waiting for an answer. "Crelm! I'm *awful* sorry. I was supposed to be here when you came in. Cap'n's gonna *skin* me!"

She grinned at him. He was a stocky Terran boy of perhaps eleven

Standards, dressed in plain slacks and shirt. There was a smear of grease on his right sleeve and another on his chin. An embroidered badge on his left shoulder bore the legend "Arbuthnot."

"I've only been here a minute," she told him. "Surely he won't skin you for that?"

The boy gave it consideration, tipping his head birdlike to one side. "Well, he still might. He *told* me to be here, didn't he? And it's rude, you gettin' off the shuttle and there being nobody to meet you." He sighed. "I really *am* sorry. I *meant* to be here."

"I accept your apology," Priscilla said formally. "Are you my escort to the captain, by any chance?"

"Oh, crelm," the boy said again, and laughed. "I'm making a rare mingle of it! An' he told me to make sure I welcomed you onboard, too!" He looked at her out of hopeful brown eyes. "Did I do that?"

"Admirably," she assured him, fighting down a rare spurt of her own laughter.

"Good," he said, relieved. He turned, waving at her to accompany him. "My name's Gordy Arbuthnot. I'm cabin boy."

"Pleased to meet you," Priscilla said gravely, trying not to stare around the wide, well-lit hallway. *This* was the ship that visited Jankalim every three years on a regular basis? The little she had seen so far would contain most of *Daxflan*. She opened her mouth to ask Gordy how many holds *Dutiful Passage* could carry, then thought better of it and asked another question instead. "What *was* that room back there? I thought I'd made a wrong turn getting off the shuttle."

"Reception room," he explained offhandedly. "For when we have visitors. Most of us just use the cargo docks when we come back on-ship."

"But I'm a guest?" She frowned. "Do you get a *lot* of visitors?"

Gordy shrugged. "Cap'n has parties sometimes. And sometimes people take passage with us—'cause we go where the liners don't, or 'cause we go there faster."

"Oh."

They entered a lift, and her guide punched a quick series of buttons. Shortly the door opened to a narrower hall, wide enough for four Liadens to walk abreast, Priscilla estimated. She smelled cinnamon, resin, and leather; she took a deep breath and held it a moment before sighing.

Gordy grinned. "Best place in the whole ship for smells. That's Number Six Hold." He pointed. "There's Cap'n's office."

Priscilla caught her breath sharply and bit her lip against a flare of pain in her head.

There's nothing to worry about, she told herself firmly. The captain wants an interview. The worst that can happen is that he has no job to offer. Time enough, when that happens, to think of another way to Arsdred.

Gordy laid his hand against the palmplate in the captain's bright red door. There was a chime, followed by a subdued "Come."

The door slid open.

Priscilla crossed the threshold on the boy's heels, then stopped and frankly stared.

Once again she was overwhelmed by spaciousness. Shelf after shelf of booktapes, bound books, and musictapes lined one wall. On another hung a tapestry worked in dark crimson, dull gold, jade, and azure, a twining geometric design at once restful and surprising. Below that was a unit bar; to one side of it was another shelf of tapes interspersed with bric-a-brac. Straight ahead, in the center of the room, two chairs faced a wooden desk supporting a computer screen and two untidy piles of hard copy. To the left of the desk was a closed door bearing a diagonal red stripe. A deep, hedonistic chair was placed at an angle to the corner, several books and a sketch pad were piled helter-skelter on the carpet nearby, while more books littered the nearer low table. The second of the set supported a chessboard. Seated on the edge of the sofa and bent over the board was a white-haired man in a dark blue shirt.

The captain was *old.* Priscilla found it somewhat easier to breathe.

Gordy Arbuthnot stepped to the table and cleared his throat. "Cap'n?" he said in Terran. "Here's Ms. Mendoza, come to see you."

"So soon? Pilot Dyson has outdone herself." The man sighed and shook his head at the chessmen. "I don't think this stupid position *has* a solution."

He rose and came forward a few graceful paces before inclining his head. "I'm Shan yos'Galan, Ms. Mendoza."

He was tall—a giant among Liadens. Silver eyes thickly fringed with black lashes looked directly into hers. Nor was he old—the frostcolored hair had misled her. His face was that of a man near her own age.

But, Goddess, *what* a face! Big-nosed, jut-cheeked, wide-mouthed, with a broad forehead, triangular chin, and thin white brows set at a slant over the large eyes. Anything farther from the usual delicacy of Liaden features would be hard to find this side of the Yxtrang.

Recovering herself with a start, Priscilla bowed stiffly in the Terran mode. "Captain yos'Galan," she said with precision, "I'm glad to see you."

"Well, you'll be among the first," he commented, and his accent was of Terra's educated class, not of Liad at all. "Though my family professes something of the sort. Of course, they've had time to get used to me. Gordy, Ms. Mendoza wants something to drink. Also, my glass is missing—and wherever it is, it's probably empty. What do I pay you for?"

The boy grinned and moved toward the bar. Pausing, he looked back at Priscilla. "The red wine's best," he said seriously, "but I think the white's probably pretty good. And there's brandy—I'm not sure about that. . . ."

"What do you know about it at all?" the man demanded. "Nipping my spirits while I'm not watching, Gordy? And who said the red's best? Your own trained palate?"

"*You* drink the red, Cap'n."

"Unprincipled brat. You don't offer brandy to a person who's come for a job interview. Strive for some polish."

"Yessir," Gordy said, not noticeably abashed by this rebuke. "Ms. Mendoza? There's red wine, white, canary, green, blue—I mean, *misravot*—and tea and coffee. . . ."

Another alarming bubble of laughter was rising. Hysteria, thought Priscilla, and suppressed it firmly.

"White wine, please," she told the boy, and he nodded, turning to the bar.

"Come sit down," the captain invited, waving a big brown hand toward the chairs and the desk. Light glittered off the stone in his single ring—the large carved amethyst of a Master Trader.

Obediently, she followed him to the desk and sank gratefully into one of the chairs. Master Trader? This ugly, too-tall Liaden was a Master Trader? And captain, too? With an absent smile Priscilla took her drink from the cabin boy.

On *Daxflan,* Sav Rid Olanek—a mere Trader—and Captain yo'Vaade split administration of ship and crew between them. That had been the one thing about *Daxflan* that had followed the routine she knew from other ships. Captain was a full-time job, after all; Trader, somewhat more than that. Yet here was a man supposedly doing *both*. And more. There were perhaps a double-dexon—twice a dozen dozen—of Master Traders in all the galaxy.

"Gordy." His clear, rather beautiful voice held a mild note of exasperation. Priscilla brought her attention back to the present.

"Cap'n?" The boy froze in the act of handing the man his glass.

Shan yos'Galan sighed and laid a blunt forefinger on the grease-smeared sleeve. Gordy flushed and bit his lip.

"There's a matching one on your chin. Are we out of water? Or soap? Is there some atavistic or religious significance attached to going about with grease on your face? Maybe you put it there purposefully, after long thought, feeling that a little facial decoration would call Ms. Mendoza's attention to you more favorably? You hoped she would be so overcome by the artistry of the smear that she would fail to chide you for being late to meet her?"

"How did—" Gordy interrupted himself and raised his eyes to the man's face. "I'm not Liaden, Cap'n."

"I have independently noted the fact. No doubt you feel it has some bearing on the matter at hand." He took his glass and leaned back in the chair.

"Yessir."

"I'm intrigued. An explanation, please?"

"Yessir." Gordy took a breath and squared his round shoulders. "Liadens consider the face the—the *seat of character*. Because of that, Liadens don't use cosmetics on their faces, like Terrans might, to—to dress up or to make themselves more attractive." He paused. The captain raised his glass and waved at him to continue.

Gordy nodded. "Also, the face has an—*erotic*—significance to Liadens. There are certain social situations where it's okay to touch between Liadens where Terran code of behavior would forbid. But only extreme intimates—like family members—touch hand to face or face to face." He took another breath. "So it follows that Liadens would be *particularly* careful about keeping their faces clean. Terrans, whose cultures don't include a strong facial taboo, are less strict."

There was a small pause while Shan yos'Galan raised the glass to his lips. "'Taboo' is rather strong," he commented. "I think perhaps 'tradition' does nicely. Liadens love tradition, while you're dealing in generalizations, Gordy." He raised his glass again, and this time, Priscilla saw, he drank.

"As far as it goes, your grasp of the information seems sound," he continued thoughtfully. "However, I'm not sure your inferences are correct. That tends to happen when you extrapolate from general, rather than specific. In any case, I have found—again, through independent observation, not to say experience—that it *feels nicer* to be clean than it feels to be dirty. Also, I have found that I prefer looking at clean faces as opposed to dirty faces. This is, I believe, a personal preference. I may be wrong. Since I am captain of this ship, though, I think I have the rank to indulge in a few harmless eccentricities. So, for the fourth time: Gordon, I would very much prefer that you endeavor to keep your person as smear-free as possible." He raised the glass again. "The next time, I'll have to dock you. What do you think might be a reasonable sum?"

The boy looked down. He rubbed at his soiled sleeve, then looked up. "Tenbit?"

"Fair enough." The captain grinned. "I detect the makings of a gambler in you. Or a Trader. We'll want lunch in half an hour or so."

Gordy blinked. "Lunch?"

"Yes, *lunch.* Did I use the wrong word? Cheese, fruit, rolls—that sort of thing. Speak to BillyJo; I repose all faith in her ability to resolve the matter for you. Now jet."

"Yessir." And he was gone, the door sighing shut behind him.

Shan yos'Galan shook his head. "It's my fate to raise small boys." He lifted his glass. "Are you ready to be interviewed, Ms. Mendoza? Or have you changed your mind?"

Priscilla sipped her wine, then met his gaze straightly. "I'm ready to be interviewed, Captain."

"Brave heart." He extended a long arm and flipped two switches set along the desk top. "Your name, please, and planet of origin."

"My name is Priscilla Delacroix y Mendoza. I was born on Sintia. I am a Terran citizen."

"Do you honor the Goddess, then?" His face was sharp with interest. "Hold to her teaching exclusively?"

"I did," she said carefully. "After all, She's part of everyday life . . . But I've been on trading ships since I was sixteen. And the Goddess isn't as powerful in the galaxy as She is on Sintia."

"Since you were sixteen," he repeated, abandoning the Goddess abruptly. "What do you know?"

She raised her brows. "I know how to cook for a crew of twenty, how to wash up for a crew of thirty-three, how to decode messages, how to code messages. I can drive a jitney, calculate weight distributions, figure loading capacities. Whenever possible, I've pursued pilot training. My marksmanship rating is ninety percent accuracy at two hundred paces with a standard pellet gun. I speak Trade, Terran, Crenish, and Sintian. I understand Liaden better than I speak it. If I have to, I can shoot astrogation."

He nodded. "Your last position?"

"Cargo master on *Daxflan,* out of Chonselta City."

"And you held that post how long?"

"Four months," she said with determined serenity. "I signed on at Tulon."

"Did you?" He raised his glass to his lips. "And what brings you to apply for work on the *Passage?*"

"I don't have any choice."

The slanted brows pulled together. "Has Mr. Saunderson still got that impressment operation going? I did ask him to stop, Ms. Mendoza, I give you my word."

For the third time in an hour Priscilla felt laughter rising. She drowned it in a swallow of wine. "I'm sorry—that was rude. What I meant to say was that I've been—dismissed—from my post on *Daxflan.* Yours is the only ship in at Jankalim now, so I'm applying here."

"I see." He sipped wine. "Your dismissal sounds abrupt."

"Extremely."

He nodded again, shifted in his chair, and rested his arms on the desk top. "Ms. Mendoza, I have a copy of your record here...." He spun the computer screen around.

Priscilla frowned, her eyes traveling automatically down the lines of information. *Ladybird . . . As You Like It . . . Tyrunner . . . Selda . . . Dante . . .*

Daxflan.

"Motherless, lying, spawn of a—" She gasped, and the rest was lost as the enormity of the thing hit her. *Ruin.* . . . She met Shan yos'Galan's eyes. "It's a lie."

"Do you want to say so officially?" He spun the screen back. "It looks pretty bad, doesn't it? 'Suspected larceny. Jumped ship, Jankalim, Standard 1385.'" He leaned back in the chair and sipped wine, his eyes on her face. "*I* don't know of any reputable captain who would take on a person with a record containing that entry— even granting the overall excellence of the rest. What happened to your earrings?"

"The second mate hit me over the head," she said tonelessly, trying to conquer the shock. "They were gone when I came to."

"Odd sort of thing for a second mate to do," he commented.

"But maybe there were extenuating circumstances. You disliked each other?"

"*I* disliked *her*. She liked me all too well." He was toying with her, drawing out the talking when there was no use in talking anymore. Priscilla tightened her grip on the wineglass, fighting to keep her face calm. On his ship, in his power . . . and who would miss a suspected thief who had jumped her last ship? Who would believe a suspected thief if she chose to tell outrageous lies about a Master Trader? He must have called up her record while speaking with Mr. Saunderson and seen that damning entry.

The man across from her shifted sharply. "And yet," he persisted, demanding her attention, "liking you so well, she hits you over the head and steals your earrings." He drank. "Forgive me, Ms. Mendoza, but *that* sounds even odder."

"The Trader ordered it," Priscilla said, clinging to serenity as if it were her last hope of salvation. Let him hear, Goddess, she begged silently. Let him believe the truth.

"Ah, dear Sav Rid." The expression on his face was one of mild puzzlement. "He will have his little joke, you know, Ms. Mendoza. But surely there were other avenues open to him, had he conceived a desire for your earrings. Why order the second mate to hit you over the head for them? Couldn't he merely have purchased them from you?" He snapped his fingers lightly. "He had offered a fair sum, and you refused to sell. Rendered desperate—"

"*Stop* it!" She snapped forward, eyes riveted on his. "Captain yos'Galan, please. It's imperative that I get to Arsdred. It's a large port—I'd hoped your ship would dock there. Any crewing duties you have—I'll work my passage to Arsdred as assistant mess cook, and you can lock me in a closet off-shift! You don't have to trust me—believe what you will. I *don't* think it's very funny to abandon someone and ruin their record, make it impossible to find—to find honorable work . . . ." Her voice had developed a quaver. Horrified, she bit her lip and clenched her hands tightly to squeeze out the shaking. "I *must* get to Arsdred."

He broke her gaze and drank wine, then swirled the remainder in the glass. "Revenge," he told the glass softly, "is a highly appropriate desire. Among Liadens, revenge is something of an art form. There are strict rules. There are certain punishments which are not considered *proper* revenge." He glanced at her. "Death, for instance. At least, not directly from the hand of the vengeful party. Should the dishonor attending a balancing of accounts prove so vast that one has no other choice—" He shrugged. "Well." He set the glass aside and looked closely at her. "I will not have a murderer on this ship."

Priscilla stared at him. "But you *will* have a thief?"

"You said it was a lie. Or did I misunderstand? Perhaps something else was a lie?"

The shaking was worse, extending up her arms and down her legs. Did he believe her? Or the record? It was impossible to read the expression on his face.

"*Daxflan*'s record—that I was stealing and then jumped ship— *that's* the lie."

"Do you want to say so officially?" he asked again.

Priscilla shook her head. "I can't prove it—how can I? 'Suspected' larceny'? His word against mine—and *he's* the Trader. 'Jumped ship'?" She produced a wan grin. "I'm not there now, am I? Though why anyone with three consecutive thoughts in her head would jump ship on a place like Jankalim, with twobits in her pocket . . ."

"And no earrings in her ears," he agreed. "But maybe you saw they were on to you and were frightened. Jankalim might have been your last chance for free flight—leg irons are so cumbersome. There are excuses for a bit of poor planning. . . ." He tipped his head. "But why *did* Sav Rid order the second mate to hit you over the head, Ms. Mendoza? At your direction, I dismiss avaricious thoughts regarding your earrings."

"I can't prove it," she said again. "I *think* they were running contraband."

"Do you? What a peculiar thing to think. You told Sav Rid, and he was—quite understandably—annoyed. Thus the second mate, the warehouse . . ."

"I'm not *that* stupid," Priscilla muttered, and wondered why he grinned. "There was sealed cargo," she continued. "I had the manifests—I knew what was *supposed* to be there. But—something seemed wrong. I didn't know exactly what. So I got the idea of checking the piloting equations, just to prove to myself that I was imagining things."

"And you found what to be the case?"

"I found the equations were so far off that the captain had to be a reckless fool. Or she had to know exactly what she was doing." She took a breath. "So I checked the densities of the cargo."

"Did you?" He leaned forward. "Now why—no, you've had some pilot training. And I'm interrupting. Forgive me, Ms. Mendoza—you checked the densities, matched them to the captain's equations, and?"

"The captain knew what she was doing. The densities didn't match the substances that were *supposed* to be in the cargo. *Daxflan* ships mostly pharmaceuticals. I started going through the list, checking the numbers . . . ." She shook her head. "I *think* there's Bellaquesa onboard. It's listed as Aserzerine on the manifest. Everything's all wrong for Aserzerine, though. Bellaquesa matches—but so does sugar. But why would you call sugar Aserzerine . . .?"

She shrugged. "It all *looked* interesting—but I can't *prove* any of it. I never *saw* the stuff. And I'll lay my last bit the data's not locked under my personal file anymore."

He nodded and leaned back in the chair again, staring blankly at the ceiling. Priscilla finished her wine and carefully put the glass aside. Now what? she wondered. She forced herself to sit loosely in the chair, hands relaxed on her knees.

Abruptly, he spun to face her. "We leave Jankalim in fourteen hours," he said slowly. "Before the two of us can discuss specifics, there are several tests required. They are rather lengthy, and, unfortunately, my presence is demanded worldside this evening. If you feel able, you may take the tests directly after lunch. The ship will extend a cabin for you to guest in, and we can speak again at Seventh Hour. Agreed?"

"Agreed."

He nodded and seemed about to speak further when the door opened to admit a clean-faced Gordy behind a wheeled cart piled high with eatables.

"In the nick of time!" Shan yos'Galan cried, flipping off the toggles. "*Now* you offer brandy, Gordy. . . ."

Shipyear 65
Tripday 131
First Shift
1.30 Hours

FORMER CARGO MASTER PRISCILLA MENDOZA leaned back in her chair, sipping at a mug of *real* coffee, the remains of an extremely edible meal on the table before her.

The tests had been lengthy—and rather odd. Among the standardized examinations had been random lists of words to define; questions regarding her personal tastes in books, music, sports, and art; and surveys soliciting her opinion on a surprising range of topics.

Priscilla sighed and sipped her coffee appreciatively. She was tired, her thoughts moving in hazy slow motion. Soon it would be time to look again at the map she had been given and puzzle out the route to her cabin. But having come to rest at last, with no immediate task before her, she was content to simply sit and sip, letting her eyes randomly scan the vast, nearly empty dining hall. She had gathered from the cook on duty that First Hour was not the usual time for people to be fed. He had laughed her apology aside and heaped a plate high, setting it on a tray with a steaming white mug.

"Start on that," he had told her, grinning broadly. "If you're still hungry when you're done, come on back and say so."

"Thank you," Priscilla said, blinking in confusion at the tray. It seemed to hold more food than she had seen at one time in months. The man laughed again and returned to his duties.

Her eyes were drooping closed. Odd, she thought drowsily, that I should feel so comfortable.

She sat up straight and drank the last of her coffee in a snap. After all, tomorrow's interview with the captain could end with her back on Jankalim, no better off—with the exception of a few good meals—than she had been this afternoon. So much depended on the tests, and on the captain. *Did* he believe her?

Why should he? she asked herself fiercely. She sighed and looked up.

A midsized Terran was standing across from her, coffee mug in hand, an expression of admiration on his round face.

Priscilla felt her stomach sink. Here we go again, she thought.

"Hi," the man said easily enough. "You must be the only person onboard who hasn't had a message to send this trip."

"That's because I'm not onboard," Priscilla told him, then grinned and shook her head. "No, *that* doesn't make sense. I mean that I'm only visiting. . . ."

"Yeah?" he said interestedly, and extended a soft-palmed hand. "Rusty Morgenstern, radio tech. Pleased to meet you, Ms.—"

"Mendoza." She took the hand and shook lightly; she was agreeably surprised when he did not try to prolong the contact. "Priscilla Mendoza. Sit down?"

"Thanks." He slouched down and put his elbows on the table, fingers curled loosely about the mug. "Who're you visiting, if that's not too nosy? And how come they left you to eat by yourself?"

"I'm not explaining things too well. What I'm doing is applying for a job. I took some tests earlier, and I'm to see the captain at Seventh Hour to find out how I did." She sighed. "The whole thing seems pointless, though. Mr. Saunderson—the agent on Jankalim—said the ship's fully staffed."

"Well, that's true." He paused to swallow coffee. "What's your line?"

"I was cargo master on my last ship."

Rusty shook his head. "Got a hell of a cargo master—old Ken Rik. Forty years older'n Satan and twice as slippery. Don't play cards with him." He drank more coffee. "But that doesn't mean much. If the cap'n figures you'll work out, there's bound to be something for you to do."

Priscilla blinked at him. "I'm sorry?"

"Well, it's like—" He pointed a finger at her. "Cabin boy. You met Gordy?"

She grinned. "He met me when I came on."

"Nice kid. Point is, we've had a couple different cabin boys. One was backup astrogator. 'Nother spent more time helping Ken Rik figure distributions than she did fetchin' wine. Last guy—seemed like all he did was play chess with the cap'n. Gordy—he's teaching the cap'n—aah, what is it? Restructured Gaelic? Some damn thing—old Terran dialect. Happens to be the everyday parley where Gordy's from."

"The captain's learning Old Terran from Gordy Arbuthnot?" Priscilla picked up her cup and frowned into it. "Why?"

Rusty shrugged. "Cap'n likes to talk."

"I noticed. But—Old Terran? And an obscure dialect, at that?"

"Better ask him—I don't know. But to get back—if the tests check out okay, you're in. And you'll work." He grinned. "*Every*body works."

"But it seems that cabin boy is filled," Priscilla pointed out.

"Cap'n'll think of something," Rusty said with decision. "More coffee?"

She smiled. "Thanks."

"No problem. How you like it? Black? Back in a sec."

He was back almost immediately, handing her a mug; he remained standing, eyeing her consideringly. Priscilla took a gingerly sip and hoped he wasn't about to say anything unfortunate.

"If you got a minute," he began as she clamped her jaw, "let's go 'round to the lounge. There's a screen there. We can call up the spec freight and you can give me lots of ideas for making money. Ought to be interesting, since you've been a cargo master and all."

Priscilla let out her breath and stood with a smile. "Okay."

"Right this way."

Matching his stride, Priscilla asked, "What's the spec freight?"

"Speculation," Rusty explained, and grinned at her blank look.

"See, every crew member who wants to pledges a certain percentage each trip for speculation. Wood, say—that's what I'm interested in. Or perfume—that's pretty chancy, but Lina seems to do okay with it. Musical instruments—I don't know. Little while back we had some Grestwellin caviar—one of Gordy's finds. Sold out next port we put in." He shook his head. "That kid's gonna be one hell of a Trader. Knows what's gonna be hot next port, even if we don't know where next port *is*—here we are."

The door slid open at their approach, and Priscilla followed him over the threshold into comfortable dimness and subdued chatter. There was a card game going on in a bright corner—Rusty waved in that direction and got two or three absent responses—and a few other people were scattered about, some in conversational clusters, some alone, with books or handwork.

"There's Lina," Rusty said, and made a detour toward a single chair where a brown-haired Liaden woman was reading a bound book.

She glanced up and smiled. "Rah Stee. They let you from your cage so soon?"

"It's later than you think," he told her, waving Priscilla forward. "This is Priscilla Mendoza. She's a guest onboard this shift. Got an interview with the cap'n next. Priscilla, this is Lina Faaldom, chief librarian."

Honey-colored eyes considered her gravely. Prompted by an impulse she could not name, Priscilla did what she had never done to Sav Rid Olanek or any of the *Daxflan's* crew—she performed the bow between equals, exactly as Fin Ton had shown her. "I am happy to meet you, Lina Faaldom," she said, with a careful ear to her accent.

The woman clapped her hands. "She speaks Liaden! See, now, Rah Stee, are you not ashamed?" She stood and returned the bow gracefully. "No happier than I am to meet you, Priscilla Mendoza." She straightened and added in Terran, "Perhaps you will prevail upon this lazy Rah Stee to learn, as well."

"Nag," Rusty said without heat. "I was going to call up the spec for Priscilla. Want to kibitz?"

"I do not know. What is it—kibitz?"

"It means to look over our shoulders," Priscilla explained. "Rusty wants me to give him ideas to make money."

"Money, money. Already Rah Stee has more money than he can gamble away. Why does he need more? But yes, I would like to kibitz. Thank you."

The screen was in the corner opposite the card game. Rusty waved his hand at the lightplate and entered his code. Lina perched on the arm of his chair, and Priscilla sat on the hassock to the left, legs curled under her.

"Here we are. Contents, Hold Six: twenty kilos mahogany; ten kilos yellow pine; fifty-eight gallons Endless Lust perfume—*Endless Lust?*" Rusty turned a pained face to the woman beside him.

"It is the *smell,*" Lina told him with dignity, "not the name."

"You're the expert. Four hundred bushels raw cotton; and thirty-two dozen bottles Essence of Themngo." He shook his head. "That kid better be right this time. . . . What do you think, Priscilla?"

"Impressive," she said sincerely. "You seem to have chosen well—mostly luxury items. I'm not an expert on woods, though. Thirty kilos sounds like either too much or too little."

"It is the artists," Lina explained. "Everywhere we go, there are the artists, always looking for something new. Rah Stee starts with the wood . . . oh, *long* ago, when the captain's father was captain. Now, we have orders. The wood becomes a—a usual thing. We are expected."

Priscilla nodded, struck by another thought. "You've got an entire hold tied up in the crew's speculative cargo? What about capacity fees?"

"Cap'n pledges that. On condition the ship gets her share first out of any profit. The ship shares any loss, too—it's a fair deal."

"More than fair." She sipped her cooling coffee. "Your captain sounds unusual."

"He is a good captain," Lina said.

"And the *Passage* is a profitable ship," Rusty added, turning back to the screen. "Most of the wood'll go at Arsdred—the Artisan's Guild put in a big order. We might pick up a few odds and ends there—not too likely, though, since almost everybody running this sector stops there. Number Six'll be empty for a while." He glanced at Priscilla. "Can't make money that way."

"But you just said the wood's an ordered item," she pointed out. "You've got a profit, right?"

"Yeah, I guess." He brightened. "Tell you what—let's try and get our shore leaves matched for Arsdred. Then we can go scouting together. Who knows? Something might turn for the spec. Or even for the ship."

Priscilla stared at him. "I might not be onboard at Arsdred, remember?" She drank the rest of her coffee and shook her head. "Do you *all* look for the ship, too? What's the Master Trader do?"

Lina laughed.

"He trades," Rusty said, his round face serious. "*We* don't trade. But anybody might see something. Cap'n's only one person—he could miss a deal just 'cause he can't be in three places at once. So as many of the crew as can go worldside. If you see something, you hotfoot to the nearest comm and call the cap'n or Kayzin Ne'Zame—first mate. If it turns out to be a go, there's a finder's fee." He blinked at her. "What's wrong?"

"Nothing. I—the last ship I was on didn't—encourage—the crew to go worldside. And the Trader did all the trading."

"Sounds like a stupid arrangement to me," the man said flatly.

"It does not make good sense," Lina agreed slowly. "The ship is everyone's venture. We all take a share of the profit. It is only sensible to work hard for a *big* profit." She looked carefully at Priscilla. "Perhaps you were not on such a good ship before."

"Perhaps I wasn't," Priscilla said dryly, and lifted a hand to cover a sudden yawn. "I'm sorry. It's been a long day. Better be finding my room. . . ." She uncoiled her legs and stood.

With a nod, Rusty signed off and moved out of the alcove. One of the card players looked up and waved him over. "In a sec," he called, and turned back. "Priscilla, I bet you threebits you'll be on the *Passage* at Arsdred."

"I don't have threebits to bet," she said ruefully. "But I hope you're right. It was good to meet you."

"See you later," he responded, and drifted off toward the game.

"You should excuse Rah Stee," Lina said, waving a hand at his retreating back. "You know where your room is from here?"

"I have a map," Priscilla began, fishing in her pocket.

The smaller woman laughed. "The map is good, but it will take you by all the main halls. I know the short ways. If it does not offend, I can show you. It is time I went to sleep as well."

"I don't want to put you to any trouble. . . ."

"It is no trouble," Lina assured her. "Only let me get my book."

They turned left from the door of the lounge rather than right, as the map directed, and pursued several short zigzagging corridors before regaining the main hail. They followed this past several closed doors, one marked GYM and another POOL, before turning into a slimmer, dimmer way.

Lina left her with a smile and a slight bow at the third door on the right. "Sleep well, Priscilla Mendoza. I will look for you tomorrow."

"Sleep you well also, Lina Faaldom," Priscilla answered softly in Liaden. "Thank you for your care."

The room was a blur to her overtired mind. She located the cleanbot and pushed her clothes into the slot, hoping that the black smear on one yellow cuff would come out in the cycle.

There was a clock on the shelf over the bed; she keyed in a request for Sixth Hour and curled into the luxuriously soft cushions with a sigh as she belatedly waved a hand at the lightplate.

She was asleep before the room was dark.

Shipyear 65
Tripday 131
Second Shift
6.55 Hours

"PRISCILLA MENDOZA?"

She started, almost spilling what was left of her coffee, and blinked at the small person who had appeared suddenly before her. The woman was a Liaden of middle years, with golden skin showing deep lines about eyes and mouth, and yellow hair going gray.

Priscilla smiled. "I am sorry. I was daydreaming. How may I serve you?"

The handsome face did not relax its austere lines. "The captain's compliments, Ms. Mendoza. He requests that you come to him, if you have broken your fast." She hesitated before inclining her head ever so slightly. "I am Kayzin Ne'Zame." The first mate.

Priscilla smiled again, despite the stiffness of her face, and pushed back her chair. "I've just finished this minute. I'll go to the captain as soon as I've cleaned up my tray." She was fairly confident of the route, having studied her map throughout breakfast.

"I shall escort you," Kayzin Ne'Zame said uncompromisingly.

Fear returned. Priscilla would be sent from the ship—or she would be required to remain—it was impossible to know which was the worse possibility. Breakfast was a handful of cold rock in her stomach; she abruptly remembered the woman she had met last night and wished they had had a chance to speak further.

Priscilla laid her tray gently on the conveyer belt and turned back to the first mate. "Thank you, Kayzin Ne'Zame. I am ready now."

THE CAPTAIN WAS BEHIND THE DESK, fingers busy on the keypad. A glass of wine sat to hand, and the previous day's stacks of paper had given birth to two others like themselves.

"Captain," the first mate said formally. "Here is Priscilla Mendoza, come to speak with you."

He glanced up absently. "Ms. Mendoza. Good morning. I'll be with you in just a moment. Kayzin, old friend, will you come to me in an hour?"

"Certainly, Captain." She executed a disapproving bow, but he had already returned his attention to the screen, and Priscilla did not think he saw. Frowning, the mate turned on her heel; the automatic door did its best to bang shut behind her.

Priscilla stood, fighting cold nausea. Biting her lip, she studied the man behind the desk, combating fear with observation.

It was a puzzle, she decided. He was so tall, his skin warm brown rather than golden. Like all Liaden men she had seen, his face was as fine-grained as a child's, without a hint of beard. The white hair and brows made a vivid contrast; the lean cheeks and mobile mouth were not displeasing.

Really, she thought, if you don't expect him to look Liaden, he's not ugly at all.

Certainly he was not an ill-made person. Beneath the wide-sleeved shirt his shoulders were level and broad, his back straight without being rigid. The big hands moved with graceful economy on the keypad, and Priscilla did not think they would be babysoft like Rusty Morgenstern's.

Abruptly he nodded, leaned back, and extended a long arm for his glass. The slanting brows pulled sharply together as he looked up. "Does Sav Rid have delusions of grandeur? Sit, sit. Have you eaten? Will you drink? Did you sleep well?"

Priscilla considered him. "I don't know. Thank you. Yes. No. Very. Did *you*?"

"Not too badly," he said, raising his glass. "Though Mr. Saunderson's idea of a party *is* a bit risqué. We played charades. And sang rounds. The youngest Ms. Saunderson attempted to elicit my promise to wed her when she comes of age." He shook his head. "Alas, it seems clear she is more enamored of adventuring about the galaxy than she is of my elegant person, so there's a brilliant match gone begging. I have your test scores. Are you interested in discussing them now?"

Priscilla made an effort to settle her stomach firmly in place. "Yes, sir."

He ran his fingers in a quick series over the keys. "Physics, math, astrogation—yes, yes, yes. Colors red, colors blue, taste in books—yes?" He glanced up. "Prebatout. You recall the question? 'How many toes should a prebatout have?' And here is Priscilla Mendoza saying, 'As many as it feels comfortable with.' I've only known one other person to answer that particular question that way."

"Have you?' Priscilla asked, hands ice cold. "Was she a suspected thief, too?"

"Thief? No, a Scout. Though, come to think of it, the two trades might have some similarities. I've never considered it in that light. I'll ask, the next time I see him. . . ." He returned to the screen, humming to himself.

Priscilla curled her fingers carefully around the armrests, refusing to rise to the bait—if it was bait—of his last comment. Let *him* talk, since he seemed to like it so much.

He moved his shoulders, gave the keypad a final tap, and leaned back. "You don't have a pilot's license? That won't do, will it? Let me see . . . forty-eight crew members, counting the captain— eight of them pilots. Too few by far. You'll have to study, Ms. Mendoza. I insist on it. Every ninth shift you'll be on the bridge for lessons."

"Wait a minute." She took a breath. "You're signing me on? As a pilot?"

"As a pilot?" he repeated blandly. "No, how could I do that? You're not a pilot, are you, Ms. Mendoza? That's why you'll need to take lessons. Certification's no problem. I'm rated master, all conditions—is something wrong?"

"Forgive me," she said carefully. "I thought you were captain. And Master Trader, of course. You're a pilot, too?"

"A little of this, a little of that. The *Passage* is a family enterprise, after all. Owned and operated by Clan Korval. And piloting runs in the blood, so to speak. I got my first class when I was sixteen Standards—been ratable for a few years before that, of course. Did my first solo on this ship when I was fourteen—but rules are rules, and they clearly state that no one may be certified until sixteen Standards. But I was saying—what *was* I saying? Oh, yes. Since I'm a master pilot, there won't be any delay once you earn your certification. Are you *certain* you haven't got a license, Ms. Mendoza? Third class, perhaps?"

"I'm certain, Captain." Things were moving too fast; the torrent of words was threatening to unmoor her fragile hold on serenity. "Just what will my position be?"

"Hmm? Oh—pet librarian."

"*Pet* librarian?"

"We have a very nice pet library," he told her gravely. "Now, details. We're nearly half done with the route. I can offer you flat rate from Jankalim to Solcintra—approximately a tenth-cantra upon docking. You'd be eligible for the low-man share of any bonus the ship might earn from this point on—finder's fees and special awards are the same for everyone, based on profit of found cargo and merit, as judged by the majority of the crew." He raised his glass. "Questions?"

She had a myriad of them, but only one was forthcoming. "Why," she demanded irritably, "do you keep waving that glass around if you never drink from it?"

He grinned. "But I *do* drink from it. Sometimes. More questions?"

She sighed. "How much will the ship charge for pilot training?"

"If you fail to report for training every ninth shift, the captain will dock you twentybits. Three unexcused or unexplained absences will be grounds for immediate termination of your contract.

Understand, please, Ms. Mendoza, that pilot training is an essential part of your duties while you are a member of this crew. I will not allow abandonment of that duty—the penalties are quite in earnest." He paused, his light eyes gauging her face. "You *do* understand?"

"Yes, Captain." She bit her lip. "It's that I've been charged for training on every other ship I served on—and pursued it during my free time. *Daxflan* denied me permission to continue training while I shipped on her."

"Sav Rid, Sav Rid." He shook his head. "However, this is not *Daxflan,* and her rules do not apply here. Now. Your supervisor—no. The ship will extend you credit for a Standard Week's worth of clothing, to be reckoned against your share at the end of the route. Please draw what you need from general stores. Your supervisor will be Lina Faaldom, who is chief librarian."

"I met her last night—"

"Yes? She will introduce you to the residents of the pet library and acquaint you with your duties there. I don't believe the work to be arduous, so you'll be expected to take on other duties as necessary. Janice Weatherbee will be your piloting instructor. If she is called elsewhere upon occasion, I will take her place. I believe that's everything. Are the terms agreeable to you?"

"Since I was almost certain I'd be back on Jankalim this morning, yes, Captain, the terms are agreeable to me." She paused, studying his face. Sometime during the interview the fear had dissipated, leaving her limp and slowly warming. "Do you *really* need a pet librarian?"

"Well, we didn't have one," he said, spinning the screen toward her. "So I guess we do. Palmprint here, please."

SHAN YOS'GALAN was tipped back in his chair, arms folded behind his head, eyes apparently resting on the crystalline mobile hanging in the far corner of the ceiling. The expression on his face was one of dreamy stupidity. He did not glance around at the hissing of the door; he did not even seem aware that he was no longer alone in the room.

Kayzin Ne'Zame knew better than to be deceived by appearances.

She sat in the seat that Priscilla Mendoza had recently vacated, her spine two inches from the chair back, and frowned at his profile.

"You've signed her on?" she demanded in the High Tongue, each syllable icy with disapproval.

"I did say that it was my intention to sign her on," the man reminded the mobile gently and in Terran. He spun the chair lazily around, unfolded his arms, and sat up. "What is it, Kayzin?"

"She is too beautiful." The Terran words were no less cold.

"But that's not her fault, is it? People can't choose their faces, can they? If they can, I want to know why I wasn't told about it."

The older woman regarded him with something perilously close to amusement. "I am, in fact, to pity her."

"What harm can it do?"

"What harm! You ask it? Or is it the game again? Do not trouble yourself, I beg you. . . ." She paused, visibly taking herself in hand. "And what harm is it—to the ship, to the crew, to your Clan, and to Shan yos'Galan—should Sav Rid Olanek prove clever as well as dishonorable? What harm, should this so-pitiful, so-beautiful woman prove to be a tool in his hands—a blade at your throat? What harm—"

"Kayzin. . . ." The big hands made a soothing motion; concern for her showed in his face.

She slumped back in her chair. "Shan, it is my last trip. I prefer it to be an uneventful one."

"There's no reason for it to be otherwise, old friend. Why should Sav Rid want to plant a—what? spy? *assassin?*—on the *Passage?* He's had his coup—and a very fine laugh. There's no reason for him to go to such trouble. No reason to think of the affair at all, except to chuckle and extend the story in port taverns as proof of Shan yos'Galan's rabid foolishness." He grinned wryly. "And he's not too far off the mark, is he?"

She gestured, speechless.

"You worry too much, Kayzin—and without cause. Circumstance, synchronicity—I don't believe Sav Rid would *wish* Priscilla Mendoza here, assuming he wished her any place at all, except, perhaps, dead. I think it more likely that he acted twice as opportunity dictated. It's interesting—but not impossible—that the victims of both actions should come together."

"It is also not impossible that Olanek has grown wary—or even that he has grown greedy. What a coup for him, should he bring Korval entire to its knees. . . ."

Shan's brows pulled together. "Do you really think he could? Not that he doesn't have the potential for being that greedy—or that reckless. Kayzin, the *Passage* proceeds as ever. For our years together and the time you spent raising me, I will attempt to keep the rest of the route as uneventful as possible. In the meantime, please try to be kind to Priscilla Mendoza." He picked up his glass and drank slowly. "And wouldn't you say it was better, Kayzin, to keep the knife— if there is a knife, of course—in our view rather than have it poised at our back?"

She smiled. "You will reward him properly?"

"Steps are being taken to bring accounts into balance," he promised, and finished his wine.

Shipyear 65
Tripday 135
Second Shift
9.30 Hours

GLASS IN HAND, Shan yos'Galan rounded the corner into the leisure section. Ahead was a slender figure, gay in raspberry tunic and celadon sash. He stretched his long legs and caught her by the intersection to the athletic hall.

"Well met, Lina."

She looked up, her smile radiant. "Shan. I'm glad to see you."

"And I'm glad to see you. As always. You're looking exceptionally lovely. Off to a party? Will you bring me with you? I promise not to brag of my exalted position. How do you find your assistant?"

She laughed. "But it is exactly of Priscilla that I wished to speak! Have you truly a moment? I know how busy it is to be captain. I hardly see you . . ."

"Languishing? He raised his glass, his light eyes mocking. "By all means speak to me of Priscilla. Do the residents approve? Is she impossible for you? Shall I send her to Ken Rik?"

"Oh, no, not to Ken Rik. The small ones are each delighted— Master Frodo to the point of purrs. You knew he would be." She stopped, frowning up into his face. "Shan? What is wrong with her—do you know? There is joy—one can feel it—but she denies . . . suppresses . . . I like her very well. Don't you?"

"It would be enough to lower anyone's feelings, wouldn't it, to

714

be hit over the head and deserted with no money, a ruined record, and no friends?"

"It is more than that," Lina insisted. "She wants Healing."

"Does she?" He sipped. "Is she impossible for you?"

"Not at all. Though perhaps *you* . . ."

"Me?" He laughed. "I'm not a Healer, Lina; I'm the captain."

"Bah!" She banished this quibble with a tiny contemptuous hand. "As if you haven't the skill and the training!" She tipped her head, considering information of which the expression on his face was only a small portion. "Shan?"

A lifted shoulder denied her. He frowned slightly. "What—perfume—are you wearing, Lina?"

"The one we bought—Endless Lust." She chuckled. "Rah Stee objects to the name."

"As well he might." He moved back a step or two. "Very potent, isn't it? I don't recall that you reported aphrodisiac qualities."

"It has none!" She grinned. "Are you certain it is the perfume?"

"Forgive me," he murmured. "I have admired you forever, Lina, but amorous thoughts were far from me this evening. If it *isn't* aphrodisiac, it's the next best thing. Did anybody explain how it works?"

"It is the smell. . . ." She sighed sharply, asked permission with a flicker of her hands, and slid into the Low Tongue, on the mode spoken between friends. "It is an enhancer of one's own odor. Thus, if you are attracted primarily, you will be more so when the perfume is used. Harmless, old friend, I assure you."

"I," the Captain said in Terran, "am not convinced. There are laws on certain worlds about perfumes and substances that—what *is* the official phrasing?—'take away volition and make pliable the will'? Something more or less pompous." He took a drink and drifted away yet another step. "Do me the favor of submitting what is left of your vial to Chemistry, Lina. I would so hate to break the law."

"It is harmless." She frowned. "It does *not* take away volition—no more than a Healer might, encouraging one to embrace joy. . . ."

Shan grinned. "I believe you may be splitting hairs. *Are* you going to a party? I would like to accompany you—purely scientific, you understand. It might be very interesting to observe the effect of this perfume of yours on a roomful of unsuspecting persons."

"I," Lina said dampingly, "am going to watch a Ping-Pong match between Priscilla and Rah Stee. You may come, if you like. Though if you persist in backing away from me in that insulting manner . . ."

He laughed and offered an arm. "I have myself in hand now. Let us by all means inflict ourselves upon the Ping-Pong match."

RUSTY WAS SWEATING and puffing with exertion, the expression on his round face one of harried doggedness.

In contrast, Priscilla was coolly serene, parrying his shots with absent smoothness, barely regarding the ball at all. Yet time after time she fractured his frenzied guard and piled up the points in her favor.

"Twenty-one," he said, his voice cracking slightly. "I don't believe it."

"No, Rah Stee, it *is* twenty-one for Priscilla," Lina said helpfully. "I counted also."

"That's what I don't believe." Rusty leaned heavily on the table, directing a sodden head shake at his opponent. "You're blowing me away! I don't get it. Half the time I don't even see the ball coming."

"That's because you have the reactions of a dead cow," Shan explained, not to be outdone in helpfulness.

The other man turned to glare at him. "Thanks a lot."

"Always of service . . . ."

"Maybe," Priscilla offered, cutting off a scorching reply, "it's because you look for the ball. I almost never do that."

"Then how do you know where it *is?*" He ran a sleeve across his forehead and sighed hugely. "Dammit, 'Cilla, I'm good at Ping-Pong. Been playing for years!"

"But not against pilots," the captain said, sipping wine.

"What's that got to do with it?"

"A great deal, don't you think, Rusty? Your reaction time's slow; you move in a series of jerks rather than a smooth flow; you fail to apprehend where an object *will be.*" He raised his glass. "Don't feel too bad, my friend. We all have our niche to fill. After all, I could hardly fill your place in the tower, or operate the—"

"Like hell you can't," the other muttered, spinning his paddle clumsily on the table.

"I beg your pardon, Rusty?"

"Never mind." He turned suddenly and flipped the paddle to Shan, who caught it left-handed, lazily. "*You* play her."

The captain blinked. "Why?"

"You're a pilot. She's a pilot. Maybe I'll pick up some pointers." Grinning, Rusty retired from the field and flung himself into a sideline seat. "Besides, I need a break. You don't want me to keel over dead from exertion, do you?"

"Now, that would be a tragedy. So young, so handsome, so wealthy—he had all to live for . . . Ms. Mendoza? Are you interested in a game? Observe that you have the advantage of youth over dissipated old age."

Priscilla swallowed a laugh. Lina frowned.

"Certainly, Captain. I'll be happy to play with you. Will you offer me a handicap?"

"You should offer one to me," he said, setting his glass aside and wandering toward the table. "Remember that I'm frail, please, and easily bruised. You'll serve?"

She nodded, and the ball was even then skimming smoothly over the net . . . to be returned with casual force, heading toward the edge of the table, barely brushing; it was caught as it struck and sent backspinning over the net, to be returned again, barely inside her play zone, then flipped by a cunning paddle edge back into his court.

"Twenty-seven, twenty-five," Priscilla said nearly forty minutes later. She actually grinned at the man opposite. "Good game, Captain."

"Fighting for every point," he agreed, laying his paddle down and moving in the direction of his wine. "Notice, please, Rusty, that I barely won. *Have* you picked up any pointers?"

"Huh? I'm gonna retire to a home for the physically degenerate." The radio tech shook his head. "You're so fast! If I hadn't heard it hit, I'd've thought you were runnin' a scam: pretending to have a game with an invisible ball."

Priscilla drifted over to Lina's chair and sat carefully on an upholstered arm. The Liaden woman smiled up at her. "You played very well, my friend."

Friend. The word was unexceptional from Lina, yet Priscilla never heard it without a small thrill of warmth. She smiled gently. "Thank you." She moved her shoulders in response to a slight twinge. "No excuse for not sleeping tonight."

Lina shifted. "You have not been sleeping? On our ship?"

Priscilla allowed herself the luxury of another grin. "I sleep better on this ship than—than I sometimes do." She moved her shoulders again, half a shrug. "It's nothing. I get by."

"In two days we are at Scandalous," the smaller woman offered, apropos of nothing. "A drop only. Then, in three days more, we are at Arsdred. Do you like us, now that you have been here a whole week?"

"Has it been a week?" The question woke echoes of Shan yos'Galan's voice in her mind's ear, and she smiled again, almost lazily. "I like you very much. Everyone's been kind . . . ." Except Kayzin Ne'Zame, of course. What ailed the woman? She glanced down and saw Lina's small golden hand resting on the chair arm at her knee. It looked strong and capable and curiously pleasing. With hardly a thought except that it would be comforting to do so, Priscilla laid her own hand over it—and flicked her eyes, startled, to the other woman's face.

Lina smiled at her.

Priscilla sighed; the sound seemed to come from very far away. Friend, she thought, and her fingers tightened around Lina's. She received warm pressure in return and smiled for the fourth time in five minutes. From across the room she heard the soothing murmur of voices: Rusty and the captain, speaking between themselves. She shook her head. "I must be more tired than I thought. . . ."

"Yes? Would you like to go to bed? I will walk with you, if you like."

Priscilla looked into the face of her friend. Goddess, it would be hard to tell Lina good-bye . . . "I'd like you to come with me," she said softly. "That would be good."

"I think so, too," Lina said, and stood, keeping their hands linked.

Across the room, Rusty suddenly sighed. "Here I thought she liked me," he complained, "and then she goes off with Lina!"

Shan glanced around absently. "I'm afraid you were outgunned. Lina was wearing that new perfume of hers."

"Was she?" He looked up, all interest. "Damn. That stuff's gonna make us *rich.*"

THEY REACHED PRISCILLA'S quarters and entered together when the door slid away. Just inside, Lina stopped and smiled up at her tall companion a little quizzically. Cautiously, she touched the bruise on the pale cheek. "I am sorry that they hurt you, my friend."

"It wasn't so bad. . . ." Priscilla murmured, gazing down into her face. Slowly, with a sense of inevitable tenderness, she bent and kissed Lina on the mouth.

Shipyear 65
Tripday 136
Third Shift
11.30 Hours
Around Scandalous

MASTER FRODO THE NORBEAR burbled happily and ran to the port opening as fast as his bowed legs would carry him. His three companions came more slowly from their cozyplaces and followed, Tiny uttering a small, dignified *bwrrr* of welcome.

Priscilla carefully measured out three portions and placed each in its appointed place. Tiny, Delm Briat, and Lady Selph fell to with a will, while Master Frodo stood by, fairly quivering with anticipation. As the last measure was placed, he extended a small clawed hand and snagged a fold of sleeve.

"Did you think I'd forgotten you?" Priscilla asked as he clambered into her hand. Master Frodo rubbed his head against her fingers.

Smiling, Priscilla brought him to her shoulder. He rolled off and sat up on hind legs, one hand clutching the curls over her ear while with the other he solemnly accepted pieces of corn and stuffed them into his cheek pouches.

"It's the tower for me today," Priscilla confided as Master Frodo broke his fast. "I'm to report to Tonee sig'Ella by Twelfth Hour."

Her companion vouchsafed no direct reply, though he let her

know by the quality of his eating that Tonee sig'Ella was not a bad sort, received everywhere by norbears of consequence.

Since Priscilla was able to verify by the sign-out that Tonee was no infrequent visitor to the norbears' hearth, this information was not startling. She thanked Master Frodo for his recommendation, however, and scratched him lightly between the ears before replacing him in the tank.

He settled to the sandy soil with a little sigh and twisted his head sideways, peering upward, one paw raised in supplication.

Priscilla grinned again. "No more for you," she said sternly, rubbing his belly with a gentle finger. "You're getting positively fat."

Master Frodo let it be known that among norbears a certain portliness of figure was considered attractive. Priscilla might, of course, think what she would. He did not like to mention it, but *she* could use a little extra corn to advantage.

Caught in the imagined dialogue, she shook her head. "I've always been scrawny," she said, closing the hatch and sealing it.

She shook her head again. Talking to yourself like a Seer. If anybody catches you, they'll have you down in sick bay before Master Frodo can give you a reference.

But the thought failed to alarm her. Lina had in fact caught her talking to Master Frodo a shift or two back. The Liaden woman's only response had been to tug on one rounded ear and warn Priscilla not to let the norbear charm her out of extra rations.

"He is a rogue, this one," Lina had explained, laughing at the creature's antics. "And you must not be taken in. He will exploit you shamelessly."

Priscilla left the pet library by way of the side door, which gave onto the library proper. Lina was at the desk, frowning at her screen, but she glanced up with a smile. Still unused to such warm and easy friendship, Priscilla caught her breath. "Everyone's taken care of," she said, striving for serenity. "I'm going up to the tower now."

"So? Call me to Tonee's attention. We have not met often this trip." She touched the back of a slim pale hand. "Shall we share Prime Meal, my friend?"

"Yes." She drew breath against the pounding of her heart.

Lina smiled. "I will see you at Prime, then. Be you well, Priscilla."

"Be you well, Lina."

THE TOWER WAS OPPOSITE THE LIBRARY and up six levels, a dome in the ship's center section exactly balancing the dome of the main bridge, six levels below. Priscilla entered a lift and punched her route, then leaned back into a corner.

Pet librarian. So far, she had spent only one shift performing the duties attached to that post. Her assignment was on her cabin-screen when she awoke, always allowing her ample time to see to the needs of the creatures she cared for. And then she was sent elsewhere: to the maintenance bay to help lanky Seth with an overhaul, to the kitchen to assist garrulous BillyJo, to the holds to pore over distribution charts with sharp-tongued old Ken Rik. And, of course, to the inner bridge for piloting lessons with Janice Weatherbee, second mate and first class pilot.

Only a week, and I must have worked everywhere but the pet library, Priscilla thought. But she found she did not mind the variety of work. Rather, it seemed to ease her in some unidentified way, even as the mix of personalities exhilarated her.

People. One might find friends here. She had found at least one friend already. And since she had had no friends at all, that was a treasure past any attempt at counting.

The lift stopped, and the door slid away to reveal a bright yellow hallway. Priscilla walked to the end of it, feet soundless on the resilient floor, laid her hand upon the door, and entered.

Instruments were flickering; one console was clamoring for attention, while a screen set in the far wall flashed orange numbers: seven in series; pause; repeat.

No human occupant was apparent.

"Hello?"

"Hahlo! Yes! A moment!" There was a harried scrabbling from behind the center console. Priscilla started in that direction and almost bumped into the person coming the other way.

"You are Priscilla Mendoza, yes?"

"I'm Priscilla Mendoza," she agreed, bowing the bow between equals. "You are Tonee sig'Ella?"

"Who else? No, we have not met—you must not regard . . ." An abbreviated version of the courtesy was returned. She had a moment to wonder if Fin Ton would have approved before her hand was caught in a surprisingly strong grip and she was pulled toward the console.

"You are a decoder, yes? You have operated the bouncecomm and know the symbols? There is a difficulty with the in-ship, and I must have time, but the messages—you perceive? Do you but decode what arrives; encode what must be sent—I will have my time; we will not fall behind. All will be well!" the little tech finished triumphantly, pulling out the console chair.

Priscilla sat and flicked a glance at screens, transmitters, receivers. The equipment was standard; there should be no problem.

"How are we getting the messages to the proper people onboard?" she asked. "If the in-ship's out—"

"I have spoken with the captain," the other interrupted, rubbing wire-thin hands together. "The cabin boy will be dispatched to the tower and will carry messages as they are ready. It should not be long. You are familiar? You will contrive?"

"I will contrive." Priscilla made the assurance as solemn as she could, despite the rising wave of laughter. She swallowed firmly. "Lina Faaldom asked to be remembered to you. She says you haven't seen each other often this trip."

"Lina!" The gamin face lit, eyes sparkling. "I will call on her—say, to beg her forgiveness!" A quick laugh was accompanied by the lightest of touches to her shoulder. Then she was alone. On the other side of the tower, Tonee was removing the cover of the noisy console.

Priscilla shook her head and turned to the task at hand.

GORDY HAD JUST LEFT with his third handful of messages. Priscilla heard the sound of the door cycling without assigning it importance, most of her attention captured by an unusually knotty translation.

Could it really be "desires your most religious custom?" she wondered, fingers poised over the keys. The message was directed to Master Trader, *Dutiful Passage*. It would be best to take a little time to be sure.

"What," demanded a heavily accented voice, "are you doing here?"

Priscilla glanced up, stomach sinking. Kayzin Ne'Zame stood before the console, and it was apparent she was in no mood to be pleased.

"I was assigned here," she began.

"You are not cleared for this work!" the first mate snapped. "Who assigns you?"

"My screen lists my duties at the beginning of each shift," Priscilla explained, keeping her voice even. "This shift, I was assigned to Tonee sig'Ella at Twelfth Hour."

"Who is your supervisor?" Kayzin asked awfully.

"Lina Faaldom."

"Lina Faaldom. And it is your belief that a librarian has the authority necessary to assign you to the tower as a decoder of messages?" There was no mistaking the sarcasm.

"She has apparently," Priscilla snapped, "had the authority to send me to the maintenance bay, the cargo holds, the kitchen, and hydroponics. Why should I assume this shift's assignment was different from those?"

"Has she?" There was an odd expression on the first mate's face. She turned, scanning the tower, eyes lighting on the hunched figure at the far corner. "Radio Tech!"

Tonee turned and hurried forward with a sigh. "First Mate?"

"How came this woman to you?"

The radio tech blinked. "Under orders, First Mate. She was expected. Twelfth Hour, so went the captain's word."

"The captain—"

"First Mate, she is required!" Tonee pleaded, as if suddenly perceiving where that line of questioning might lead. "She has been of utmost assistance. The in-ship is nearly repaired. Before we leave orbit, I promise it—but you must not take her now! The messages—surely you know the need!"

It was apparent from her expression that Kayzin *did* know the need. She looked from Tonee to Priscilla, rigid at the console, then inclined her head. "A question of clearance, Radio Tech. However, since you have the captain's word, there is no more to be said." With that, she turned on her heel and left the tower.

Priscilla and Tonee exchanged glances before the little tech flung both hands out in a gesture of wide amazement.

"You work well. When we leave orbit, the screens will be clear. The first mate . . ." There was a ripple of narrow shoulders. "Her temper is chancy, a little. Do not regard it."

With another delicate pat on the shoulder, Priscilla was left alone to conquer bewilderment and return to the matter at hand.

Shipyear 65
Tripday 137
First Shift
1.30 Hours

ଉଉଉଉଉଉଉଉଉଉଉଉଉଉଉଉଉଉଉଉଉଉଉଉଉଉଉ

PRISCILLA WHIPPED ABOUT—and froze. The alley behind her was full of men and women, hands ominously clenched, righteousness shining from each grim face. She fell back, forgetting the danger behind—

Until with a jerk the precious bag was torn from her grip and she was dealt such a blow between the shoulders that she fell to her knees in the alleyway.

She was up in a flash, facing Dagmar with fury. "That's mine! Give it back!"

"Yours?" the other woman sneered as Pimm tel'Jadis came laughing to her side. "That ain't the tale I heard, Prissy." She jerked open the bag and thrust her hand within, rummaging about. Then, uttering a crow of triumph, she raised high a fist in which were clutched the seven silver bangles of a Maiden-in-Circle.

The crowd shrieked.

The first rock caught Priscilla on the thigh as Dagmar brought a fist across her face.

The second rock slammed solidly into her right arm, breaking it with an audible crack.

The third took a rib, and she screamed, rolling into a ball on the

726

filthy alley floor, trying to protect her head while the rocks struck with greater and greater force, and the crowd cried out her names: Liar! Coward! Unperson!

"Priscilla!"

She felt hands on her, and she struggled.

"Priscilla! No, *denubia*, you must not. . . ." The voice was familiar, concerned.

"Lina?" She lay still, hardly daring to believe it.

"Of course, Lina. Who else?" The hands were soft on her face, her hair. "Open your eyes, *denubia*. Are you afraid to see me?"

"No, I . . ." She achieved it and beheld her friend's serious face. "I'm sorry, Lina."

"And I. Such *terror*, my friend. What was it?" The kind hands continued their caress; comfort like a healing warmth enclosed her. Priscilla sighed and shook her head.

"It was nothing. A bad dream."

"Yes?" Lina ran light fingers along Priscilla's jaw and down the slim throat, then laid her hand flat between rose-tipped breasts. "A very bad dream, I think. Your heart pounds."

"I dreamt—I dreamt I was being stoned." She shivered, drew a breath, and tried to recapture inner peace.

"Stoned?" Lina frowned. "I do not think—"

"It is the custom on my—on the world I'm from—to throw rocks at a criminal until she—until she dies."

"*Qua'lechi!*" The smaller woman sat up sharply and reached to trace the line of her friend's brow. "No wonder you were frightened." She tipped her head. "But this thing was not truly done to you?"

Priscilla managed a smile. "No, of course not." There, she had found the well-worn way to serenity and set her spirit feet upon it. "I'm not very brave," she told Lina softly.

As Priscilla's lashes drooped and her breathing evened, the Liaden woman frowned. Tentatively she unfurled a mental tendril, as one might with a fellow Healer, extended it along the least dangerous of the lines—and nearly cried out as Priscilla reached the place she had been seeking and firmly closed the door.

☆ ☆ ☆

THE LIBRARY DOOR SLID OPEN, and a tall, broad-shouldered person ambled to the center of the room and stood sipping from his glass, quietly regarding the figure hunched over the master terminal. It was perhaps five minutes before she sat back with a sharp sigh and spoke with the ease of long acquaintance. "Are there Healers among Terrans, old friend?"

He considered it, coming forward. "Not formally, I believe." He bent over her screen, frowning at the upside-down characters. "You want 'empath,' my precious. It's listed under 'paranormal.'"

"Paranormal!" Lina's head was up, eyes flashing.

"I didn't put it there," Shan pointed out mildly. "I only offer information. That's where it was when I searched it."

And, Lina realized, he would have done just such a search a few years ago. She smiled. "Forgive me. There was hard work done, if little accomplished. I am—edgy."

He bowed slightly. "I might offer aid."

"So you might." She smiled again and reached to touch his stark cheek. "I thank you, bed-friend and colleague. Grant me grace and offer another time."

"So I will." He drank wine. "Don't stay up all shift, please, Lina."

"Bah! And what of you! Or does the captain never sleep?" She chuckled, then sobered abruptly. "Kayzin was complaining to me that Priscilla is assigned where she has no right to be."

"I heard." Shan shook his head. "What did she want me to do? First she tells me this is her last trip and I must not ask her for decisions concerning future trips, then she takes me to *severe* task for daring to follow her instructions! I tell you, Lina, it's a hard life the captain lives!"

"Alas," she managed around a mouthful of laughter.

He grinned and raised his glass. "Search well, Master Librarian. Sleep well, too."

"Sleep well, Shan."

But he was already gone.

Shipyear 65
Tripday 139
Third Shift
16.00 Hours

THE *DUTIFUL PASSAGE* broke orbit smoothly and proceeded down the carefully calculated normal space lane to the Jump point and passed without a quiver into hyperspace.

Priscilla ran through the last check, reaffirmed destination and time of arrival, locked the board, and leaned back, barely conquering her grin.

"Not too bad, Mendoza," Janice Weatherbee said from the copilot's seat. She glanced at the chronometer set in the board. "Quittin' time. See you 'round."

"Okay," Priscilla said absently, still watching the grayed screen. It was not the simulation screen this time—it was the prime piloting screen on the main bridge, and she had done it all. She, Priscilla Delacroix y Mendoza, had plotted the course, worked the equations, chosen the coords—done everything, out of her own knowledge and ability.

She closed her eyes against the screen, cherishing the solid wedge of belief in her own ability. For this little time, at least, it seemed not to matter that she was outcast and lawfully nameless, with no more right to call herself Mendoza than Rusty Morgenstern had.

"Sleeping, Ms. Mendoza? It's a very comfortable chair, I grant, but someone else might wish to use it."

729

She opened her eyes and grinned at the captain, who stood with one hip braced against the ledge and a glass of wine in his hand.

"Sorry, Captain. I was indulging in vulgar self-congratulation."

"Well, that's encouraging," he said, grinning back. "I was prepared to believe you had no faults at all. But now that you admit to gloating, I'm sure we'll get along very well together. Janice is a bit laconic, is she?"

"Maybe she's trying to make up for you," Priscilla suggested, then bit her lip in horror.

Shan yos'Galan laughed. "Could be. Could be. *Some*one should, I guess. Are you working a double shift? Even so, you're allowed an hour to eat—ship's policy. And there's really not much to do here now, is there?" He glanced vaguely at the gray screen. "Seems to be in hand. Why not take a shift or two for yourself?"

"Thank you, Captain," she said. "I will. Good shift."

"Good shift, Ms. Mendoza." He raised his glass to her.

SHE WAS TO MEET LINA AND RUSTY for Prime at Seventeenth Hour. Priscilla turned left, away from the lift. There was time for a walk to stretch legs cramped by hours in the pilot's chair.

Hugging her recent accomplishment to herself, she wandered down a quarter mile of hallway, took a down-lift when the way deadended, and smiled at dour old Ken Rik when she stepped off one level below.

I feel good, she ventured, probing the thought as if it were a shattered bone. A mere quiver of pain answered, to be quickly blotted out by another warm thought.

I have a friend. The first real friend since her girlhood on Sintia. The friendship existed independently of the sudden physical relationship. She'd had bed-mates from time to random time, and it was very nice to be loved and petted and—made comfortable. And it was wholly delightful to be permitted to return that grace as best as she was able. But this was not the thing that was precious, that prompted her now to reexamine the plans she had laid out for herself.

Again she heard the sleepy voice of her friend: "Priscilla? Go back to sleep, *denubia*. All is well."

All is well. For the first time in many years she allowed herself to think that it could, in time, *be* well. If she remained a member of this ship, with its odd captain, and clumsy Rusty Morgenstern and Gordy and the old cargo master and Master Frodo and Lina—of course, Lina. . . .

Perhaps if she stayed there . . . if she put Sav Rid Olanek and Dagmar Collier out of mind and concentrated on a future full of friendship, where all might be well . . .

"What are you doing here?"

The sharp voice brought her up short. She blinked at the unfamiliar hallway to which her unheeded feet had brought her, then looked back at Kayzin Ne'Zame and inclined her head. "I'm very sorry. I was thinking and lost my way. Is it restricted? I'll go away."

"Will you?" The first mate was tight-lipped with anger. "You will just walk away, is it so? I *asked* what you are doing here. I expect an answer. Now."

"I am sorry, Kayzin Ne'Zame," she said carefully. "I gave you an answer: I was walking as I thought, and lost the way."

"And you so conveniently lost the way in such a manner that you come to the main computer bank. I will have truth from you, Priscilla Mendoza. Again—what do you here?"

"I don't think that's your business," Priscilla flared. "Since you won't believe the truth, why should I keep repeating it?"

"You!" If she had been angry before, the mate was livid now. "How much does he pay you?" she demanded, her accent thicker by the second.

The Terran looked at her in blank astonishment. "One-tenth cantra, when we reach Solcintra—"

"Have done!" There was a pause while Kayzin looked her up and down. The set lines of her face did not alter; she opened her mouth to speak further, then closed it, eyes going over Priscilla's shoulder.

"Go!" she snapped. "And mind you do not lose your way to this place again. Do you hear me?"

"I hear you, Kayzin Ne'Zame," Priscilla replied evenly. She inclined her head and turned away.

Shan yos'Galan was leaning against the wall, glass of wine held negligently in one hand, arms crossed over his chest.

Priscilla took a breath. "Good shift, Captain."

"Good shift, Ms. Mendoza," he said neutrally. She walked past him and down the intersecting hallway.

He turned to Kayzin. "Correct me if I'm wrong," he said softly. "The crew is allowed access to all portions of the ship?"

"Yes, Captain."

"Yes, Captain," he repeated, his eyes holding hers effortlessly. "Priscilla Mendoza is a member of the crew, Kayzin. I can't think how you came to forget it, but please strive to bear it in mind in the future. Also, it is just possible that you owe an apology."

She drew a deep, deep breath. "Say that you trust her!"

"I trust her," he said flatly, giving her the grace due an old friend.

"You are besotted!"

"Quite sober, I assure you," he said in icy Terran. Then he switched to the High Tongue, that of Lord-Instructing-Oathsworn. "I act, having given consideration to laws of necessity."

Kayzin bowed low, pride of him glowing through her mortification. There were those who said that Er Thom yos'Galan's lady had foisted a full-blooded Terran upon him as his eldest. If those could but see him, standing there, with the eyes spitting ice and the face just so! Who could behold him thus and say he was not Korval, blood and bone?

"Forgive me, Captain," she murmured. "It shall be as you have said."

"I am glad to hear it," he replied in Terran.

Arsdred Port City
Local Year 728
Midday Bazaar

ARSDRED PORT ROARED. It pushed, yodeled, shoved, sang, shimmied, stripped gleaming naked, and swathed itself head to toe in bright colors and glittering gems. Much of the noise—and most of the color—was contributed by the people behind stalls, before storefronts, and beside carts piled high with Goddess knew what. These were Arsdredi, dark-skinned Terrans, doe-eyed, hook-nosed, and voluble. They wore layer upon layer of gauzy, brilliant cloth and hawked their wares, sweatless, in the glare of the midday suns.

Some of the clamor, to be sure, was generated by those for whom the wares were displayed. Thronging the narrow streets were members of half a dozen races: Terrans of all description; graceful Liadens, dark-lensed Peladins, hairless Trimuvat, silent Uhlvore. Priscilla started, catching a gigantic figure out of the corner of an eye, wondering if even the Yxtrang stopped here—but it was only a towering Aus, golden-haired and full-bearded, head bent as he addressed a booming remark to the tiny woman skipping at his side.

"Firegems, pretty lady? The finest here—for you—so pale your skin, so black your hair! For *you*, beautiful lady, what else but azure? A mere twentybit—sacrificed on the altar of your beauty! Only try and see how it becomes you."

"Cloth, noble lady? Scarves? Crimson, gold, serpentine, xanthin, indigo! Wear them about your head, twist them 'round your waist—a fair price, noble."

"Porcelains, lady? Guidebooks . . . Ices . . . Incense . . . Gemstones . . ."

Peace.

Priscilla rounded a corner into a less traveled thoroughfare, breathing a sigh of relief. The roster had granted her leave this first day in port. Rusty and Lina had drawn time together on the third, a circumstance that brought a frown to the Liaden woman's face while Rusty shrugged. "Maybe next time."

Secretly, Priscilla was relieved. A leave-companion would have quickly discovered the state of her finances. She was pleased not to burden her friends with that particular information and perhaps be forced to endure kindhearted offers of a loan or, worse, an outright gift.

It was better this way, she thought, strolling along the hot little street. A day of rest before a trying tomorrow. For the roster's other news had been that she was to assist Cargo Master yo'Lanna with the worldside unloading next shift-worked.

She had come to the first cross street when a familiar voice intruded upon her.

"Hi, Ms. Mendoza! Is this your day, too? Want to partner?"

She turned, smiling down into Gordy Arbuthnot's round—and exquisitely clean—face. "I'm afraid I'd hold you down," she said carefully. Then she added more briskly, "You aren't here *by yourself,* are you, Gordy?"

He grimaced. "Well, sort of. Cap'n says he knows I got enough sense not to get in trouble, but that accidents happen an' my grandad'd break his nose for him if I came by one. So, we compromised." He tugged something off his belt and held it out for inspection: a portable comm.

"I've got the cap'n's direct beam-code. If I get in a scrape—even a *little* one—I'm supposed to get on the beam and *yell.*" Gordy sighed, then looked up again, trying to put a good face on it. "I guess that's not too bad, is it, Ms. Mendoza?"

"It sounds," Priscilla said truthfully, "very generous. And

reasonable. A great many people, you know, would think you were only a little boy."

"Well, that's true," he agreed. "Even Ma said something like that when Grandad told her he'd got everything fixed with the cap'n, and she's usually—reasonable too. But Morgan'd been talking her ears off about how Shan wasn't *really* related to us—and Liaden, besides. I guess," Gordy concluded rather breathlessly, "that kind of thing'd be enough to make *any*body unreasonable."

"It certainly sounds like it would be," she agreed with amusement. "Is the captain related to you?"

Gordy nodded as he clipped the comm back to his belt. "Shan's ma was Grandad's sister. So we're cousins—Shan and Val Con and Nova and Anthora. Well, at least," he said scrupulously, "not Val Con. He's a fosterling. But I call him cousin, too. And he's *Shan's* cousin, so I guess we're related, some way." He grinned at her. "Want to partner?" he asked again.

Priscilla shook her head. "I think I'd rather just roam around and get my thoughts in order, rest a little. I'm scheduled to help Ken Rik tomorrow."

Gordy laughed. "You better rest, then. Ken Rik's okay, but he likes to make people squirm. Good at it, too. Tell you what: I'm due at the shuttle Last Hour, shiptime. Let's go up together, okay, Ms. Mendoza?"

"Okay." She smiled at him. "You might as well call me Priscilla. Everybody else does."

"Cap'n doesn't," Gordy pointed out, moving off. "I will, though. See you later—Priscilla."

"See you later—Mr. Arbuthnot."

That drew another burst of laughter. Priscilla shook her head, still smiling, and turned left down the cross street, away from the voice of the bazaar.

IT WAS A LITTLE PAST NINETEENTH HOUR, shiptime. Priscilla, feeling very well in a lazy sort of way, had quit the municipal park some moments before and was sauntering down a thin avenue that curved in the general direction of the port.

Most of the shops along this way were closed, though she passed a brightly lit window displaying an extremely ornate chess set carved of red and white woods and set with faceted stones. She paused, considering the set and comparing it to the chessmen she had seen upon the captain's board. Those pieces had been carved of ebonwood and bonebar, but very plainly—a set for a person who played the game, not for a collector of the exotic.

She continued on her way. The next window, under a sign that read TEELA'S TREASURES, was crowded with an eye-dazzling collection of objects. A carved ivory fan lay next to a tawdry firegem tiara; a gold necklace with a greenish tinge lay as if flung across a bound book of possible worth and definite age; while a cut-plastic vase hobnobbed with an eggshell porcelain bowl down on its luck.

Fascinated, Priscilla bent closer to the window, trying to puzzle out more of its contents. A carved wooden box with a broken hinge; an antique pair of eyeglasses, untinted; a—her breath caught in her throat as she spied it, balanced precariously atop a stack of mismatched flowered saucers: a blown-crystal triglant, caught by the artist in a mood of pensiveness, wings half-furled, tail wrapped neatly around its front paws. A charming piece—and hers!

Hers. And of the few things she had been able to bring with her from Sintia, it had been the most treasured. *She* had commissioned the work, paid for it with the labor of her own hands. *She* had built the velvet-lined box in which it had been lovingly displayed.

Perhaps the thief had thought the box worthless.

Priscilla stalked stiff-legged into the shop, twobits clenched in her fist. Fifteen minutes later, she came out, carefully tucking the paper-wrapped figurine in her pocket. Broke, she reminded herself, trying to call up fear.

But all she felt was warm contentment. She had the triglant. She had a berth on the *Passage*. She had a tenth-cantra waiting for her when they docked at Solcintra. It would suffice. She had a friend—perhaps even three. That was so much more than sufficient that she barely had room for the grief of leaving her other things in the hands of the proprietor of Teela's Treasures.

She took the first cross street, hurrying now toward the port. To her right, a shadow moved. She spun.

"Hello, Prissy," Dagmar said, grinning widely. She took two steps closer.

Goddess, aid me now . . . "Good-bye, Dagmar," she gritted through, her teeth. She made to pass on.

The bigger woman blocked her way, grin widening. "Aw, now, honey, you ain't gonna let a little thing like a headache come between us, are you? I was just following orders, Prissy. And I sure am glad to see you again."

"I'm not glad to see you. Good-bye." She turned away.

Dagmar grabbed an arm and yanked Priscilla forward, while her other hand found a breast and squeezed.

Priscilla swung with all the force in her, slamming five knuckles backhanded across the other woman's leer as she twisted, just managing to get free.

Dagmar lunged, grabbing a handful of shirt. Priscilla continued her twist. The fabric tore, and Dagmar pitched backward, scrabbling for support.

It was time to run. Priscilla dived forward.

IT WAS EASY.

Dagmar was bigger—and no doubt stronger. Certainly she was more accustomed to this kind of business than was her prey.

But she was *slow*.

Priscilla had the measure of the game now. Moving with pilot swiftness, seeing with pilot eyes, she landed an astonishing number of blows, though the ones she received were telling.

She ducked back, slammed a ringing blow toward the ears that was only partially successful, and suffered a numbing crack to her right shoulder.

Several more passes and she saw how it might be ended—quickly and to her advantage. She began the spin to get into position—

The hum warned her, and she snapped backward, rolling heavily on her right side, wishing she had had the sense to run before.

Dagmar had pulled a vibroknife.

GORDY WAS LATE.

He streaked across the municipal park, causing consternation among the local duck-analogs, and careered into Parkton Way. He passed the window containing the chessmen without a glance, though he did slow as he came abreast Teela's Treasures, out of respect for the policeman half a block ahead.

A side street presented itself, wending portward. Gordy took it—and froze in disbelief.

Before him was Priscilla Mendoza, shirt torn nearly to the shoulder, bent forward like some two-legged, beautiful, and quite deadly predator, carefully circling a larger, broader woman, who circled in her turn.

The position of the two changed sufficiently for Gordy to see the rest: The larger woman held a knife.

Gulping, he turned and ran back the way he had come.

PRISCILLA CONSIDERED THE KNIFE dispassionately. It could be done. She was fast. Dagmar was slow. Her objective was only to dispose of the blade—*she* was no knife fighter.

Priscilla moved.

Dagmar twisted—so slooow—and Priscilla's fingers swept through hers, dislodging the evil, humming thing and sending it spinning into the shadows. The larger woman finished her twist and slammed heavily into her opponent, trying to grab and hold two slender wrists in a big hand, hugging her tight, and Priscilla could not breathe. . . .

"Here now, here now! That'll be enough of *that* kind of carrying on!" Strong hands grabbed and pulled—and breath returned.

Priscilla sagged backward, too grateful for the boon of air to resent the hand irons so competently slapped into place. Dagmar, she saw presently, was in worse shape. She had apparently taken a stunner charge and was retching against the wall, her face already beginning to purple.

The cop finished affixing irons and turned away—and his eyebrows went up with his stunner. "All right, my boy, fun's over. Give it to me, please."

Gordy blinked, reversed the vibroknife, and held it out. The cop took it gingerly, then jerked the comm from the boy's belt and clipped it to his own.

"That's mine!"

"Then you'll get it back after the trial. Hold out your hands."

"I won't wear irons." The round chin was rigid.

"Then you'll go unconscious, over my shoulder." The cop considered him. "Might drop you, though."

Gordy looked over the man's shoulder at Priscilla. She managed a ragged smile and a nod. He held out his hands.

~~~~~~

THE EXHIBITS WERE ON A TABLE against the far left wall: a vibroknife, a portable comm, a pile of glittering shards that had once represented a triglant at rest.

The prisoners were to the right. The slender woman and the boy sat next to each other, as far away as possible from the bulky woman with the battered face. Sedatives had been administered to all, in keeping with the magistrate's order. Though there had been no renewal of hostilities, the arresting officer was keeping a sharp eye out. One never knew with outworlders.

Priscilla fought the tranquilizing haze, struggling for clear thought. They were waiting, the cop had said, for the arrival of a ranking officer from *Daxflan* and from *Dutiful Passage* so that the trial could commence.

Kayzin Ne'Zame, Priscilla thought laboriously. She dislikes me—here's a Goddess-sent opportunity for her to be rid of me altogether.

Lina. What would Lina think? Would Priscilla be allowed to speak with her, explain what had happened, before the *Passage* left orbit? She caught her breath, her mind suddenly clear of fog, aware of a nearly overmastering desire to fling herself down and sob.

Fool, she told herself harshly. You should have run.

There was a rustle of robes in the outer hallway, and Gordy shifted next to her. "Maybe that's the judge," he said drowsily, "I sure hope so. Crelm, Priscilla! Do you know how late we are? Shan's gonna *skin* me!"

Her reply was cut off by the arresting officer.

"All rise for Magistrate Kelbar!"

She stood; she started when Gordy slipped his hand into hers, and then squeezed his fingers.

"That's you, too!" the cop was telling Dagmar, who mumbled something and climbed to her feet.

Magistrate Kelbar swept into the room, an imposing figure in his sun-yellow robes of office. Out of stern brown eyes he considered the three of them before seating himself with a flourish upon his throne. He waved a hand in a languid gesture that the cop translated sharply.

"Prisoners sit!"

Dagmar grunted and slouched back onto her bench. Priscilla sat quietly, though Gordy heaved a sigh.

Let it be done quickly, Goddess, Priscilla prayed.

As if in answer to that thought, the door was opened from without, admitting a small, fair man.

Sav Rid Olanek had been called from a party, Priscilla thought: His shirt was shimmering rose silk; the pale trousers surely were velvet. Jewels glittered in his ears, on his hands, and from the buckle of his belt, and around his throat was a titanium collar worth double the pay she would never collect at Solcintra.

Recognizing a person of consequence, the magistrate snapped his fingers at the prisoners to rise and swept forward. "Good evening, gentle sir!" he said in affable Trade, extending a wide hand. "I am sorry to have had to summon you here. A small matter, I am sure, and easily settled, once your honored colleague arrives. I am Magistrate Kelbar."

He was accorded a flickering glance from bright blue eyes, and the barest possible bow. "I am Sav Rid Olanek, Trader on *Daxflan*, out of Liad," he said coldly. "I am afraid you may be too optimistic, however." He pointed at Priscilla, who returned his gaze with determined serenity. "*That* person is a desperate criminal. She is without doubt a thief. What else she may be—"

"Good evening!" a voice called in cheerful Terran, preceding its owner into the room by a heartbeat. Sav Rid Olanek bit off the rest of his sentence, and Priscilla felt Gordy shift next to her.

It was not Kayzin Ne'Zame, after all.

He wore a shirt barely less bright than his hair, and soft black trousers. His belt buckle was merely silver, its design changing from a fanciful bird to an impossible flower as Priscilla watched. An amethyst drop exactly matching the color of the gem in his master's ring hung from his right ear.

He was the most welcome sight Priscilla had ever beheld. It'll be all right now, she told herself, and didn't even wonder why she thought so.

He smiled at the magistrate and bowed easily, then came forward with hand outstretched. "I'm Shan yos'Galan, sir. Am I very late? Forgive me, please. I was at Herr Sasoni's—but perhaps I should say no more. Except that I was on the verge of concluding a very— interesting—piece of business, so it was fortunate your message reached me when it did."

The magistrate actually laughed, taking the more slender hand in his. "But this is dreadful!" he cried. "Surely you were able to procure her key for later use? I should never forgive myself, sir—"

"No matter," the captain interrupted easily. "I'm sure we'll be able to clear this matter up in a moment or two, and I'll return— what *is* the matter, by the way, sir? I—" He turned his head, eyes alighting, apparently for the first time, on his glaring colleague.

"Good evening, Sav Rid," he said politely in the Liaden High Tongue.

"You!" the other snarled.

"Well, of course, me. I couldn't very well be anyone else, could I? Has this little inconvenience put you out of temper? I'm sure we'll be shut of it in a moment. The magistrate seems very amiable, don't you think? As I just said to him—but I've forgotten, you don't speak

Terran, do you? A sad pity, since so many other people do, but no doubt you have your reasons."

"I do, and they are not yours to inquire into." Trader Olanek waved his hand in their direction, though his eyes did not leave the captain. "You might wish to turn your limited understanding to the matter at hand. It may be that you have undervalued the inconvenience."

"Yes?" The silver eyes swept the three of them vaguely. "Well, I must say, your crew member—I assume she is yours—looks as if she's taken rather a tumble. In her cups, perhaps. But you're too experienced a Trader to allow a little drunken sport among the crew to spoil your whole evening."

"Gentles?" Magistrate Kelbar said in firm Trade. "If we may get on with the hearing? I am certain we would all rather be elsewhere." He resumed his seat with another flourish and waved the prisoners forward. "Will you two gentlemen please identify these persons?"

Trader Olanek pointed. "That is Dagmar Collier, second mate on *Daxflan*."

"And, as her superior officer, you are willing to speak for her?"

After a slight hesitation, the Trader said, "Yes."

"And the two remaining," the captain said cheerily, "are mine, sir. The young gentleman is Gordon Arbuthnot, cabin boy on the *Dutiful Passage* and my kinsman—"

"You mean to say you acknowledge that connection?" The Trader's High Liaden carried outrage. "It's full Terran! Have you no sense of the honor due your Clan?"

"Well, we're *half* Terran, after all," the captain said mildly. "You knew that, didn't you, when you propositioned my sister? And he's a good lad."

"You cannot be serious."

"He is under Korval's wing." The captain's inflection shifted subtly, his voice nearly cold. "Do not mistake me."

"Pah! Korval's wing unfurls too far for health. Does the same apply to the bitch beside him?"

She stiffened, outrage erupting—

"Priscilla!" the captain snapped, and she stilled, cheeks flaming.

"You keep it on a short leash," the Trader commented. "How much do you pay it? Or does it serve for the pleasure of looking at your beautiful face?"

The captain shook his head. "On Priscilla Mendoza's home world, Sav Rid, you would have just now uttered an insult demanding your death for Balance. It's fortunate, isn't it, that her knowledge of our tongue is a scholar's? But I am forgetting my manners again! You are acquainted!" The light eyes were on her. "Have you no greeting for the honored Trader?"

She stared at him. Did he really expect her— And then she smiled, recalling another of Fin Ton's lessons. Loosing Gordy's hand, she bowed low.

"Forgive me the situation, Master Trader," she said in her careful High Liaden, "and believe me all joy to see you."

"What!" Sav Rid cried, visibly shaken. "How is it possible that—"

"Gentles," the magistrate said. "I must insist that we keep to the matter at hand."

"Of course, sir." The captain was contrite. "Do forgive us. My colleague is an avid student of lineage and sought enlightenment regarding Gordon's place in the family tree. To continue, indeed. The lady with the torn shirt is Priscilla Delacroix y Mendoza. She is under personal contract to the captain of the *Dutiful Passage,* serving as librarian, pilot, and apprentice second mate." He smiled. "I'm quite happy to speak for both of them."

What was this? Pilot? Second mate in training? Priscilla tried to recall the precise phrasing of her contract, but the magistrate's voice defeated the effort.

"As all three have someone in authority to speak for them, the hearing now commences. What we know is this: Yonder knife is the property of Dagmar Collier. We have taken imprint readings and find it to be so. She does not deny it.

"It is important to note that two other sets of prints are found on the hilt, besides those of the arresting officer: those of Gordon Arbuthnot, and a faint, very blurred set which we believe to be those of Priscilla Mendoza." The magistrate paused to clear his throat importantly.

"We will hear from the arresting officer."

The cop's statement was brief and to the point. He had been hailed by Gordon Arbuthnot, who cried that there was a fight in Halvington Street. Arriving on the scene, he had found "those two persons there" in close embrace, the larger apparently engaged in squeezing the smaller breathless. The arresting officer was of the opinion that this project was near completion and so had administered a judicial stunner blast to the larger person, hand-ironed both combatants, and turned to find Gordon Arbuthnot with "that knife, there, sir," in his hand. So, in the interest of fair play, Gordy had been ironed as well, and all three brought in. The officer paused, scratched his head, and added that he had also taken from Gordon Arbuthnot a small rectangular object with a belt clip—very likely a portable comm and no harm to it. But at the time he had seen no reason to take unnecessary chances.

"Quite right," the captain said approvingly, and the cop grinned shyly.

The magistrate motioned him back. "We will now hear from Dagmar Collier."

Dagmar came forward slowly and darted a glance at Trader Olanek. He did not meet her eyes.

She made a woeful attempt to square her shoulders. Her voice when she spoke was hoarse, the words mushy. I hope I broke every tooth in her mouth, Priscilla thought.

"Prissy and me are old friends," Dagmar was telling the magistrate. "Used to serve on *Daxflan* together. It was just natural for me to go over and say 'hey' when I saw her walkin' down the street." She shrugged. "Must've been drunk, I guess, Your Honor, 'cause she just hauled off and hit me."

There was a short pause before the magistrate asked dryly, "Is that your statement of the affair?"

Dagmar blinked. "Yessir."

"I see. We are willing to hear you again, should something else occur to you after Priscilla Mendoza speaks."

Priscilla stood forward. "Ms. Collier and I were never friends," she began hotly. "She has stolen from me and sold my things to a—a *thrift shop* on Parkton—"

The magistrate raised his hand. "That is not the issue at trial here. Please limit your remarks to the incident in Halvington Street."

Priscilla bit her lip. "I saw Ms. Collier in Halvington Street," she began again, "as I was on my way back to the port. She spoke to me. I returned the greeting and tried to pass on. Ms. Collier blocked my way and grabbed me—I *believe* she intended rape, but that may be unjust. At the time it seemed exactly what she meant, and I—" she broke off, her eyes seeking the captain's. "I lost my temper," she said wryly. He nodded, and she turned back to the magistrate.

"I tried to defend myself against what I thought was an attack. Ms. Collier continued to block my way and at some point pulled a knife. I *did* disarm her, but she grabbed me. Which is how I came to be in the absurd situation from which the officer rescued me." She sighed. "That is my statement, sir."

"Very clear, Ms. Mendoza. Thank you."

"I would like to point out," Sav Rid Olanek said abruptly, "that the animosity between these two individuals seems of long standing—"

"Exactly," the captain interrupted. "in which case, Magistrate, I venture to say that each has had ample opportunity to vent her spleen. A fine, of course, is in order, for breaking the peace. But, since it is highly unlikely that they will meet again soon . . ."

Magistrate Kelbar beamed at him. "I am sure you can be trusted to control the members of your crew during the rest of your time in port, sirs. My trust in your discretion prompts me not to demand that both individuals be rendered ship-bound for that period. They will, of course, be confined to the port proper. And, there *is* a fine." He coughed gently. "For engaging in fisticuffs in a public thoroughfare: one hundred bits each. Drawing a deadly weapon: two hundred fifty bits. Possession of said weapon without Arsdred certificate of permission: six hundred bits. Resisting arrest—" He looked up and smiled, first at Gordy, then at the captain. "I think we might dispense with that. Transport fee: fifty bits each.

"So then, owed from Dagmar Collier, through her superior, Sav

Rid Olanek: one thousand bits. Owed from Priscilla Mendoza, through her superior, Shan yos'Galan: one hundred fifty bits. Owed from Gordon Arbuthnot from his superior, Shan yos'Galan: fifty bits. You may pay cash at the teller's cage as you leave, gentles." He arose and sailed from the room, the arresting officer in his wake.

Shan considered Olanek's set face. "One thousand bits," he murmured in sympathetic Trade. "Will it put you out of pocket, Sav Rid? I can extend a loan, if you like."

"Thank you, I think not!" the other snapped, jerking his head at his crew member.

Shan sighed. "So short-tempered, Sav Rid! Not sleeping well? I do hope you're not ill. At least we know you don't have a guilty conscience, don't we? By the way, Ms. Mendoza seems to have lost a very special pair of earrings. Do you know Calintak, on Medusa? Wonderful fellow, very good-tempered. And the things he can fit in just a *little* bit of space: built-in sensors, trackers—that sort of thing. If you're ever in the market for something, since you wear so *much* jewelry . . ."

Dagmar Collier was hovering close, eyes riveted. "Sensors?" she asked with a kind of fascinated dread. "How small a space?"

"Oh, are you interested? He's quite dear, you know—but hardly any space at all. An unexceptional earring, for instance, is all the room he needs to work in. An artist—"

"Oh, have done!" Sav Rid snarled, turning on his heel. "Pay him no mind, he's a fool. Now, come!" He was gone, Dagmar following.

Shan shook his head and held out a hand to Gordy, who came and slid his own into it. "Well now, children—Ms. Mendoza?"

She was at the exhibit table, picking up the shards of crystal, one by careful one, and settling them in her palm.

"Crelm!" Gordy muttered, and went to her side. "Priscilla, what're you doing? It's busted."

She did not look away from her task. "It's all I own, anywhere, and I'm taking it with me." Her tone was perfectly flat, with an absence of emotion that raised the hairs on Shan's neck. He stepped forward quickly, pulled a square of silk from his sleeve, and dropped it in front of her.

"You'll cut yourself, Priscilla. Use this."

"Thank you." Her voice was still flat, though he fancied he detected a quiver of *something.* . . .

Hand in hand, he and Gordy waited until she had finished and tied the silk into a knot. Gordy took her hand, and, so linked, they went out to pay the cashier.

Shipyear 65
Tripday 143
First Shift
2.00 Hours

"YOU WILL DO ME THE FAVOR, won't you, Gordy," the captain murmured, "of neglecting to inform your mother that you've been arrested?"

"Was I?" the boy asked hazily. "I mean, I wasn't *really.* They didn't do anything to me."

The man laughed. "Arrested, I assure you. The details may vary by world, but the larger outlines remain constant: irons, hearings, magistrates, fines—not at all the kind of thing mothers enjoy hearing of, even when it's carefully explained that you were completely without blame. Which reminds me—how did your imprints come to be on that thing?"

"Priscilla was losing," Gordy explained. "And the knife was just lying there. I was trying to figure out how it worked. . . ."

"Yes? To what end, please?"

"Well, I thought if I cut Dagmar's arm, she'd let go."

"It's a theory," the captain admitted. "Report to Pallin Kornad after breakfast, please. I see it's time you learned how to protect yourself."

"Yes, Cap'n." He paused. "Shan?"

"Yes, *acushla?*"

"Is it—can I tell Grandad I was arrested? I didn't do anything

749

wrong. . . ." This last was spoken, it seemed to Priscilla, with considerable doubt.

A boot heel scraped on the pavement as the man went down on one knee, eyes level with Gordy's.

"You will *absolutely* tell your grandfather," he said firmly, his big hands on the boy's round shoulders. "He will be proud of you. You acted with forethought and with honor, coming to the aid of a shipmate and a friend." He cupped a soft cheek. "You did very well, Gordy. Thank you."

"Yes." Priscilla heard her own voice from far away. "Thank you, Gordy. You saved my life."

He blinked at her over his cousin's shoulder. "I *did?*" She nodded, not sure what her face was doing. "She really was winning. I couldn't breathe. You did exactly right."

She should, she thought vaguely, find something more to say, but it was unnecessary; doubt had vanished from the young face. He grinned. "I'm a hero."

"You're an impossible monkey." The captain stood and held out his hand. "And you're well behind your time to return to the ship. Come along."

They walked a little way in silence. The drug was gaining the upper hand again, and Priscilla stumbled; she caught herself and asked over Gordy's head, "What was that about your sister?"

"Sav Rid's little joke," the captain said easily. "It amused him to propose marriage to the eldest of my sisters."

"What!" Gordy was outraged. "That—person? To *Cousin Nova?*"

"Indeed, yes. Exactly Cousin Nova. Why? Do you think Anthora might suit him better? I admit it's a thought. He so fair and she so dark. . . . But he was more enamored of fair with fair. You can't really blame him, Gordy; it's merely a matter of taste."

"What did you do?" Gordy demanded awfully, ignoring this flow of nonsense.

The man looked down at him. "What could I do? I was from home. Besides, Nova is well able to take care of herself. Simply told the fellow she'd rather mate with a Gehatian slimegrubber and sent him about his business." He sighed. "I'm afraid he didn't take it in very good part. Well, how was she to know he had a horror of the creatures? I'm sure she would have thought of something else just as revolting to compare him with, if she'd had the least idea. Very resourceful person, Cousin Nova. The more I think on it, the more certain I am that you're right, Gordy! Anthora would certainly suit him far better! A pity he didn't see it that way and allowed himself to be enraptured by a mere pretty face. Perhaps we should suggest—"

"Pretty!" the boy choked. "Cousin Nova's *beautiful!*"

"Well," the lady's brother conceded, "she is. But I wouldn't let it weigh too heavily with you. Gordy. Sort of thing that might happen to anyone. And she's really quite clever."

They came at length to the cradles and crossed to their shuttlepad in silence. A shadow loomed at the door, bringing two fingers up in a casual salute. "Evening, Cap'n."

"Good evening, Seth. Two passengers for you. Take good care of them, please; they both seem a bit yawnsome—is that a word?"

"Bound to be," the lanky pilot returned good-humoredly. "Not going up yourself?"

"Business, Seth. Duty calls."

"He has to get her key," Gordy said helpfully.

"Brat." His cousin sighed. "Don't forget Pallin next shift, Gordy."

"No, Cap'n—at least, *yes,* Cap'n. I'll remember."

The captain laughed and began to move away, then checked himself and came back, fishing in his belt. "My terrible memory! I knew there was something else. Ms. Mendoza!"

She started. "Captain?"

He was holding out a flat rectangle, a card of some sort. She took it automatically.

"Do take care of it, Ms. Mendoza," he chided gently. "It's really not the sort of thing you want to leave lying around. Good evening." He was gone.

Priscilla frowned at the card, but the uncertain light or her sedative-fogged eyes defeated the attempt to identify it. She put it in her pocket with the knotted kerchief and followed Gordy into the shuttle.

GORDY WAS ASLEEP WHEN THEY DOCKED. The snap of the board being locked jerked Priscilla out of her own doze, but even the most stringent effort she was able to make would not rouse her companion from his.

Sighing, she fumbled her webbing loose, then opened his. Her several attempts to pick him up should have roused one dead, she thought foggily, but Gordy only grumbled a few sleep syllables and tried to curl farther down into the chair. Priscilla rubbed her forehead with the back of a hand and tried to apply her mind to the problem.

"Out for the count," Seth commented from beside her. "I gotta get back down. Can you carry him, or should we call Vilt?"

Priscilla gave him what she hoped was a smile. "I can carry him. Getting him up is the problem."

"Naw. Not when somebody's that far out." He bent, grabbed an arm, heaved, turned, and offered Priscilla an armful of boy.

She took Gordy and allowed herself to be escorted to the door of the cargo dock. It slid open for her, and she stepped into the corridor, blinking a little in the directionless yellow light.

Before her she saw, with the vivid disconnection of a dream, a bronze-winged dragon hovering. No. It was a painting on the wall, a smaller reproduction of the design in the reception room. Under Korval's wing, Priscilla recalled. She shifted her burden and began the long walk to the crew's quarters.

She had made it, staggering only now and then, to the top of the corridor where Gordy had his room, when she heard quick steps behind her and an exclamation.

"Priscilla! Is that Gordon? What has—is all well, my friend?"

"Well?" She considered Lina muzzily. It took several seconds to formulate an appropriate response. "Gordy's all right. It's mostly that stupid stuff they injected us with at the police station. Makes you . . . makes you groggy. Half asleep, myself."

"Ah." The other woman fell in beside her. "The police station? Does the captain know?"

Priscilla nodded, then paused to regain her balance. "He came to bail us out—dear Goddess!" She stopped, arms closing convulsively around Gordy, who muttered. "Dear Goddess," she said again, though not, Lina thought, prayerfully. "One hundred fifty bits! Out of a tenth-cantra? And the clothes . . . ." She took a hard breath and began to walk again. "Broke. No money at all."

Lina's worry increased, but she refrained from pursuing questions, merely remarking that they had reached Gordon's room and lifting his hand to lay it against the palmlock.

Priscilla laid him on the bed, pulled off his boots, straightened the blanket, and pulled it up. Lina stood by the door, watching and saying nothing.

The boy disposed comfortably, Priscilla glanced around the room, and nodded slightly, then bent and ruffled the silky hair.

"Ma?" Gordy inquired from the depths of sleep.

She started, then completed the caress. "It's only Priscilla, Gordy. Sleep well."

Lina followed her out, stretching her short legs to keep up with the pace her friend set, even half-drugged.

At the top of the hall Priscilla made to turn right. Lina caught her arm. "No, Priscilla. Your room is this way."

"Have to go to the library," she protested. "Now."

"Not now," Lina said with decision. "Now, you must rest. The library will be in place next shift."

Priscilla shook her head. "Have to see my contract."

"Your contract? Priscilla, it is—*conselem*—an absurdity! What good does your contract do when you must sleep? You are signed until Solcintra. You may look at your contract any time these next four months. Come to bed."

"He lied," Priscilla said flatly, a decidedly mulish look about her lovely mouth.

Lina sighed. "Who lied? And why must— The captain lied?" She stared up at her friend. "That is not much like him, *denubia*. Perhaps you misunderstood."

"I'm very tired," Priscilla said clearly, "of misunderstanding. I must see my contract."

"Of course you must," Lina agreed. "It would be very bad to have misunderstood the captain. Let us go to your room and access the file from there." She slipped her arm around the other's waist.

Priscilla stiffened and moved away—a very little. Lina's eyes widened, but she said nothing, only withdrew her arm. And waited.

"All right," Priscilla said presently, the mulish look much abated. "Let's do that. Thank you, Lina."

"I am happy to help," Lina said carefully as they turned left down the hall. "What happened, my friend?"

There was a long pause before the taller woman shook herself and answered, "I was attacked on the street. Gordy tried to help, and we all three got arrested. They called the captain out of a party to—to speak for us."

"Most proper," Lina said, and stopped, waiting for Priscilla to lay her palm against the lock.

It seemed for a moment that she did not recognize her own door. Then she shifted and placed her hand in the center; when the panel slid away, she entered, with Lina trailing after.

"Most proper," Priscilla repeated, standing in the middle of her cabin and staring around as if she had never seen the place before. She spun.

"It cost *one hundred fifty bits* to *speak* for me!" she cried with an unexpected but wholly gratifying flare of passion. "One hundred fifty! And I'll have earned a tenth-cantra by the time we reach Solcintra, *and* I already owe the ship for my clothes—and all my things—my things are gone. . . ." Abruptly she sat on the bed, running violent fingers through the curly cloud of her hair.

Lina came forward, daring to lay her hand on a rigid shoulder. She frowned at the startled jerk. "I did not attack you on the street," she said severely.

Priscilla looked up, apology in her eyes. Lina smiled, lifting the tips of her fingers to a pale cheek.

"Of course I did not. I have been very well brought up." She tugged gently on an errant curl. "Of this other thing: The ship has a—*legal fund*. Since *you* were attacked, I think the fund will pay the expense of your bail. It is a thing you should speak of with the captain. Was he angry with you?"

Priscilla blinked. "I don't think so. Does he get angry?"

Lina laughed. "If he had been so, you would not be in doubt. So, then, I would not worry about my wages. It is very likely that they remain intact. Now, allow me to call your contract up." She went to the screen.

Behind her, Priscilla stood, moved unsteadily to the mirror shelf, and began to pull things from her pocket. The knotted silk she placed carefully to one side of the usual oddments. Patting her pocket to be sure it was empty, she felt a flat thickness—the card the captain had given her at the shuttlepad. She pulled it out and examined it, her breath catching.

"Lina!"

The Liaden woman was at her elbow instantly. "Yes?"

Priscilla held out the card in a hand that was not at all steady. "What is this, please?"

Lana subjected it to a brief, two-sided scrutiny and handed it back, smiling. "It is a provisional second class pilot's license in the name of Priscilla Delacroix y Mendoza. *Ge'shada*, my friend, you have done very well."

"I've done very well. Done well. . . ." Priscilla stared and suddenly threw back her head, uttering a sound so shattered that no one could have called it laughter. Then she bent double, torn with sobs.

Lina put her arms about her and probed with a Healer's sure instinct, evading weakened defenses and slashing at the protected reservoir of pain.

Priscilla cried out and went to her knees. Lina held her closer, withdrawing somewhat, content for the present to have the storm rage.

After a time, the sobbing eased and she coaxed her friend to the bed. When they were lying face to face, she probed again, projecting on all possible lines.

Priscilla stirred, sodden lashes lifting, then extended a tentative finger to trace the lines of her friend's face, exhausted wonderment on her own.

"I see you, sister," she murmured. Then her hand fell away, and she slept, bathed in warm affection and comfort.

๛๛๛๛๛๛๛๛๛๛๛๛๛๛๛๛๛๛๛๛๛๛๛๛

"BUT WHY CAN'T WE SELL THE PERFUME HERE?" Rusty demanded, staring at Lina over a suspended forkful of ice-toast.

The Liaden woman sighed. "It is—bah! I have forgotten the word. It is to *force* one to love another, a . . ."

"Aphrodisiac," Priscilla supplied, looking up from her own breakfast. "Aphrodisiacs are illegal on some planets. I guess Arsdred's one of them."

Rusty scowled at his plate.

"Rah Stee, do not!" Lina was laughing. "You will spoil your food! It is not so bad. We will sell at another port." She shook a slender finger in mock severity. "You believe I have given us a loss! But I claim the dice for more than one throw. You will see, my friend: the perfume will sell—and at high profit!"

Rusty looked dubious, and Lina laughed again.

"Priscilla?" a breathless young voice asked at her elbow. She turned her head to discover the cabin boy, clutching a box.

"Good morning, Gordy," she said, offering him a storm-beaten smile. "I thought you were supposed to be learning self-defense first thing this shift."

"Crelm!" he said scornfully. "I did that an hour ago!" He held out the box, plainly expecting her to take it. She did, full of wonder.

"Cap'n's compliments," he said formally. "And his apologies for sending you planetside alone." Gordy tipped his head. "He said he was a fool, Priscilla, but he can't have meant me to tell you that, do you think?"

"Very likely not," she agreed. "So we'll pretend you didn't."

"Right. Gotta jet. Morning, Lina! Rusty!"

She sat holding the box in her lap until Rusty inquired, a little impatiently, if she wasn't going to open it.

"Yes, of course," she murmured, making no move to do so. *Allowing me planetside alone? A test, Goddess?* she wondered. *To see if I would choose revenge, after all?* It occurred to her to wonder if the captain's watch over her had been rather closer than she had supposed. She shook her head and reached for a blunt-edged jelly knife.

The sealing tape broke easily. She laid the knife aside and unfolded the flaps. The box contained several objects, each wrapped in bright gossamer paper.

Very slowly, she pulled out the first object. She unwrapped it as slowly, refusing to acknowledge what weight and shape told her until her eyes added irrefutable evidence.

The object was a rosewood comb, intricately carved with a pattern of stars and flowers, the tines satin-smooth from years of being pulled through a waist-length cascade and, more recently, a brief, unruly mop of hair.

Priscilla took a breath, laid the comb aside, and returned to the box. One by one she uncovered them: the brush and hand mirror that matched the comb, several fired-clay figurines, a thin folder of flatpix, a brass-bound kaleidoscope, four bound books, nine music-tapes, and three thin silver bangles.

Priscilla held the bangles in her hand for a moment before laying them with the other things. Once, there had been seven: the full complement of a Maiden-near-Wife. Four she had sold at different times, as need had dictated. They would have been worth far more as a set, sold to a collector of the occult. She never let one go without a wrench that was almost a physical illness.

She laid the bracelets carefully beside the other objects. In the bottom of the box was one more item: a small red velvet box. Frowning, she picked it up.

"What is all this?" Rusty demanded, breaking the silence that had fallen on the three of them.

"My—things," Priscilla. said hesitantly. "My personal things that were left behind on *Daxflan.*" She held out the red box. "Except this. I don't know . . . ." She lifted the lid.

Earrings.

Not *her* earrings, which had been ornate and old. These were new, not at all ornate, just simple hoops; their plain design was deceptive, for the weight and sheen said platinum, and the individual who had crafted them had signed each with a proud flourish.

Priscilla looked at Lina. "They're not mine."

"Ah."

"Why?" Priscilla whispered.

Lina moved her shoulders. "He sent apologies. Perhaps he felt you were owed. You should, perhaps, ask."

"Yes. . . ." She closed the lid carefully and put the box with the rest of the items.

Rusty picked up the kaleidoscope and peered through it. "Nice," he murmured.

"Mother, look at the time!" Priscilla cried suddenly, pushing her chair back. "I'm as bad as Gordy! And Ken Rik *will* skin me! Lina—"

"I will take care of them," her friend said, picking up the mirror and beginning to rewrap it. She looked up with a fond smile. "Go. Give Ken Rik a kiss for me."

"You do it, if you want him kissed," Priscilla retorted, and was gone.

Rusty picked up a piece of tissue and clumsily crumpled it around the kaleidoscope. "Funny sort of thing for the cap'n to do," he said thoughtfully.

Lina glanced up. "Do you think so?"

"Yah, I do." He looked at her closely before returning to the remains of his breakfast. "And don't try to bamboozle me into thinking you don't think so, either. We been on too many rounds together for that to pass."

"Well," Lina said conscientiously, "there are many reasons why he might do so."

Rusty grinned and drank the rest of his coffee. "Knew you were fuzzed," he said triumphantly, pushing back his chair. "You think of more than one, come on up to the tower and tell me what it is."

KEN RIK had done no more than glare at her rather breathless arrival. He slapped a clipboard in her hand and set her to supervising the emptying of Hold 4, adding a caustic rider to the effect that he hoped she knew enough to balance the load properly for the shuttle.

Priscilla rounded her eyes at him. "Thank you," she said in an awed whisper. "I would never have done it without a reminder. Lina said you were kind."

The old man looked at her suspiciously, saying he knew very well Lina had said no such thing. But Priscilla thought he sounded somewhat less cross.

Hold 4 contained the agricultural plants *belmekit* and *trasveld*, both stasis-held items; both on their way—so the clipboard informed her—to the warehouses of one Herr Polifant Sasoni, Offworld Bazaar, Arsdred. The last pallet came up on her board as "samples." She followed the jitney bearing it to the shuttlebay, her mind on breakfast.

Ken Rik took the clipboard, rechecked her figures, approved the weight distributions with a sniff, and waved her into the shuttle.

Automatically, Priscilla started for the copilot's place, to be sharply called to book by her companion.

"Are you a moonling?" he demanded, dropping into the co's chair himself. Priscilla stared at him until he snorted in exasperation and pointed at the board. "Come along, woman! Don't waste my time."

"You want *me* to take us down?"

"No, I want the shuttle to fly itself," Ken Rik snapped with relish. "I am told you are a pilot. You will, therefore, pilot." He folded his arms over chest and webbing, leaned back, and closed his eyes.

Priscilla webbed into the pilot's chair. Slowly at first, then with more assurance, she ran her fingers over the board, calling up rotations, distance, wind speeds, upper atmosphere. Then she chose her approach, cleared the site, and signaled ready.

They left the *Passage* in a neat tumble, skimming toward the planet in a matching arc, hit atmosphere a little later with the barest possible bump, and slid into the approach approved by Arsdred Port. The wind gave her a little trouble, but she managed to hold the craft steady, her teeth indenting her lower lip, her hand unfaltering over the board.

In a glass-smooth glide, they settled on the pad. Priscilla rechecked and locked the board, then flipped the toggles that unsealed the hatch and snapped her webbing loose.

Ken Rik was already standing. "Not too bad," he allowed grumpily, "for a first attempt."

Priscilla grinned. "Praise, indeed."

"Hmmph," Ken Rik said, and turned away.

Arsdred Offworld Bazaar
Local Year 728
Dawn Bazaar

"IN ADDITION," said the fat man in the electric purple overrobe, "we have fourteen dozens of the finest quality firegems in a multitude—a double rainbow!—of colors. It is certain that the honored Trader must feel impelled to acquire so worthy an item."

Shan took a careful puff on the hookah that his host had so graciously provided for him. The smoke was narcotic—mildly to the individual across from him, rather more than that to even a large Liaden well fortified with anti-intoxicants.

"Firegems," he said, blowing a thoughtful smoke ring. "But surely the honored merchant jests. Why should I wish to purchase firegems of any quality, when all the galaxy carries them? More profitable to ship ice. Or atmosphere."

The fat man smiled with unimpaired good humor. "I see the honored Trader is a man of discrimination, with an eye for the beautiful and the rare. Now, it happens that we also have in our warehouses Tusodian silks of the first looming, *elbam* liqueur, essence of *joberkerney*, *praqilly furleng*, tobacco such as we now enjoy. . . ."

The honored trader yawned and blew another ring. "Herr Minata, do, please, forgive me! When Herr Sasoni spoke of you—of your warehouses, the rarities—but I misunderstood! My command of your language falls short. A thousand apologies for having wasted your time, sir! Believe me, your most obedient. . . ." He stood, bowed with more courtesy than abjectness, and turned to go.

"Master Trader!"

He turned back, concern apparent in his face. "Yes, Herr Minata? How may I serve you?"

The fat man dropped his eyes and toyed with a fold of his robe. "Perhaps we might speak again," he suggested delicately.

"That would be pleasant," Shan said with apparent delight. "We will have our pavilion in Ochre Square within the port, as always. Anyone will tell you the way. Please do come. I will be most happy to see you there."

He bowed again and turned away. This time the merchant let him go.

Outside, Shan took a deep breath of double-baked air and allowed himself a moment of self-congratulation. *That* fish was well netted and no mistake. *Praqilly furleng*—essence that was mere perfume for some, and a religious necessity for others—Tusodian silks . . . a vivid mind-picture of Priscilla Mendoza draped in diaphanous garnet silk presented itself for his inspection.

That will do, he told himself sternly, banishing the picture and merging with the flow of pedestrians heading toward the Outworld Bazaar. The sample case would be down by now, and Ken Rik would surely have something choice to say if his captain were not present at the raising of the pavilion in Ochre Square.

THE SHIPMENT had been taken to Herr Sasoni's warehouse and handed over to a capable-looking young man who inspected the packing and gravely counted the crates before signing the receipt and handing it back.

Returning to Ochre Square and Ken Rik, Priscilla maintained a sedate pace through the bustling pedestrian and jitney traffic, prolonging her first opportunity for quiet thought since the previous evening's encounter with Dagmar.

The second class provisional in her pocket had proved to be neither counterfeit nor imaginary. Sworn to by Master Pilot Shan yos'Galan, it had been issued and registered at the Arsdred branch of the Galactic Pilots Commission yesterday.

A pilot—even a provisional second class pilot—could always find work, she thought, steering her jitney carefully through a crowded corner. The red and yellow plastic card in her pocket represented a solid, respectable future; it represented a breathing space, if she required one when they hit Solcintra, before looking about for another berth.

She slowed as she reached another knot of traffic, then stopped as it became apparent that the driver of the jitney stuck sideways across the thoroughfare was going to be some time in righting his error. Sighing, she leaned back and ran her eyes absently along the crowded street.

What a difference from Jankalim! The air was filled with the whine of jitney motors and the deeper throbbing hum of the monotrains running on the maze of catwalks and rails that roofed the whole of the port. And, of course, voices: raised in conversation, song, argument.

Priscilla yawned and reached for the thread of her thoughts. She had not yet reviewed her contract. That was the first thing to be attended to, next off-shift. Then she would speak with the captain.

With her eyes on the bustling, bright crowds, it occurred to her that she had several things to speak with the captain about. That he should restore her belongings was a puzzle. Lina had said something about owing, but that made no sense. She was Terran; no Liaden could feel honor-bound to balance accounts with her. And if honor had not prompted him to return her things, what in Her name did a gift of earrings mean?

Priscilla sat up suddenly, eyes sharpening on the crowd, catching sight of a familiar bulky figure just turning the corner into Tourmaline Way.

Dagmar.

Her hands clenched the steering rod convulsively even as her breath hissed out between her teeth. Stop it! she ordered herself sharply. That one who has been in the service of the Goddess should feel hatred for a fellow being . . .

She swallowed hard and sent her thoughts back to the comfort of her friend—to meet with mockery even there. Done well, Lina?

"C'mon, honey—move that thing! Coast's clear!" Priscilla shook herself, automatically shifted into gear, and sent the jitney forward again, resolutely declining to think of anything at all.

"TOOK YOUR TIME, DID YOU?" Ken Rik asked, though not with the air of one who expected an answer. "Found the warehouse-man amusing?"

"There was a jitney jammed across Coral Square," Priscilla said tonelessly, sliding out of the seat and offering him the clipboard.

He took the board and glanced at her sharply. Priscilla shrugged. Sharp glances, after all, were not unusual in the old cargo master.

"All right," he said after a moment. "Help me with the samples. When the captain arrives, the pavilion will be raised."

"And the captain *has* arrived, so work may proceed without interruption," concluded that gentleman, walking toward them with a grin. "Thank the gods. I was certain I was late and living in terror of a tongue-lashing, Master Ken Rik!"

"You're a bad boy, Captain," the old man said repressively.

"My expectations fulfilled! Thank you, old friend. Now—" He spun slowly on one heel, surveying the immediate neighborhood. "Wonderful, a temporary-permanent next door. We shall ignore it, secure in the knowledge of our superior taste. The southeast corner, I think, Ken Rik, and we'll have the *nerligig* for catching eyes. Herr Sasoni's order has been safely delivered?"

"Priscilla Mendoza has just returned from the warehouse. The trip down was unexceptional."

"Unexceptional?" Priscilla demanded. "You told me it wasn't too bad."

Ken Rik sniffed and burrowed into the depths of the sample crate.

"Carried away by exuberance," the captain explained. "It's the sort of thing that happens to Ken Rik rather often. My father had to speak to him frequently."

The subject of this palpable untruth turned his head to glare. "Are you going to help raise this pavilion or not?"

"Absolutely! Nothing could induce me to miss such an undertaking! I was only just now having the most delightful chat with Merchant Herr Minata. We could have gone on for hours, so at one did we find ourselves on all matters of importance. But no, I said to him, making my excuse, I *must* go and help raise the pavilion, for Master Ken Rik rules me with an iron hand."

A small sound escaped Priscilla, somewhere between a sneeze and a cough. The captain looked at her curiously.

"Are you well, Ms. Mendoza?"

"Perfectly, sir. Thank you." She took hold of the slippery pavilion cloth and kept her eyes lowered.

"Now," Ken Rik said, shoving a portion of fabric into the captain's hands, "we begin."

It took some time to arrange the corners to Ken Rik's satisfaction. Eventually it was accomplished; the valves were closed, and the pavilion began to inflate.

Priscilla, standing a little way back and watching the first wriggling upheaval, caught sight of a tip of bronze against the bright yellow fabric and inclined her head, as if welcoming a friend.

"Is Korval the dragon or the tree?" she wondered to no one in particular.

"Neither," the captain said. "Or both. The Tree is *Jelaza Kazone*, originally the cipher for Clan Torvin—Line yos'Phelium. The Dragon is Megelaar, for Clan Alkia—Line yos'Galan. Together they're Clan Korval."

She frowned a little. "Two clans merged to make one?"

"Oh, well," he said, smiling, "they really didn't have a choice. Cantra yos'Phelium was the only member of her clan on the colony ship—when it landed on Liad, you understand—except for her unborn child. Tor An yos'Galan was in the same fix. At least, he wasn't pregnant, so perhaps his fix was worse. She had been pilot; he'd been co. When they finally raised a world—landed the ship safely—she asked him to raise her heir, should something happen to her. He accepted it, poor child, ready to abandon Alkia to the void and become Clan Torvin. But Cantra seems to have been a fair-minded sort of person, among her other faults, so Torvin *and* Alkia ceased to be, and Clan Korval emerged." He moved his shoulders. "Family history. But you asked for it."

"Yes, I did. Your Clan was made when the ship landed on Liad?" Priscilla was still frowning; it seemed a very long time.

"A young House," he said cheerfully. "An upstart. There are some who trace their ancestry back to the Old World. Sav Rid's family, for instance—"

"Captain?" Ken Rik said from the seat of the jitney. "I'll go to Thessel's now and see if there's news. Unless you would rather go?"

"I," the captain said, "would rather get my hands dirty setting up the *nerligig*. By all means go to Thessel. And *do* say all those polite things she seems to find so necessary to her comfort."

Unexpectedly, Ken Rik grinned. The jitney slid easily into the flow of traffic, heading west.

The captain wandered over to the sample case, rummaged about for a few moments, and emerged with a toolbox in one hand and a dark *nerligig* in the other.

Dropping the toolbox, he sat on a crate before the slowly inflating pavilion and put the *nerligig* on his knees.

"Might as well put waiting to work," he murmured with the air of quoting someone. "Why don't you take a walk, Ms. Mendoza? There's nothing for you to do here right now."

Priscilla hesitated, nettled by this casual dismissal. But his head was bent over the mechanism, and he was to all appearances absorbed in making the necessary adjustments, so she eventually stalked away.

Ochre Square was a crowded, busy block under the shadow of the monotrain station. Over the buzz of the track, the jitney traffic kept up a perpetual whine. Priscilla considered the other Traders' displays and tents from a distance that said she was not a potential customer. Several things tempted her, and she regretted her lost money. Presumably Dagmar had kept the cash she had found in Priscilla's cabin.

Shan was still concentrating on his work when Priscilla came leisurely back toward the fully inflated pavilion with its striking dragon and tree design. It was comforting, she thought suddenly, to see him there, patiently working, the big, clever hands manipulating the tools with precision.

Frowning, she shook her head. There was no reason at all for her to be comforted by the captain's presence, yet twice now she had distinctly had that sensation. She was not altogether certain she approved of it. Irritably, she looked away.

The jitney was driverless. It was speeding, helped along by the double load gripped in its front claw. And it was on a collision course with the *Passage's* tent.

Later, Priscilla was never sure if she had run or merely flung herself across the distance that separated them. She struck the captain with brutal force and knocked him rolling from the crate, rolling herself as he twisted away, hearing sounds of destruction from too near at hand until she caught up, gasping, against the wall of the temporary-permanent.

She came to her knees, horror-filled.

He lay a little distance from her, his back against the wall, his eyes closed. If he was breathing, he was going about it very quietly.

"Captain?" she whispered. She laid her hand along his cheek.

The slanted brows contracted, and the dark lashes snapped up. "Don't do that, Priscilla."

"All right." She dropped her hand and looked at him uncertainly. "Are you hurt?"

"No," he said shortly. "I'm not hurt." He sat up and looked past her, his silver eyes enormous. Priscilla turned.

The pavilion was gone, tangled crazily about something that surged and tottered and whined like a netted *wilmaby*. A crowd was beginning to gather.

"Your arm please, Priscilla," said the captain, eyes still on the wreckage.

She rose and offered a hand. He accepted the aid and linked his arm in hers, his hand curved lightly about her wrist.

"Captain?" she said softly, hating to say it but certain it should be said. "I saw Dagmar earlier, on Tourmaline Way. . . ."

"She has a right to be here, Priscilla; this is the port. Ah, a policeman. How nice." He started toward that official, and, arm-linked, she went with him.

Shipyear 65
Tripday 143
Second Shift
10.30 Hours

THANKFULLY, THE LIBRARY WAS EMPTY. Priscilla had no wish to speak to anyone at the moment, not even Lina. She located an isolated screen by the door to the pet library and sat down, fumbling with the keys.

The interview with the policeman at the port had been interesting. Disentangled, the jitney was identified by an emaciated gentleman in cherry and white robes as belonging to his employer, one Herr Reyes. He had noticed its absence approximately twenty minutes before and had reported the disappearance to the police before undertaking a rather lengthy walk back into the city. By coincidence he had been turning into Ochre Square as the Tree and Dragon suddenly shrieked, shuddered, and folded in on itself.

A quick examination by the policeman at the site showed that the steering rod bore no imprints at all.

At that point Priscilla had opened her mouth. The captain's fingers tightened briefly on her wrist. Priscilla closed her mouth.

This happened three more times during the course of the captain's conversation with the cop and once as he was speaking with a visibly shaken Ken Rik. He then gave Priscilla into the cargo master's care and instructed him to escort her to the shuttle.

"What!" she cried. *"Why?"*

The captain returned her stare calmly. "You've had a hard shift, Priscilla. Take the rest of it off and come to me at Prime. Be back as soon as you can, Ken Rik. There's a bit of cleanup to do. I'll be speaking with Merchant Reyes's clerk." He had turned away.

The screen chimed, bringing her back to the present. She fed in her request, then waited a few anxious moments until the proper file was retrieved and displayed.

SERVICE RECORD. PRISCILLA DELACROIX Y MENDOZA.

She began to scroll through it impatiently. Suddenly she hit PAUSE and went back a screen.

STANDARD 1385, TULON. TEMPORARY BERTH DAXFLAN, CARGO MASTER TRANSSHIP JANKALIM AS AGREED DUTIFUL PASSAGE, PILOT (PROV SEC), LIBRARIAN. NOTATION: COMMAND POTENTIAL; SECOND MATE TRAINING INSTITUTED.

She read it twice, each time going back to the beginning and scanning every line to the end. There was no mention of thievery or of jumping ship. *TRANSSHIPPED JANKALIM AS AGREED.*

At the end of the file she paused again, staring at the certification from the registry office on VanDyk.

It was dated one Standard Week ago.

"Impossible," she told the screen.

The words persisted. She read them again and keyed in her next request.

CONTRACT SIGNED BETWEEN PRISCILLA DELACROIX Y MENDOZA, FIRST PARTY, AND SHAN YOS'GALAN AS CAP- TAIN, DUTIFUL PASSAGE, SECOND PARTY. FIRST PARTY SHALL AGREE TO PERFORM DUTIES INHERENT IN THE POST OF PET LIBRARIAN AND ALSO TO UNDERTAKE PILOT TRAINING ONE SHIP WATCH OF EVERY NINE, WITHOUT FAIL, AND ALSO TO UNDERTAKE ANY ADDITIONAL TRAINING OR DUTY DEEMED REASONABLE AND JUST BY SECOND PARTY.

Priscilla leaned back. There it was. She briefly and belatedly recalled advice given a much younger Priscilla: "I tell you what, youngster. Don't you ever sign a Liaden's contract. I don't care how careful you read it. If he won't sign yours, let the deal go. Safer that way."

Still, there was nothing wrong with undergoing second mate's training. She would have appreciated being told, but she was sure that he had meant it for the best.

It was not until she had cleared the screen and left the library that it occurred to her to wonder why she *should* be sure of it.

PRISCILLA EXITED THE LIFT and walked resolutely toward the captain's office. She was dressed in the yellow shirt and khaki trousers she had worn when she first walked down this hall. In her pocket was the provisional second class. The rest of her belongings were in the cabin that had been hers, the clothes neatly folded and stacked beside the scrounged plastic box. She must remember to tell the captain to offer the bracelets to a collector. The price they would bring as curios would go far toward paying her debt to the ship.

She rounded the corner by Hold 6 and nearly walked into Kayzin Ne'Zame.

The first mate recovered first and swept a surprising bow, as deep as one would accord the captain, augmented by an odd little flourish that mystified Priscilla entirely.

"We are well met, Priscilla Mendoza," she said in a light, quick voice much unlike her usual manner of speech. "I have been remiss in offering you an apology for my behavior several shifts gone by, when we spoke near the central computer." She took a breath and looked up. "Pray forgive it. I was discourteous and in error."

Priscilla blinked, collected herself immediately, and bowed in turn, though not as deeply, nor did she attempt to copy the flourish.

"Do me the honor of putting the incident from your mind, Kayzin Ne'Zame. I shall do the same."

The Liaden woman inclined her head. "You are kind. It shall be as you have said. I leave you now."

"Be well, Kayzin Ne'Zame," Priscilla murmured, laying her hand against the captain's door.

"Come!"

He was standing, hands hooked in his belt, his bright head bent over a chess problem. It was a new one, Priscilla saw, and she wondered if the other had had a solution, after all. He glanced up as the door closed and smiled. "Hello, Priscilla. Did you rest well this past shift?"

"I visited Master Frodo for a while," she said, hesitating between desk chairs and couch.

"A very restful companion. I've always found him so, at any rate. Ken Rik labels him terminally cute. But Ken Rik likes snakes. What may I give you to drink?"

"Nothing, thank you, Captain." She decided on one of the chairs before his desk, drifted over, and perched on the arm.

"Nothing?" The slanted brows drew together as he crossed the rug. "Are you angry, Priscilla? Or am *I* angry? If it's me, I assure you that I'm not. And if it's you—but surely you knew I had to send you away? It would have been unforgivable to keep you by, especially when I'd put you in so much danger already."

"You put me in danger?" She stared at him. "It's the other way around, Captain. *I* put *you* in danger. Which is why I would rather not accept a drink. I'm not stopping long." She forced herself to meet his eyes calmly. "I think it would be wisest for me to leave the *Passage* immediately."

"Do you?" He paused. "What a very odd notion of wisdom. If you were staying long enough to have a drink, Priscilla, what would you prefer? Purely hypothetical, of course." The light eyes were mocking her.

"Idle speculation, since I'm not staying that long," she said crisply. "I came only to say that—"

"It would be wisest for you to leave the *Passage* immediately," the captain interrupted, holding up his hands placatingly. "You *did* say it. I heard you. Now, Priscilla, please pay attention—this is very important. You might at least have some consideration for my feelings in the matter. I'm thirsty, and you're telling nonsense stories, which you could as easily tell while having a glass of wine with me like a civilized person." He tipped his head. *"Do* strive for some courtesy, Priscilla."

She felt laughter rising and clamped down, with limited success. A small sound woefully reminiscent of a hiccup emerged. "Red, please," she said, glaring.

"Red," he repeated, moving toward the bar. "An excellent choice, as even Gordy will tell you. Though, of course, there's nothing wrong with the white or the jade or the *blue."* He was back and handing her a cut-crystal glass. Her fingers curved around the stem automatically. "And the red won't ruin your taste for Prime—you will have time to dine with me, won't you, Priscilla? I agree that I should have first found if your schedule was clear, but it did seem rude to ask you to come to speak with me at dinnertime and then rob you of dinner."

She sipped her wine and tried again. "Captain, surely you must see that the longer I stay with you—with the *Passage—* the more danger you're in? If I'm gone, then you—"

"Priscilla, you have a woeful tendency toward single-mindedness," he interrupted, sitting on the edge of the desk and swinging a leg.

She clamped her jaw and stood. "Thank you for all you've done, Captain, but I really must be going."

"You can't do that, Priscilla; you have a contract. You're bound to this ship until Solcintra. That's four months, as the route runs. You don't have the buy-off fee, do you? I didn't think so." He raised his glass. "It looks like you're stuck, child. Might as well sit down and finish your wine."

"I'm not a child!"

"Well, I can't be expected to know that, can I, if you persist in acting like one? You really must try to curb these tastes for melodrama and resignation."

"Melodrama!" She glared at him, her fingers ominously tight about the glass. "At least I'm not high-handed and—"

"High-handed!"

"*High*-handed," she asserted with relish. "And dictatorial. And *obstinate*. As if you couldn't see why—"

"High-handed! Of all the— Priscilla, when we reach Solcintra, I engage to introduce you to my brother's Aunt Kareen. Call *me* high-handed! Before that, you'd best improve your grasp of the High Tongue—your accent's *execrable*. And another thing! How dare you profess yourself all joy to see me? Have you no sense of propriety? I hardly know you."

"Nor will you know me any better," she stated, suddenly calm. She set her glass on the edge of his desk. "Because I'm leaving. Contract or not. Sue me."

"I won't. But I will arrest you, if you force me to it." He was in front of her, his face quite serious. "Priscilla, have some sense. Don't you realize you saved my life this afternoon?"

She gaped, aware of a strong desire to take him by the shoulders and shake. "Do *you* realize it? You act like—Captain yos'Galan, if you know it, then *let me go!* Surely you see that the sooner I'm gone, the sooner you're safe! People will stop trying to kill you—"

"No, wait." A big, warm hand closed around one of hers. "Priscilla, please—a favor. Come sit down . . . here's your wine. Now, if you please, tell me what happened at the port today."

She sat carefully, accepted her glass, and took a sip, steadying heart rate and breathing, embracing serenity. "You know what happened, Captain. You were there."

"I was there," he agreed, back at his station on the edge of the desk. "But I'm Liaden. You're Terran. From what you've said, it seems clear we think that two different things occurred." He leaned forward, eyes intent on her face. "Tell me, Priscilla. Please?"

She took another sip and looked at him straightly. "Today someone deliberately tried to kill you by aiming a jitney at you, jamming the rod, and jumping out. By the grace of the Goddess, I was close enough to knock you out of the way." She took a breath. "I believe—though I have no proof—that Dagmar Collier made the attempt. I also believe that it was ordered by Sav Rid Olanek, striking at you because you gave me sanctuary. So, if I leave the *Passage,* show myself to be a free agent, no more attempts should be made on your life."

"There it is," he said softly, brows pulled slightly together. "Why sacrifice yourself to keep me safe, Priscilla? Assuming all of what you say is accurate, of course."

"I brought danger to you," she said patiently. "It's only just that I take it away again. It's what is honorable."

"Is it?" He raised his glass, reconsidered, and lowered it. "Then I'm afraid we have a conflict of honors. The code I was raised to says that, having been so careless as to have necessitated your saving my life, I am very much in your debt. Setting aside the fact that allowing you to go would be murder, if my assessment of Ms. Collier's character is correct, I owe you the protection of this ship—of my resources, say rather. To send you away—unprotected and unprepared—to decoy danger from me is lunacy. And also highly dishonorable. It makes far more sense, is within the limits of honor—and duty!—to stay where it is relatively safe and work to balance what is owed them!" He did drink this time, slowly, then lowered his glass and shook his head.

"The fact is, Priscilla, you don't know the rules. I grant that the admission of Ms. Collier and yourself into the game alters things somewhat, but not enough to matter. Certainly the larger points remain constant. Am I being sinister enough, or should I wrap myself in a cloak and snigger?"

"Can you snigger?" she asked with interest.

"Probably not." He grinned. "But I'll do my best if it takes that to convince you to let me have my high-handed, dictatorial, and—what was the other one?"

"Obstinate," Priscilla supplied, though she had the grace to blush.

"A fairly accurate reading of my faults. Though you omitted inquisitive and meddling. Your suspicion of Sav Rid does him less than justice, by the way. I don't think he ordered me eliminated. It's my belief Ms. Collier was acting on her own initiative. Sav Rid has his limitations, even in stupidity. And it would be extremely stupid to murder me." He drank. "Besides, I don't think I scared him that much."

She blinked. "Were you trying to—oh, the earrings?"

"The earrings. But that seems only to have frightened Ms. Collier into an indiscretion. Lamentable. Sav Rid really ought to screen his people more carefully. I saw Ms. Collier's record—idle curiosity, you understand. She had been a marine. Dishonorable discharge. Personnel complications." He tipped his head. "I said that she used to be a Marine, Priscilla; please pay attention. How close did you come to killing her?"

"I didn't—" The lie choked her, and she looked down, then looked back at him. "She's so *slow*. But I misjudged the knife, so she almost killed me, not the other way around."

"An error of inexperience, I believe. I doubt it would happen again. Forgive me, Priscilla, it had seemed a good idea."

This was more than usually convoluted. She put it away for later thought. "What are the rules, Captain?"

"The rules are—" He paused and looked at her consideringly. "Whose life did you save, Priscilla?"

"Shan yos'Galan's," she said, wondering.

"Did you? Good. It makes things somewhat simpler. Now, what—oh, the rules. Wouldn't you rather have the story first? I always need something to hang the rules on, don't you? My dreadful memory. But maybe yours is better."

"It's awful," she told him seriously. "I'd better have the story."

He grinned. "Not too bad, Priscilla. With a bit of practice you should be quite convincing. More wine? No? Oh, well." He finished his glass and set it aside, lacing his fingers around a knee.

"For the sake of argument," he said pensively, "we'll say that the story begins with Clan Plemia, Sav Rid's family. A very old, most respected House. And also one that's fallen on hard times these last hundred Standards or so, which makes money . . . oh, not as plentiful as it once was. Fortunes rise, fortunes fall, and Plemia's case, while no doubt uncomfortable, isn't *dire*. There's every reason to expect that a bit of careful husbandry will bring them about. In time." He paused, then shrugged.

"Unfortunately, Sav Rid doesn't seem a patient man. He wishes to restore Plemia to its pinnacle *now*. I assume that he cudgeled his brain and finally hit upon the happy plan of taking a lifemate. He possesses lineage, address, a comely face, an elegant person—an extremely eligible individual in all ways. It need not be said that one of Plemia might look where he chose."

Priscilla smiled. "Which is how he happened to propose to your sister."

The captain grinned. "Well, it does make a certain amount of sense, you know. Nova's of age; she might choose whatever husband or lifemate suits her. She has lineage, address, a comely face, an elegant person—and is, incidentally, of course, quite wealthy. There was no reason why they shouldn't have been very happy with each other."

A sound escaped Priscilla, neither a hiccup nor a sneeze—a chuckle, low and obviously delighted. "But she sent him off with a flea in his ear."

"So she did. But she was sadly provoked, you know. The silly creature wouldn't take no for an answer—kept asking and asking. The final time, he paid a morning call for the sole purpose of pleading his case once more. He sighed. "We none of us have gentle tempers— very hotheaded family, the yos'Galans; and the yos'Pheliums are worse. At any rate, the morning call was the nether end of too much, and she threw him out." He looked at her earnestly. "I wouldn't have you think less of her, Priscilla. She really did try very hard to be civil."

"I'm sure she did. It's irritating when people won't believe what you tell them." Her grin faded. "But if there's a—vendetta—it would be on Trader Olanek's side, wouldn't it, Captain? If he wanted to believe your sister had insulted him?"

"I should have warned you," the captain said, picking up his empty glass and sighing, "that it's a rather long story. Will you have some more wine? Thirsty work, talking."

"I'd have thought you'd be used to it."

"You wrong me, Priscilla; I'm often quiet. Reports are that I hardly ever talk in my sleep, for instance." He was at the bar. She turned in her chair, considering the fit of his shirt and the worked leather of his belt, the gentle bell of cloth from knee to instep. He always dressed with immaculate simplicity. She saw now that the fabrics were costly, the tailoring precise—not readymades from valet or general stores.

He turned around, brows twitching. "Yes?"

"You had said your clan—Korval—is an upstart?" She stopped short of all she wished to ask, unsure of the polite way to do so.

He grinned and handed her a glass. "Oh, we're respected enough. After all, we trace our lines to Torvin and Alkia, and thence to the Old World. It is, of course, to be regretted that my father should have seen fit to allow Terran blood into the Clan, but there's nothing wrong with Terran blood that I know of. Does its job just as well as anyone else's blood. Purists may frown, but not many Clans can recite a lineage that doesn't include the odd Terran or two. My brother tells me that the Clutch-turtles simply call everyone 'The Clans of Men' and let it go at that. In a little while—according to *their* view of things—we'll all be one race. No Terrans. No Liadens. No half-breeds." He raised his glass. "Ready for Chapter Two?"

"Please."

"Again we start with Sav Rid, I think. Why not? He and Chelsa yo'Vaade, both of Clan Plemia. Chelsa isn't too bad a pilot but doesn't have any brains to speak of. She does what Sav Rid tells her to do. A pity.

"Also important to this story is Shan yos'Galan, who is, please remember, a fool." He paused, brows twitching. "You said, Priscilla?"

"I wanted to know how a fool became Master Trader," she repeated.

He grinned. "It's easier than you might think. And my father would settle for nothing less from me." His face became more serious. "Several people hold the opinion that Shan yos'Galan is a fool, Priscilla. There's a certain advantage to that. Several other people believe that Shan yos'Galan is *not* a fool, if it comforts you, but Sav Rid isn't one of them.

"To continue. In the course of his trading, Sav Rid took on

a quantity of mezzik-root—highly perishable, but also highly profitable, if one happens to be going to Brinix. Sav Rid was, hence the root. He, in fact, jumped out of Tulon System, pegged for Brinix. And returned just an hour or so after the *Passage* docked at Tulon Prime. I met Sav Rid at the trade bar a little time after that and heard his tale. *Daxflan* was urgently required elsewhere on business of Clan Plemia. The mezzik-root would pass its time before he had any hope of delivery. Would I be going near Brinix? Would I consider buying the shipment at a flat figure, thus helping a fellow Liaden and enriching myself?"

He shrugged. "It was an opportunity, and I took it. It does occur that one is suddenly called away on Clan business and must dispose of cargo as it's possible. I knew nothing of the honored Trader except that he had annoyed my sister—easy enough to do. She's seldom completely in charity with *me,* for instance. The price was paid, the load transferred. Other business completed, the *Passage* jumped out-system, pegged for Brinix—which was found to be under medical quarantine and expected to remain so for the next local year, far past the time when the mezzik-root would have started to deteriorate." He paused to drink.

"The tower manager was polite—and astonished. *Daxflan,* under Captain yo'Vaade, had been in orbit not many days since and had promised to deliver news of the quarantine to Tulon."

Priscilla took a breath. "How much did you lose?"

"Forty cantra. But I did enhance and improve my reputation as a most wonderful fool, which must be counted a gain." He shook his head.

"By the time we got back into Tulon, the story was all over the trade bar. The report had been delivered two minutes after the *Passage* jumped out. *Daxflan* was gone, having hired a new cargo master."

"All that for—Balance—for being insulted by your sister?" Priscilla was frowning.

"Now there," the captain said, "I'm not at all certain. Nova is old enough to mind her own honor. If Sav Rid had a quarrel with her reading of his character, then his satisfaction lies with her. He might have assumed that I forbade the match, as Head of Line, you see. I didn't, and probably wouldn't have, if she'd set her heart on him. It never came to me at all; I learn everything after the fact, and in pieces—which, come to think of it, is the only way you learn anything from him—from Val Con, who was kind enough to show Sav Rid the door on the occasion of his morning call." The movement of his shoulders was not quite a shrug.

"For whatever reason, a debt is owed—has been owing. Sav Rid's belief that I am too foolish to be considered an able—" He stopped, brows contracting. "Here's a thing that doesn't happen often," he murmured. "Forgive me, Priscilla; my Terran seems to be lacking. Can it be *debt-partner?*" He sipped wine, considering the carpet with absent intensity.

"Say debt-partner," he decided after a moment. "It makes less nonsense than the other possibilities."

Priscilla shifted in her chair. "This happened at Tulon?"

He glanced up. "Yes. At the beginning of our run."

"And you still owe him for—dear Goddess—forty cantra?" The amount of the loss was staggering.

"Forty cantra's the least of it. I owe him a lesson to treat me with courtesy and respect, not to mention honesty." He sipped, eyes on her face. "These things take time and planning, Priscilla."

"So it was lucky that I came here asking for a job," she said, making the connections rapidly. "I could be a very useful weapon."

"Now, Priscilla, for space sake, don't get into hyper again!" He was in front of her, hands spread-fingered and soothing. "I'd have given you a job if Sav Rid were my best friend! Only a lunatic would turn down someone of your potential." He grinned at her. "Foolish, yes. Crazed, no. And it's not a question of giving. You're earning your pay."

"Am I?" she demanded, refusing to give in to her desire to be mollified. "And when will I start training as second mate?"

"You've started," he told her, lowering his hands slowly. "Ken Rik thinks very well of you. So does Tonee. And Lina. And Seth, Vilobar, Gordy, BillyJo, Vilt, Rusty, and Master Frodo. If you keep on at this rate, you'll have the expertise by Solcintra. You already have the ability. Are you angry, Priscilla? Don't you want to learn the job?"

"Of course I want to learn it," she said irritably. "I just would have appreciated being told instead of finding out by accident."

"High-handed," he said mournfully. "I'll try to curb it, but don't expect miracles. I've been this way a long time."

"You're not much older than I am," she told him severely. "How did you manage that trick with my record—dated last week! And no mention of theft or jumping ship."

"Oh." He drifted back to the desk, hoisted himself up, and recaptured his glass. "More high-handedness, I'm afraid, Priscilla. Please try to bear with me." He drank. "I contacted the captain of *Dante* for a more specific recommendation, took every word as truth, and pin-beamed your updated record to VanDyk with a notation that it superseded all previously dated information."

He grinned at her. "Sav Rid had ruined your record within the sector; but he's tight-fisted, and the courier bounce to VanDyk will take months. Just imagine his unhappiness when he finds his report of your nefarious activities returned to him marked 'Superseded by Data Attached.' Do you think he'll file an official complaint? And risk a hearing into the specifics of your so-called crimes? Will he insist that his very negative report be inserted next to all those glowing ones?" He raised his glass in salute. "I think not."

"You pin-beamed . . . Captain, do you know how expensive pin-beaming is?"

"No. Tell me." The silver eyes were laughing at her.

She frowned, rediscovered her glass, and took a healthy swallow.

"Don't worry about it, Priscilla We've got a pin-beam on board—Rusty's favorite toy. One of the services the *Passage* offers the more backward of our ports is the use of the pin-beam. For a fee, of course. I'm well paid, by contemplating the expression on Sav Rid's face when he reads 'Data Attached'— Dinner at long last!" he interrupted himself as the door chimed.

Gordy grinned from behind the serving table. "I'm on time," he pointed out with considerable pride. He parked the table and came around to Priscilla. "Now you're a hero, too."

"No," she said with decision. "I'm *not* a hero, Gordy."

He tipped his head, clearly puzzled, and turned to the captain. "Shan? Isn't she?"

"She just said she wasn't, didn't she, Gordy? People have a right to define who they are, don't they? If Priscilla doesn't want to be a hero right now, she doesn't have to be. It's probable that she's hungry. Very difficult to be heroic when you're hungry."

The boy laughed and went to the table to begin unfolding leaves, and releasing odors. Priscilla suddenly realized that she was very hungry.

"Ken Rik said to tell you the *nerligig* works fine," he said over his shoulder.

The captain stared at him. "It does? He tried it on all settings?"

Gordy nodded. "The case is pretty dented, he said, but since it's for attention getting, that doesn't matter." He paused to glance at his cousin. "He really did say that."

"Of course he did. Ken Rik doesn't believe in curbing his tongue for anyone. I'd be seriously concerned for his health if he started now. Besides, he met me when I was younger than you are, and twice as clumsy. No doubt that makes it occasionally hard to proffer the appropriate respect. What about the tent? Has he gotten a new sample case together? And he'll—no, never mind; I'll wander over and speak with him later. Is prime ready yet?"

"Whist, now, Johnny Galen," Gordy murmured in an exaggerated accent.

The captain laughed and drank wine. "Intolerable puppy. I bear that from your grandfather. But I'm bigger than you are. Please try to keep it in mind."

"Bully," Gordy said, settling plates amid an amazing amount of clatter.

"High-handed," the captain corrected, and grinned at Priscilla, who dropped her eyes.

Gordy stepped back. "Ready. Should I stay?"

The captain glanced at him in surprise. "Did I ask you to

dinner, Gordon? Forgive me, the invitation slipped my mind. I seem to recall a report that you've fallen behind in your studies, a circumstance your grandfather, my uncle, would not forgive me. We're due for a review, aren't we? At breakfast."

Gordy swallowed visibly. "Yessir."

"That bad?" He raised his glass. "Well, better see what you can catch up on beforehand. And mind you're in bed at a reasonable hour. I won't need you anymore."

"Yessir," Gordy said again, looking so comically crestfallen that Priscilla had to forcefully swallow the rising laughter. "G'night, Cap'n. G'night, Priscilla."

"Good night, Gordy," she said, smiling at him warmly.

"Good night, Gordy." The captain reached over to the boy and ruffled his hair lightly. "*Do* sleep well."

The boy smiled up at him, made an awkward bow, and departed, the door hissing closed behind him.

"Now, then, Priscilla, if you'll pull up the chairs, I'll serve us. I hope you're as hungry as I am."

A little time later, the edge of hunger blunted, she leaned back and considered the top of his head and the thick, well-cut hair gleaming in the room's soft light.

"Johnny Galen?" she wondered.

He glanced up, smiling. "It's my Uncle Richard's fancy that Liadens are the 'little people' of Old Terra's legends. Thus, Arthur Galen, Johnny, Nora, and Annie Galen. And their foster brother, the king of Elfland."

"Oh, no!" A chuckle escaped, but she didn't notice.

"Oh. yes," he assured her. "Complete with 'my liege' and 'your highness.' Pretty comical, actually. My father finally did manage to put a stop to it, but I think he had to resort to threats."

"But he let himself be called Arthur, and you Johnny?"

"Well, no, not exactly," he said, reaching for his glass. "He didn't *answer* to 'Arthur,' you see, so if Uncle Dick really wanted to speak with him, he had to use 'Er Thom.' I don't mind 'Johnny'—my mother called me 'Shannie' more often than not—and Anthora was *always* 'Annie.' To the best of my knowledge, Nova never did answer to 'Nora.'" He sipped. "I hope Val Con doesn't feel he owes balance for the king routine. I rather doubt it. Whatever his faults, Uncle Richard is a master storyteller. And Val Con's addicted to stories."

Priscilla frowned down at the table, then glanced up. "Captain? What is a debt-partner?"

He set his glass aside and picked up his tongs, readdressing dinner. Priscilla hesitated, then returned to her own plate, wondering if she had offended.

"A debt-partner," the captain said slowly, "is one with whom you are engaged in a balancing of accounts." He glanced at her quickly from beneath his lashes. "There are, as I mentioned before, many rules governing revenge—Balance—and how it might be achieved. One of them is that Balance is only owing *respected persons.* Animals, for instance, may not claim debt-right." He paused, watching her face carefully.

"It," Priscilla whispered, her spoon forgotten halfway to her mouth. "He called us 'it,' Gordy and me."

"So he did," the captain agreed carefully. "One of the least attractive things about the High Tongue is that it's so easy to deny worth." He looked at her closely. "*I* didn't call you 'it,' Priscilla. Of all the people in the galaxy, I'd be among the last to do so. But Sav Rid believes that people who aren't Liaden aren't—people." He raised his glass and took a sip. "What he had done to you on Jankalim, he would never have ordered done to another Liaden. Even one he considered a fool of the first order, completely careless of his personal honor, the honor of his Line, and of his ship." He grinned. "He thought he'd gotten away clean, Priscilla. Imagine his depression when I not only turn up to bail you out, after he thought you safely disposed of, but uttering threats about earrings, guilty consciences—little enough. But he knows he's gotten away with nothing. He may still doubt my ability to do it, but he knows I'll attempt balance."

She laid her spoon down carefully. "But an—animal—has no recourse."

He sipped, eyes on her. "But you're not an animal, are you,

Priscilla? Aren't you a person? Isn't respect due you? You can be an animal, if you choose to say you are. Or you can show him quite clearly that you are a resourceful, intelligent *person,* worthy of the dignity accorded all persons." He set the glass down, his big mouth tight.

"He has stolen from you—possessions, money, personhood. And you speak of taking on the role of an animal, sacrificing your life for mine. Priscilla, don't you see that you are owed? How *dare* he order violence against your person? How *dare* he steal the money you earned, the things you own, your reputation? And by what right did he place your personal honor in jeopardy in the first place, hiring you as master over a cargo of contraband?" He held out a hand. "Wouldn't you rather stay, Priscilla? We'll bring him payment together."

With no hesitation at all, she slid her hand into his.

"Yes," she said clearly. "We'll do that."

Shipyear 65
Tripday 143
Fourth Shift
18.00 Hours

෨෨෨෨෨෨෨෨෨෨෨෨෨෨෨෨෨෨෨෨෨෨෨෨෨෨෨෨෨෨෨෨

PRISCILLA LAID HER HAND AGAINST THE DOOR. It slid away to a soft "Enter" from within.

Smiling, Lina bounced up from her seat at the desk. "Priscilla! How are you, my friend?"

"Fine." Priscilla smiled back, sliding her hands into the small ones stretched out to her. "You're busy? I'm not on urgent business."

"No, come and talk with me! If I look at that terrible report another minute, I shall develop a *severe* headache." She laughed, tugging on Priscilla's hands. "Save me!"

They sat on the bed, Lina cross-legged in the center and Priscilla on the edge.

"So, now, what is this not-urgent business?"

"I'm afraid it isn't going to make any sense," Priscilla apologized, toying with the quilt. "At least, I can't think of a sensible way to ask it. Lina, isn't Shan yos'Galan the captain?"

The smaller woman blinked. "Of course he is. Are you having a joke, my friend?"

"I said it didn't make sense," Priscilla pointed out. "I just had dinner with the captain—" She stopped. Lina folded her hands together, waiting.

"I had dinner with the captain," Priscilla repeated slowly. "As I was leaving, I asked him about having returned my things. He said the ship bore the expense of buying them back, that I was to consider it my bonus for having been put in danger." She paused, frowning a little. "Then I asked about the earrings, because they *weren't* mine."

"And?" Lina prompted softly.

"He said the earrings were a gift from Shan yos'Galan, and the captain had nothing to do with it."

"He said so?" Lina moved her shoulders. "Then it is true."

Priscilla sighed. "Yes, I'm sure it is. But Lina, if Shan yos'Galan is the captain . . ."

"Surely you know that the captain speaks—acts—for the ship," her friend said carefully. "Yes? So, Shan speaks for himself. It is—I do not know the Terran word. Shan yos'Galan has many . . . roles! He is captain, Master Trader, pilot—three voices with which to speak on the *Passage*. On Liad he is also Lord yos'Galan. He only made certain that you understood which face he used—from which role he acted—when he gifted you."

Priscilla stared at her. "It makes a difference? But he's the same man, no matter what title he's using!"

"Of course he is. But the captain has specific duties, responsibilities, different duties than the Master Trader. A pilot has yet another set." Lina chewed her lip uncertainly. "It is only *melant'i*, Priscilla." She sighed at the blank look on her friend's face and tried once more. "It is true that Shan yos'Galan is the captain. But the captain is not Shan yos'Galan."

"I'll work on it," Priscilla said, smiling apologetically. "There might not be a Terran word, Lina." She tipped her head. "Is my Liaden accent horrible?"

"No. Who said it was? You are very careful and listen hard, but it is true you are just learning."

"The captain—at least I *think* it was the captain, but it might have been Shan yos'Galan—told me my accent was execrable and that he was going to introduce me to his aunt—his brother's aunt."

"To Lady Kareen? *Illanga kilachi*—no. Priscilla, did he *promise* that he would do so?"

"He said he would *engage* to," she said, somewhat amused. "How awful can she be?"

"You cannot imagine. She is very proper—ah, he is bad! We will practice, the two of us, very hard. And tomorrow I will choose enhancement tapes. You can sleep-learn? Good. Also protocol lessons." She looked up at her friend, hands fluttering. "What made him say such a thing? To Lady Kareen—"

"I told him he was high-handed," Priscilla confessed.

"So he now wishes to show you what that is." Lina grinned. "You are well served, then. However did you come to say something so rude?"

"It slipped out right after he told me I had a tendency toward melodrama."

Lina laughed. "It sounds as if you had a fine dinner! Compliments all around."

"Protocol lessons are a necessity," Priscilla agreed, smiling. She sobered. "Lina? Why is it wrong for me to tell the captain—the Master Trader—that I am all joy to see him?"

Lina looked at her in horror. "You said that? To Shan? In public?"

"And in the High Tongue," her friend admitted sheepishly. "Am I beyond redemption?"

"No wonder he gives you earrings!" Lina cried, taking her hand. "Priscilla, you must never do so again! It is a phrase reserved for . . . a brother, perhaps, or an individual one has grown up with . . . a lifemate."

"Really? I'm glad I said it, then. It was exactly right."

"Priscilla," Lina pleaded. "It is most improper! You must not do so again."

"All right," she agreed sunnily. "I don't think I'll ever need to again." She laughed then, very softly, and Lina held her breath. "Poor Sav Rid!"

LINA FOUND SHAN IN THE GYM. Just inside, she stopped to watch him swing the paddle, strike the ball, spin, connect, dive, connect—faster and even faster, the ball a white blur trapped between wall and paddle, the man moving with lithe intensity, never missing, never pausing.

After a moment, she walked forward, angling toward the wall, then heard the ball strike just beyond her shoulder.

"Lina! Are you courting suicide? You could have been hit!"

"No," she told him calmly, changing her course. "You are far too quick for that, my friend."

"Accidents happen." Shan walked to meet her, paddle in one hand, ball in the other. His hair stuck in wet points to his forehead, lending him a slightly satanic air; he was breathing hard, and the wine-colored shirt showed darker patches. Lina set aside a spurt of fond sympathy; she stopped at precisely the proper distance and looked sternly up at him.

"You are meddling!" She spoke in the High Tongue, as senior to junior.

"I always meddle," he returned in mild Terran. "You know that."

"You will cease to do so in this instance. Immediately." Her words were still in the High Tongue, commanding, as was proper.

"Dear me," Shan murmured, looking down with a fine show of bewildered stupidity. "Do you mind if we sit down?"

She laughed and turned with him toward the side benches. "You are impossible!" she told him in Terran. "You deserve to be scolded!"

"Often," he agreed cordially, flipping paddle and ball into the wall slot and dropping into the first chair he came to. He thrust his long legs out before him. "Scold me."

She frowned. He was in a chancy mood. She began tentatively. "Shan, it is serious. Please. You could do harm." She extended a mental tendril.

She was met with opposition, the familiar Healer's barrier. He rarely took such complete refuge; never in all their years of friendship had he done so with her. Not at the time his mother had died so tragically, nor when Er Thom yos'Galan had turned his face from kin and from duty to follow her.

Lina withdrew the tendril and considered him quietly. "It is a bad thing," she offered, "for Healers to argue over a proper approach. Most especially when Healing has begun."

"I agree," Shan said.

"That is good. Now, I will tell you that I am puzzled. We spoke, did we not? And it was agreed that I should proceed, though Priscilla was drawn as much to you as to me. You insisted, old friend, saying you were captain, not Healer."

"True. I do not act as Healer in the matter."

Lina stifled a sigh. This was Shan at his least tractable, showing the streak of stubborn reticence that characterized Korval at the fore. In a way it was a blessing—if she could not read him through the protective barrier, neither could he read her. The Wall, like so much of healing, was reciprocal.

She considered that last thought. One did tend to become entangled with those one Healed. Priscilla . . . He may have feared reciprocity, having felt the strength of her—even half-crazed with pain. And if he had been drawn enough to fear the Healing process . . .

"What is it that you want, old friend?" she asked.

He stirred. "I want to be her friend."

So. "And her lover!" She put a lash to that. If he did not yet know . . .

"I am not," Shan said carefully, "made of stone. You will have noticed this."

"Better you should have taken her to Heal yourself, then! The bond was there, from the beginning! Healing across sex is more rapid—you know that! Why—"

"And have her think herself hired to be the captain's slut? Thank you, no." There was Korval ice in that.

Lina blinked and gave a flickering thought to her own protections. "Why should she have thought so, old friend?"

Shan sighed. "She came to me—as captain—for protection. One Liaden had already robbed her of status as a person. It would not have seemed at all wonderful to her if another continued—" He shifted irritably. "Priscilla's Terran, Lina. She wasn't raised to *melant'i*.

I *am* the captain to Priscilla. She believes it. It would have been nothing short of rape, a violation of trust so basic. . . ." He took a breath and ran his fingers through his hair, standing it up in sticky spikes. "I was in error, old friend. I act as Healer in the matter, in that I refused to act as one."

"I am Liaden," Lina said softly. "I am her superior."

"You are also friends. And I believe that the amount of influence a senior librarian exercises over a junior is somewhat less than what a captain may exercise over a crew member."

There was a silence that grew lengthy. Then Shan leaned forward abruptly and took her hands between his.

"I want her to be well. Joyful and complete. That most. I want her friendship, but I don't—won't—force it. A pair of earrings? Call it restitution for another wrong done her by Trader Olanek, if you like, Lina. If it will make all easier—"

"You have already said they are your gift to her," she reminded him. "But I do not think harm was done." She smiled warmly. "It is a good thing to have friends."

"I think so, too." He leaned back. "I leave the Healing in your hands. My word on it."

"So, then," she said, satisfied. She brought a finger to the side of her head. "I had almost forgotten the other. She did not mean it, Shan, when she welcomed you in esteem. I have explained, and it will not happen again. You must not be angry with her."

"Angry with her?" He laughed. "I'm delighted with her! She would have done no better if I'd coached her beforehand. What a devastating setdown for poor Sav Rid! The look on his face! I could have kissed her."

"You must not encourage her to behave improperly," she scolded him. "You talk of being her friend! It is important that she learn to behave with propriety. Especially if you will present her to Lady Kareen!"

"Yes, Lina," he said with wholly unconvincing meekness.

She shook her head. "No, *that* will not do. I know you. Priscilla and I will work on her accent, and she will use sleep tapes. Lady Kareen will find her above reproach."

"A matter of your own pride, in fact?"

She laughed and stood. "Completely impossible. Good night, old friend." She touched his cheek, very gently, noting that the Wall was yet in place. "Sleep well."

Shipyear 65
Tripday 144
First Shift
1.30 Hours

HE DID *NOT* SLEEP WELL. Nor did his interview with Gordy do anything to mend his badly frayed temper. He had begun by snarling at the boy, and his mood was not improved by the realization that he sounded rather like his father in that tone.

Irritably, he crossed to the bar and poured himself a glass of morning wine. There were a few things to attend to here before going worldside to begin a local week of trading. He dropped into his chair and spun the screen around.

Buzzzz!

Shan looked up, not quite placing the sound.

Buzzzz!

Brutally, he rearranged the mob of documents on top of the desk and eventually uncovered a shiny blue pad set with two unmarked keys. He depressed one at random. "Yes?"

Buzzzz!

Shan sighed and pushed the other key. "Yes?"

"Cap'n? Rusty here. Sorry to bother you."

"Rusty? Aren't you scheduled for world leave today? I thought you'd be dancing in the streets with a lover on each arm."

"Well, I'd planned on it," Rusty said seriously. "But when we hit port, there were two—oh, individuals—waiting for us. They say

795

nobody from the *Passage* is allowed on-world and that they're coming up." There was a tiny pause. "They say they've got a warrant, Cap'n."

"Do they? What are we to do with that very interesting piece of information, I wonder? And what does it have to do with the crew's leave? Do strive for clarity, Rusty—I'm afraid I'm a bit dense this morning."

"Well, they say they want to see you. I guess they'll explain it personally."

"Wonderful. What sort of . . . individuals, Rusty? Ambassadorial? Mere policepersons? Concerned citizens?"

"Ummm . . ." Rusty's voice drifted, then came back. "Didn't Cap'n Er Thom used to say that if your host wore a dagger, you should wear a dagger and a dirk?"

"It sounds very like him."

"By those rules, you ought to wear three daggers and a machete."

Shan grinned. "And these very formidable persons wish to call on me? How pleasant. Do me the favor, please, Rusty, of asking Seth to bring our visitors up as quickly as possible. Gordy will meet them and serve as escort. You needn't bear them company, if you'd rather not."

"Right you are. I'm not losing *my* breakfast. I'll catch a lift with Ken Rik, since they're evacuating him, too."

"Marvelous. Thank you for the call, Rusty. You always have such cheerful topics of discussion."

The other laughed and broke the connection.

Shan spun in his chair, hit the toggle that would summon Gordy, opened a drawer, and began to sweep papers into it.

The door opened to admit a subdued and rather pale cabin boy. "Yessir?"

Ruefully, Shan stretched out a hand. "Forgive me, *acushla*. My dreadful temper. I swear I didn't mean it to sound half as fierce as it did."

Gordy actually produced a grin, albeit a faint one. "That's okay. I should've been workin' at it all along. Guess I deserved to get my head bit off."

"That for me!" his cousin cried, snapping his fingers with a grin. Sobering, he shook his head. "An emergency, Gordy. Run to Selna and get a piece of the sample wood—so." He squared it off in the air with big, capable hands. "On your way back, stop and ask Calypso for the loan of his antique. Jet!"

Gordy was gone.

In an amazingly short time he was back, armed with the required items, which he placed on the pristine desk.

"Good," Shan said, surveying things. "Another task. Shortly there will be two individuals in the reception hall. Please bring them here."

"Yessir," the boy said, moving toward the door.

"Oh, Gordy!"

"Yes, Cap'n?"

Shan grinned. "Take your time."

THE VISITORS WERE NOT PLEASED. They followed Gordy with rustling aloofness, their sulfur-colored robes brushing the sidewalls, and kept their hands on the hilts of their swords. They came finally to the red door—after having traversed the length of the ship twice, had they but known it—and Gordy activated the annunciator.

"Come!" Shan's clear voice was followed by a peculiar heavy *thump* just as the door slid open.

Gordy stepped into the room. Shan was lounging back in the chair behind the desk, which was clear except for a block of oak with a wooden-handled hatchet buried in it. He raised his glass and lifted his brows.

Mindful of the proprieties, Gordy bowed. "Cap'n yos'Galan, here are Budoc and Relgis come to speak with you."

"Good day, gentles. A pleasant one, isn't it? How might I serve you?"

Relgis, who was bald, stepped around Gordy and executed a grudging bow. "Good day, Captain," he replied in hoarse Terran. "We are officials of Arsdred Court. It is my duty to inform you that we carry papers denying your crew access to the planet surface for the amount of time required for the municipality of Arsdred to inspect and verify your cargo. Under this same order, you are banned from trade activities until such time as investigation retires charges brought against the *Dutiful Passage*, tradeship, and Shan yos'Galan, captain and Master Trader." He paused to glare sternly from beneath bushy eyebrows. Shan sipped wine.

"The charge," Relgis continued in a goaded voice, "is smuggling illicit pharmaceuticals and proscribed animals."

"The *Dutiful Passage* is accused of running contraband?" the captain inquired in the mildest possible tone. "May I know the name of the accuser?"

Relgis looked at him with suspicion, apparently formulating a reply. Into the silence stepped his partner, saying with ponderous affability that no such thing as *charges* had been leveled at ship or master.

"Relgis made a slip of the tongue, sir. The thing is, a complaint has been lodged with the court, citing *suspicion* of contraband. I'm sure you'll agree that this is a very serious thing."

"Oh, I do," Shan said, raising his glass, "Especially when suspicion names my ship."

Budoc had the grace to look discomfited. "Well, of course you're bound to feel that way," he allowed after exchanging a startled glance with his partner. "I'm sure it will be inconvenient for you to deny your crew leave and forfeit a few days' trading. But if you're innocent—as I'm certain you are—then there's no harm done, is there? You'll be allowed to go about your business, just as you normally would."

"The municipality," Relgis stated, revolted by this conciliating speech, "must be certain of either the truth or falsity of a suspicion of contraband. We cannot be too careful."

"I see. Any other suspicions, sir? Or is this the awful whole?"

Once again Relgis found that tone of vacuous amiability disconcerting. Budoc took over, clearing his throat noisily.

"We also bear a warrant for the detention of one Priscilla Delacroix y Mendoza, of the crew of the *Dutiful Passage*. She is to be questioned under deep probe and held, pending arrival of further information."

"On what charge?" Shan queried gently, leaning forward and setting the glass aside.

"Suspected thievery." Relgis was back in the game.

"Really?" Shan looked at him with interest. "Now *I* have found her to be scrupulously—no, make that excessively—honest. Who accuses her?"

"Trader Sav Rid Olanek brought the matter to the attention of the court, sir. When the balance of his information arrives, determination shall be made as to whether the matter would be most properly handled by local or galactic authorities."

"And if she's innocent?" Shan asked, resting his chin on his left hand. His right lay next to the wooden block.

"If she's innocent," Budoc said magnanimously, "she will be released."

"Which will," Shan said dulcetly, "do her a great deal of good if the *Passage* has moved on in the meantime." He ran an absent finger down the hatchet haft. "What is she suspected of stealing from Trader Olanek? The clothes on her back? She had nothing else when she came to me."

The two officials exchanged glances. "No doubt that will be included in—"

"Trader Olanek's further information," Shan concluded. "Of course. May I see the papers you carry, sirs? I must say that I think it extremely unlikely that Ms. Mendoza is a thief. As to allowing her to be removed from this vessel and placed in a detention block for—how long before this information comes forth? Stupid of me, but I don't seem to recall . . ."

"We didn't say," Relgis said quellingly. "No longer than ten days, local."

"Captain," Budoc added, with a warning glance at his partner.

Relgis glowered, produced the papers from the depths of his robe, and handed them over with scant grace.

"Thank you," Shan said, receiving them in the spirit in which they were offered. He glanced at the hovering cabin boy. "Gordon, fetch Ms. Mendoza, if you please."

"Oh, no you don't!" Relgis snapped, leaping between Gordy and the door in a swirl of fabric. He fingered his sword hilt menacingly. "A very sly idea, Captain, but it won't work! Send the boy for her! Warn her, more likely! Next we'll be hearing from him that she's escaped!"

"Escaped?" Shan blinked at him, striving for his best look of foolish interest. "Now, where would she escape to, I wonder? I do seem to recall rather clearly a statement to the effect that none of my crew would be allowed worldside." He picked up his glass and took a thoughtful sip. "Of course, the *Passage* is a large ship," he conceded. "But not that large, do you think? I'm sure you could run her to ground if she took a notion to hide from you."

Perceiving a sheen of dew on Relgis's bald pate, he relented somewhat. "Go for Ms. Mendoza," he instructed Gordy gently. "Say that I wish to see her immediately. Please do not mention the presence of these two persons."

Gordy goggled at him, then recovered enough to bow and mutter "Yessir" before turning toward the door.

Speared by a glance from his partner, Relgis let him go.

Shan had another sip of wine and began a leisurely perusal of the court's documents.

IN JUST UNDER FIVE MINUTES, the door chime sounded.

"Come!" Shan called, eyes still on the documents he had already committed to memory.

The two officials turned, hands on swords, ready to confront the desperate criminal herself as she stepped unescorted into the room.

Relgis preserved his countenance. Budoc visibly gaped.

Priscilla gave each a friendly, though curious, smile and stepped around them. "You wanted to see me, Captain?"

He glanced up, sternly subduing the pang he felt upon seeing her ears yet unadorned. "Good morning, Ms. Mendoza. I'm sorry to have to call you to me so abruptly. These gentlemen, however—" He nodded at Budoc and Relgis and paused, frowning. "My terrible manners! Ms. Mendoza, these are Relgis and Budoc, officials of Arsdred Court. They have come to deliver this paper to you." He held it out.

She took it, directing a sharp glance at his face before beginning to read. Her cheeks flushed, then went white. Shan overrode the impulse to hold out his hand to her; instead, he picked up his glass and brought before his inner eye a Wall.

"Will he never stop?" Priscilla cried, slapping the paper onto his desk. "He hounds me, names me criminal, leaves me for dead—and now has me arrested! Questioned under deep probe! What good can he think it will do him? Trader on a ship crewed by lechers and motherless fools!" She spun, approaching the two officials with a tigerish tread. Relgis gave ground by a step. Budoc licked his lips.

"Whose palm was greased?" she demanded awfully. "*Suspicion* of theft? Information *forthcoming?* And I'm to be detained and questioned, treated like a thief on the strength of information that will never arrive, and so I swear!" She straightened haughtily. "I'm not going anywhere with you."

"Well," Budoc said carefully, "you've got no choice, miss. We've got the warrant, and you've got to come. It's the law."

Priscilla sniffed. "This is a Liaden ship. You have no authority here."

"*You're* Terran," Budoc pointed out with a fair semblance of rationality.

"I should perhaps explain," Shan broke in apologetically, "that Ms. Mendoza serves on this ship because of a personal contract between her and the heir apparent of Clan Korval."

There was a moment's silence. Then, in accents between dread and wonder, Budoc asked if that wasn't the Tree and Dragon Family, trade representative for Trellen's World?

"Exactly the Tree and Dragon." Shan beamed at him. "Precisely Trellen's World. The contract between us extends back nearly two hundred Standards. How clever of you!"

That information might have impressed his partner, but to Relgis it conveyed nothing more than a blatant attempt to thwart the Law. He stiffened his resolve and advanced upon Priscilla's position by one step.

"Be that as it may," he said sternly, "the law is still the law. This woman's Terran, and she goes with us." He shifted his eyes to the man behind the desk and thrust out his chin. "She's not Liaden, even if this heir or whatever it is, is. We don't have a warrant for her contract—we've got a warrant for her!"

"Heir Apparent," Shan corrected gently. "Not, praise gods, the Heir. Ms. Mendoza is correct, you know. A personal contract of this kind assures her of the Heir Apparent's protection. Which amounts to the protection of Clan Korval. And Clan Korval is a legal Liaden entity." He finished his wine and set the glass aside. "An interesting point, isn't it? I'm sure the lawyers would be able to argue it for much more than ten local days, don't you?"

"Now, Captain," Budoc said nervously, "be reasonable. No one wants to get into that kind of protracted debate. Think of the expense! Better to just let her come along with us. Maybe the judge will allow her back right after the questioning—in light of her contract, you know!" He licked his lips again. "I'm sure we can work something out."

"Are you?" Shan asked. "Good. I think so, too." He picked up the disdained warrant and made a show of frowning perusal. "There doesn't seem to be anything here about bail," he murmured, feeling Priscilla's gaze bent on him in speculation. "An oversight on the part of the judge, no doubt. Who *was*—oh! Judge Zahre? What a delightful circumstance!" He smiled with exquisite stupidity at the two officials and avoided Priscilla's eye.

"We'll have everything settled soon!" he said gaily. "I'm acquainted with Judge Zahre. What a fortunate circumstance!" He flipped a toggle on the panel by his desk.

"Tower," a crisp voice informed him.

"Good shift, tower. Are you busy? Would it be possible for you to find Judge Abrahanthan Zahre of Port City, Arsdred, for me? I'd like to speak to him."

"Right away. Captain. Route the call to the office screen?"

"That will be perfect, tower, thank you. Do hurry. We have guests, and I seem to be wasting their time."

"Yes, sir." The connection was cut.

Shan nodded to himself and called the commlink from its slot, then turned to the infoscreen and tapped in a quick series. Out of the corner of his eye he saw Priscilla drift over and perch on the arm of the nearer chair, dividing her attention between the two officials and her captain.

Budoc and Relgis exchanged glances and remained uncomfortably silent. Relgis nurtured the hope that the judge would drop one of his thundering lectures on the heads of both captain and crew member.

The commlink buzzed gently.

Shan spun his chair, tapped the violet key set along the left margin of the screen, and inclined his head to the austere individual in ruby-colored robes. The other man also wore a ruby turban, held by a glittering *nelaphan* brooch. His eyes were dark and deep-set, and the authority of his nose exceeded that of Shan's own.

"I am Judge Zahre," he said emotionlessly.

"Yes, sir," Shan agreed easily. "We are acquainted, though I doubt you remember me. My father, Er Thom yos'Galan, and I guested you aboard *Dutiful Passage* several Standards ago, upon the occasion of your honesty's succession to office."

The face in the screen thawed somewhat; the lips bent a trifle. "Indeed, I do remember you, sir, and most kindly. How does your father do? It would honor me if you and he would dine at my residence, if the length of your stay permits it."

Shan took a breath, hardly aware that it was deeper than the one before it. After so many repetitions, the phrase had become merely rote, and the inward voice that had keened "My father is dead!" was now but a wordless flicker of pain.

"I regret to be the first to inform you," he said evenly, pulling the words verbatim from the High Tongue, "that my father's heart ceased its labor nearly three Standards gone by."

The lines about the judge's mouth grew deeper as he bowed his head. "It grieves me to hear it. I am richer for having had his acquaintance, though it was for so brief a time."

"I will tell my family you said so, sir. Thank you."

The older man nodded. "Now, tell me what I may do for Er Thom yos'Galan's son."

Shan smiled. "A misunderstanding has occurred. At least, I

think it must be a misunderstanding." He held the warrant up so that the other could read it. "This was delivered by two officials of Arsdred Court—Budoc and Relgis. It's a warrant for the detention and questioning of one of my crew members, Priscilla Delacroix y Mendoza. Apparently Trader Sav Rid Olanek accuses her of theft."

Judge Zaire nodded. "I remember him. I admit I did not like to let him swear out such a thing and then immediately depart the sector, but he pleaded urgent business and paid penalty and swear-charge. All was according to law, as he promised further information by bouncecomm, within ten local days. I performed my office, as set out in the book."

"I am certain you did," Shan said soothingly. "However, there are several points of which you could not have been aware. One is that Trader Olanek has taken Ms. Mendoza in severe dislike. I am not certain of the cause. It is a fact, however, that far from her stealing from him, he has stolen from her. A member of his command has within the last local day sold personal articles belonging to Ms. Mendoza at a shop in Parkton Way—Teela's Treasures. The proprietor is Frau Pometraf. She has a very good memory."

The judge inclined his head. "I am grateful. The information, of course, will be verified." He looked up, his deep eyes shrewd. "You have yet to say what I might do for you, Shan yos'Galan."

"A small thing, correction of an oversight." He rustled the paper. "There doesn't seem to be any mention of bail here, sir. Now, Ms. Mendoza is an important member of my crew. I can't spare her for ten days. Not for ten minutes! What shall I do?"

The older man's lips twitched, though he gravely agreed that it *did* seem to be an oversight. "You must understand that a warrant has been sworn to, sir. The law must be served."

"Of course it must." Shan spun the infoscreen around. "I had nearly forgotten! This is Ms. Mendoza's record, sir. Now, I ask you: Is it likely that a person possessing such a record would sully her honor by stealing?"

After a longish pause, the judge said, "I believe bail of one cantra—cash, of course—is sufficient to this case. You will guarantee Ms. Mendoza's presence, should the matter in fact go to trial?"

"Korval guarantees," Shan said formally, and jerked his head at the gaped-mouth officials. "These two gentles may take the money with them? It will be secure?"

"Relgis and Budoc are completely trustworthy."

"I'm sure they are. No thought of their venality crossed my mind, sir. It's only—a cantra, you said? You're certain they won't want an armed guard to escort them?"

Relgis made an outraged noise; the man on the screen smiled.

"I believe that no guard will be necessary, sir. I appreciate your concern."

"One cannot be too careful," Shan said earnestly. "What with innocent persons being attacked by ruffians in the streets of the city." He sighed and spread his hands. "You've been very kind, sir. I find it necessary to impose upon you still further." He held the second document up.

The judge scanned it quickly and shook his head. "This matter is out of my jurisdiction. However, I am acquainted with Judge Bearmert, who is among those signed. Allow me to call him and ask if he will speak with you."

"You're very kind, sir," Shan said again. "Forgive me the trouble."

"There is no trouble. It is my duty to see that the Law is served, not that the innocent suffer." He bowed stiffly. "Be well, Shan yos'Galan. Will you come to dine tomorrow evening?"

"I would like nothing better, sir. But I believe that the ban on my crew visiting your pleasant world applies to me as well."

"Nonsense," the judge said crisply. "I will send my yacht for you, sir. You will be conveyed directly to my home. You will experience no difficulty."

Shan grinned. "In that case, of course. I'll be delighted."

"Good. Until then." The screen went dark.

Shan thumbed the yellow stud, and the screen slid back into the desk. Absently, he pulled open a small drawer on the right side and fished out a battered lacquer box.

"Cantra," he muttered, and dumped the box over.

Coins *tinged* and tumbled, rolled in tight circles, and sped away to catch against the block of wood supporting the hatchet:

Terran bits of all denominations, Liaden coins, local money of half a dozen worlds, several rough-cut citrines, and a loop of pierced malachite.

"Cantra," Shan murmured again, conscious that Budoc was drawing closer. With clumsy care, he selected ten tenth-cantra from the jumble of money and beckoned the man still closer.

"One, two, three . . ." He counted all ten carefully into the sweaty palm and nodded. "Ten, are we agreed?"

"Yes, Captain," Budoc breathed.

"Good." He pointed at Relgis. "You, sir. A receipt, please."

Relgis glowered but did as he was bidden. Shan flipped a toggle by the desk. The door chimed instantly and slid away on his word to admit a grim-faced Gordy.

Shan smiled. "These gentles are leaving now, Gordon. Please conduct them to the reception hall and arrange for refreshment. Seth will conduct them worldside in good time." He turned his smile to the officials, striving for complete vacuity. "Thank you so much for your visit, sirs. I enjoyed it immensely. Good day."

"Good day, Captain," Budoc said, bowing low. Relgis sniffed and bowed, silently and slightly. Both turned and followed Gordy out.

The door closed, and Priscilla stood, holding out a hand. "May I refill your glass, Captain?"

He considered her warily. "Thank you, Priscilla. The red, please. And pour yourself something."

Priscilla stared a moment at the hatchet in the block of wood, then turned to busy herself at the bar.

"It's Pendragon," she announced suddenly.

Shan frowned at her neck. "Pendragon? Oh, the fellow with the table. One of Val Con's favorite stories, I recall. Named one of his infernal felines Merlin." His frown deepened. "It's only Uncle Richard's fancy, Priscilla. Coincidence. Dragon-analogs are fairly common around the galaxy, you know."

She nodded and handed him a glass before settling into the chair across.

"One hundred fifty bits the night before last, a terrible scare yesterday, a cantra today. What am I going to cost you tomorrow?" Her tone was mild, but her eyes were very bright.

Shan considered the Wall; he left it in place and raised his glass. "I don't expect you'll cost me anything tomorrow, Priscilla. You didn't really cost me anything today. Sav Rid's thought was to cause me discomfort—so it seems I'm taken seriously! How gratifying." He sipped. "He has accused the *Passage* of running contraband. That's creative of him, isn't it? We're to be investigated—by officials of Arsdred Court."

"Unless the friend of your friend brings his authority to bear," she said dryly.

"Well, I don't think he will, do you? It's worth a try, of course. No sense rousing Mr. dea'Gauss until we need him. My sister the first speaker prefers our man of business to stay close to hand. His tact and finesse are a good balance for her temper, you see. By the way, you were magnificent."

"I thought that was it." She considered him for a moment out of half-angry black eyes, then shook her head and smiled a little. "*Are* you Heir Apparent to Korval?"

"Of course I am. It's not the sort of thing one lies about, after all. You could find yourself in a great deal of trouble if you did. Besides that, if you want truth, I'd rather not be Heir Apparent. Especially with Val Con adventuring around the universe, busy being a scout and making no push at all to place an heir of his body between myself and destiny." He sighed. "I'm afraid I wouldn't be a very good Delm."

There was a pause while Priscilla tasted the wine, her eyes on the hatchet. Shifting her gaze to his face, she asked, carefully, he thought, "Will you do me a favor?"

"I'll certainly *try*, Priscilla," he said with matching caution. "What is it?"

"I wonder if you wouldn't make me a list of all the people you are, so I know who to ask for."

He grinned. "I'm afraid it might get a bit lengthy. And a few are so close that only a Liaden would make a distinction." He set the glass aside and began to count on his fingers. "Head of Line yos'Galan. Heir Apparent to Korval. Guardian to the Heir Lineal—that's a joke. Brother to Val Con, Nova, Anthora. Cousin to Val Con. Guardian to Anthora. Father to Padi. Master pilot. . . ."

He sighed. "This is too tedious, Priscilla. You could call me Shan if you get confused, and I'll sort it out for you."

"Why don't I just call you Captain?"

"I *knew* you were going to say that," he complained.

Surprisingly, she grinned and pointed at the hatchet. "What's the idea?"

"My father used to say—so I was informed earlier—that if your host wears a dagger, you should wear a dagger and a dirk. I think he might have meant it in some other context, but Rusty did me the favor of calling it to mind this morning when he told me of the presence of our visitors." He wrenched the hatchet free, sending two sundered chunks of wood skittering across the polished desk top.

"My brother, now, says there's nothing will give one pause like the sight of a naked blade." He extended it, and Priscilla leaned back in her chair. "He's right, I see. That's comforting. I thought I would give our visitors a visible reminder of might." He grinned. "Liaden tricks, Priscilla. Forgive me."

She shrugged. "It worked, didn't it? And *they* were using tricks, too. Blustering and acting as if all justice were on their side."

"High-handed, in fact."

"I'll never live it down." She sighed. "Will it help if I say I'm sorry?"

"*Are* you sorry? You might ask me to forgive it, if you think I'm offended. But Liadens don't in general say that they're sorry. It's an admission of guilt, you see. Asking forgiveness acknowledges the other person's right to feel slighted, hurt, or offended without endangering your right to act as you find necessary."

She blinked at him. "Which is why Kayzin Ne'Zame was so infuriated with me when we met at the main computer! I kept saying I was *sorry*. . . ." She sipped, working on the concept in silence.

Shan toyed with the weapon, turning it this way and that, taking note of its balance and the feel of it in his palm. Laying it aside, he took up his glass again and sipped, allowing himself the luxury of watching her face.

As if she felt his eyes on her, she glanced up, a slight smile on her lips. "Is there anything else, Captain? I'm supposed to be having a piloting lesson."

"Teaching me how to run my ship?" He waved his glass toward the door. "Go back to work, then. And thank you for your assistance."

"You're welcome, Captain," she said serenely. "It was no trouble at all."

Arsdred Port City
Midday Bazaar

MR. DEA'GAUSS LEANED BACK IN THE SEAT and allowed himself a moment of self-congratulation. Progress thus far was satisfactory. Not, he reminded himself, that he was in any way reconciled to being shipped harum-scarum off Liad and flung out into the galaxy with barely an hour's notice. If his heir had not just recently entered into a contract marriage that tied her to the planet, Korval would have found itself represented by the younger, less-tried dea'Gauss; and so the elder had informed Korval's First Speaker.

Lady Nova had acknowledged that statement with a slight tip of the head and continued outlining his task in her calm, clear voice. Mr. dea'Gauss experienced a reminiscent glow of warmth in the region of his mid-chest. She was a great deal like her father, and competent beyond her years.

She'll do, Mr. dea'Gauss thought with satisfaction. They would *all* do eventually. It was simply a sad pity that so powerful a clan as Korval should have been left untimely in the hands of persons too young for the duty. Even the eldest, Shan, now Thodelm yos'Galan, had not attained his full majority. And young Val Con, the Delm-to-be, was barely more than a halfling, no matter how gifted a scout he might be.

The old gentleman laid his head against the cushion. It was his duty to insure that all continued as it should during this period of readjustment, just as Line dea'Gauss had kept Korval's business for generations—to mutual profit.

They were intelligent children, after all, he reminded himself with a shade of avuncular pride, and quick to learn. He and his would be unworthy indeed of the post they had held so long if Korval were to lose ground before Val Con placed the Clan Ring upon his finger.

The taxi glided to a stop. Mr. dea'Gauss opened his eyes and glanced out the window. Satisfied, he gathered up portfolio and travel desk, slipped the proper Terran coin into the meter's maw, and exited the cab as the door elevated. He blinked once at the din and the colors and the smells of the Offworld Bazaar, then turned his steps with calm dignity toward the shuttlecradles.

There was an armed guard before Cradle 712. Mr. dea'Gauss was untroubled; he had expected no less. What did puzzle him was the presence of two additional individuals engaged in vociferation with the guard.

"I don't care," the fat woman with the jeweled braids was saying loudly, "if you've got orders from the Four Thousand Heavenly Hosts! I am Ambassador Grittle of Skansion! You've seen my identification. You've verified my identification. I have urgent business onboard the *Dutiful Passage—*"

"Off limits," the guard interrupted laconically. "Judge Bearmert's orders."

The fat woman's face turned a curious purple color that contrasted not unpleasingly with the silver lines drawn around her eyes. The second individual addressed the guard.

"I am Chon Lyle, sector agent for Trellen's World. It is imperative that I be allowed onboard the *Dutiful Passage.* Clan Korval is the licensed representative of Trellen's World in matters of off-world trade. A charge of illicit dealing brought against its flagship must also be thought a charge brought against my world."

Mr. dea'Gauss's brow cleared. Unmistakable, here was the hand of Korval's First Speaker. He stepped forward, affording the guard a tip of the head, as was proper for a person of consequence addressing a mere hireling.

She surveyed him with boredom. "Don't tell me. You want to get up to the *Dutiful Passage.*"

"Precisely," he said, undeceived by the apparent readiness of her understanding. He proffered a piece of orange parchment folded thrice. "I have here a manifest from Judge Bearmert allowing me that privilege, and also whomever I deem necessary to the commission of my duties." He moved a hand, encompassing ambassador and agent. "These persons are such. Pray verify the document. I am in haste."

The guard sighed, took the paper, and unfolded it with a flick of the wrist. Her eyes moved rapidly down the few lines, then returned to the top and moved downward more slowly. Eyes still on the page, she unhooked her belt-comm, thumbed it on, spoke into it briefly, then listened. She nodded.

"Okay, shorty," she said, handing the paper back to Mr. dea'Gauss, who folded it precisely and replaced it in his sleeve, "you're legit." She craned her head around the entranceway. "Hey, Seth! Customers!" Then she took up her official stance again, arms folded under her bosom, legs wide.

A tall, rat-faced Terran appeared at the edge of the ramp and glanced at the three before bowing to the elderly Liaden. "Yessir?"

He was awarded a slight smile and an actual, if shallow, bow. Korval employed persons of worth. It was as it should be.

"I am Mr. dea'Gauss, Korval's man of business. Lord yos'Galan expects me." He indicated his companions. "These are Ambassador Grittle of Skansion and Agent Chon Lyle of Trellen's World. His lordship will be most gratified to receive them."

Seth nodded and stepped aside. "Welcome aboard, sirs, ma'am. We'll be lifting as soon as the tower clears us."

Shipyear 65
Tripday 147
Third Shift
15.00 Hours

ᘓᕲᘓᕲᘓᕲᘓᕲᘓᕲᘓᕲᘓᕲᘓᕲᘓᕲᘓᕲᘓᕲᘓᕲᘓᕲᘓᕲᘓᕲᘓᕲᘓᕲᘓᕲ

"THAT CARGO IS SEALED!"

The taller of the two inspectors turned and sighed down at the cargo master before repeating for the ninth time that their duty was to inspect and—

"Verify the holds, goods, equipment, and general cargo of the *Dutiful Passage,* out of Solcintra, Liad, under the captaincy of Shan yos'Galan, Master Trader," Ken Rik singsonged, and threw up his hands in exasperation. "I *know.* I also know that this cargo is sealed. Do you understand what sealed means?

"Sealed means—one, that this cargo was delivered by the agency that leased the hold, made secure to their satisfaction and sealed with their lock.

"Two. It means that, having sealed the cargo at their end, the agency expects—has paid for the certainty—that the hold will still be sealed when the cargo reaches its destination.

"Three. It means that, if you two—people—unseal that hold, the *Dutiful Passage* will lose a shipping fee of approximately fifteen cantra—that's five hundred twenty-five thousand bits to you!—and very likely ten times that amount in commissions she will not receive for shipment of sealed cargoes in the future."

The taller inspector sighed. "I am aware of the exchange rate, sir. I am also aware of my duty. Surely you understand that in cases of contraband, to rely upon the ship's own records is sheer folly."

Ken Rik gasped. "How *dare—*" The Terran words were insufficient, he realized suddenly. Setting his jaw, he marched forward, placed himself before the hold in question, crossed his arms, and rooted his boot heels to the floor. "This hold is sealed," he said with a calmness his captain would have instantly recognized as highly dangerous. "And it will remain sealed."

"Quite proper," a dry voice said from the left. "Unless, of course, one of these individuals is a certified representative of the company whose seal is upon the cargo."

"Mr. dea'Gauss!"

Korval's man of business bowed. "Mr. yo'Lanna. I am pleased to see you well."

"And I'm pleased to see *you,* sir," Ken Rik said, throwing a grin of pure malice over his shoulder at the inspectors. "How may I serve you, Mr. dea'Gauss?"

The other man considered. "I will need a place to work. I apprehend these persons are inspectors from, ah, *Arsdred Court?*"

"Indeed, we are," the taller one asserted, coming forward with hand held out. "I am Jenner Halothi; my associate is Krys William. It is our duty to—" He cast a wary eye in the cargo master's direction. "—search this vessel for contraband and illegal goods."

"But not, I think," Mr. dea'Gauss said, ignoring the hand, "the holds sealed by companies independent of Korval or the *Dutiful Passage,* unless a representative of that company is present." He surveyed the inspectors with the air of one sizing up the opposition. "The purpose of this, of course, is twofold. The representative will be present to oversee the unsealing and search of the cargo and will be able to make testimony that it is, in truth, the proper cargo. Also, should the cargo prove to be—or to contain—illegal items, you, sirs, will have your culprit. Is there a representative of—" He glanced at the device on the hatch. "—Pinglit Manufacturing Company on board, Mr. yo'Lanna?"

"No, sir, there is not," the cargo master replied happily. "There is, however, Ambassador May of Winegeld, Pinglit's world of origin. Also Ambassadors Sharpe, Suganaki, and Gomez, from trade-linked planets."

"Excellent, excellent." The old gentleman's eyes were seen to glow with what Ken Rik knew to be the light of battle. "If these gentles will but follow—Mr. yo'Lanna, I regret. Is there a place I may work?"

"You may use my office, sir," Ken Rik offered with exquisite cordiality. "This way, please."

"With all due respect, Mr.—umm—dea'Gauss?—we have our duty."

"Of course you do," he agreed. "We each of us have our duties. At this present, however, yours must wait upon mine." He executed a stiff, barely civil bow. "Attend us, please, sirs."

SHAN YOS'GALAN rounded the corner with lazy haste, a glass of wine in his right hand and a large green plant cradled in his left arm. Suddenly he stopped, plant fronds swaying over his head, and blinked with consummate stupidity.

"Have the inspectors gone, Ken Rik? Or is it time for your midshift tea? Please don't think I begrudge you anything, but—"

Ken Rik grinned at him. "Mr. dea'Gauss is here."

"Is he? How delightful for us. Has he been shown his room? Oh, are you going visiting? Silly of me—of course you are. Very proper, since the two of you are such fast friends. A game or two of counter-chance, a few glasses of wine, a bit of gossip. But the *inspectors,* Ken Rik?"

"Mr. dea'Gauss is with the inspectors. He came directly to the holds, looking for your lordship, and has taken matters into his hand. I am sent for a ship-to and a colorcomp, that he may do his work the better."

"You left the inspectors *alone* with Mr. dea'Gauss?" Shan grinned widely. "Poor inspectors. Should I succor them, do you think, Ken Rik? It wouldn't do if a charge of cruelty to those of limited understanding were lodged."

"Mr. dea'Gauss summoned four ambassadors pertinent to the

present situation to my office, where he is instructing the inspectors. I think they'll be safe enough for this while." He sniffed. "Did you know that we've engaged the services of a local accounting firm to tally the losses to port and to ship while the *Passage* is off limits?"

Shan regarded him with awe. "Have we? That was clever of us, wasn't it? How did we do it?"

"We put an advertisement," the older man explained, a bit unsteadily, "in the port business publication."

Shan gave a shout of laughter, the plant shivering alarmingly in his arms. "Oh, dear. Oh, *no!* In the port business paper? Ken Rik, we have a blot upon our immortal souls: We've brought an expert to an amateur's game! Speaking of which, I believe I should be present, as referee. My lordship wouldn't miss such a show for—never mind." He held the plant out. "Do me the favor of taking this along to Ambassador Kelmik's quarters. She tells me that she cannot feel comfortable without a bit of greenery about."

Ken Rik sighed. "How are matters in the pet library?"

"Lina and Priscilla seem to be holding their own. Really, we have a most remarkable crew. When I left, the inspectors were bloody, but game. Neither of the ladies had yet been touched."

"Nor will they be," the cargo master predicted with delight. "Please tell Mr. dea'Gauss that I have not forgotten him, and that he will have his equipment very soon."

"I will, indeed," Shan promised, moving off with his big, loose stride. Ken Rik grinned and proceeded toward the guesting hall, plant fronds bouncing over his head with each step.

"ALSO," Mr. dea'Gauss was telling an attentive audience when Shan entered the cargo master's sanctum, "it must be taken into account that persons employed by Clan Korval receive wages that are between ten and fifteen percent higher than wages received by persons employed in similar positions on other vessels. This, of course, means greater in-port spending on the part of Korval's crews. I expect to have the precise extrapolations in—your Lordship." He rose immediately and bowed low.

Shan stilled a sigh and inclined his head. "Mr. dea'Gauss.

I am happy to see you. Forgive that I was not on hand to greet you personally when you came aboard."

"Your lordship is gracious. It is understood that there are many demands upon your attention. Mr. yo'Lanna has seen to my needs. I believe it is not overoptimistic to state that matters progress well and an end to this misunderstanding will be speedily attained."

"I am sure we all hope for that," his lordship responded gravely. "Please continue. It's always an inspiration to watch you at your work."

Mr. dea'Gauss acknowledged this with a tip of the head and reseated himself. Shan drifted to the left, exchanged polite smiles with the four ambassadors, and took up a position where he could watch the faces of the inspectors and Mr. dea'Gauss's workscreen.

"We should shortly," Korval's man of business resumed, "have a response from Pinglit Manufacturing Company. If they agree to the proposal offered—that is, your Lordship, to allow the presence of these four persons, Ambassadors May, Sharpe, Gomez and Suganaki, to equal the presence of one of their agents—then we will proceed with the unsealing and inspection of Hold Forty-three. In the meantime, sirs . . ." He turned to the befuddled inspectors. "I shall require from you a list of areas inspected and a certification for each."

"Certification, sir?" queried the shorter one—Inspector William, Shan recalled—with trepidation. "What sort of certification?"

Mr. dea'Gauss regarded him from under drawn brows. "Why, certification that you found nothing illegal within the stated area, of course. I do not ask if that was indeed the case. It could not have been otherwise."

Inspector William exchanged a glance with his partner.

"Was it otherwise?" Mr. dea'Gauss demanded.

The shorter inspector swallowed. "No, sir, of course—that is to say, we found no illegal substances in the holds thus far inspected. However, sir, it is our instruction to search the vessel entire and issue certification at the end."

"Insufficient," Mr. dea'Gauss judged, turning back to the screen. "Also, I find it incredible that two teams of inspectors are assigned to this task. A vessel the size of the *Dutiful Passage*—it is laughable. And while you pursue your efforts, Korval loses on the order of—" He touched a key with the reverence another man night reserve for stroking the cheek of his beloved. "Seven cantra per trade-night. Arsdred Port loses four point eight cantra per trade-night. This does not include the loss to those merchants who have offered guaranteed delivery for the goods we carry, based on our reliability. We must have at least two more teams of inspectors."

"I," Ambassador Suganaki said quietly, "would consider it an honor to be allowed to supervise one of those teams. It is absurd that the crew bear all the burden when there are so many of my colleagues here, pledged to aid. I am sure the crew has its scheduled round of duties, which must go on, regardless."

Shan bowed. "I thank you, ma'am. That's exactly the sort of assistance we do require. If I'd had any indication that the *Passage* was to have been boarded in this way, I would have signed on extra crew at the beginning of the trip."

"It is, of course, an unlooked for and unprecedented event, Captain," Suganaki agreed gravely, though there was a twinkle in her eye. "Perhaps an announcement at the reception this evening will alert my colleagues to the need." She turned to Korval's man of business. "It is possible, I think, sir, that even *four* more teams may not be excessive. The *Dutiful Passage* is a large ship."

"A worthy suggestion, Ambassador. My thanks to you. I shall inquire of Judge Bearmert how best to obtain additional inspectors. Now—" The in-ship buzzed, and Mr. dea'Gauss tapped the speak key. "Yes?"

"Tower here, Mr. dea'Gauss," Rusty's voice said formally. "Pinglit Manufacturing Company agrees to your suggestion. Hard-copy verification arrives via courier ship soonest. If there is anything else they may do, they beg you not to hesitate."

"Excellent, tower. My thanks to you." He cut the connection and gazed around in satisfaction. "Let us repair to Hold Forty-three."

MUCH LATER, after the inspectors had departed for the night, Shan walked with Mr. dea'Gauss toward the guesting hall.

"I have a message from the first speaker, your lordship," the old gentleman murmured in the High Tongue. "She bade me inform you that the clan bears all expense in this situation, since the blow seems aimed at Korval entire, not only at the *Passage*—or yourself."

Shan nodded absently. "The first speaker, my sister, is generous."

His response was most proper. Mr. dea'Gauss cleared his throat as a prelude to speaking further. It was not often that one found his Lordship so biddable. He did not at the moment recall that every period of docility he had previously observed in Shan's career had been immediately followed by some mad start. "I have also a message from Lord yos'Phelium."

The big mouth curved in a smile. "Do you? And what has my brother to say?"

Korval's man of business paused. The message was an odd one—flippant to the point of outrage. However, it seemed certain that young Val Con had inherited his father's devious directness, and Mr. dea'Gauss believed the true message lay far within the one he was bidden to deliver. Carefully, striving for the original phrasing, he said, "He asked me to tell you that he believes a successful scout and a successful thief must share certain vital characteristics. He thanks you for the suggestion of an avocation and asks further what he may be honored to steal for you first."

Shan laughed. "Renegade. He should have been drowned at birth. How long does he stop at home?"

Mr. dea'Gauss allowed himself a sniff to indicate his disapproval of this manner of speaking of Korval's Heir and replied stiffly. "He had been on Liad a bare quarter *relumma* when he was suddenly recalled to his duties as scout. He left the planet, I believe, the very day I was called before the first speaker. It was only by chance that I was privileged to see him for a moment and exchange greetings."

Shan considered him. "Suddenly recalled by the scouts, was he?"

"Yes, my lord, and a sad blow it was to Lady Nova. She had invited Lady Imelda to guest. I believe she looked for a contract marriage in that direction, so that his lordship might fulfill his duty to the Clan."

"Is she feeling better now?" Shan asked solicitously.

Mr. dea'Gauss blinked. "I beg pardon, your Lordship? Is who feeling better?"

"My sister. Of all the ladies she might have tried to force down Val Con's throat!"

"Lady Imelda," the old gentleman said severely, "is from a good clan. She is honorable and quite complaisant."

"*Quite* complaisant. And neither stupid enough nor brilliant enough to pull it off. Val Con would have been at the screaming point within a *relumma*." They paused by an indigo-colored door. "I will give you any odds you name, sir, that that sudden recall by the scouts came after a personal request to be recalled."

There were several answers to this, none of them proper. Mr. dea'Gauss maintained an icy silence. His lordship grinned and bowed. "Your room, sir. I trust you will find everything exactly as you wish it. The ambassadorial reception will be at Twenty Hours. I hope to see you among the merrymakers."

There was nothing for Mr. dea'Gauss but to make his bow and enter his room.

Shan moved toward his own quarters, his long stride eating distance while he frowned in thought.

It was true that the lad must do his duty to the clan. Everyone must provide the Clan with his or her personal heir. Even Shan, the reprobate, the cynic, had given Korval a daughter who would in time take his place at the head of Line yos'Galan; at the head of the *Passage* . . . . Damn them both for being at such loggerheads! If only Nova would try to enlist Val Con to the task of discovering some suitable lady, all might yet come out right.

Shan sighed, stopped in the middle of his sleeping room, closed his eyes, and breathed deeply and evenly, as he had been taught so long ago by the Master Healers. Slowly, the worries—familial, professional, personal—stilled.

One thing at a time, he reminded himself with forceful calm.

An image of Priscilla as he had last seen her, the light of battle in her face as she confronted two harried inspectors, rose before his inner eye.

With a groan, he dropped onto the bed and closed his eyes.

You want too much, your lordship, he told himself. Try to be worthy of her friendship. If you're very lucky, you'll manage it.

He rose from the bed and wandered toward the 'fresher, stripping off his clothes as he went. He stepped into the needle spray, resolutely turning his thoughts to the coming reception and what profit might be earned from it.

Shipyear 65
Tripday 148
Fourth Shift
17.00 Hours

⤷⤶⤷⤶⤷⤶⤷⤶⤷⤶⤷⤶⤷⤶⤷⤶⤷⤶⤷⤶⤷⤶⤷⤶⤷⤶⤷⤶⤷⤶⤷⤶

"YOU MUST HAVE A DRESS!"

"Lina—"

"No!" the small woman cried, taking her friend's hand. "You attend the reception properly attired. I will hear no more!"

Priscilla stood her ground and bit her lip. "Lina, I'm sorry—*truly* sorry. But I don't have any money, my dear. None. And I'm already into my wages for the cost of the clothes I'm wearing now. A—party—dress . . ."

"Bah!" Lina flung up a tiny hand, then swung close, pressing lightly against the taller woman's side. "I shall provide the dress, and you shall wear it to please me, eh?" She smiled. "All is arranged!"

Priscilla smiled and shook her head. "I can't ask you to do that, Lina. Why should you—"

"Why should I not?" Lina interrupted. "We are sisters—you said it yourself! Should I allow my sister to go improperly clad? And far from asking, you make it astonishingly difficult to gift you!" She laughed and pulled on Priscilla's hand, urging her to the entrance of the general stores. "Come, *denubia*. You must learn to accept a gift with grace."

The Terran woman chuckled. "Another protocol lesson? Next you'll be telling me to wear the earrings the captain gave me!"

"And why should you not?" Lina demanded. "The design is pleasing; I think they will look very well on you. Shan is honorable—he does not gift and then cry 'owed!'" She looked up into her friend's face. "The earrings are *yours,* Priscilla. A gift, freely given. No hurt can come from wearing them." She pulled her companion through the first storeroom, past the working clothes and everyday boots, past even the festive tunics and softshoes, into the room beyond, where dream fabrics drew the eye from all directions and the air smelled of Festival-time.

"I don't think . . ." Priscilla began, staring about her like a thing half-wild.

"Bah!" Lina said again, allowing no time for refusals. "Why should you not have a dress that becomes you?" She came close once more and extended both a hand and a mental touch of comfort to still the beginning panic. "Priscilla, you are lovely. It is added joy that you are so. Why not pleasure yourself—and those who see you—by wearing beautiful clothes? The occasion demands it!"

But Priscilla was no longer listening. She bent and stroked Lina's hair lightly, then slid a hand beneath the small chin and tipped her face so the light fell on it. Lina met the sparkling black gaze calmly, all Roads open and clear, the Wall at her back.

"You are of the Circle," Priscilla murmured, perhaps to herself. "I can feel the warmth coming out of you, like a hearth fire, my friend. And before—the pain—then the healing. . . ." The hand withdrew; Lina kept her face tipped fully up, eyes steady.

"Are you Wife, Lina? Or Witch?"

"I have been a wife—twice by contract, as is proper. And I am mother of two sons: Bey Lor and Zac. By trade I am librarian; by training I am Healer. I do not know what a Witch is, my friend."

"Healer?" Priscilla frowned. "A Healer is—Soul-weaver, we say, on Sintia. When someone is sick in spirit. . . ."

"When one does not accept joy," Lina agreed. "Shan says the proper Terran word is 'empath.'" She hesitated. "I am not sure. It seemed from my readings—for a Healer may not aid everyone. There are those I cannot feel at all. And there is training to be undergone, protections to be learned, techniques to be mastered."

"Yes, of course." Priscilla was still frowning. "But I—"

"You," Lina interrupted, "were fighting joy, denying both laughter and the possibility of kindness. It could not continue so! I had the means to aid you. Why should I not?" She swayed close, regardless of other persons in the room, all Roads open yet. "Priscilla? Sisters. You said it. I do not deny it."

There was a flare of pain like thrown acid, followed by a surge of joy nearly as searing. Lina put her arms around her friend's waist and hugged her tight, feeling Priscilla's arms pull her tighter.

"Sister and friend. . . ." After a final, nearly bone-crushing squeeze, Lina felt herself released and realized that the Roads bore the other woman's clear, singing happiness; she retained enough wit to shut herself away from the intoxication.

"Come," she said, smiling and taking Priscilla's hand. "Let us choose you a *magnificent* dress!"

LONG AFTER LINA LEFT, Priscilla stood before the mirror, oscillating between terror and delight.

The dress *was* magnificent: black shimmersilk, shot with random silver bolts that glittered and danced as she moved. The fabric covered her from knee to neck, from shoulder to wrist, meticulously reproducing every line it adhered to. The slit on the right side made her accustomed stride possible while allowing a tantalizing glimpse of creamy thigh. Goddess knew how much it had cost. Lina had not answered when Priscilla had asked.

She frowned at her reflection. She wore her three remaining bracelets on her right wrist, and a blue enameled ring borrowed from Lina on her left hand. A silver ribbon wove like lightning through her storm-cloud curls. Yet there was something missing.

Slowly she went back to the wardrobe and rummaged within. The velvet of the box was warm in her hand. She worked the catch on her way back to the mirror, then carefully hung a hoop in each ear and stepped back to observe the effect.

In a moment she nodded, which set the hoops dancing; laying the box aside, she left the room.

RUSTY FRANKLY STARED before coming forward and offering his arm. "'Cilla, you're gorgeous. How 'bout a cohab contract?"

She grinned. "You've been in the tower too long, friend."

"Well, that's true," he said morosely. "Between the cap'n and Mr. dea'Gauss, I thought I'd never get off that damn beam! We've got the fourteen prime points covered, I swear."

"Sounds rough," she sympathized. "Try coming to the pet library and defending Master Frodo's right to live."

Rusty snorted. "Busybodies. Why don't they find something real to do? As if we'd ship contraband! Must've lost all their aces to try and pin that on the *Passage.*"

Just then Lina approached, arm in arm with an elderly Liaden gentleman in formal dark tunic and strictly correct ash-colored trousers. "Priscilla, here is Mr. dea'Gauss, Clan Korval's man of business," she said with a stateliness made tolerable by her smile. Turning to the gentleman, she repeated the formula. "Mr. dea'Gauss, here is Priscilla Mendoza, my good friend."

Both pet librarian and man of business bowed.

Straightening, Mr. dea'Gauss was seen to smile. "Lady Mendoza, I am delighted to make your acquaintance. Lady Faaldom has spoken most warmly of you."

"I am happy to meet you, Mr. dea'Gauss," Priscilla said cordially; she added a diplomatic rider. "I am certain that Lina's friendship must be a bond between us."

"So I thought, as well," the old gentleman said, delighted to find her so well spoken. He inclined his head to her escort. "Mr. Morgenstern. How do you go on?"

"Pretty well, sir," Rusty returned as if he had not spent the greater part of his day executing the old man's instructions. "How are you?"

"I find myself in the best of good health, thank you, sir, in spite of the fact that I have recently been constrained to travel. Ah, there is Ambassador Kung." He executed a nicely gauged bow between Priscilla and Lina. "I beg to be excused. Duty must ever come before pleasure."

"Pity Ambassador Kung," Rusty muttered as Mr. dea'Gauss moved off after his quarry.

Lina laughed. "Ah, he is not so bad, the old gentleman. He

sincerely tries to care for people. It is not his fault that he loves work more."

"If you say so," Rusty said doubtfully. "At least he's not as strung-up as Lady Whatsis—Kareen? You remember that run we had her and her son? I don't think Shan showed his nose in the halls the whole time she was here! Even Captain Er Thom looked nervous."

Lina smiled. "But it was only for a few weeks, after all. And the rest of the trip was very nice. Bah! Now *I* must ask to be excused! I did promise to speak with Mr. Lyle. And it is true that we should be pleasant, since we wish them to work for us." She executed the bow between equals and slanted a grin up at Priscilla. "Lady Mendoza. Mr. Morgenstern."

Rusty shook his head and sighed down at Priscilla. "Well, she's right. I'd better find that silly woman who was so excited about the pin-beam and show off my manners." He raised a hand, grinning ruefully. "See you later."

Priscilla looked about her. Mr. dea'Gauss was in earnest conversation with an emaciated and exceedingly tall Terran. Janice Weatherbee and Tonee had engaged the attention of three or four lesser officials; the conversation was liberally laced with laughter. Ken Rik listened politely to a fat woman with a painted face and a multitude of jewel-tipped braids, while Lina smiled winningly up at a clearly captivated gentleman who was, Priscilla supposed, Mr. Lyle. Rusty had disappeared into the crowded back of the room. And she did not see the other person she was looking for.

Irritably, she shrugged her shoulders and moved at random into the crowd. What difference did it make to her if Shan yos'Galan chose to absent himself from the reception?

"It would, of course, be unfortunate," Ambassador Gomez was saying confidentially to an elder in the robes of an Arsdredi, "should Clan Korval send word to its allies and trade-partners that it no longer stops here."

"Generations to recover," another person murmured as Priscilla eased by. "Economic tragedy . . . second-rate port . . ."

Was Clan Korval as powerful as that? she wondered, slipping by

Janice and Tonee with a smile. Could they ruin a spaceport? Make thousands jobless? By refusing to stop? Merely by letting it be known that they would no longer stop there? It seemed incredible. And yet Shan yos'Galan had lost a middling fortune at the hands of Sav Rid Olanek and claimed the money as the least part.

He's a truthful person, Priscilla thought. He'd have told me if the coin-loss was desperate.

Spying a lone ambassador, important in beribboned tunic and sash-belt, she smiled and bowed. "Good evening. I am Priscilla Mendoza, of the crew of the *Dutiful Passage.*"

The ambassador, it turned out, had a thirst for knowledge. He wished to know everything concerning the *Passage,* her captain, Clan Korval, the pet library, and the crew. Priscilla obliged him, editing where it seemed appropriate, thankful for once that the possession of a comely face allowed her room to be just a trifle stupid. While she could not feel that her interpretation of the role was as inspired as Shan yos'Galan's, it was perfectly adequate for the audience.

The patterns of the party altered, partnering Priscilla's ambassador with one of his own. Liberated, she moved off. She saw Seth bent almost double, speaking into Tonee's ear; Rusty was near the bank of green plants with Kayzin Ne'Zame, his stance formal as he spoke to a half circle of listeners.

And leaning against the far wall, beneath the very wings of the dragon, closely attending a blond woman in ambassadorial dress, was Shan yos'Galan. He wore a blend of Liaden and Terran formality: ruffled white shirt, brocade jacket, dark, form-fitting trousers. The amethyst drop hung in his right ear. Priscilla was aware of a feeling of relief and took an unconscious step in his direction.

He glanced up, his big mouth curved in a smile. Priscilla froze, feeling her face flush.

"Ms. Mendoza?" The voice at her elbow was unpleasantly shrill.

She turned and smiled at the fat woman of the many braids. "Yes? How may I serve you, ma'am?"

The woman smiled, creasing the intricate pattern of her facial decoration, and made a jerky forward motion, which Priscilla interpreted as a bow. "I am Ambassador Dia Grittle of Skansion. Cargo Master yo'Lanna tells me you are a native of Sintia."

Her smile felt stiff on her face, and she was certain that she had lost color. Fortunately, Ambassador Grittle did not appear to notice.

Priscilla cleared her throat. "Indeed I am, ma'am. . . ." She let the sentence trail to a tiny note of inquiry.

The ambassador nodded sharply. "Thought as much when I saw you walk in. Got the look of your mother."

Priscilla took a breath, forcing air down her constricted throat. Not here, Goddess, she prayed. Not *now*.

"Lady Mendoza. Ambassador Grittle. Forgive the interruption. I have here one who is anxious to meet you, lady." The speaker was Mr. dea'Gauss. Priscilla felt her knees sag in relief. Silently she thanked the Goddess.

The smile she gave Korval's man of business was genuine. "Of course, sir." Ambassador Grittle muttered something inarticulate but no doubt proper. Mr. dea'Gauss bowed, indicating the gentleman at his side.

"Priscilla, Lady Mendoza, may I make you known to Judge Abrahanthan Zahre."

The gentleman stepped forward, his ruby-red robes rustling, and held out a smooth, thin hand. "I am pleased to meet you, Lady Mendoza. Especially as it affords me the opportunity to make my apologies in person."

"Apologies, sir?" Priscilla's forehead puckered, then cleared. "The warrant!" she exclaimed, striving for a look of vacuous enlightenment. "I had forgotten, sir. Please do the same."

"You are kind." The judge bowed, smiling. "But I do wish you to know that it is not my practice to brand one a thief on such flimsy evidence as was presented to me by Trader Olanek. He was very persuasive, it is true. But I serve the law, and I hold myself responsible. That warrant should never have been issued."

"Warrant!" Ambassador Grittle was staring at the judge in what seemed to be disbelief. "You issued a warrant! Did you take no time to *think*, sir? Did you take no time to consider with whom you dealt?" She took a deep breath, her voice rising ever more shrilly over the room at large. "To think that a *Mendoza of Sintia* might be a thief—it is an outrage, sir! We of Skansion are trade-partnered with Sintia. I am myself acquainted with the Mendoza family. It is an insult, sir! And one nearly past bearing! Of all—was there bail set?" she shot at the white-faced and rigid Priscilla.

"A cantra was set as bail," the judge murmured in a moment, "and has been paid by *Dutiful Passage*. Clan Korval guarantees Lady Mendoza's appearance, should the matter go to trial." He smiled faintly. "Which I am certain it will not."

"A Mendoza of Sintia needs no one to guarantee her word!" the ambassador snapped. She reached into the velvet pouch hung at her ample waist, produced a single dully shimmering coin, and slapped it in the judge's hand. "Skansion doubles the bond! Thus do we stand by our allies!"

Priscilla ran her tongue over dry lips, then opened her mouth to say—what?

Again Mr. dea'Gauss rescued her. He stepped forward and offered the ambassador his arm, smiling coolly. "Lady Mendoza is fortunate indeed that her home-world has so staunch a trade-partner. Allow me to procure a glass of wine for you, Ambassador."

Priscilla inclined her head to Judge Zahre, then raised her eyes to find him smiling in real amusement. Her own lips bent in response. "Now I must beg *your* pardon!"

His smile widened into a grin. "Without cause, Lady Mendoza. *You* were not rude." He glanced over her shoulder. "I see that refreshments have arrived. Allow me to escort you."

"You're kind," she said breathlessly, "but I—I must see someone just now. Perhaps we'll talk again later."

The judge's face turned quizzical. "Yes, perhaps we will." Bowing formally, he left her.

Moving with pilot swiftness, pilot grace, she slipped through the press of people and into the corridor. She strode down the hall, turned a corner, and leaned against the wall, listening to the pounding of her heart.

That dreadful woman! Who had heard? The entire room, most

likely. And she claimed acquaintance with Anmary Mendoza! Allmother, what shall I do?

"Good evening, Priscilla. Asleep? It's a terrible crush, isn't it? My lordship isn't good for much of this kind of thing. I'm a sad trial to my sister—no manners, no address."

She opened her eyes, breath snagging. "Captain."

"Sometimes," he agreed, light eyes mocking. "Don't you like the party? Mr. dea'Gauss seems very impressed."

Her face relaxed a little, her mouth curving toward a smile. "I didn't have the nerve to tell him I'm not a lady," she confessed, striving for lightness. "I'm afraid it would embarrass him."

Shan laughed. "Mr. dea'Gauss never errs in these matters. I suggest you accommodate yourself to ladyhood." He tipped his head. "That won't be so hard, will it, Priscilla? After all, a Mendoza of Sintia—"

Her face went white, eyes widening, one hand moving up and out, warding him away. "No."

"Priscilla!" He snapped forward, hand outstretched. "Priscilla, it was a joke! I—I never wanted to distress you!" He took another step as he bit his lip. "I'm *sorry,* Priscilla."

Her hand wavered, fell, and closed about his. "It's all right," she said unevenly. Her hand trembled in his as she took a ragged breath. "Please, you mustn't ask. . . ."

"I don't ask. I have no right to ask, Priscilla. It was only a joke. You looked as if you needed to laugh so badly." He smiled ruefully. "My wretched tongue!"

Her mouth wobbled on the edge of a smile. "Ambassador Grittle. . . ."

"Makes you stop and wonder, doesn't it? How could she have become an ambassador? Do you think she might have assassinated someone?"

"There's a chance, if she did." The smile was there, finally; nor did she take her hand from his. "Maybe someone will assassinate *her.*"

Shan laughed. "We can hope." Then he sighed. "My Lordship is expected to return to the festivities. Will you come with me? Or are you retiring?"

She removed her hand, though the smile remained. "I'll stay here for a moment or two, I think. Then I'll go back."

"All right," he said, moving reluctantly away. At the corner he turned back. "Priscilla?"

"Yes, Captain?"

A shadow crossed his face but was gone before she could name it. He bowed slightly. "It was nothing. I'll see you later, Priscilla." She was alone.

Leaning against the wall, she closed her eyes and breathed in the way that was taught to every Initiate: breathe in serenity, breathe out confusion. Breathe in strength, breathe out weakness. Breath in hope, breathe out despair.

In a little while she opened her eyes, stood away from the wall, and went back to the reception.

Shipyear 65
Tripday 155
First Shift
4.00 Hours

SHAN GROANED AND ROLLED OVER. One long arm swung out, smacking the alarmplate unerringly. Obedient to this prompt, the cabin lights came up and music began to play. Loudly.

"Give me a break," he muttered, sitting up and running his fingers through his hair. The music abated somewhat, a boon to his pounding head. "Damn that stuff! Floats you on a cloud, then hits you over the head with a rock. Why would *any*body want to smoke it?"

The room offered no answer.

Well, it had been a profitable week of trading, with the Arsdredi seemingly bent on recouping every cantra of "loss" the port business paper had kept such careful track of. It was merely a sad pity that profit had not yet been known to cure a headache.

Shan groaned again, and the pounding intensified as memory returned. Mr. dea'Gauss wished to speak with his lordship this morning on business concerning Clan Korval. Wonderful.

He placed his feet carefully and stood, grimacing. Perhaps it's not too late to resign as a lordship? But there was no conviction in the thought. His brother and sisters needed him, so a lord Shan would be.

"A shower," he told himself firmly. "And breakfast. Coffee. Lovely, hot coffee."

BREAKFAST had been the right idea. Coffee had been inspired. Armed with a second steaming mugful, Shan moved back toward his office, nodding to and exchanging greetings with the crew members he encountered.

The good news, he reflected, laying his hand against the plate, was that his interview with Korval's man of business must of necessity be brief. The *Passage* had received permission to leave Arsdred orbit in one ship's hour.

The bad news was that Mr. dea'Gauss could pack more well-mannered moralizing into an hour than a Moreleki proselytizer. The phrase "business of Clan Korval" was especially ominous.

Unless he very much mistook the matter, Shan was in for a masterly rake-down.

It was odd, he thought, setting his cup on the desk and disposing himself comfortably in the captain's chair, how lordhood's vaunted powers and privileges did nothing at all to protect one from the righteous nagging of those who held one's best interests at heart.

The door chimed, and Shan sighed. He toyed briefly with the notion of remaining silent, then regretfully decided that it would not be seemly and picked up his mug. "Come."

Mr. dea'Gauss walked three steps into the room and bowed low, as agent to lord.

Shan inclined his head and took a sip of scalding coffee. "Mr. dea'Gauss. How delightful to see you looking so well! Adversity always did agree with you, sir. Please, sit down."

"Your lordship will have his joke, I suppose," the older man said repressively. "The business I come on is quite serious, however. I am certain that your lordship will give me the closest attention for the next several moments."

"Of course." Shan murmured politely.

Mr. dea'Gauss regarded Shan steadily, feet flat on the carpet, hands folded, spine stiff and inches from the back of the chair. "In the course of following the instructions laid upon me by Korval's First Speaker," he said crisply, "I found that which seems to indicate that you have undertaken debt-balance with Sav Rid Olanek of Clan Plemia. I ask if this is so."

Here it comes, Shan thought. He inclined his head slightly. "It is so."

Mr. dea'Gauss exhaled sharply. "It is perhaps unfortunate," he suggested, though Shan failed to observe any note of delicacy in his tone, "that your lordship took it upon himself to enter into such an enterprise without first consulting those of us who are more knowledgeable in affairs of this nature. If I had been apprised of the situation at its first occurrence, Balance might have been quickly and, I will say, cleanly achieved. As it stands—"

"As it stands," Shan interrupted, allowing an edge of irritation to be heard, "I am captain of this vessel. As captain, it is my duty to guard her honor, the honor of the crew, and my own honor *as* captain."

"Very true," Mr. dea'Gauss agreed. "However, the situation is not so clear. It is not your responsibility as captain to plunge ship and crew into debt-Balance without making the First Speaker aware. It is the first speaker's duty, after all, to protect the honor of the clan. And I believe this to be a strike at Korval entire." He paused, rubbing his hands together dryly. "You are aware, I think, that Sav Rid Olanek had previously given your sister, the first speaker, cause to feel that she was owed?"

Shan drank coffee and shrugged. "I think the case is that my sister, the First Speaker, gave Sav Rid Olanek cause to feel that *he* was owed. But, yes, I was aware. It did not appear to alter things significantly."

"Wherein," the old gentleman said with asperity, "lies the meat of my comments. I have grown old minding Korval's interests. It is vainglory for one as young and as inexperienced as yourself to think he might take up so weighty a matter, unaided by older, wiser counsel." He paused. It occurred to him that perhaps this was not the best tone to take with Shan, who was well known for his unpredictability.

"It is true," he continued in a more conciliating mode, "that your Lordship is yet young. Experience comes with age, with observing the actions of one's elders and studying their thoughts. It is my dearest wish to aid you, your Line, your clan. I have done so my life long. If I speak too freely, it is from the knowledge that youth errs most greatly when it strives to do what is most proper."

There was a pause long enough to inspire Mr. dea'Gauss with the fear that he had indeed badly overstepped himself. It was within Shan's power—and certainly within the scope of his character—to refuse the aid offered and send his man of business straightaway back to Liad. In such a case, Mr. dea'Gauss's interview with the First speaker could only be painful. Nova yos'Galan had a clear sense of her duty as First Speaker in Trust. She would not brook failure.

"So, then," Shan said conversationally. "What do you want from me, sir? Shall I give the captaincy of the *Passage* over to your capable self? Or call a halt to the Balancing with what has already been done and hope that it suffices?"

Shan's unpredictability, Mr. dea'Gauss reminded himself carefully, could run both ways. "I hear from all only that you are a most excellent captain," he answered quietly. "A Trader of the first rank. For this present . . . If your lordship would apprise me of what steps have been taken?"

"Pin-beams have been sent to four hundred twenty-eight worlds, issuing social and civil warning and citing *Daxflan's* unfortunate link with port violence. To date, three hundred have responded positively, via pin-beam and bouncecomm. The Trade Commission has likewise been notified and responds with thanks and a promise to investigate." He paused. "I trust you find these efforts not completely ineffective."

Mr. dea'Gauss drew a careful breath. "I will, of course, desire to study your lordship's records, for my own edification." He considered a moment before venturing further. "Lady Mendoza is partnered in this enterprise?"

"Lady Mendoza," Shan said, his mouth suddenly tight and grim, "has had her person abused and her honor jeopardized—by order and by direct action of Sav Rid Olanek. You may find the details in her file." He leaned forward, tapped a one-fingered sequence into the keypad, and rose to his towering height. "If you will sit at the desk, sir, you will see what efforts have been made thus far. I hope you won't find them entirely without merit." He bowed slightly. "I'm sure you'll forgive me, sir. Duty calls me to the bridge. The *Passage* leaves orbit shortly."

"Certainly, your lordship," Mr. dea'Gauss said, coming to his feet. He bowed as Shan swept out of the room and then moved behind the desk, pulling a notecorder from his sleeve.

"LEAVING ARSDRED ORBIT," Rusty said pensively. "'Bout time. I tell you, 'Cilla, I don't think I've ever been so sick of a port before. Lost money hand over fist—well, not the *ship*. Kayzin was saying at breakfast that the port-profit appeared to be adequate." He grinned. "That means the cap'n made a killing.'"

Priscilla gave one of her nearly noiseless laughs. "But that's good news, isn't it? Your share will be more at Solcintra. And you didn't lose money on the spec cargo, did you? I thought the wood was preordered."

"Yeah, that's all okay. Point is, we had to pay a stiff fine to— umm, convince the inspectors that Lina's damn perfume wasn't illegal in *some* places, even if it is on Arsdred, and that we never had any intention of trading it on Arsdred." He stopped, a riveted expression on his round face. "You know what, though? We'd been going to try and trade some here, except the cap'n nixed it. Whew! Close one! I tell you what, 'Cilla: Shan's damn good."

"Well," Priscilla said as the door to the bridge slid aside to admit them, "he *is* a Master Trader."

"Sure is. What're you doing after shift? Want to pick up Lina and have a picnic in the garden? My treat."

"That sounds good. But Lina might have other plans."

Rusty set his coffee cup on the comm island. "I'll check before we get started. See you later, Pilot."

"Carry on, Radio Tech." She continued across the bridge, past Navigation and around Meteorology to Piloting. Smiling, she slid into the chair and inclined her head to Third Mate Gil Don Balatrin. He returned an absent half bow.

"Early, aren't you, Mendoza?" Janice Weatherbee asked; she, too, was early. "Might as well start calculating." She leaned back in her chair and folded her arms over her chest elaborately, her eyes ostensibly on the blank screen over the copilot's board.

Priscilla nodded, slid her card into the slot, logged on, and began to run the figures, building an image on her screen. She checked it frowningly, made several adjustments, checked again, and nodded. A slim finger touched the send key and the image coalesced on the coscreen. Priscilla leaned back and deliberately closed her eyes.

"Looks okay to me, Mendoza. Feed it and lock it."

She nodded, stifling a sigh as her fingers flew across the board. "Looks okay to me" was an accolade when Janice said it. It's childish, Priscilla thought, but it would be nice to hear that I'd done this or that *well*.

A chime sounded, and the minor hum of voices faded, to be replaced by one voice, clear and soul-warming "Good morning, all. Station reports, please. I assume everyone's ready to leave?"

THE SCREEN WAS A UNIFORM GRAY except for the red digits in the bottom right-hand corner, busy counting the "real time" they spent in hyperspace.

Priscilla shifted in the pilot's chair, conscious of a glow in the vicinity of her stomach. From orbit-break to Jump-entry, the piloting had been hers. Janice had sat, watchful, throughout the shift but had given neither instruction nor assistance.

Janice stood and stretched. "Okay, Mendoza. I'm gonna run down and snap a cup of coffee. Should be back before Jump-end. If not, you go ahead. This place is a real backwater. Nothing tough. You want anything?"

"No, thanks."

The second mate nodded. "Okay. Back in a couple minutes."

"YOUR LORDSHIP? May I speak with you a moment?"

Shan sighed and stopped, waiting for Mr. dea'Gauss to come alongside. "Good afternoon, sir," he said politely. "How may I assist you?"

"A few words on the matter lying between Korval and Sav Rid Olanek, your lordship. I have taken the liberty of ordering credit checks on *Daxflan* at all ports in this sector. This is in the nature of a supportive effort to your lordship's own tactic."

Shan raised a hand. "Mr. dea'Gauss, I regret. We are due to break into normal space in less than five minutes. Duty calls me again to the bridge."

"Of course," the old gentleman murmured. "May I walk with your lordship?"

There was no escape. Shan inclined his head. "Certainly, sir." He began to move, sternly suppressing a desire to continue at his usual long stride.

"I am certain," Mr. dea'Gauss said, "that your lordship will inform Lady Mendoza of the action I have taken. Also, it is necessary to ascertain whether she has notified her House of the fact that it is partnered with Korval in a venture of honor. I retain the impression that upon Sintia, Mendoza is a House of power, enclosing a varied *melant'i*. It would be wise to establish amicable relations." He paused, and Shan nodded absently. Matching the old gentleman's pace had kept him from reaching the bridge before Jump; the Jump alert sounded peacefully.

They rounded a corner, entering the long hallway that led to the bridge. Mr. dea'Gauss cleared his throat as the tingle of pretransition raced though the ship.

"Your lordship has done quite well in the initial moves. The warnings will cost Trader Olanek much in time, in flexibility, in money. Of course, in this, as in chess, which I believe your Lordship studies, it is important for us to cast our minds ahead, considering the possible countermove open to our opponent."

The Jump-quiver came. From nowhere, from everywhere—the

shriek of a siren. Above Shan's head, a lightplate snapped from yellow to red—and Shan himself was suddenly gone, running flat out toward the bridge.

THE DIGITS IN THE CORNER OF THE SCREEN told their final tally and faded as the break-Jump chime rang across the bridge. Priscilla extended a hand toward the board.

COLLISION COURSE the red letters screamed. Abruptly her hands were flashing over the keys, calling up defense screens, demanding data as her eyes scanned the instruments, assessing what it was, how big, how fast and—

HOSTILE ACTION

Second screens up, Jump alert, coords locked back in, coils— Hurry up, coils! She saw it now, the screen providing maximum amplification: a tiny ship, bristling guns, in position for a second run-by. Coils . . . coils—up!

Her hand was at the Jump control, eyes on the distance dial. There was enough room—just. Now. . .

"Well done, Priscilla." A big hand closed around her wrist, pulling her away from the switch even as he slammed into the copilot's chair and rammed his card into the slot. "Series A29, shunt 42—second screens up? Of course. . . ."

Priscilla's fingers flew in obedience, assigning control to him; she heard him snap an order to Rusty for a visual and another to someone unknown, regarding Turret 7.

"Hurry up, please, Rusty."

"Got 'em, Cap'n—your screen."

The image filled both their screens: the bridge of the other vessel, smaller than the *Passage* by several magnitudes. A man was at the board. From off-screen, a woman's voice, initially inaudible, was becoming rapidly clear: ". . . tell Jury to start her run?"

"You will observe," the captain said from Priscilla's side, "the position of the gun turret on our off side."

The pilot of the other ship looked up in shock, made lightning adjustments to his unseen board, and swore. "Tell Jury to hang where she is!" he snapped over his shoulder.

"A wise choice," the captain said gently. "I hate to belabor the point, but I believe we now have five turrets trained on your vessel. Do correct me if I'm wrong."

The man took a deep breath. "You're right." He glanced behind him as another man came into the screen, a man older than the pilot, hard-faced and calm.

"What goes, Klaus?"

Wordlessly, the pilot pointed at something out of the range of the watchers on the *Passage*. The boss considered for a moment before turning back to the screen and inclining his head.

"Nothing personal, Captain. A contract."

"A contract," Shan repeated. "With whom?"

The boss grinned and shook his head "Confidential. But I'll tell you this: he wanted you out of the race real bad."

"Did he? I hope you got your money in cash and up front, sir. No?" He shook his head at the look of sudden dismay on the mercenary captain's face. "That was careless of you. I suppose you're sure that you have the right ship?"

"He gave me your break-in pattern, a time frame for arrival, approximate mass—real approximate."

"But he gave you no name? And you didn't ask—no, why should you? This is the *Dutiful Passage,* sir. Clan Korval. Tree-and-Dragon Family. Stop me when you hear something familiar."

"*I Dare.*" The voice of the unseen woman was breathless with awe.

"A student of heraldry? Exactly. 'I Dare.'"

The other captain seemed uncomfortable. His eyes strayed from the screen back to the pilot's unseen instruments, then came back to the screen again. "All right, Captain, what's the deal? You've got weaponry and the mass to back it. You gonna use it?"

"That depends on you, doesn't it? I suppose you wouldn't be betraying a confidence if I asked if the name of the man you dealt with was Olanek or the ship *Daxflan?* You needn't say yes, only no."

There was silence.

Shan shook his head. "I hope you got at least half of your money in advance, sir. No? Forty percent? Thirty? *Twenty-five?*" He laughed suddenly at the acute distress on the other man's face. "I'm ashamed of you sir! Didn't your mother tell you never to sign a Liaden's contract? Twenty-five percent down on a job that would mark you all for the rest of your lives? Ask your crew member there if she believes a family with 'I Dare' for a motto would let you rest if you'd completed your mission successfully."

The mercenary captain shrugged. "There wasn't a contract," he said sheepishly. "It was a gentleman's agreement. But I know where to find him."

"No doubt you do," Shan said cordially "I should perhaps mention that *Daxflan* is also capably armed. And the captain is counted a very fair shot."

The boss bowed his head. "What's the price?"

"Get out of here," the captain snapped, his voice suddenly hard-edged and cold. "We have your ships recorded and filed. The information is being pin-beamed this moment to the Federated Trade Commission. I advise you to take up a different line of work."

The boss glanced over his shoulder. "Tell Jury and Sal to scram. We'll do the same, if the captain'll deflect his guns."

THE LAST SHIP REACHED ITS JUMP POINT and blinked out of existence. Priscilla's instruments showed empty space around the *Dutiful Passage* for several light-minutes in all directions. In the chair beside her, Shan yos'Galan took a deep breath and spoke, voice glacial. "Second Mate."

There was a slight hesitation before Janice answered from directly behind them.

"Captain?"

"You will report to the captain's office immediately before Prime. You will bring hard copy of your contract. Dismissed to quarters."

Priscilla caught her breath at the other woman's shock; she thought for a heartbeat that one of them would cry in protest.

The second mate cleared her throat. "Yes, Captain." And Priscilla heard her go.

Relief flooded through her, shocking in its intensity, mixed with outrage, pain, and near-manic glee. She gripped the arms of the chair, seeking serenity, buffeted by emotion. Adrenaline high, she told herself, keeping to the search for the path.

"Ms. Mendoza."

She took a breath and found her voice. "Yes, Captain?"

"On behalf of this ship and of Clan Korval, Ms. Mendoza, all thanks. I could have done no better in your place, given the resources at your command. I only hope I would have done as well." He pulled his card from the slot and tucked it absently into his belt. "There will be a meeting of the crew immediately after Prime. I would like to see you in my office following it, please."

"Of course, Captain." The inner chaos was subsiding somewhat. Daring to turn her head, Priscilla met a pair of quizzical pale eyes even as the feeling hit her again—differently, though as intense—an overwhelming impulse to fling back her head and laugh, to embrace the man beside her. . . .

Just as she knew she must be lost, she found the pathway. She flew down the inner way, found the door, and slammed it hard behind her.

Beside her, Shan sighed sharply and snapped to his feet, spinning to face the incoming relief pilots. "Your boards," he said curtly.

Vilobar bowed. "The shift changes, Pilots." Priscilla pushed herself out of the chair, still giddy from too much emotion experienced too quickly. But she found her path blocked by the captain, who was glaring down at Mr. dea'Gauss.

"Well, sir?" Shan demanded.

The old gentleman inclined his head. "Shall I draft a message to the first speaker, your lordship?"

"I believe," Shan said icily, "that is the captain's duty. I thank you for your concern."

Mr. dea'Gauss bowed low. "Forgive my presumption, your lordship. It is, of course, exactly as you say."

"I'm pleased to hear it," the captain snapped, and swept by, heading for Communications.

Priscilla watched him leave; realizing that she was watching, she moved her eyes, cheeks flaming, but found her instinctive step away hindered.

Mr. dea'Gauss bowed to her, not as deeply as for the captain but with a hand flourish indicating profound respect. Priscilla forced herself to be still, to form the proper Liaden phrase.

"Mr. dea'Gauss. How may I serve you?"

"It is I who wish to serve your ladyship. Will you accept my aid in contacting your family? They should, perhaps, be apprised of what transpires." He looked at her closely. "I ask indulgence, my lady, if the offer offends."

Priscilla stared at him blankly, then recovered herself and inclined her head. "You are all kindness, sir. I thank you for thought and offer, but no. There is no need to trouble House Mendoza with my affairs."

Mr. dea'Gauss hesitated fractionally. Then, recent contact with Lord yos'Galan having rendered him wary, he bowed again with no less respect. "As you will, my lady," he murmured. He stepped aside to let her pass.

Shipyear 65
Tripday 155
Third Shift
12.00 Hours

"NO," Gordy answered Lina, "I don't." He took an appallingly large swallow of milk. "I guess I'm just dumb, or way too weak. No matter how hard I try, I just *can't* hold on. Every day I go to the exercise room, grab on to the bar, and Pallin tries to pry me loose." He sighed. "Does it every time. And he keeps saying I've got to think about my strength being a river, all running down my arm and pooling in the hand that's hanging on, but you know what? That don't—doesn't—make any sense at all! Rivers don't hang on."

"Indeed they do not," Lina agreed seriously. "But perhaps Pallin only wishes you to understand that strength is a fluid thing. A—a variable."

Gordy stared at her blankly. "That doesn't make sense either," he decided. "You're either strong or you're not. I'm pretty fast, but Pallin says I've got to learn to hold on before I learn how to hit back or run."

"Ah," Lina murmured, momentarily stumped. She picked up her teacup and glanced at the third member of the dinner party.

Priscilla sat with her hands curved around a cup of coffee, her eyes plumbing the dark depths. She had put her dinner aside untasted and had appeared lost in her own thoughts. But now she looked up, giving the boy frowning attention. "I know something that might help," she said softly. "It might sound silly to you, but it works."

"I'll try *any*thing," Gordy said, thumping his glass on the table for emphasis. "Nothing can be sillier than trying to think about a river making you strong."

Priscilla smiled faintly and sipped coffee. "To do this," she said slowly, "you should close your eyes and sit up straight, but not stiffly, and take two deep breaths."

He followed her instructions, shifting to set both feet on the floor and squaring his round shoulders.

Lina froze, regarding both with Healer's senses. Gordy radiated trust and boy-love, untainted by alarm. And Priscilla . . .

Gone were the grays and browns of unjoy, the coldness of unbelonging. Priscilla was a flame—a torch—of assurance, compassion. It was as if a door hidden within a dark and joyless cellar had been flung open to the full glory of a sun. Lina watched as Priscilla extended herself and surrounded the child's love and trust, saw her pluck one well-anchored thread of confidence from the glittering array of Gordy's emotions and expertly begin the weaving.

"Now," she said, and it seemed to Lina that her voice had also taken on depth; a vibrancy that had not been there a heartbeat before. "You're going to become a tree, Gordy. First think of a tree— a strong, vigorous tree at the height of its growth. A tree no wind will bend, no snow will break."

The boy's brows pulled together. "Like Korval's Tree."

"Yes," Priscilla agreed, still in that supremely assured voice, "exactly like Korval's Tree. Think of it alive, with its roots sunk deep into the soil, pulling strength from the ground, rain from the sky. Think hard upon this prince of trees. Walk close to it in your thoughts. Lay your hand upon its trunk. Smell the greenness, the strength of it." She paused, watching Gordy's face closely.

Lina carefully set her cup aside, watching the weaving with amazement. A Master of the Hall of Healers would do exactly what Priscilla was . . .

The boy's face went from concentration to pleasure. "It's my *friend*."

"Your friend," Priscilla reiterated. "Your second self. Walk closer. Lean your back against the trunk. Feel how strong your friend is. Lean closer; let the Tree take you, make you one with it. Feel how strong you are—you and your friend. Your back like a trunk, the strength running in you drawn up from the deep—clean, green, absolutely certain strength. You're so strong. . . ."

There was a small silence as Gordy sat, face joyful, wrapped in love, taking the image into himself. Lina heard the image strike home then, with a chime so pure that outer ears could not have heard it, and felt it click into place in the next instant. Priscilla withdrew slowly; Lina could see nothing in the fabric of the boy's pattern to indicate the new weaving.

Beside her, Priscilla extended a hand to sketch a sign in the air before the boy's face.

"It's time to say good-bye to your friend now, Gordy. Take another shared breath . . . take a step . . . another . . . you may come to visit as often as you like. Your friend will always welcome you."

She picked up her coffee cup and took a sip. "Don't you want dessert, Gordy?" she asked, and her voice was entirely normal.

The boy's lashes lifted. He grinned. "Pretty good," he said, still grinning. "Do it for me again tomorrow?"

She lifted her brows. "Me? I didn't do anything, Gordy. You did it. All you have to do is close your eyes and think about your Tree whenever you need to renew your strength." She smiled. "Try it on Pallin tomorrow."

"Crelm! Won't he be surprised when he *can't* yank me loose?" Gordy laughed, then glanced at the clock. "Guess I won't have dessert, though. Got to get to the meeting room and make sure everything's okay before the crew gets there. See you later, Lina! Thanks, Priscilla!" He was gone.

"Will it work?" Lina asked carefully.

Priscilla smiled. "It usually does. A small spell, but very useful. It's one of the first things an Initiate's taught when she's brought to the Circle for training."

"Spell?" She was unsure of the word. Inwardly, Priscilla had shielded the flame, not hidden it. Lina wondered if her friend yet understood.

"That's what it's called at—on Sintia," Priscilla was saying apologetically. "A spell. Other people would call it hypnotism, maybe, or voice tricks and psychology. Whatever the right name is, it *does* work. The image is so easy and so strong." She smiled again.

"Is it so important for an—Initiate?—to be strong?" Lina wondered, feeling her way, taking care to keep all incoming paths open in case the other should reach out, Healer to Healer.

Priscilla sipped coffee and nodded. "Learning to make decisions, learning to use your voice, the power symbols . . . and later, the larger magics that might require the woven concentration of ten or twelve of the Circle. It's very important to be strong."

Lina tipped her head, groping for the best phrasing. The chime announcing the end of the Prime sliced across her thoughts.

Priscilla stood and held out a slim hand. "Come to the meeting with me, friend?"

Lina smiled and slid her hand into her friend's larger one. The inner roads were empty. Priscilla would not approach her that way. "Of course," she murmured, standing. "We should also save a seat for poor Rah Stee. He is always late."

JANICE HAD BEEN STOIC.

Yes, she understood the reason for her dismissal. Negligence of duty was a serious matter. No, she did not think she would accept a position as shuttle pilot on one of Korval's lesser ships, though she appreciated the captain's offer. She had friends on Angelus, fourth planet in the system they had just entered; she thought she would pay them a visit before looking for another job. After a small silence, she offered the opinion that Mendoza was a damn good pilot—ripe for first class.

Shan nodded, counting out the coins that bought back her contract. Janice informed him that she was packed and could leave the *Passage* immediately. She had no good-byes to say.

Again Shan nodded as he flipped a toggle and spoke quietly to Seth in the shuttlebay. Janice's departure was scheduled for Fourteenth Hour. They would be within shuttle distance of Angelus then.

The door chimed, and he whirled about, snapping to his feet. "Come!"

Kayzin Ne'Zame entered the room, checked, and bowed profoundly. "Captain."

"If you've come to remind me that I'm to attend the crew

850

meeting, Kayzin, you'd no need. My memory is quite sharp, though I daresay it will begin to deteriorate very soon."

Covering her shock, her face neutral, she bowed again.

Shan sighed sharply and strode past her to the bar. Glancing over his shoulder as he poured a cup of *misravot*, he strove for a happier tone. "Kayzin? Will you drink?"

"Thank you," she said formally, "but no." She waited until he turned his face to her fully before continuing. "If it does not offend, Captain, I ask to walk with you. There is a thing to be discussed. A matter of reassignment of duty, to accommodate the lack of a second mate."

"Very well." He moved to the door and bowed her through before him. That was highly improper; rank earned *him* that privilege. But what could she do when he waved at her so imperiously?

"The case is," Kayzin pursued through her prickling hurt, "that the third mate does not wish promotion to second. He feels he lacks the proper qualifications, that his reaction time is insufficient to demands such as those present upon the bridge this shift just passed." She paused. Shan said nothing.

"I agree with his assessment of his strengths—and his weaknesses. He is willing to extend his hand to those duties of administration for which the second mate is responsible." She looked up at him gravely. "It is the first mate's recommendation to the captain that this be done. For a short time. And conditionally."

"The captain hears," Shan said unencouragingly. "The conditions?"

Another nuance had developed in the symphony of emotion that was Kayzin. A chilly fogging . . . embarrassment, Shan identified, and was amazed.

"In view of the first mate's imminent retirement," she said levelly, "and the lack of a second mate, coupled with the third mate's inability to step into that position, it is in the best interest of the ship that another be trained in the line of command as soon as may be. I request that the captain assign Priscilla Mendoza to the first mate, that she may be strenuously schooled in the duties of the second."

"Reasoning, please."

"She has the ability. You yourself placed her in a training position. I admit that track is not as rigorous as this proposed will be. However, it has been my observation that Priscilla Mendoza possesses a strong character, quick understanding, and sure judgment. I believe she may do well for the ship, were she but offered the means. And if she does not," Kayzin shrugged, "the ship is no worse off than it is at this present."

"There is a phenomenon which Terrans call 'personality conflict.' The captain has seen indications of this phenomenon between the first mate and Priscilla Mendoza."

"The first mate has mastered herself."

Shan nodded. "Your recommendations have merit. They will be put into effect tomorrow First Hour, assuming Ms. Mendoza's acquiescence. The captain will require from the first mate a daily report of training and progress—or lack." He paused at the door of the meeting room and bowed. "Forgive my hapless tongue, old friend. I regret having caused you pain."

Her relief was like a puff of Arsdredi smoke. She smiled and returned his bow. "It is forgotten."

"By both," he answered properly, and preceded her into the room.

SHAN LEANED BACK IN HIS CHAIR and sipped. The room was full. Those of the crew whose duties prevented their physical presence watched by monitor from their stations. The general hubbub indicated good spirits and confidence.

He considered his inner Wall, then carefully allowed the merest slit to part its impenetrable fabric.

Hot, scintillating, brilliant iciness assaulted him. He took a breath, narrowed the slit, and began a Sort of the larger threads, flickering among webs of burning color, neither apart from nor completely of them.

Satisfied, he closed the slit, took some wine, and held it for a moment in a mouth dry with effort. The crew was outraged, of course, by the attack. But there was no trace of panic, of terror. They were certain of their ship—of their captain.

He wished he shared their certainty.

He moved a hand, and the room's lights dimmed as the central screen glowed to life. The crew's chatter died.

"You are all aware," Shan began conversationally, "of the day's *second* Jump alarm. I'd like you to watch a tape of what led up to the pilot's activation of the alarm." From the corner of his eye he saw Priscilla start. Lina reached out, and the taller woman settled back, her expression wary.

"We're at minus twenty seconds of the final transition from the scheduled Jump. Pilot Mendoza is at the board. Now—normal space."

COLLISION COURSE the screen shouted as Priscilla's hands flickered, hitting the screens up. "First defense barriers active." HOSTILE ACTION "Second screens up, coords fed, alarm on. We're waiting for the coils to come back up. Coils up and we're ready to go." On the screen his own hand stopped completion of the exercise. The action froze and faded as the room lights came on.

"Reaction time," Shan said for the benefit of the pilots watching. "From time of first warning to full defense: one and one-half seconds. From full defense to Jump-ready, two seconds. We were ready to depart twenty-four seconds after the initial alarm. Most of that time was spent waiting for the coils to renew themselves."

The silence in the meeting room was broken by the soft flutter of pilot hands over imaginary boards as pilot brains counted seconds.

Over to the right, Seth stood. Shan nodded to him.

"Yes?"

"I move that Priscilla Mendoza be given an up-share bonus. She got us out of a tough one. That bomb was right on the drive sections. Would've done real damage if it'd hit."

Rusty was on his feet before Seth was off his. "Second."

"Third," Ken Rik said. "And a call for ship-points, Captain. The debt lies there."

Gil Don Balatrin seconded that diffidently.

Shan nodded. "Any comments? Disapprovals? Discussions? No? Show of hands, in favor?

"First Mate?"

"Unanimous, Captain."

"So I counted, also. Thank you." He initialed a paper on his pad. "Recorded and done." He smiled slightly over the room. "Also recorded and done—two points hazard pay for all crew, payable at Solcintra. More business?"

There was none.

"Thank you. Dismissed."

Shipyear 65
Tripday 155
Third Shift
14.00 Hours

THERE WAS TENSION IN THE AIR, prickling the short hairs on her arm. She focused her attention on the tapestry over the bar.

"Brandy, Priscilla?"

She started, then managed a smile. "Thank you."

"You're welcome." He handed her the glass and went by, heading for the desk.

She followed and settled into the right-hand chair, with the tension still singing around her.

The captain took a sip of his drink. "Gordy tells me you've taught him to be a tree," he commented. "I don't say it's a *bad* idea, Priscilla. I only wonder how his mother will react if I deliver him into her arms all green and leafy."

Laughter escaped her, softly. "No, an inner tree. Pallin keeps telling Gordy to think of his strength as a river. But Gordy believes that strong is strong, without variation."

"I see." The light eyes were speculative. He inclined his head. "It was kind of you, Priscilla. Thank you for your care of my kinsman."

She moved a hand in a gesture learned from the tapes Lina had provided. "It's not a *kindness*. I like him. He reminds me of Brand— my younger brother—the last time I saw him."

"My sympathy to you. But perhaps you'll find he's grown into a young gentleman when you go home next. I remember when that particular metamorphosis overtook Val Con." He laughed, and the tension shimmered. "*Truly* terrifying."

She laughed also, softly and unconvincingly. Sipping, she noticed an undercurrent of warm admiration such as she had not felt since her days as a Sister at Temple.

"The reason I asked you to come to me," the captain was saying, "is to discuss the new administrative structure of the ship."

She waited.

He sighed. "Janice Weatherbee has left us, leaving the post of second mate vacant. A problem, you will admit. The third mate has been approached and has graciously—one might say with comic haste—declined the promotion. The first mate has thus applied to the captain for another trainee." He leveled a blunt forefinger. "You."

"Me?" She stared at him. "I'm not qualified to be second mate."

"Did I say you were? I do beg your pardon, Priscilla. What I meant to say was that Kayzin had asked me to assign you to her so she could teach you to be second mate. What *is* the phrase? My dreadful, dreadful memory—aha!" He snapped his fingers. "On-the-job training."

To tension and admiration was added confusion. Priscilla drank. "I don't—why me?"

"Why not you? You were in the track already, after all. I do admit that the training Kayzin proposes will be more demanding, but it's the same training. Merely a difference in intensity." He stopped. "Kayzin is a very good teacher, Priscilla. She's been on the *Passage* for over fifty years, first mate for thirty. And she handled much of my own training, thankless task that it was."

Priscilla took a breath. "She dislikes me."

"No. She distrusted you, I believe. But I also believe that it's passed. Even if it hasn't, Kayzin is not one to let mere personal prejudice stand in the way of doing the best she can for the ship." He sipped, eyes quizzical. "Well, Priscilla? Do you want the job?"

Want the job? Like she wanted breath. Shocked, she looked

within and found the same surety that had allowed Gordy to find the Tree. "Yes," she said.

"Good. Now, then, there are a few things to be explained." He paused, then nodded. "First, it is imperative that you acquire your first class license. You will come to the bridge every day immediately following your duty shift. I'll teach you. There's no reason why you shouldn't be a first class pilot by the time we reach Solcintra."

She considered it. "Shan?"

The tension altered in some indefinable way, though the warmth was constant. "Yes, Priscilla?"

"Won't it work out . . ." She sighed and began again. "The captain."

"What of the captain, my friend?"

"If I'm to report for piloting lessons on my first off-shift, won't the captain be pulling a triple shift?"

"Occasionally." He grinned. "The captain's made of stern stuff. When I was learning the ship, I often ran double shifts, between tutoring from Kayzin and tutoring from my father—and then stayed up half the sleep shift studying for the next day." He tipped his head. "Do you object to the captain's instruction, Priscilla?"

"No, of course not. . . ." She felt an echo of tension and an echo of warmth. The echo would overwhelm her if she did not take care.

"Fine, then that's settled. Other points: Second mate signs a standard ship contract. That means you'll no longer be under my protection, but under the protection of the *Dutiful Passage*. . . ."

Not under his protection? Panic added a sheen of ice to the echoes. No longer to be under Korval's wing, where there was comfort and friendship and aid? To be cast out? To be—

"Priscilla." His voice was a flame of common sense, licking at the ice. "The *Passage* is owned and operated by Clan Korval. A ship's contract guarantees you assistance that a personal contract with Shan yos'Galan cannot. You will, of course, read it before you sign it."

"Yes, of course . . . ." Feeling foolish, she drank.

"You'll want to know the rate of pay." He tapped on the keypad as he turned the screen to face her. "Second mate draws three cantra flat for the short run, plus one-half ship-share. Bonuses and increments—not applicable at present. You will, of course, be starting at the low end. We've got four months to go, so that's prorated . . . plus the amount owed under previous contract . . . crew's hazard pay . . . ship's points, can't forget them . . . oh, and the up-share . . . subtract ship-debt. Well, some of this can't be finalized until we hit Liad, but I think that's everything, Priscilla: the minimum. Is the sum agreeable to you?"

It was staggering. The glowing amber letters named more money than she had ever seen at once. Enough to repurchase her bartered bracelets three times over. She could buy a Hundred Hours for Lina and herself, and still there would be money for clothing, for books, for tapes, for lodging, for food. It might be more money than she had made in her life . . . for one trip!

"That can't—*can't*—be right."

"Can't it?" Shan frowned and turned the screen around. "Well, then, let's do it again. Base pay for second, prorated. . . ."

She felt wave after wave of emotion: admiration, nervousness, exhilaration, exhaustion. Priscilla felt herself expanding under the assault, taking it in, sending it out, over and over. The exhilaration built, as it had not built since she and Moonhawk . . .

Moonhawk was dead.

And the echoes came faster, where there should never have been sound. Where there could be no motion. Dear Goddess . . . she pictured the Tree. She took a breath, hearing Shan's voice as he muttered the figures over and leaned into the familiarity—the comfort—of it. The Tree had worked. The Gyre might work, as well.

She began the opening sequence and felt the image click into place and take on its own momentum. Thank you, Goddess. She would need to be in her quarters within the hour. Sleep was the room beyond Serenity: the end of the Gyre's dance.

"No, Priscilla, I'm afraid the figure is correct. You do have to realize that this is the short run, and that we're less than four months out of Solcintra. If you renew your contract at the end of the trip, you'll net more. Simple matter of mathematics. You'll be on from beginning to end, and the next trip's the long one. Takes a year to finish the circuit. Priscilla?"

She had passed through the First and Second Doors. The next was the Door to Serenity, where she would abide awhile before she came to Sleep.

"The sum is more than adequate, Captain," she murmured. "I was surprised because it seemed like such a lot of money."

"Oh, well, the *Passage* is the flagship of Korval's fleet, after all. You wouldn't want us to pay on the same scale as an ore shuttle, would you?"

"No, Captain." Serenity was in sight . . . then achieved. Priscilla took a relaxed breath and a drink.

Across from her, the captain stiffened: he shook his head sharply and stood. "I think those are the important points, Priscilla. You'll begin your training with Kayzin at First Hour. I will see you on the bridge for pilot training at Sixth. There will be a copy of the second mate's contract on your screen when you wake. Good night."

Such abruptness was hardly like him. But he must be tired, too, she thought, and offered him a smile as she bowed.

"Good night, Captain."

THE DOOR CLOSED BEHIND HER, and Shan's knees gave way. He hit the chair with a gasp and hid his face in his hands.

He mastered himself with an effort, levered out of the chair, and turned toward the red-striped door to his personal quarters. Then he stopped.

Turning away, he crossed the room and went down the hall.

The crew hall was quiet and dimly lit: a blessing to his pounding head. He found the door by instinct and laid his hand against the plate.

For a moment he despaired. She was not there . . . The door slid aside. Honey-brown eyes blinked up at him. "Shan?" Then she slid her arm about his waist and drew him within. "My poor friend! What has happened? Ahh, *denubia* . . . ."

Allowing himself to be seated on the bed, he pushed his face into the warm hollow between her shoulder and neck and he felt the Healing begin.

"She shut me out, Lina. Twice, she shut me *out*."

Shipyear 65
Tripday 155
Fourth Shift
20.00 Hours

THE CONTRACT WAS EXTREMELY CLEAR; attached was an addendum providing the amount the second mate was due at Solcintra and the formula by which it had been figured. The addendum stated that the sum was not fixed and would be refigured upon final docking using the same formula and taking into account any additional bonuses, finder's fees, ship-points, or debts.

Priscilla placed her hand against the screen and felt the slight electric prickle against her palm as the machine recorded the print. *Beep!* Contract sealed.

Her hand curled into a loose fist as she took it away from the screen; she stared at it. Then, grinning, she turned to put on her shirt.

LINA'S DOOR WAS OPENING as Priscilla rounded the corner; she lengthened her stride.

"Good morning."

"Priscilla! Well met, my friend. I thought myself exiled to eating this meal alone, so slugabed have I been!"

It had done her good, Priscilla thought. Lina was glowing; eyes sparkling, mouth softly curving, she radiated satisfied pleasure. "You're beautiful," she said suddenly, reaching out to take a small golden hand.

Lina laughed. "As much as it naturally must grieve me to differ with a friend, I feel it necessary to inform you that among the clans one is judged to be but moderately attractive."

"Blind people," Priscilla muttered, and Lina laughed again.

"But I have heard you are to begin as second mate in only an hour!" she said gaily. "*Ge'shada, denubia.* Kayzin is very careful, but she is not a warm person. It is her way. Do not regard it."

"No, I won't," Priscilla agreed, looking at her friend in awe.

"It is a shame that you will not have time to come regularly to the pet library now," Lina was rattling on. "You have done so much good there. I never thought to see the younger sylfok tamed at all. Others have remarked the difference there as well. Why, Shan said only this morning—"

Priscilla gasped against the flare of pain, and flung away from jealousy toward serenity—

To find her way barred and a small hand tight around her wrist as Lina cried out, "Do not!"

She froze, within and without. "All right."

"Good." Lina smiled. "Shan and I are old friends, Priscilla. Who else might he come to, when he was injured and in need? And you—*denubia*, you must not shield yourself so abruptly, without the courtesy of a warning! It *hurts.* Surely you know . . . surely your instructors never taught you to treat a fellow Healer so?"

"Fellow—" She struggled with it and surrendered to the first absurdity. "Do you mean you're open *all the time?*"

Lina blinked. "Should I huddle behind the Wall forever, afraid to use what is mine? Do you deliberately choose blindness, rather than use your eyes? I am a Healer! How else should I be but open?"

Priscilla was bombarded with puzzlement-affection-exasperation-lingering pleasure. She fought for footing against the onslaught and heard her friend sigh.

"There is no need to befuddle yourself. Can you close partially? It is not this moment necessary for you to scan every nuance."

She found the technique and fumbled it into place like a novice. The pounding broadcast faded into the background. She took a breath, her mind already busy with the second absurdity. "Shan is a . . . Healer? A *man?*"

Lina's mouth curved in a creampot smile. "It is very true that Shan is a man," she murmured, while Priscilla felt the green knife twist in her again. "It is also true that he is a trained and skilled Healer. Do I love you less, *denubia*, because I also love others?"

"No . . . ." She took another breath, pursuing the absurdity. "It—on Sintia, men, even those initiated to the Circle, are not Soulweavers. It's taught that they don't have the ability."

"Perhaps on Sintia they do not," Lina commented dryly. "Shan is Liaden, after all, and Sintia's teaching has not yet reached us. Those of us who may bear it are taught to pay attention, to use the information provided by each of our senses. Shan is not one of those who may do nothing but learn to erect the Wall and keep their sanity by never looking beyond; nor am I. And it hurts, *denubia*, to be in rapport with someone, only to be—without cause and without warning—shut out. You must not do so again. An emergency is another matter: you act to save yourself. Should you find that you must shield yourself from another Healer, it is proper to say, 'Forgive me, I require privacy,' before going behind the Wall."

Priscilla hung her head. "I didn't mean to hurt him. I meant to *shield* him. I thought I was generating a—false echo, because I was tired."

Reassurance, warmth, and affection flowed in. Priscilla felt her chest muscles loosen and looked up to find Lina smiling.

"He knows that the hurt was not deliberate. The best balance is simply not to do it again." She held out a hand. "Come, we will have to gulp our food!"

Trealla Fantrol, Liad
Year Named Trolsh
Third *Relumma*
Banim Seconday

TAAM OLANEK took another appreciative sip of excellent brandy. Nova yos'Galan had been called from the party some minutes ago. "Business," she had murmured to Eldema Glodae, with whom she had been speaking. Olanek allowed himself the indulgence of wondering what sort of business might keep the first speaker of Liad's first Clan—why, after all, dress the thing up in party clothes?—so long from the entertainment of which she was host.

True, there was Lady Anthora, barely out of university and comporting herself with the ease of one ten years her senior. She was at present listening with pretty gravity to Lady yo'Hatha. He toyed with the idea of rescuing the child from the old woman's clutches, but even as he did, Anthora managed the thing with a grace that filled him with admiration. Not the beauty her sister was—too full of breast and hip for the general taste—but no lack of brains or flair.

No lack of that sort in any of them, Olanek admitted to himself. Even the gargoyle eldest had wit sharp enough to cut.

Their fault—collectively and individually—lay in their youth. Gods willing, they would outgrow, or outmaneuver, that particular failing without mishap, and Korval would continue bright and unwavering upon its pinnacle.

While Plemia continued its slow descent into oblivion.

Olanek sipped irritably. It seemed somehow unjust.

"Eldema Olanek?" a soft, seductive voice said at his elbow. He turned and made his bow, no deeper than was strictly necessary, but without resentment. That she should address him as First Speaker rather than Lord Olanek or Delm Plemia was worthy of note.

He smiled. "*Eldema* yos'Galan. How may I serve you?"

"By your patience, sir," Nova murmured, pale lips curving in what passed for her smile. "I deeply regret the need. Is it possible that you might allow a moment of business to intrude upon your pleasure?"

Odder and odder. He inclined his head. "I am entirely at your disposal." Clearly Nova wished to treat with him as a colleague. Now, why should Korval wish to discuss business with Plemia when they moved in such different spheres? And why at such a time, in the midst of this vast and enjoyable entertainment? Why not a call to his office tomorrow morning? Surely the matter was not so urgent as that?

Still, he walked with her from the room, declining to have his glass refreshed. They went side by side and silent down the wide hallway to another, where the woman turned right.

This portion of the house was older, Olanek saw. Its doors were of wood, with large, ornate knobs set into their centers. Nova yos'Galan stopped at the second, turned the knob, and stepped aside, bowing him in before her.

The gesture was graceful—one could not accuse Korval of flattery. What could they possibly gain? Olanek inclined his head and passed through.

He stopped just inside to consider the room. It was a study or office, warm with wood and patterned crimson carpeting. Korval's device, the venerable Tree-and-Dragon, hung above the flickering hearth. He took a step toward the fire, heard a rustle, and turned instead to face his host.

She gestured an apology—a flicker of slender hands—and moved to the desk. Olanek followed.

"If you would have the kindness to read this message. I should say that it has been pin-beamed and arrived only recently."

GREETING FROM CAPTAIN SHAN YOS'GALAN TO ELDEMA NOVA YOS'GALAN, the bright amber letters read. It was a formal beginning for a message from brother to sister, surely—but this was business. Olanek sipped his remaining brandy and read further.

Finished, he stood silently. When he did speak, it was in icy outrage and in the highest possible dialect. "Plemia is not diverted by the jest, *Eldema*. We demand—"

"No," she interrupted composedly, "you do not. It is conceivable that my brother could frame and execute such a jest. It is not conceivable that he would bring formal charge in this manner, as captain of the *Dutiful Passage*, begging guidance from his First Speaker." She drew breath, and the sapphire rope glittered about her throat. "My brother is not a fool, *Eldema*. He understands actions and the consequences of actions. As was shown, I think, when he was himself First Speaker.

"You should know that Mr. dea'Gauss was on the bridge of the *Passage* at the time of the attack. I leave it to you to judge whether he, at least, would be party to such a thing, were not every reported particular correct."

"I would speak with Mr. dea'Gauss."

"Of course," she replied calmly. "I have sent word, recalling him for that purpose."

"It might be wise for you to recall your brother's ship as well," he suggested ominously.

She raised her brows. "I see no cause. The route is nearly done. Captain yos'Galan has received the tuition of his First Speaker, as requested. For this present, of course." She looked at him out of meaningful violet eyes. "It does not need to be said that Plemia will act with honor and good judgment, listening with all ears, seeing with all eyes. Korval depends upon it."

To be thus schooled by a mere child, when he had been First Speaker—aye, and Delm!—longer than she had had breath! He gained control of himself, essayed a small sip of his dwindling refreshment, then inclined his head.

"Plemia wishes only to make judgment for itself, as is proper, before negotiating further with Korval." He paused. "I would ask, if Korval's First Speaker has not yet in her wisdom done this thing, that Captain yos'Galan be . . . entreated . . . to stay his hand until the precise circumstances have been made clear to all concerned."

Nova yos'Galan inclined her fair head. "Such was the essence of the First Speaker's instruction to Captain yos'Galan. I am certain that Plemia will instruct Captain yo'Vaade in like manner."

"Of course," he said through gritted teeth.

The woman bowed and smiled. "Business is then completed, *Eldema*. My thanks for the gift of your patience. Do enjoy the rest of the party."

Somehow, Olanek doubted he would.

Shipyear 65
Tripday 155
Second Shift
6.00 Hours

KAYZIN NE'ZAME was a thorough teacher—and a determined one. Priscilla's head felt crammed to the splitting point already. And there was so much more to learn!

She was in a hurry, lest she be late for her piloting lesson with the captain.

The captain! She dodged into the lift and punched the direction for the core and inner bridge. Rattled for the last six hours by a storm of information, she had nearly forgotten about the captain.

He was a Healer—a Soulweaver—though no man she had ever heard of was master of that skill. He was constantly open, always reading, aware. . .

Aware of her emotions. From the very beginning, he had scanned her and touched her feelings—and knew her as intimately as a . . . Sister-in-Power.

No! It was not done. It was improper, blasphemous! The power to read souls came from the Goddess, through Her chosen agents. Moonhawk, who was dead, had been such an agent, and Priscilla Mendoza her willing vessel. To use the power consciously, without divine direction. . .

The door slid open, and Priscilla escaped into the corridor; she dived into the first service hall she saw and froze, heart pounding.

Mother, help me, she cried silently. Help me . . . I'm lost . . . .

The Tree, the Gyre, the Room Serenity, the Place of watching—each had she used within the past day. She, who was nothing and no one, save that once a saint had lived within her.

Heedless of time, she closed her eyes and quested in the Inner Places, where the Old One's soul had sung in time gone past.

Moonhawk?

Silence surrounded the echo of the thought. There was no one there but Priscilla.

Priscilla knew no magic.

Magic had worked. She held to that thought and opened her eyes. Three times—four!—magic had worked. And the promise she had given Lina had held no taint of unsurety. She would not close the captain out. She would hold the Hood ready to muffle any strong outburst and spare him as much pain as she could.

The hour bell sounded, and she gasped.

Tarlin Skepelter, on her way to Service Hall 28 to replace a faulty sensor, was treated to the interesting sight of the new second mate running at top speed away from her, toward the inner bridge.

"NO! COMPLETELY USELESS!"

She knew it before he said so and barely caught the blaze of self-fury in time to muffle it. Beside her, the captain snapped forward and swept his big hand across the board. He was out of his chair in a blur and towering over her.

"Are you *angry*, Priscilla?"

She winced at the volume and kept a firm hold on the Hood. "Yes."

"Then be angry! You're a better pilot than that! *Gordy's* better than that! Of all the inexcusable, sloppy, *ground-grubber* piloting I have ever seen—"

"And I suppose you could do better—keeping the board in half your mind and watching for echoes, too!"

"Did I tell you to watch for echoes? I told you to mind that board, Pilot! If you can't keep your whole mind right there and nowhere else, we'll suspend all lessons, now! I'll not have this ship endangered because the pilot at the board was thinking about something besides the business at hand!" He was a glittering buzz of anger. Priscilla fielded it unconsciously, even as the hold on her own rage slipped.

"I didn't ask to be on the board with a full-open empath! What am I supposed to do? Forget about the spill? What about—"

"Yes! That's precisely what you're supposed to do! Damn it—" He slammed into the copilot's chair and flung his hands out. "Priscilla, am I made of glass? Will I break, do you think, at the touch of a little well-earned self-rage?"

She was silent, seething without attempting to contain it.

The captain sighed, his pattern now containing less anger than frustration overlaying interest-admiration-warmth-friendship. "I'm not wide open, Priscilla. I don't need to be. You're coming through quite clearly without it. Also, I am not a cretin. I can adjust the level of reception, if things are so intense I find my mind wandering. Further, I am a pilot! I've worked with *dozens* of people since I began training. One of the finest pilots I ever knew was terrified every moment of duty. Another I worked with fairly often was as nearly asleep as she could be, no matter what the emergency—and her reactions were perfect. Ask her why she had done a certain thing, though, and she'd panic. . . ." He shifted, offering a smile. "I'm not fragile, friend. My word on it."

It was a temptation to extend herself, to grasp his warmth and cuddle it about her. She shook her head. "I—Lina said that—Healers are open, except for emergency. On—I was taught to remain closed unless Soul-weaving was required, and to return to Serenity once the duty was done."

His response was outraged puzzlement. "Then how do you make love?"

"It's not for that!"

The captain moved his shoulders. "Forgive me, Priscilla. It seems our training has been very different. For *this* training, however, please be assured that I can take care of myself—except against slamming doors! You are here for lessons in piloting. The next time we meet, I expect your mind to be only on piloting! If you choose to remain outside of Serenity, then don't try to damp every little twitch of irritation or jubilation. If you wish to be closed, then please make sure you are behind your Wall before you arrive."

He stood. "Today's lesson is done. I'll see you tomorrow, Priscilla."

Trealla Fantrol, Liad
Year Named Trolsh
Third *Relumma*
Cheletha Sixthday

TAAM OLANEK WAS FINDING THE WAY to truth uneasy. Even the testimony of so irreproachable a witness as Mr. dea'Gauss was insufficient to rescue him from his quandary.

In charity, Nova sat silent, though they had covered the salient points again and again. She found patience for the task by recalling the countless times Shan had befuddled her. When the charm of these palled, she could begin to list the occasions on which he had sent their father into fury with his ways.

All the world knew of the unpredictability of Thodelm yos'Galan. Recrimination was useless, of course. To remind Shan of his position as Head of Line yos'Galan was to invite a blizzard of outrageous behavior, all calculated, one would swear, to bring her to the blush.

But it never had been said that Thodelm yos'Galan was less than honorable.

Still, she thought, how much easier, in Taam Olanek's place, might it be to suppose that Shan had crossed finally into dishonor than to believe that Plemia had fired upon Korval?

"This person Mendoza," Olanek said to Mr. dea'Gauss now. "I do not properly understand, I think. Who is she, sir? What is her claim in the matter?"

872

So, they were at last beyond Shan and into deeper questions. Matters were progressing, she assured herself. Well and good.

Mr. dea'Gauss cleared his throat. "Lady Mendoza is of a high House on the world of Sintia, in the Thardom Sector. Ship's records indicate that she has been offered reasoned harm by Clan Plemia, in the person of Sav Rid Olanek. Or by those to whom he stands as lord. Verification is being sought. I am certain, however, that we will find the records from the *Dutiful Passage* accurate." He paused.

Delm Plemia inclined his head with Nova's silent approval. A lesser person would have murmured "Of course" to Mr. dea'Gauss in such a face. Plemia merely awaited further explanation.

It came. "There appear to be considerations of *melant'i* involved. Lady Mendoza is of Terran extraction; thus, it may be some while before matters become sensible. Word has been sent to House Mendoza, informing them of the situation as it was before my return to Liad. A response has not yet reached me. In the interim, Lady Mendoza is content to walk Korval's path, so I speak for her, as well."

"Her position?" Olanek pursued. "Some *melant'i* must be obvious, sir. For an instance: here it is said that she serves under personal contract. Do I learn from this that Captain yos'Galan extends the protection of Korval entire to a pleasure-love?"

A reasonable question, Nova admitted, from one unfamiliar with Shan's habit of rescuing every lame puppy and kitten in the galaxy. Certainly nothing so untoward that Mr. dea'Gauss should stiffen and draw sharp breath.

"At the time of my departure," he informed Plemia in accents of ice, "Lady Mendoza served the *Dutiful Passage* in the capacities of apprenticed second mate and second class pilot. It was she who was the pilot of duty when the attack came against the *Passage,* and she who prevented damage and life-loss. That she honors Captain yos'Galan with her friendship is clear. Lady Faaldom enjoys like regard. The person we speak of could bestow no honorless esteem."

Great gods, what a paean! Nova very nearly stared at Korval's man of business.

Taam Olanek gestured peace, light sliding off the bright enamel work of his Clan Ring. "I meant no disrespect to the lady or to the captain, sir. In the service of clarity, the question demanded asking. You yourself mentioned complications of *melant'i*."

Mr. dea'Gauss inclined his head. "*Melant'i* enters in another guise, sir. Information from House Mendoza will no doubt make matters there obvious. Are there other questions that demand the asking? Is there a way in which I might serve you further?"

Olanek wiped his screen with a sharp wrist twist and sighed. "I believe the questions remaining are those best asked of my kin. *Eldema*, I will go to *Daxflan* and ascertain what has, and what has not, been done. I ask, in the interest of both Korval and Plemia, that Mr. dea'Gauss be allowed to accompany me."

"I am," the old gentleman murmured, as one giving just warning, "Korval's eyes and ears."

"For that reason do I crave your company, sir. You are known as a person of long sight and careful counsel. In such a tangle as this, it is wisdom to see that Plemia will require both."

"Korval," Nova said calmly, "has no objection."

Mr. dea'Gauss caught her eye for a brief moment; almost it seemed that he smiled. He inclined his head to Olanek, gesturing his willingness to serve. "I am ready to travel at Plemia's word."

Shipyear 65
Tripday 171
Third Shift
14.00 Hours

PRISCILLA CAME TO HIM WITH PILOT GRACE, one slim hand extended, a smile of dawning delight upon her face. Scarcely breathing, he waited, dizzy and joy-filled. She had erected no Wall, shut no door—and this her choice, freely made! He turned his face into the caress, eyelashes kissing her palm even as he moved outside his own defenses.

There was an intake of breath, expelled on soft laughter. "Shan. . . ." Her hand slid along the other cheek, cupping his face for enrapt inspection. The feeling sang between them, soaring unbearably. He felt his heart pounding and knew that hers kept pace.

She kissed him.

For a frenzied heartbeat he simply stood there, prisoned in reflected rapture, then he felt her question and turned his mouth more sharply; he stroking her body closer to his as their shared songs twisted each about the other, creating one.

An alarm began to scream.

She started—and was gone, even as he tried to hold her. "Priscilla!"

His own cry woke him, though the alarm's din was louder. Snapping around in the tumbled bed, he slammed a violent palm against the shutoff and collapsed, eyes screwed tight against the rising lights. "Damn, damn, damn, *damn!*"

The music came up: Artelma's "Festival Delights," rendered with passion on the omnichora, by his brother Val Con.

"Damn," Shan said once more, and headed for the 'fresher.

SOME TIME LATER he passed through the dining hall on his way back from the cargo master's office. Ken Rik had been a bit less testy this morning. Perhaps he was getting over his pet at Mr. dea'Gauss's abrupt summons back to Liad.

Priscilla and Rusty were sitting with their heads together at a corner table. Belly tight with jealousy, he helped himself to a cup of coffee and a ripe strafle melon.

Healer! he jeered at himself. You can't even control your own emotions. And what does she project that you dare be jealous? Friendship? Those small bursts of appreciation, of comfort perceived, of desire . . . He drew a hard breath and bit into the fruit with a snap. Those are the sorts of things one might feel about anyone. Do strive for some conduct, Shan.

"How do, Cap'n!" BillyJo greeted him from the door of the galley. "You'll be havin' a real breakfast, won't you? Can't live 'til luncheon on an apple."

He grinned at her, talked a few moments about kitchen operations, accepted the sweet roll she pressed upon him, and refilled his cup. He left the dining hall by the side door, resolutely keeping his eyes away from the private corner.

The message-waiting light was blinking on the captain's screen. He put the sweet roll on the edge of the bar and hit GO as he slid into the chair

No more pin-beams from his sister, he noted. That was one fear laid to rest. He sipped coffee and scanned the directory. Nothing urgent. Well, tag the letter from Dortha Cayle. Maybe this time they had a deal. What was this?

A pin-beam from Sintia, directed to Mr. dea'Gauss?

He queried the item, frowning, found it was in reply to a message sent, and called it up, his memory stirring. Priscilla was from a powerful family, wasn't that it? Mr. dea'Gauss had wished to apprise them of circumstances.

TO DEA'GAUSS CARE OF TRADE VESSEL DUTIFUL PASSAGE. FROM HOUSE MENDOZA CIRCLE RIVER SINTIA. RE QUERY PRISCILLA DELACROIX Y MENDOZA. DAUGHTER OF HOUSE BEARING THAT NAME BORN (LOCAL) YEAR 986, COMMENDED TO GODDESS (LOCAL) YEAR 1002. MESSAGE ENDS.

He stared at the screen. "Commended to the Goddess"? *Dead?* His heart stuttered as he thought of Priscilla dead, then he shook his head sharply.

"Don't be stupid, Shan."

He cleared the screen and demanded Priscilla's filed identifications as well as those requested from Terran census as a matter of mindless form.

The figures appeared side by side on the screen: retinal pattern, fingerprints, blood type, gene map.

The woman who called herself Priscilla Delacroix y Mendoza *was* Priscilla Delacroix y Mendoza, to a factor of .999.

A Mendoza of Sintia. . . . He remembered the clammy wave of desperation, Priscilla's colorless face, her hand, warding him away: "You mustn't ask. . . ."

But Mr. dea'Gauss had asked, damn him, and the answer returned was worse than none at all.

He had an impulse to destroy the message. But he knew that was childish—and useless. If a reply did not arrive within a reasonable time, Mr. dea'Gauss would merely query again.

Well, she was rather active for a corpse. He sipped coffee, staring at nothing in particular. Save the captain. Save the ship. . . .

"What in space can she have done?"

He sighed and finished his coffee.

The easiest—simplest—explanation was that she had run away. It was not hard to see how Priscilla might have become disillusioned in a rigid societal structure, with all power belonging to the priestesshood.

So, then. The young Priscilla departs; her family declares her dead, for honor's sake. What choice, after all, would they have? The local records reflect the "fact."

But Terran census, above mere local politics, still carries one Priscilla Delacroix y Mendoza alive, alive—oh.

Simple. Comforting. Even logical. Except something was missing.

"She could be a criminal," he told the room loudly. "I don't believe it. Lina wouldn't believe it. Mr. dea'Gauss, with no hint of empathy about him, wouldn't believe it. Ah, *hell. . . .*"

Local crimes were varied and interesting, as any space traveler could attest. A felony on one planet was conduct that on the next would not cause even the mildest of middle-class grandmothers to blanch.

Ostracism. A crime earning that punishment would have to be extreme.

From world to world there was some variation in the most heinous crimes. Not much.

Kin slaying. Rape. Child stealing. Murder. Mind tampering. Enslavement. Blasphemy.

Murder? She had certainly been ready to wreak mayhem upon Sav Rid Olanek. He retained a vivid memory of that initial interview, with its racket of fury, terror, and exhaustion. Murder was possible.

Kin slaying?

Child stealing?

Mind tampering? Enslavement? She was an empath—and a powerful one. Those crimes, too, were possible.

Blasphemy?

He sighed. Wonderful word, blasphemy. It might mean anything.

An exact definition of her crimes was required—for the ship, and for the clan. Korval owed her much. It was vital that the person to whom the clan was in debt be known—in fullness. Priscilla Mendoza had demonstrated aboard the *Dutiful Passage* a *melant'i* both graceful and strong. She had not, however, come into existence two months ago, much as he might wish it. The captain of the *Passage* could order the necessary actions, or Mr. dea'Gauss could order them, for the good of Korval. In either case, Shan yos'Galan's wishes and desires meant nothing. Necessity existed.

Hating necessity, he tapped in a new sequence and turned to issue instructions to the tower.

Shipyear 65
Tripday 171
Fourth Shift
16.00 Hours

"PRISCILLA?" Gordy interrupted apologetically. "Morning, Rusty. Priscilla, I was thinking. Could you teach me to be a dragon?"

Rusty glowered; she caught the flicker of his irritation and let it pass.

"Dragons are possible," she admitted, considering the radiance of the boy's anticipation, "but very difficult. Some people work for years and never achieve the Dragon. It requires study and discipline." And the soul of a saint? Lina had been at pains these last busy weeks to demonstrate how empaths conducted themselves in the wide universe. *Melant'i* figured prominently in these lessons. Souls did not.

At her elbow, Gordy sighed. "But *you* know how, don't you?"

Did she? The Dragon was a spell of the Inmost Circle—but Moonhawk's soul was an old one. She had known the way. . . .

Before her mind's eye the pattern rolled forth; the Inner Ear caught the first rasp of leather wings against the air. She took a breath and reversed the pattern.

"Yes," she said, around her own wonder, "I know how. If you truly want to learn, I can begin to teach you. But there's a lot of study between the Tree and the Dragon, Gordy, and no guarantee that you'll be able to master it."

"Could Rusty be a dragon?" Gordy asked, trying perhaps to establish a range.

"I don't *want* to be a dragon," that person announced with spirit. "I like being a radio tech just fine. Don't you have someplace you need to be, kid?"

"Not right now. I've gotta help Ken Rik in twenty minutes. Priscilla, how come not everybody can learn this dragon thing? The Tree's easy."

"So it is." The Tree, the Room Serenity—anyone might learn these. The larger magics? Lina claimed no soul but her own. "The Tree is a very simple spell, Gordy. Only a good thing. The Dragon is both—a weapon and a shield. It's not to be used lightly. You could live a whole life without knowing need great enough to call the Dragon."

He frowned. "You mean the dragon is a good thing *and* a bad thing? That's as goofy as Pallin's river."

"Paradox is powerful magic. The River of Strength is a basic paradox. The Dragon is immensely complex, Gordy. You must learn to balance the good against the evil, the strength that preserves against the fire that consumes. You must be careful that the fire does not consume your will, or sheer strength override your . . . heart. You must not—soar—too close to the sun."

Rusty's uneasiness pierced the wordnet. She pushed away from the table and smiled at them both. "Or be late for your piloting lesson with the captain. Talk with me more later, Gordy. If you're still interested. Rusty, thank you, my friend. I won't see you at prime, I'm afraid. My schedule's blocked out for the next two shifts."

He whistled. "That's some piloting lesson."

"No time with Kayzin Ne'Zame today." She grinned. "A vacation."

Rusty's laughter escorted her to the door.

SHE REACHED THE SHUTTLEBAY before him. Just.

"Good morning, Priscilla! On time, as usual."

"Good morning, Captain."

He stopped in his tracks, swept a bow that the carryall slung over his shoulder should have made impossible. "Second Mate. Good things find you this day. I perceive that I am in disgrace."

"As if it would matter to you if you were!" she retorted, receiving the first rays of his pattern with something akin to thirst. Two weeks ago she would have wondered at such temerity. It was incredible how quickly she had come to depend on a sense that could not be hers.

"It would matter a great deal," he said, waving her into the bay before him. "Nice day for a shuttle trip, don't you think?"

It was at least reasonable. The *Passage* was currently in normal space, ponderously approaching Dayan in the Irrobi System.

"If, in the judgment of the master pilot, one requires more board-time in shuttle," she said.

"High in the boughs today, aren't you? Practice makes perfect, as Uncle Dick is wont to say. Roll in, Priscilla. Won't do to be late."

He dropped the carryall by the copilot's chair and slid in, his eyes on the board as he adjusted the webbing. Priscilla strapped herself into the pilot's seat, feeling his excitement as if it were her own: sheer schoolboy glee at finagling a day without tutors or overseers, the thrill of some further anticipation riding above his usual pervasive delight. And a glimmer of something else, which she had first taken for his well-leashed nervous energy but now perceived as an edge, almost like worry.

"Board to me, please," he murmured, hands busy over the keys.

Obedient, she shunted control of the ship to the copilot's board and leaned back, watching.

Lights glowed and darkened; chimes, beeps, and buzzes sounded as he ran the checks with a rapidity that would have dizzied any but another pilot. Air was evacuated from the bay; the hatch in the *Passage's* outer hull slid down, and they were tumbling away. Shan laughed softly, executed a swift series of maneuvers, cleared screens and instruments with the same flourish, and reassigned the board to her.

"Screen, please."

She provided it, wary now that it was too late.

The *Dutiful Passage* was ridiculously far away, big as a moon in the bottom left grid. Irrobi's four little worlds hung placidly beneath her.

Shan pointed at the second planet. "I want to be there, please. In—" He paused for a swift silver glance at the boardclock. "—eight hours, I wish to be docking at Swunaket Port. See to it." He spun the chair, snapped the webbing back, and reached for the carryall. At his touch it became a portable screen and desk. Radiating unconcern, he began to work.

Priscilla clamped her jaw on a caustic remark and began the dreary task of determining where exactly they were in relation to where the captain wished them to be.

Dayan
First Sunrise

"**SWUNAKET PORT, CAPTAIN.** The pilot regrets that we have landed five Standard Minutes beforetime."

He looked up, blinking absently. Since his pattern for the past two hours had been the steady buzz of concentration—as perhaps when one played chess—this ploy failed to deceive her.

"Still steamed, Priscilla?" The absent look faded into a grin.

She willed her lips into a straight line. "It was a *rotten* trick."

"I remember thinking so when my father pulled it on me," he said sympathetically. "Other things, too. Most of them sadly unfilial. You did quite well, by the way, especially when we hit that bit of turbulence—all the lovely hailstones! Really, the local weather has cooperated beautifully!"

The laughter caught her unaware, filling her belly and chest, heart and head, and, finally, the cabin. "You are a dreadful person!"

Shan sighed and began to reassemble the portable desk. "My brother's aunt, my eldest sister—now you. I bow to accumulated wisdom, Priscilla."

"I should think so!" The webbing snapped back into its roller as she stood. "The pilot awaits the captain's further orders."

He set the box aside and stood, stretching with evident enjoyment. "The captain does not require the pilot's services at present, thank you. He does, however, desire the second mate to accompany him to a certain place in the town where business is to be conducted."

She regarded him suspiciously. "What sort of business?"

"Come, come, Priscilla, I'm a Trader. I have to trade *some*time, don't I? To preserve the illusion, if nothing else."

He bowed slightly, ironically. "And I have need of your—countenance—here. I will be walking a proper distance behind you. The address we go to is in Tralutha Siamn. The name of the firm is Fasholt and Daughters." He waved a big hand, ring glinting. "Lead on!"

SHE STOPPED IN THE SHADOW of the gate, Shan close behind her, and stared into the street.

Bathed in the butter-yellow light of the smaller sun, women hurried or strolled, singly or in pairs. Behind each, at a respectful three-pace distance, came a man or boy, sometimes two. One elderly woman strolled by on the arm of a younger one, both expensively jeweled and dressed, followed by a train of six boys, each heartbreakingly lovely in sober tunic and slacks.

Priscilla frowned after them. The boys radiated a uniform contentment. Playthings, she thought. Well cared for—perhaps even beloved—pets.

"Well, Priscilla?" His voice was very quiet, with mischief and something more sober spilling from him.

She turned her head to glare. "Am I suppose to own you?"

He nodded. "But don't repine." He felt the fabric of his wide sleeve between two judgmental fingers, tapped the master's ring and the intricate silver belt buckle, and stroked light fingers down a soft-clad thigh. "You obviously pamper me."

She flushed. "I can't think why."

"Unkind, Priscilla. I'm counted not unskilled. Also, I'm a pilot, a mechanic, a good judge of wines, fabrics, spices—"

"And an incurable gabster!" she finished with half-amused vehemence. "If you were mine, I'd have you beaten!"

The slanted brows lifted. "Violence? You might damage the goods, exalted lady. Best to attempt to barter for one less noisy if this one's voice displeases you."

"Don't," she begged him, "tempt me." Back stiff, she turned and marched off.

Head down to hide his grin, Shan followed.

LOMAR FASHOLT WAS ROUND-FACED and rumpled; her tunic was a particularly pleasing shade of pink. She smiled widely and dismissed her daughter with a nod as Priscilla entered her office.

"A good day to you, Sister Mendoza," Lomar said heartily, coming around the gleaming thurlwood desk and extending a fragrant hand. Priscilla took it and grinned with relief.

"A good day to you, also, sister."

Lomar laughed gently, her eyes going over Priscilla's shoulder. "Shannie! What a sight for old eyes you are! Have you decided to marry me, after all? Your room stands ready."

He laughed and came forward to bow: the bow of honored-esteem, Priscilla saw. "It's good to see you, Lomar," he said gently. "How many husbands do you have now?"

"Eight—can you believe it? But it's no use, Shannie, I can't *not* make money! And the more I make, the more husbands they insist I take." She shook her head. "The newest is only a cub, the same age as my youngest daughter! What do they—" Her hands fluttered. "Oh, well, I've set him to be schooled, poor lamb. Though it's hard to find tutors who don't feel it below their dignity to teach a boy. But here I'm rambling on, and you both standing! Come, sit down."

"I don't think I'd do well, do you," Shan pursued, "as the ninth? There are certain freedoms I'm accustomed to." He grinned and slouched into a chair, legs thrust out before him. "Besides, I have a minor skill at making money, too. How many husbands can you support?"

"Oh, a few more, certainly. Though not as many as they'll insist upon. If I were twenty years younger, I'd leave this silly planet and set up somewhere else. I don't know why my daughters stay—true speech!" She sat, embracing them with her smile. "Well, I thought you'd say no, my dear, but one can hope. You'd certainly keep me laughing. Why are you here, Shannie?"

Priscilla caught the flicker of his puzzlement before he replied.

"I'm here because I have items to trade. Korval has traded with Fasholt these last two generations."

"And will do so no more. I'd hoped my message was clear." The round face turned sad. "It's true, isn't it, Shannie, that your family— your Clan—is headed by a man?"

He frowned and straightened a little in the chair. "Val Con is Heir Lineal, surely—Delm-to-be. But the yos'Pheliums aren't traders, Lamar; the yos'Galans are. Two different lines."

She considered that for a moment, then: "Who is the mother of your—Line—then, Shannie? No, that's wrong, isn't it? I don't know the right word."

"Thodelm," he supplied, his puzzlement increasing. "I am. Lamar, what is this? Have we slighted you in some way? Have you complaint of our policy, our price? Surely it can be mended. We've dealt together so long."

"Do you think I don't know it? Long, mutually profitable, and always such pleasant visits! Your father, always willing to sit, take a glass or two, and tell me about goings-on in the wide galaxy. You the same as he . . . ." She smiled wistfully. "Things would have been better, Shannie, if you had been a girl."

Shan was sitting very tall, intent on the woman's face. "Lomar, I'm at a loss. I've been male all my life, and my father before me! The trade has always gone well."

"Didn't I say so?" She sighed, radiating grief and affection. "It's a new law, Shannie. From the temple. The thrice-blessed have instructed us to have no trade with any families but those who are properly headed by a female. To trade with no ship, except when captain and Trader are women." She fidgeted with an oddment of stone on her desk, then looked up sharply. "It's *law*, Shannie."

"Lomar." Shan was speaking very carefully. "The contract between Clan Korval and the Fasholt family dates back to our grandmothers. It reads—if memory will serve me today—yes: 'Between Petrella yos'Galan, or assignees, and Tuleth Fasholt, or assignees.'" He moved his shoulders—not quite a shrug—and smiled. "Assignees, both."

"I know," she said, shaking her head. "It seems to hold some hope, doesn't it? I put the case forth, adding that it is the custom among outworlders to consider women and men equal." She grimaced. "The thrice-blessed were quite clear: trade is permitted only with those families or ships which are now headed by women. Because outworlders follow unnatural custom is no reason for us to do the same."

"After all," Shan said softly, "the Goddess made us all in Her image."

"Don't blaspheme, Shannie."

Priscilla stirred. "That is what we are taught—on Sintia."

The older woman smiled sadly. "This is not Sintia, sister. Here we follow the temple's instructions. Or find ourselves broken into bits and scattered, mother from daughter, and sister from sister, across the world."

Priscilla raised her hand and traced the Sign to Forefend in the air between them. Lomar nodded.

"So, I hope, as well. But it seems that my wishes are not to be fulfilled in this lifetime. Perhaps the next turn of the Wheel will find me in a happier time."

"So might it be," Priscilla murmured and Lomar bowed her head.

Shan cleared his throat. "Is it permitted by the—thrice-blessed?—that I speak to you of an item which belongs to a member of my crew? Lady Faaldom, who is Head of her Line—and female! Priscilla will attest my word. Or shall we go away?"

She considered him. "Is this item truly the possession of Lady Faaldom, Shannie? Why didn't she come to me herself?"

He looked, Priscilla thought, a little hurt. "Of course it's Lina's cargo. I said so, didn't I? As to why she didn't come herself, why should she? I'm Master Trader, she's librarian. It's reasonable that I speak for her in the matter."

Lomar shook her head. "If she's sworn to you, Head of her Family or not—I'm sorry, Shannie. The law is the law. I don't dare."

With a flash of vivid concern, Shan leaned forward abruptly, extending a hand across the desk. "Lomar, come away!"

She reached out and patted his hand. "There, now, dear . . . What a good boy you are, Shannie! But it will be all right."

"It will not be all right!" he snapped. "You know and I know that it will become less and less right. Cut off trade with half the galaxy? It's insanity—worse! Suicidal. You'll starve. If the luck rides your shoulder. If not—a society that enslaves half its population? Lomar, what happens when the slaves see the masters are weak?"

"Revolution," Priscilla said in a low voice, feeling prophecy stir within her. "War. Hatred. Death."

"I have read history, sister." Lomar sighed and stroked Shan's hand again. "Should I go without a bit to buy a guidebook, Shannie? My assets must be liquidated. That takes time, careful planning. And my daughters. It's not possible. Not now." She sat back. Priscilla thought she looked older all at once.

Shan sat poised, tension singing through him. Then he, too, sat back, sighing. "Of course. You'll do as you think wise. Do you have my pin-beam code, Lomar?"

She laughed a little. "Your personal code and the code for the *Dutiful Passage*. Why?"

"A favor, for the friendship we hold each other. When you're ready, call me. Transport will be provided. Also, I'll engage to be second partner in any business you care to establish."

She laughed. "Absurd creature! Why, again?"

Shan did not even smile. "Your credit is here. To set up elsewhere, you'll need local credit. With me as your second partner, there will be no problem." He did smile then, tiredly. "You do make money, Lomar. I know it. Why shouldn't I lend you aid in return for a profit I don't have to work for?"

She shook her head. "But you're local on Liad, Shannie. I don't—"

"Korval's credit," he interrupted gently, "is local everywhere. Except, perhaps, here."

There was a brief pause before she spread her hands. "A silent partner, then. For; say, five years? Ten, it had better be. Then I'll buy you out."

He nodded. "Easily arranged. But a mere business matter. The important thing is that you move you and yours as soon as may be—forgive my presumption, old friend. Line yos'Galan will be happy—joyful—to guest you for a time, so you may look about and make informed decisions."

"You're a good boy, Shannie," she said again. "I'll remember. Now, my dear, I'm afraid I'm going to have to bid you both good-bye."

"Have we endangered you, sister?" Priscilla asked as they moved toward the door.

Lomar smiled and patted her hand, too. "Bless you, child, things aren't that bad yet. But it's best not to push what Shannie calls 'the luck.' Walk in Her smile, now, both of you."

PRISCILLA SET A RAPID PACE through the morning streets, with Shan's uneasiness feeding her own. She felt the chill of worry at her back, eclipsing his warmth.

Mother, grant us safety, she prayed.

The port gate loomed, and she increased her stride, breathing a sigh of relief as she crossed into the outworlder's preserve. At her back, Shan's worry diminished somewhat.

Thank you, Goddess, she breathed silently. Then she sensed startlement—and outrage like a zag of lightning.

She spun in time to see the white-robed woman shake Shan sharply.

"Creature! How dare you pass by without obeisance?" Her staff snapped toward his head, calculated to cow, not to strike. Shan's fury flared, and the woman shook him again. "What are you called, soulless?"

"Frost, exalted lady." The quiet voice was in sharp contrast to the din of his rage.

"Frost, is it? Exalted lady, is it? Have you no manners, creature, or are you too stupid to know one of the temple when you see her?"

Priscilla felt a surge of bruising power. *Aspect!* She extended herself, deflected the other woman's intention, and felt her own expansion. . . .

"Enough!" she snapped.

Both spun, staring.

"Frost," she snapped. "An apology to the thrice-blessed. And then behind me!"

For a heartbeat she thought he would not play along. Then, stiffly, he bent, forehead brushing knees.

"Forgive this one, thrice-blessed. No insult was intended your holy self."

It was scarcely the most abject of abasements, with the highborn fury crackling from him like electricity. Nor was the thrice-blessed appeased. Her staff whipped out, slashing the air between him and escape.

"Forgiven, indeed. After punishments, as it is written. A public scourging—"

"I had said enough!" Priscilla cried, projecting stern authority, soul-strength, and awe. "Would you mete violence to this person, with the Mother's own mark upon him?" She extended a hand and traced the sign, glowing, before Shan's face for the other to read.

"This man is more than you can know. He has power, as a temple-sister might have it! Depth of learning, skill of use—a mystery. And more!"

The priestess was fairly caught—the wordnet enveloped her, glittering. Priscilla pulled strongly on awe, mystery, belief, and began to weave—then became aware of something else: a single, sustained note, building passion and power, swelling, scintillating, magnificent—a lance of greatness overwhelming in its majesty.

It was Shan, projecting on all levels.

Within the wordnet, the thrice-blessed gasped; she raised a hand to shield her eyes from his radiance.

The note built further as Priscilla made adjustments. He must be caught, held in the echo of the thrice-born's trap . . .

The note paused, then glissaded, power fading with each downward thrum, until the last hung, vibrating rainbows . . . and was gone.

The thrice-blessed hung in her net of glamour, reverberating mystery. The man was merely a man, radiating nothing.

"So have you seen," Priscilla intoned, loosing the net carefully.

"So have you heard. So shall it be. We live in blessed times, young sister, when mysteries and miracles abound. Look closely at all you see and trust that the Goddess holds each of us protected."

"Ollee," the priestess murmured. "I am blessed beyond counting, having beheld this wonder. Elder sister, I ask pardon. And your blessing."

Priscilla's hand rose and traced the proper signs at eyes, ears, and heart. "In Her name, forgiveness, as She forgives each of Her children. Walk in Her grace. Live well. Serve long."

The other effaced herself, and Priscilla turned, motioning to Shan. Unhurriedly, and without looking behind, they walked away.

SHAN COLLAPSED INTO THE COPILOT'S CHAIR, his head thumping into the headrest. He opened one silver eye. "I would appreciate warning, please, Priscilla, the next time you feel the need of such support." His voice held a thread of amusement, another of exhaustion. His pattern . . . his pattern—was gone.

No! She sat, graceless, and reached along the inner ways, seeking his warmth as a blind person would seek the sun's touch upon her face. The questing encountered smoothness, cool and slippery, like a mirror, denying without repelling. And he must be beyond it. . . .

"Priscilla?"

She brought her attention to the outer ways, striving for calm. "I didn't think to ask. I thought—I was afraid you'd been caught in the echo."

He snorted. "I haven't been caught in an echo since I was twelve years old, Priscilla. Give me credit for some ability."

"Yes, of course . . . ." But this was a nightmare, with him before her and she unable to hear, unable to *know* . . . "Shan—"

He leaned forward and extended a hand, the master's ring flashing its facets. "I'm here, my friend."

There was concern in his voice and on his face, while within there was only the horrible, unyielding coolness. She gripped his fingers, feeling that warmth. It was not enough. "Shan. . . ."

"I'm tired, Priscilla," he said gently. "It's been a long time since

I've needed to travel outward along all roads. Grant me rest." He considered her face, squeezed her hand. "I'm in your debt again."

"Please," she began, and drew a breath. She found a phrase in High Liaden. "Pray do not regard it."

He sat back, his fingers slipping out of hers. "Kayzin is a thorough teacher, I see." A quick glance at the board took in the white proximity light. "The *Passage* is in orbit. Wonderful. Let's go home."

Home. Even with him locked behind his private mirror she felt a sense of relief, and heard the sound of need.

"Yes, Shan," she said, and then, in urgent correction, "Yes, Captain."

Shipyear 65
Tripday 177
Second Shift
9.00 Hours

KEN RIK STARED IN DISBELIEF. "Prepare Hold Thirty-two to receive cargo?" he asked finally.

Shan raised his eyebrows and looked down his nose for good measure. "You're up to the task, aren't you, Ken Rik? Or is Hold Thirty-two already full?"

"No, it's not full," the old man snapped. "As you well know. You're not taking on that—ah, damn this language!—that *lanza pel'shek! His* cargo!"

"I'm not? Well, I'm pleased to know that, Master Ken Rik, thank you. But, do you know, I had the impression that I *was* going to take it." He paused, then delivered the punch line gently. "I had the further impression that the cargo master takes orders from the captain."

Ken Rik had tears in his eyes. "Shan—he tried to kill the *Passage.*" He spoke in the High Tongue now: elder to youngling of a different Clan. "Now you take up his cargo, guarantee delivery! Your father—"

"Would have done exactly the same!" Shan finished in ice-coated Terran. "This is outside of Balance. The goods are needed—required—on Theopholis. The port master appealed to us because of need. We guarantee delivery—because of need. We're going to

Theopholis, aren't we, Ken Rik? Have some sense, for pity's sake! A pretty set of sharks we'd look when it came known that the *Passage* was petitioned at Raggtown and refused to take the load."

"Yes, of course." The words were nearly whispered, but they were in Terran. He bowed the bow of one instructed to instructor. "Forgive—"

"Oh, bother, you annoying old man! You've been ripping up at me for years! Don't, I beg you, begin to act properly now!"

Ken Rik laughed. "It would be something of a strain, I admit." He made a second bow, as subordinate to superior. "With the captain's permission, I will now go to prepare Hold Thirty-two for cargo."

"Thank you, Ken Rik," Shan said gently. "I'd appreciate it."

Master's Tower, Theopholis
Hour Of Kings

PORT MASTER ROMINKOFF eyed the elderly gentlemen. That they stood there at all spoke of resourcefulness as well as resources. The amount of cumshaw required to pass two persons up the ladder of subordinates and into her presence was no doubt large. She made a mental note to find out the current rate. One liked to know the value of one's services.

The younger of her two visitors bowed, not deeply. "I," he said in careful Trade, "am Taam Olanek, Delm Plemia. My clan possesses a tradeship, called *Daxflan,* which was to have been in port at this present. I find it has not arrived."

The port master sat up. Perhaps the old gentlemen had not paid so much, after all. "I am in agreement with you, sir," she said urbanely. "*Daxflan* has not arrived."

"I had hoped," Taam Olanek, Delm Plemia, pursued, "that you might teach me what you know of circumstances. I have learned from other persons here that berthing space was reserved—that it was not canceled. That there are goods awaiting?"

"And goods awaited," she finished, shedding a little of her urbanity. "Just so. You seem to know all I can teach you of the situation, sir. *Daxflan* is late by some four local days. Reassure yourselves that nothing ill has overcome it, however. I have had reports of her within the sector, doing business at certain—ahh, *free-duty* ports. It appears previous commitments have not been recalled."

She steepled her fingers in front of her. "This is unfortunate. It is, of course, unfortunate for you, but it is even more so for Theopholis. Among the things *Daxflan* was to deliver are two shipments from Raggtown, consisting of medical supplies imperative to the conclusion of our vaccination program, and the jewelry the regent will wear at his coronation next week. Our last information from Raggtown is that those shipments are still in the warehouses, awaiting pickup."

There was a moment's silence, during which the port master wondered if her explanation had been too rapid for the old gentleman to follow.

He bowed. "The situation is very serious. Plemia has guaranteed delivery. There will be delivery. If you would allow me use of your facilities, I will make arrangements to employ a subcontractor for the delivery of the goods from Raggtown."

Well, now. *Here* was something. The port master inclined her head. "I will have you escorted to the beam room, sir. One moment." Her hand approached the keypad, but hesitated as the door to her right clicked open, admitting a breathless adjunct.

"Port Master," he began. The belated sight of the two gentlemen gave him abrupt pause.

Master Rominkoff raised her brows. "Continue."

"Yes, Port Master. We have had a pin-beam from the tradeship *Dutiful Passage*. It tells us they carry the shipments from Raggtown." The adjunct took a deep breath and finished his message. "Anticipated docking time is within the next local day."

"So, then." She smiled at her visitors. "It seems the problem is solved for us, sirs."

But Taam Olanek did not seem appreciative of his good fortune. He rounded on the adjunct, his face set in anger. "How does *Dutiful Passage* carry *Daxflan's* cargo?"

The boy blinked and looked for guidance. She nodded. "The port—the port at Raggtown, gentle," he stammered. *"Dutiful Passage* was asked to transmit the goods that were urgent, that were perishable. There was room, and the—the captain did the kindness. . . ."

"Quite proper," the second gentleman murmured surprisingly,

and the first spun to stare at him. "I suggest that we await the morrow. Captain yos'Galan will certainly be happy to lay every detail before you."

There was a moment of singing tension before the first gentleman bowed to due second. "Even so," he said softly. He turned back to the port master and bowed more deeply this time. "I thank you for your kindness and ask forgiveness on behalf of my clan. Contracts must, of course, be honored. I pledge that they will be so, in the future."

The port master thought without sympathy of *Daxflan's* Trader. The wrath in the old gentleman's eyes was well earned.

"I am glad that the present crisis has been resolved in so timely a manner, of course. It will not be forgotten that your first thought was of that, sir, and of the solution." She stood and bowed to both. "It has been a pleasure speaking with you. May we meet again."

"May we meet again," the second gentleman echoed, performing his bow with precision. He offered an arm to his companion and guided him gently to the door.

The port master nodded at her adjunct. "Inform me when *Dutiful Passage* takes orbit. I think I should greet Captain yos'Galan—personally."

Raggtown
Local Year 537

THE SUM WAS ENORMOUS. standing at the Trader's shoulder, Captain yo'Vaade was hard put to maintain her countenance. The trade at Drethilit had not earned them half so much, besides having gone to the port master to pay for the unused berthing. And the goods were gone as well, so there would be that loss, and another bill was awaiting them at Theopholis.

"What do you mean," Sav Rid demanded, his voice beginning to rise in that way she dreaded, "that my cargo is not here? You give me a spurious invoice and in the same breath say that the goods are not in your warehouse? Where are they?"

The warehouseman shrugged his wide Terran shoulders. "You didn't show, the client got worried, asked somebody else to take the stuff along. Shipped out yesterday."

"By what right—*who?* What ship took my cargo? Because I say it is nothing less than theft!"

Again the man shrugged. "That's between you and your client, Mac. Tree and Dragon took the stuff. Now, about the—"

"Tree and Dragon," Sav Rid repeated blankly. Then he shouted, the Trade words nearly unintelligible. "yos'Galan! Thieves, whores, and idiots! My cargo! Mine! And you release it to yos'Galan? Fool!" He shredded the bill, flung the pieces into the man's startled face, and stormed away, looking neither to the right nor to the left. Chelsa yo'Vaade hesitated, tempted—strongly tempted—to let him go.

Then she spun back to the warehouseman, tugging the *nireline* ring from her finger and stripping the heavy chased bracelet from her arm. "They are old," she said quickly, pressing them into his hands. "It will be enough, if you sell to a collector of antiquities." She left him then, running.

Sav Rid was striding across the shuttle field, Second Mate Collier hulking at his shoulder. He had not been unguarded, then. Chelsa was aware of a certain relief as she laid a hand on his sleeve. "Sav Rid? Cousin, I beg you—let it go. It is—you have let it prey upon your mind. End now. Cry Balance."

"Balance?" He shook her off, lips tight, eyes glittering. "*Balance?* In favor of that frog-faced, half-Terran lackwit? yos'Galan is the reason we lose in every endeavor we undertake! yos'Galan steals our cargo, slurs our name, hounds us from port to port—there can be no Balance!" He held out his hand, fingers clenched tight. "I will crush them—both of them! The idiot and his whore sister!" He paused. "And the Terran bitch who puts her cheek to his!"

Chelsa's stomach clenched with fear—of him? for him?—as she cupped his shaking fist in her hands. "Sav Rid, it is *Korval!* Let be. Let it all be," she pleaded suddenly, her eyes tear-filled. "Let us go home, cousin."

"Bah!" He jerked away, his rings tearing her palms. "Korval! A pack of half-grown brats, born to wealth and ease—no more! But you are like the rest—say *Korval,* and they tremble lest they offend." He spat into the dust and marched off, the second mate keeping pace. "Coward!"

The tears spilled over. She struggled for a moment, then achieved control and started slowly after him.

Crown City, Theopholis
Hour Of Knaves

DAGMAR FINGERED THE KNIFE and gave her quarry a little lead time—but not too much. She had almost lost them, right at the beginning, when she had still figured that there was some kind of sense to their explorations, before she had understood that they were simply following the boy's whim.

She eased out of the doorway and sauntered after them, picking up speed as they turned a corner. The boy was tugging on the woman's hand—they were heading toward the port. Slowly, doubling back on their own tracks now and then, they were completing a rough circle. Dagmar lengthened her stride.

Soon. Soon Prissy would pay for setting the white-haired half-breed on *Daxflan,* eating their profits—eating *Dagmar's* profit. Dagmar's share. Yes, her share. Without her, the Trader would not have thought of shipping the stuff. She had been the one who had showed him how profitable it would be for the ship, and for his precious clan. She had been the one with the contacts at first, the one who had shown him how to play the game. So she got a piece of the action. A sweetheart bargain. What a Liaden would call Balance.

They had stopped again. Dagmar slid into an alley mouth, then edged out to watch. Prissy was laughing and pointing to something in the window of a shop six doors distant. The boy had his nose pressed against the glass.

It would be the boy. She had decided that. Satisfying as it would be to hurt Prissy, to purple that white skin, to snap fragile bones . . . Dagmar wiped wet palms down the sides of her trousers, savoring the thrust of desire that the image imparted. Maybe. . . .

No. She would take the boy. That would cause the deepest hurt—both to Prissy and to her half-breed lover.

They were moving again. Dagmar fingered the knife and let them get a little ahead.

DILLIBEE'S DIGITAL DELIGHTS, the sign read. Gordy checked and drifted closer to the glassed-in display, joy flowing out of him in a purr so strong that it was a marvel the outer ears did not hear it as well. Priscilla smiled and rested her hands lightly on his shoulders. He wriggled comfortably, his attention on the gaudy goings-on beyond the glass.

Five minutes went by without a sign that his rapture would soon pass off. Priscilla squeezed his shoulders. "Let's go, Gordy."

"Um."

She laughed softly and ruffled his hair. "Um, yourself. The shuttle leaves in exactly one ship's hour. Your credit with the captain may be up to missing it, but mine isn't. Let's go."

"Okay," he said, still gazing at the display.

Priscilla sighed and walked away by a step or two. "Gordy?"

"Yeah, okay."

Shaking her head, she went farther down the block, adjusting her awareness so that the matrix of his emotions remained clear.

A bolt of terror impaled her as his voice wrenched her about.

"Priscilla!"

Pilot-fast, she was moving back toward the woman and the struggling child. A scant two steps away, the woman twisted, her shoulder against a garland-pole, the boy held across her thigh with one hand as the other snaked to the front over his shoulder and held something that gleamed beneath the uptilted chin.

"Freeze, Prissy."

The gleam was a vibroknife, not yet live.

Priscilla froze.

"Good. That's real good, Prissy. You stay right there." Dagmar grinned. "Where's the white-haired boyfriend? Not gonna bail you out today?"

Fury and terror poured from Gordy. Priscilla shut him out. She opened a thin hallway: her heart to Dagmar's. Then she heard, tasted and saw kill-lust, fear, rage, and desire, a fragmented cacophony that held no pattern but shifted, froze, and broke apart again and again.

Dementia.

Gordy twitched in Dagmar's grip, then gasped as it tightened brutally.

"You be a good boy," she snarled, "and I'll let you live." She made a sound like a laugh. "Yeah, I'll let you live—a minute. Maybe two."

Seeking a tool, Priscilla groped within and found a rhythm; she picked it up even as she felt another stirring and saw a flicker of light and darkness, outlining the Dragon's broad head. The vast wings unfurled as she passed the spell-rhythm to her body; she swayed to the right, not quite a step.

"Stay there! You want this kid to have as many seconds as are coming to him, Prissy, you freeze and stay froze!" Dagmar grinned and moved the knife but did not thumb it on. "An' don't you look away, honey. I want you to tell the boyfriend exactly what it looked like."

"All right," Priscilla agreed, her voice pitched for magic, the words like strands of sticky silk. "I'll watch, Dagmar. Of course I will. But should I tell him everything? That might not be wise. If I tell everything, then they'll have you, Dagmar. They'll know who you are. They'll know where to find you." The faraway wings filled, then hesitated. She dared another half step, her eyes watching Dagmar's eyes as her heart watched Dagmar's heart.

"Best to let him go. Let him go, and they'll let you go. Let him go and be free. Let him go and rest. Rest and be peaceful. Free and at peace. Let him go. Walk away. No hunters. No hunted. Let him go. . . ."

Dagmar's pattern was smoothing, coming together into something reminiscent of sanity. Far off, the Dragon hesitated, wings poised for flight.

A heavy-hauler slammed by in the street beyond, shattering the circle she had woven. The knife straightened in Dagmar's hand.

"Freeze!" she hissed.

Priscilla stood calm, her eyes on her enemy, not allowing her to look away. "Dagmar," she began again, taking up the thread of the weaving.

"Boyfriend buy your stuff back, Prissy?" Dagmar across her words. "He did, didn't he? Except not earrings. Not the earrings. Nobody'll see them again. Bugged, were they? Not now. Took a hammer, pounded 'em to dust. Spaced the dust." She gave a jagged bark of laughter. "Let him try and trace that! Tryin' to follow where we're goin'. Tryin' to catch us sellin' the stuff—but he didn't! Not so smart, after all, is he?"

"It was a trick," Priscilla murmured against the sudden whirlwind of a Dragon in flight. She was cold. She was hot. She resisted, trusting yet to the power of voice and words. "Only a trick, Dagmar. He wanted to scare you, that's all. Like you've scared me. I'll tell him how it was. I'll tell him you mean business. That you wanted balance. That you have balance. The score's settled now, Dagmar. You can let the boy go. Let him go, Dagmar. A little boy. Only a boy. He can't hurt you. Let him go and walk free."

Footsteps in the street beyond cut the fragile strand. Dagmar shifted her grip on her hostage. "Little public here. Move it, boy. Nice and slow. Prissy, you stay put 'til I tell you to move."

"No!" Gordy twisted, and one hand shot out to grip the garland-pole. In her mind's eye, Priscilla clearly saw a Tree, green and vital, roots sunk through paving stone, soil and magma, to the very soul of the world. . . .

Dagmar swore and yanked at Gordy, her already mad pattern splintering into a thing hopeless of order. She yanked again, then gave it up—and thumbed the knife to life.

Priscilla heard it hum, low and evil.

And within, the sound of wings was like thunder as a hurtling body blocked out heart and sight and sense and soul, screaming like a lifetime's accumulated fury—Dragon's fire!

Master's Tower, Theopholis
Viscount's Hour

⌒⌒⌒⌒⌒⌒⌒⌒⌒⌒⌒⌒⌒⌒⌒⌒⌒⌒⌒⌒⌒⌒⌒⌒⌒⌒⌒⌒⌒⌒⌒

IT WILL BE INTERESTING TO SEE how she contrives to send Mr. dea'Gauss away without me, Shan thought, sipping wine. The port master's desire washed him with warmth, and he curled into it shamelessly. Mutual pleasure was intended, neither hinged upon old friendship nor waiting on richer desires—the very thing he needed.

Healer, he instructed himself wryly, heal yourself.

The wine was excellent.

"Confess then, Captain," the port master drawled lazily. "You're intrigued by the proposition."

That was a masterly move. They had been discussing a possible investment of her own, the talk shared evenly between himself and Mr. dea'Gauss. Shan smiled, slanting his eyes toward her face in a sweep of black lashes.

"I am always intrigued," he answered audaciously, "by a lady's proposition."

She laughed, well pleased with him. "Perhaps you and I might meet to discuss the matter more fully." She inclined her head, including the old gentleman in her smile. "Mr. dea'Gauss must accompany you, of course. I'm sure we will both require his counsel."

He raised his glass. "The trading will keep me—tomorrow, the next day. You understand, ma'am, that there are persons I must see, in the normal course of business."

905

"Of course," she said appreciatively. "Perhaps I should stop by your booth in the Grand Square in a day or so. By then you may know your commitments more fully."

"Why, that would be lovely!" he exclaimed, smiling widely. "I'd be delighted to see you there, ma'am." And so he would, though he would be more delighted to see her this night—as she yet intended.

"Then naturally I will come." She began to add something more, then checked herself as the door to her right opened, no doubt admitting the third course.

But the individual who stepped into the room bore no tray, pushed no cart, and looked not a little worried.

The port master frowned. "Yes?"

"I beg your pardon, madam," her aide said formally. "Precinct Officer Velnik calls on your private line. He assures me the matter is one of urgency."

After a moment's frowning hesitation, a hand flick directed the aide toward the wallscreen. She turned back to the table. "Do excuse the interruption, sirs. This post has many privileges. Privacy is not one of them. It will be but a moment. Please do not regard it."

"That's quite all right," Shan assured her, smiling sympathetically. Mr. dea'Gauss inclined his head.

The precinct officer looked nervous. As well he might, Shan thought. The port master's displeasure was plain on her face.

"Well?"

The officer swallowed. "I'm sorry to disturb you, Thra Rominkoff," he said breathlessly. "It seems routine on the surface. But the boy insisted we call. Says he's the ward of a—Captain yos'Galan?"

Shan stiffened, all attention on the screen.

The port master nodded sharply. "He is here. Is the boy injured?"

Relief flooded Velnik's face. "No, Thra Rominkoff, he's just fine. But we've got a dead Terran female—"

No! And then he was expanding in all directions, an explosion of seek-strands, streaking past the port master's pattern, and Mr. dea'Gauss, and the liveried servant here, and those in the kitchen beyond, stretching, stretching as no Healer could, trying to read the city beyond the walls, searching for one signature, one life— *Priscilla!*

In his far-off body something snapped, followed by pain and more pain as the search slammed hard against its limits, rebounded . . .

He dropped the shattered stem next to the sharded crystal bowl in its puddle of bright wine and blood, and wrapped a napkin around his hand as the port master spun back to the screen, snapping her fingers.

"Quickly! Who has died?"

"Dagmar Collier, Port Master." The man was stumbling over his own words, his eyes flicking from Shan to the woman and back. "Native of Troit. Second Mate on *Daxflan,* out of Chonselta."

Which should not be here! Shan swallowed his curse and saw the thought reflected in the port master's face.

"Bring the boy here," she instructed the precinct officer.

He shook his head. "We have the woman who killed Collier, Thra Rominkoff. She confesses. But murder requires a formal trial, since rehabilitation is the fee—"

"No!" That was out before he could stop it.

The port master slanted a quick glance at Shan's face and returned her attention to the screen. "The woman who confesses is a friend of the boy's? He refuses to come away without her?"

"Yes, Thra Rominkoff."

"Port Master." Somehow he had control of his voice against the tearing pains in hand and head and the terror in his heart. "The person in question is a member of my crew. Am I not allowed to speak for her?" Rehabilitation. Gods, rehabilitation *here.* "It is possible that she does not understand. She is not native here. And perhaps not all of the—circumstances—have been made clear to the precinct officer."

She nodded. "It is, of course, your right to speak for your crew member, Captain." Her eyes were back on the officer. "We shall arrive within the hour. So inform the captain's ward. And arrange for the guard to pass us without delay."

"Port Master." He gave a formal salute, and the screen went dark. The port master rose.

"A medkit," she snapped at the frozen aide. The woman scurried off, returning in a bare moment. Mr. dea'Gauss took it from her and himself applied the lotion, sealed the sharp edge of the cut, and wrapped it in soft cloth, radiating concern.

The old gentleman's pattern set Shan's teeth on edge with anguish: the complex spill of rage, puzzlement, and—admiration?— from the port master nearly had him in tears. Painfully, he began the sequence to seal himself away, to leach the worst of the pain from the rebound shock so that he might unseal himself in an hour, perhaps even to some purpose.

"My car awaits, sirs," the port master said, concern her face.

"You are all kindness, ma'am." He managed the formula, stood, and made his bow.

"Nonsense!" she snapped. "It is my duty to monitor what goes on in this port, Captain. That includes seeing justice done." She indicated the patient aide. "Melecca will see you to the car. I will join you very shortly. There is an urgent matter I must attend to." She was gone in a swirl of bright fabric.

"*Daxflan's* in port," Shan murmured to Mr. dea'Gauss as they followed Melecca to the car. "That's interesting, isn't it?"

"Very," the old gentleman agreed. He sighed.

Precinct House
Crown City, Theopholis
Hour Of Demons

෨෨෨෨෨෨෨෨෨෨෨෨෨෨෨෨෨෨෨෨෨෨෨෨෨෨

THERE WERE FAR TOO MANY PEOPLE in the room. Port Master Rominkoff paused to sort out the crowd. The young captain never broke his stride.

"Shan!"

The boy was smallish and pudgy, running pell-mell toward them. The young captain went down on one knee, caught the child as he skidded to a halt, and returned a hug just this side of savage.

"Gordy." He set the boy back, ran his hands rapidly over the plump frame, and touched a smooth cheek. "You're all right, *acushla*?"

"Crelm!" the boy snorted. "*I'm* okay." The round face clouded. "Shan—they wouldn't listen! I told them—I did! They wouldn't fix her arm and—"

"Hush." He stroked the boy's cheek again, then laid a gentle finger over his lips. "Gordy. Just relax for a moment, okay?" The small body lost some of its tension, as if those words were all it took. "Good. Where's Priscilla now?"

Tears filled the brown eyes. "I tried to make them not—" He took a ragged breath. "They put her in a cage."

"Here now, young man!" the precinct officer said, approaching warily, his eyes flicking from the port master's face to the man and boy, then back to her face. "Not a *cage!* Just a holding cell, I promise!"

The captain rose smoothly and inclined his head. "A holding cell," he repeated softly. The precinct officer ran his tongue over his lips. The port master forbade herself the smile.

"I am captain of the *Dutiful Passage,*" Shan continued clearly. "Ms. Mendoza is a member of my crew. I am here to speak on her behalf, as set in the trade compacts. You will liberate her from the—holding cell—and guide her here so that all may be done . . . lawfully."

The port master denied the smile more sternly. Really, the young captain pleased her more and more.

The precinct officer was shaking his head. "I'm afraid I can't do that, Captain. She's a confessed murderer. We asked her twice, according to law. She understood the questions and answered them. Twice. She talked crazy about other stuff, but not about that. The law says in those circumstances, we hold the prisoner for a next-day trial. It's most likely the judge will rule rehabilitation in light of the confession, and lacking witnesses—"

"What do you mean, lacking witnesses?" the captain demanded. "The child says he told you what happened—and that you refused to listen!"

Officer Velnik held up a hand. "Not admissible, Captain. He's underage."

"On his home-world," came a dry voice from the port master's side, "Master Arbuthnot is of an age where his testimony is considered admissible."

"I'm sure it is, Mr.—ah?"

"dea'Gauss," the old man supplied, going forward. "I am the man of business for Clan Korval, of which Captain yos'Galan and, by wardship, Master Arbuthnot are members. Pray elucidate the reason for your refusal to admit testimony from a witness of sound mind and honorable character. You have yourself cast doubt by stating that Lady Mendoza spoke irrationally of subjects other than the specific mischance. It behooves you to place before a judge all interpretations of the event that are available. Justice could hardly be served in any other way."

"See here—"

It was time for the port master to take a hand. "Mr. dea'Gauss raises a valid point and asks a pertinent question," she drawled from the doorway. "Why is the boy forbidden to testify, Velnik? I have monitored trials where children much younger than he appears to be have spoken and been heard."

"Thra Rominkoff, it is law that all witnesses in cases of violent crime must testify under the same drug administered to the accused. Persons under majority—nineteen Standard Years—may not be compelled to submit to the drug."

"What drug?" the young captain asked very quietly.

"Pimmadrene," she replied. "It's been used for many years. The ego is temporarily dissolved, which nets quite truthful answers." She considered the precinct officer. "And yet it does still seem to me that I have seen very young children testify. The law speaks of 'impel.' What if free choice is offered?"

He moved his shoulders. "The parents gave permission for the drug in the cases you mention, Thra Rominkoff."

"Or guardian of record?"

He bowed.

"But it is dangerous?" the captain asked quietly.

"Dangerous? No. The doctor adjusts the dose to body weight and stays by to monitor. But it's unpleasant. Not the sort of thing to force on a person who can't—a child. The side effects are dizziness, stomach cramps, fever, disorientation. Some people go blind for a few days, but that's not common. Doc over there could tell you specifically."

"I'll do it," the boy said suddenly, and tugged on the captain's sleeve. "Shan? Tell them I'll do it. I'm your ward. Grandpa told me!"

"*Acushla*, think carefully. The side effects sound very bad. And the intended effect isn't good, either. I'll do what you tell me to do. It's your decision. But be sure, Gordy."

"Shan, it's *Priscilla*." He grabbed on to a big hand, looking up worriedly. "They said—do you know what they're going to do to her, if the judge says she's got to be—to be rehabilitated?"

"I know, Gordy. Hush."

But Gordy would not be hushed. He hung on to the captain's

hand and looked at Mr. dea'Gauss, making the explanation to him in a voice that washed against every wall in the room.

"They said—since she's a *murderer*—she'll go to the organ bank. They'll float her in a tank and feed her through tubes and stuff until somebody maybe needs an eye. Then they'll take one of Priscilla's eyes. And she'll float some more 'til somebody needs another eye, or a kidney, or a lung, or a leg, and they'll cut her up, piece by piece. . . ."

"Gordy!" The captain was on his knees, pulling the boy tight against his shoulder and rubbing his face in the sandy hair. "Stop it, Gordy. Please."

There was silence.

The boy pulled back, lifted a tentative hand to the man's stark cheek, and snuffled. "Shan, you better tell them I'll be a witness. They can't—Priscilla's *good.*"

"Yes," the captain murmured, coming slowly to his feet. "I know that, too."

He bowed to the precinct officer very slightly. "It has been determined that my ward will testify at Ms. Mendoza's trial. Please tell us its time and location, as well as the proper manner in which to present ourselves."

"There is no reason," the port master cut in, "why the trial should not be held at once. I am empowered to act as judge in affairs of the port—as soon as my robes arrive and a room is made available." She glanced at the desk officer, who hurriedly placed a call.

THE ROBES WERE HEAVY ON HER SHOULDERS. Perhaps it was their unaccustomed weight: she rarely took part in such affairs, usually letting things run the legal course in their own time. Perhaps it was the boy's involvement, or the young captain's. They sat together by special permission, the giant, white-haired Liaden austere, and the boy with his empty, drug-toned eyes.

She sighed heavily, rang the bell to order, and read the preliminaries without expression. Having established the identities of those present, she glanced at the monitor; she nodded satisfaction and looked back at the boy. His face was slightly damp, eyes wide open, pupils dilated black with a thin ring of brown iris.

"What is your name, boy?"

"Gordy." His voice was blurry, like a sleep-talker's.

The port master consulted the card and frowned. She addressed the boy again. "All right, Gordy. What is your full, *legal* name?"

"Gordon Richard Arbuthnot."

She nodded. "What is your planet of origin?"

"New Dublin."

"In Standard Years, what is your age?"

"Eleven."

"What is your father's name?"

Silence.

She frowned. "Gordy, what is your father's name?"

"His father," Mr. dea'Gauss whispered in her ear, "is dead."

"I see." Damn this drug! It was clumsy—misleading. "Gordy, what *was* your father's name?"

"Finn Gordon Arbuthnot."

That was another match. "What is your mother's name?"

"Katy-Rose Davis."

And another. She turned her head. "Doctor, have we established that the drug is in force?"

"Yes, Thra Rominkoff."

"Excellent. We shall proceed with the testimony."

She paused to order her thoughts, mindful of the drug's limitation. "Gordy, when did you and Priscilla Mendoza arrive on-world?"

"First shuttle."

First shuttle? What sort of time was that? "Approximately Regent's Hour," the young captain said softly, and she nodded her thanks. "Why were you with Priscilla Mendoza, Gordy?"

"We were leave-partners."

"You were assigned to each other?"

"No."

She sighed. "How did you become leave-partners?"

"I asked Priscilla if she'd be partners, and she said okay."

"Who chose where you went in town?"

"I did."

"You chose to be in Nietzsche Street?"

"Yes."

"Why?"

"It looked interesting."

"Did Priscilla Mendoza ask you to go down Nietzsche Street?"

"No."

"Did Dagmar Collier ask you to go down Nietzsche Street?"

"No."

"Did Priscilla Mendoza kill Dagmar Collier, Gordy?"

"Yes."

She swallowed a curse at that simple damnation; she heard Velnik shift beside her, and saw the young captain's lips shape one word. She gave it voice.

"Why did Priscilla kill Dagmar, Gordy?"

"To save me."

On the other side, Mr. dea'Gauss leaned forward infinitesimally, his attention centered on the blurry young face.

"Were you in danger, Gordy?"

"Yes."

"How did you come to be in danger?"

"I didn't come when Priscilla said to."

The port master made a mental note to explore drugs other than Pimmadrene for use in interrogation.

"Gordy, I want you to tell me exactly what happened from the time you didn't go with Priscilla in Nietzsche Street to the time the arresting officer came."

"Priscilla said the shuttle was leaving in a ship's hour and if my credit with the captain was up to being late, hers wasn't and we had to leave. She went two steps away and said 'Gordy?' I said 'yeah,' and she went further away and I was getting ready to go with her when I got grabbed and it was Dagmar and she yanked and held on when I tried to run and held us against a pole and held me over her knee and Priscilla was running toward us and Dagmar had a knife and she said 'Freeze, Prissy.' And Priscilla stopped." There was a tiny pause as the boy licked his lips.

"Where did Dagmar hold the knife, Gordy?"

"Across my throat. Under my chin."

"All right, Gordy. Priscilla stopped. Then what?"

"Dagmar said Priscilla had to stay there. She asked where Shan was. I tried to get away again, and she—she hurt me. She said if I was good she'd let me live for a minute or two." There was another small pause. The port master snapped her fingers, never taking her eyes from that damp face.

"She said Priscilla had to watch. To tell Shan what it looked like." An aide arrived with a glass of water. The port master waved her to the boy.

"Rest a minute, Gordy, and drink."

He did, draining the glass thirstily.

"All right, Gordy. Dagmar said Priscilla had to watch, so she could tell Shan what it looked like. Then?"

"Priscilla started to talk. I don't remember what she said, but it made my head feel funny. She talked and walked forward a little bit and Dagmar's arm got loose and I thought about running away but then there was a noise in the next street and Dagmar's arm got tight again and she made Priscilla stop. Priscilla tried to talk some more, but Dagmar asked if Shan had bought Priscilla's things. She said she broke Priscilla's earrings into dust and then spaced the dust. She said Shan wasn't smart and that he wouldn't catch them selling the stuff.

"Priscilla started to talk again and my head felt funny again and then there were footsteps and Dagmar tried to make me go with her 'cause it was too public, she said. But I was scared and I didn't want to go with her and I grabbed on to the pole and held on and thought about the Tree like Priscilla'd taught me and Dagmar turned on the knife. I heard it hum and I was scared and I hung on and thought about the Tree and I heard a—roar. Like a big animal. And Priscilla was running fast—faster than Shan runs and Dagmar let me go and Priscilla—it was so *fast!* She grabbed Dagmar and twisted and did something with her hands. I heard a snap, like a stick breaking. Dagmar fell down. Priscilla stood for a minute and then she fell down, too." He swallowed.

"I went and kicked the knife away from Dagmar and then I tried to make Priscilla get up. It was hard and I thought she was—I thought she was dead. But she woke up and called me 'Brand' and her voice was all funny, like it hurt her to talk. Then she stood up and told me to go back to the *Passage*. I told her Shan wouldn't like it if I left her alone when she was in a scrape and she hugged me and threw a stone into the window of Marcel's Tailoring Emporium. Then she said she'd killed Dagmar and the cops would come in a minute and arrest her for murder. She told me to leave again, but I wouldn't. Then the cop came."

The port master leaned back in her chair and counted to twenty-five, eyes closed. She opened her eyes.

"Precinct Officer Velnik," she said very carefully. "I will now see the recording of Priscilla Mendoza's . . . confession."

The woman was slim, middling tall by Terran standards, doubly dwarfed by Velnik and the arresting officer. Her hair was short and black and curly, her face dirt-smeared; her eyes were enormous, ebon—and exhausted. "Priscilla Delacroix y Mendoza," she answered the precinct officer. Her voice was a ragged whisper.

"Planet of origin?"

"Sintia."

"Are you employed on a trading vessel?"

"Yes."

"State the name of the vessel, its home port, your rank."

"*Dutiful Passage*. Solcintra, Liad. Pilot, first class pending. Second mate."

"Did you kill the woman Dagmar Collier?"

"Yes."

"Did you deliberately murder the woman Dagmar Collier?"

"Yes."

"Where did you kill Dagmar Collier?"

"In front of Dillibee's Digital Delights in Nietzsche Street in Crown City on Theopholis."

"When did you kill Dagmar Collier?"

"One hour ago."

"Did you attempt escape after you killed Dagmar Collier?"

"No."

"Why?"

"There was no place to go."

From the young captain came a wordless protest. As if cued by that slight sound, Precinct Officer Velnik asked Priscilla Mendoza, "Why didn't you return to the *Dutiful Passage?*"

"No murderers are allowed on the *Passage.*" The captain drew a sharp breath. "Your name," the precinct officer pursued, "is Priscilla Delacroix y Mendoza?"

"Yes."

"Did you intentionally kill the woman Dagmar Collier?"

"Yes."

"Describe your actions that brought the death of Dagmar Collier."

"I called the Dragon. When it was with me, we roared and threw a fireball to distract Dagmar's attention from Gordy. Then I broke her neck."

There was a slight pause while precinct officer and cop exchanged glances.

"You, Priscilla Delacroix y Mendoza," the precinct officer said carefully, "broke the neck of Dagmar Collier, fully intending to bring about her death?"

"Yes."

"Are you a native of Troit?"

"No."

"What is your legal name?"

"Priscilla Delacroix y Mendoza."

"What is your planet of origin?"

"Sintia."

"Did you kill Dagmar Collier?"

"Yes."

There was a small pause. "Where is the Dragon now?"

"Above the Tree."

"How much is two plus two?"

"Four."

"Have you said any lies since you were brought here by the arresting officer?"

"No."

"Did the dragon kill Dagmar Collier?"

"No."

"Who killed Dagmar Collier?"

"I did."

"YOU SEE," Velnik said to the room in general as the lights came up. "Dragons, trees . . . ."

"The Tree-and-Dragon," Mr. dea'Gauss cut him off, "is the shield of Clan Korval. It depicts a dragon, guarding a full-leafed tree. The motto is 'I Dare.' Lady Mendoza is quite familiar with the shield. It is displayed prominently on the *Dutiful Passage.*"

"So they had meaning for her; she was self-aware."

"Yes," the port master snapped, coming to her feet. Velnik retreated a step. "She knew what she was doing. The boy is alive. The person he names his potential assassin is dead. Priscilla Mendoza was not asked *why* she willfully and intentionally killed Dagmar Collier, Precinct Officer. Your interview was less than thorough."

Velnik licked his lips and came to rigid attention.

"Doctor, is the serum you gave Mendoza still in force?"

He shook his head. "It runs through the system pretty fast. She'll be on the downside by now." He glanced at the bench. "Can't give her another shot for two days. That's a medical fact. She mightn't recover."

She nodded. "It won't be required, thank you. My ruling in this case is that Priscilla Delacroix y Mendoza is found not guilty of murder. Defense of a child is not a crime here! Arresting Officer, bring Priscilla Mendoza here, so that she may be released into the care of her captain."

Mr. dea'Gauss caught the young captain's eye. *"Daxflan—"*

"My office is currently dealing with that difficulty, sirs," she said, turning back. "Granting even unheard of levels of inefficiency, it should at this moment be sealed in close orbit. And there, I think, we may all let it wait until the morrow."

The old gentleman bowed. "It is as you have said, madam. I should mention that the feud between Lady Mendoza and Dagmar

Collier is one of long standing. Dagmar Collier threatened her lady-ship and Master Arbuthnot with violence once before to my certain knowledge. On Arsdred."

"I would appreciate receiving the particulars of that event, sir. Also—Captain. I am deeply ashamed that my inefficiency has caused this circumstance. Dagmar Collier should never have been in this port. I am responsible, and I am grieved. Please consider me at your disposal in the resolution of the matter."

"You're very kind, ma'am," he replied, smiling wearily.

"Port Master," the arresting officer said, arriving alone and looking very nervous. "Port Master, she—won't move. I open the door and call, but she just sits, Port Master."

"I'll come." The young captain slid away from the boy, beckoning to the old gentleman. "By your kindness, sir."

"Certainly." Mr. dea'Gauss sat carefully and slid an unaccustomed arm about young shoulders, enduring the head resting upon his chest.

"Let's go," the captain snapped at the cop as he strode by. She had to run three steps to catch up.

Precinct House Detention Hall
Crown City, Theopholis
Hour Of Fools

〜〜〜〜〜〜〜〜〜〜〜〜〜〜〜〜〜〜〜〜〜〜〜〜〜

THE ROOM WAS MERCILESSLY BRIGHT—shadowless. In the center of the cot huddled a ragamuffin creature, legs crossed, arms hugging her waist, head leaning against left knee. She was trembling minutely and constantly.

"Let's go, Mendoza!" the cop called briskly, unlocking the cell port.

The bundle of misery did not stir.

The cop licked her lips and tried again. "Come on, Mendoza! Your boss is here!"

Nothing.

Shan laid his hand on the cop's arm. "Leave us. I'll bring her."

She began to shake her head, lips parting to prate some senseless law.

"Go!" He augmented the command with a lash of fury. The cop jumped—and fled.

The anger was blue-hot in him—Korval rage. With an effort he contained it, banked it, and shut it away until it might be used. Calmed, he went to the edge of the cot. "Priscilla."

She flinched, and he caught his breath; he calmed himself again and hunkered down before her, his hands resting on the edge of the mattress. "Priscilla, it's Shan."

"Shan." There was anguish like a knife in the ragged whisper. "Shan, there wasn't enough time to be sure!"

Her agony caught him by the throat, even shielded as he was.

The next moment he had cast protection aside, spinning a line of comfort, of love. . . .

He was met by terror-desire-longing-grief-shame-love—a whipping windstorm of emotion, punishing in its intensity. He gasped, fingers clawing into the mattress as he scrambled for the line he had spun for her—he gripped it, following it back into himself by painful jerks, and finally called up the Wall.

It slammed into place with a force that drew a soft moan from Priscilla, though she did not lift her head.

"My dear friend. . . ." Slowly he unclenched his hands. "Priscilla, please look at me."

She was silent, motionless but for the constant shivering.

"Priscilla?"

"I'd rather—talk—to you. Please, Shan . . . They're going to—to kill me. I—can you stay with me? Please . . . Until they come . . ." She drew a shuddering breath. "You keep—going away. . . ."

He forced his brain to work, to consider that last. "Have I been here before, Priscilla?"

"I think—yes. I was talking to you—trying to tell you . . . I tried to—to reach *athetilu*, but you were closed and I tried to—to hold you and you went away and I thought I'd made you angry . . . ." She moved a fraction, tightening her arms about her waist. "*Cama se mathra te ezo mi. . . .*"

Sintian. He was losing her, crippled as he was, not daring to step beyond the Wall. Shaking, he extended a hand and stroked the bedraggled curls.

"Priscilla, *please* look at me. I grant I'm hardly a feast for the eyes, but it would spare my feelings."

She gave no sign that she had heard him. Then, slowly, almost clumsily, she unbent and sat straight, her right arm cradled in her left, her eyes bottomless ebony pits in a filthy, exhausted face.

He smiled and dropped his hand from her hair to her knee. "Thank you. Now, since I seem prone to this fading in and out—your hand, please, Priscilla."

It took a moment for her to manage the movement, but she held a quavering left hand out to him.

"Good." He tugged the master's ring from his finger and slid it onto her thumb, where it perched precariously. "If you find I've gone away again, notice that you have my ring. I'll come back for that, at least, won't I?"

She considered it. "Yes."

He sighed, holding her hand lightly. "What a brute I am! It's a wonder I'm allowed your friendship at all, Priscilla; I marvel at you. What's wrong with your arm?"

"I burned it."

"Throwing fireballs?"

She jerked. His fingers tightened on hers, and she relaxed, licking her lips. "Yes. I'm not—accustomed—to throwing fireballs."

"I'd think not. Are you well enough to walk?"

"Yes."

"Good." He stood. "Let's go."

She stared up at him, her hand moving in his. "Go where?"

"To the *Passage*. You're hurt and sick and tired, and I'm tired and Mr. dea'Gauss is tired and even Gordy's tired." He grinned. "The port master's tired, too, but she doesn't come with us."

She tried to pull her hand away. He did not allow it.

"I can't."

He frowned. "Can't?"

"Shan. . . ." Tears welled out of her eyes and spilled over, making streaks down her face. "Shan, I killed Dagmar."

"Yes, I know." Bending to take her other hand, he found her face close, so that he might lay his cheek against her— *Priscilla, I love you. . . .* He fought the emotion and found the control to address her gently. "I'm *sorry*, Priscilla. It should never have come to that. You should never have had the need. Forgive me, I've taken poor care of you."

"You said—"

"I said 'no murderers,' may my tongue be damned! But self-defense isn't murder—nor is protecting the life of a friend." He took a breath, cooling the sharpest of the pain. "Please, Priscilla—for the friendship we have between us—allow me to take you to the *Passage*. You need care, healing—a sheltered place to sleep. When you are able, I will personally escort you anywhere you choose to go. Let me aid you."

There was confusion in her face and in her eyes. She was silent.

He raised a hand to touch the platinum hoop in her right ear and stroke the curls above it. "Please, Priscilla."

"The trial. . . ."

"Has been performed. Gordy testified. The port master sat as judge. You are acquitted of murder. No one is going to come and take you away to die. Only Shan is come, to take you home."

"Home." Her hands clutched his, then relaxed. She looked into his face, her expression unreadable through the grime. "Please, Shan, take me home."

"Yes, Priscilla."

She staggered when she stood, clutching his arm for support. "Are you well enough to walk, my friend? Or shall I ask the port master to provide a chair?"

"No." She straightened, face set.

"Very well." He slid his arm around her waist, turning her toward the door. "Mr. dea'Gauss," he predicted with a merriness he did not feel, "will be appalled."

IF MR. DEA'GAUSS WAS APPALLED, he hid it well. The bow he performed was profound. "Lady Mendoza."

She inclined her head, which was all that dizziness and Shan's arm about her waist allowed. "Mr. dea'Gauss. I'm pleased to see you."

"You are kind." He glanced at Shan. "The physician has given Master Arbuthnot a drug he feels may counteract the worst of the side effects, or at very least allow him to sleep through them. He has also provided a printout of the structure of both drugs."

"Well enough," Shan said calmly, as if it were no surprise that Gordy should be lying so white and quiet upon the bench.

"I don't—" She shifted, half intending to go to the boy. The arm tightened about her fractionally, and she turned to look into silver eyes. "He was all right! They were going to send him to the *Passage.*"

"But he would not go without you," a new voice explained.

"Afterward it became necessary that he be given the drug, that his testimony might be heard."

Priscilla blinked, clearing her vision. The tall, handsome woman in glittering evening dress smiled formally and bowed. "Ms.—Lady—Mendoza. I am Elyana Rominkoff, port master in the regent's service. Allow me to present my apologies: this should not have befallen you in the city under my care. When you are rested— at your convenience!—please contact me, that we may sit together and discuss fair recompense."

"Yes, of course," Priscilla mumbled, unable properly to attend to what the woman said to her. She was sinking into an indigo blur where the only realities were Shan's arm about her and the warm strength of his body steadying hers. Abruptly she pushed at the creeping indigo and reached out, tapping that near source of energy.

Strength flowed unstintingly from him to her, clear and bracing. She straightened as the room came back into focus and inclined her head to the woman before her. "Port Master, forgive me. I am— unwell—at the moment. I will call you, and we will talk."

"That is well, then." The woman shifted her gaze beyond Priscilla, smiling with warmth rather than mere formality. "Captain yos'Galan, remember what I have said. I am entirely at your disposal in this matter. My eyes and ears are yours to command at any hour." She bowed then and moved back, cutting off his reply with a wave of her hand. "At this hour, you have folk to care for. My car awaits you. If you allow, the precinct officer will carry the boy. Lady Mendoza, Mr. dea'Gauss holds your license and your papers."

"Thank you," Shan said gently. "You're all kindness, ma'am."

The walk to the car was blessedly short. Priscilla settled into the seat, Shan's arm still about her waist, his strength buoying her. She curled her fingers around her thumb, gripping his ring tightly. Then she reached within and turned off the tap.

The last thing she remembered was resting her head upon his shoulder.

Shipyear 65
Tripday 181
Third Shift
14.00 Hours

HE POURED UNSTEADILY, brandy splashing the bar top and, incidentally, the cup. Gritting his teeth, he managed to fill the thing halfway and set the decanter decently back into the rack.

Priscilla was in sick bay, under Lina's capable eye, and Gordy was there too. Both were asleep and abed—which was where he should be, working through the exercise that would grant his pounding head relief and rest. Brandy was not the best cure for an empath in his condition.

He sipped, frowning in momentary puzzlement at the stain on his cuff. Blood.

Yes, of course. Must remember to send the port master a set of crystal. Stupid Shan. Doesn't know his own strength.

Sav Rid Olanek. Gods, to have his hands about Sav Rid Olanek's slim throat. . . .

And then? He jeered at himself, drinking again. The flaming ice of Korval rage stirred behind the barriers he had built about it. And then he would pay balance with his life! Shall he threaten lady, foster-son, ship?

Priscilla. That punishing outage of self-hate, terror, and confusion. A trace effect of the drug? Or something more permanent? Lina would know.

He stopped himself on the way to the comm. Lina would know, sooner or later. And when she knew, so would Shan yos'Galan. He would do nothing now but distract her from an essential task.

"Go to bed. Shan," he told himself.

But he tarried, sipping his drink, staring sightlessly at the tapestry above the bar.

When the annunciator chimed, he jumped.

"Come!" he called.

Mr. dea'Gauss entered, papers rustling in hand, face full of import. It was indicative of his weariness or the value of his news that he broke at once into speech, neglecting even his bow.

"Your Lordship, I have received the report of Ms. Veltrad, whom you sent to Sintia on the matter of Lady Mendoza. It is—"

"No!"

Mr. dea'Gauss blinked. "I beg your lordship's pardon?"

"I said," Shan explained, voice thin with strain, "no. No, I do not wish to hear Ximena's report. No, I do not wish to hear the name of the crime Priscilla is supposed to have committed. No, I do not wish to find the report on my screen next on-shift. No, I do not want Ximena to call or visit so that she may tell me in her own voice what she has reported. No."

Mr. dea'Gauss took stock. Shan stood near the center of the room, holding a quarter-full glass in his bandaged hand, the blood-stained ruff falling gracefully about taut knuckles. The stark brown face might have been hewn from strellwood, and there was a slightly mad look around the silver eyes.

"The report from Sintia," he began again, "indicates that—"

"*No!*" Shan was across the room in a blur, was towering over Mr. dea'Gauss, his face set in cold fury, the syllables of the High Tongue crackling. "I do not hear you! Go."

Mr. dea'Gauss gave no ground. He had seen this before—from Er Thom yos'Galan. The proper answer had never included giving ground.

He drew himself up and took a firmer grip on his papers. "Will you hear it from me? Or from your First Speaker? It is a matter of ship's debt. The captain's attention is required."

For perhaps a heartbeat Shan was utterly still. He turned, went to his desk and sat, placing the glass precisely aside.

"yos'Galan hears," he said in the High Tongue, Thodelm-to-Hireling.

Mr. dea'Gauss walked forward. He was not waved carelessly to a chair. Shan's face was expressionless, waiting. Mr. dea'Gauss bowed.

"Thodelm, it becomes my knowledge through the words of Ximena Veltrad, who was offered coin in return for verified truth, that Priscilla Delacroix y Mendoza was ostracized from her world for the crime called 'blasphemy' ten Standard Years gone by. The details of this crime are covered most fully by Ms. Veltrad's report. I wished only to assure you at this present that Sintia's *melant'i* suffers greatly by the reported incident. Lady Mendoza's actions were, as always, above reproach."

"And yet someone reproached her. Strongly." The High Tongue exuded no warmth. "You will explain this paradox."

"Yes, Thodelm. I am not conversant with the depth of the situation reported by Ms. Veltrad. My understanding is that Lady Mendoza, as an apprentice in Circle House—what is called there a 'Maiden' or novice priestess—called recriminations upon herself for an act of heroism. I confess that I do not understand why the saving of three lives should have caused these recriminations. Ms. Veltrad's report indicates doctrinal, rather than rational, causes. In any wise, Lady Mendoza was called before the masters of the craft and offered a chance to disown her act and be properly chastised. Lady Mendoza refused to recant. She was then stripped of her goods and her title, and banned from the craft. In order to keep face, her House cast her forth as well." Mr. dea'Gauss paused, considering the icy eyes. "Politics, Thodelm. Not Balance."

"So." Shan drank the rest of the brandy slowly, then replaced the glass. "yos'Galan has heard. You will leave the report with me. Have you anything else that I must hear at this present?"

"No, Thodelm."

"Good. You are dismissed."

Korval's man of business bowed, then turned away.

"Mr. dea'Gauss."

He turned back. "Thodelm?"

Shan smiled wearily, his bandaged hand resting on Ximena's report. "Sleep well, sir. And thank you."

Mr. dea'Gauss felt absurd relief as his lips bent in reply. "Sleep well, your lordship. You are quite welcome."

Shipyear 65
Tripday 181
Third Shift
16.00 Hours

ഝଊଊଊଊଊଊଊଊଊଊଊଊଊଊଊଊଊଊଊଊଊଊଊଊ

SHAN LIFTED HIS HEAD, groping after the sound. Surely . . . Ah. The door chime.

"Come."

The door parted, and she entered, slight and small, her face Liaden gold. "Old friend."

"Lina." Memory returned with a force that shuddered pain through his misused head, and he was half out of the chair. "Priscilla—"

"Resting. And well." Her small hands flickered, soothing. He sank back as she came around the desk. "More—she is herself. We spoke. She is rational; she knows what has transpired; she knows that necessity existed and that she acted as best she might." Lina sighed. "Much of the confusion you reported must be counted an effect of the drug—and of despair. Life has taught her to expect neither rescue from trouble nor surcease from pain. Healing had gone far, but that lesson is not easy to unlearn."

Shan had closed his eyes. Now he opened them, and Lina felt shock at the depth of weariness there. "She'll be all right," he murmured, his beautiful voice blurred and uneven. "Thank you, Lina, for coming to tell me. This is your rest shift, isn't it?"

"And yours, as well," she said briskly. "Priscilla sent me to make sure you slept. You were angry, she said, and hurt."

He rubbed his forehead absently. "Stupid. Trying to scan the whole planet. . . ." He tapped a sheaf of papers. "Had to read Ximena's report. Mr. dea'Gauss . . . An act of heroism. She'll have to stop that, Lina. Get herself hurt. Saves three lives, using some sort of thing she wasn't taught yet. But she said the old soul—give 'em old souls, the Initiates, with the old names attached. Priscilla's soul was named Moonhawk. Very powerful lady. Much respected. Said the old soul had done it, for the glory of the Goddess and—and . . . who knows? Long and short, she gets thrown out. All very well and good to have a tame *dramliza* on your hands, but when she starts demanding her due, that's dangerous."

Lina frowned, noting the empty glass by his hand. "Is Priscilla a wizard, Shan?"

"Very good chance. Should see her—no, I hope you don't see her. Does things above and beyond us mere Healers. Got a definite flair. . . ." He rubbed at his face again. "Gods, gods, she's *strong*."

She leaned forward and stroked the warm, thick hair. "Shan. Come to bed."

He blinked at her. "Bed?"

"You are tired. You must rest, let yourself heal. How much brandy have you had?"

"Half a beakful," he muttered, and then grinned. "But it's quite a beak, eh?"

She laughed, between frustration and relief. "Come to bed, *denubia*." She grabbed the unbandaged hand and tugged. "Shan, have pity! I have promised my *cha'leket* to see you resting. Would you have me turn my face from her need?"

"*Cha'leket?*"

"Priscilla herself named me sister. I find my heart agrees. *Will* you come to bed?"

"Since you ask so nicely. Not likely to do you much good though, my precious." He wobbled to his feet but would not lean his weight upon her. Unsteadily, he laid his hand against the inner door.

She coaxed him to lie flat, unsealed the tight dress shirt, then sat stroking his hair and murmuring, weaving a net of warm comfort and loading it with the desire to sleep deeply and long.

After a time his eyes closed, his breathing lengthened.

Lina continued her weaving and stroking until she sensed that he had reached the first depths, where prime healing begins. She slid from the bed and spread the coverlet gently over him, dimmed the lights, and disarmed the alarm. Kayzin had agreed that the captain's rest should not be interrupted untimely.

Affairs ordered to her satisfaction, Lina bent and stroked his cheek. "Sleep well, old friend." And then she was gone.

Crown City Theopholis
Judge's Hour

THE CAB PULLED TO THE EDGE of the pedstrip and stopped. The driver looked over his shoulder and said something in a barbaric garble. Sav Rid stared at him coldly.

"The vehicle can go no farther," the driver announced in abrupt Trade. "Pedestrian traffic only inside the port. The fare's fivebit."

Sav Rid extended the proper coin silently and exited the cab. Behind him the driver spat between his teeth and muttered, "Louse!" But the action was beneath Sav Rid's notice, the single word in Terran.

He walked cautiously through the crowded port, intensely aware of his lack of guard. Dagmar Collier had not been at the rendezvous point this morning. He wondered what might have happened to the creature, then put the thought away with an impatient shrug. Who, after all, really cared? If Dagmar Collier chose to jump ship before the run was through, that was certainly its own affair. *Daxflan* would make good use of the unclaimed wages.

A man was coming purposefully toward him down the pedstrip: older with more gray than black in his thinning hair. Sav Rid froze.

His Delm continued briskly forward, then stopped at the proper distance and inclined his head. "Kinsman. I give you good day."

He managed a bow. "As I give you good day, kinsman and delm. It surprises me to find you here, so far from home and House."

"No more," the elder said dryly, "than it surprises me to find you here, when the port master reports *Daxflan* absent."

"We hold orbit about the fourth planet out, my delm. It has been found more—convenient—to use another vessel to bring goods from *Daxflan* to prime orbit."

"Indeed." Taam Olanek extended an arm, smiling coolly. "Walk with me, I beg you. I am curious about this so convenient method. Have you subcontracted your cargoes to others, Sav Rid?"

They walked a few paces in silence.

"It became necessary," Sav Rid murmured, "for *Daxflan* to purchase a subsidiary vessel to act as shuttle from *Daxflan* to berth. The method is quite simple, sir, and serves us well."

"Am I to understand," Plemia demanded, "that you have made *Daxflan,* in essence, a *warehouse?*"

"Exactly so," Sav Rid said, pleased.

His Delm drew breath. "I see. Forgive my question, kinsman, but such a purchase as a trading vessel . . . It seems that I surely would have noted the passage of a so large a voucher across my desk. Yet I recall nothing."

Sav Rid smiled, triumphantly oblivious to the worry in the other's face. "It was a small matter, sir; there was no need to resort to credit vouchers. We paid cash."

"Cash," Plemia repeated tonelessly. He was silent a moment or two as they walked. Then he straightened abruptly, renewing his grip on Sav Rid's arm. "It only now returns to me, kinsman—the matter of which I wished to speak. I have heard from the port master that a member of your crew—one Dagmar Collier—has been found dead in the city outside the port."

"So, that is what became of it," Sav Rid said calmly. "I had wondered. Well, it always had a quarrelsome nature."

"Had she?" Taam asked softly around the sudden ice in his throat. "And how long had Dagmar Collier served you, kinsman?"

Sav Rid moved his shoulders. "Two or three trips, I believe."

"Ah." Taam stopped, whirling on the other. "Sav Rid, a woman who has been in your service these four years has died! Do you not at least go to the precinct house and claim the body, that it might be sent properly to her kin?"

There was honest puzzlement in the young face. "No, why

should I? I doubt it had kin. It was Terran, you see," he explained more fully in the face of his delm's further silence.

"Terrans are not all kinless folk, Sav Rid," Taam murmured, his eyes filling as pity unexpectedly overtook dread. "They are people, even as we are." Still there was only puzzled confusion in the eyes watching his. He touched the smooth cheek gently. "And if they were not, my child, *we* are people. It is our burden and our pride to behave with honor, always."

"Yes, surely. But a Terran, sir. . . ."

"Never mind, child. It will be attended to." He took Sav Rid's arm again and resumed the walk. "I hear from Korval that you and young Shan attempt to Balance some puppy accounts. Are you not too old for such mischief, Sav Rid?"

The arm in his had stiffened, as had the young face. "It is not mischief, sir; it is earnest. I will have yos'Galan on its knees—hideous brother and first sister! Aye, and young Val Con, as well! How dare he treat a guest so? It was sheer insult, sir! They gave no consideration to that due one of Plemia! They will learn—and not soon forget! 'Korval,' Chelsa bleats, with fear in her face! A rabble of ill-raised brats! There is Balance owing, sir, and it will be obtained. That I promise!"

"I see," Taam said again sadly. He took a breath. "Then you will not be averse, I think, to this other news I bring. Korval demands a meeting, in sight of port master and witnesses, to establish Balance and put paid to all accounts. The time is set for this local evening, if you find yourself able to attend."

"Korval demands a meeting!" Sav Rid laughed. "But they must, after all! How could they allow the idiot eldest to ruin himself?" He disengaged and bowed gravely. "I will accompany you with the greatest pleasure, sir."

Shipyear 65
Tripday 182
Second Shift
8.30 Hours

SLEEP RECEDED, and she opened her eyes. The room had an uncertain familiarity—not her own quarters, nor yet the prison cell. . . . *Sick bay,* memory provided. Lina had sent her into sleep, riding the wave of one resounding note, to wake when the healing reverberation was at last still.

How many hours? she wondered without urgency. She stretched, catlike, where she lay, noticing the cramp in her right hand, her thumb tucked tightly into her fingers.

Slowly, she eased the tension, the great amethyst of the master's ring sparkling in the room's dim light. Priscilla smiled. Goddess bless you, my dear, for bringing me home.

She stretched again, relishing the sensation, then sat up, pushing the thin cover away. Time to be about, whatever time it was. And she was *starving*.

The door to her left opened with a soft sigh. "Morning, gorgeous!"

She started, then grinned at the gangling medic. "Vilt. Do you always terrify your patients when they wake up?"

"Makes sense," he pointed out, taking her arm and beginning to unwrap the gauzy dressing. "If they're gonna have a heart attack, might as well have it here, where there's somebody to take care of 'em."

"Who?" she wondered, and he laughed, laying the dressing aside.

"Go ahead, do your worst. Just remember who runs the inoculation program around here. Arm looks great. Damnedest burn I've ever seen, though: inside, between wrist and elbow." He shook his head. "How'd you do it?"

She looked him in the eye. "Throwing a fireball."

"That a fact? Lucky you didn't lose some fingers. Better use a glove next time."

"Goddess willing, there won't be a next time."

"If you say so. How's the throat?"

"Okay."

Vilt shook his head in mock severity. "Think I'm taking your word for it? Open up, gorgeous—and don't even think about biting."

She submitted resentfully. Vilt made a thorough and, she suspected, leisurely exam, then grunted and stepped back.

"Looks good. Be careful of the voice for a couple days, just in case."

"Let the captain do the talking," she suggested.

He laughed again. "He will, anyway. I've known Shan since I was apprentice medic on this ship and he wasn't any older than Gordy. Been talking nonstop all that time. Likely born talking. His mother was a linguist, which probably accounts for it. Genes, you know," he explained sagely as Priscilla chuckled. He stepped back, abruptly sober. "All right, gorgeous, pay attention. Sometime between leave-time yesterday and arrival time, you lost one-tenth of your mass. The kitchen has been provided with special menus, just for you. You will eat everything on your tray until you've regained that weight. And just to keep you honest, you'll weigh in before you begin each duty-shift." He glanced at his watch. "A tasty, high-caloric breakfast will be here in three minutes. After you've eaten everything on the tray, you can use the 'fresher across the hall. Lina put fresh clothes in there for you. Any questions?"

"No."

"Great." He slapped her shoulder lightly and grinned. "See ya later."

"Vilt!"

"Yah?"

"Is Gordy okay?"

He snorted. "That kid? Been up for hours. Demanded to see you. Lina took him off to help in the pet library. Said you'd call him there when you woke up."

"I'll do that, then."

"You'll eat that breakfast before you do anything. Aha!" He stepped triumphantly to one side, allowing the orderly to push the meal cart up to the bed. "Enjoy!"

PRISCILLA STEPPED OUT OF THE DRY CYCLE, running her fingers through unruly curls and frowning at her reflection. Her teachers had ever been anxious about her slenderness, saying that her body—Moonhawk's vessel—was not robust enough to endure the working of larger magics.

True enough, by the mirror's testimony. Fourteen pounds lost meant countable ribs and jutting hipbones, the knobs at wrist and collar painfully apparent. She cupped a breast, sighing. She looked like a disaster victim. She turned sharply away to rummage in the closet.

The fresh clothes were unexpectedly fine. Priscilla wondered where Lina had gotten them, for they had the air of things hand-made to personal specification rather than bought from general stores. Wonderingly, she unfolded the silky shirt, noting the flaring collar and the wide, pleated sleeves gathered tightly into ruffled cuffs. Its color was a pure and shimmering rose. The trousers were river-blue and soft. Velvet? she wondered, running light fingers down the nap. They belled slightly at the knee and fell precisely to the instep of the new black boots. She ran the tooled leather belt around her waist, fastened the rosy agate buckle, and turned again to her reflection.

"Thodelm," she breathed, touching the collar that framed her face and lent blush to her cheeks. Lina had provided clothing that the head of a Liaden Line might wear when about the business of the Line.

Hesitantly she approached the mirror, and put out a finger to trace the features of her own face: the slender brows, the straight nose and startling cheekbones, the stubborn chin, the full mouth, and all around them the tumbling mass of midnight curls, relieved at each ear by the pure curve of a platinum hoop.

"Priscilla Mendoza," she said aloud.

On her hand the borrowed amethyst glittered—and that was wrong. She was not Master Trader.

Nor was she outcast.

She stared into the purple depths, considering that thought. "Moonhawk is returned to the Mother."

Truth.

And what did that truth mean, after ten years, a double-dozen worlds—a death? What did it mean here, in the place her heart called home, surrounded by friends, buoyed by a power she thought had fled?

Lady Mendoza, the old gentleman invariably addressed her with profound respect. Lina had not found it unusual that her friend possessed power, only that she had not been taught courtesy in its use. Shan. . . .

But it was not possible to think clearly of Shan. Certainly he regarded her abilities, like his own, as natural and acceptable. "How do you make love?" she recalled him asking, and she put a hand to a cheek suddenly flaming. Don't do that, Priscilla. . . .

Last night . . . How much had been drug-dream, how much true actions? He had come—she wore the proof on her hand even now! He had brought her home. What else besides these was fact?

Disturbed, she turned slowly and left the 'fresher.

In the hall she hesitated. It was time she reported for duty. Yet Vilt had not released her, and the finery she wore was not meant to withstand a second mate's rounds.

"Hello, Priscilla. Can you spare me a few moments?" Shan's voice interrupted her thoughts.

"All the moments you like," she told him gladly even as she groped for his pattern.

It was subdued, though she caught an indefinable jolt of something as he paused and looked at her closely.

"Are you well, Priscilla? Tell me the truth, please—no heroics."

"Well," she caught doubt and drifted an unconscious step forward, smiling reassuringly. "I lost some weight—strong magics have that effect. Vilt has me eating the most incredible amount of food! But I am well. In fact, I was getting ready to sign out of here and go back on duty."

"Duty? Priscilla . . . ." He paused, glancing about. "Is that the room you were in? Do you mind if we speak there? I . . ."

Something was wrong. She expanded her scope, trying to read it from his pattern, but received only a discord of pain, bitterness, anger, despair—a medley so unlike Shan that she would hardly have known him had her outer eyes been closed.

"Of course."

He stood aside to let her enter first, then closed the door behind them and dropped into the single chair. Uncertainly, she sat on the bed.

The silence was uneasy; scanning was worse than useless. She pulled the Master Trader's ring from her thumb and held it out.

He stared, despair increasing: taking the ring, he sat holding it between thumb and forefinger, toying with the lights among its facets.

"Have you decided," he asked, looking at the ring, his voice husky, "where it is I shall take you?"

She stared at him, ice blossoming in chest and belly.

"Why," she managed, "should you take me anywhere?"

"I gave my word," he told the amethyst. "You only said you would stay until you were—*well*, Priscilla."

Through the isolated, tangled scenes of the night before, she recalled it and licked her lips. "You said you—had come to take me home."

"Did I?" Still he did not meet her eyes, but stared at the ring in his hand. "I will then, Priscilla. But you must tell me where that is. Home."

"Shan!" Anguish knifed through her; she made no attempt to damp it, and felt his answering surge of concern as he at last raised his face.

"You don't want me to go!" she cried, knowing it was truth. "Why—"

"It doesn't matter what I want, Priscilla! What matters is what you want! If there is a place that is home to you, where you know, if you are in need, that there is someone—anyone!—who will aid you, I'll take you there. See you safe—settled. . . ." His voice cracked on the unaccustomed harshness. Instantly the black lashes flicked down, shielding him.

He took a breath, then another, his emotions an unreadable riot. "That a member of this ship's complement should feel there was no place to go when she was in direst need . . . I am ashamed, Priscilla. I've failed you as a captain . . . and as a friend."

"I want to stay." Her words came as barely a breath of sound. She gripped the mattress and tried again. "Captain, please. You never failed me. I failed, by not learning soon enough . . . by not understanding what it means to be a crew member." Tears ran her cheeks, unheeded. "Shan, by the Mother! The *Passage* is my home. Don't—don't make me leave!" She drew a shuddering breath and loosed the mattress to wipe her face with shaking fingertips.

"Really, Priscilla, you might tell me in advance if I'm expected to provide handkerchiefs for us both."

She gave a startled gasp, groping perhaps toward a laugh, and took the proffered cloth. "Thank you."

"Don't give it a thought. I have dozens. I just don't happen to have them all with me at the moment." He leaned back, his face less bleak, his pattern showing a glimmer of what might be hope.

"The ship would miss the services of the second mate," he said carefully. "The captain's information is that the second mate progresses excellently in her training, taking over more responsibilities each shift. The first mate is pleased. The captain is also pleased."

Melant'i. She drew a deliberately even breath, relaxing tight chest muscles as she recalled sleep-lessons and Lina's tutoring. "The second mate wishes with all her heart to continue serving the ship and the captain."

Relief like a draught of ice-cold water cascaded from him to her. "Good. You will take your duties up again in four shifts." He raised a hand to still her protest. "There is a meeting at local midnight in the port master's office, Priscilla. Since you are intimately involved, it's best that you be there. Also present will be Delm Plemia, Sav Rid Olanek, Port Master Rominkoff, Shan yos'Galan, Gordon Arbuthnot, Mr. dea'Gauss, and Lina Faaldom, as observer."

"Balance?"

"Balance, indeed. Which reminds me, Thodelm. Mr. dea'Gauss wishes to meet with you in a very few moments now to ascertain the extent of debt owed you by Plemia and Korval—"

"Korval owes me nothing!" she cried. "If anything, I owe Korval for giving me a job, for—"

"Priscilla, do be reasonable. If you hadn't been on this ship, there quite possibly wouldn't be a ship right now, whether or not there was a captain. Ship's debt exists. As well as a personal debt."

"No," she said stubbornly. "I won't take payment from you. There's no debt now, if there ever was one." She leaned forward, extending a tentative hand. "Shan? You gave me—a life. I gave you a life. Balance."

He hesitated, then put his hand into hers. "Balance, then, Priscilla." He smiled. "You drive a hard bargain. Mr. dea'Gauss awaits us. May I escort your Ladyship to the meeting?"

"No," she said, gripping his hand and drinking in his lightening pattern with giddy joy. "But you may escort your friend."

Shan grinned and stood. "Much better, I agree." He flourished the bow between equals. "After you, Priscilla."

Master's Tower, Theopholis
Witch's Hour

രാഷ്ര്രാഷ്ര്രാഷ്ര്രാഷ്ര്രാഷ്ര്രാഷ്ര്രാഷ്ര്രാഷ്ര്രാഷ്ര്രാഷ്ര്രാഷ്ര്രാഷ്ര

TEN MINUTES BEFORE THE HOUR.

Taam Olanek sternly forbade himself the luxury of fidgeting with the papers before him. It was not expected that a delm betray uneasiness. At his right hand, Sav Rid sat silent. He still did not grasp it, Taam knew, pity warring with anger. He wondered briefly what had caused the younger man's madness, and set wonder aside. It hardly mattered.

Across the room, Mr. dea'Gauss was in quiet conversation with Port Master Rominkoff. The balance of the group had yet to arrive.

The door buzzed and was opened by the guard stationed there. Taam Olanek felt his breath snag.

A plain-faced Liaden woman in the costume of Thodelm entered, a tow-headed Terran child at her side. Taam Olanek's breathing eased. Of course Korval would arrive last. It was proper.

"I'm not sitting at the same table with him!"

The child had stopped, eyes fixed on— *Me?* Taam thought. No. On Sav Rid.

The woman had her hand on the boy's arm and was speaking in gentle Terran. "Gordon? We are here to settle past difference. You know this. To do so we must sit and speak together."

"I'm not," Gordon said through clenched teeth, "sitting at a table with him. He called me 'it,' and he said Priscilla was a thief."

With a feeling of infinite sadness, Taam Olanek rose and went across the room. A child, Sav Rid? he thought.

He and Mr. dea'Gauss reached the spot at the same moment. Asking permission with a flicker of fingers, Taam bowed to the child: elder to young person of rank. The boy eyed him narrowly but returned the bow properly, then straightened and stood waiting.

"I am," Taam said, speaking the unaccustomed tongue with great care, "Taam Olanek. The person you object to is one who will obey my word. Will it satisfy you, young sir, if I pledge that my kinsman Sav Rid will behave with fitting courtesy during the time we meet together?"

The brown eyes looked into his: a weighing glance. Taam returned it calmly. The boy looked to Mr. dea'Gauss.

"Is that true?" There was no insult in the tone; he was merely requesting information. Taam Olanek found himself amused.

Mr. dea'Gauss inclined his head. "The word of Delm Plemia is above reproach, Master Arbuthnot. What he has said will be."

"Okay." The boy inclined his head. "Thank you, Delm Plemia."

Taam bowed graciously. "Thank *you*, Master Arbuthnot."

Mr. dea'Gauss indicated the patient woman. "Plemia, here is Thodelm Faaldom Clan Deshnol."

He inclined his head. "Thodelm, I am pleased to meet you."

She bowed, as Head-of-Line-to-Delm-of-Another-Clan. "I am pleased to meet you, Plemia." Neither voice nor face betrayed her thoughts. Her behavior was most proper.

As observer, Thodelm Faaldom sat at the bottom left of the table. The boy sat to her right, near Mr. dea'Gauss. Sav Rid eyed both coldly; he made neither overture nor introduction.

The hour struck on the clock above the door, nearly covering the sound of the door buzzer.

The woman was tall, though not much taller than Shan yos'Galan, who walked just behind her right shoulder, and black-haired and slender. But for its paleness, her face might have been Liaden. She wore calm authority like a silken cloak over the clothing of Thodelm.

Gliding, she crossed to the port master and bowed as between equals.

Pilot, Taam Olanek thought, seeing the woman's grace mirrored in her white-haired escort. He understood now Mr. dea'Gauss's moment of outrage. Pleasure-love she might be, but this regal lady was no one's plaything.

"Port Master," she was saying, her voice soft and deeper than one expected, "I'm happy to see you again. Please accept my gratitude now for your kindness to myself and my friend."

The port master smiled in momentary pleasure, then waved a dismissing hand. "You owe me no gratitude, Lady Mendoza. My duty was clear. I believe there are still amends to be made; we must meet again before you leave."

The black-haired woman murmured assent and stepped aside.

Shan yos'Galan made his bow to the port master. "I'm pleased to see you again, ma'am. Please accept my gratitude as well, to be flung aside with Lady Mendoza's."

She laughed. "A lesson in manners, Captain? Very well, I accept the gratitude of all—including the boy's, though he hasn't offered it. Perhaps he's a realist." She indicated the rest of the table. "We are all gathered now. Mr. dea'Gauss?"

Korval's man of business rose to his spare height and bowed profoundly to the two just arrived.

"Thodelm yos'Galan. Thodelm Mendoza. Here are Elyana Rominkoff, Port Master; Taam Olanek, Delm Plemia; Lina Faaldom, thodelm and observer; Gordon Arbuthnot, foster-son and witness; Sav Rid Olanek, Trader."

Plemia inclined his head. Beside him, Sav Rid shifted and snapped, "*Lady* Mendoza!"

The woman's face remained coolly serene; she might not have heard. Certainly yos'Galan had heard; the light eyes glittered steel.

Plemia turned his face. Deliberately, using the Command mode of the High Tongue, he instructed for the ears of all, "You will exercise fitting courtesy here!"

Impossibly, Sav Rid looked hurt. "Certainly, sir."

Taam sighed to himself and saw a flicker of a reaction cross Lady Faaldom's face. At the top of the table, Lady Mendoza sat, Lord yos'Galan at her right. Plemia very nearly sighed aloud. Korval thus demonstrated its support of Thodelm Mendoza's demands and sub-ordination of its claims to hers.

"It must be known," Mr. dea'Gauss announced, "that a pin-beam has been received from *Eldema* yos'Galan. It reads thus—" He plucked a sheet of hard copy from the pile before him. "'In the present affair between Plemia and Korval, it shall be that Thodelm yos'Galan speaks with the very voice of Korval. I, Nova yos'Galan, First Speaker in Trust, Clan Korval.'"

yos'Galan inclined his white head, his ugly face austere. "It shall be done as the First Speaker instructs."

Mr. dea'Gauss laid the sheet aside. "For the purpose of balance, it shall be considered that Priscilla Delacroix y Mendoza is indeed Thodelm. Since she has chosen to disassociate herself from House Mendoza, Sintia, she must also be considered Delm Mendoza Offworld—"

"Offworld?" Sav Rid cried, cutting the old gentleman off. "Outlaw, more like!"

"Sav Rid!" Plemia allowed irritation to be heard. "I remind you again that I will have courtesy from you, for every person here."

"What difference," the younger man demanded, eyes glittering fever-bright, "if the bitch chooses to style itself thodelm? Our business is with Korval, which has the ill judgment to allow the fool to speak for it—"

"*You are silent!*"

A wave of heat washed past Taam's cheek, gone even as he understood the words to be in the High Tongue—Ultimate-Authority-to-Rankless-Person—and recognized the voice to belong to Thodelm Mendoza.

Beside him, Sav Rid opened his mouth, throat working. No sound emerged.

"Your delm," the woman continued in faultless Liaden, "will speak for you. When your words are required, you will be permitted speech."

"Most proper," Mr. dea'Gauss murmured.

Taam looked quickly around the table. Shan yos'Galan was expressionless; the port master was puzzled but unshaken. Gordon

Arbuthnot's brown eyes were stretched wide. Lady Faaldom was staring at the black-haired woman, awe and consternation in her face.

"Korval," Lord yos'Galan said in quiet Trade, "acknowledges a subordinate position in these negotiations. Debts owed Lady Mendoza are by far the greatest and must be met. We support her claims and are guided by her thoughts."

"Just so." Plemia inclined his head, carefully not thinking about the impossibility of what he had just witnessed. Beside him, Sav Rid sat mute and shivering.

"Thodelm Mendoza. I have seen information provided by Mr. dea'Gauss regarding your grievance against Plemia. Also, I have heard privately from my clansman that which convinces me of the justice of that grievance. Without doubt, Plemia owes. The amount must yet be ascertained. I am interested in hearing your thoughts on this."

The black eyes considered him calmly. "Sav Rid Olanek must be removed as Trader on *Daxflan* immediately."

He stiffened. "That is a Clan decision, Thodelm."

"Then it is a decision I require of the Clan," she returned serenely. "Sav Rid Olanek is unfit. If he were examined by the Trader's Guild tomorrow, sir, he would be found wanting and his license revoked. More." She lifted a hand, forestalling his protest. "I tell you now, sir, your kinsman gave scant attention to the honor of his crew—Liaden as little as Terran. His cargo included illegal pharmaceuticals: Bellaquesa, I will swear to; others I might guess. He is a danger to the honor of your Clan, the honor of your ship . . . and to himself." She glanced at the man on her right. "Is it permitted that I ask Lady Faaldom to speak—as a Healer?"

"If Plemia agrees."

Taam inclined his head. "Plemia agrees."

"Healer Faaldom."

"Lady Mendoza?"

"I feel that Sav Rid Olanek is not—rational. Are you able to form an opinion? Would you tell us what it is?"

The Healer gave the softest of sighs. "My opinion parallels

your own. Sav Rid Olanek is deranged. The pattern is one I have only occasionally seen, most often in connection with ingestion of harmful drugs. Bellaquesa addiction, for instance, might cause such a pattern."

"Can he be Healed?" There was hope in the Terran woman's voice. Taam Olanek looked at her in wonder.

The Healer hesitated. "It is beyond my skill."

"Beyond everyone's skill, Lina?" She spoke insistently, and Olanek felt his wonder grow.

"On Liad, perhaps. The path would be a long one, I think, and tedious." She sighed once more. "If Plemia desires, I will provide names, an introduction."

"You are kind, Healer. My thanks to you."

"You will need that list, sir," Lady Mendoza informed him. "My second demand is that he be Healed."

"Thodelm," he said with dignity, "you do not need to demand it. The child shall have what he requires."

She bowed her head. "Forgive me, sir. I meant no offense."

"None was taken, Thodelm. May I know what items further go to balance Plemia's debt?"

"It must be recalled," yos'Galan said smoothly, before the lady could speak again, "that several attempts have been made on Lady Mendoza's life—which is the life of her House, entire. The first attempt must be laid directly upon Sav Rid Olanek, who ordered Dagmar Collier to strike. The second and third incidents must also be laid upon Trader Olanek for his inability to control the actions of one sworn to his service."

"There are practicalities as well," Mr. dea'Gauss put in. "Unpaid wages, contract fee, clothing, hazard pay, recompense of personal indignities suffered while employed on *Daxflan,* family heirlooms lost—"

"Korval," yos'Galan broke in, "owes for the heirlooms, sir. Evidence indicates they were destroyed in retaliation for words spoken by Captain yos'Galan."

Mr. dea'Gauss made a notation. "So then. The sum owed, were there no further balance to be established: two cantra."

Plemia inclined his head. It surprised him that the woman should have drawn so low a wage, that she should have possessed so little. "Plemia agrees to a payment of two cantra in Balance for these things."

"Lady Mendoza," yos'Galan said gently, "has declined her right to Trader Olanek's life as Balance for his attempts on her own. The life-sum agreed upon by the Council of Clans for a first class pilot is three hundred cantra. It must be remembered that Lady Mendoza is currently the sum of her Line and Clan. It is to be assumed that one in her position would desire to establish a solid base for her House. Three children, I think, is not an unreasonable number. Nor is it unreasonable to suppose these offspring would inherit pilot reactions. Nine hundred cantra, then, for the children unborn."

Twelve hundred cantra.

"A just sum," Plemia murmured around the sinking feeling in his stomach. "Precise Balance is intended. However, if Lady Mendoza permits, I would propose this alternate plan: Plemia pays a sum of fifteen hundred cantra, over four Standards, the money to derive from *Daxflan's* profits—"

"No!" she said sharply. "I want no money from *Daxflan.*"

Wearily he raised his eyes to hers. "Lady, I assure you, not all of *Daxflan's* profits come illegally. A guaranteed payment of three hundred seventy-five cantra per Standard would be made, even should *Daxflan* fail to earn that sum. Is this plan acceptable?"

She looked at him for a long moment, then glanced beyond. "Mr. dea'Gauss."

"Thodelm?"

"If Clan Korval permits, sir, I would like you to take charge of these—details. The sum of twelve hundred cantra at once or fifteen hundred over several Standards is agreeable to me. Otherwise, it would be—comforting—to know that you act in my interest."

"Korval raises no objection," Lord yos'Galan put in, "if Mr. dea'Gauss feels he can undertake the task."

"I accept the commission, Thodelm Mendoza. I am honored to give service." He inclined his head. "Perhaps Delm Plemia and I might meet on the morrow and discuss the matter more fully."

"Certainly, sir. At your convenience."

"We come now," Mr. dea'Gauss said, "to that owed Korval. There is deliberate loss engineered by Sav Rid Olanek. There is the paid attack upon the *Dutiful Passage—*"

"Korval," yos'Galan broke in, "makes the following demands for balance: From Plemia, twenty cantra toward the loss on the mezzik-root purchase. Captain yos'Galan will likewise pay twenty cantra to the ship, to remind him to hear more fully. Also, Korval does likewise insist that Trader Olanek be removed from *Daxflan* immediately and sent home, that Healing may commence.

"Last, Captain yos'Galan would speak with Delm Plemia and Captain yo'Vaade regarding the management of tradeships and the planning of trade routes. Plemia may reap profit from the discussion."

Taam Olanek felt himself adrift. He managed to incline his head. "Plemia agrees to all terms of Korval's Balance."

"So be it," Mr. dea'Gauss said formally, and made notation.

"I believe that Master Arbuthnot also holds a just claim," Taam ventured, still unsure of what had occurred.

"Me?" The boy looked up in surprise. "Shan? Does this—does Delm Plemia owe me something?"

"You were in quite a bit of danger through the Trader's mismanagement, you know, Gordy." From the mildness of the tone, yos'Galan might have been discussing a rather mediocre play.

The boy frowned and shook his head. "The only thing he owes me is an apology for calling me 'it.' But if he's going to see a Healer, I guess he'll learn better, so that's okay. Dagmar's the one put me in danger, and she paid as much as she can." Surprisingly, then, he inclined his head, speaking in tolerably accented High Tongue. "Thank you, sir, but I believe our accounts are in order."

Taam bowed his head. "Thank you, Master Arbuthnot. Should you have need, Plemia's name is for you to use."

"Thank you," Gordy said again in response to a glance from Lady Faaldom.

Plemia glanced at the port master. "Madam, I would ask assistance. *Daxflan* must be searched, and all illegal substances must be removed. Is it possible you could instruct me in the proper procedure?"

She nodded gravely. "Delm Plemia, I would be honored to assist you. Allow me to call on you tomorrow midday for the purpose."

"You are kind, madam. I thank you."

"I believe," Mr. dea'Gauss said dryly, "that the meeting may be adjourned." Seeing no dissent, he turned down his papers.

At the head of the table, both tall thodelms stood, bowed, and glided toward the door. On the threshold the woman turned and raised a hand, tracing an invisible pattern in the air.

"Sav Rid Olanek," she announced in the High Tongue, "you may speak now."

Then they passed through the door and were gone.

Taam Olanek felt a sigh pass him, as if a bubble had given way. Beside him, Sav Rid burst into tears.

Shipyear 65
Tripday 287
Third Shift
16.00 Hours

ACTING FIRST MATE MENDOZA strode toward the captain's office. Hold 6, empty for the past two months, tantalized memory with the odors of leather, resin, spice. She took a deep breath, then sighed it out with a grin. It was hard to believe that they would establish orbit about Liad in five hours; hard to believe that so much had happened in five months. From pet librarian to acting first mate—she nearly laughed as she laid her hand against the captain's door.

He was frowning at the computer screen, his mental signature laced with irritation. At her entrance he looked up, irritation fading. "Hello, Priscilla."

She smiled, relaxing into the familiarity of his inner self. "You wanted to see me?"

He grinned. "Very good. When in doubt, hedge. The captain has several things to discuss with the first mate. Also the first mate was to have discovered what Lina Faaldom was going to do with that damn perfume of hers."

Priscilla laughed. "She's got a buyer in Chonselta City. They're going to package a distillate and sell it for a cantra the quarter ounce. The name is 'Festival Memories.'" She stopped because Shan was laughing.

"Oh, no! Shameless, shameless! She'd have done better to turn her hand to trading than librarying, Priscilla. 'Festival Memories,' in fact! The woman's dangerous." He leaned back, grinning hugely. "She's reserved a quantity for the crew, I hope?"

Priscilla nodded, lighthearted with his pleasure. "Anyone who wants part of their profit in perfume may take it that way, up to two bottles."

He chuckled. "Wonderful, wonderful. Pour yourself a drink, Priscilla, and come sit down."

She moved to the bar. "What are you drinking?"

"Nothing at the moment. But I would like a brandy, if you'd be so kind."

She poured them each a drink, brought him a glass, and settled into the right-hand chair.

Shan sipped, his light eyes on her. "Have you decided what you will do, Priscilla?"

"Do?"

He waved an apologetic hand. "Of course, it's true that you're rather well off now. You might choose to do nothing at all. But I'll tell you frankly, Priscilla, doing nothing is a very boring line of work." He sipped thoughtfully. "Not that there aren't a great many people who don't seem to find it arduous at all. My cousin Pat Rin, for an instance. The first jewels, the most fashionable companions . . . Why, if he didn't play the wheel with suspiciously consistent luck, he'd have no money at all to call his own, and live within his quarter-share he could not."

She smiled. "I don't think I'd do well as a gambler."

"Well, neither do I, frankly. But there are other things you might be about. Buy a house, a bit of land, start talking to people— lay the foundation for possible contracts and alliances."

"To set up my clan," she surmised.

"Exactly to set up your clan. Nothing wrong with that, is there?"

She sipped her drink, considering him. Emotive patterns told too little. He was not desperate, but there was a—tentativeness— mixed somehow with the desire she had found herself responding to more and more of late.

"I thought I'd invest my money," she said quietly. "Mr. dea'Gauss kindly offered his services."

Shan raised his glass. "I see that Korval will have to begin casting about for a new man of business. Mr. dea'Gauss is clearly smitten. I had hoped it would prove to be merely a case of calf-love, Priscilla, I confess."

She laughed. "More likely he thinks I'm too young to manage my own affairs! He helped me gain funds and status; how can he leave me alone to botch things now?"

"A fair summation of Mr. dea'Gauss's *melant'i* in the situation," Shan acknowledged. "But you still don't tell me what you'll be doing, Priscilla."

"Have you heard from Kayzin Ne'Zame?"

The slanted brows pulled together. "She brought *Daxflan* safely home and continues to work closely with Plemia to revise ship's procedures and work out a route that will not unduly tax available resources. I believe she had hopes of showing him the advantages of belonging to a cooperative, with which project I wish her luck. Plemia was rather resistant to the idea when I brought it up in our discussions."

"Does she think she'll be able to finish her work there in time for the *Passage's* next voyage?" More tentativeness. She knew it for her own.

Shan was surprised. "Kayzin warned me some time ago of her intention to retire at the end of this trip. Most properly, as Mr. dea'Gauss would no doubt agree. In a way, it was good that *Daxflan* and all its troubles came along. It gave her thoughts a new direction, away from—endings." He sipped. "Kayzin's captain was my father, Priscilla. They ran this ship together thirty years. It's not easy for her to see another in his place, even though she helped train me for just that purpose. She only stayed this long to be certain I was able. Her last duty to her captain."

"You'll be needing a first mate and a second?"

"Indeed I will. Which brings us back at last to my original inquiry, Priscilla. Have you thought of what you will do? Your contract runs out in—what? A day?"

"Fourteen hours," she replied, her mind racing. There was so much she did not know, so much training she would need; and there were people on the *Passage* who had been there all their lives, child and adult. Kayzin Ne'Zame, working on the ship for fifty years, at the captain's side for thirty of them, a captain she served even after his death. . . .

Shan sipped brandy. She sensed tension in him, and restraint. The decision was hers. *Goddess, I'm a fool. How can it be easier to conceive of looking at his face, hearing his voice, sensing his moods for all of thirty years, than to consider myself without those things for even a week?*

She licked her lips. "If—I would prefer not to renew my contract as second—" she sensed shocked pain from him, quickly damped, as she hurtled on, "—and to sign a new one, as first mate!"

She was swept by singing triumph and a tangled knot of other feelings, from which she isolated lust, and relief, and joy, and something that seared so she could not find its name before the whole concert was controlled and shackled into the merest background hum.

"Thank you, Priscilla."

Her heart was pounding; she was gasping with the force of his emotions, her own powerfully evoked. *Mother, the echo . . .* she thought. But it was no echo.

"Priscilla?" He was before her, radiating concern. "Forgive me."

"No." She set the glass aside, hand questing. He took it in his. "Shan. . . ."

"Yes, Priscilla?"

She translated it from the High Tongue, because protocol said it was done this way between Liadens, and it was imperative that he understand, that he not think her grasping or unaware of her place as someone all but Clanless. "Will you share pleasure with me, Shan?"

His fingers tightened as astonished joy flickered between them, weighted, though, with something else. Seeking, her inner eye perceived a wall, thick and impenetrable, with only a tiny slit in its smooth surface. As she watched, the slit enlarged, eating the wall until it was gone and there was only—Shan.

The impression was not just sound now, or pattern, or even an occasional whiff of elusive spice. It was all: a woven whole spread before the inner senses—Shan without defenses, open for her to know completely.

Priscilla cried out, jerking to her feet, gripping his shoulders. "No! Shan, you mustn't!"

Then there was sadness, though not despair, and the inner landscape faded, becoming again the barely breached Wall as she sagged against him, craving what she had just denied, and pushed her face against his shoulder.

"Priscilla, I ask your forgiveness yet again." His voice was very gentle in her ear. "I didn't want to distress you."

She drew a shaky breath and stood away. "I—" Words failed her. Goddess, she thought, twice a fool.

He sighed and guided her to the couch. Sitting beside her, he took her hand. "When I came to get you from the precinct house in Theopholis, Priscilla, you said something." She tensed. What *was* real from all she thought she remembered of that night?

"What you said," he pursued gently, "was, 'Shan, there wasn't enough time to be sure.'"

She relaxed. She did remember that. "True."

"It might still be true, Priscilla. There's no need for haste. And many reasons to be . . . sure."

She struggled with it, trying to balance the Liaden concept of pleasure-love with what she felt in him even now, with what she herself felt. "I asked . . . pleasure. And you want it!"

"Priscilla, my very dear." He raised her hand, lips brushing her palm, cheek stroking her fingertips. "Of course I want it. But not at the expense of your certainty. I'd be a poor friend if I made that trade." He sighed. "And I've already made you angry with me."

"Not angry," she protested, knowing he could read that lack in her. "It's—Shan, it's *wrong* to—to open up so far. To let someone see your—allness."

"Even when that someone is my dear friend? Even when I wish to give the gift?"

She opened her mouth, then closed it. "It is how I was taught," she told him humbly. "I never thought to question it." She had the name of the searingly bright emotion then, and felt tears forming. Too little time, indeed . . . .

He sensed her understanding and nodded. "There are other reasons not to rush, as I said. Consider your new position, for one matter. Will you have people say that you are first mate because you and the captain are lovers?"

Her chin rose. "It's our business, not theirs!"

"Theirs," he corrected. "It's a matter of *melant'i*, and of ship's administration. The crew must know that the two people who run this ship are honorable, are trustworthy—are *capable*. That proved, you may take any lover—and as many!—as you wish. You do have an extensive amount of training to undergo, you know, before you'll be up to Kayzin's level."

Impossibly, she laughed. "As if I didn't know it!"

He grinned, relieved and admiring. "Will you be staying on Liad, Priscilla?"

She nodded. "I'm guesting with Lina until I find a house of my own."

"Good. Then you'll be able to get a firm grounding during the time we're docked. And the next run is the long one—one full Standard. Enough time, I'd think, for everyone to know what works and what doesn't." He squeezed her fingers. "We might not make a very good team in spite of it all, Priscilla. That happens sometimes."

"We're a good team," she said, startled to hear the Seer's lilt in her voice. "We'll be a better one. The best."

The silver eyes glinted mischief. "You sound sure of yourself, Thodelm. Would you care to place a small wager? Say, a cantra? Issue to be decided at Solcintra docking, next run-end."

"Done." She grinned, surprised at finding herself so easy, and read the same deep serenity in Shan. On some level, then, they understood each other. The pattern of the Goddess's dance would see to the rest. She gripped the big hand tightly, then let it go and stood. "Sleep well, my friend."

"Sleep well, Priscilla."

She moved to the door.

"Priscilla!"

"Yes?"

"May I call on you at Lina's, Priscilla? It might aid certainty."

She smiled, peace filling her utterly. "I'll be all joy to see you."

Liaden/Terran Dictionary

A'nadelm: Heir to the nadelm

A'thodelm: Head-of-Line-to-Be

A'trezla: Lifemates

Al'bresh venat'i: Formal phrase of sorrow for another Clan's loss, as when someone dies.

Al'kin Chernard'i: The Day Without Delight

Balent'i Kalandon: Our local galaxy

Balent'i tru'vad: The starweb of all creation

Cha'leket: Heartkin (heartbrother, heartsister)

Cha'trez: Heartsong

Chernubia: Confected delicacy

Chiat'a bei kruzon: Dream sweetly.

Ckrakec: (derived from the Yxtrang) Approximately "Master Hunter"

Coab minshak'a: "Necessity exists"

Conselem: An absurdity

Delm: Head of Clan (Delm Korval, Korval Himself/Herself)

Delmae: Lifemate to the Delm

Denubia: Darling

Dramliza: A wizard. PLURAL: dramliz (The dramliz . . .)

Dri'at: Left

Eklykt'i: Unreturned

Eldema: First Speaker (most times, the delm)

Eldema-pernard'i: First-Speaker-In-Trust

Entranzia volecta: Good greetings (High Liaden)

Fa'vya: an aphrodisiac-laced wine sold at Festival

Flaran Cha'menthi: "I(/We) Dare"

Galandaria: Confederate? Countryperson?

Ge'shada: Mazel tov; congratulations

Glavda Empri: yo'Lanna's house

I'ganin brath'a, vyan se'untor: Play with the body, rest the mind

I'lanta: Right

Ilania frrogudon palon dox: (approx) Young ladies should speak more gently

Illanga kilachi: (no translation available)

Indra: Uncle

Jelaza Kazone: The Tree, also Korval's Own House. Approx. "Jela's Fulfillment"

Lazenia spandok: Son of a bitch (REAL approximate)

Lisamia keshoc: Thank you (Low Liaden)

Megelaar: The Dragon on Korval's shield

Melant'i: Who one is in relation to current circumstances. Also who one is in sum, encompassing all possible persons one might be.

Menfri'at: Liaden karate

Mirada: Father

Misravot: Altanian wine; blue in color.

Nadelm: Delm-to-Be.

Nubiath'a: Gift given to end an affair of pleasure

Palesci modassa: Thank you (High Liaden)

Prena'ma: Storyteller

Prethliu: Rumorbroker

Qe'andra: Man of business

Qua'lechi: Exclamation of horror

Relumma: Division of a Liaden year, equaling 96 Standard days. Four relumma equal one year.

Thawla: Mother (Low Liaden; approximately Mommy)

Thawlana: Grandmother

Thodelm: Head of Line

Tra'sia volecta: Good morning (Low Liaden)

Trealla Fantrol: The yos'Galan house.

Valcon Berant'a: Dragon's Price or Dragon Hoard, the name of Korval's valley

Valcon Melad'a: Dragon's Way, the Delm's Own ship

van'chela: beloved friend

va'netra: charity case, lame puppy

zerlam'ka: kinslayer